# Love's Register

Leslie Tate

**TSL Publications**

First published in Great Britain in 2020
By TSL Publications, Rickmansworth

Copyright © 2020 Leslie Tate

ISBN / 978-1-913294-59-5

Cover image:
Tahiti viewed from Mo'orea. Photograph by Bruno Leou-on
Leslie photo: Jemma Driver

*To Diana*
*from*
*Leslie Tate*

To Lillian Howan, author of *The Charm Buyers*,
a novel set in Tahiti,
who helped me with the Oceana sections.

# LOVE'S REGISTER
## FAMILY TREE

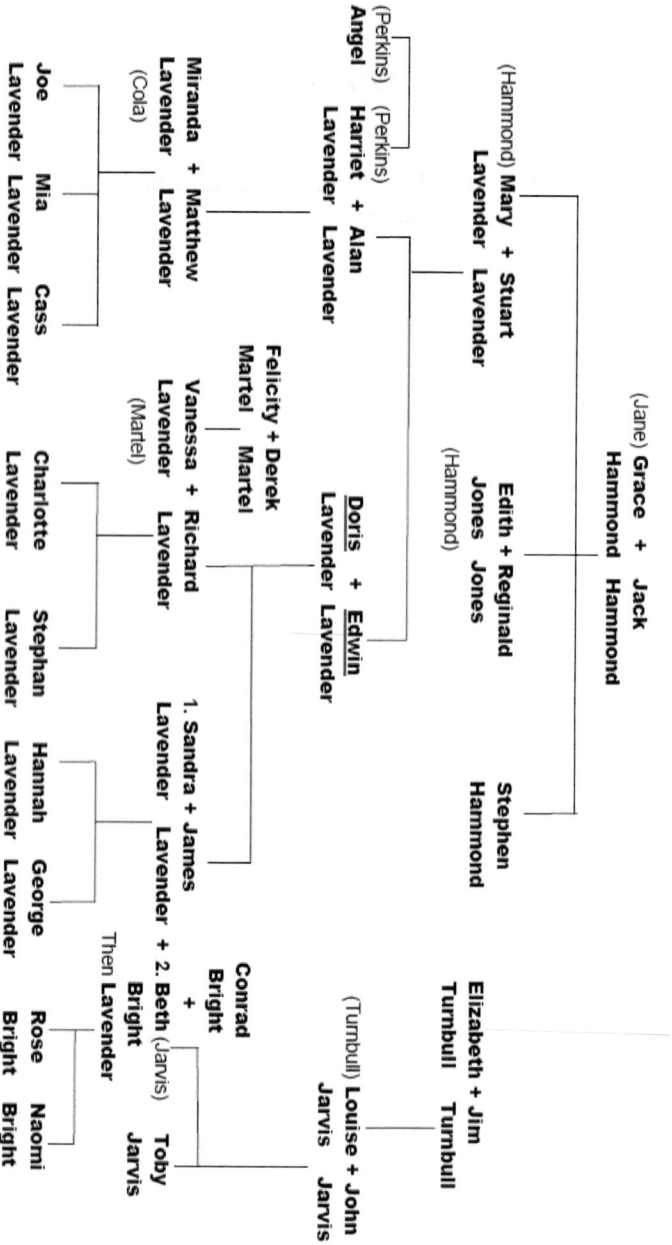

(Jane) Grace + Jack
Hammond Hammond

(Hammond) Mary + Stuart
Lavender Lavender

Edith + Reginald
Jones Jones
(Hammond)

Stephen
Hammond

Elizabeth + Jim
Turnbull Turnbull

(Turnbull) Louise + John
Jarvis Jarvis

(Perkins)
Angel
Lavender

(Perkins)
Harriet + Alan
Lavender Lavender

Doris + Edwin
Lavender Lavender

Miranda + Matthew
Lavender Lavender
(Cola)

Felicity + Derek
Martel Martel

Vanessa + Richard
Lavender Lavender
(Martel)

1. Sandra + James
Lavender Lavender + 2. Beth (Jarvis)
Bright Bright
Then Lavender

Conrad
Bright
+
Toby
Jarvis

Joe        Mia        Cass
Lavender   Lavender   Lavender

Charlotte   Stephan
Lavender    Lavender

Hannah     George
Lavender   Lavender

Rose       Naomi
Bright     Bright

See end of book for *Notes*

4

# ONE

As a young man, Joe Lavender often wondered who he was. As son to Howling Matt he'd fronted the Lavender Blues Shakers – but that was in his head, and maybe he'd moved on. Because if his thoughts were real, they came from somewhere else. And, as he told Mia and Cass, his life was undercover, or not all-there.

Get busy the teacher told him. Put yourself out there. Tick all the boxes. Be pro-active and make yourself known. In his mind he could hear it – speeches from the coach, the team leader, the accountant and advisor, BE A WINNER they said.

Welcome to the machine.

In his pre-teen years Joe played big bro and prof. With Mia he looked up names of insects and plants. With Cass he talked, seriously. Together they were the Lavender Kids camping out with crazy-hipsters Matt and M. And Joe sang along to Dylan and The Kinks.

But then came Joy Division, with Joe in black lying on the floor. He could hear things going crash. The world was full of broken glass. And his thoughts were tunnels into nowhere.

Then at 16 Joe heard Thom Yorke sing, "I wish it was the Sixties." Listening to that lost aching voice, Joe heard his own inner thoughts in caps and tags sprayed on walls. It was sad; it had wings. Everyone everywhere was broken.

All his friends were like that. For them Radiohead signalled pills and soul-loss and voices in the head: "I wish, I wish, I wish that something would happen." Not for them those simple truths when kids fought the system in wild naked moments resisting the man.

For them it was heads down and get used to it, because life wasn't like that. In any case his dad had told him about the Sixties with its fat cats and rip-off merchants and big-money hippies. By the Eighties, Matt said, they'd all given up or had passed away.

I hope I die before I get old.

What his old man said didn't surprise Joe. He'd grown up listening to the *Fillmore Sessions* and *Live at Leeds*, drumming on the table to harmonicas and guitars. To *Young Man Blues* and *Satisfaction*. But behind that was the ego trip and the sell-out.

How I wish, how I wish you were here.

Even then, it had all been about appearances. If the revolution had ever happened, it was a big bang moment, mainly in the head. And as Thom Yorke said, it was much harder to do that now.

Failure was part of Joe's inheritance.

♪ ♪ ♪

### York, 1969: The Making of Matt, Joe's Dad

As a young man, beginning at college what he'd later describe as his *Hendrix days*, Matthew Lavender took pride in his newfound ability to understand others, diagnosing their problems by extension from himself.

In the world of late-night talks, grouped around tables with coffee cups, candles and milk bottle joss sticks, or squatted on carpets with background drumming and acoustic guitars, Matthew listened closely, offering his insights with a sympathetic nod, a line saved up from Nietzsche or Blake and talk of us and them. He knew and he showed – and showing, being there, putting in a word, a gesture, a fine speculation, well, wasn't that what he did?

"You've read all these?" asked his room-mate Paul, counting the volumes of Freud and Jung piled up on the desk. "And these?" he continued, adding those in corners, balanced on the bedhead and scattered, dice-like, over carpet and chairs.

"Helps," said Matthew, and in answer to the unspoken question: "Know thyself."

He might have added what he'd got to know of others, through deep talk and truth talk in small group confessionals, because that helped too; it named and gave relief. And to put a case in words, that was how he coped; saying made him real. It strengthened his position to pick and choose and edit his own feelings, to lay claim on weakness and present his own hurt – which he did with judgement, where necessary, to share and blend in.

And knowing others' problems taught him how to shape it, to conceal by telling all. Yes, that was true, he'd been there too; people had their hang-ups, his were as he'd told them, he answered with experience, no one sussed him and talking was a comfort.

Because Matthew was a reader of books, of people, of feelings, of life. He was deep into problems and kept himself busy analysing, reviewing all the evidence to understand the affections and map the secret heart, searching into mind stuff because he knew it helped.

It also helped that he was tall. Six foot and vigorous with grey-blue eyes and hair to his shoulders, well-known to the porters, the bar staff, the cleaners and students right across campus, Matthew was a presence, an enquirer, a young blood fired up. Mercutio with glasses or Tony on the run. But he also played Hamlet, bluesy and barefoot with buttons missing as he drifted silently on early morning soul watch, pacing the walkways between plate-glass dining halls, concrete dormitories and the artificial lake.

He was on the scene with hey there greetings, yeah talk and cool, then bodies on the sofa with star chart and kaleidoscope, or passing around chocolates while turning the pages on Escher and Richard Dadd. Suzanne by the River and Mellow Yellow ... The Magic Roundabout ... Bambi ... Daisy chains and ethereal voices. What Paul sometimes spoke of, with headphones buzzing to Bloomfield and BB King, as sweeter-than-sweet.

And it was Paul, speaking softly as he squatted on the carpet, who'd first turned him on. "Breathe deep," he'd urged as the joined-up papers coloured like toast. "Relax, hold and count," he'd said as he passed on the joint.

"You high?" he enquired soon afterwards as Matthew, now restless and sweated by holding and counting, began to feel the lift.

"It's OK," he added later as Matthew signalled doubt, "you're good, very good."

And it was Paul in the end who told him, pausing for effect, how proud he was to see him so switched on.

Soon they were known. As Paul Dalveen and his friend Matthew they were blues aficionados, super-cool and easy, wearing bath shrunk Levi's and tie-dyed headbands; as Matt Man and P they were careless, unshaven, and as the turned-on-two serving Earl Grey and substances, they were where to be.

But it wasn't open door – certainly when smoking – with incense burning, scented candles and talk of busts and raids, or shadows in corners hunched over dice throws and Matthew reading from *The Book of the Dead*. Their pad, their hangout, with hellfire posters and psychedelic albums, like the *Old Town Record Shop*, was one of those spots where true freaks gathered and weird things might happen. It was a dream space capsule, with multi-coloured light bulbs, art books, postcards and tinted glassware. For this was strange heaven, and those who attended did so in a whisper, almost like conspirators or church-types praying.

Something was happening.

But what, and with what purpose? And why, asked Matthew, if it was happening, did he feel, when he heard it, out of breath somehow and in search of something more?

"Don't think in answers," was their friend Jay's pronouncement, "just be."

Matthew's eyes widened. "Be?"

Jay remained silent. In the dark his saintly, emaciated face con-cealed behind hair strands might have been taken from a Murillo deposition. "Whatever you like," he responded finally, "a leaf, a cloud, a joint, an image in water."

"Come again?"

"Transformation," returned the other loftily.

"You mean that, Jay?"

Jay pondered, oblivious. "A portion of the whole."

Frowning slightly, Matthew glanced around the room: talking, smoking, dreaming, they were all elsewhere, or had withdrawn. In any case Paul's friend was by now all too familiar. Because Jay was special, his fame went before him. It was legend: his bean sprouts in plastic, inch-slice scrapings, two-second dips with herbal tea bags; his algebra on shirt sleeves and see-through socks. People all knew. *Jay Bird* they called him, remarking on the bag spills; the acid tabs in eggcups and half-eaten fungi; the recycled platefuls of beans on toast.

8

Leaning forward Matthew picked up a book, opening it at random. "For everything that lives," he read out with a soft ironic grin, "is holy."

Jay's expression was that of a traveller observing landscape. Then, impassive: "Think in waves."

Matthew sighed. "Jay. You realise it's first week back? What I mean is, it's not exactly …" Something was telling him to give it a miss. It barely seemed worth it. Not so soon after Christmas with parents.

When Jay responded, linking drugs to transcendence, Matthew ended shrugging, eyes to the ceiling, "Hmm. How about cloud nine?"

"Yeah sure, metempsychosis, anamnesis, whatever," Jay intoned.

Afterwards Matthew wondered if he'd been too harsh. He could hear himself talking like his father, probing. Maybe in the rush to judgement he'd missed something?

"Has he always been like that?" he asked Paul next day, after confirming their history as school friends, blues fans, students at the Tech.

"He's deep, like his family. His father writes about quantum physics and his mother's God squad."

Matthew had a flashback to a fragile-looking woman in embroidered cottons peering around a gathering, asking Jay politely if he'd seen her son.

"He's into Floyd isn't he?"

Paul checked his hairline in the mirror. "Could say that."

"Careful of that axe."

"More like several species of small furry animal."

Matthew smiled; he enjoyed these exchanges. The words were quotable and might prove useful in lonely-boy rock songs, or to pad between action when he wrote his book. There were others, of course, his hip-cool-phrases used for effect: *We are the people your mother warned you against … Everything they say we are, we are …* but not at this time, close on midday, bagging up roaches and returning albums to their crumpled inner sleeves.

"He's not wrong, you know," put in Paul, fingering the edge of a polished-up record.

Matthew, balancing a book-pile, mimed surprise.

"I mean when he talks about *being,*" Paul continued.

"What, you believe him? The omniscient one?"

"Not exactly. Though I do know he has ego in bucketfuls."

"So, he's part of the problem. Or maybe, according to you, part of the solution?"

Paul considered, staring into vinyl. "I guess he's into the contemplative. Not *doing* all the time." He slid the record onto a matt-black turntable. "A Maharishi type. All part of the bigger picture."

"And you'd see that as cool?"

"Well, yes. Cool is … can be progressive. Kinda classic, or minimalist."

"Like you," said Matthew and immediately regretted. Coming out like that – fixing and flat-voiced like his father – well, his friend Paul just didn't deserve it. And in any case that wasn't what he meant.

Or was it? Because big man Paul was so – comfortable and contained? Likely-laddish? Mr Kind-heart, really? – "You'd be Paul, and I've heard," was the first thing he'd said when his room-mate had walked in.

Paul had ridden it like an actor on curtain call, looking around with a half-surprised grin. "Amazing how news travels," he'd said after Matthew had recounted the pre-meeting stories of late nights and debauchery. Nor did he seem at all fazed by coffee-swilling, out-loud Matthew sounding off about parents. "They fuck you up," Paul said, ducking to the mirror in the built-in wardrobe. And he was cool, but not so offhand, in telling what was needed, the in-things and the latest to make Matthew more assured, more up there and with it.

Because Matthew arrived straight, with short hair, baggies and oversized jumpers; so straight, so uncool in fact, that he had to be given treatment. Beginning with hair, grown with sideburns, no grease, no cream and casual centre parting; then wardrobe, smocks with cravats, Doc Martens, shades and below-the-heel Levi's; next language, bad; music, underground; cigarettes, menthol; reading, comics; followed by a name, Matt or M, and travel (extensive), plus star sign and paranormal experiences.

Then came getting stoned: being wiped or blocked or right out of your head – which had to be studied and involved, said Paul, attention, panache, and a special kind of practice. Everything in order, everything laid on, as in climbing a staircase or dressing for a dance.

"You can always tell," said Paul, "people who do, and who don't." A remark he returned to with minor variations in a variety of settings, picking up on clues – a voice tone here, interest taken, knowledge made evident in hair length or talk – as he measured those met in common room or seminar, cruising for experience, for what he called form. He put himself around, searching for likelies, for those who'd scored. And he knew what to look for: some sort of mark, an edge of hardness, an inadvertent gesture observed in passing that indicated pride in things that shouldn't be. Darkness lived through; a feel for being lost. All this in the bars and the meetings, in the parties and gatherings and lakeside walkouts, all noted and collected in systematic fashion without, apparently, any reference to his newfound friend.

*Who do, who don't.* The phrase still held: four beat and simple like a chorus in a song. It returned to Matthew now, talking as he sorted, clearing the room. It held through the music as Paul increased the volume on the black metal record player. Pure sound. Astronomy Domine. Darkness visible.

"Cool," observed Paul, examining the scissor marks on a cut-down packet of Gitanes. Reaching forward he turned the volume higher. Rising and falling, the notes thickened, filling up the room.

Outlined now by the still-dark window, Matthew glanced over and pulled back the curtains, opening to the world.

$$\ddagger \ \ddagger \ \ddagger$$

Paul and Matthew went visiting. Just back from parents, they needed to be out: to call and be seen, to check, show interest, exercise judgement and take in developments. And today they intended to be where it mattered; they'd a patch they had to work.

Most days they simply wandered and played themselves as tourists; the world, they felt, was an event worth watching. Walking, inspecting, they took their turn around campus, enjoying what they found. Often, they did surprise, tried out different groups: bar crowds, politicos, food freaks and dope heads and those, like them, who chose their own image, were conscious of difference and followed inclination, led by the flow.

Some days they played *spottings*, identifying trends, calibrating interest and who was eyeing who, or they gave out *signals*: Hi There and See You as they drifted the walkways in transit between lectures; usually there were connections: people who had tickets or access or might cut deals, and always there were the dailies: people of importance whose names just presented, appearing as given when deciding where to go.

So today Matthew proposed calling on Theresa. At the mention of her name Paul, as expected, was agreeable; Theresa Theron had approval. Pale and slight with a planetary expression and dream-soft eyes, she'd achieved, almost without trying, an elevated status that placed her in the forefront of those who do. Speaking at a whisper, reporting on voices and half-hidden contacts, she mood-shared about life. There were dealings and familiars, unseen matters, and things that just occurred, mostly at night, and often in the arms of soul mates like Paul.

Leaving their pad, they descended a staircase with views of other blocks. Several windows were curtained. There were doorways and walkways bounded by grass; beyond that asphalt, and a fence with upturned bottles spiked on post ends. Reaching ground floor, Matthew led down a corridor smelling of porridge and pulses. They passed through a kitchen where an unshaven male was staring at a white-grey clothes lump stacked on a radiator. There were coffee stains on plastic, posters with burn marks, chocolate-smeared curtains and hollowed-out candles floating in the sink. They emerged at the porter's desk, all keys and polished wood. Passing through the common room they waved and greeted. The J-block crowd was there, studying the fine print on a laminated notice. Led by a bearded male and an olive-skinned woman, they appeared to be lip reading the announcement in a state of outraged bewilderment. Words like *lackey* and *soggy liberal* hung in the air. On the other side, large-bodied males watched on-screen football with expressions that shifted from mild anticipation into doubt, progressing through pain and disbelief to hands in the air then dumbstruck silence.

After a brief exchange with a small group of hairies grouped around the window seat they passed out through double doors. Outside was mild. The sky was brushed silver, speckled with grey. In one corner, green mud streaks peppered by stubble hinted at spring. The cracks in the path held bottle tops, hair grips, matches.

As they approached the lake, they encountered Jay squatting on a bollard fingering a guitar. Behind him a dog moved uneasily. His voice echoed against concrete, a half-tone down. They waved and greeted. Startled, Jay checked left and right then his eyes softened as words were exchanged. Sensing another chorus, Matthew engaged long enough to satisfy decency before walking on. "Strummers," he muttered as they passed across the bridge.

Theresa's door was on the top floor and well set back; it took time to climb to and even longer to open.

The girl who appeared showed no surprise; her eyes were unfocused and face rather still. She greeted them with a nod and pulled back the door. A hooded purple cloak served as a dressing gown. The garment beneath was long, Victorian and flowery. She waved them in as if they'd arrived to fix an appliance. Her room was cave-like and half-curtained with papers everywhere and a desk lamp that flickered. "Got essays," she explained. They exchanged greetings then briefed each other on holidays and parents. There were presents to discuss, doing time with family, anecdotes, dreams, and things more private. As they sipped their coffee and exchanged stories, Theresa moved into confessionals. She described how close she'd been to dropping out, talking about pressure and forces brought to bear; about time on the other side and false projection. Her voice, though breathless, remained flat and bald as if she were reporting from a battlefront. Her narrative used the word "shit" as noun, verb, comparative, superlative and occasional interjection.

Matthew watched her, distanced slightly, like a child through a keyhole. She appeared so set, so much *of herself*, and yet, looked at closely, he wondered who could tell. Part of him was persuaded – and had been from the start – that Theresa was on his wavelength. In her

13

he'd detected something like a call, a signal in passing, at least when they'd first met.

"Blue and green," she'd said, referring to his surname.

"And purple passages," he answered. "Don't forget those."

They were sitting side-on, triangulated by Paul, in the big-windowed dining room that fronted the lake. "I can see you," she said, apparently reading from somewhere just above his head. "You're clever and aware, a traveller."

Matthew, sensing the challenge, deflected. "That's not what *he* thinks," he said, nodding towards Paul. Waving a spoon, he continued, "I'm Mr Straight y'see. Good ol' country cousin."

Paul laughed and asked for a second opinion. Theresa declined to comment. "It's image," said Paul. "Once we've got that …"

Matthew examined his reflection in the spoon. "Like that?" he asked, holding up the back. "Or that?" reversing to the bowl.

"Both," replied Paul.

"One half blue, one half green," put in Theresa.

"The man's into purple," Paul said.

"Deep purple," added Matthew.

Theresa eyed him. "You really like that music?"

Matthew wrinkled up his nose. *"Shades of Deep Purple* … some of it." He glanced across at Paul. "British psychedelia, yes?"

Paul nodded, staying silent.

"But less blues, more kinda purple."

Again, his friend agreed.

Theresa stared out through glass. "Deep purple, yes ..."

And after that, when he thought about Theresa, Matthew always saw her seated looking out, gazing into purple that shaded into blue.

Which was why he still wondered as she talked about dropping out, whether it was possible that she'd never read him – not that part, anyway – she'd never understood. Could it really be … his hours by the lakeside, her image in water and dreams of being close … Surely she could sense it, like call and echo, or buckets in a well?

Though of course he'd kept it hidden for fear of losing all. Because this was what he lived with: a kind of secret inner chamber, a cobweb

14

in darkness; a cough beneath the stairs. And as for her call? Well, one day perhaps, when she listened.

"And the shits want me out," Theresa ended sadly. As she rose and moved to the window she brushed against Paul. "When you're second year," she added, drawing back the curtains, "the shits'll do that."

Paul followed, round-faced and attentive, ready to play rescuer: "How many essays to go?"

Theresa prevaricated; not many it seemed. He touched her on the arm saying nothing. She turned and his hand passed down to curl around her waist. It seemed she didn't mind.

For a second Matthew wondered whether he should leave. The room had become theirs. Everything had narrowed: the lamp with its papers, the bed that he sat on and the window at the end. Certainly, he was there, real and actual, but only as an adjunct, a figure painted in.

"You OK?" asked Paul.

Matthew nodded. He could fit to others; as sidekick he was willing. "I'm cool," he replied.

Paul grinned, moving to one side as if they'd just been dancing. "Time we split," he said, and Theresa agreed, mentioning essays. She was, she said, more together now. By the time they left Theresa was writing, the desk lamp was switched off and a yellow-white brightness was spreading through the room.

Outside on the bridge as Paul and Matthew considered their next move, they heard themselves being called. It was Sally Jenkins just out from lunch, arm in arm with a girl in a trench coat.

"Hi …" the single syllable drawled out slowly, sounded flirty. "You going our way?" It seemed they were, or at least they'd no objection. As Sally joined them at the railing, they eyed her, grinning; she had their attention. For her, Matthew's boyish interest was something to be enjoyed, while Paul, being smoother and more knowing, gave less advantage.

Sally angled back her head. Red-haired and freckled, wearing stretched polyester, she under-topped both by something like a foot. "Oh my, ever so sorry!" she exclaimed, turning to her companion, "Miranda. Miranda Cola."

The friend, who was tall and vaguely athletic, greeted with *"Ciao"*, adding, when given their names, that she knew them already. She spoke with emphasis and a wide-mouthed smile. Her delivery was quick and bold and wryly unapologetic.

With the introductions over, Sally briefed both males on their intended destination. "We're off to the Friendly Society. There's a talk, invitation only, and because I've asked you, you'll both come of course."

Paul and Matthew stood undecided; neither seemed bothered. After words of encouragement, talk of plans and a degree of coquetry their consent was obtained. Taking charge Sally led off, joined at the hip to Miranda. Matthew and Paul followed, exchanging pleasantries and talking agreeably about their visit to Theresa.

They travelled the back route, at first along the lake where over-flow stains had spread across concrete, past a couple feeding ducks, Jay on his bollard, and around by the kitchens where head-high gratings hummed and blew warmth. On the way, the men were greeted by people who knew them but they'd forgotten, while the women provided names. Rejoining the main walk-through, they saw up ahead a fenced-off section where a large, arrowed sign directed to a perimeter path. It took them past brick piles and open trenches. All around were pipes large enough to be crawled through: in the middle they were stacked up, container-style, but beyond that they jutted out at all angles like a derailed train.

When the path forked, they turned right led by Sally and climbed to a terrace. "Take a look from here," she called. "It's a bit mad. Something's going on."

They gathered by a bench, looking down.

Below they could see workmen inside a fence waving tools and shouting obscenities; outside, a student gathering. It seemed a dog had entered and was running wild. There were glimpses of flaking yellow helmets and an unkempt collie being chased or coaxed. At each appearance of the dog the crowd, panto-like, sent up a cheer, but the workmen who followed were booed like Wicked Queens. Dog: applause. Workmen: whistles. Both sides: laughter. The contest continued with asides and shouted encouragement until word got around that the owner had arrived.

"Jay," said Matthew dryly.

Jay Nielsen was crouched at one corner, peering through the wire mesh fence. Hooded, with one knee bent, he appeared to be praying, like a prophet seeking guidance. He stretched to see, and the guitar pinned across his back slid off. Unchecked, it bounced heavily from knee to pavement, landing with a dull crash. The dropped instrument lay chiming like a broken cuckoo clock. It went on shuddering and chiming until, taking notice, Jay leaned over to pick it up. He examined it at arm's length, turned it over and shook it like a money box, then struck up a chord. As he launched into song the dog came running and jumped up excitedly, then belly-crawled beneath the fence, barking.

"You know him well?" asked Sally, waving towards Jay who by now had strapped on his guitar and was ambling back towards his bollard.

"Everyone knows him," Matthew replied. "Jay's king of the college. Number one freak."

"Don't you feel at all sorry for him?"

"Not if I can help it."

"You don't mean that."

"What's there to be sorry for? Jay is Jay, simple as that. Why should we all run round making excuses – or apologising – for what anyone does?" He looked across at Paul who nodded. Sally, whose attentions were fixed on Matthew, offered her best smile. Then Miranda cut in, "So why apologise? Why bother at all?"

Matthew grimaced. "What's that? Why *bother*? Where's that coming from?"

"You should know."

"I should?"

"It seems you know things."

"Ah, I see. And that just won't do. Apology required."

"Maybe. You could try."

"Well, say I'm not bothered, I'm really *not* bothered. What then?"

17

Miranda bristled. "Not bothered? Or not sorry?"

"Both. Or neither. Whatever comes naturally."

"And you don't apologise, ever, I suppose."

Matthew feigned a smile. "Sorry, didn't quite hear that."

"Mr No-Apology … Mr Never-Say-Sorry …"

Matthew went loud, "Sorry? Sorry? What'y say?" Watching for effect he dropped to conversational, taking a mock bow. "I'm sorry? Oh, I do beg your pardon. Please, after you. No, no, after you. Oh, ever so *sorry*. Please don't say sorry, say pardon."

"Yeah, that's right," Paul cut in. "It's cool man, just cool." His eyes began to soften. "In any case, it's not what Jay does. Jay just *is*."

"And he lives in a cave with several species small and furry. But please don't feed the animals."

Miranda shook her head. "You think you know him and can fix him with a word." She hesitated. "But he's part of what – what we all are."

Matthew shrugged. "And all things bright and beautiful."

Miranda turned away and busied herself grimly with the buttons of her coat. When Sally took her arm, she allowed herself a smile.

"OK, time to move on," said Paul quietly. Sally directed as Matt and Paul formed up and, steered by gesture, they left the terrace. Nothing more was said. They walked downhill past a precast metal sculpture, by notice boards and litter bins and half-plastered walls then descended beneath an overhang to arrive at a windowless office labelled *Student Union*. A corridor inside led to an open whitewashed hall with a half-curtained platform and steel and canvas chairs.

The talk had begun, or had finished already. A small group of listeners were posing questions to a round-faced man in a braided purple suit. Entering from the back Sally and Miranda slipped in sideways, while Paul and Matthew sat further forward. The suit-man led; arms short, head large, breathing quickly, he fielded their questions stepping back and forth like a singer. The questions were about faith – all kinds of faith: long-term and short, in God, in college, in justice and prayer, in and out of marriage, in government and UFOs. Suity had faith, he believed what was evident, he liked, he didn't, he heard and saw and he discovered, he'd appreciate if his listeners wrote that down. Sometimes rewording, he appealed for different answers, threw out a challenge, picked up on expressions, on truth-tell and look and audience examined for what was in their hearts.

When he homed in on Matthew the response was brief. "Religion? That's nothing man."

Suit-man begged to differ. He knew, had words, had been there, with reason.

"No use to me," said Matthew curtly.

The other stepped forward, declaring. In his heart, if only he could hear.

"It's shit."

Suit began to quote by chapter, verse and number.

Matthew cut in, "God is dead. D-E-A-D. Dead."

Suity felt so much sorrow, it grieved him to hear it.

"For Christ's—"

Suddenly, before Matthew could finish, Miranda leaned forward and shushed him. "Enough. Some of us came here to listen."

"To him?"

"Not to you, anyway."

"What, you believe all this crap? You believe it? And this phoney? SOS and feel sorry – sorry for everyone?"

"*Basta*. Mr No-Apology … Just listen. Listen."

"With mother?"

"To God."

"Can't hear him. Too much chatter. Too much of you, and this man."

"And of you. Far, far too much." Miranda stood up. Her fingers were shaking as she gathered up her coat; her gaze had turned inward and her wide, expressive mouth had narrowed to a line. Colouring, Sally rose to join her.

Matthew, tigerish, turned on the man: "That's what I can't stand about you lot. All that fake sorrow, fake humble, feeling sorry for the world. I can see it now in your eyes, you feel for me, don't you? Think I've something wrong." He laughed. "Go on, feel sorry for me. *Please*. I'm a poor lost soul."

As suit-man danced and called upon his God, Matthew rose and crossed to the doorway. He stood there flushed, breathing hard. His face was wild, hair in a tangle, eyes unfocused. As Suity tailed off, Matt snapped his fingers, "Shit, man. Religion – who needs it? What kind of sob story's that?"

Leaving, he raised a V-sign to the ceiling. His voice ran on, cursing and laughing, as he retreated down the corridor and out beyond the basement door, singing.

# TWO

### *Mary Lavender, née Hammond: Matt's Gran Speaks*

From the start I could tell Matty was a Lavender, just like his dad. Two sides of a coin, peas in a pod, though they'd never admit it. How do I know? Well, you could say that's the way with our family. Something about standing with your back to the wind and sand drizzling the sea wall. I remember when my Alan first brought Harriet home. "You'll soon be a Lavender," I told her. It was a tease, but she didn't smile. I knew she was thinking *mother-in-law* with a fish-faced look, like those Andy Cap cartoons. Yes, I nearly said, welcome to the tribe.

It's in the blood, that's what people say. For Alan, it goes back. I think of him and me as sea lavender: a few frilly heads on soft green stems, the leaves small, up to the knees in mud. It's a line, one that runs back like a wave on the turn, stirring from the bottom. Put your hand in and you'll feel the cold.

I saw it in Matty, sitting with Alan on the beach. Copying his dad, back to the camera, basking in the sun. Matty-chatty, the cartoon boy digging in the sands. The lad who burned and flaked like pastry, because that's family too.

Of course, when I say a Lavender that's what I've become. I've been grafted on. Harriet's a Perkins and my side's Hammond, but it's all one type. You can tell us by our talk, we say it to your face, straight. What we think is what you hear. Contrary, you might say, but it's a kind of holding out. And that makes us shy, like kids.

But first, my life as a Hammond, beginning with JH, my dad. Jack the Hammer, as we called him, or Jack-and-whose-army. That was when he did his I'm-in-charge thing. "Just remember who you are," he'd say, cutting through our talk, "you're better than *them*." Because he hated us being part of what he called the "tittle-tattle mob". They were the herd. Sheep, he called them. "Be yourself," he'd say, making baa-ing noises. "You're not that daft. You're with the wolves."

When he said it, I thought that was him to a T. He'd a way of popping up without warning, ducking through a door or jumping round a corner and saying something shocking. I mean grumpy-shocking like Mr Punch. He'd make out he was crazy or could see something you couldn't. I knew it was panto, but serious as well. There was a force behind it, like a knock to the head, as if he was jailer about to lock you up. Because he knew how to make you scared, and he played on it. So, he'd close in and look, breathing noisily. "Watch out," he'd warn, running his tongue around his lips, "I'm on the prowl." I think he was caught up in his own tough-talk. To him, it was all about action and taking it on the chin.

I remember the first time when I came home late and he was there waiting just inside the door. "Is that you Mary?" he called when I rattled the letterbox. His voice sounded muffled, as if he was half asleep. When he opened the door, I kept my eyes down holding back the words. "What time's this?" he demanded, follow-ing me to the stairs. I wasn't quite sure what he might do next. His eyes were set hard and his chin was jutting forward. I think he'd been waiting for hours. He yanked out a large metal stopwatch and pushed it towards me, pointing to the hands. "And don't give me your tales!"

I stepped back. "But Dad …"

"Don't!" he called, reaching for a leather strap hung on the coat stand. Seeing his arm in motion I squealed and ran. As I struggled upstairs, he swiped across the back of my legs. "Don't!" he shouted as he lunged and struck. He kept on hitting as I crawled to the landing. Even as I pulled out of reach, he managed to land one last stinging blow. It felt like a match head striking on flesh.

Next morning, I talked with my sister. We'd shut ourselves in the backyard shed. Edith's eyes moved slowly up and down as she examined the back of my legs, looking pained. "Did you cry?" she asked.

I shook my head.

She signalled me to be quiet and put an ear to the door. "It's all right," she said, stepping back, "he's gone."

The shed was cold. It was a brick square with high-up window-slits, gaps around the doorframe and a hole in the roof. The walls were cobwebbed, plastered one end, and hung with tools on nails. At the back was an old bath full of sea coal. We sat at the front on a large wooden trunk. Beside us there was a box full of kindling and chopped-up logs. The air smelled damp.

"We will leave," said Edith. "Like Stephen. Just go."

I looked at her, wondering. She had her ghost face on. Her eyes were starey and the set of her mouth was hard. If I'd seen her in a picture, I'd have thought she was a Victorian governess.

"Leave?" I asked. "Where to?"

Edith pushed forward. "It doesn't matter. We start out and keep walking. There are places."

I knew she meant it. She was only eighteen months older than me but she'd left twice already. The first time I only knew she'd gone when a friend had brought her back. The second time she'd walked after Dad had strapped her. I'd heard the shouting, then seen from the window as Edith led along the street. Her head was high and her chin was out. "Hit me then," she called, rolling up her sleeve. "Go on!" she cried, baring her flesh. When he hesitated, she stood for a moment glaring, before dropping her shoulders and walking off. I could feel the eyes watching behind net curtains. "Edith!" I heard him shout. He followed her yelling. It was like some awful, penny-dreadful story, only this was real and Edith kept going.

So she was serious when she told me we'd leave. But I said we must tell Mum first.

"She can't stop him."

I leaned over and reached into the box at my side. "Then we'll help her," I said, pulling out a stick and waving it like a wand.

"With that?"

I looked at my stick. It was squared off and knotted at both ends. The middle bulged out around a hole. "Why not?"

"Not with that stick."

"What's wrong with it?"

Edith poked a finger through the hole. "Too weak," she said, pulling with the other hand.

"Don't," I said, gripping harder.

The stick shook like a tuning fork.

"That's *his* word," she cried, twisting.

As I pulled the other way the wood bowed out. Then with a raw, breaking, splitting sound, it tore around the hole.

We both fell back. Edith was staring at her part of the stick. It had snapped like a wishbone. She held it up as if it was a prize. "You'd think," she said, "that we could do better than this." She barked out a laugh and I waved my stick. It flashed through my mind how silly we must look.

Afterwards we were red-faced and teary, like drunks. "You have the sticks?" I said and Edith nodded. When we left the shed, she raised the two halves, now joined into one. "We have to stay sisters together," she said, "and not show the cracks." Then we hugged.

When she heard what had happened, Mum surprised us.

Edith told her over breakfast after Dad had gone to work. She dropped it in as an aside, expecting nothing. "Back of the legs," she said, glancing at me.

I kept eating. I wasn't going to show how I felt.

"Six times."

I shook my head. "Five."

Edith repeated her figure. "Not that it matters," she added, quickly staring at Mum, who hadn't reacted.

Grace put down her cup. "Five times?" Before we could answer she pushed her plate to one side, gently. "Is it true?" she asked, turning to me. When I nodded, she checked the back of my legs and stood up. "I might have guessed," she said, waving both hands. "Go now. I'll see to it."

As I left, she stopped me. "It won't happen again, depend on it." Her voice had dropped to a whisper. I was reminded of walking barefoot, stepping on hot sand. Behind that dreamy, soft-spoken smile my mum was ready to do battle.

That evening, what I saw through the doorway made me breathless. She was facing him over the dinner table, staring him down. When he tried to argue she held up her hand. "I will leave," she warned. The three words, said slowly, shocked me.

"You what?"

"I-will-leave."

He put down his fork. "Talk sense, woman."

"And I'll take them with me."

"You're kidding."

"And *this* is why," she said, holding up the belt.

"What—"

"So, *Don't.*"

"Who's been telling tales?"

"The marks."

"What marks?"

"I've seen them."

"And?"

"And so will everyone else. When we leave."

"You can't do that."

"Unless you stop, I will."

His shoulders dropped. "What's the matter woman?" he grumbled. It seemed, at that moment, I shouldn't be listening. I can still hear her reply. "You, James Hammond. That's what's the matter."

Even now I wonder if I made it up. There's a voice inside that keeps telling me it's not so. Mind, something like that must have been said, but I'm not quite sure how much. Anyway, whatever they said it was a turning point. After that I do have a memory, listening from upstairs, of them arguing, often. First him niggling and shouting, followed by her saying no. Then he'd go silent or out into the yard, grumbling. Between them it was a raw, blustery, back-and-forth business, carrying on for years. Like a fight between armies. Or the sea when it's dangerous.

# THREE

Cass Lavender was old for her age. Someone had once told her that she'd skipped three stages in growing up. She'd walked at one, talked soon after, wore glasses at six and now, at twelve going-on-thirteen she was writing her autobiography.

People called her *Super-Cass*, a name she earned by coming top in most subjects and turning in near-faultless performances in anything written.

And yet there was a gap inside, a kind of disengagement, as if she was about to jump up and dance but had thought better of it.

Her music was Mozart, studied in the head. When she moved on to Chopin, she was Sparky at keyboard with her piano talking back. "Play," she whispered, and her hands got busy. "Play, play," they said.

Cass remembered facts and figures like screenshots. They came without warning, appearing on the walls and ceilings like tickertape. At the flick of a switch they were there, then gone. Everything had its time and place. To her, life was a board game where the rules were being drawn up.

Words were her friends. They were in the habit of finding ideas. When things were difficult, they came to her rescue. Words were her protectors. Whatever she did was shaped by them.

At school Cass was all smiles. She was free-and-easy Cass, full of life, who took pride in being clever. It kept her away from the other self, the double-diligent girl who busied herself with study-ing and being oh-so adult when all she really wanted to do was to play, play, play …

♩ ♩ ♩

Matthew was lying low. After the Friendly Society word got around; there was chatter, rumour and talk behind doors that people like Miranda knew how to spread. At the gatherings he'd felt it: people were rating, examining, discussing his performance. The world was a glasshouse; a crowd had gathered; an accident had happened, or he was the wedding guest and the tale was beginning. Or simply that they'd caught him.

It pushed him back to his own worst moments: odd thoughts and embarrassments, things he'd rather blank. Words of course: body parts, obscenities, imprecations heard and stored for later, dictionaries, films in title; and those bare-wound memories that hurt when they touched him.

One such was the book, a library loan given by his parents. On the cover the words *Feelings: A Young Person's Guide*; inside, it was large print with diagrams and arrows. Produced offhand and presented without warning it had lain for days, after one quick flick through, at the back of a cupboard concealed inside a box. His purity was offend-ed. How could they suppose, he'd wondered soaking in the bath, that this was what he wanted? It all felt soapy; a thing he held away, out of modesty, squeezed behind flesh. And the book just drew attention. It was misplaced and unsightly, more than was required – monstrous, really that they should do it this way. And what he knew, he knew. Next to nothing. Better kept hidden then produced when asked for, passed back unread.

Another was the pictures, grainy and bordered, stored beneath his underwear and shifted often, showing women in costumes posing on the beach. Cut from newspapers their expressions said it all: soft-cheeked, fruity, or barefaced and full-on, they were his encounters;

playmates he spoke to all night, in a clench. Like the early morning girl watched for at the bus stop, the smart one with beret; or the girl three doors down: Madonna behind curtains. Then the doorway secretary plumped up in skirts, the face-girls at counters, the girls at parties wearing black line and red.

And he wished he could approach them, show he'd got the knack, the words that smoothed the way. If only he could do it, put aside the stops and starts and random hesitations, speak clear and true and hold down his blushes for fear of going wrong. Because between him and asking out girls stood a sense of being tarnished, of bad faith and belittlement and pitying glances. Those things he'd been told, or overheard in classrooms with fingers poking desk holes and questions in corners and words he didn't know. Tips for how to do it with big leery *did-yous*? and *dare-yous*? and talk of all the way. And behind that the drift, the sense of something wished for, in a world kept under where the greatness of his longing, and efforts not to show it, would earn its own reward.

He wanted to be decent. If there was a God – something he doubted, but sometimes felt imminent – he wanted to do things on the level, be upstanding and go with girls cleanly, without a second thought. He'd do what was allowed, and his passion and sufficiency would make him whole. In any case he was different and believed in being straight. He'd share and give himself, unguarded before God. It should be simple service.

Then at fifteen his first girl had happened. Or at least he'd seen her – short and assured with girl-round features and big-waved hairdo – and followed her once to a house on its own: a grey-brown semi with unclipped borders and off-yellow porch lights. Seen there at the door, she'd drawn out a key; it shone like a coin.

While passing, he kept his head down, disguised as a traveller moving through. But when he checked back from the corner the porch was empty and the girl, if she existed, had spirited into air.

For months he'd followed, picturing her on buses arriving at odd moments, then circling to the girls' school where she joined with those around, fused into gym slips, hair bands, white and black cottons and grip-marks on flesh. Her life was his: gifted with awareness, quiet in corners where she sat reading Keats, or jumpy and hair-spread, running the track. And how well he knew her! Brown collar up, hands behind her back, curl on forehead – then pictured in her house, downstairs on her own, rising to the landing and into her room. And there he stopped; watching and hoping, not really daring.

And once – once only – he'd had a chance to speak at the end-of-year party, gathered in a hall with her there, bright and shiny in heels and a dress.

And he'd wondered what to say, what line to take; how to approach and talk as required and how to follow up. Always there were codes and things expected. He'd stepped up to audition only to go blank.

All of which, when he looked back now, seemed rather foolish, a life he'd left behind. He'd been without *it* or any kind of front. And he wondered as he and Paul sat about in common rooms talking of image and being on the scene, how much he showed his boyish inexperience, the things he didn't do.

At the gatherings he was careful; he was Mr Nice Guy with something now to prove. Good with people, he tuned in, he accommodated and brewed up coffee. There to give support, he *supposed* and listened and made himself willing, to score against Miranda.

Then Sally came to visit. She arrived without warning, calling her name as she entered. Wide-faced and curious, her colour was up. She looked around quickly as if it were a shop. "Hi guys, just me."

Matthew greeted; surprise made him watchful, showing nothing. Paul, on the other side talking to Theresa, appeared not to notice.

Their visitor, speaking nicely, checked herself in then sat, hands together. Her hair fell in ringlets, rich brown to russet, swept around one shoulder and forward to her breasts. Broad-hipped and busty, she filled the chair. When Matthew suggested drinks, she was happy to have coffee. She thanked him when he delivered, stirring her cup vigorously. When asked for her news she frowned. She'd been so busy, back home briefly, things had happened – major, rather – and though she didn't want to trouble him (here she went silent, glancing at the table) she'd just come round to talk.

Matthew followed carefully, limiting his response. Though delivered deadpan, his interest seemed to satisfy. They talked for a while about deadlines for essays and gossip going around, progressing to matters personal. When Matthew mentioned home, Sally took him up. She wanted to know more. "I've been thinking," she asked pronouncing slowly, "did you – do you – have someone?" She waited then clarified with a prompt, "I mean, before you came here?"

"Well, I don't know whether I'd call it that ..."

"Together. *With* someone."

"Like them?" Matthew said, pointing to Paul and Theresa who had fallen asleep on the bed. Before she could answer he added, "You could say – that's one way of looking at it."

"I thought so."

"But it's not that simple."

Sally established, nodding as audience, that the girl wasn't current. "Did she like you?"

"I'm ... I don't really think so."

"I think she loved you."

Head to one side, Matthew considered; her words didn't touch him.

"And you?" said Sally. "How did you feel about her?"

"Well, several things. It's complicated."

"But you did *feel*?"

"Oh yes, a great deal. Too much perhaps."

"And did you love her?"

"Not that word. Not in that way."

"How then? Tell me."

His gaze searched the room: "Not love, really. A kind of embarrassment. Like I was someone else. An observer in a way, in a story."

Sally fixed him with a look. "I had someone, till last weekend. But it's over."

Matthew turned away, directing his gaze to a small side table positioned close by. The table was arranged with what he and Paul called "equipment". Leaning forward, he laid out a pair of cigarette papers, licking the edges to join them.

Sally persisted, "Will you tell me her name?"

"A name?" he replied, flaking tobacco and resin into his joint.

"Promise I won't repeat it."

Matthew continued, sticking the papers together then shaping one end to a wick. The other end he stuffed with a cut-down cigarette packet, coiled like a spring. Silence.

"Was she beautiful?"

"A bit, in a conventional kind of way." He fitted the joint like an inhaler to his lips and lit up. After sucking hard, he offered her the end. It was as if something hung in the balance and this might help.

Sally shook her head.

"You don't do that?"

"I can't," she said, moving to get up.

"You don't have to. Really, you don't. You can smoke or not smoke, it's up to you."

"Just can't." She looked at him strangely. "I mean I can, but not here, there are … reasons. Things have changed." She paused at the door, head on one side. "I need to talk." Her voice wavered, "Maybe tomorrow? You'll come round?"

"I can't either," he said then, leaning forward, corrected himself: "I mean I can, I'd like to, if …" Rising, he inhaled again and counted. At seven his expression cleared, releasing to a smile. On the outbreath he looked into her eyes. "I'll explain. Tomorrow. When I come round."

The next day, Matthew rose early. Sally's call and her open invitation had caught him by surprise. He needed to adjust, to get his head around what had happened and work out what to do. While she, it seemed, wanted conversation (which could mean bright-talk, book-talk or soul-talk about life) he'd things to get on with. What his father would call real-life business.

Sitting at his desk, he went through his plans, listing options and ticking off his *dues*. Overdues mainly: books to the library, money to his friends, ideas for writing, plans for leaving home.

And behind that an awareness of things on the move, of paths leading off, and a slightly breathless feeling that he'd lost direction, arriving at a viewpoint where it all fell away.

In any case he decided, as he pulled back to his papers, there were things now pressing: an essay only just started, quotes to find somewhere, coffee for recovery, and feeling comfortable.

The essay was 5,000 on the English novel: its beginnings, a few choice examples and subsequent development in Fielding, Richardson and Defoe. By now it was well past deadline, so much so that its arrival – promised, predicted and given out as imminent – had become an act of faith. "It's in the picture," was the mantra that he'd offered at seminars, meaning it was visible, like the artist's signature, if you knew where to look. At first his tutor had smiled when she asked what he'd done, but slowly she'd hardened, moving from puzzlement and questioning glances through hard-faced appraisals, to arrive at dead-pan and long-held stares. Now, when he reported on progress she simply looked.

But Sally had believed him. They were both free spirits. She'd even echoed his formulation, declaring, "It's in there somewhere," as if she understood.

So, Matthew, though only half awake, still felt he had the essay awaiting recovery stored in his head. It existed, like his own projected book, in a space marked Special, a theoretic ground out there at a distance where things were still in process. And like his book it felt better waiting, as a project, and could remain so forever, in sketch form and not quite attempted. For this was *his* time to do and be, without too much denial. It was also a breather; a break and necessary preparation to lead towards reckoning and end his putting off.

For by now, the essay was a must. Theresa had warned him: the shits would make him do.

Still hopeful but unsettled, Matthew considered. This was the actual, hard-edged like the window, a matter of focus. He glanced across the desk: its surface was littered, like his brain. There were books half-opened, pen tops and packets, notes in a bundle, with envelopes, dog-eared postcards and ink stains everywhere. Turning in his seat, he adjusted. He'd skimmed the books – which he counted as a plus – memorising plotlines, fixing on characters and jotting down thoughts. They were where to start: no crits or cribs, the writing on its own.

But other thoughts pushed in: minor irritations and flashes of unease over what might happen next. There was too much going on. He tried turning pages and shifting position then lounged, shuffling between papers. There were so many words: single words, phrases in brackets (and brackets within brackets), titles, word counts and unfinished introductions. But nothing developed.

He decided to use tactics. Standing, sipping coffee, he kept himself alert. He gazed out of the window counting students passing, then turned back to the room. The light on his side was a constant fascination: white to grey it shone like oil on canvas. On the other side was dark.

When he moved, he held his breath. At toilet breaks he yawned and gazed in the mirror, reviewing things with Sally. She represented – what? Maybe just friendship with no real passion, a kind of holding off. Though the other thing, the flesh thing, left him feeling dazed. Was Sally all she seemed? And was she good enough? In any case, supposing he declared, what markers did he have and had anything really happened?

Returning to his desk, he observed his room-mates. Still asleep, they'd separated further. There were shifts and sighs, arms out, heads back and long exhalations. It was as if they were extras playing dead whose breathing gave them away. Because, fond as he was, he found them sometimes hard to live with. Wonderful certainly, but also quite distant. Or to put it another way, like Jay they seemed to run their lives by signals from above. In fact, he wondered sometimes just what happened between them. At the moment things were on, meaning hours sat together, silent on bed ends, or long-term in the dining hall where they played out an image: pure inaction, in a manner chosen. They were the steadies, and by their stillness they impressed.

Still his essay stalled.

What was it, he wondered, drawing around his thumb. Of course, there was *that* – here he viewed a dark-haired girl on the walkway – but not, he'd decided, for characters such as him. In any case it was a bother, with too much undercover, a thing so private he'd rather go without.

He held up his thumb sketch. It was see-though like a watermark; flesh made paper. A thought occurred: should he take a break, go to Sally's early and make trial of what she'd said? He pictured her now, brown-eyed and alert, opening the door. "Yes," she'd say and they'd walk out into landscape: together in sunlight, like a poem from a book. Boy meets girl with nothing more to say.

"Matt."

Paul's call surprised him. Replying in kind he moved back from his desk. The mood had passed, his essay could wait.

In the other half of the room, Paul and Theresa had surfaced, switching on a lamp and propping themselves on vertical pillows. Vaguely ceremonial, they sat facing forward with Paul rolling up and Theresa watching. Their pose reminded him of photos in a book. There was something archaeological about them, as if they were a dynasty coupled – or at least as much coupled as cool would allow.

"Sleep OK?" asked Paul, stretching and pulling on a vest.

Matthew said he had. He returned Theresa's greeting with a slight hesitation; there were wishes still dormant, words unsaid. One day perhaps.

Soon Paul was getting up. Theresa followed, dressing by arrangement in a break between coffees while Matthew went shopping. As he walked, he replayed the latest gathering, his schoolboy fancy, the book still to write. Reaching the shop, he picked up some powdered milk and white sliced bread then returned, noticing the crocuses as he skirted the lake. He took his time, walking the long way, toying into thought. *In case*, of course … though if he was honest, they'd never really cleared it. Because when Theresa stayed there was usually some moment, a thing done in blackness, and her gasps held down, as if underwater. Better, he thought, as he paced the walkway, if he lived his own life and switched off his thoughts. In any case he'd learned now how to position, to do and show and put himself around.

On his return Theresa was laying out cards and Paul was rolling up.

"Kept this back," his friend said, peering like an artisan at a black, pebble-sized lump balanced on a spoon. "Best Moroccan Gold." Watching carefully, Paul lit a candle and grilled it from below. "Blow your head off," he muttered, testing its bouquet. The lump glowed yellow then cooled through lilac and brown to unpolished jet. As it cooled, Paul passed one hand over, testing. He waited, rocking to and fro, before sprinkling it in twists on a bed of tobacco. Finally, he folded it in and spread what remained, smoothed to the edges like breadcrumbs.

Taking the papers, he licked and sealed, lit it from the candle and passed it around. "House special," he said.

An offhand Theresa breathed in and held, then passed it to Matthew, who steadied himself, before inhaling deeply. Something dark and blue travelled down inside him. Already he was tunnelling, diving into cool, yet always there was pressure, the hand sweats and tingles, the fear of going under.

The joint passed around. Each time he accepted Matthew breathed in, sinking further. Level by level he dropped. His friends by now were fitted out with halos, both curious, child-like and quietly comedic. They'd only just entered, blown in by a gale. He saw them from a distance through one-way glass; they were all at odd angles, drawn out of shape. He knew them well. Free spirits he loved.

Whiteness filled him. His head, which was full hard and expanded, became see-through, almost painful, like the sun. A cold sun, seen through a veil, hung there in the room. He smiled at the puppets with their mouths pushed wide, and hands that twitched. Beautiful and ludicrous, their gestures were well-meant; they amused him.

Now he was returning, his friends' voices echoed, booming underwater. Grey, shifting threads held him safe. There was relief as after rain, and something universal. Everything was in place. The sun returned, milk-white and hazed; brightness filled him, his bubble was climbing … any moment now his face would pop out, the waves would dance and he'd swim back shoreward.

His mind came back. Here he was, studying. Of course, he knew it all, it made perfect sense. There was nothing could touch him. The essay didn't matter; his novel was unwritten; Sally could wait.

# FOUR

When I look back, being a Hammond was like sitting on the beach watching the sea. We did that a lot. Most of the time it was wet or windy, but then there'd be a shift and the sun would come out. There was always some change, something you hadn't bargained for. One minute wild, the next calm, you never quite knew.

But whatever the weather we stuck it out. And afterwards, when we trooped back to have tea, I remember the warmth in the room.

So being a Hammond wasn't always bad. There were times we were together, weekends mainly, when family took over. Even when we argued, we knew what came next. When Dad was angry Edith and I backed each other up, and when he was happy it brought us close. Then he was little-boy-playful, at least on the surface. "Chop, chop," he'd say, popping his head around the kitchen door. But behind his words I could tell he wanted something. It was as if he was on stage, and he needed notice. "Watch me cutting," he said, beckoning us to the door. I went first, with Edith behind me. It was our job to look and his to show. So we stood on the step as he worked, splitting the logs. "If I chop a log in half, then chop again into four, then into eight," he called, "how many chops to make a million?"

Of course, I didn't know and Edith wasn't interested. It was one of his number games, like dealing cards, throwing dice or working out distances. "Powers of two?" he beamed and I smiled back as if I knew the answer.

I remember how I smiled too when he showed me how to chop. A stiff, pasted-on grin with a hint of panic. That was later, when Edith and Mum had gone to the shops. "Like this," he said, cupping his hands around mine. He'd jammed the axe, head down into wood. "Lift," he said quietly, as we rocked back together. I could feel the weight, straining through his arms. "Now down," he said.

When the log struck concrete, it felt like being strapped. The crack came first then the bang, juddering my whole body. "Again," he called as he hauled back and swung. This time the blow was red hot. I was climbing the stairs, straining beyond reach. "One more," he hollered, swinging. There was a splitting, tearing noise and the sound of metal, sparking. The blade hit concrete and the log rolled open. "No," I cried, shaking. "No, Dad, no."

He grinned, "That's you done then?" There was a sudden drop in feeling.

I nodded.

"Now, let's see." He walked me back to sit on the step. "You all right?" he asked, crouching. His voice had gone quiet. I could feel his breath on my cheek and for a moment we were close.

He placed a hand on my forehead then straightened. "You'll manage," he said, picking up his axe. Swinging it like a hammer, he split the logs. Every so often he'd stop and check I was watching.

When Mum and Edith came back, the wood was chopped, Dad was in the shed stacking it, and I was in the yard, sweeping. I was gripping the broom handle hard, like a walking stick. In my mind his hands were closed around mine. I could still feel the axe blows running up my arms.

I remember him around the house, unscrewing doors, mending chairs, building cupboards. "Jack's got the knack," he'd say and ladder his way up to the gable, where he'd bang in nails singing *Clementine*. He'd have a go at anything, cleaning out chimneys and digging drains. And once, when a pipe burst, he re-plumbed the whole bathroom, working overnight. That was when he was happiest. Making plans, crawling into corners or exploring the loft. What he needed was jobs, lots of them.

It was later that I put together a very different Jack, talking to his foreman.

36

Dad was a porter at the docks. He was on casual, waiting for work unloading cargo and stacking wagons. But to be hanging around spare made him twitchy. He was there to get on with it. Everyone knew him. He was the small, short-haired man arguing with his mates. The one they called Jack Sprat but behind his back, Bolshy. The truth is they wanted rid of him. But for him it was all cat and mouse. At home he'd put on panto-act voices where he'd raise one eyebrow then fix the wall with a hard stare. "You reckon," he'd say, unsmiling. Or he'd step up to us, snorting and snapping his fingers. Then he'd walk away, head high, daring anyone to follow.

What I know now is that the docks put him down. He was given a number, told to get cracking and paid in tokens. When I think of him like that, I see him as he was. A short man in a black and white photo, hands in pockets, waiting by the wall. He stands on his own with puddles at his feet. Behind him are the cranes and a Union Jack. When I look, I feel his loneliness.

Then Edith met a boy. His name was Reg, he was older, and he lived with his parents. Reg had a sharp squirrel-like face, bleary eyes and a pencil moustache. His second name was Anthony, his last was Jones, and when he came round we were special. Suddenly we were going out, accompanied by Mr R A Jones. He'd escort Edith, usually in a line with Mum and me, as VIPs on parade. What I didn't really realise was how awkward he felt. There was a deliberate slowness about him. I think he was all at sea, and feeling it.

One day we were out walking, Reg, Edith and me. It was late afternoon and we'd gone beyond the seafront, passing up a slope to the fairground. We knew we were out of bounds, but the risk didn't matter. This was our fancy-free moment and we weren't going to lose it.

When the fair came, it brought in what Dad called the riff-raff. They were the grubby, weather-beaten types who stood by watching as people spun and dived and squealed. You could tell by their silence that they weren't that bothered. They wore chains about their necks and greased their hair. Sometimes they smoked, stubbing out their rollups in sand. Their hands were fidgety but their eyes were still and calm. They seemed to be waiting for something to happen.

We walked around chit-chatting, having a good look. We had the fair pretty much to ourselves. I can hear us now, laughing and delivering speeches about what we planned to do. Edith was the loudest. Her talk was for everyone, but I'd a feeling it was directed at Reg. She talked about how we'd make our names, the places we'd go and how we'd spend our money.

It was when we were passing by a tent that a man stepped into our path. "Who's this?" he asked, nodding towards Reg. He was short and pale and looked at us oddly, with a stuck-on kind of grin. For a second I was thrown until I heard his voice. "Stephen," I said, without thinking. "What are you doing here?"

As I said it, I realised this was my brother. He was standing there, larger than life. Like the Prodigal Son he'd returned, and I was glad.

Stephen glared. I could feel he was shaky underneath. "Who's he?" he said. His question seemed to hang in the air, blocking our path.

Behind him, the fairground was busier now. There was music, a dog barking and the rattle of an engine starting up.

"Please Stephen, don't speak like that," I said, wishing I could hug him. I remembered him at home, a bright-faced boy with a quick, jumpy manner who questioned everything.

Edith cut in. "Reg is a friend, and a lot better mannered than you'll ever be."

"And what does *Dad* say about him?"

"He doesn't say anything. Reg is with us, part of the family."

Stephen's lip curled. "Call yourself a family? Him shouting and you dodging, is that what family means?"

"But you're different, I suppose?"

The fairground behind was busier now. Things were moving. There were bangs and shouts, engines revving up, and a lumbering, scraping, grinding noise of metal on stone.

"Not a Hammond," he said, pushing out his chin. Before Edith could speak, he fixed her with a stare. "No, don't say anything. Come this way, I'll show you."

What happened next seems strange, even today. I remember him leading along a cinder track between oil cans and tents into a fenced-off area. In the middle were three large tractors, with their engines running. "The powerhouse," he said, shouting over the noise.

"And those generators," he added, pointing towards three metal boxes, "are mine. I fixed 'em up." He crouched down, watching the movement of three thick metal belts. They stretched across the area like washing lines.

"And I keep 'em on the go," he said, rising. He didn't seem bothered by the smell of petrol and the rattling, chugging sounds that filled our ears.

"Stephen, what're you doing here?" I called.

"Doing? Everything," he said, waving his hand around the area.

"Why aren't you with us?"

"I'm *wanted* here."

"But you have to come home."

"This's where I live," he said, pointing around. "I drive, fix everything, and I put up these ..." At the end of the compound there was a line of wooden boxes that looked like beach huts.

"You *live* here?" asked Edith as he led us to the huts.

Stephen glowered.

She laughed. "You built this rabbity hutch thing?"

His eyes were set hard and his chin was jutting forward.

"And you call that home?"

I can hear his answer, now. It came out harshly, or perhaps it was the machine, because suddenly he was yelling. I heard the word *don't* and saw him raise his arm. Then he threw back the door to one of the huts. "Look," he cried, "that's home." On the inside was a bunk bed, a basin with a mirror and a fold-up chair. At the back I saw a small, barred window and a soapbox table. It was like a prison cell.

But what struck me straightaway was the colour. Across the floor, all around the walls and right across the ceiling the hut was covered in a strange, oily, glowing purple. It looked like the inside of a cave. Or the sea on a storm day, seen from below.

# FIVE

At 14 Mia Lavender went through a phase where she called herself *Cat*. It was all part of her my-human-bugs-me feelings. She was on the side of the wild things.

As *Mia-Ow!* she pictured herself as an all-weather feline, stalking in the garden. Out there was her patch, her Super Furry Animals territory where she danced with fleas and hopped with birds and burrowed with worms. It was squirmy and squiggly and full of chewy stuff.

On other days Mia explored her life as someone else. When she was like that the world was an experiment where the answers could be surprising.

For instance, when she cut stems to dunk them in water – and kept them there, sitting on her windowsill for weeks. She watched how they sprouted. Their grey, thread-like bodies made her shiver. Once grown they sprouted, like frog legs. They were her *gist*, her weird inside. At times like that she was close to what the textbook called a self-replicating being.

For Mia, living like that made her aware of things unseen. That was when she walked alone in the dark, hearing the calls. Whatever made those ghostie noises, their world was different. Their gibberings and twitterings came from far off. They were her guides.

♯ ♯ ♯

"You came," said Sally, "as required."

Matthew smiled. It was late afternoon ten days later and they were sitting alone in the *Old Town Record Shop* taking bites out of samosas on white cardboard plates. He'd carried them up three flights of stairs, together with carrot cake, an earthenware salad bowl and two mugs of tea. The chairs were canvas, the table was wood, and the tray he'd used, edge-taped in black over bright red plastic, was propped against pipes. Tape loop music was ascending from the shop below where, five minutes earlier, Sally had led up in sandals and a midi, carrying a shiny pink handbag. Her voice had gone ahead, talking to the stair-head, throwing out thoughts about horses. As she climbed her calves shook, looking rather cold. Her exposed flesh was pale and freckled like hazelnut ice.

"I did," confirmed Matthew. "At your service ma'am."

This was their third old town meeting. They'd started going out after Matthew had visited, arriving early evening at her room. The warmth of her welcome had surprised him. It was, she said, just the right thing. Curled up in the chair, she'd told him what she was like: she was sad, she was happy, anyone could read her. Though she didn't go too far – for life was private, not a thing of gossip, at least for girls like her – she hoped he understood.

They'd talked till late then walked out by the lake. Side by side they looked, without touching. Here it was silent, the air was chill, and the night sky was cloudless. A fine haze of stars was visible south-ward, with the moon at quarter. The lake was very still.

They'd stopped by the bridge gazing east. On the walkway borders ice-feather patches had spread; behind them a bird rustled in the bushes. Further off an engine was revving. A faint pink glow, almost ashen, was rimming the horizon.

Sally, who was coatless, shivered. In the half-dark Matthew could distinguish an outline, and a thickness of hair falling to her breasts. She was leaning forward, like a swimmer over water. Again, she shivered. Realising, he removed his jacket and hung it around her shoulders.

When they parted at her door, she passed back the jacket and thanked him. The lining was still hollowed out. All the way back, as he walked into dawn, the jacket felt air-soft and warm.

It was Sally's idea to meet in town. She didn't want the attention and stories, the not-nice assumptions. It would keep them as they were, free of implications, above all that. Matthew was agreeable. He'd already noticed a change in Sally, the mask had slipped and her doubts were on show. There was something rather boyish about her talk of riding races, a family she distrusted, her need to go apart. "Am I posh," she'd asked him that first night, "nose in the air, really?" He had to tell.

But now, meeting in town, she was happier. Outside campus there was life, separate and without pretence. Town was an island on its own, without watchers, where she could tell him what she wanted.

"The record shop's the sort of place," said Matthew, "where no one's bothered."

Sally, who was dipping into salad, looked across the table. "Who do you suppose might come here, Matt?"

"You, me, it's very select. A cast list of two."

"But we can't really be the only ones all day, every day." She glanced around at the multi-coloured posters lining the walls. With so much warmth and colour and drama, the world surprised her. "I mean, how can you explain it?"

"It's always been like this."

"With no one, absolutely no one?"

"Well, occasional freaks, travellers, poets."

"One wonders how they survive."

Matthew considered a few suggestions but decided not to say. He remembered Jay and his dog. "You don't mean that," she'd said, and he'd noticed her finality, her way of cutting off, while not perhaps intending. And here she was, woman-smooth and oblivious, looking beautiful.

They ate in silence. Sally sampled carefully, sorting what she fancied, consuming the best and banishing the discards to her plate edge. Matthew ate quickly without much attention.

Sally looked up. "Are you on your cake already?"

Matthew nodded, pointing to his mouth.

"Oh, I see," she said, sounding a bit off.

"You happy?" he asked when he'd swallowed. "You're not put out?"

Sally equivocated.

He tested again: happy or not?

Sally stared down at her plate.

"Because I can, you know, go slower," he continued, "but you have to say. I can't do without saying."

"Of course," she said, coyly, "we all need things said."

No answer presented; it seemed perhaps there wasn't an issue. Like a break in the music the mood passed over.

Sally finished eating and leaned back in her chair. Something about being here, she said slowly, felt quite strange. She panned around the room and her eyes were drawn to one large poster. Pointing, she asked him what he thought. Matthew, who'd already noticed it, picked up a napkin and polished his glasses. His expression was thoughtful; he was his own man.

"Do you understand it?" she asked.

Matthew stood up. The poster was white at centre, broadening into hot-red then yellow, then black. Above the middle, an exploding ball was rising from a stupa. Beyond that the orange-red sun was throwing out circles of cupids, dancing genii and witches on horses. A thick black border acted as a frame.

"I've seen it before. I believe it's a group, or maybe it's a picture. Not sure which."

Sally seemed quite surprised. So, whose idea was it then? Did it go by a name?

Adjusting his glasses, Matthew stepped closer. There were words mixed in with the wash of colour, repeated in capitals across the upper border. Speaking slowly, he read them out: "Hapshash and the Coloured Coat featuring the human host and the heavy metal kids."

"What on earth does that mean?"

"It's a kind of joke."

"Do you like it?"

"Depends how you look at it." He glanced from her to the picture. She'd taken on an air of being blocked or constrained, an edginess of attention as if she'd been ignored. It reminded him of talking politics with parents.

"But you don't," he said, staring at a point just above her head.

"Don't what?"

"Like it." Suddenly he turned impish. "But I've an idea, we could try something." In response to her question he pushed two chairs to the centre of the room. "It's a viewing," he said, placing them apart, both facing the poster, "You look, and say."

Sally wasn't sure, she needed explanation.

"It's a crit. You eyeball the picture for, let's say, half a minute then give an opinion."

At his insistence Sally came forward to occupy a chair. Moving stiffly, she said she wasn't certain … perhaps another time? Using his best voice, Matthew guided. He was the performer calling from a stage. Twice she sat then rose, flicking back her hair and turning her eyes to the stairs. Like a horse in a starting-box, she had to be coaxed.

"Thirty seconds," he said, sitting down beside her, "then we tell all. Just what we saw. But no bullshit, as rude as you like."

Their first viewing ended after twenty seconds with Sally ducking out. "I can't," she said, giggling, "no thoughts at all." The second viewing she was silent while Matthew took over, speaking about highs and lows, Ginsberg, individuation and believing in fairies.

"You make it sound deep," she said when he'd finished. "But I'm not sure you believe a word of it. Maybe it's just a noise, something big and grand to make people sit up."

Matthew considered. "It could be me," he smiled wryly, "doing purple."

It seemed she understood.

"Now your turn," he said. "And don't mind me, just say what comes. The first thing that pops into your head."

Sally shivered. "I can't."

"Give it a try."

"No, no," she answered, glancing towards the staircase, "the thoughts won't come."

"Think of it as fun. I won't say a word … Promise."

Sally rose and crossed to the window. "I wish it was that simple," she said, gazing at the rooftops. "We all just stand up and say our piece, out on the surface, over and done with. No secrets, like you." She turned to show profile.

Matthew breathed in sharply,

"I know," she continued, pouting, "*you* think I'm being girlie."

Matthew denied.

Sally crossed back to confront the poster. Her colour was up. "And I don't really like this *thing*." She turned about the room. "It's the worst picture here, awful." In the silence that followed she stepped along the wall, examining, as if it were a line-up. "I like this one … this's so-so … it'll do. Oh God, that's dreadful. Yes, yes … hmm interesting," continuing to the end where she paused.

Camera-like, Matthew's eyes followed every movement.

"Have you seen these?" she asked him, turning. On the bench, at the end, was a collection of wooden reliefs, hand-size and unfinished. They lay there in heaps, like unused dominos. Picking up a few, she crossed to the table and lined them up. Matthew sat opposite, content to play audience. "Animals," she said, pointing and naming. Some she paused at where the carving was worn, others she held up, a few she finger-traced like artefacts from a dig, in the end she named them all.

Matthew was impressed. "I see you know your species."

Sally agreed.

"And you like them, yes?"

She smiled.

"And they like you?"

Child-like, she nodded. Matthew looked. His gaze was accepted. Eye to eye for the first time, he felt himself blushing.

They both glanced away.

"What colour is my hair?" asked Sally quickly. "I need your opinion."

Matthew stared.

"Is it red or brown?" she added, tugging out her hair grips and unwinding her hair.

Matthew noticed the curve of her neck and her well-rounded face. Her arm was uplifted as if she'd been bathing.

45

"What would you say?" she continued as her ringlets fell below her shoulders.

"Red …" he said, thinking coral, rosewood, ginger.

"You can touch it, if you want to." Her large brown eyes were turned towards the window.

Matthew reached out, drawing his fingers slowly down to the hair-ends. He noticed her bra-cups showing. "I want to," he said.

Sally let him stroke then, shifting to one side, excused herself. Sliding from her chair she crossed to the stairs and suggested that they go. Before they left, she picked up one of the animals, touched it to her lips and slipped it quietly into her shiny pink handbag.

♪ ♪ ♪

All that spring Matthew and Sally met up. Usually twice a week, they hung out in town, beginning at the record shop. Being there was special, and meeting freely on their own terms, well, what could be simpler or better? They were alone in a you-me space they called their own, where everything mattered.

Physically they were shy; a doubt lay between them. To reach out and touch – how certain was it? Better to take time, to meet and talk; and who cared anyway what they did? Like tourists they were free. And each time they met there was something just ahead, a quiet crossing path and road not travelled where they stepped out on their own.

Some days in the morning if the record shop wasn't open, they'd walk down shopping streets and alleyways, past half-timbered buildings and old stone walls. They'd wander together along pavements with steps down to basements, or stop in church squares with plaques over doors and wrought iron gates. Giving themselves up to whim and inclination, they'd view The Minster, or pass along the walls behind school and guildhall, then pause by a kiosk to buy a bag of sweets. The town was their playground where they'd peer over walls at secret gardens then sightsee around the market looking at the cheese rounds and seafood behind glass.

On days when it rained, they sheltered in the library and viewed The Great Hall – briefly, in passing, because this was university. On dry days there were gardens, now showing bulbs, where they sat on benches or climbed the castle mound; while cold days were for cinema or walking the arcades.

Their favourite was the river, downstream and tree-lined, at a spot beyond the town. Here they walked close, sometimes nearly touching.

"The water's up," said Matthew one day as they followed the towpath beneath a bridge. Beside them as they walked the river was brown, churning and backing as it swept beyond the arches. On one side there was a wire mesh fence and a derelict factory, on the other, ivy over brickwork and a warehouse with a crane.

They continued some distance in silence. Sally was in black, tight across her chest, with boots and knitted skirt and a sheepskin on her shoulders. Matthew wore his hair swept back, barefaced and plain in steel-framed glasses. Sally advanced quickly, busily; Matthew moved in strides.

"I can tell," Sally said, "you like the river high." Her voice was uppercase, with emphasis.

"True. It's kinda whoosh-whoosh. Boyish."

They arrived at a section where the river's continuous roar echoed between walls, mingling with their words. Sally pointed to some splintered wood turning in the flow: "You see what happens when it rains."

"That's something."

She advanced to the bank. "But isn't it dangerous? What if you fell in?"

"Me? I can't swim."

"I meant *one*, if someone fell in."

"I believe people have. Quite a few in fact … Some not by accident. Suicides."

Sally's eyes searched the path. "That's so awful. When you think, we've walked here and not realised." Her face tightened and she caught onto a tree, tugging at a branch. "Do you know where they …?"

Matthew wasn't sure.

Sally was insistent. Where had he heard it?

Matthew gave it some thought – probably the papers.

"Because I'm not going anywhere without knowing," she declared, gripping the wood. "It's like stepping on someone's grave."

Matthew grimaced, looking around. The riverside was windswept, bare beneath the trees, green beside the water. To the left was a redbrick wall, behind were the bridges. A track ran ahead to a bend; beyond that the river widened, opening into fields. "But you always know really," he said quietly.

Pushing at her branch, Sally winced.

"I'm certain you can tell about places," he added. "It's a gut thing."

"Maybe for you."

"Because your body knows. If you listen."

"I'm not sure mine does."

"OK tell me now, have you ever shivered, I mean in *that* way, when you've been here?"

"Not that I'm aware of."

"Well then …" He added a few riders about rescues, the high rate of survival and a story of a dog, then looked towards the river and asked how she felt.

"A bit happier," she conceded, facing forward. "You've just about done it."

They walked on to the bend. He noticed her hand and wondered if he should hold it. It hung there like a blossom, white and unfolded, ready to be taken. Perhaps he should ask her? Or simply reach out and take what he could? He wondered, but Sally seemed oblivious and rather than disturb her he decided to wait. She seemed quite distant, wrapped up in this business about suicide. He regretted what he'd said.

Reaching the bend, they debated whether to go on, with Matthew willing but Sally uncertain. Now there was a gap; it all seemed weighted. In their minds they were part of something larger: a step they couldn't take.

A ray of sunlight struck weakly through the branches, gleaming on water. This was the town edge where the river went its way. Vein lines of silver shifted across grey.

Matthew checked again. To return now felt awkward; another walk, another stop, but nothing definite. It left him feeling vague and rather lost. He was, it seemed, exposed and unable to make progress – and he wondered how long it would carry on this way.

The sunlight strengthened; it shone off-white, spotting through the trees. For a moment it was ice-bright, then grey. A wind got up; light and tingling, it played against their faces. With it came The Minster bells, striking the hour. "Time we went," declared Sally, backing a few paces. Blown about her clothes, her hair showed red against black.

As Matthew followed, he noticed, set back in a corner, a small drift of daffodils with their heads bent forward. Around them, river water had flowed across the path, submerging the stems; they looked like castaways awaiting rescue. Touching Sally's arm, he took a breath. "I'll get those," he said, moving forward. In them he'd found an aim, a kind of rationale. It gave him purpose.

The pool was uneven and deeper than expected. As he pushed towards the centre an invisible obstruction caught against his toe. He stumbled before continuing, upright and careful. On reaching the daffodils he stooped, tugging them back and forth, as if he was pulling hair. "I wandered lonely," he called out, tightening his grip and pulling harder. The plants strained and coloured beneath his fingers. "When all at once," he declaimed head down, baring his teeth. He carried on reciting, dragging the plants in all directions like a dog on a lead. As he arrived at the words, "When on my couch I lie," a stem tore away and he stood back, swearing. Holding up his catch he checked for damage: three lime yellow heads showed above a mess of green. It seemed he'd had enough. As he waded shoreward, he held his trophy aloft calling the last stanza like a battle cry.

Arriving at Sally he held out the flowers. Straight-lipped and dutiful, he stood there waiting, like a runner with a torch. As he stood his jeans ran water.

She nodded her approval.

Ironic, he bowed and offered: "Then my heart with pleasure fills."

Sally accepted: "And dances with the daffodils."

# SIX

It's only now that I really see where it was heading.

At the time there were tide charts and bird flights and tracks in sand, but nothing that certain. One day was dry, the next was foggy. There'd be gales and rain then sudden warm patches when we'd sit out like tourists on the beach. But of course, whatever it was, it never lasted. The wind got up, someone would complain or something would break, and the trouble would start. I can still see us now. Mum and Dad fighting, Edith taking umbrage about something said, and me taking cover in the tent. It was like living in a war zone.

You have to see the funny side. There we were, struggling, like wasps in jam. In it, up to our necks. As if someone had shouted fire and we were pushing to get out. I call it all v all, fighting on all fronts.

Of course, at that age I didn't really see it. Not properly, not as it was. You could say it all washed over, or it only half-happened. It's like standing on rocks, watching a pool filling up. Something shifts as you touch the surface. Suddenly it's shivery and there are cold ripples around your hands. And you begin to wonder who's moving, you or the water. But then you glaze over and stop seeing anything and it all runs together, or it leaks through your fingers. You never quite know.

Now, where it was heading seems clear.

After a few days the fairground left and Stephen went with it. I'd given a man a letter for him. "Storm Boy?" he said, holding up the envelope, "I'll tell him." I noticed the nickname. Once, when he'd used it speaking to Mum there'd been trouble. Dad had overheard and had given him a talking-to, going on about pride and the family name. Stephen had turned red, saying he'd walk out. He said it twice, like he meant it, and kept on arguing. I thought there'd be a fight, but then Dad's voice fell. It was wrong, he said, to let down the family. He kept on talking about shame and upset, ending in silence. I think he was all choked up.

Looking back, I realise that's how he got his way. He'd switch without warning from angry to hurt and you never quite knew which he'd be. It's what I call the hot-cold treatment. And of course, he was soon back on the attack, picking on appearance and calling Stephen his "big mistake". It was all part of their long-running battle over clothes and football and drinking and nights out with friends. Everything Stephen wanted was always shouted down.

And the letter? I asked Stephen to write, giving my best friend's address.

For a month I heard nothing till a note came, saying he'd left the fair and gone travelling. What that meant I didn't find out until I got a postcard. Someone was paying him to dive into wrecks. I was surprised, but checked the writing. It was small and messy and sloped to one corner. I couldn't help noticing the picture on the other side. It showed a full moon rising over a liner. The ship, sailing on an ice-white sea, looked like the *Titanic*.

Another note came after a couple of months. It mentioned a few jobs that didn't last, like picking fruit and bailing hay. The note didn't warn me what would happen next.

It began one morning with our weekly coal delivery. The coal we used was dug from the beach. It was cheap and sludgy and came in sacks that leaked like paper bags. The coalman would hump them into the shed, tipping them out into a large tin bath. Then the coal would lie there draining, smelling of seawater. Later my dad shovelled the mixture into buckets to stand by the fire. When it burned it fizzed like sherbet.

That morning, when the lorry arrived, I heard shouting. When it started, I didn't take much notice. The alley was always full of tradesmen calling their wares. But this shouting was different, more of an argument at closing time. Thinking of the fairground, I stepped outside. There I saw Dad standing face to face with a new delivery man. At first, I wondered what was happening. I knew he had no time for coalmen. He'd said so often, calling them "no-goods" and "thickos", though I noticed he was jokey to their faces. But this wasn't him putting on an act. He was inches away from a short, muscly man with a pencil moustache. On both sides their chins were thrust forward and their eyes were glittery. It was when I heard the word *don't* shouted twice, I realised that the coalman was Stephen and they were squaring up.

My brother stepped away, twisting his arm to dig into a sack. His face was puffy, like a Guy Fawkes mask. "See this!" he called, scooping up a mixture of coal and sand. For a second I thought he was going to throw it, and my mind flashed back to play-fights on the beach. I saw the sand flying and the water splashing up. "Don't say anything!" Stephen shouted and then, quite unexpectedly, he ground the coal into his own forehead. "Don't!" he repeated, grabbing two more handfuls and smearing both cheeks. "Here," he said roughly, gripping a sack by the corners, "take it and burn it." He dumped the sack in front of Dad, scowling. Then he climbed into the cab, fired the engine and drove off.

The other thing that happened was Edith left.

It doesn't seem surprising now but at the time it was a shock. It began, as these things do, with a row. But this one was different, because it blew up over the kitchen table. Usually, at tea time Mum talked family and we'd be silent, while Dad made noises about work. But this time things were going well. Dad had just fixed a leak, and he and Mum were getting on. In fact, it almost seemed like somebody had staged it. We all had full cups, with a butter dish, scones on plates and home-made jam. It could have been tea at the vicarage.

"Dad," Edith said, "I want to tell you something. It's about Reg."

I wondered how she did it. Speaking like a teacher, straight into his face.

"Him? Can't it wait?"

"It needs to be now."

"Ah, but if I'm not suited ..."

"Dad, listen."

"Well, what about him?" he said, fingering his plate. He was in that sleepy-voiced mood where nothing seemed to matter.

"You have to get to know him, Dad."

That's when the surface began to break. "Why's that young lady?" he asked, pushing out his chin.

"Because he's a good man."

"Good-hearted, I'd say," put in Mum.

"You know, for sure," he said, curling his lip.

"Whatever *you* think," Edith said, "he's a friend."

"Him? Not to me he isn't."

Edith flushed. "Yes he is."

"How so?"

"You'll find out."

Dad looked around the table, checking our faces. "Find out what? You hiding something?"

"Nothing to hide," said Mum.

"What's this about then?"

"Me and him," called Edith, rising. Her voice was stiff and she was breathing hard. "We're engaged."

Dad turned white. "What ..."

"Jack," warned Mum, "don't go spoiling."

"Say again."

"I'm engaged, to Reginald."

"To *him*?"

"That's right."

"You serious?"

"That's her choice," cut in Mum. "Now leave it."

Putting down his head, he gripped the table. "She doesn't ask, just does, and you expect me to leave it? What happened to family, and to fathers?"

For a moment I thought he was ill. His face had stiffened and his voice had dropped.

"Dad, are you all right?" I asked.

Raising his head, he pointed at Edith. "It's you Edith Hammond that needs to leave it. Give up this stupid business. And now."

"He's my fiancé."

"And I'm your father."

"You want me to choose?"

"You can't."

"I can't ...?"

"You heard."

"But why can't I choose?"

"Because you're a Hammond."

Edith stood up. "I'm not anymore. That's over. I'm leaving."

I can still hear her saying it. The words came out tightly, cutting the air. She was looking straight into his face again.

"You go out that front door," he waved towards the hall, "and you don't come back ... ever."

"Ever?"

"That's right. Ever."

"Very well," she said, stepping out to the hallway. She was staring straight ahead.

Dad got up. His face had clouded and his hands were shaking. Mum got up too, blocking the doorway. In the hall behind her I glimpsed Edith, climbing the stairs.

"Jack," Mum cried, "let her go!" When he let out a threat, she pointed towards the yard. "The wood needs chopping."

Before he could reply she waved towards me. "And take Mary, she doesn't need this."

There was a pause, then his body seemed to fold. Like a storm at sea, it had all passed over. Reaching out, he led me to the door and sat me on the step.

"Watch, Mary," he said, quietly. "You and I, we can trust each other." As he drew out his axe, the last thing I remember was the sound of his breathing and the front door closing.

# SEVEN

Joe Lavender fronted a band called OUTASIGHT.

There were four of them: Suzi on drums, Lauren on lead guitar, Joe who sang, and Karl on bass.

Joe came on stage in a white robe decorated with squares and circles. His head was shaved.

When their music began, it was Suzi and Lauren who struck up. Joe took the mike, wrapping the lead around one arm and rolling his eyes as if he was having a seizure.

"I'm not me," he chanted, moving the mike so his voice came and went. "I'm inside, inside, inside."

"We're not ourselves," sang Suzi, harmonising.

"We're in orbit," put in Karl, in a slow robotic drawl.

It was then, or about then, that Joe usually started pacing the stage, pitching up in a wild falsetto.

For him, OUTASIGHT were The Bonzos crossed with Tangerine Dream and Joy Division.

At the end of the set Joe lay down on stage making tick-tock noises. Lauren and Karl joined him, chanting IT'S OUTASIGHT, IT'S OUTASIGHT.

Joe was shifting his outstretched limbs between two positions. He looked like Leonardo's Vitruvian Man.

Suzi kept drumming.

♯ ♯ ♯

The term end was approaching. All around campus there were phone calls and discussions, talk of seeing family, last-minute messages, essays being written, adverts for lifts. In a matter of days the lectures would end. There'd be final gatherings, addresses would be given, cases packed, kisses exchanged and the campus would go quiet.

Everyone had a story about what they'd get up to. For Paul it was blues nights and working in a record shop, for Theresa minding children and maybe Amsterdam, Jay would sleep, Sally aimed to ride and Matthew had his reading, his music and long poetic walks away from his parents.

And for Matthew in particular, the last few days needed to be special. "What will you remember," he asked Sally as they walked in the park, "about this term?"

Sally wasn't sure.

"Is it the walks?"

She gazed across the lawn and out towards the skyline, as if she was picturing them walking there together.

The sun was high, unseasonably hot, and a number of townies were sprawled on the grass. There were boys in shorts and girls in skirts, grouped in gangs, tangled as couples, or lain out side by side like sleepers. Matthew noticed one particularly self-absorbed couple where the boy had his hand inserted beneath the girl's blouse. His face was boy-blank and masterful. Every so often he applied his mouth to hers. She seemed not to notice.

Matthew pressed: "Which spot will you remember? The record shop? The river? The Minster maybe?"

Sally remained doubtful.

Again, he prompted.

She gazed downhill, frowning; they'd arrived at the terrace. From here there was a vista, taking in the flowerbeds, a few large trees, the old town walls and beyond them office blocks and the long curving roof of the steel-arched station.

"The Friendly Society."

Matthew pulled up. Sally, too, had halted, placing herself by some steps and a worn stone balustrade. Behind her he could see the self-absorbed couple.

"You liked that?"

"It was important."

He noticed how she stood; half directed forwards, half somewhere else. "I thought you lined up with Miranda."

"At the time I did." She dropped her eyes. "Miranda's a nice girl. You were very rude."

"So was she. But God, that preacher!"

"I think you both got rather carried away."

Matthew felt the sun warm against his neck. They were seated now on the steps, with Sally below him. The couple on the lawn lay side-on, squeezed together, the boy slightly higher. He was feeling flesh.

"I don't like bullshit."

Colouring, Sally wound one finger into a ringlet of hair. "I know," she echoed sadly. It was as if she'd set a task, some sort of trail for him to follow.

"I want—" said Matthew, looking directly at the couple behind her. The girl's flesh was showing, white around the back and midriff.

Sally, eyes down, appeared to tire. "It's all about feelings," she said, pausing. "Because feelings aren't straightforward. They're not always what you might *want*. They're more complicated. You see, I need to be – more myself – more unexpected if you like. To understand *me*, you'll need to listen."

The sun wavered slightly, fringed by cloud. The couple on the grass had shifted up, leaning on their elbows. Their faces had become Bacchic: fixed and calm and not quite human.

Sally rose and placed herself centre step, facing the view. "I need to walk," she said. "You can come if you like."

He agreed and they left, passing down the lawn towards the river and the route back to campus.

At first, they were together with Sally just ahead, walking quickly. With the sun now behind her, she appeared to be focused on her own shadow. Whatever she was feeling it wasn't fit to share. They passed by buildings with high stone walls, gateposts, carvings and patterns in wood, arriving at a church with boarded-up windows, set back from a shopping street in a small cobbled square. Here Sally did a turn. "You go on," she said, suddenly, "I need a break."

When Matthew offered to wait, Sally shook her head; it was better this way, she said. At her insistence he set off on foot, feeling as if he'd lost his way. They'd drifted and now, led by denial, stayed out too long. It reminded him of a high summer moment when he'd played all day between sea and sun, and the dizziness afterwards, staring blankly over bleached white sand.

Back at campus, people were clearing out. There were doors left open, bins in corridors, boots and sleeping bags in kitchens, stray socks everywhere, and messages in chalk on concrete and brick. Everyone felt it; a space had opened out; there was loss, there was drift. Marks on the carpet were evidence of clearance, walls had been stripped and windows opened. The common room was littered with paper-scrap cartoons, half-finished board games and felt tip scrawls on cork board and plaster. The notice boards were full: there were records up for sale, notices of lifts and holidays for two, adverts for festivals and Christian services and a collection of notes with handwritten messages saying *Help Me ... What Now?* and *How-Sad-I-Feel.* It had all become a show: a drama of withdrawal.

For some, like Matthew, it opened up a gap. Walking the lake, smoking or simply crashing out had kept him with his friends, in the moment. He knew them all, they were his family; their loss would set him back.

"Makes you think," he called out to Paul as they stood together, gazing across campus watching students leave.

They were at the top, side by side on the flat college roof. At Matthew's suggestion they'd dressed before coffee, climbed the back stairs and walked out to the view. From here they could see builders climbing ladders; a taxi drawing up, a girl on a bike; a cleaner, a porter, a gardener with a fork and ducks by the lake. Like a market-place Bruegel, it was crowded.

Paul, who was smoking, exhaled in stages. His large heavy face registered interest. "It's Jay," he said, nodding.

On the walkway below a tall, emaciated figure was plodding slowly uphill. Half-turned, he was dragging on the bar of a supermarket trolley. The trolley, which kept sticking, had odd-sized wheels and a length of metal rising like a flagpole at the back. It was piled up with clothes and assorted foodstuffs. Each time it stuck, Jay braced and threw himself forward. His eyes were fixed on a point just beyond his boots, showing nothing.

"Where's what's-his-name, that dog of his?" asked Matthew.

"You mean Alpha Centauri? They had to put him down."

"Overdose?"

Paul nodded.

By now Jay, blank-eyed and weary, had almost reached the top; his face was that of a hibernating animal.

Reaching his goal, Jay unhanded, then gazed off somewhere, considering. His expression was hieratic; it seemed he'd lost all connection. Leaning on a bollard he allowed things to happen.

The trolley began to roll. Gathering pace, it circled backwards and left the pavement, tilting sideways with one wheel ploughing into mud. Some fruit, some cereal, and an avalanche of pulses spilled across the ground.

From above Matthew called for Jay to do something. He laughed and he shivered; this was absurd. "Can you imagine?" he murmured. He entered, briefly, the mindset of Jay. Who was this man: madcap, bonehead or saint? And oddly, as he thought it, his mind went back to his own lost times, his long hours watching and waiting at the window for things that couldn't be …

Jay looked around; something had happened. Leaving the bollard, he returned to his trolley where he stood and listened. There were angels, laughter and people he knew, calling. Child-like and dazed, he followed their directions – *do this* they cried, *for me*. Gathering what he could, he sniffed and examined; he held it in his hands. Bending forward, he scooped up life: mud here, mud there, bean sprouts rotting, holes in plastic. On hands and knees he bowed down and tasted: bits of creation, portions of the whole. The world was all before him.

# EIGHT

The man at the station barrier was tall. His grey-blue eyes were deep-set and thoughtful; his face, thrust forward, was long-jawed and pained; his mouth, held firm, was dogmatic, and his expression, which was serious, hovered between enquiry and doubt. There was about him an element of command, or distance; he wasn't with the crowd. Standing tall behind others, with slicked back hair and black-framed glasses, he gazed towards a point beyond the platform. He'd business to attend to.

Mr Alan Lavender eyed his electroplated wristwatch: sixteen-thirty. Either the train or his timepiece was at fault. Looking upwards he followed a pattern of struts and girders, arched on top. The station was an achievement, Stevenson's finest. It went up like a cathedral, curved like a liner, echoed like a vault.

An announcement crackled and boomed like distant breakers. The words were inaudible. The air smelled of oil and newly-painted metal. Nesting birds were twittering on ledges. Out beyond the station a signal was green. A detached double page with newsprint and pictures blew across the line.

The train came into view; expanding quickly, it filled the station. As it entered, the platform vibrated and a high-pitched scraping ran along the line. Its weight could be felt closing the gap. Easing to a stop, it shuddered, the slam doors opened and bodies filled the platform.

When Matthew appeared Alan raised his umbrella, handle upwards as if to secure him. Their greeting was drowned by an announcer, welcoming passengers on The North East Pullman.

"Did you have a good journey then?" Mrs Lavender asked as they settled in the living room with three large cups of tea. She'd brought them on a tray with a pot in a cosy, a silver milk jug and a plate full of cakes and chocolate biscuits. As she lowered the tray to the knee-high table, Alan lit up. His cigarette was long and grainy and blue around the filter; his fingers were nicotine-yellow.

Matthew said a few casual words about his journey. Sitting on the stool that had been his since early childhood, his body sprawled like a puppet, dangling in all directions. Like Gulliver he'd grown, or his parents had shrunk. Now, in worn-down jeans and jacket with long brown hair, he looked more like a hermit than their son.

A discussion of journeys led to talk about line-works and Sunday services. Things it seemed were as bad as ever, if not worse. There was outrage in it – what governments didn't do and value for money – and behind the upset, a note of appeal.

"Eat up," Harriet urged, "you've got awfully thin."

Matthew aimed his gaze at the polished wood tabletop, arranging his food. Reaching and placing, he covered the plate with a Swiss roll plus several digestives and a few chocolate fingers. He wondered where to begin: a spread arranged nicely like a teashop window, or period photo.

When Alan asked about his studies, Matthew moon-gazed at the ceiling until Harriet asked him sharply if he'd heard.

"Things to do," said Matthew, sampling the Swiss roll.

The appeal turned uppity – what *had* he still to do?

"This and that."

So when would he do it?

"Don't worry. It'll get done."

And was he *sure* he was OK?

Matthew dropped his head and occupied himself breaking up biscuits.

A pause followed as his mother busied herself, pouring a second cup of tea. His father, leaning forward, lit another cigarette. The appeal returned as they talked about the weather, world events, worries and illnesses, with a voice tone that was needful, wanting better days.

For Matthew, the stool beneath him was something to hold on to. A small patch of space from which he could view them, an island of his own. Because already he was losing ground; there were details to attend to, timings and arrangements, facts they had to know, and a flood tide of enquiries about this-and-that business, all of it conducted with an edge of discomfort and a world-weary smile.

"I'll unpack," he said finally, glancing towards the door. His mother responded by pointing to the biscuits. When he refused, she tried more tea followed by coffee, then cocoa if he liked, and when that was declined, cake or scones. To reach the door he had to insist he'd had quite enough, ignore further offers and, picking up his backpack, head off his father's move to act as porter and carry it upstairs.

Next morning, he rose late. The curtains were undrawn and for a second he wondered if his mother had been in. Frowning slightly, he peered at his wristwatch then put on his dressing gown. Turning towards the window he paused. The view was to the north; it extended to the fields and a water tower. Closing to the glass he widened the angle: east and west. He checked around, gauging the sky, seeing the big picture. Although there were clouds, it was half sun and half grey, a canvas lightly shaded. Close up, on the outside, the paint had flaked, exposing patches of undercoat blue; some feet below the garden was sprouting, off-pink and creamy on blue-grey branches; beyond that there were roofs, with chimney-cowls and aerials. In the distance there was sun, beaming intermittently on a long straight road that led towards the horizon.

Dressing slowly, he checked his pockets before sliding the door over thick-pile carpet. Moving carefully, he descended, one hand out, holding the banisters. A mirror he passed showed an unshaven face with centre-parted hair. For an instant he was there unseen, a fly on the wall.

Entering the dining room was like stepping into custody; it felt both cold and crowded. The table was six-foot-long, with one leaf extended. An embroidered tablecloth, dotted with placemats, covered a fat brown felt. The walls were shiny, embossed with broad stripes in pink and white. They were hung with a double line of gilt-framed pictures. The collection included sunsets over hills, flowers in vases, highland cattle, a Lowry, a seascape at dawn and Urquhart through mist. In one corner, a glassed-in showcase held some books, a few Toby jugs, and a photo of Harriet arm in arm with a girl her age, the pair of them gazing out to sea from a breakwater.

He sat and poured some lukewarm tea and spooned up cereal. Directing his attention, he could make out his mother busy in the kitchen, closing cupboards and running water. His father would be sitting with a book in the living room corner, smoking. Already Matthew could sense them preparing their say, with questions to answer, things to get straight. They'd want to know everything: his day plans, intentions, commitments, strategies and departure arrangements; nothing less would do.

Harriet appeared. Thin and teacherly, she checked he'd had enough.

Matthew nodded.

And had he slept?

Again, he nodded.

And did he need more food?

Matthew was fine.

Or a fresh pot of tea?

"Everything's fine … just fine," he repeated, with effort.

His mother hung fire, watching. Her blue-grey eyes were slitted; her cheekbones high; hair wound back and secured.

Taking in her gaze, Matthew sat back, spoon-less. Sorting through the feelings that rose to the surface, he inspected vaguely: the brown-fleck carpet, the tie-back curtains, windowsill cacti – everything on hold, everything framed – and now her there waiting for an answer … he ought to fill the gap. "Going for a walk," he said, and immediately regretted it. The less said the better; now she'd have to know everything.

As predicted the questions began, mostly detail, mainly about timings, all of them closed. She needed warning, for making food, to know when he'd be back … it was only reasonable … she hoped he could say … the least he could do.

He tried to hold his ground. He was doing just that. Yes, doing what she wanted, telling.

A contest began with Harriet asking, then asking again when Matthew put her off, probing what he wanted, what he might be hiding and why he didn't answer. Most of all she wondered what was wrong. In the end the appeal returned, hedged around with apologies – which was where she chose to pause, talking weather, clearing the table, conceding slightly.

Climbing to the bathroom afterwards, preparing for his walk, Matthew could hear her, high and breathless, reporting what he'd said. She was using his name with a heavy second syllable. It was as if she were an usher reading from a charge sheet, calling the next case.

He moved past a metal fence and gates; through daylight, yellow-edged and grey. Walking the estate with redbrick and grass patch and knee-high hedges. Along by the bus stop, the garage, the route well-known. A cyclist passing and a lorry spreading dust. Walking into grey, past cars and a bus, observing detail: blue bonnet and red, taking corners. First one foot, then another.

Now all alone, passing signposts and tarmac into fields, Matthew as a poet, I-am-a-camera, storing impressions. Crows, black in branches, high up, wheeling; the sky still grey. Long level land with a water tower showing. Past rust-metal gates and tyre tracks all around. Turning from the road to enter into green.

In step with Wordsworth, observing and recording: hawthorn, elder, old man's beard. A farm track abandoned with stone posts and wheels. Outcast and explorer; walking off the map.

Deeper now, past broken walls with ivy and cracks. Close up and fascinated by airfield huts. Looking what's to see: metal frame twisted with holes and views out to runways. Something to think about, a military zone. Narrow path followed with the water tower ahead: white-grey concrete, highpoint marker.

Now turning in, hidden, to a tree belt. Damp and still. A copse with ivy and last year's leaves. Blind spot behind bushes, outside life.

Now look and listen, then drop all clothes. All shame discarded, piled onto a stump. Bathing naked with pink cold skin. Air, soft against nothing, can't catch me. One hand pumping, breathing short. Barefoot on earth without inhibition. Adam.

Soon to the top then last yard sweating. Quick finish off to end-of-race spurt. Now fearful looking around … who me? Impossible, too adult for that. A relief, a secret and shameful. Never to repeat, nowhere to run.

"Did you have a good walk then?" Harriet asked as they sat down to eat.

Matthew went quiet. What if she knew? For a second he wasn't there. Someone had reported; there were police enquiries, stories going around.

Harriet asked again. Coming to himself, Matthew nodded.

She checked on his route and Matthew evaded; when asked about the weather he was non-committal; on timings he was careful; when it came to other walks he couldn't really say … and he'd no plans, it seemed, to do anything, either all hours walking or leisure days at home. More was less; he could still keep them guessing.

They moved on to family, talking about illnesses and who'd got what. For this, he was their child who might one day learn about family – which, for the moment, they talked about as given, without specifics. Only occasionally did they touch on what they'd done for others, visits made or, closer even, what he one day might do for them.

Even at this, their standard provocation, he remained low-key. He'd a new life at college; things they didn't know; it really didn't matter.

In the break that followed the meal took over. A distance set in, bringing back silence. Now they were occupied, he could allow his feelings. His head was full of lines from protest songs. He could hear his own late-night phone voice reporting to Sally: the walls of opinion, the unrelieved negatives, the attempts to run him down.

He told them while eating he'd a college book that had to be studied before next term – modern, great and difficult: it was a classic.

At the mention of greatness Alan leaned forward. "Reading Churchill's History," he declared. "Now that's what I call writing." He pointed to four large black and gold volumes that filled up a shelf in the glassed-in showcase.

Matthew frowned. What *was* it, he wondered, that his father wanted? He stared towards the books. "You reading that lot?"

"Second time through," Alan said pointedly. "Do *you* good to read. Educational."

"Not for me."

"You should, it's important."

Matthew looked away. "Don't think so."

"What do you mean?"

"I wouldn't ever want to read something like that."

"Why on earth not?"

"Propaganda's not my thing."

His mother inhaled sharply.

"Those books," his father declared, "were written by a man you need to thank. A great man. One who saved this country. Without him you wouldn't be here today."

Matthew shifted forward, shoulders hunched, sighting down the table. Not that one again. Why *did* his father have to talk like this?

In the argument that followed battle lines were drawn – one side in protest, alleging blindness, an obsession with the past; with queen and country and war dressed up as some kind of kindness – and the other side in shock: tight-lipped and dogged, refusing to back down.

For both, they'd heard it all.

And even when they paused, breathless, or when Harriet called time, their dispute, lacking resolution, kept up its own momentum. Alan was a warmonger, Matthew knew nothing, Harriet wanted quiet. For all three it was final – and like war, once it was started there was no going back.

It continued of its own accord, going off all evening. Each time there was quiet, something more was said and before they could stop it another round began. It crept into everything with asides and re-minders and points in addition, leading to stops and head-shaking silence with feelings underneath.

"You're both so obsessive," Harriet said at the end of one exchange.

"Not me," returned Matthew.

His father glared. "Meaning, of course, me. *I'm* the problem."

"If you say so, Dad."

Alan held his gaze. "That's just the sort of answer ..." he began before tailing off.

The next day was similar: Matthew defiant, his father injured, both sides militant.

"The world's changed," said Matthew when his father expressed disgust at a picture in the paper. "It's not like you think."

"You both ought to listen," said Harriet when the two men clashed over alleged war atrocities and numbers slaughtered.

"It doesn't really matter what I say," complained Alan, concluding yet another run-in, "it's always wrong."

At bedtime, exhausted, they agreed a kind of truce, a standstill moment with no more try-ons, no more challenges and nothing left to say.

For the rest of Matthew's stay the house took on a frontline feeling. Daily there was pressure, with talk in corners and unexpected gestures that didn't quite add up – so Matthew felt there were watchers, someone was onto him, and that everything said was, like a carefully plotted thriller, subject to scrutiny as proof of something wrong.

The appeal returned, signalled by a sigh, a cigarette left burning, another cup of tea. Everywhere had its phrases, its ought-tos and put-upons, its burden of complaint.

In his bedroom he played his tracks. The Animals, The Kinks, Jagger in a strut; Roy Harper, declaiming; Hendrix, repeated; The Who recorded live. He lay back smoking, studying the ceiling, thinking what to do, his next move and further, and how to keep it up. He pictured them at table with their eyes on his hair length, mouths compressed, fingers restless. Long before they said it, he knew just what they thought. If this was poker he could, if he chose to, call for them to show. With so much hidden, so much to declare; there had to be a reckoning.

In his mind, when they spoke, he kept the upper hand. Didn't they know? He was building up a score, a lead they couldn't match. When they tried him with remarks, he returned them in kind:

*Maybe.*        *If you only listened.*        *It isn't always me.*

At table he was jumpy. What did they suppose, or care, or notice – if anything? What could they do, and did it really matter? When pressed on the stool, he gave one-word answers. Each question was a goad, a tease, a deliberate provocation. And it was just before bedtime, when he came across his mother in police-search mode fishing through his jacket that he told it as it was. "Like hell," he said when she claimed he'd misunderstood.

"None of your bloody business," he told his father when required to stop.

"Total bollocks," he shot back when she made out it didn't matter.

"Fucking police state," were his last words as he strode off upstairs, then repeated twice on the stairhead when challenged by his father. Full force on the landing, he'd said it all.

Next morning when he left, Matthew took with him a closely written letter composed overnight, carried in a bundle pushed to the bottom of an inside pocket. Pages long, it described his college life, his friendships, his books and music, his lifestyle now. Using different inks and scored through often, it told how he'd grown, how far he'd travelled, how different he'd become.

This was *him*. What they'd better get used to. Not their little boy.

The letter ended with a page about living separate – in term time at college, holidays at friends' – with a postscript on family life, on things passed down, and a final request that his father should carry out his threat made in the hallway to draw up a document and legally disown him.


# NINE


Other people's parents were different. When college began, they were there in cars or helping on platforms, with cheque books and smiles, taking turns with cases or giving out cigarettes; they all seemed relaxed and easy to get on with.

Other people's parents arrived without fuss, after one or two holdups and not much trouble, then parked quite easily or completed by taxi. They appeared still fresh, smiled as they drew up, stepped out unruffled wearing light summer jackets and toe-pointing shoes or Swedish-type head scarves in expensive-looking lace. Calm and as-sured they acted as adults and took things in their stride.

Some struck Matthew as surprising: Theresa's for accent, South African, she said; Paul's for age, quite near retirement, and talk of giving parties; Jay's and Miranda's for warmth; most of all Sally's who, when he met them over lunch, spoke low and paused often, conceding to their daughter when she cut in with anecdotes or launched into impressions of what she called "the set".

"Are they always like that?" Matthew asked the next day, returning to the subject as they walked the old town walls.

"Like what?" she countered, breathing hard.

"Different. Not what you might expect."

"You think that about mine?"

"They're not like mine, that's for sure."

"You think mine're *easy?*"

"Maybe, by comparison."

"You should try."

"It seemed like they meant well."

"To you. That's how they present."

He saved his answer until they reached the city gate. "OK then, they're average, polite, middle-class Brits."

Sally shook her head. "They're upper. Jolly good *types* … Queen and country and full of it. I know."

He wondered. Sitting at their table he'd seen how she behaved: cutesy, reactive, but also rather cold. "These are my parents," she'd said, then sidelined them for an hour with her need to interrupt, her comments and corrections and issues taken; it seemed they'd done her wrong.

Matthew looked out across the old town roofs. The sun was high, glinting on the slates. There were spires and towers and chimneys with aerials over flat roofs and black metal fire escapes. The old town was a jumble. It seemed like something placed there, a mock-up of sorts, like a Fritz Lang film set.

He walked back across the gate tower, treading carefully. He could feel Sally watching, standing to one side. Again, he saw her, at odds with her parents. She was looking for advantage.

They were close in now to the Gothic Minster: grey stone and buttresses, square-built at centre with a Decorated tower. The wall-walk ahead ran around the south beyond the transepts to the east end, where tiered scaffolding rose against stone. The construction was grand and blocky and surprising: a ship of God. Shading his brow, Matthew panned around. Between church and walls his eye was drawn to a bleached wooden cross; behind it was a scattering of graves. A dust-grey path led through to a sunken garden with gravel in a square, hoops around earth and a dried-out fountain.

He turned to find himself alone. Already Sally had pushed on, exploring the wall walk.

Matthew caught up, wondering at her mood. He flanked her or walked behind, calling his remarks. As they circled The Minster he pointed out features, keeping up a flow of one-line observations. He felt like a small boy prattling to his parents.

Sally stopped at a gatepost where some steps descended towards the sunken garden. A sign marked them private. At this point the city wall ran along a ridge that dropped both sides: outside the town over grass; towards The Minster, through briars and tangled rhododendrons. "Had enough," she announced flatly, avoiding his gaze. She was holding onto the gatepost like a swimmer to a rock.

In response to Matthew's question she put her head to one side. Her hair covered both shoulders like a red-coiled cloth. "The quick way," she said, indicating the steps.

In the descent that followed Sally led, saying nothing. She moved at will, ignoring Matthew. At the bottom of the steps she angled sideways to zigzag down the slope, clinging onto branches. Underfoot was loose, a mixture of rock and granulated earth, flaking in places to a crumble. Dust puffs skittered sideways from her shoes. The leaves above screened against sun.

Sally found a dry leaf-free gulley and picked her way down, moving like a tracker. Matthew followed, knees bent, using both hands. This, he realised, was a chase; she wanted to prove something.

Halfway down, buckthorn covered with creepers blocked the path. Sally picked her spot, using sticks and hands to prise them back. Her strength surprised him. Breathing hard, she pushed each tangle to one side, stepping beyond it before letting go. Each release kicked up a dust cloud, causing her to cough. Matthew, in following, moved up quickly and pinned back the suckers with a fallen branch. Thinking how he must look, he shuffled forward, pushing on his branch like a broom handle.

It was near the bottom that Sally, while stepping over something, heeled into air and lost her footing. Her arms went up and she slid to one side, sprawling into brambles. When she realised what had happened, she gave out a shriek. "It hurts!" she protested.

Matthew pushed forward. "Are you all right?" he cried.

Sally repeated her protest. She was lying side-on, struggling. Her knitted top was snagged from below; there were scratch marks on her hands and dust spots in her hair. "Don't touch me!" she shrilled, when Matthew tried to lift her.

He fell back and watched as she dragged to one side forcing down the branches. "No, no – not there – now get off – off – just get off," Sally repeated to herself, like a child regulating her own actions.

Moving stiffly, she cleared the thorns and dusted herself down. In answer to his enquiries she frowned. "That way," she said brusquely, ducking forward to peer through branches. Her hair had spread and her limbs were shaking. About her now there was a force of separation. "Don't look," she said, "I can't bear it." Her face was set and cold, peering ahead. Matthew said nothing.

Sally continued peering and staring as if she'd seen combat. She felt around her sides and squeezed both hands before resuming her descent. "Hurts, hurts," she muttered as she pushed her way down through a screen of bushes. One more drop, some roots, a tangle of green and suddenly she was free, emerged into sunlight at the bottom. Matthew followed to take up a position at her side. "The Traitor's Yard," he said, the name appearing from somewhere in his head.

They'd come out at a corner of the sunken garden. The central fountain was drained dry. Around it there was gravel and a square of metal-framed hoops dividing earth from path. A few etiolated stems struggled in the borders, tied in by string to flaked bamboo. Four peeling benches occupied the corners.

As they stepped into the square a single bell note sounded. Ringing once, twice, it held briefly as an unfinished phrase, curling like smoke over water. Then suddenly a tumbling, crashing, thundering sound fell about their ears, ringing and reverberating from gravel to stone.

Sally winced, raising her hands to her ears. Her mouth mimed a question. In reply Matthew waved towards the central tower, laughing. "Great, isn't it," he called. Sally shook her head. Her eyes now were fixed on a point somewhere in the distance. Round and brown, they showed pain.

For Matthew this was arrival; it was as if after months of drifting they'd finally reached land. "Fantastic," he cried, walking the square. He crouched down to the path, playing with a stone. "Like the sea," he called to Sally, who had shifted back to huddle on a bench. Scooping up gravel, he examined for size. "The sea. When it rains. A downpour."

He continued counting stones then juggling them between his palms. For a second he was tempted – *she loves me, she loves me not* – then, shaking his head, he stood to listen. The bells were all around; ascending and descending, they filled the air. They were tidal, overlapping, successive.

He held up a stone: a throwaway line. "That's us," he cried, "as we were." He leaned back and threw, high and vertical. The stone went up, hung, and descended like a cricket ball, smacking into his palm. "Now watch," he called. Turning, he sighted the wall and their descent through bushes. "Us now," he called, raising the other arm. Again, he threw, this time at an angle, and a volley of stones went up and out. They carried to the bushes, dropping like a flock of birds to land unseen.

He turned: all around was bell-toned, echoed. Everything was sound, pure bell-sound. The earth, the borders, the stones in the path, even his own thoughts were changed and shaken by the sound. He glanced at Sally, indifferent now. He noticed her eyes, small and selfish, her spots and freckles, the twist of her mouth. Suddenly she was sitting, schoolgirl and pudgy, at a table with her parents, offering nothing; nothing to him.

He turned the other way, disgusted. One phrase only occupied his mind: *nothing more to say.* Pointing to his route, he moved to the edge of the sunken garden. When she called, he shook his head. Choosing the path to the church front he began the long walk back. Behind him and on his neck and shoulders the bells fell, cool and yet fiery, aching, shivery, touching like rain. Under their pressure he felt, for the first time, alive and composed, able to breathe, buoyed up like a swimmer.

Afterwards in the letter that he wrote, first in his head mixed in with the bells in the distance and things he should have said; then on an envelope found in his pocket; then later at his desk with statements of intent and comments in the margin, Matthew felt he'd made a start on something, a draft or sketch that might perhaps develop to a chapter in his book.

The letter he'd planned had been final. But then, as he walked, he began to elaborate, to rerun different incidents, something he'd forgotten, some sort of grace-trick or *merci*, a card turned up. It could be just a break, an interval between halves; there were always second chances.

When he arrived at his room Paul was out – the note said overnight – so Matthew charged up with coffee, put out a notice and sat with pen and paper, preparing.

The letter required depth and rationale. What had happened was over and done with. A part of him felt he'd proved himself, and a voice in his head kept adding a phrase, something formulaic used once with Sally … it was true, so why make apologies?

He applied himself to getting it down. As he wrote, gradually gaining speed, he gave himself licence to sidestep training, to go for fluency and accept what came. No time for structure, meaning or defining terms, less still for word count, references and positions taken, this time he'd deliver and make it stick. It would, he hoped, be something to look back on, a door into expression. And yes, that was it: the real life and the actual, all plugged in.

His job was the saying, and levels of exposure.

Something he achieved through *feelings*, announced each sentence, with highs and lows and flights of poetic fancy, which later he redrafted, picking out details of who did what; then rewrote parts into step by step descriptions. His hand was aching but he kept on, trying out capitals then italics with boxed-in sections and notes in the margin, as he veered between styles, from fact to fiction to diary to some kind of manifesto.

He wrote all day and on overnight, accompanied by music. The task, with its variables, kept him on a high. By version ten the desk was full, by fifteen it had spread to shelf edge and chair, by twenty he was crouched, matching papers on the floor. It became a treatise, a compilation worked-at past dawn in loose leaf and note form, to end up doubled-sided, typed into eight straight pages, no paragraphs or breaks, piled beneath his bed.

Exhausted, he slept, dreaming in words. When he woke, his body felt empty and achy while his thoughts ran on. As the words crowded in, his certainty grew. Of course, he knew: what was lacking was obvious, now he could see it, it had to be told.

Taking the letter, clipped and folded and fitted to an envelope, he unhooked his jacket remembering how he'd used it late night at the lakeside. Slipping the envelope into a pocket, he set out for Sally's. The lights were coming on as he passed across campus. The air was still, cool around the water, warmer down the walkways and warmer still as he stepped beneath an air vent. It immersed him in thought. He passed through doors and tiled lobbies, along a corridor and up an open staircase, walking with purpose. As he neared her door, he was busy composing, running through a script. The words were loose, an intonational pattern with one main subject, appearing undercover in many disguises, a next-door radio left running in his head. And he knew, as he stood there, that what he had to say was in there coded, gathered into place like the poems he'd once memorised, often without meaning, early in childhood.

He knocked and she appeared. Greeting hoarsely, he asked to come in. At first nothing registered. Then her expression flashed surprise – could this be? She stood looking, until Matthew repeated his request, adding the word "talk". Then, as if she was responding to something hidden, Sally stood aside.

Inside was low-lit and private, almost like a shrine. It was arranged, thought Matthew, with an eye to being seen. The walls and shelves were lined with pictures of horses and snapshots of Sally posing with her friends. There were cushions with mirrors, a William Morris throw and a hand-carved cross. Soft toys filled the bookcase with pink and blue fluff. There were also signs, mainly around her desk: screwed up paper handkerchiefs; a notepad, empty; a bottle of sherry; two bars of chocolate, half-eaten. In one corner, a slatted wooden chair had collapsed to a frame; its cushion lay discarded. The chair back was jammed beneath the wardrobe handle as if to bar access. This was what happened, thought Matthew, behind the façade.

Once in and seated, he felt the charge: a sense of things withheld. There was a strangeness in the air; a gap had opened up.

Sally offered tea or coffee, checked about milk – she only had powdered – if he wanted she could find biscuits, she always had fruit. He watched as she filled the mugs. Her movements were practised. She was absorbed, it seemed, in her own actions. When she passed across his tea Matthew thanked her, managing his responses, judging what to say.

For a while Sally did the talking. She ran through her news, updating on holidays, this term's essays, friends back from travelling and couples splitting up.

Matthew followed what she said, as if from a distance. He could feel things drifting.

While she talked Sally kept one hand cupped around her mug. From time to time she took a sip, then continued with her story. The mug was large and Sally's hand barely reached around. Matthew, sitting opposite, wondered how long she would hold it. In one scenario he imagined her spilling tea or hurling the mug in his direction; in another it was spiked and intended for him; in the end he simply watched without expecting anything. When her talk ended, it came as no surprise that her hand slipped away.

"That's it, all I can manage," she said, sitting back, looking pale. "Your turn."

Matthew asked what she'd been doing.

"Nothing much. Just the usual, really."

He tried her on Miranda and going to lectures.

Sally shook her head.

And had she, like him, been thinking?

"I'm trying not to do that …"

Matthew understood. He felt the same way.

Around them now there was pressure, as if they'd just met. It held them, like strangers bound in by protocol.

Matthew enquired further: was she surprised to see him?

She was and she wasn't. "Though I did think *what on earth* when I saw you at the door," she added.

"And now?"

"Oh, it's OK. I'm fine with it."

Matthew was glad. "Because we need to talk," he went on, dropping in a phrase from his pre-rehearsed speech.

"Yes, I suppose so, if that's what you want."

He nodded. "I've been thinking. There's a pattern we've got into. It's like we're always on the case, trying not to say things, then something happens and we're running round in circles trying to patch it up."

Head to one side, Sally considered. "Is that really how you see us?"

"Why not? It's called games people play."

"But is it really so? Or is it just a theory?"

"You mean I'm making it up?"

"You could be," she said smoothly.

"You believe I'm like that?"

"There's something going on."

"And you, of course, know it all."

"Listen, Matt, why are you angry with me?"

"Isn't it obvious? *O wilt thou leave me so unsatisfied* – you know that one from Romeo and Juliet?"

Sally's fingers returned to her mug. "You mean …?"

"I think," he said, switching into calm, "there's a reason. It's what we don't talk about, what's *really* there. We try to avoid it. But we know it's always there."

Sally's hand became a lid, palm down, covering her tea. "I'm not sure. You seem to be implying something about me."

"Suppose I am, is it true?"

She part-removed her hand. "If you mean what I think, you've got it all wrong."

Matthew flushed. In the speech he'd rehearsed she didn't say this, it closed off options. Already it felt like there'd be no backing out.

76

"I have passions," she continued, "if you know how to treat me."

His breathing slowed; he felt her challenge like a torchlight probe, illuminating areas he didn't care to name.

Her other hand now was resting just above her knee. Small and squat, it crossed the boundary between skirt-line and flesh. She held it there, curled into a ball, like a half-asleep animal.

"I want to stay," he announced, feeling the exposure, "and sleep together."

Sally nodded, her voice tone rising, "I thought that's what you meant."

"Is it OK?"

"Yes, of course, *I'd* like ... If you can, and you want."

He did, but couldn't say it. Suddenly he realised that his body felt all hollowed out. With one hand he touched the letter still lodged in his pocket. So ironic, he thought, this was the moment where his life had run itself on. Take it or leave it, he was beyond all that; there was nothing to hold on to, no previous. Everything before felt foreshortened somehow, as if he'd been deep underwater holding his breath and now, at last, he was rising to the surface.

Sally shifted forward. Smiling archly, her half-closed eyes were fixed on his. "And so to bed," she said quietly and Matthew watched as she put aside her mug and rose from the sofa, tossing back her hair, and held out her hand.

Next morning, as he left, Matthew had a picture of himself and Sally pillow-propped in bed (and her with both breasts showing). In his mind's eye they were both flushed, with Sally speaking brightly. How he, Sir Matthew had read the encyclopaedia (at least twice), the dictionary (and swallowed it), the entire D H Lawrence scriptures (what was it she asked, about that man? Was it the consumption, the goatee, the rant that wouldn't stop?) anything heavy or unheard-of, and the entire life works of the psycho-analytical circle.

Joking, laughing, they'd done what they had to. They'd got through their first night.

Then Matthew's turn, mimicking her parents (posh), warning *their baby* to keep away from long haired freaks who'd climb in through windows and whisper what they *shouldn't* (slit-eyed, weaving) to draw her into bed (tongue out, snaky) then, tickling and wrestling, kiss her in a clench …

# TEN

For me, the day Edith left was a turning point. The odd thing was how calm we seemed. I can see us now, posed like actors in a silent film, with Mum blocking the door and me on the back step, eyeing Dad. Even he seemed to be playing a part. He made himself busy chopping wood and whistling *Clementine*. Outside in the alleyway, the tradesmen were shouting. Next door a dog barked. The gulls on the roof were calling. It was all too everyday-and-normal. The truth dawned later when I looked around the bedroom. Edith had gone, her room was empty, and I was alone.

In the months that followed it was quiet. I didn't do much, except go to work. That kept me busy, I mean busy-busy, like a worker bee. It was there that I learned about the acts people put on, and how they really are behind closed doors. Like the boy with the emperor, I saw what was hidden.

I'd been taken on part-time at a dentist's. Working at the desk and sometimes around the chair was an eye-opener. Maybe I should say jaw-dropper. It certainly made me sit up. It's the stuff you might see in a comic strip. Everyone in a panic, putting on an act. There were patients who arrived looking calm then acted like drunks. There were silent fighters who swore then cried, those who went stiff, those who slept, and a few who took ill and never came back. I began to wonder if anyone was what they seemed.

Then one day a man came in who wasn't like the others. He was tall and slim with a boyish face and a quiet kind of gaze. His speech was what I call good, with a pause between phrases. In the chair he lay still, watching the dentist. His eyes were blue and calm and when the drilling began he switched his gaze to the ceiling. During the treatment, which I knew was painful, he lay back like a statue with a far-away look. He did jump once from a nerve hit, then waved it off. In a sense, I knew he was looking at me, not straight-on, but from the corner of his eye. I could tell there was interest.

Afterwards he was calm. Perhaps too calm, as he sat up, asking if we'd done. What happened next seemed to follow on. He put on his jacket and "we" became him and me as I led out. At the desk we arranged an appointment with a single, giveaway smile. The look was what I remember. It filled me with a lightly-glowing feel, like moonlight on water. And the glow stayed with me all day as a secret smile. You could say I was afloat in a dreamboat.

After he'd gone, I checked the records, learning what I could. He lived in the town, worked in housing, was seven years older than me and seemed to be single. His name was Stuart Lavender.

When he came back the next day, what surprised me was how much he'd changed. He was wearing a tie and jacket with his hair slicked back and a buttonhole carnation. His voice was different too. It sounded a bit wobbly. He told me he'd come to change his appointment. It was early, I couldn't read his mood, and I found myself struggling. I felt like the actress who's forgotten her lines. I think he knew, and when we'd filled in the diary he spoke, touching his carnation.

"I've a favour to ask."

"A favour?"

"Something I'd like you to consider."

If his voice sounded shaky, my body was riding the big wheel.

"Yes," I replied, hearing my own breathing.

"I'd like you to have this," he said, taking out his flower. He held it up. The pink and white petals were folded like paper. "It's yours," he continued, looking serious.

My mind went blank. A big white wave was carrying me up.

"If it pleases you," he added.

Realising what he'd said, I took it. I could feel myself smiling. It was like stepping out from land into a small, brightly-painted rowboat.

Stuart returned every day, after work. We walked to the park and, when it rained, stopped off at *The Captain's.* It was a café with a garden at the back of the newsagent's serving tea and cakes. In those days we described it as being *on the town.* It wasn't big-time or swanky, but a corner table with clean cups and mats in a room we called our own.

Sitting in *The Captain's* I came to know Stuart not as a patient but as a man who'd come through the war in ships with a medal. Mind, what we talked about was mostly people and work, but there was something deeper, as well. A private, unspoken trust in who we were. I understood his feelings and he listened to mine.

At the start, that trust went with us, everywhere. So we walked to the station and stood by the ticket office watching the trains. To us they seemed strange, and exciting. We chatted about where they'd come from and where they might take us. Their routes were through towns and cities whose names I'd never heard of.

The next day we went down to the docks, taking peeks inside the boats. We talked about voyages and where we'd like to go. Stuart named some places from songs and I told him about Stephen's postcards.

It reminded me of Edith talking at the fair. But we were more private.

Another time we walked along the lanes and out to the head-land where we stood by the lighthouse, without speaking. On our way back we did a circuit by the links and behind the church. We walked in step, following our feelings. We were like sightseers or day trippers. And wherever we walked the town was ours.

We'd begun courting, of course. In those days it meant saying very little and seeking out places where people didn't go. There was an awkwardness about it, as if we were up to something. Of course, I was a good girl and wouldn't allow anything, and Stuart was respectful. With us it was more about getting out and about without being spotted. I think we saw it as an adventure.

Then Stuart decided he'd like to meet Dad. Remembering Reg, I warned him. But he wouldn't be put off and a visit was arranged through Mum. She'd joined us on the odd walk and got on well with Stuart. She seemed to admire him. Whenever they met she called him "his nibs" or "sir" and even, once, "Mr Stuart L, VIP". I think she was kidding a bit, but in another way she meant it. Maybe out of guilt or to make a point about Dad, but also because she loved me. And when she set up the meeting, she gave us our orders. I was in the clear, Jack was cautioned, we were both told to talk and be on best behaviour.

When he arrived, Stuart surprised me. He entered and said hello with a thin-faced stare then sat, facing Dad. As I watched, I flashed back to Edith. He'd the same quiet directness, but more cocky, more male. Stuart had been in the forces, so he didn't run away.

There was a pause before they began talking, but then Stuart made a joke of the sort Dad liked. From then on they talked. Real talk, complaining about work, arguing politics and rerunning the war. They were against the same things, didn't believe anything, had seen it all before. I think really, behind the big talk and claims, they wanted to get on. At the end they stood by the door and shook hands. And from then on that was how it was.

Then the blow fell. It happened suddenly, like that moment in the yard chopping wood, or the belt across the legs. And like both, I felt the pain for years afterwards, like a scar beneath the skin.

Dad came home early one afternoon. There'd been no work but he was whistling his songs. I could tell there was something up because he'd brought home a bottle of booze. When Mum objected, he went out with me to sit in the yard, filling up his glass. The weather was September-ish with a nip in the air. Maybe it was the cold or his mood, but I thought I saw his hand shake and the drink spill. It was only a few drops, but I heard him use language. He never did that, not in front of us. Even something muttered wouldn't pass his lips, so I knew it was serious. He was rocking back and forth and staring at the sky. I remember the cold, his hand shaking and the cry of seagulls on the roof. In the distance, the sky was darkening.

Then Dad made a noise. A horrible, deep-in-the-throat noise as if he'd been struck. It sounded like a boxer being winded. I tried to stay calm but the noise got louder as he slid to the ground. He was groaning and shaking like a man being beaten. When I reached him, his face had gone blue and his breathing had stopped. Something awful was happening in front of me, but it meant nothing. I simply cried out without thinking, as if I was a hurt animal.

Then the spell broke. Mum came running and we tried to pull him up but his body was stiff. It felt like lugging a bag of sea coal. Mum shook him, calling his name. When he didn't reply Mum sent me to get the neighbours. I ran and shouted and they telephoned, but by the time the ambulance came he was on his back, staring blankly at the sky.

My dad had passed away.

# ELEVEN

When Matthew told him about Sally, Paul wasn't surprised. "We're pleased. It's good news – for you both," he said, sounding formal, as if the announcement was from family and printed in the newspaper. Under questioning he explained that "we" meant him and Theresa who had suspected for months but didn't want to say. When asked, he couldn't quite say why they'd kept quiet. If he did approve, it came with silence and a knowing smile. He did divulge later, as he dressed for the evening, that they'd both wanted to give them space and keep things together. And his *real* view? Sally was good – straight, mind, but a good match for Matt.

In any case, Paul had added, when smoking at Theresa's, there'd been quite a change.

"Change?" grinned Matthew.

"Could say."

"Mornings, you mean?"

"Yeah. It made us think—"

"But really you *knew*. Yes?"

82

Paul nodded.

Matthew laughed. "Smile if you had it last night, eh?"

"So people say."

"And it's what they *say*," concluded Matthew, bowing forward with a photo-fixed smile, "that makes the world go round." A phrase he repeated the very next evening at Sally's to explain how Paul and Theresa had known all along (on the basis, he said lolling in a chair, that when it came to it, people were fascinated by other people's hang-ups and what they did or didn't do in bed).

The original decision to go public was agreed to by Sally as a result of sightings by neighbours on her all-female corridor. He'd been spotted sneaking in and out like an intruder. It only became an issue for two of her neighbours when he'd walked into the kitchen one morning, barefoot and shirtless, minus glasses. "Hi there," he'd called, wrapping himself up in a towel he'd taken from the radiator. "Does Sally have a cupboard here?" he'd asked, and went in where they showed him, banging about like a workman hunting for matches. He'd sworn repeatedly, the women said when they petitioned Sally afterwards, he'd acted like a jerk, smoked out the kitchen, taken no notice when they'd been forced to leave the room.

"You'll have to be more careful," Sally warned, "things get talked about."

"Yeah, word goes round. Like it did with Miranda."

Sally, who was dressing, looked at him in the mirror. She had to admit that with his hair to his shoulders, his classic features, parted lips and nervous expression, he looked just like a poet.

"It's territory," he continued. "I mean, I can see their point. Probably got it from their parents. They think I'm uncouth."

Reaching for his glasses he checked along her bookshelf, pulling out a volume of Wordsworth. His long delicate fingers flicked through the pages till he found the poem he wanted. "Remember the river – *and dances with the daffodils*?"

When Sally, despite herself, allowed a smile, he cleared the chairs, placed a rug beside the desk and crouched down at its centre calling out lines, interspersed with swear words, while tugging at imaginary daffodils.

"Oh my," said Sally, "if those women could see you now."

"You mean the Mirandas? The ones who spread the word?" Turning to the coat hooks he reached down her umbrella. He twirled it about and launched into a mock sword fight while calling out obscenities, taking both parts in his argument with Miranda.

Sally grinned. "Maybe she had a point."

"OK, OK. Re-enactment drama number three," he cried, arranging the chairs in a fence-line then imitating Jay searching for his dog. Halfway through the dog-search he broke into song, strumming his umbrella; next he did scat, then noises, then Townshend smashing his guitar, ending on the floor playing Sally in the undergrowth.

"I'm not sure I like that one," she said, spluttering with laughter.

"Not sure I do either. Put my foot in it there."

He replaced the furniture, singing.

"OK, babe," he called out when Sally had finished dressing, "time for you an' me to go cat go."

Sally, looking puzzled, asked him to explain.

"Meet the nosy neighbours," he said and launched into a chorus of *Johnny B Goode*. He ended, slyly, "And just don't you worry. I'll do the talking. You'll see, I can charm 'em."

"You're not serious?"

"Sure am, gal," he said, making whinnying noises as he rode his umbrella around the room. "You 'n' me, my Dixie chicken." Matthew capered to a stop, discarding the umbrella. He bowed and put out his arm. When she hesitated, he urged her not to shy away: he'd do it, if she came too.

"Well, I do admire—"

"No, don't even think about it. Just do it." He pressed her arm into his and steered towards the door. "Magical mystery tour, first stop the kitchen."

They emerged, passing through off-white walls and a wired glass door into blue-grey strip light. Once through it seemed clearer; they'd made their first move.

During breakfast, shared in the kitchen with two suspicious neighbours, Matthew was perfect. He presented himself as Matty, winning the women round with smiles and enquiries, then following up their answers with pleasing attentions and an interest in what they said. When he left, their goodbyes were clear-voiced and smiley.

"So, now you see how happy they are," he said, checking Sally's room for things left behind, "I hope you'll agree there's only one thing to do."

"To do?"

"Yes, top of our list."

"And what might that be?"

"Get it out in the open," he said, pocketing a few coins. "Tell everyone, the whole bloody world if necessary. Don't let them make the running, get in first with *our* version."

"Do you really think so? Aren't you overreacting somewhat?"

"By now I reckon those two women will have told two more. Next step is four, eight, and so on. Won't take long."

She coloured.

"It's the only way," he continued. "Just say it. Who knows what the story will be if we don't get it out there before them."

"I suppose, looked at that way ..."

"It's how things are." He checked his pockets, adjusted his glasses and glanced towards the window. "So now it's time to talk. I'll do it if you like – tour all our friends, spread the news."

In reply, Sally simply nodded.

The act of telling friends, most of it conducted by Matthew calling and talking like a door-to-door salesman, made things more definite. It changed things and established them as an item. People were pleased for them, thanked him for honesty and vowed their support with talk of living life and going where it took them; though all rather more formally than Matthew had expected. But it registered. They were a couple who'd got it together, established as steadies with one name between them: Matthew-and-Sally or Sal-and-Matt, with their own allotted place up there high on the bill; they were the latest.

And for Matthew it changed things. He'd waited this long, believed himself unfitted, and now quite suddenly, he was dating. So, at his insistence, they re-walked the town, looked around the record shop, the market, the route down to the river, but this time linked and touching and sometimes kissing, then walking hand in hand.

"You see?" he said when they crossed the park, passing a young couple lying on the grass.

"See what?" she asked, gazing blankly.

"See you, see me," he laughed, looking at her hair.

"Boy meets girl," he explained when questioned again. "In any case, it's easier now."

"Easier?"

"Yeah, going out together – now we can say it – feels pretty good."

Half-closing her eyes, Sally laughed, as if in acknowledgement.

At university, too, it all seemed freer and simpler, now people knew. Walking, talking, they put themselves around as steadies in the making. And for a while, when they appeared at gatherings, they were the beautiful two.

They were of course on show. Watched from all sides and required to be *with it*, to lie on beds in Kama Sutra tangles – which felt like putting pieces in a very difficult jigsaw – listen and express liking for the latest psychedelic tracks, share weird stories, and take part in getting high.

But for Sally that kind of high didn't come easily. When the smoking started, at first she just missed, passed on discreetly or didn't inhale. If asked to go further, she spoke about her fears, adding she wasn't there yet. Then, when Matthew gave his reasons – there wasn't any danger, everyone did it, they called it turning on – she tried, but broke out coughing, dropping the joint where it burnt through a blanket. She couldn't do it next time, wasn't so inclined. Her attempts that followed were no more successful, ending in discomfort and a twitchy kind of chatter where she spent her time shifting around cushions and readjusting clothing between walk-outs to the loo and talking horses.

It was Jay who turned her on. Their friendship had begun when he'd shown the group what he called deep space meditation achieved, he said, like digestion, by not doing anything.

"Can anyone do that?" asked Matthew. "Digest themselves?"

"Give him a chance, Matt," said Sally. "I want to hear what he says."

When Jay talked of yogic flying, she took his side against a clipped and nasal Matthew who was interviewing God as he crash-dived his plane. And she studied the shapes and Leonardo-like equations that Jay drew on misted glass as he talked about psychotropics and the effects of THC. "So, it's herbal," she said pointing to a scrawly outline streaked with drip lines that looked like a spider climbing a palm.

Jay confirmed.

"And you could in theory cook it?"

Jay mentioned hash cake. Sally asked about ingredients and if he'd got a recipe. A pocket search produced a broken ruler, a dog whistle, a log table and a yellow-edged notebook which, when opened, yielded the recipe in capitals with several variations, each occurring within a Platonic-style dialogue, bordered by snake signs and anatomical drawings.

Jay explained that he'd copied the text from a booklet found in the *Old Town Record Shop*. The idea pleased Sally. Just the sort of spot, she said, where surprises and odd things could happen. "Perhaps it's one of those special places …" she added, with an upward inflection as if it were a question.

It turned out that Jay had a photographic memory of everything in the shop: titles of sections, names of artists, posters, details of furniture and what he called *specials*: those in attendance, the spirits of the place. "The shop belongs," he said, expressionless. "I've talked with them." In answer to Sally's prompt he gazed off smiling into space, "Hamadryads … they own the aura."

"What, for profit?" Matthew cut in.

Sally pulled a face. "Matthew, please—"

Matthew returned to debating the influence of blues on rock with a thoughtful-looking Paul.

Sally switched back to Jay and the recipe, asking him to read it out. When Jay began slowly, as if he was translating a scientific thesis, she sat and listened, becoming by degrees puzzled, twitchy, then pained and interventionist, ending with appeals and a hand across the page. Yes, she wanted it, but not that way. Another attempt led to a section read in chorus but soon diverging, as an overlap appeared. There were two more efforts involving coaxing, coaching and being led by example, until finally, Sally appropriated the volume and completed solo. When she'd finished there were smiles: they'd done really well, it didn't seem so hard. Maybe if they worked together, him tasting, her baking, perhaps they could make it?

Jay didn't appear to recognise any connection.

"OK, I shall cook it," she concluded brightly, taking his silence as consent.

Hash cake became established as a Sally speciality. Cooked with various toppings and flavouring added, it became her take on getting high.

"Hmm, good. Very good," said Matthew when she served up on a tray and they all partook, with glasses and water jugs provided. "Like Christmas pudding," he said between mouthfuls, couched like a Roman on the bed. Sally offered seconds, dividing what remained by the number of takers. Waitress-like, she passed around with the tray then returned to feed Matthew.

Matthew adjusted the pillow, holding himself in readiness. When Sally served up he took down a few mouthfuls then volunteered return service. Sally showed willing, "Like a filly," she said, guiding his cake hand till it levelled with her mouth. Side-on and watchful, she nibbled and swallowed, then reclined against the bed head awaiting results.

Usually dramatic, the effects when they began were often revealing. Her system, it seemed, was a lightning conductor as she turned on all over. Sometimes she *was* her dream (not an action she said afterwards, a noun-state, quite literal, a reflection of being real), at other times she was what she called "altered", and sometimes, at the high point, she had blue blood. "Lavender's blue," she sang back quietly, looking over Matthew teasingly.

"That's Theresa's line," he responded glancing around, "when we first met."

Sally sang, her song ending, as Matthew told her later, with the Q word. "And this is where I'm at home," she added, her eyes turning circles, taking in the faces, "and these are my people."

At their Halloween party, Mia and Cass appeared wearing black sheets with insect-like feelers and red glass eyes stuck to their foreheads.

"Whoo!" cried Mia, "let's prank Joe."

"Joe? Where's he gone?" asked Cass.

"Bro! Where are you?" called Mia, poking her head out into the garden.

It was dark and no one replied.

They set off down the path moving slowly, holding each other's feelers.

"Can't see," said Mia. "Maybe it's an animal trap?"

"Joe," called Cass, "where are you?"

Still no reply.

"I'm listening," said Mia. "Can't hear anything. Could be he's dead."

"Don't say that."

"I mean playing dead. Like an animal. I do that a lot."

"You do?"

"In The Wild Things I do, yes."

"But where is he?"

"Here," said Joe suddenly, stepping out from behind a tree. He had fangs and claws and was wearing a wolf suit. "Hey, what animal are you?" he demanded, pushing his face close to Mia's.

"I'm a spider. But I can fly."

"Can you eat yourself?"

Mia shook her head.

"So who are you?"

"I'm family."

"Like Addams Family?"

"Yeh. Altogether ooky."

"I'm more like Rocky Horror." put in Cass.

"Listen. Tonight, I'm Howling Wolf," he said, throwing back his head and making blues guitar noises, "Whoo hoo. And I eat the moon."

"And you're a fruit bat," said Cass, pointing to her sister.

"Yoyo. I'm with the beasties," replied Mia.

Joe laughed. Then he led them singing *Thriller* followed by *Season of the Witch*.

‡ ‡ ‡

*Everybody must get stoned.* The words became for Sally an injunction, a sing-along chorus. When Dylan sang it (with behind him what she heard as ghosts or admirers laughing and joining the refrain) it acted as a prompt, a chant, a magic form of utterance. Of course, it was everybody; they must, certainly; and as for getting stoned … "All join in," she called (or thought she called, or hoped, or imagined herself directing, later, with her fingers beating time) then heard herself at midnight, warbling and slurring in an off-key loop like a New Year's Eve reveller.

When she got stoned—

The song, imagined, foot-stamped and clapped with long level chorus and arms linked together or played back in her head: the song, the anthem, the ditty, well, that said it all. Drawn out and chanted, it beat up to that word, hit hard in protest, bannered what it thought. I get, you get, we get, they must be getting, the PM, the President, the moon-shot crew, everyone, everyone. All up there, getting it with a smile. It made them so important: like her they were proud.

And when she got stoned – really on a high, squiffy, so far out of it she just didn't care – *they* had to listen; Victoria or Elizabeth, she made the rules. As their monarch she'd have it just-so: the lamps and vases moved around and placed, light bulbs changed, books in order and pictures straightened up.

She was at centre, there was no middle ground.

Then what she did came up quickly, in a rush, or remained forever hanging. Things just occurred with no forward planning: either she was still, lain out prone with an ear to the speaker as it whispered *Tomorrow Never Knows*, or breathless and heightened, shifting around furniture like surplus stock.

Oh yes, when she got stoned.

"I'm hungry," she'd announce and fill up on crumpets, overspread with syrup and a mixture of jams, all of different colours, or she'd pick and mix between paste spreads, Marmite and peanut butter. Then she'd play at wild card, try out lucky dips: fruit with coffee, chickpeas with sherbet, pasta with mousse. Or she'd throw together opposites, go for schlock: dark chocolate ice cream drizzled over toast, meringues with grated cheese, sugared fried eggs, dried fruit and spinach layered between baps.

Before gatherings she wondered, speaking in the gaps and interregnums and rests between sessions, where it all came from. This newfound life with its transports and strangeness (or was it something narrower, something she'd worked up to, a deliberate kind of fit?) this upsurge of colour and drama, well, was it really her? Could she be doing this? Or had she perhaps been led, allowed herself without really noticing to arrive at an edge, a step off into nothingness where everything before her was one-way and airy, a dream perhaps she'd not be able to wake from?

By day she prepared. Then she was on hold, doing business, playing catch up and working on essays, sometimes separate, sometimes with Matthew. Now they were steady they felt themselves obliged, required like parents to look out for each other. How the other came across was what they rated – the moves, the clothes-sense and details of expression – heading off criticism by getting in first.

*Coupling*, Matthew called it. "Like dogs and owners," he said, teasingly, "after years, you can't tell 'em apart." And when Sally objected, referring him to horses, how each came with pedigree and character, he played the role of listener, nodding and agreeing without, she suspected, very much interest in what she'd really said. Somehow, without ever stating it, he gave the impression that he knew better. It was as if, after making some commitment, he didn't want to honour it, and nothing was accepted, or ever allowed to stand. He was, she thought sometimes, Matthew-I-Am.

There were gatherings too with Jay. Times as voyagers, set-fair travellers who acted for each other: Sally as navigator, on lookout, Jay gone galactic, flat-voiced and imperturbable, reporting from the void.

Later as familiars, sharing something coded, a steadiness of purpose. So they talked of immersion and deep space flotation as they moved without thought, like swimmers, outdoing even Paul and super-cool Theresa. Like them they were impressive.

When challenged by Matthew she said it didn't matter. Jay was just a friend, nothing more. And yes, maybe she did have him as her – what might one say? – *project*, if you like. He was someone who appealed, a little boy blue. She felt quite protective.

"You mean he's sweet?" There was an edge to the question. *Sweet* was suspect, a word to pull a face to, a slop word, one of those markers referred to by Paul and Matthew as "turn off talk". Paired with "fluffy" it declared the speaker, who was usually female, at best wrongheaded, certainly muddled and possibly in need of therapy.

Sally sighed. "No Matthew. Jay is Jay, simple as that."

Matthew narrowed his eyes. "That sounds kinda familiar."

Sally, who was baking, pointed to a packet of dried fruit on a high shelf. "Needed for the mixture," she said and Matthew passed it down, holding the bag as if it were an exhibit. Sally tipped in the fruit, folding it under with a large wooden spoon. She added glacé cherries while listening to Matthew who was formulating theories, using as his example how she treated Jay. "He's not a pet, you know, and he's not a child either. He's one hundred percent responsible for the mess he's got himself into."

Sally kept busy, adding in scrapings from a tin of drinking chocolate. "I don't understand. What *is* it about Jay? Why are you so angry with him?"

"Anger doesn't come in to it. Now if you said I'm on his case, well, that's different."

"I just don't see what he's done that's so awful."

"There's a bubble he's blowing. He thinks he's the balloon man, inside some sort of other dimension."

She shook in spices and some powdered hash from a small plastic bag. "But he's not doing anything to you?"

"Jay wants notice, he *spreads*. People like him think they're the centre of the universe."

"Don't an awful lot of people think that, in some way or other?"

"Not like him, he's so bloody perfect. *Don't touch me I'm a holy man*. Sits there smiling like he's in a daisy field, just waiting for someone to take a photo."

Sally pressed down the mixture and committed it to the oven. "But he is sweet," she said tipping back her head and smiling, "very, very sweet."

Matthew grimaced. "Oh shi—" he began then stopped himself mid-sentence. "OK, OK," he continued stiffly, "I get it. Joke, of course."

"Sweet is sweet, simple as that."

Matthew stood back, affecting calm, like a detective closing a case. "Assuming that doesn't turn your stomach."

"Well, Matt, it doesn't turn mine," she countered, adjusting the oven and glancing at her watch. "And now," she added briskly, "there's a cake to deal with." And she ended by running through timings and putting him on cake watch while she went off and studied.

That evening was a turning point. For Sally it became clear that, whatever Matthew said, when she did things like talking, sitting, or simply being, it was easier with Jay. Together they were big dog little dog. With Jay she felt admired, all thought and giving. Because just being there, silently sitting in a corner, eating, drinking or defending against Matthew, had built up a connection (a pact she called it, a special relationship) and she saw in his actions, the true face of simpleness, flower-like and helpless, a gift he had for soul.

"He's gentle," she told Miranda, who she'd met the next day by accident on the dining room terrace. "And deep," she went on, "very deep, I'd say. One of those people who you always feel really *understands*, if only you could get them to tell."

Miranda nodded. Dark-eyed and thoughtful, she echoed Sally's words. With him, she said, it was all about depth. "Or highs," she said suddenly, frowning. She added that though she'd given up on church, she'd still a sense of him being closer to what people called God.

Sally shielded her eyes, looking across the lake. The fountain was drifting colour spots in an arc. Every so often it dropped, bubbled from below then sprang back to life. As the arc rose again, a thin cloud of spray carried to the terrace. Drawing in her shawl, she turned towards her friend. "He's not like other guys."

Miranda thought so too. She felt he was different, of interest, not as people said.

"Sounds like you know him," Sally said, shivering slightly as the wind touched her legs.

Miranda leaned forward, talking about Jay. As she spoke, her long black hair shone in the sun.

"So actually, you and him go back some way?"

"You could say."

"And?"

Miranda flashed a smile. "Meaning, I take it, you want the full story."

Sally confirmed and her friend, speaking quietly, began with what she knew. She described the youthful Jay who'd attended the same school. "Even then he was different," she said, "you could see he was sensitive. Very good at maths and science of course, not so good with people." Miranda paused, gazing over water. "I think that's when he started taking – huge amounts, as you know – because of the bullying. They really gave him stick."

"Was it that bad?"

"I think so, lots of name-calling and rudeness, and sniping all the time. Often from boys who were clever, who turned against him. Probably to avoid being next in line. Anyway, whatever the reason, his so-called friends were the worst."

"And you think that when people upset him …"

"It pushes him, yes."

"Especially if they're close."

"Absolutely."

"Or belong to the same circle."

"You've someone in mind?"

"You can probably guess."

"You don't mean …?"

Sally sighed.

Miranda flared up, "Him, of course. Mr No-Apology, Mr Never-Say-Sorry."

Sally looked down, saying nothing.

"Well you know what I think," Miranda fired off, "he's just the sort—"

Sally said she knew, only too well.

Miranda's voice began to shake: "I can just see him doing it. He'd have to have his say. Mr *Vanità*, the one who knows everything, going after Jay. That's *him*, thinking he's clever, thinking he really knows." She paused, frowning into air, then noticing Sally's silence pulled herself up. "I'm sorry, I suppose I shouldn't be saying this. I know it's not nice."

Sally shook her head; she preferred honesty, really.

"But it's how I feel," Miranda added, "the truth, warts and all." She turned towards the lake where the fountain had reduced to a low-level bubble. "Anyway, I think you're wasted on his sort. Just think about it, you know you can do better."

When they parted, hugging, Sally thanked her friend. "You understand," she said, hearing her own voice repeating her thanks like a chorus. And as she walked back from the terrace she reran her last words, timing her steps to reinforce the rhythm of her thank you incantation.

That evening a quietly inscrutable Sally, pushing in mouthfuls of her best cake yet, got so stoned that it wasn't till the next morning when she bit into honey on lightly sugared biscuit that she remembered the sweetness of her one-second contact, mouth to mouth, with a barely conscious Jay.

# TWELVE

"Thank you for *what*?"

Matthew was standing on the town-end footbridge looking down at the shadows of buildings seen moving in deep clear water. He was leaning against a chest-high ledge with bars between him and the river below. The bars were tall and the high-roofed bridge was built wide as if to take an army. Both ends were approached by oversize steps, the central boxed-in walkway was fortress-like, while gaps below showed through to a heavy central pillar and piers both sides, all plated in grey-green metal.

Behind him Sally said nothing.

They had stopped, at Matthew's insistence, after walking the market, the park and out along an arm of the river towards the factories and railway sidings that straggled to the north. It was a close, airless day and they'd drifted without contact, mainly in silence. Sally, who had proposed the walk, claimed she "wasn't touchable today" and had led, apparently without aim, until the bridge. Halfway across, Matthew, who was admiring the view, called for her to stop. It came out rather harshly, almost like a challenge. But when Sally had returned to join him, he'd told her that however short he sounded he really didn't mean it. For him, it was just that the walk didn't feel comfortable.

In reply, quite without prompting, Sally had offered her apologies. Regrets too, that she'd repeated when questioned (why? he'd asked himself, just what had brought this on?) and also her thanks, which was when, after some hesitation, he'd asked her if there was something still to come, and if there was, she just had to say it.

Sally had replied without particulars, creating an impression that there was indeed something but, like the weather, it remained uncertain. An apology followed and more about feelings.

Matthew straightened, pushing back his hair. "I just don't get it. All of a sudden it's sackcloth and ashes, but I'm not sure why."

Sally sighed. "It's how I feel."

"I spy the English disease. *Peccavi.*"

"Sometimes, Matt, I just don't follow you."

"We're a nation of grovellers and apologisers. The English are so N-I-C-E."

"You've been reading too much Lawrence again."

"Which may be true, but I happen to think it myself, regardless of D H."

"Well I'm more into Jane Austen."

"That might explain a thing or two."

"Sorry?"

He flashed her a look. "I hear the magic word."

"I meant pardon. *Répétez, s'il vous plait*," she said, wearily.

"OK, point taken. What I mean …" He paused to consider, then shifted tack: "No, take that back, I should just stop before I go any further. What I *really* mean is, I've made a resolution. No more clever-boy stuff." Deepening his voice, he placed both hands on imaginary lapels: "Matthew Lavender, take one hundred lines, *I must stop being flip.*"

He quickly looked her over. Her expression had calmed and abstracted, turning vaguely inward; like the sky, she had clouded. She asked him why he did it. "It's defensive," he replied, lowering his voice, "the snappy catch answer. Get in beforehand and head things off by saying them first."

Sally shifted forward to stare across the river. He noticed her breasts, heavy in cotton, and the lace around her bra. Her blouse was cut away and her back-piled hair, pinned up to a bun, showed thick and red against her bare white neck.

"There has to be an answer," Matthew continued, gazing into air. "As it is, we've gone backwards. Back to the avoidance thing."

Below, the water moved slowly, darkly pooled and mirrored between redbrick and concrete. Matthew smiled wryly. "It's like all those essays. In there somewhere."

"You could say that." Sally fixed her eyes on the slow drift of images shifting over water. "Look Matthew," her voice began to waver, "we need to talk." Behind her now, the sunlight had weakened and high-level clouds were sealing up the day. "There's a problem."

Matthew remained silent, wondering what was coming. Part of him was absorbed, almost proudly, in measuring what he'd said; another part wished he'd not said a word; yet another part was watching as if on camera, awaiting her next move.

"You must understand, I do still like you, Matthew …"

The word *but* hung in the air; there was more on the way.

"You see, I've always said I'm not that easy."

He could feel her closing in. She was weighing up her chances.

"I don't know how to say this …"

*Then don't* he thought fiercely, the idea flaring like a match. *Please don't*, he repeated, hoping to deflect. He really didn't want this, but already he could feel it, she'd brought him here – how could she do it? – not by chance, but like a stalker, with intention.

"Go on," he said, quietly, surprising himself. Suddenly he was calm, almost glacial, more alive now than ever before. Maybe this was for the best.

"I need to … I've decided. We have to split up."

*Split up.* The words remained out there, ringed round by silence. She'd said it so he knew, it was that simple. "You've decided?"

Sally nodded.

For an instant he saw himself, long-haired and stooping, shaking his head. Did she really mean this? Uncomprehending, he echoed back her words: was there, he asked, no other way?

Again, she nodded. This was what she wanted.

Suddenly he flared: "Split up – for good – is that what you *really* want? Over and done with, just like that? No discussion?"

She moved back stiffly, refusing to be drawn.

"So, that's it, is it? Thanks but no thanks. Ended. All in the bin?" He felt himself sweating; this was all wrong. What hurt most was the lack of explanation. She'd done this to him, judge and jury, with no word of warning. He threw out one arm. "It's another bloody whim, isn't it? Sally and her *feelings*. Queen Bee Sally, who's got to have her way."

Sally denied. This was *him*, his words just showed.

Matthew dropped silent. A gap had appeared, a walk through to nothing. Things were breaking up.

"I don't want this … these problems," she declared, frowning. "I'd thought we could be friends, but now …"

This was a door closing in his face. His voice, when it returned, sounded far off and strained. "What is it? You think I'm arrogant, is that the problem? Too much I-am?"

Sally didn't answer. The sun returned, calm and unwavering, like a camera focused. It spread, clear and hard, bright against metal, shifting slowly over cold water. It played across the buildings, the bridge, across her red-coiled hair and lightly-freckled flesh.

Matthew saw that her head had turned away. Her hurt, like his, was tightly stretched and close to the surface. Now, more than ever, he wanted her affection. "Can't we just try?"

As Sally shook her head, a new burst of sunlight spread across the bridge. With it, out of nowhere, came a hot hard thought, a curtain opened. In a moment it took over and suddenly he knew. "It's Jay, isn't it."

She denied. How could he think that?

"But it is. You two together, that's what this is about."

Once again, she denied. This was impossible.

"All those times, whispers in corners, getting stoned together. It's you and bloody Jay, you and that bloody bastard Jay, I know it." He raised one fist like a hammer then swung it down hard, striking the bridge. The metal rang out, bell-like and jarring, as his fist ran blood.

Surprised, Matthew pulled back, examining his hand then pushed it in her face. "OK, you fancy Jay – yes or no?" Sally shrank back. "Come on, let's hear it, yes or no, you and Jay?" Sally stayed silent, avoiding contact. "Yes or no? Yes or no?" A trickle of blood appeared on his wrist, spreading to his shirt cuff. "See, you can't deny it. You and that bastard Jay. You and him. What a pair of shits."

He dropped his shoulders and walked away, fist to mouth, crying. As he reached the bridge-end her voice rang out, shaky but clear, "Listen, Matthew, I'm going to tell you, so you know. The whole truth. The fact is I *am* with Jay, but it's not about him or me, it's about you. You're the reason. I've just had enough, I don't want to be with you any longer."

As she called, Matthew carried on walking, head down. His legs were shaking and his chest felt hot. In his heart he'd shut off. A memory came up of schoolboys yelling, and in his mind, a stone flew by. He wanted to turn and charge, fists flailing, and knock them to the ground, but a voice inside coached him to keep walking and they'd soon lose interest.

Her call had ended, the air had stilled and his mind had returned. Flushed and alone, Matthew turned along the towpath, retracing his steps without looking back. Like the boys she wasn't there, they'd not been together, nothing had happened and what she'd called after him, that too, was cancelled. He really didn't like her.

He walked, apparently without purpose, blinking and shivering in the afternoon sun. Passing through park gates, Matthew saw bare earth and dryness. A brown-grey path led uphill to where the boy-girl couples were positioned on the lawn. Their statuesque closeness and coded defiance seemed directed at him. Behind them was the stone terrace with steps up to where he and Sally had sat. He felt the sun's rays hot against his neck. Climbing, he ached. As he passed out to the road his movements slowed and became furtive, as if he'd been sentenced for something he didn't do. At the crossing he felt exposed: there were exhaust fumes, noise, colour in flashes and the scent of blocked drains. As he searched on the other side for a break in the old town walls, Matthew willed himself forward like a runner near the tape. Finding a gateway, he passed through to a raised-up pavement that led towards The Minster. He pushed himself on, past an overhanging gatehouse and a terraced row. As he entered the square, he noticed there were people with guidebooks holding up their cameras. Facing the façade, he gazed unseeing at saints occupying niches, streaked with droppings. In his head he heard the bells. Was that, he wondered, what had turned her?

He sat on a wall and examined his fist. The skin was red and swollen. He noticed the small dried scabs and smears of blood. When he opened it, his hand felt stiff. His mind kept replaying Sally's last words, the bare metal echo, the sun, and the slow-moving river. In his heart he felt the shock. He'd not seen it coming. It had crept up behind him to enter unannounced. Everything he relied on was being stripped away.

He wondered how long he should stay there. It was best, he supposed, if he kept himself moving. Distraction, action, occupational therapy, that's what people said. A breeze got up and he started taking notice. His eye was drawn in, admiring the grey stone curtains and interlace windows. Even now, after so many viewings, The Minster took his breath. This was something larger.

As he moved around the square, he found himself imagining her there. He saw her walking back, boarding a bus and sitting at the window fixed in thought, with eyes not for him. Of course, he should have seen it. Sally looking out, Lady of the Lake with hair down to her arms, tossed back and careless. How could he bear to see her – her and *him* – be there in a gathering, act not bothered with them together, touching? How could she do it (was it, he wondered, a choice made to spite, a thumb-nose thing, an artful provocation?) and especially and deliberately of all people, with Jay. It didn't bear thinking about. She'd let herself down. What was it with that guy? She'd chosen a nothing, a man of no qualities, a blank-eyed starer who was only half there – and, yes, bastard as he was, got just what he wanted – how *could* she do it and not care? For he knew and hoped and wished, and told himself slowly, with a shiver and a sun-like stare, that she'd soon come to regret it.

"Pardon me, can I ask your help?"

Surprised by the soft American voice, he looked around to see a short, black-haired girl standing on her own, holding out a miniature camera. "Would you be so kind as to take me," she said, nodding to a spot just to one side, "in front of this wonderful building?"

Broad and firm, her face was both dark and lit from within. Something about her was asking for attention.

Matthew felt her warmth. "Yes, of course," he agreed. It seemed she'd caught him quite by chance, like a stranger on a corridor, and his defences were down.

She passed across the camera. It was smooth and black with a silver-plated lens and contoured sides, and felt like a gift. He weighed it like a pebble in his hand. "Mind, you'll have to show me how to use this thing," he warned, examining for controls, front and back.

"Sure can, it's pretty simple." Her hands showed how. Soft and expressive her voice moved with them, explaining button, adjustment

101

and viewfinder. "And this, over the head," she said finally, helping him with the strap. "You OK?" she added, regarding him closely, like a nurse checking for symptoms.

"You might not want to know," he said quickly, and fell silent, wishing he'd been more guarded.

"I figured there was something, soon as I saw you."

"You did?"

"Things show, we all put out these unspoken messages. And the more we hide, the more we show."

Matthew wasn't sure. In his head, he heard a small voice of protest. He wondered what she might be putting out for show. "The photo," he reminded, waving to the area in front of the façade. Turning her head, the girl nodded. As they walked, with the girl in front, Matthew took her in. She was short-set and stocky and big round the hips where she bulged out like a Rubens. She walked at her own pace, moving with purpose.

On their arrival, she smiled and struck a pose. She wanted two pictures, then three. There was sun, there was light, the building was so grand, she seemed to enjoy it. "It's been what you Brits call nice," she said afterwards, as she reached for the camera. "Nice building, nice meeting you. Very nice." They faced each other, and it seemed for a moment that they might take paper-scrap addresses, promise to meet some other time … then Matthew asked her name. She beamed, chin up, like a child receiving chocolate. "Robyn. Robyn Loretti," she said, running it together, then asking him the same. When told she asked again, then re-asked for spelling and to enjoy it. His surname – really, had anyone told him? – it fitted him so well, "Kinda warm and Mediterranean, but English too."

They filled in a few details: both first-year students, Matthew from the North East, Robyn from Boston, then agreed to her suggestion for a coffee. "You know a good place?" she asked, glancing at the buildings that boxed in the square.

"I can think of one," he said quietly, leading off. As they walked Matthew asked himself if this was really happening. He wondered how he'd tell it, how he'd write it in his book, and where *they* were going now, or not going … It all felt so up and rushed. Was this, he thought, just a quick-change moment, all talk and best behaviour? He could see the whole scene with Sally, hear himself shouting then the walk into nowhere with nothing left to say. It had all just happened somewhere at a distance, almost without him. And now, like a weather change, Robyn and the photos …

On the journey he told her they were going to the *Old Town Record Shop*, calling it *alternative*. "That's great," replied Robyn. She was full of observations: the British, their difference, their way with words, these streets they went through, an author she'd just read, while declaring herself open to whatever Matthew said. They passed by walls and gateways and timber-built houses that he named for style and dated where he could; at some she asked to stop, at others she took photos, all were of interest.

At one stop, a dragon's tooth doorway with Robyn asking questions, she'd reached out and touched him, sliding down his arm to grip his hand. "No pressure," she'd said, as if she'd read his thoughts.

Her hand was small and warm, and though again he wondered, he told himself this time it was real. He'd stepped into her glow.

At the *Old Town Record Shop*, they unhanded briefly to order from a menu chalked up on a board, then carried out their coffees to a caved-in sofa set out on the pavement. They sat there touching, remarking on the weather, the dried-up pot plants, the lopsided buildings. It was as if they were on view, like sitters for a picture.

Soon they were mouth to mouth. When they broke, Robyn was flushed. She spread her arms, sliding herself backwards to lie between cushions. Small grey lumps of sofa bulged out around her. "Oh yeeeees. Oh yeeeeeah," she cried softly. "And was that fine. Oh, was that fine?" Matthew grinned. Part of him was proud, stirred by her call, and part simply thankful, while another part wondered how much she really meant it.

Returning to upright, Robyn pulled him close. Noticing his silence, she smiled: "You look like you lost something. I mean before we met."

"Little boy lost, you mean?" he replied slowly, thinking of Blake.

Robyn kissed his cheek then asked about more drinks. Checking his preference, she collected their mugs and disappeared briefly, to re-emerge mugless, expressing her surprise. "Closing," she told him, and stood peering in through the dirt-streaked window.

"Welcome to England," Matthew said dryly.

"Seems weird, the way they do it." She turned back to the street. "You'd think they didn't like you."

Before he could answer Robyn touched his arm and said she'd like to go.

"Where to?"

"The cathedral, we'll take more pictures."

Matthew stood up and she put out a hand, which he accepted gladly. "To the God house," he said, drawing her with him, stepping from shadow into glare. "And photo call."

On the way there, he'd a feeling he was moving through streets that seemed quite strange. He was on a journey where anything might happen – and the route he was taking, though well-worn and familiar, was at the same time completely unknown.

At The Minster, the afternoon light had thinned out. It angled softly, spreading over arches and stone. Where it touched glass there were pinks and blues; reaching the square it spread like wine across a cloth; its beams were yellow over grass, brown over cobbles and ochre across tarmac.

In one corner Robyn was placing her subject, hand on camera. She wanted him, she said, next to the best statue. Matthew, pointing to Jesus, stuck out his tongue.

"Cut! Cut!"

"Did I do something wrong?"

"Only everything."

They started again, this time with Matthew standing by a carving of a long-robed figure seated at a desk, holding a book.

"You know who it is?"

"It's Saint Matthew."

"How do you know that?"

Matthew pointed to a figure at the top of the panel. "It's his sign, the angel."

Robyn joined him to look more closely. She peered up at the stone, as if admiring formations in a cave. "The man with the angel," she said slowly, raising her camera. "He's you. Or your pa."

"Not him. My old man's Jeremiah."

"Excuse me?"

He explained the reference.

"So, you don't get on with your pa?"

"Not much, we agree to differ." He scowled up at the statue. "If my dad was here, he'd want to know first how it was made, second the material, third the tools, fourth the cost and fifth how they put it in place. *The facts*, as he'd call it."

Robyn lowered her camera. "You mean he wouldn't get it. Not as a statue."

"Not a bit of it. He's an engineer. In his eyes it's just a *thing*. He's only interested in what he calls the *practical*, meaning an object of use if you're fighting a war."

"And you'd argue otherwise."

"Could say."

"Sounds like you're pretty mad at each other." The finality of her words pulled him up; she could see what mattered.

"I sometimes think he just wants to provoke. You wouldn't think it, mind. He's dead serious, to look at."

"But it's a game?"

"Yeah, it's like he's setting traps."

"Your pa gets you going ..."

Matthew acknowledged; he knew what she meant. He was, he said wryly, a textbook case.

"Father and son," she said, examining him closely, "most guys have that."

It seemed she had his measure, or some part, anyway. With the sun in his eyes, he wondered vaguely how far it showed. He wanted to ask – there were so many questions, points she might have noticed and things left hanging.

Her gaze descended to his hand. "Does it hurt?" she enquired, speaking objectively, careful not to touch. She added, before he could reply, a question about the cause.

Matthew passed it off. It wasn't important.

Robyn thought otherwise, she wanted him to tell.

Again, he stalled.

She insisted. Seeing him like that, she simply had to know.

"You really want to hear?"

"It's your story, so it's important." She kept up her gaze.

"I see I'm going to have to tell."

"You are."

He told his story briefly, as if it didn't matter. The version he gave was truthful, to a point; strong on action, it minimised feeling. He'd had a fling with Sally but he was beyond that now. "You might call it bloodletting," he concluded, dryly.

Robyn grimaced and bagged up the camera. "It showed. I felt the vibe." She put her face up to his, stretching for a kiss. When Matthew responded, flat-tongued and searching, she slipped one hand up behind his neck, prolonging contact.

When they broke, she was breathing hard. "I want you, Matthew," she hissed fiercely.

Again, he felt the warmth, this time as a pressure. She had him in her sights. "Here?" he asked, looking around quickly. Anything was possible, he wanted her to know.

Robyn peered into brightness. "I'd rather we went somewhere on our own."

Matthew waved forward: "The sunken garden. At this time of day, it should be empty."

"I'd like that."

They crossed the paved square to a wall, and a metal gate; it opened to a touch. On the inside there were tombs and a whitewood cross. A path led forward through grass-square patches and stunted bushes to the central gravel area with hoops all around and benches in corners. While they were walking, the bells rang the hour.

They arrived on the last note. Here it was darker; the evening was coming on. In the middle, where they stood, the air showed blue; beyond that, towards the walls, it lightened towards grey, while behind, to the church side, the shadow stretched deeper, blue-grey into black. "Let's sit," she said quietly. Side by side they took their places; they were like partners preparing for a dance.

She drew him to her and angled up a knee. "I like you here," she said, taking his hand and pushing it down her jeans. "Go on," she said, breathing hard. Matthew felt her flesh, loose and folded, and the slack between her thighs. She was butter-smooth and delicate.

Slowly, he began rubbing. "That's nice," she said, loosening her waistband and unbuttoning. Pushing his hand from outside the jeans, she urged him on. "Harder," she whispered. "There, and hard." She was moaning now. With her body leaned back, she gripped and rocked and pressed against his hand. In response to her whispers he pushed in harder, feeling the shivers and flutters in her body, raising the pace as she urged him to do more. "Yes," she cried, arching her back. She cried again, wordless now, as he quickened to a rush, pumping hard, till suddenly she gave way, snorting and exhaling and panting to a stop.

Afterwards she lay still. Her breath had dropped to almost nothing and her face was calm.

When Matthew removed his hand she woke and stretched, like a swimmer breaking water. "Your turn?" she asked, smiling. Matthew shook his head. "Not now?" she said gently, then sat up looking around. As she fastened up her jeans the bells rang again, this time briefly. "You know what that means?" she asked.

Matthew took a breath. "Maybe a service," he said.

She stood brushing herself down, and took him by the arms to raise him from the bench. "You're so cute," she said as he rose to meet her, blinking slightly, as if he was emerging from a bath. She slipped one arm into his, manoeuvring to leave. "And now," she said, pulling out a key, "I hope you'll be my guest." Her voice dropped a tone, "Because I've one more night here, then tomorrow a plane flight."

*A plane flight*. He wondered if he'd heard her right. "You're leaving? Tomorrow?"

"That's right."

"And that's it?"

"A plane flight, yes."

He felt the edge rising in his throat, "Can't you change it?"

"Impossible. It's to America."

"So, it's one night," he said with a sudden hot chill of warning.

"That's right, I'm going home. It's booked." She flashed him a smile: "Will you come back to my hotel? I'd love you to, before I leave, it would be wonderful."

"I can't," he said, withdrawing his hand.

Robyn tried again. She would write and phone, think of him daily, come back to visit.

"No," he said suddenly, feeling the cold climbing in his chest, "under no circumstances." As he said it the whole thing registered. She'd selected him, seen him in the square, asked for a picture – how obvious was that? And now it turned out it was nothing, a whim, a throwaway, over at the start. Already he could hear them: promises, goodbye expressions, then silence. Nothing in the mail, no words on the telephone, only distance, wishes, stories in the head. "No," he repeated as a shiver ran through him.

She showed him the key, holding it out like a present. "I'd fig-ured—"

Matthew shook his head.

"I thought you liked me," she said. "It seemed like we were set."

Standing by her side Matthew looked down at the key then back and up at the outlined Minster. There were lights now inside, yellow and distorted. Soft-edged and ephemeral, they glowed in darkness. "See those lights?" he said, pointing.

Robyn looked, saying nothing.

"You think they're cute?"

Robyn remained silent.

"When you think of us," he said, his voice now monotonously insistent, "just remember those, seen through glass. Something you wanted, but didn't understand." He turned and began to walk. About him now, the air had cooled. When she called, he pressed on across gravel, crunching hard. It felt like a shift, a scene change in the dark.

When he reached the gate, he looked up at the windows. The words of a song ran through his head. *You've lost that loving feeling.* He paused by the doorway with his hand on metal. The lights, half seen and distant, what were they? He imagined them as moons, as stones, as coins in water. He stood there in shadow with night approaching, hearing *'Cause it's gone, gone, gone.* The windows held him. Like his thoughts they were dark and light and strangely indifferent. Nothing else was real.

It was the bells that changed things.

This time it was the sound they made, like plate glass dropped or water coming down, and their force.

The bells and what they stood for. For Robyn it was surprise and things in a mass; for Matthew, like Whittington, what they said.

When they began, they stopped him at the gate. He replayed the *1812* with its canons and applause. They filled the air with echoes and stories going around.

As they continued, ascending and descending in overlapping layers, Robyn came to join him. She was quietly watchful like a child in a corner.

When the bells ended, Robyn spoke first, "Don't go."

"I could – did – say the same to you."

"But I haven't any choice, otherwise I'd stay."

In the dark he looked thoughtful. "I suppose it's more …" he paused, hoping she understood.

"You mean I won't keep in touch?"

He nodded.

"I'll write every day."

"I hope so, but let's face it—"

"Face what?"

"Human nature."

"Matthew," she said, her voice-tone rising, "can't you believe?"

Matthew pressed both palms together, looking down. He wanted to, of course, but needed time.

"We can fix it. Now," she said.

"But how? You're still leaving."

"Matthew, will you promise?"

"Promise?"

"I mean the real thing, so it's permanent. An engagement, *our* engagement."

He wondered if he'd heard her right. "You want to get married?"

"Hmm, I do."

The words wouldn't come. You *do* he thought, testing his feelings.

"And you?" she asked.

Even in the dark he could feel how she glowed. He hadn't imagined what she'd said.

"Promise," she said, her face set forward.

He allowed himself to answer, "I do. I promise."

Robyn stepped forward. "Matthew, that's so great." They kissed; this was who they were; they'd fixed on each other.

Afterwards, in the square, the bells returned, this time without force, high up and drifty, moving slowly. One ring, two, an overlapping phrase then silence.

"That's for us," she said.

Matthew saw her watching. She had angled back her head, with one arm around him, as if he was a find. "Yes, the bells," he echoed then stopped himself suddenly. "But you don't want it like that, in church, do you?"

Robyn shook her head.

"I'm glad," he said, leading off, "I really couldn't handle that."

At the edge of the square they stopped and Robyn asked him if he'd be willing to come back.

Matthew hesitated.

She pressed his hand close between her palms. "I'd like you to."

Matthew laid his other hand, like a game of pat-a-cake, lightly across hers. "OK, let's go," he said and checked which direction to walk.

She pointed and they set off, arm in arm, passing down the High Street across the river and beyond the walls. Their route was quiet, with the odd stray tourist, couples strolling and a few remaining window shoppers taking peeks at illuminated displays. With Robyn now directing, they walked to the ring road, turning right along an avenue with soda-yellow lighting. At the end was a gate and a floodlit sign above a long level building with porthole windows and a line of conifers planted against brick.

"Your hotel?" he asked and Robyn nodded. "I think I know it," he said quietly.

"How's that?"

"It's where my parents stayed, last time they were here."

"No. Really?"

"I'm almost sure of it."

Robyn let out a low, whistling breath.

He asked to see the key, checked both sides like evidence, then returned it with a sigh. "I should've realised."

Her eyes searched his face. "Realised what?"

"Same hotel, same room."

"Well, is that weird?"

"You could say."

"Does it put you off?"

Matthew felt himself shiver. This didn't feel comfortable. "Let's walk," he said, holding himself in. It was almost as if his father stood there watching with his electroplated wristwatch, recording every move.

They walked to a deserted garden with twisted railings and a slope down to the river. It was paved, and lit by a street lamp. In one corner, outlined, was a fenced-in Roman wall with a plaque and a cordon of small trees. Behind them, tucked in like a hide, the branches enclosed a small wooden bench. It was here, where the street lamp didn't reach, that they settled.

For a while they talked about their histories and the things that turned them on, then kissed. Matthew, who had recovered, and wanted to prove it, explored her breasts and down to her thighs, touching where she guided.

"That's great," she whispered as her hips began to move, pushing back and forth. She kept moving, fluttering towards closure, sighing as he worked. "Oh yes," she hissed, taking in air. Then she bucked wide till her hips ground down and legs went apart, to arrive, quite suddenly, as if she'd just landed.

Matthew, when she woke, had fitted his hand to hers. Robyn stirred then fingered him backwards, fate-line, life-line, tracing to his wrist. "I dig your hand," she said slowly.

"You do?"

"It's so beautiful."

He looked down, slightly puzzled.

"And it's mine. Mine now, no one else's."

"Private property, no trespassers?"

"That's right."

"We're each other's, for keeps?"

"Sure. You want that?"

"Sure I do."

"And Matthew," she said, pointing towards the river, "forget what happened with her. It's a new start."

After a pause she asked him about the other girls, the ones before Sally.

"Dreams," he said dryly, "and poetic licence."

She asked him to kiss her then drew him down to a hold. When they parted she was breathing hard. "I want you to come back. Forget your parents, we'll change the room."

"It's OK, this's fine. Nothing else needed."

She pulled herself up. "It's all right?"

Matthew was satisfied.

"Seems strange to me," she said, sitting forward.

He said he felt happy.

"How do you mean? Remember we're engaged."

Matthew smiled. Of course, he knew.

"But don't you want more?" she cried.

Yes, he said slowly, but not now, not *here*.

"Then where?" she sang, *appassionato*.

When Matthew didn't answer she told him that she wanted him. He had to understand. Whatever it took, he had to come inside.

Still he didn't answer.

She broke from the bench and stood, staring. "Is it my body? You don't find me sexy? Is that it?"

Matthew fired up, "No, it isn't that. Not that at all."

"What is it then? Is it something you want me to do?"

He could see her shaking. In her voice now there were questions, things she had to know. He couldn't put it off. "It's nothing to do with that. It's me. I don't find I can—" His pause said it all. Glad of the dark, he sighed. "OK, so now you know … You see, with Sally it didn't really work. We put off and put off, and then when it started it was all so big-dealish. Thunder, lightning, earth moves, all that. But in the long run I just couldn't *make* it happen, however hard I tried, not all the way, not for me."

As his words took effect, Robyn shifted around to half-kneel on the bench. "Gee, I'm sorry. You must think I'm awful."

"Not really, I can see how you took it."

"No, you're being kind. The truth is, I rushed it."

She sat and placed one arm lightly around his shoulders. "The man with the angel," she said, as she pushed in closer. "Don't worry," she whispered, "I understand …" and she continued, with lightly placed emphasis, telling him quietly that what mattered was their vow.

She ended on feelings, how they'd come this far, it was just so special. "In any case, what really counts is—" She paused then told him once, twice, then again with emphasis, repeating to herself like a newly-learned catechism, how much she loved him.

They stayed out all night. Now they'd declared, they could talk without pressure and explore the town, enjoying the feeling that they were here on their own. Sometimes they simply wandered, touring the back routes and old town passageways, then walked to the river where they talked about their engagement as they lay out on grass. Later they returned to The Minster and slept on a bench with their arms around each other. When an ambulance passed, they stirred and checked the time before falling back to sleep.

Dawn, when it came, was a curtain lifted. As the bells rang six, the dark drained off and the rooftops came into view. Bird notes sounded, short then long. A breeze got up, blowing papers to their feet; there were lorry sounds, shouts, and milk bottles rattling. They rose and stretched before retracing their footsteps to the hotel. As they arrived at the gate the sky began to flatten: grey-white and silver, it shone like water.

Matthew stood outside while Robyn packed. He waited by the gate, thinking what he'd say. A song about leaving sounded in his head. She had to go early / it was here so soon / his eye could see it all. The sun was rising and grey wisps of cloud were brightening into pink. In just a few hours … He planned out his letters, their last words on the platform, their next time's greeting. It was all so new, a jump into life. When Robyn reappeared holding a rucksack, he felt quite tingly as if *he* was the one going on a journey.

At the station she checked her ticket, found the carriage and climbed in with her sack. Returning to the platform, she talked him through her route. It wasn't till the end, when she kissed him from the step and whispered about their vow that he began to feel he'd lost her. And when the train slid off, receding around a bend, it brought things home. Suddenly he felt empty, yet proud as well and in an odd way hopeful.

He began writing straightaway, working on a letter. At first, he kept it private but after telling Paul, he realised how unlikely it all seemed – if he didn't know otherwise, he'd assume he'd made it up. So he retraced his steps and wrote about his feelings then, after posting his letter, kept up his spirits by picturing her reading it. But as the days went by and nothing came back he began to wonder why, so he read up about lost post and telegrams and checked on maps, perhaps absurdly, counting off time zones. He even tried using a phone number she'd given, but either the dial code was wrong or the college payphone wouldn't let him through.

But then a letter came, a carefully folded record in blue-black italics covering back-home observations and day-to-day routines. It ended suddenly with a note added, she said, just before posting. It explained that their snapshots had failed. He mailed straight back, an outdoor picture, asking for the same. It took some time, and when she sent a photo Matthew was surprised to see her heavily made-up in a low-cut dress, posed by a lake. She was done-up like a model. He studied what she'd written, looking for tone and the Robyn he knew, because the girl he'd been with seemed to have fitted herself into a portrait of the sort that he, as a youth, had hidden in a drawer.

The emptiness continued, a pullback into silence. What people said about him and Sally didn't much touch him. He kept himself apart, caught up on essays, wrote often, and became so detached he read his own actions like a character from a book.

It was only when he saw his parents that his situation registered. It came out on a visit, with talk of *putting things behind us*, when he took them to the *Old Town Tea Rooms* to sit outside, screened off by bushes in a walled-in garden.

They were wary but indulgent, braced up, and only slightly fussed by timings and how they'd get back. "So, you're settled now," his mother said, rubbing at a tea stain that she'd dripped on cloth.

"And studying," his father added with a nod.

Matthew confirmed. He could tell they were on best behaviour. They'd kept off the *subjects*, the probes about health and what he'd do next, the politics and opinions, the views on youth and how it used to be, war-talk, money-talk, work-talk and family-talk, and hadn't even mentioned hair length or guitar sounds or posters showing flesh. In return he'd humoured them with grades, his tutor's approbation, his next year's intentions, and now was bracing – eyeing the polished table with its red-checked tablecloth – preparing to tell all.

"There's something else—"

Behind his father he could see a nearly-blown rose. Pink and blowsy it overspread the wall. A faint sweet smell hung around the courtyard, either from the tea things or the thickly-layered blooms.

"Don't worry, Matthew," his mother put in, smiling, "no need to tell us anything. Unless you want to."

Matthew took a breath. "I think it's best …" He wanted to say more, but felt at a loss, surprised into doubt by her unexpected offer.

When his mother added that they'd decided it was best if they treated him as an adult, he glanced at his father seeking confirmation. Alan nodded briefly, like a bidder in an auction.

Matthew took a breath. "I appreciate that. It's better for everyone."

The rose scent now was milk-sweet and tangy. There were bees visiting the blooms; they circled in the sunlight, oblivious.

Braced against the chair back, Matthew tried again. "I'd like you to know – and I hope you can deal with it – something important's come up." He could feel his own hush rising inside. Against it he was determined he'd not go under or pass it off lightly, something must be said. It was as if this was a quiz show and he was in the hot spot weighing up his words: how best to say his piece, and the reception that might follow.

Again, his mother assured him that he didn't have to tell.

A new wave of rose scent wafted from the wall. It fused with the bees, the sunlight, his blush still hidden and the declaration still to come. "Yes, important—" he stalled, echoing himself. Realising suddenly that his father had lit up, he caught a whiff of smoke. The rose scent and the smoke, intermingled, sweet and pungent, brought up a scene playing in the garden with his parents watching. He saw himself centred by his father's camera, a sand pit boy standing to attention with a this-is-me smile. He was their son, they had to understand.

"I'm engaged," he said. The words came out, brief and factual, like a throwaway greeting. He wondered for a moment, what more could he say? A flash came back of Sally with her parents, the brightness and disappointment, the faces without contact. "Engaged to be married," he added when a blank-faced Harriet echoed back his words. He gave a few facts, her name and country, mentioning Boston then left it.

They all fell back into silence. In the afternoon garden there were sounds of plates clashing, chair-shifts, voices, bees in roses.

When his mother began, her voice was short-breathed and terse, hot around the edges; she was speaking low, as if in church. There was something suffered, a near-the-edge feeling, as if she was in prayer.

He'd hurt her and it showed. She continued probing, trying to take it in. There was something final in her firm clipped syllables, check back on facts, stages of questioning and disbelieving stare. This was all too much. She wanted to know how long this had been going on, the girl's full name, age, what kind of family background and why on earth he hadn't told them. As the story came out, her voice tone rose. She didn't like Americans, couldn't believe his haste, wondered what was behind it (and was it some kind of joke?) was amazed and alarmed and deeply disappointed. Frankly, she was astounded.

Matthew played it straight, batting back her comments. At each escalation he became shorter and surlier. Like a cornered politician he denied, he rebutted, he wasn't having any. Whatever tack she chose he had his own position, his dignity, his rights. "It's my choice," he said finally, bristling. "I'm old enough."

"In theory, yes," said his father.

Matthew took exception. What gave *anyone* the right … And did he really realise just how rude he'd been?

His father, too, wasn't having any. He'd say what he liked.

"Whatever comes out," said Matthew, dryly.

Harriet cut in, "I don't understand how you can sit there saying all this. Is there something else, does this girl have a hold over you, is she pregnant or something?"

"Even if she was," Matthew began, then switched. "No, it's a choice. My choice, that's all."

"But to get *married*," Harriet returned, glacial now, "have you any idea, Matthew, what that means?"

It seemed he didn't.

"It's not what you think, Matthew, it's not just a game."

"You mean like your marriage?"

"I'll thank you—" Alan shot back, glowering.

"Not to speak?" Matthew enquired.

"Matthew," Harriet called, warningly, "I don't think you've thought about this at all. Marriage isn't all play. It takes time and effort."

"And a certain maturity," his father put in.

Matthew snorted. "By which you mean *this*?"

In reply to Harriet's query he looked her over pityingly: "Treating me *this* way – oh so mature – like an *adult*, you said."

"This is different."

"Of course, of course. It's different, it's always different. And I'm different, very, very different from anything you think."

Alan began to rise. He'd heard quite enough. "Washing my hands," he said, speaking, it seemed, to an invisible audience.

"So, you intend going through with this … this business," threw in Harriet as she rose to join her husband.

"I do."

"Well, I can only hope," Harriet said, "that you don't live to regret it." As she turned to leave her voice dropped to a whisper, "Don't do it, Matthew. If you have the slightest doubt, don't do it."

Matthew didn't answer. Sucking in his cheeks, he followed them inside to stand around the cash desk and watch them pay the bill. He said he'd pay his share, but his father insisted. Grey-faced and silent, Alan did the honours, counting out one note, two, and reckoning up in coins. He took the receipt, checked his watch and exhaled heavily. There was a train to catch, work on Monday, his wife's feelings.

Harriet had turned white. Lips set, hair swept back, her eyes had widened to appeal. She wished this hadn't happened, hoped he'd think twice, wanted only what was best for him. "It's not what you think," she repeated, frowning. They left then, muttering.

Matthew, feeling empty, returned to the garden where he ordered coffee, pulling out a pen and a half-finished letter that he placed on the table. He straightened in his chair then, pressing hard, began writing, pausing often to inhale scent, to reread his own words and watch without seeing as a bee stumbled blindly among the pink and white roses.

# THIRTEEN

After Jack's death I became a Lavender. Of course, I didn't know what was going on or what that meant, but I can still feel the change. It was strange and hard, and for a long time I struggled. Everything went blurry and quiet, as if I was walking alone in a fog. I was lost, trying to find my way through a wall of feelings. They filled me up.

To begin with, there was grief. It came in waves. But for a while I didn't feel anything, I was numb. I'd been scared and shocked by how he'd looked and everything I did seemed hollow. Next, I felt all churned up. I'd imagined death as out there somewhere, something small and specky, like a ship on the horizon. But this was so close it made me scared. I didn't want to think about what I'd seen. There was my dad laid out like a board, with a stone-faced look. He'd gone, to be replaced by a picture in my head. In that picture was a gravestone, flowers and people in black. It made me feel bad. At night I could hear my mum crying, and I blamed myself for not doing something to save him.

In any case I had a secret, one it took me years to face. To be honest, even now I don't find it easy. The truth is that I often pictured him being washed out to sea. I told myself I shouldn't, but it kept coming back. I was dreaming of him going under, of his body behind glass with his mouth wide open. Even after his death I kept seeing him everywhere. I couldn't shake the feeling he was there on the street, watching. He was just around the corner threatening to jump out. It added to the idea I'd done something wrong. And I didn't dare tell anyone, not even Edith.

It wasn't till months after the funeral that I began to understand. My feelings had changed. It was as if I'd been locked up in a cold, dark room and now I'd stepped outside. I was on the shoreline walking to the headland. The sun had come out and I'd a strange feeling that I was up there with the seagulls looking down.

Of course, it didn't really happen, but for a moment I could see myself small. I was the woman walking in silence, studying the beach. I was hunting for things buried, for stones and shells and feathers and dried-out wood. And then, as I looked, I felt a shadow pass over. The shadow was warm and alive and moved right through me. It filled me like a breath. And I knew at once what it meant. It was something about life and death that I'd known all along, and I'd learned it from my mum through her love for something small …

Mum had always been good with plants. She grew them in pots that she watered twice a week. Some were squeezed into eggcups, others were paper-wrapped and kept in the shed and a few were planted in earthholes around the yard. When they were small, she protected them from snails and called them names like *bright thing* and *little one*. As they got larger, she picked off bugs and supported them with sticks. Every morning she checked their health and asked them how they were. In a way, her plants were part of the family.

When Dad passed away, she cleared a patch by the wall. She left it bare for a while until one day she asked me to help in the yard. We'd been out at weekends on the sands, coming back with shells and stones and one big rootball of sea lavender.

She placed the stones and shells around the patch. Then we dug like navvies. When the hole was ready, she stepped back. "You don't find this often round here," she said, pointing to the lavender. It had sprawled to one side, looking as if it had been trampled on.

"Does it flower?" I asked.

"In marshland, yes," she replied, heeling it in. "But here, it needs help."

As she straightened, I asked what she meant.

"You have to look after it. It's, you know, different …"

"You're calling it *different*?" I said. I think she knew straightaway, without saying anything, who I was quoting.

"Different is different," she replied, stepping back. "But you have other things to think about, now."

"You mean ...?" I was staring at the plant. I could see she'd ringed it round with a double row of stones. "Yes, you're right. It's different."

"And needs looking after."

"So how do I do that?" I asked.

Mum went into the shed, bringing out an old teapot without a lid. "By sprinkling it with cold tea and a bit of seawater."

"You want me to do that?"

"Every day."

"With tea and seawater?"

"A little and a little."

"Won't it die?"

"We'll see," she said, "I want you to try."

So, I watered it. At first it straggled like a mop head. It was damp and messy and I found myself wondering if it might die. It didn't seem to like where it was planted. The leaves drooped and began to shrivel. When a blackness appeared, creeping up the stems, Mum fingered the leaves then told me to leave it. "Sometimes they need a fright," she said.

We gave it a few days, cutting leaves and pruning out the black. Mum sprinkled ashes around the roots and watered it again. "Kill or cure," she said, stepping back. It seemed to be dead. It was yellow all around and flat to the earth. But then next day, a shoot put its head up. When I saw it in the sun it looked like a flame. It was tiny and see-through.

I told Mum and she came straightaway. "It's come back," she said quietly and crouched down. "See, there's life here." Her voice was low and breathless. She pointed to the shoot and smiled, "It's a sign."

That was all she said but, inside myself, I knew what she meant. In the middle of the plant, where her finger was pointing, there was one small flame appearing from blackness. I looked, and I knew.

# FOURTEEN

*Going out by air mail* was how Matthew put it when telling his friends about Robyn and the big parental split. He didn't say engaged, went vague when asked how many times they'd met and promised something soon when pressed for a picture. In private he was upbeat. There was a craziness about it that he rather enjoyed. If it was sudden, he'd still kept his balance, had it reckoned up, and if it was absurd, then only he knew it. Of course, Paul had the full story, the first unguarded before telling could disguise it, but after that there were various versions, all slightly different, where whatever had happened belonged to living free, to festivals, love-ins and the body beautiful.

"She's rich?" he was asked by one of the J-block crowd.

"Heiress, loaded. Old Bostonian," beamed Matthew, warming to his part.

"Turned on?" asked a hairy.

"Buzzing," he replied, smiling.

There was also the meeting with his parents and his low-key response – a pokerfaced account delivered straight like a TV newsreader – which people took as a mark of maturity. He showed he was bigger, had his own vision and was more laid back than them. In any case he'd the right, as everyone told him, to choose who to be with and how he lived his life.

"What's her star sign?" Theresa had asked, as she turned up pictures from a well-thumbed pack that she'd arranged in lines, claiming that the cards were "showing interest" and "taking his side".

"It's whatever *you* decide," she'd said later, working with a sequence that she said was "convergent".

Matthew, as he watched, felt recognised.

She advised him, speaking slowly with one eye on her card-piles, to act from conviction and lay things on the table. "Don't let the shits stop you," she concluded. "Say it as it is. You're Matt."

The Matt she referred to was high on the list for deep-thought and angle, and had established across college a rep for doing different. He'd read it, knew it, had *connection, experience,* and now, with this thing about Robyn, had his own special status, a story to live up to.

So, although he played it down, people still took sides, speaking of Matthew as someone who'd stood up and made his contribution, one of those who did.

His experience had become a part of the newfound freedom, of soul up front and mind expanded, of closeness to being and deepened understanding. A wide-open world where the young were authentic, doing things on impulse, with expression, saying what they thought. For this was their right, an important statement. It belonged out there in an all-public space where people went barefoot, swore, made love, took pleasure: an all-out world, a drama of allowance.

As a story it sustained him and kept him writing letters that he posted daily, while Robyn, after an initial flurry, established hers as twice a week, though sometimes only once if her letters arrived together.

They both reported on parents – on his side the breach, on hers acceptance and a liking for his photo – and while Matthew dived into feelings, Robyn began low-key, writing more in general. But gradually her letters moved from the everyday factual to saying what she felt. The weather, a visit to a gallery, passages from books, it all sparked memories, made her think of him. Because she wanted him alone and beautiful on a trek through woods to an outback cabin owned by her uncle where he'd see the real America and be in touch with life.

With all her letters he read them several times, examining them for markers, a crossed-out word or a corner folded down. He kept them, like his parent's cheques, tucked away in a half-zipped pocket then later archived, filed centre shelf on the piled-up bookshelf. Their magic held him, not so much the words, but the thought of being chosen.

And when he wrote, he gave her purple: his ups and downs and free-form poetics about flower-life, music and archetypal dreams. And he read in her replies the promise of love, soon to be actual, the long-term thing.

Then, within a space of days, the story changed. It began with a letter about *subjects*, but faint on feelings, without the usual vows or talk of commitment. Next came a note, written just before sleep, pleading busyness and ending unsigned. Then a very long letter, arriving next day, bundled into rolls with dated entries, some typed, some handwritten, with a request that he read it carefully, a preface about being honest, coupled with a warning that it might seem sudden, and a hope that he'd understand.

In it she used the words *beautiful* and *poetic*, linked to their meeting and how she first saw him. There was much about happiness and doing your own thing. There were other words too – *realistic, doubtful* and *rethought* – leading to a section with words like *decision* and *better this way*. On the last page she told him what she should have said earlier, how someone had asked her, and now she knew her answer it made things impossible, and that Matthew shouldn't come over because she'd realised that in truth it just couldn't be.

Before he reached the end, Matthew wasn't there. This took back everything. His breathing had slowed, his thoughts had gone away. He could hear already his phrases telling Paul, the story around college and his parents passing judgement. He glimpsed himself being picked out and stared at. The boys were there behind him, threatening what they'd do.

When he'd read it all, he walked. He set out in a line, straight across campus and along by the river, reading snatches and checking back on passages with a feeling that what was happening must be somehow false, a weirdness of the heart. When he passed beneath a bridge he felt it as pressure, a roof closing down. Each step was an effort, a challenge. At one point he imagined jumping into water and his body washed up with her letter in his pocket and a half-finished poem, ink-run and crumpled, penned in reply. When he climbed to a road he looked around like a stranger, left and right, before setting off. Directionless, he walked. He was sad, he was lost, he didn't have connection. A blur-wall surrounded him as he passed through town.

And when he arrived at The Minster he'd a sense of exclusion, of life without purpose, as if he'd lost his footing, and he knew he must do something, even if it hurt, to put himself in touch.

He stood facing the facade then drew out the letter. He bent back the pages and took out a pen. At the spot they'd taken photos, he read back some words, saw her smiling and scribbled them out. Circling the square, he read more, swore, dug deeper and blanked another line. At the corner by the gate he hacked in further, this time a paragraph that he scrubbed completely. By the time he reached the sunken garden he'd taken to crosses, overscored comments and swear words in boxes. On the bench he pressed harder, tearing into paper. When the bells began – a few without order, ringing on and off – he scanned several pages, crossed them through, then picked up a stone to act as a paperweight and pinned them to the bench.

Sighing, he dug into his jacket to draw out her envelope. It was cream-white and shiny with a gummed flap and blue wavy lines across its upper edge. Glaring, he cancelled his address, wrote in Robyn's and wedged it between the bench slats. His fingers shook as he pouched it open.

Inside was a page that had slipped from the bundle. He drew it out and held it up, butterfly-like, before tearing, at first in half, then into quarters, then subdividing further, to end up with paper-shredded scraps that he pressed into the envelope. Returning to the letter he released it, one page at a time, from its paperweight. Moving mechanically, he repeated the process, dicing each sheet into halves, quarters, eighths, sixteenths, and pressing in more, till the envelope bulged like a waste sack.

Sealing up the flap, he set off. A shadow came with him hidden in his heart. Ignoring the glances from tourists and children, he crossed the square, the park, and out along the river, retracing past journeys to the sidearm running north. Holding his envelope, he walked forward with a sense of being guided.

At the north arm he remembered: *nothing more to say*. The water here was sluggish, deep at the centre, with outflow channels and foam in patches. He walked past factories with graffiti-ed metal gates, fire-blackened doors and broken fences. Where the towpath narrowed his thoughts seemed to jam. He'd brought this on himself by too much trusting.

A dip brought him out to a platform, a head-high fence and steps up to the footbridge where he'd split with Sally.

The sky was cloudy and the air was still as he stepped out on the walkway. His feet rang on metal as he sought out where they'd been. He'd a sense of something gathered, large and heavy, centred around his heart. He'd business to unload. At the middle he stopped, looking down at the water, and unsealed the envelope. Stirred by his fingers, a few stray bits spilled over. Stooping to retrieve them, he topped up the envelope and pushed it through the bars. Watchful, he upended and shook out its contents. A snowfall of paper tumbled downwards. As it landed, it spread out like a veil. It lay there, spot-white and powdery, then turned and expanded to slide off downstream. Some bits collected, lodged like foam against the bank, other bits spread and moved centre stream, while most hung still, caught within eddies trapped below the bridge.

He watched for a while, hearing his own breathing. It was over. The envelope was empty.

By now the papers had drifted beyond the walkway. They were shifting slowly, curling and branching like dye on water. A long white tail, bunched at one end, was moving, suspended on the flow. Even as he watched, it was putting out side shoots, like stems across glass.

He returned his attention to the bridge. Here was loss: a hollowed-out absence. It made him feel unreal. Here he was bound in by calculation, by *fact* as abstract, in cold dimension. The world felt hard and heavy and ungiving. This was the world of *things* that his father believed in.

He knew what followed, the walk to the post office, the queue, the stamp and the letter posted empty. He imagined its receipt, how she'd know from the writing, would unseal quickly then, as she realised what was missing, understand her loss.

His head felt tight. In his mind there were voices, drilling on a note: *Bye bye baby*, flattened, and repeating.

He wondered where it led. The sun had now emerged and the river was clear as the papers drifted off. The boxed-in walkway showed yellow-white and black. As the water glinted, he saw himself watching at the bus stop, hoping to glimpse the girl he'd seen whose eyes were not for him.

*Bye bye baby.*

He looked around for marks: his fist on metal, the bloodstains and letter-bits scattered. He glanced downstream to where the sun's glare was spreading. Perhaps it really didn't matter: the sunlight without tone, the river running slowly, the gestures into air. It had all just drifted, gone off separate and pulled itself apart.

One last look – to put it all behind him, or fix the place in memory – as he turned towards town, walking the long walk to post box and college, then late-night gatherings listening to people talking and diagnosing others with the four-beat call of a blues song sounding in his head:

*Bye bye baby*
*Bye bye baby*
*Bye bye baby, goodbye.*

# FIFTEEN

I married Stuart in a small service at our local church. Of course, I was nervous. When I woke on the day, I wondered what was happening. During the morning I was alive and all of a flutter. Edith was my bridesmaid and while she dressed me my mind was racing. I imagined something going missing, I wasn't looking right, and what if he got cold feet and didn't turn up? Then there were the bits and pieces, the zips and fasteners, the bouquet, the order of service.

Before we left Edith checked my hemline. "Look at you," she said, twisting a flower into my hair, "you're a picture."

I smiled and in the mirror she smiled back.

"Today's your big day," she said. "And you're ready."

"I hope so," I said.

She took my hand. "Don't worry, Mary, I'm with you now. It's what you always wanted."

I nodded.

"And I want you to know something," she said, lowering her eyes. Her cheeks had gone red. "I've thought about how I left. It wasn't good."

I tried to speak but nothing came out.

"And I'm sorry. It can't have been easy."

I really don't remember what we said next. But I do know the feeling, and what we did. Her words had freed us and suddenly we were hugging. It took me back to the stick in the shed. What had been broken had come together and we were sisters again.

She peered out of the window. "Well, looks like time's up," she said, pointing to the car at the gate with Stephen inside. "It's your day, lucky girl, so smile and let's be having you."

But behind her words I thought she sounded sad.

When we entered church and everyone stood up, I'd a feeling that I'd been there before. At the front were parents and behind that family. At the back the seats were all empty. It reminded me of Dad's funeral, with only us and his foreman there.

But our marriage was different. Stuart came forward, I let him lead, and we stood and listened. It was more than real, and oddly chatty. There was a warmth around us and a sense of together-ness. As the minister spoke, I could see us together in *The Captain's*, talking. It was as if there were two conversations going on at once. But of course, the minister's words won out. They were calmly beautiful and came from somewhere else. And when we said our vows, we were facing each other.

We didn't have a honeymoon. Instead we lived at home with Mum, calling it our hols. Mind, for Stuart it *was* a big break while for me it was more of a change. As a newly-wed I'd joined the grown-up women with households to run and I walked the streets with a special, here-I-am feel. Even though I'd not had children and we were living with Mum, I was growing.

The next change was Newcastle. We'd moved for Stuart's work. He'd studied as an architect and been put in charge of a new estate. We went there as outsiders, living in a flat and later in a house that he designed himself. It wasn't easy. Newcastle those days was big and busy and I soon began to feel homesick. The centre was dirty, I didn't know my way around and the faces in the streets seemed not quite there, as if they were in battle.

In a city like that we didn't really fit. We lived on a hill not far from Stuart's work, looking down on smoke and cranes and ship-yards. To us, it was all space and lightness, a top-of-the-world feel. To them, we were standoffish.

But the big change was marriage. Being with a man wasn't what I thought. My doubts began to surface, not all at once, but bit by bit. I tried to shut it out but if I was honest, I knew things were wrong. It's like watching the tide. If you look out to sea nothing's happening, but if you look at the beach it's gone in hours.

So, marriage wasn't easy. There were differences between us, things creeping in and the small stuff at the start soon took over. We'd differences over words, their meanings or how they'd been said. There were niggles about food, about money or where I'd put things, with lots of pauses and hard-to-read looks. But mainly silence and what I called *the wall*. The wall went up most evenings after work. And when that happened, although he was there, really he wasn't. His face went hard and his eyes glazed over. Like that, nothing seemed to touch him.

When I brought it up, he asked me what I meant. At the word *wall*, he looked puzzled. When I explained, he went cold. After that, whenever I mentioned it, he either said nothing or claimed I'd made it up. I'd a feeling that whatever I said he didn't really listen.

It was in his nature, of course. He was the man who knew what he wanted and had his answers ready, talking about "putting things in order" and "one step at a time". Like this he was clever and snappy and a man of the world. He was the boss, the one who gave orders and sorted out problems. He dealt with bills and

129

checked on wages, setting people on and laying them off. But looking back now I see him on his own, gazing out to sea. Because the real Stuart Lavender was hidden. I mean of course the man in the beach snap or alone on a cliff. He'd a big sad longing inside him, like an airman or an adventurer. I suppose it was the war, but it went back further. Inside him there were dark, strange places where he cut off altogether. He was a Lavender, blue on the surface, shading to violet, and I was his wife.

But, of course, it was a marriage. I'd given my hand and in those days that was it. We always kept our word. I knew that from Grace, she'd stood by Jack. So I lived in Newcastle, looking out across a big city with a feeling of loss, as if there was a gap all around us, or I was on my own. I wanted out, to go AWOL, sneak off in the night. It was what you might call my dream of no return. But the marriage came first. I'd given my vow. And unlike Edith or Stephen I couldn't run away.

# SIXTEEN

Welcome to The G-G-Generation Show, the #b4Igetold where we dig deep into the Sixties. This week we turn the spotlight on children of hippie parents. And hey! we're here to interview *Lavender Blues*, a young pantsdown comedy act #3shadeslurve who get off, so they say, on oversharing.

I asked Joe, Mia and Cass about their gigs and how their parents *re*-late to what they do.

Cass: Our parents? It was their idea. Reality TV. About us all.

Mia: Ha ha ha. Yes, Matt and M sit front row and heckle. Or they write academic articles about what we do, or should've done.

Joe: They've got into it now. But it was crossed legs at first and deep breaths. Lots of NIMBY. "I didn't say that, did I?" that kind of thing. But you only stay red-faced for ten mins max. After that you float off into space.

Mia: S ... happen, man.

Gen Show: So why call it confessional stand-up and why the f*** do it?

Joe: Suppose we get off on #doit. Blagging it, like our parents did. Going onandonandon about being us, or being them.

Mia: Actually, we're performing seals, grey ones with thinking caps – get it? – saying HELLO everybody, wakeywakey. Time to thinky-think.

GS: *Think?* About what?

Cass: Anything. UFOs, I Ching, levitation, fairy rings, getting laid, anti-war marches, whatever our parents got up to.

Joe: Or down to. Like being out of your depth, feeling silly and acting hip. They worked hard to cover.

Cass: Yeah, and ego-tripping. And looking down their noses at straights, right!?

GS: Really? And they still do all that?

Mia: Oh no. But they say they thought they were special. Like the whole world was watching, all day every day.

Cass: Yay. And we're just laughing at ourselves 2day. Poking fun at what it's like to grow up spoiled rotten.

GS: OK, right now folks, we've a few ads coming up, but hey, just stay listening! AFTER the break we'll give you a lot, lot more about the real live show …

♪ ♪ ♪

That summer Matthew went away. He had to as cover, to guard against discovery and not go under. So he took to living apart, went with what happened, and only put in an appearance at important gatherings, or when someone with problems wanted his opinion.

The letter had arrived in the last week of term, which made his retreat less obvious – lost in the talk of travelling, farewell parties and summertime festivals. His status was established as Matt-with-the-American going out by air mail who'd fly there over summer when he'd earned the bread. If he ducked out of socials people talked about his parents, about letters to Robyn or maybe seeking work, and if he went quiet his friends talked of giving him space, or simply let him be.

131

Paul helped, giving out that there were essays and a novel coming up, while Theresa said that he was adjusting, he felt his exposure and he needed to spend some head-time getting things together.

And it was Theresa who advised him, after using the shit word on Robyn in a *dictation* (a slow, meandering beat-talk ramble with disembodied expletives, shifting pronouns and oracular asides) and several exchanges conducted through her cards, that he mustn't tell anyone, especially his parents. "Don't let on, just make out you'll be in America."

Matthew was surprised. Glancing at Paul, who was plugged in to headphones, he asked how he could do that. When his friend didn't answer he added that America was the one place at the moment he didn't want to go.

Theresa smiled. "No need to, I've already sussed it." She gathered in her cards and stretched to a drawer, pulling out a red and purple box. The lid was brown and came separately. She reached to the bottom to extract a letter that she viewed against the light, smiling to herself, as if she were trying on clothes in a mirror. The letter was blue with a sprinkling of stars and coloured angels. She pointed to a rainbow symbol and described where it came from: a friend's place in the country where Matthew could spend the summer and no one would know. It was a commune, a kind of workshop where people dug poetry and theatre; she was sure he would like it. "They're very open, good to visitors," she said. "They were with me."

Gazing at her card-pile she described how she'd gone there as a schoolgirl, all lollipops and minis, to get herself turned on. "They don't do that now," she continued, picking up the box and running one finger along a dragon-shaped pattern channelled around the edge. "They made this for me," she added, smiling and folding in the letter. The lid didn't fit so she asked him to close it, which Matthew achieved after several attempts, by jamming it back like an ill-fitting hat. Theresa examined it then slipped it into a drawer and air-gazed into space while addressing them both: "Paul, you can get a van – yes? And Matt – you just say when and we'll go look. You'll dig it, man."

They travelled two days later. Matthew had packed a rucksack and a leftover cricket bag with clothes, books, equipment and a few choice albums. He'd put it together as a fall-back, in case he chose to stay. Paul and Theresa had a soft bag each. They all loaded the night before, then left early, smoking rollups and passing round a flask of black coffee.

For Matthew, going on a journey was a relief. He'd been hurt, and now he needed out. Because he'd started to go down, replaying his words and analysing his actions for what could have made a difference and where it might have led.

If he'd only tried that, or not done *that*.

*That* included recognising stops, watching for signals and getting in early with challenges and questions. With *that* he might have got back with Robyn or stayed with Sally. Although even with *that*, he'd a feeling it wasn't going to happen. For he saw that what he called his "letter love" had held him suspended without foundation or any real connection, in a strange kind of vanity, like a child pulling faces at its own reflection.

The sun was low, at first straight ahead and later to one side. The road was patched, narrow in places, and Paul drove slowly with the windows wide open. There were speakers growling blues while Matthew talked theories and Theresa dozed. As the sun rose higher, Matthew brightened. He hummed back a chorus and spotted different birds. When overtaken by cars with children he mad-clown waved, then peace-signed an ambulance, making nee-nor noises. When some bikers passed, he slipped into Steppenwolf then angled sideways, slotting himself head and shoulders out of the passenger-side window. Using his handkerchief, he buffed down the windscreen.

"You're mad," laughed Paul.

"Watch this," said Matthew. Holding the wing mirror, he reached across to flick off dirt from the far-right corner.

"Completely loco," his friend called, turning up the music.

They passed by a fenced-in airfield and out across farmland on a long straight road that led towards a flat-topped moorland escarpment. Theresa, who had revived, guided from memory. She directed them to a spur and a cone-shaped valley that rose to the moors. They made their way up, changing sides, driving past cool meadows, wild rhododendrons and overhanging rocks.

The commune lay near the valley head. Located by a ruin, it was reached along a track by a ribbon-thin stream and up past a plantation. They climbed through clearings to emerge at a hill farm surrounded by bracken and drystone walls. During the ascent Theresa sang. Her voice surprised Matthew. It was pure-toned and repetitious, but clear and flute-like. It felt like she was piping them in.

They came in sight of some low wooden huts. Set back on a ledge with trees as backdrop, the huts overlooked a field with what remained of a monastery on a mound to one side. As the van approached there was movement: a head, a tail, then legs of different sizes crowding to the huts. They arrived to a greeting by several large dogs, some hens and a herd of brown-haired goats. The animals ran forward, surrounding the van.

"Are they friendly?" called Matthew, winding up the window.

Paul grunted and inched slowly forward with the animals bleating, barking and cackling on all sides.

"Don't worry," called Theresa, "I know them all."

When they stopped, she stepped out first naming and shushing them, choir-like, into order. Her voice ran on as she stroked and patted them. She was at ease, contained within her past; this was her story.

As Paul and Matthew descended from the van, a man hailed Theresa. He was short and balding with patchwork leggings and a fixed expression. His face was round and wrinkled, pink around the edges and rather olde-worlde. Theresa introduced him as her good friend Eric.

"Welcome," he said, "this is our home. We want it to be yours." He continued speaking slowly, directing his voice towards Matthew. As he talked his face remained still and self-absorbed, like a child in prayer.

Moving stiffly, he led them on a tour, talking about *my people* and the tribes of the commune. Paul and Matthew followed him while Theresa guided her animals to a field, rejoining later. On the tour they viewed the wood and plaster huts, meeting several residents, all of them busy carving, painting or drawing shapes on cloth. In one hut, the largest, Eric introduced Fallon, his Queen, who was busy brewing tea on a cast-iron range. She was short like him, with her hair in pigtails, betel-yellow teeth and a high Mayan-like forehead. Her smile when she saw them was veiled but appealing. "You'll join us?" she asked, indicating a man and two women already drinking from large earthen mugs. She appeared to be addressing a back-row audience, a foot behind their heads.

Eric, who announced he'd business to attend to, left them with Fallon, issuing instructions to make them welcome. "You know how it is," he said, "I may be some time ..." and he moved to the door, slowly shaking his head.

In his absence they finger-picked salad and sampled different brews, mostly what Fallon called "vintage", a brown-grey liquid that tasted of tannin and cloves. There were smiles and nods but no names given and precious little conversation. It reminded Matthew of eating with parents.

When they'd had their fill, they pocketed a few apples, picked up their bags from the vehicle and followed Fallon. She led to two adjacent huts daubed with mud and surrounded at knee height by a log-roll stockade.

"Your cabins. They're protected," she said, pointing to a Horus-eye painted on each door. Behind them was an overgrown garden with a rusted wood-saw and a half-collapsed bench.

"Follow the path," she said, leading behind a shed to a dried-up pool and a hole in the ground with newspaper and flies. "For guests," she said airily, ignoring the smell. On their return she told them about the timings of meals and then, promising to come around when Eric was back, left them to settle.

The afternoon passed with Paul and Theresa stretched out together on bamboo recliners that they'd found in the shed, while Matthew walked on his own exploring the woods. He circled uphill, keeping within earshot, stopping to examine the moss on rocks and multi-coloured fungi. The wood was mixed, with holly in patches, bare ground with gorse, and overgrown areas sprouting ivy and brambles. As he walked, he drifted. Already he felt calm. Here in the quiet he could hear his own breathing. There was no one watching and he chose a footpath that took him through rocks and waist-high ferns, skirting the border between deciduous and pine. He felt glad to be alone.

On his return Matthew found a folded piece of paper pinned to the door. It told him that they'd waited, but now they'd gone to supper. He checked his watch then headed downhill, retracing his footsteps to reach the main hut. Peering round the door, he saw Paul and Theresa on a low wooden bench surrounded by residents on scattered cushions. An upbeat Eric was speaking. Sat forward on a cassock in an oversized chair, he announced where they'd come from, apparently oblivious of Matthew's entrance.

"And so to tea," he concluded with a wave. Fallon rose and circulated with a kettle pouring grey-yellow liquid into pint-sized mugs. When everyone had been served, Eric stood, brandishing a torn-off scrap of paper.

"Ah," murmured Fallon, "the piece." The room fell silent.

Eric announced that he'd reworked a poem that he wanted to deliver in honour of their guests. His listeners smiled and leaned forward. Eric explained that he'd found his inspiration in something that had happened, a small event taken from childhood. His audience nodded. Speaking slowly, he described his experience, a moment of truth occurring regularly on the toilet. Another group nod. He proceeded to tell about the tiles, their height and colour, numbers in a row, then about the cistern – its make and its noise, unlidded – then counting the bristles on the toilet brush, describing the lino, the door, its handle, then on to frosted glass, cracks in the ceiling and the blue thing down the toilet. When he'd finally finished listing and those around had expressed their appreciation, he held up his paper that was, he said, the very latest version that he'd read, just as it was.

His listeners sat up.

What followed was conversational: five lines, with pauses, unrhymed, delivered in a mumble. The lines, bare and undecorated, could have been taken from a route map or a postcard sent home. They were almost without colour, didn't sound meant and belonged to notices on the wall, *Reader's Digest* or gossip on the phone.

When he'd finished, Eric looked about with a half-bemused smile. Applause followed quickly and shouts of bravo. There were cries of approval, calls for more, then a sudden hush, and another reading. This time a woman called Denise wearing brownline glasses who began her poem squatting. She read in a drone from a hard-backed scrapbook, like a monk chanting timetables. The words were technical and specialist, about scientific measurement and episodes from history. There were sections dealing with dentistry, others on Zen, then prosthetics as an art compared to origami, plus a number of lacunae quoting Eric's poems and a passage about soil-types with tips on growing lettuce and how to deal with slugs.

Two men followed, the first appearing with a roll of perforated paper that he read from staccato, the other hesitant, staring blankly, filling up the gaps with quiet one-liners and lugubrious smiles. The first talked of concepts and boundaries crossed, the second of sadness and the uselessness of words. Both had supporters: a red-faced man declaring for the first, and an overweight woman, ooh-aahing and thrilled by feeling, brought to her feet by the second reader's set. "That's so special," she said when her hero paused between stanzas. "Beautiful, beautiful," she cooed when he resumed at a mumble. "Such a big heart," she declared as he shuffled off finally, grinning to himself.

The first half ended with a flat-voiced woman wearing overalls and a cap. Waving for quiet, she walked to the front to take on her audience. Short, with large brown eyes and a teasing expression, she introduced herself as Clarry, a visitor who published poetry and worked as an illustrator. After reading from a notebook she plugged her workshop: an early evening walkabout for sketching nature.

In the break that followed, other residents entered and lined up at a table filled with raw veg, berries and a dough-like preparation smeared with hummus. There was talk of macrobiotics and eating mushrooms.

After sampling briefly, Paul and Matthew stepped outside to smoke. They lit up by a birch tree, then walked to a distance while Theresa herded the animals to a sunspot in the field.

"What d'you think?" asked Paul.

"Seems like a case for earplugs."

"You don't go for the poetry?"

"The what?"

Paul inhaled, gazing downhill towards Theresa who was petting a large black dog. There were shadows now gathering, extending from the ruin. Where Theresa stood, she was close to what looked like a slowly lengthening pool. A storm of insects had lifted just behind, sketching a nimbus to her head.

Paul breathed out and smiled. His attention circled from the monastery to the cabins, ending with a quick appraising glance directed to his friend. "Will you manage here all right?" he enquired quietly.

"Of course I will."

"You sure?"

"One day at a time, I'll do it."

The air now was hazy. In the field below Theresa and her animals were walking uphill, pushing through flattened grasses, returning to the pens.

"She likes it here," said Matthew.

Paul agreed. An unspoken question hovered in the air. Matthew drew down sharply then heeled his cigarette against a rock. "And I will too," he said, contriving to sound definite.

"You won't get to thinking?"

"No," Matthew said, firmly, "not about Robyn anyway. I won't let that happen."

When Theresa arrived, he suggested they went back in, gave themselves up, accepted what was on offer and listened to the poetry.

By the following afternoon when Paul and Theresa were leaving, Matthew was deep in thought. The commune wasn't what he'd expected. It was full of people who seemed to have been there forever. They lived in a world set apart: an unreal, head-in-the-clouds bubble where their purpose was to please. He could see it in Fallon with her urge to give service and in the others in their willingness to be led. But what *they* called feeling and meaning he called a mess. He didn't feel he belonged.

There was also Eric and what he called poetry. Not just poetry but a whole arts evening about what he, as link-man and controller, described as *shared direction.* Beginning, in the second half, with words that rhymed using rhythm and imagery, and a lot that didn't. A poetry of incident and detail, of flies on windowpanes, daisy heads, splinters and spiders in the bath. Then long, ranting stand-up poems thrown out by breathless performers, followed by pure-ice poems read with deportment, joke poems, vignettes, and slice-of-life poems – during which Matt posed as The Thinker, elbow on one knee and eyeballs showing blank.

Later there had been music (*more direction* said Eric, *praise for who we are*) with deadpan wailers and Dylan-type droners repeating lyrics about war and generation. Then you-and-me mumblers groaning darkly through two-note refrains about love and dreams and parting. Later still the folkies, with one hand-cupped ear, sun-and-moon lyrics and hillbilly accents. Then their finger-picking accompanists, trying out instruments – a tone-flat accordion, a rattly tambourine, pipes that wheezed and assorted stringed plonkers, vibrators, resonators and untuned elastic bands; the whole run together in a mud-mix of half notes, foot stomps, twangs, snaps, apologies, flat-toned asides and heavy, stertorous breathing.

"Wish me luck," said Matthew, watching Paul as he climbed into the van. It had taken all morning and several cups of coffee to recover from the show.

His friend pushed back into the dented leather seat. "Earplugs, remember?"

"It might take more than that."

Paul checked his hair in the rear-view mirror. "This has to be better than parents."

"The least bad option."

Theresa appeared. Taking her place next to Paul, she wound down the window and gestured for Matthew to look across the field. The animals, she said, would look after him.

139

Paul started the van calling, pilot-like, above the engine: "Don't do anything I wouldn't do."

Matthew laughed. "So I'm absolutely free, yes?"

They shared a boyish grin.

"There might be a few limits."

"No axe man stuff?"

"That's OK, I'll come and stand bail."

Paul let out the clutch and the van bounced off through the trees and back to the track that ran beside the stream. It swayed and rattled, giving out sounds of guitars growling and voices hitting notes. Matthew waved and Theresa waved back. His last glimpse was the back doors disappearing downhill with red-orange flashes shading into green.

That afternoon he determined to keep well apart and play the waiting game. Returning to his hut he drew out a bowl and filled it from the standpipe, splashing his face before sitting out in a deckchair with a notebook and a biro. At first he doodled, rising once to seek out a novel that he skimmed without interest. Then he sat back looking skyward. There were thin banks of cloud closing in. In the trees there were nesting birds calling in bursts. Somewhere at a distance a plane was climbing.

After chewing on his pen, he began to write. Sketches only, flash-thoughts, phrases in the head. He imagined his friends driving down the valley and mapped back their journey, remembering what they'd said. Raising his head, he took in the view. A wood, a slope, a grass patch, leading to the monastery. Soft light over stone with midges. Thin cloud and shadows. A field of dreams.

A breeze touched his face and he thought of Robyn. She'd hit on something hidden and left him feeling numb. It had happened without warning. He'd made that commitment and then – what then? Well, of course, she'd set him up. She'd dipped in and tested before losing all interest. She'd simply had her fill.

Glancing at his writing, he shivered. Purple, as usual, with a thin line of grey hidden under gold. Himself made up, grand and elaborate, straining to impress. Reach for the sky and your trousers fall down.

He pictured the college, seeing its lake with ducks around the margins and students on the grass. Smoking, dreaming, they'd talked of freedom and far-out experiences. Looking for enlightenment they'd made up their own high. And he saw himself there, not quite with them and not quite apart. He'd lived it, stepped off the ladder, and now was moving on.

Rising, he stretched and put aside the notepad. The air was cooling and the breeze had strengthened, scattering the clouds. From behind the trees long bars of sunlight were quartering the landscape. Shifting forward, he walked out to the field. His eye caught the monastery as he pushed through grass. The remains of its tower showed above the trees. Rough-cut and crumbled, it leaned in places. An arch on one side was clothed in ivy. A crow's nest at the top looked like a hairpiece.

At the back of his mind he'd decided, at least his next move. It was what he wanted. He'd give it a go, join in to show willing, and try Clarry's workshop.

When he arrived, Matthew was surprised to find Clarry on her own sitting behind the tower sketching a plant. Her short-framed body was leaning sideways, studying her subject from more than one angle. A few loose strands of hair curled out from beneath her cap.

"Is this the workshop?" he asked.

"Not anymore."

"You mean it's changed?"

"It's off. Eric didn't want it." Her voice was calm and distanced, but also quite challenging. "It's not unexpected," she added, when Matthew showed surprise.

"Any particular reason?"

"Control. *His* decision, simple as that."

"And that's it," he answered, fitting to her mood.

"Sees me as a threat," she said, packing away her sketchpad.

"He would."

"But I'm glad you came."

"Oh?"

"Yes," she said softly, looking him in the face.

Colouring, he looked away.

"You're Matthew, yes?" she said coaxingly.

He nodded, wondering what might happen next.

"Was there a reason you came here?" she asked.

"A reason?" he echoed, sounding puzzled.

"Yes, why? Did something drive you?"

"Escape," he answered quickly, without a second's thought.

"From parents?"

"That's right."

"And a girl perhaps?"

His silence said it all.

Clarry checked her watch. "You hungry? There's food, if you come back to my cabin."

Matthew took a breath. It was that simple.

"Well yes, that would be nice," he said, steadying his voice.

Clarry gazed down the slope. From where they stood a pearl-grey moon was rising in a clear sky. "Look," she said, touching his arm, "it's bigger tonight." Following her gaze, he nodded then checked around the view. The wood behind had darkened. By them was the tower and below that the field. Long aisles of shadow were running from where they stood, cutting paths across the grass.

"Back to yours?"

By way of an answer Clarry fitted her arm in his and they set off along a ridge, glancing occasionally at the blue-grey moon.

When they reached her hut, the breeze had returned. Colder now, it made him more aware. He backed away slightly, withdrawing his arm. "I want to know the deal," he said, frowning.

"Of course, you're bound to." Her words sounded practised: this was normal, she understood his feelings.

"OK, so where does this lead to?" he asked, nodding to the door.

"To whatever happens next."

"You mean it's a story?"

"More of a workshop."

He weighed her words, gazing into air. "You writing something?"

"In the head, perhaps."

"About a young man?"

"Could well be."

"And is he wild?"

"Very."

"Ah, Rake's Progress …"

"That's one version."

"And how does it turn out?"

"He escapes."

Matthew grinned.

"If he's willing, that is," she added, "and not afraid."

Leaning forward, Matthew eyed the door. "OK, I'm ready. Now, let's see, this young man's name …?"

That night she showed him how. After eating in the half light, they held hands and chatted before taking themselves to bed. Passing through a curtain, they canoodled lightly then began their moves. Slow moves undressing, led by feel, with Matthew wondering vaguely how much he could manage, and whether for him the act would need forcing.

In the dark she smelled fresh, with a hint of something herbal. "Don't worry," she said, sensing his mood. Her hand was there, helping. She reached around and guided, coaxing when he faltered. He'd got to relax, she whispered, just allow it to happen.

Gradually she worked and teased him till he was hard. "Yes," she murmured. "Oh yes," tucking herself under. Once in, he was hers. "That's it," she exclaimed, shaking. She jerked and squirmed and began calling. Her calls became quicker, taking on a panting, forcing tightness, rising to a cry as she pushed towards climax then arrived with a shout, a kick and sudden yelping sigh.

After lying still, she pulled up and kissed him. "That was good," she said. "Now you. Just lie back." She turned, rolling to one side and pressed him to the mattress. Climbing on top, she hitched and positioned, teased him with tongue and finger before slotting inside. "It's easy," she called blithely, as if she was on a swing, "just enjoy."

Feeling the lift, he wanted to say yes. There was a *no* close behind, but the *yes* grew louder, turning into cries as he saw himself running forward, shouting on the beach. He drove himself on, repeating *yes*. He mustn't look back or the *no* would catch him. The tide was in and he was singing out his word, but before he could be heard, the need took over. The wind got up and his body had swollen. He was there at the top hearing the shout and running in the sun. And then it was all happening, he was hot and glowing and giving himself up. And when he came, it was quickly.

"Better?" Clarry asked afterwards, smiling. She added a few random thoughts, then dozed off for the night, in need of nothing more.

Stretched out by her side, Matthew drifted. He felt he'd got there. It was as if a door had opened and he'd walked out into the woods. When it came, his sleep was a drift into something dark and fleshy and sweetly impulsive.

Waking before dawn they washed, wrapped themselves in blankets, and Clarry lit a lamp. Turning out a cupboard, she produced biscuits with goats' cheese and honey. While Matthew ate, she boiled a kettle and dressed in a corner throwing out remarks about taking chances and paths that crossed. While she moved around the cabin she spoke of life's pleasures and lucky dips. She also made it clear, speaking without sentiment, that this was a one-off. She'd wanted, that was all.

When they stepped outside it was cool and the moon was still visible. Smaller now, it was milk-white and shadowed. Its surface was pitted with off-greys and blues.

Clarry stood smiling. "It won't be long," she said nodding to the east. A faint rim of sunlight was unfolding slowly, flattening and widening, filling up the air. "Waxing gibbous," she announced, turning to the moon. Already it was fading. "Of course, it'll still be there, all day, but we won't see a thing, except shades of blue."

Matthew felt her distancing. Whatever happened now, he'd had his experience, nothing could touch him. "What next?" he asked.

"I shall leave and go home."

"You're not staying?"

She shook her head.

"Had enough, eh?"

"Episode over," she said. "Next phase begins."

He gazed moon-wards, considering what she'd said. "It's time to make a move – yes?"

Clarry confirmed. The moon now was gauzy and blurred around the edges. "But, with sixteen hours left," she added, "it'll be quietly."

Matthew looked around with a sense of recognition. Whatever she meant, it seemed it must be so. The morning was clearing, they'd been together briefly, their lives were moving on.

♯ ♯ ♯

Welcome back to The G-G-Generation Show.

For folks just joining us, I have with me Cass, Joe and Mia Lavender. They've been telling us what it's like to be at their *Lavender Blues* STANDUP SHOW. Now, guys, I hear you've a new act out and it's a blast, as we say. OK, let's hear about it. First-up, does this show have a name?

Cass: Not till now, but #ITSABLAST sounds cool.

GS: All right. Who's kicking off? What about you, Mia? Tell us what you do …

Mia: That's easy. At the start I'm Fat Freddy's Cat with BIG whiskers. They shake as I move, making me look a bit insecty. I'm wearing striped pyjamas so I'm the clown-cat as well. It's fun. Someone gives me a clown horn and I'm circling the stage honking like a goose. I've a big tail that swishes across the floor as I do it. Then I quick-change into an all-white costume and I mime in slowmo. It's a Sixties piece by Lindsay Kemp, called *The Fool*. There's lots more, but you get the idea …

GS: What about you, Cass?

Cass: Well, let's see. I start as Vanessa Redgrave on voiceover mixed with Honor Blackman. In one part I'm the Queen, but then I get more hip-American and arty. There's a lot of swearing in that bit.

GS: And you Joe?

Joe: Whatever. It varies. Say I start solo, I pick up the mike and pretend my dad's in it. "Is anybody there?" in a séance voice, that kind of thing. Of course, he's reading a book. "Dad," I say, "hey man, read me a story." Then I loop the mike cord over the stand and drop it down, still talking. Next, I lie underneath, swinging it above me, telling the audience I'm on the couch. I say I'm c-c-crazy, loony, loco, hahahahaha, I share some oedipal stuff, and answer myself, in his voice. It's deep, like he's God, and mine's high and squeaky. But then he has a go over stupid stuff like whose turn it is to put out the rubbish. Yeah-yeah-yeah. So I squeal and squeal till he gives up, saying I'm just like he was at that age. When I get up, I tell the audience how small he makes me feel. I look sad ☹, carrying on about how he's done it all and left me nowhere to go. When I get to singing *I am your son, but I wish I knew you* and the audience are feeling really sick I walk off stage. And that's it.

GS: Lol. That's Cat Stevens – yes?!

Cass: Father and son, he's always singing it.

Mia: That's when he's not joshing. Dad and him. *Anything you can do …*

Cass: The thing is Mum knows where it goes back to. *My Way*, she says.

Mia: OMG that's a song IDL. I mean *really, really* IDL.

Joe: It's way, way before Sinatra. I've looked into it with Mum. The families did it. Telling their kids be individual, stand up for themselves.

GS: WHOAH. So, the *me generation* were …

Cass: Just like dear old dad.

Joe: Yay. Meet the new boss. Same as the old boss.

GS: What about your act? What else? Tell.

Mia: Well, later in, Cass and me do a happening. I get two stepladders with a plank between them and sit on top singing *Nellie the Elephant*. Then I read the phone directory. It's a poem.

GS: A poem?

Mia: OK, listen. whiiish yogunsun arima bobobo hakkyho mungum thressssssss …

146

GS: WTFDYM?

Cass: It's a sound poem. And while Mia's going on, I'm mopping the floor with a cabbage. Or spreading jam on pillows. Or trying on lampshades. Or standing in the corner doing nothing.

Mia: And then I go into the audience and we all do a sound poem together. Clap-clap-clap, glonkow unsaat vooooox bephat p-p-p-pym and Jabberwocky stuff.

GS: So how does it all end? Can it end?

Joe: We dance.

♯ ♯ ♯

Over the next week Matthew, who'd taken to sitting out beside his hut at the high end of the commune, was spoken about often. His name came up at gatherings where they talked about him with interest and a degree of concern. Questions were raised about whether he felt welcome, so he found himself visited. Eric called daily and Fallon usually followed, inviting him to tea. He was provided with food, invited to view artworks, read-to over meals, asked to take part in the naming of trees, shown cushion-stuffing, body painting, cake decoration, worm counting and how to trace ley lines. Matthew was their project.

"I'm grateful," he told Eric, and he meant it as long as he'd the freedom to keep himself apart. "It's a wonderful place," he continued, gazing up the valley. His words set off a song in his head: *I can see for miles and miles and miles and miles and miles.* The music and the view went up to the horizon. Beyond that the cream-grey clouds were spreading slowly.

Eric didn't look up. He wanted, he said, the place to be Matthew's, a home from home. "Trust us," he said, and his eyes strayed sideways, searching the grass for something more to say.

Matthew thanked him.

Eric smiled vaguely. "There's a reading this morning," he said with a hint of invitation.

Matthew merely registered.

"You are welcome any time. Whenever you're ready."

"I've heard," countered Matthew, "there's another part to the commune."

His mentor paused, weighing his reply.

"Is that true?" Matthew asked.

Speaking slowly, Eric confirmed. When questioned further he pointed to a path that led, he said, to the adjoining valley. "People call it The Colony," he said airily.

"And what do they do there?"

The response was equivocal; it seemed very little.

Matthew nodded. With each half-answer his attention had sharpened. "Do you guys not get on?"

Eric seemed not to hear.

Matthew's eyes swept the valley like an explorer. "Sounds interesting." He cut across Eric's reply with a smile. "That's where I'll be," he said, waving forward, and set off down the path, calling back to Eric to enjoy his reading.

The route around the hillside circled through pines. It was broad and rutted, with a verge on both sides. The open parts were covered with cotton grass and mosses and bracken in clumps. Everywhere was damp.

Passing from sunlight into shade, Matthew considered what had happened. One night, and he'd grown. One night and away, with no case to answer. She'd come and gone and left him free. And he wondered as he walked, if he'd really turned the corner and this was his new outlook, the way he'd come to be.

He walked past a firebreak edged with firs. In the centre, where a long line of pylons looped downhill, it dropped to a river and a blue-green haze. He stood and looked, then continued forward with the trees now closer. As he gazed along the rows he smelled the wood-damp, where the forest slept. It was cool and quiet like a closed-up room. He imagined it in stories with wolves and strange lights. He looked for things hidden, as if this was a journey and he was taking notes. There were ghosts and insects, bark with fungi and sun-shafts into earth.

At a bend in the path the mood dropped away. The trees thinned out and the scenery changed. Here he could view the adjacent valley. It spread down from the moors in a wash of vegetation, light green to turquoise, wood-brown to khaki – and suddenly the air felt warm. As he descended, ivies took over, the trees became squat, and occasional patches of Himalayan balsam appeared around the path.

Reaching a fork, he paused beside a small green pool where insects hovered. At the edge there were clumps of water-crowfoot and yellowing reeds. Birds sang, their voices magnified by the stillness all around. To one side, the trees thinned out. As he walked on, he noticed a large, asymmetric house that he took to be the colony. Set back in a field, it was surrounded by tyre tracks. As he struck towards it his eye was caught by some cairn-like objects, appearing in the grasses. He stopped to study one. Built of layered stones and tapering at the top, it looked like an obelisk made of broken tiles.

As he glanced back to the house, he saw a large-bodied woman approaching. Dressed in a caftan, she wore her hair in a straw-coloured plait down her back. She closed on him quickly with a spring in her step and a toothy smile. Her eyes were large, blue and inquiring.

She greeted him from some yards off. Her voice helloed and welcomed him as she waved one baton-like finger, naming the house, the field and the valley. It felt like the prologue to a play.

"And I'm Jenny Deane. Pleased to meet you," she announced, stretching out her hand.

He returned her greeting, feeling her gaze like a mirror to the sun.

"You're staying with the commune?"

"That's right."

"And you know this is the colony?"

"Hmm, so I'd heard." He looked around, "Nice place – beautiful. But why *colony*?"

"I suppose, because it's for *artists*."

"Self-styled, with leader?"

"Just artists. Doing our best ..."

He nodded slowly. It seemed they shared a view.

Jenny checked where he'd come from, his town and university, adding with a smile that she'd heard they called him Matt.

Matthew gave his name in full then asked about the cone.

"It's a sculpture, made from gathered stones."

He examined it, stepping round.

"Do you like it?" she asked.

"Interesting question," he said slowly. Her energy made him careful.

"Say what you feel."

He asked if he could touch it. Encouraged by Jenny, he ran his hand lightly across the top and crouched down to sight along the courses. He peered through a crack, inserting a finger, then lay out on the grass, viewing like a mechanic from below. "Ant's eye view," he said then stood up, smiling. "It's great. I'd not expected ..."

Jenny raised one eyebrow.

"It's a surprise, and a change," he said, wryly.

"You mean after ..." she said, nodding in the direction of the other valley.

"Yes them."

She asked how he'd coped.

"There are ways. It's like dealing with toothache. However bad you think it's going to be, expect worse."

"Factor of ten, that sort of stuff?"

"Off the scale."

Jenny laughed dryly, pressing him for details.

Matthew gave a few examples: a phrase from Eric's poem, the odd quote from Denise, impressions of strummers and out of breath folkies, ending with a summary of what he'd said to Paul. He kept Clarry out of it.

She found his talk of axe men amusing. "And a gobful of rocks for our *leader*?" she suggested casually, looking at the sculpture.

He grinned and began counting cones.

"Nine in all," she said, raising her voice as she gestured around the field. "See, there and there, and over there. I made them with visitors and my family."

He asked about shape and how long they lasted.

Jenny pointed to a cone with one side cut open. "Things develop," she said, leading him over. "Either at the time or afterwards."

"And that's part of it?" he said, crouching down.

"Exactly so. This one's all structure, like anatomical drawings."

Matthew leaned closer. "It's interlocking," he said, peering inside. In the layered stones he could see the interiors of caves and low-roofed huts: "Reminds me of the things I used to build with kits. They fitted like this does." Moving position, he closed one eye to sight along the break. "But they had mortar and plans."

Jenny's voice dropped, "Whereas this just *is*."

He stepped around and back. This was a different mode, a place set apart where norms were suspended. He glanced at Jenny, who was watching, keeping connection. It was as if there was a shield, an air-wrapped silence and they were both inside it, contained by life.

"Yes, it *exists* …" he said, looking around the field. It was brown and yellow, full of different grasses. Their dried-out seed heads shone in sunlight. And between the grasses, standing, thrust up like herms: Jenny's statues.

"You talk like they're alive," he said, playful now.

"Well, we've named them."

He wondered briefly if he'd missed something.

"They're the planets," she continued, turning a circle and naming each one.

He followed as she turned. The sculptures were positioned loosely in a line. He could see how they fitted. "So, it's astrological?" he asked, with a tongue-in-cheek smile.

"No, just space. Space and time and how things happen."

Matthew felt her closing. All at once she was part of something larger. Not just a watcher, but out there, with her sculptures, in the business of becoming.

And he knew that he was going to like her.

Jenny asked him in and they crossed the field to stand before the house. It was thick-walled, whitewashed and built out into dogleg extensions, each with recessed windows divided into squares. Reaching the front door, Matthew heard the voices of children calling from inside. Entering, he smiled. The house was full of chatter and movement.

Jenny led the way over bare boards and rugs, turning a corner into a kitchen with a range. At one end were some chairs around a paint-stained table that filled up a large-windowed diner.

"My brood," she said, gesturing towards three young girls busy doing art. At one end of the table, crouched forward, was a bearded, thin-faced Afro-Caribbean man. He was shoulder to shoulder with one of the girls, guiding as she drew. With his sharp, attentive eyes and square-framed glasses, he looked more like a teacher than their father.

"Meet the prof," Jenny said, "Leon Deane: Matthew Lavender."

The hand Matthew shook was lithe and slight with a turn of pressure that surprised him. "You were looking at the planets," Leon said.

"You know?"

"A man has his eyes." He glanced round proudly at his girls. "And two eyes good, four pairs better."

"Five pairs, with glasses," said Jenny, laughing.

Leon reached over and took her by the hand: "And this is she, my woman."

The girls began to call. They wanted help, could Daddy just show them, and did the man do pictures?

Leon returned them to task then introduced Matthew to his daughters, Rosa, Jasmine and Daisy. They were bare-armed and paint–stained with long oval faces and mischievous eyes. Together they'd covered the table with loose-sheaf books and off-grey papers that they'd streaked and spotted with colour dots and glued-on stars. There were paint pots everywhere, brushes in water, piled up magazines and crumpled silver paper. In one corner Leon held custody of the scissors, packed in a box together with glue and assorted coloured pencils.

Matthew joined in, asking what they'd done, and the girls demonstrated. There were small blobs that were eyes, flower heads in pastel, lots of sheep, monochrome houses, red-hatted grandmas and large sprawly washes that the girls called sky, or sea-with-sun, or desert island views.

Rosa liked trees. She made them in splodges with candelabra arms and sun-ray auras. On the arms she drew fairies and owl-grey objects that she referred to as her friends. Between humming and shifting her chair, Rosa asked where she should put things and what she should call them. As she worked, she twisted the bobble that fixed her hair in an upward ponytail. Jasmine beside her, whose hair sprang out in two thick bunches, leaned forward often to re-dip a brush or rummage through papers to extract something shiny. Her leans caused Rosa to wriggle and cry, "Not there!" as her older sister drip-smeared paint or dislodged paper. Jasmine, who seemed oblivious, continued with her artwork, filling up a sketchpad with horse heads, ballet shoes and round-faced portraits of teachers from her school.

With Daisy it was different. Head down and hair out (which she wore soft Afro), she had her own world. Her pictures were of space-ships landing on planets with odd and eccentric multi-limbed crea-tures, framed and captioned in cartoon series. There were maps she'd drawn of journeys through unknown habitats with cellar drops and back stairs and hideouts underneath. Two finger walkabouts by rock falls, tracing the prints of long-extinct animals. Strange beast hunts using telescopes and brooms. And a collection of faces in boxes with stalk heads and aerials stuck into flesh.

Daisy wanted Matthew to join her. He was her supporter, there to sharpen pencils and use his big teeth to prise open boxes and unblock the glue. For her he was special.

Which didn't suit Rosa who wanted attention. And didn't suit Jasmine who didn't want Rosa. And didn't suit Daisy who just needed Matthew. And didn't suit Matthew who had to be everywhere.

Then Leon took over. "Hush," he insisted, using both arms, tent-like, to enclose all three. "Volume down," he continued, repeating his phrase twice, each time more gently. As the girls subsided, he led them into breathing, counting as divers to see how long they could hold. Then, returning them to task, he became their stockman issuing powder paints, supplying brushes and carrying water from the sink. "They want," he said, waving Matthew closer, "we give."

He also acted as referee, giving time out and warnings. Particularly with Jasmine who, as the session progressed, took a liking to everything of Rosa's. If her sister had a pen it became Jasmine's; any special paper was subject to forfeit; a brush, a rubber, anything small was hers for the taking.

Reaching for her arm, Leon intervened. "A word," he said, looking her in the eye. "Everything's by shares," he began, his voice tone balanced between gentleness and warning.

Jasmine said nothing.

"Take air, for instance – you remember?"

The girl looked down, embarrassed. He coaxed her and she returned a few words.

"That's right, *shared*," he confirmed. "And sun is everyone's, yes?"

Jasmine nodded.

"And earth …" he continued, listing examples, including her sister.

When his talk ended, Jasmine returned to her art, sharing and passing things to Rosa.

"You see?" said Jenny, as she poured out honey-sweetened tea, passed around in bowls, with a plate each of cherries. "He's my good man. These girls listen up."

Leon grinned. "Or they'll be beaten, by their mother."

Jenny's reply was pre-empted by Rosa with an appeal about Jasmine, who counter-claimed loudly and a small dispute set up, till both parents shushed them.

"Count time," said Leon, and led the two girls into calling out numbers. When they'd run through twice, he asked who was thirsty and did they want some eats?

It required both parents, backed up by Matthew, to take orders, equalising slices and levelling drinks before dishing out. Leon cleared space, pushing back papers and pots, while Jenny directed the meal.

After firsts, and selected second helpings, with yawns and fidgets and attempts to leave the table, a change was suggested. They'd been too long indoors and needed to get out. Leon said the word, Matthew echoed, and a chorus of approval led to a move outside.

Emerging in a line with the two men behind them, the girls started forward. A track downhill led to a copse, taking them from sunlight into tree-lined interiors. The shift under cover was sudden. They were in the woods, and edgy.

"Ya ya," called Jasmine, "is there anybody there?" She dodged around Rosa, waving her arms and walking tall.

Her sister bristled. "Ya ya ya ya," she repeated, throwing out her chest.

Daisy at the back made weird ghostie noises.

The path turned a corner and dropped to a scooped-out bowl with beech trees above and some minor open quarrying, now disused. At the centre was a thick rope with a bucket seat hung from an overhanging branch. To one side, a wooden construction built out from rock held up the branch.

"I'm king of the castle," cried Jasmine as she ran into the dip. Rosa and Daisy followed at a distance with Matthew close behind. Leon stood back, lifeguard-style, watching from above. "This's mine," called Jasmine, seizing the swing rope and drawing it to one side. Standing on the seat, she threw her weight against the rope to kick off like a rider. "Push me!" she cried as she swayed back and forth. "Push!" she repeated as she gradually lost speed. "Push-push!" she called, idling at the centre of the dip.

At the top of the slope, Leon held up three fingers and Matthew, clowning slightly, squared his shoulders. Rehearsing internally, he descended to the girl. When he arrived, she had lowered herself backwards to occupy the seat. "Now Jasmine," he said, attaching her buckle strap, "you get three pushes, that's all. Then it's your sisters' turn."

The girl stayed silent.

He repeated, and she nodded.

"Agreed?"

She murmured, vaguely.

"Say it – 'Yes'."

"Yes."

"And again, so you mean it."

"*Yes.*"

"OK then, watch out!"

He caught on to the seat and stepped back, raising her from behind to shoulder height. "Wheeeee!" he cried, hurling her forward like a javelin.

Jasmine shrieked as she travelled out on a curve, returning at speed in a big looping arc. "Higher!" she yelled as she levelled to his shoulders. Matthew watched her through an arc, then gripped and threw her forward, propelling her body to an even bigger loop. "Higher!" she squealed, leaning into the movement.

"Last one!" he warned as he heaved and sent her climbing, slingshot-style, wheeling into air.

As she dipped and rose, Jasmine yelled out. Her shout at the top hung and lengthened then, as the rope moved backwards, suddenly cut off.

She carried on swinging, gradually slowing down. He knew she was preparing. When she arrived at the centre, Matthew walked forward.

"It's mine," said the girl.

He watched her, expressionless.

"My swing."

As Matthew stood, still quiet, she shifted in her chair.

"Mine."

He remained silent.

"It *is* mine."

Still he said nothing.

She tried once more before lapsing into silence.

Matthew waited, then reached out suddenly. "Get down," he said, flat-toned and calm.

Surprised by his assurance, Jasmine released the rope. She wriggled up, allowing herself to be lifted, before beginning the dismount. When she arrived on the ground Matthew crouched on his haunches, level with her face. "Well done," he said quietly, "that was great, Jasmine."

She smiled doubtfully.

"Really. It was great," he repeated.

The girl stood for a moment, apparently undecided.

"I mean that, Jasmine, you're just great ... Now, share – yes?"

She flushed and without saying anything waved to Rosa and Daisy. "Yours," she said, pointing to the swing. "I'll give you push."

For the next half hour till Leon called lunch, Jasmine swung her sisters. She guided from behind while superhero Matt pushed high and long. When they finished, the girls led him happily back through the woods holding each arm, calling and whooping as if he were their hostage.

Looking back later, Matthew came to realise that this was the moment when he changed from first-time visitor to some sort of mascot to be paraded: a kind of big bear hero.

"Thank you," said Jenny, when they arrived at the house, "I hear you were a hit."

"Welcome, Clark Kent," Leon said quietly, as the girls began to chatter.

"From now on," added Jenny, "you're theirs." And she passed him, as if in recognition, a plateful of cherries and a bowlful of honey-sweetened tea.

*† † †*

For the rest of his stay Matthew spent his time switching between centres, first sparring with Eric and listening to his followers, then visiting Jenny and Leon, eating cherries and playing with the girls. He surprised himself how well he adapted. He'd a foot in both camps, and as he moved between them, he saw himself changing, shifting with the times, while hearing the words of *On the Road Again*.

When he realised what was happening, Eric asked Matthew to put in a guest appearance at the art show in the studio. "We value your eye," he said. "Come."

Matthew had resisted, but was won round by Fallon who had asked it as a favour, if only for the others who'd made things about the commune. "It's about us and from us," she said, "to you."

Wild man Matt heard her words as music – The Beatles, pre-Sergeant Pepper – while Matthew from the colony was curious and went along to see.

When he arrived, the studio was busy and cluttered. It was housed in a marquee with bamboo partitions, moveable clothes rails and a channel down the middle where a stream discharged over hollowed-out plastic. The mud-yellow water steamed like a drain. There were boards to tread on with sink-spots in between, fence posts with panels, tied-together poles and upended bed frames. On these were the art-works, hung using clothes pegs, with artists in attendance and Eric looking on.

"Put it higher," he called, directing construction like a foreman on a site. "Change it altogether," he cried, fingering the frame of a still life with veg. "Swap, swap," he insisted, pointing to a pair of blobby cartoons.

As Matthew moved around he was shown things, waved to, given theory, angle and practical demonstration. If effort and belief were enough, then everyone working was producing masterpieces. They were doing their own thing, opening doors, shaping dreams, finding a language to signal into silence – though looked at in detail, thought Matthew, their art appeared at least flawed, if not in need of burning. Much of it was messy, a great deal was rough and parts were like jigsaws or DIY offcuts; all needed work.

There were copies of Van Gogh, smeared and splodged with ground-in food stains, water lilies glazed with something like shoe polish, dream-eyed women with outsized shoulders and stunted arms and legs, mud-thick views of the commune and animals, numerous lifeless head and shoulder portraits (mainly of Eric) with pork-pie faces and elasticated skulls, and a flood tide of abstracts, all washed-out and faded, resembling carbon copies left out in the rain. There were craft things too: broom handle sculptures with rust bits and nails protruding; what looked like oil-blackened bread, sliced and curled at the edges; sludge-coated crackers and creosoted objects broken into lumps and smelling of old socks. There were wire mesh constructions with snapped cross struts and dents; objects inside objects, mainly cardboard, dripped and stained, looking and smelling like supermarket cartons, and a junk shop collection of discarded furniture, its drawers all stuffed with loose plastic sheets, torn-up tissues, toothpicks, match-sticks and grey-green smears that resembled snot.

As he toured with Eric, Matthew held back. When asked he spoke quietly, choosing his expressions not to offend. "Fine, fine," he said, though he could have meant the weather. "I see," he added, his eyes elsewhere. "That yours?" he asked, knowing already the answer to his question. "You did that?" he said, his voice tone level, not harsh or flat, but not too encouraging.

And the artists who'd made him welcome saw him nod, switching between diffidence and engagement.

"No wild man," he told Jenny afterwards. "Seems I held it in."

"Oh yes, I can just see you, a true Brit. Stiff upper and buttoned."

Matthew laughed. They were following a track downhill to the bottom of the valley. It cut a tunnel through trees, leading to a clearing and a riverside view.

"Did you enjoy *any* of the exhibition?" called Jenny as they came in sight of Leon and the girls. They were standing by a bend observing a large oval object turning on the flow.

"All of it. Loved it. Just so *artistic*."

Jenny smiled and descended silently to the riverbank. Matthew went with her, stopping a few feet back, watching from behind. Now he could see it, Matthew recognised the object from a photo he'd examined, hung beside the stairs. It was built out of branches with a raft-like base and dome on top that was slowly opening like fold-out card. The bark, he noticed, had rubbed itself off where it swelled out into knots; in other places it was sprouting. He remembered from the caption what they called these constructions – *The Endurance, The Beagle, The Discovery* – how they built and launched them, with dates and times and estimated progress. He also remembered a wallet full of photos that showed how they wove them together from fallen branch-es, cross-tying the base with bindweed and grass.

Leon was taking photos of the object floating out. As it inched downstream it circled like a model on a wheel. At the bend it shed a few loose branches, then drifted to the middle and swept out an arc. As it turned, the insides unfolded like paper flowers.

Jenny joined the girls, who were standing very still, watching every move. Crouched forward, with his eyes fixed on a spot just above the waterline, Leon looked like a diver preparing to go under.

As they watched, the base began to dip, the projecting branches opened further and the object foundered. It hung for a moment in a pocket of calm then collapsed, spilling out wood.

It felt like something offered.

The girls cheered as the branches bunched and collided and filed off downstream. Jasmine moved closer to her father as he took snapshots from all angles. "Look Dad, there!" she pointed as a side shoot detached and swept past the bank, drawing in other branches. It turned through a long slow curve, advancing like a snowplough. Several more detachments, the base, and a wash of splintered wood passed in convoy, leaving only a rough mess of bark and leaves stuck together.

When Matthew stepped forward, the girls welcomed him, hanging on his arms. Leon and Jenny were standing side by side gazing calmly at the V-shaped foam lines.

"Did you give it a name?" he asked, following their gaze.

Leon smiled and put one arm around his wife's shoulder. "I believe the woman's on the case."

"Jury's still out," Jenny replied.

Matthew laughed. "I name this ship …"

Jenny extended her arms, calling the girls to her. "A photo, with everyone," she said, drawing Matthew in. They grouped by size, with the river in the background.

As Leon raised the camera Matthew asked again, face forward, smiling, "Any name yet?"

"I have two," said Jenny quietly. Her words ran into Leon's cry of "Cheese!" the girls' suppressed giggles and the shutter clicking, once, twice. As the girls fell back laughing, Leon leaned forward for a close-up. "Too close! Too close!" they squealed, until Matthew put his arms around them and shushed them.

In the pause that followed Jenny spoke. "The Lifeboat," she said, as if she'd just thought of it. "Or *Kon-Tiki*," she added.

Matthew nodded then, steering and marshalling, pushed the girls into a photo group. When they were in the frame and standing tall, he pointed to the river. "OK, we're on stage, this is theatre and the play's called The Brave Rescuers!" he cried. "Listen, the audience are clapping, it's the final curtain, so let's take a bow." And he led the girls forward and back, arms linked together, as they waved and curtseyed while Leon worked the shutter, freeze-frame-clicking, catching every movement like a light switch snapping on.

Later, after supper and goodbyes, Matthew walked the hillside path with a farewell blues song running in his head. The woods were in shade as he pushed through the grass, hearing the call of a distant bird. During his walk he felt the flow, inside and out, like a footpath leading on.

When he arrived at the hut Matthew found a message signed by Fallon that a man had phoned, talking over loud music and a van would be here to take him somewhere – college, she thought – within the next week.

In fact, Matthew's send-off came sooner. A follow-up call advanced the date and the whole commune, who seemed to have his movements carefully charted, swung into action. They busied themselves putting everything in place as if they were roadies setting up a gig. Within a day the art tent was cleared, low-level benches were placed around the walls and a children's paddling pool was positioned at the centre, filled with a brown-yellow liquid that smelled like tea. A broken clothes horse was placed in one corner, bunches of carrots and some cut saplings were hung down one side, and a sign put out: *Welcome to the Play*.

At the appointed time the commune gathered, wearing cowls and habits and paper-cut pendants, awaiting the big show.

Sitting next to Paul, who had just arrived, Matthew looked around coolly curious, affecting indifference. He pointed out speakers at each

161

end, suspended from the tent frame. "Earplugs at the ready," he said, nodding towards Eric who was crouched at a turntable with a record in his hands.

The speakers crackled and hummed, then began to groan. As they started to broadcast Paul and Matthew fell silent. There was a long introduction with recorded bird song, an alarm, footsteps approaching, a door slam, a burp and what sounded like a toilet flushing. Then came voices in a mumble, backed by strings, building gradually, adding pipe sounds, clock chimes, hammers hitting metal, cars revving up and a clanking, rattling sound of glass on glass, chinking and jingling like bottles in a crate.

When a blank-faced Eric, after wandering the benches with a faraway smile, took up position on a cushion-pile, an actor appeared, wearing a loin cloth and sandals. He was followed by a group, one in a headdress covered with body paint, one in pyjamas, two in tied-together bin liners and a group wearing convict uniforms with paper bag visors and cardboard tridents.

"This is an enactment!" cried the loin cloth man, seizing a carrot and holding it aloft.

The others followed suit each calling their own variation, the last one shouting something that sounded like "Dreadful!" and running to the paddling pool where he crouched in one corner, whipping up foam and spraying it on the cast.

"And we're the enactors!" they cried, circling the tent waving their carrots.

A dog ran in followed by some goats. They pushed up to the actors, licking and butting and nibbling at their clothes. Attempts to herd them ended with a turning, bleating, barking mass of animals milling around the tent, during which a woman's toe was trampled. She blanched, cried out and had to be sat on a bench with Denise rubbing in some blue-black ointment that smelled of sweat and mouldy cider vinegar.

The performance continued with a phase where the carrots were used as batons in jog-trot relay races; a mock parade waving bits of the clothes horse; a period of calm where the actors staked saplings into earth chanting their own names; a floor level period rolling in mud; a *What's the time Mr Wolf?* section involving tiptoed approaches and mimed gunshots, leading to a pool-centre climax with bodies streaming brown-yellow liquid, wet shaggy head shakes, shrieks, splashes and mouth-blown streams squirted into air.

During the intermission Paul and Matthew left, spluttering and coughing, blaming the pollen count. Paul led the way to the van, holding a tissue to his mouth. When they'd reached the vehicle, he removed it and burst out laughing. His chest was heaving and his eyes were damp. "Unbelievable, just unbelievable."

"Well, now you've seen it all. The commune in action."

"But this …"

"Yes, pretty much a classic."

"Surely they don't think—"

"What? That it's good? That it's art?"

"That it's anything. I mean, have you ever—"

"Ah, but it's real. An *experience*. A once-only."

"Let's hope so."

"Remember, Eric must have given his approval."

"But do you really think they believe in what they're doing?"

"Oh yes, very much so. They take it seriously."

Paul fell silent, pulling out a packet of Gitanes. He flicked back the top and offered one to Matthew, who declined.

"You not smoking?"

"Not since I came here. Got out of the habit."

Paul stared, made to say something then lit up. While he smoked, Matthew leaned on the van. Between them now it was low-key and relaxed; they took things as they were.

Paul asked about the stay: "You been not saying much, I guess?"

"Yes, don't ask me how. But I've kept my eyes open, it's been what you might call interesting."

Paul exhaled, asked a few more questions and gestured to the tent. "So, what about the second half?"

Matthew wrinkled up his nose. "We could pretend. Play innocent."

"No one told us, that kind of thing?"

"Or we spent too long in the toilet."

"How about we got lost on the way back?"

"Yeah. Make out we forgot."

"But it's kinda fascinating, you wonder what they'll do next."

"Or we could say we got abducted by aliens."

Paul grinned. "But seriously, Matt, don't you reckon maybe we ought to?"

"Ought to what?"

"Go back in, see what they're doing."

"Do I have to?"

"You might feel obliged."

"Ah, you mean, *thank you for having me* ..."

"If you want to see it that way. And as a gas."

"I suppose I'm in their debt."

"Honour bound."

Matthew considered. "Can you bear it?"

"If you can."

"OK then, once more unto the breach?"

"Whatever. Whenever."

When they returned the play was just starting. Matthew looked in before leading across mud to take a seat near the door flap. In their absence the tent had been cleared and a tiered square of pyramid-style building blocks had been placed in the middle. The pyramid was uneven, with one side sloped using planks, another side cliff-like, while the two other sides were angled step-wise into Colosseum-type gangways. The actors were positioned near the top wearing off-white sheets and cardboard box helmets. When they lifted off the boxes their faces showed white with black-lined lips, glitter in their hair and electric-yellow forehead flashes.

"Waiting for the UFOs," called one. "Look and learn," he added, darkly.

"See, the astral plane," cried another.

"Contact is made," chorused two women at the back.

"The mothership is closing," two more returned.

"Ola! Ola!" the men all chanted, jazz-handed.

"Yazam! Yazam!" the women replied, bowing forward and back.

"Yuh! Yuh! Yuh!"

"Tulah! Tulah! Tulah!"

Suddenly the whole cast turned and pointed prophet-like to the entrance. A long painful silence followed. There were sounds of heavy breathing, a fly buzzing, a voice chatting beyond the tent flaps, birdsong and giggles. Then the tent flaps rose and a group of children carrying tools, cutlery and rusted metal bowls marched in to take up position, standing at intervals right around the tent. Organised from behind by a man in a boiler suit they laid out a long line of bowls then, at a signal from their leader, raised their implements above their heads and brought them down, metal against metal, with a bone-shaking, jarring, cacophonous crash. "Send out the signal!" the man cried and the children hit again, hot and hard, beating out a random hammering tintinnabulation.

"Oh, man," yelled Matthew, "jet plane taking off."

Paul, looking pained, mouthed his distaste.

"You're right," hollered Matthew, "just such fucking shit …" At that moment the hammering stopped, cancelled by gesture by the leader, and Matthew's last word, "… yeah!" rang out.

At the centre of the pyramid the whole cast stood up. Seizing upon Matthew's word they began one-two hand clapping, shouting, "Yeah!" and stamping. They continued jumping and stamping, calling, "Oh yeah!" as the children bowed out. They'd just set up a recall two-beat shout of, "Oh yeah! Oh yeah!" when the blocks began to slip. As their feet heeled down, the pyramid shifted, pushing out a wall of loose blocks. The apex sagged and imploded down the middle, sinking in pieces to the floor. The cast sank too, arms in the air, calling for rescue, and as they went down the audience stood up. Both groups struggled, those on the floor unsteady and heaving like drunks on ice, their audience on tiptoe, craning for a view. The speakers blared a big shouty tune and they braced against each other, swaying to a chant. And as the cast clambered up, using each other and the blocks as leverage, their watchers sank down, pointed seat-wards by a stone-faced Eric. For a moment they hung, some up, some down and some in between, looking to others for guidance. Then, with a yell, three of the actors attempted a break, scaling the wall to overlook the audience. They stood grouped at the edge and sang a few notes.

The speakers cut off. The group stalled, clowned for a moment and lined up to bow. As they angled forward, the remaining blocks lurched to the floor, skidding and bouncing, taking all three with them. Head down like surfers they helter-skeltered, sledging over debris and loose planks to arrive with a crash, sprawled and dishevelled, at the feet of Eric.

In the silence afterwards, with all eyes fixed expectantly on Eric, Paul and Matthew slipped out through the tent flap, laughing and shaking their heads.

"Call that art?" cried Matthew, pushing out his chin.

"Ought not to be allowed."

"Disgusting."

On the way back to his hut Matthew reran the performance, grinning to himself as he pictured various highlights. At the hut he left a note thanking Fallon and finished packing, checking the drawers and underneath the bed before rejoining Paul. They returned to the vehicle avoiding the tent, Paul with backpack and Matthew carrying a cricket bag and an army surplus rucksack.

They were setting off together, heading for home like just-escaped prisoners.

As they drove off in the van, Matthew had a done-that seen-that been-there kind of feeling. It took him back to his life at home, to short hair, Brylcreem and thick-rimmed glasses with still life pictures and questions in the air – and it connected, like the glassed-in photo of his mother gazing out to sea, with meanings that he'd long since outgrown.

# SEVENTEEN

Alan was born in Newcastle, in a white, bare room at *The General*. In those days it was set back behind a high brick wall. You were led in through double doors and down corridors to a bed with a number. *The General*, as I soon found out, was an ex-military hospital. For two long weeks I was warned against coughing, scratching, told lights out at six and regularly given tellings-off. It felt like I was under arrest.

When I got out, I was calm on the outside but worried underneath. I wanted to be a good mother. That meant I had to feed and wind him, get up in the night for nappies and later for teething, then smile the next day. And if I felt tired or anything went wrong, I'd to keep it to myself. Not a word to anyone, that was how we were brought up. We saw it as a job, something we did without thinking, and because it was right.

I loved him, of course. I could feel his little moods when I squeezed his hands. At night I listened to his breathing, standing by his door. And when he was awake, he smiled as if he knew me. I called him my little man. He'd a way of peering around with a quiet, thoughtful, *what's-this* kind of look. Even though he was a baby I could see he was my Alan.

When Edwin was born, Alan was two and we'd got used to living where everyone could see us, above the city. It was as if we'd changed sides and joined the owners. In a way, I suppose we had. Stuart's job had changed too. He was in charge of building a new warehouse and the men he gave jobs to had known Jack. They called him the gaffer and hated him. Stuart didn't say much, of course, so all I knew was the locals weren't friendly and the door-to-door sellers never came by.

I brought up the boys, backed up by Grace. She came round when she could, with the help of my brother. He'd returned and was working as a mechanic. Sometimes they both came, but mostly him. Mum talked about him now as the man of the house. I was glad they were together. My Stephen, The Prodigal, had come home.

For me, Mum's visits were a lift. When she came, we cleaned and cooked then went out in the garden. We'd a fenced-off patch that we called our nursery. It was where we planted the seeds and bulbs she brought in brown paper bags. She called them our "other children". During spring they sprouted small, flame-like flowers on creeping stems. In summer they were green, in autumn brown and all through winter they hid themselves away. Mum helped pick them and arranged them in water. We cooked with them and dried them and boiled some up into jam. And each year our patch grew bigger as we planted more. In the end the whole garden was a nursery.

We often talked about the boys. From the start Alan was tall and clever like his father. When he was young, he'd pick a flower and study it, squinty-eyed. He'd hold it up to the light and wink, but not in fun, more slowly, as if he wanted the flower to wink back. He didn't say much. Words for him were pointers, naming what he found. Not just flower names but parts of the body, things around the kitchen and tools in the shed. As he got older, he drew up lists of countries, matching them with capitals and battle dates and famous leaders.

Edwin was the kind of boy who'd pick flowers and throw them away or tear them to bits and eat them.

But my mum knew how to treat them both. With her, the rules were simple. If they were good then she was nice, if they weren't then neither was she. Of course, they also knew they'd be listened to. Or, to tell the truth, Mum listened to one, kept tabs on the other.

So, with Alan she went out in the garden and they talked. Usually, it would go something like this …

"What's that?" he'd ask, pointing.

"It's a flower."

"What flower?"

"That one's a rose."

"But what is it?"

"A rose, my dear."

"But what's it made of?"

"Ah … petals, leaves, roots. Lots of plant things."

"And what're they made of?"

"Well—"

But with Edwin she took a different tack. He needed to be told, and kept busy. She called it "watch the birdie". If she saw him getting into trouble she'd call "Tchk-tchk," and hold up her hand. If she heard him being rude, she'd cut in with "Not now." And when he put out his tongue or jumped in puddles she'd shout "Edwin," in a way that stopped him.

But she did go wrong once. It was when we were out walking. Edwin tried to run off and she said Jack's word. She spoke, and it was out. "Don't!" she cried and blushed.

My reply came up like a wave from below. "The word is don't, Edwin. Don't," I said calmly, as if it didn't hurt. As I said it, I reached out to Mum. The hand I took was firm and steady and squeezed mine twice.

With Grace there the boys grew quickly. You might say they grew apart. People who didn't know were surprised they were brothers. At school Alan learned things fast, read lots of books, was top in maths and science, while Edwin went for sport. In class they sat apart. Right through school Alan did the listening and Edwin talked. They were the same but different, and you could see it in their eyes. Alan had his father's, grey with streaks of blue. Edwin's eyes were brown, like mine. Alan wore glasses and studied things close-up while Edwin looked forward, like a runner. One was shy, the other was a clown. I suppose it comes down to how you see the world.

When the war began Stuart joined up. He wasn't that fit but his time in the navy got him in. He said it was the least he could do. In a way, once he had a leaving date our marriage became easier. Although we didn't know it, a line had been drawn. We said good-bye with a cheek kiss as he boarded ship. It didn't seem much of a send-off, not the sort you'd want to put in a story. Alan cried while Edwin fidgeted and only Grace gave him a hug. I think of Stuart now, tall and blue-eyed, going up the gangway with a nod and a wave towards us.

He was killed in action. An officer told me his ship went down. No survivors. Missing, presumed dead.

The words left me empty. Although there'd been trouble, this stopped everything. I'd nothing to hold on to, nothing I could say. It felt like failure, my failure. The marriage hadn't worked, that's why it had happened. I'd let everyone down.

The worst part was telling the boys. I held them as I said it and held on afterwards. They were quiet, then tearful, then angry with me, angry with themselves, angry with Stuart. For a while their grief brought them together. But even in this they were different, and a gap opened up. Edwin, who was loud and unsettled and very up and down, soon got back to sport and going out. But Alan didn't speak about it. He'd sit and brood, and when I asked, he'd say it didn't matter. He'd read war stories, taking them to bed and using a torch beneath the covers. Sometimes, when we visited Grace, he'd go barefoot into the sea and look out sadly. He was a boy without a father. In fact, it wasn't till after the war, when he met Harriet on a visit to the coast, that Alan became himself again. It was their marriage that saved him. And, of course, his pride in having Matty.

I think of the years that followed as my first, real, happy family life. It was post-war, and my duties were over. I moved back to the sea to live with Grace. Like an upstream salmon I'd returned to my element. I'd gone full circle. Edwin joined the railways, married Doris and gave me two bright grandsons, Richard and James. Their visits were very special. Mind, they took some looking after when we sat out in the backyard. But Matty was good with them, he had a way with small children. He played lookout on our walks, showed them flowers and talked about adventures. He was tall, enjoyed being leader, and all three were wild and clever and very Lavender-ish. I watched as Matty played *let's pretend* hiding round corners. He was Robin Hood, James was Little John and Richard played Will Scarlet.

Between them, they made up a story. In it they were explorers, Matthew, Richard and James, running all over. Small boys crossing sand hills, burrowing on the beach, chasing the tides. They were by the sea, enjoying life. And I loved them.

‡ ‡ ‡

Mia showed Cass a collection of seed packets. "I'm planting," she said. The packets were postcard-size, brightly-coloured and sealed at the top. She was carrying them in a box.

"What're you planting?"

"Runner beans, peas, violets."

"Why those?"

"For their stories."

"Ah, now let's see if I can name them. You've got Jack and the Beanstalk and The Princes and the Pea, but what's it with violets?"

"They're Thumbelina's bed."

"Oh, that's good." Cass began leafing through the packets. "Hey, you've got Lavender here."

"Yes, I was going to try it. I'll plant it in a sunny spot."

"If it grows, will that be our story? The Lavender Kids, something like that?"

Mia shook her head. "Lavender is about sensitivity. Plants have it, you know. They're HSPs."

"What's that?"

"Highly Sensitive People."

"Like us?"

"Only if we listen to what's alive. It's all around us."

"So, the Lavender story is about being aware and tuned-in and touchy-feely stuff – right?"

"And worms," said Mia.

"Worms?"

"I've read about them. The world needs worms."

"Yes, Darwin knew that."

"Hang on, Cass, what's Darwin got to do with it?"

"If it's worms, just about everything. He spent 40 years feeding and counting them and testing their hearing. But mostly, he measured their loam."

"Loam?"

"Worm casts. Soil recycled through their bodies."

"Well, plants need worms."

"And we need plants."

"You are what you eat, eh?"

"And we're Lavender Worms and HSPs, it seems."

Mia laughed, holding out her box. "Time we did some planting," she said, leading to the end of the garden. "Lavender first."

Working carefully, they cleared a patch and picked up some digging sticks. After scooping out a trench, they scraped away the loose earth with their fingers. "Take a whiff of that," Mia said, opening the Lavender packet and tipping seeds into her palm.

"Hmm. They smell like they've been dried in the sun and bottled."

"Strong stuff, eh?"

"Like medicine, I'd say. Warm. dark and intoxicating."

"And they'll grow," Mia replied. scattering them along the trench.

'Like us," said Cass.

$$\mathcal{J}\ \mathcal{J}\ \mathcal{J}$$

In the first week back, before lectures started, Matthew made it known that there'd been a break with Robyn and the trip to America was off.

"We took a decision," he said, adding as an afterthought, "it's best this way."

If asked, he had his patter about how they'd learned things by letter and both thought again, delivered offhand as plain and simple fact. He mentioned *warning signs* but then admitted he'd not seen what was coming. "But it's no big deal," he added, "life goes on."

*Getting real* he called it. The phrase got about (as in "What's real now" and "Matt Man's getting it") and soon became a buzz, a self-directed warning that he offered tongue-in-cheek, with hip talk, peace signs and lead-break classics performed on air guitar. "Hello university," he called, rock star-like, climbing on the bed. "Hello people, hello world, hello universe," he continued, waving. "Everybody must get real," he sang with dead flat intonation and a long pause afterwards while he glanced around at friends. Though when he spoke of *getting wiser* or *getting in touch* or *getting self-aware* he didn't pass judgement or hold himself apart.

With Paul there and Theresa, he found himself able to put things to one side and mend the breach with Jay. He even saw Sally and invited her and Miranda round. It all seemed settled, he'd rejoined the tribe.

Though the new term wasn't easy because suddenly there were deadlines and tick lists on registers with talk of seeing panels and being kicked out.

"Best play the system," said Paul, "just give 'em what they want."

Which Matthew accepted as a new kind of challenge. "OK, I'll try it and see what I can do," he said.

So he cast himself as a top-grade *student*, used abstracts and commentaries and looked up references, planning all his essays, filling them with quotes and following written guidance to show he knew his stuff.

"The truth is, I don't want to be second best," he told Paul one day, walking by the lake, "even when it's writing to formula."

"You care what they say?"

"I suppose I do."

"For me it's where you draw the line. If you do just enough, then that says it all."

"But isn't that the same?"

"Not really. I just churn it out, the bare minimum. You have to do *better*."

Matthew raised one hand against the early evening sun. The lake was still and the fountain in the centre had ebbed to a slow, bubbling flow. He could hear, issuing from the dining room, the sounds of students leaving and tables being cleared.

"I think we're both combative," he said, blinking in the glare.

"But in different ways."

"Different, but the same."

"Yeah, two top dogs."

Hearing voices, Matthew looked around. Two women were approaching, one short and round-faced, the other taller, long-limbed and dark. "Isn't that Sally?" he asked, frowning.

"With back up," said Paul, glancing towards Miranda.

The two women came closer. They were wearing black, ankle-length robes studded with multi-coloured beads. Their necks were encased in white and gold lace. Walking in step with eyes to the floor, they were talking hard.

"Carnival queens," Matthew said, turning away to avoid being heard. Paul nodded, sharing a grin.

As the women drew level with the lake end, Sally touched her friend's arm. "Hi there!" she called, directing her words to echo off concrete; her face showed pale with awareness.

Paul returned the greeting. "You out to take the air?"

Sally confirmed and Miranda added that they came here daily, then the four stood facing.

"Is this something new?" asked Matthew, pointing to the clothes.

"Not new, but different," Miranda replied. "You wouldn't understand."

"It's interesting," Matthew countered, directing his remarks to Sally.

She smiled. It was enough.

"Good image," echoed Paul, playing his part.

Miranda frowned. "It's more than that."

Matthew persisted with his one-way comments, "You didn't see us, but I was watching as you walked. It's a big change, very striking."

"Yes," said Sally, "people do look." Her colour rose as she set her head sideways to peer across the lake. "I thought you wouldn't be interested."

"Why?"

"I don't know, I just imagined you wouldn't. You'd see it as nothing. Shrug it off, or label it as unimportant."

"Which is how men operate," Miranda put in.

"Of course. Guilty as charged."

Miranda shook her head. "It's not as funny as you think." Drawing in her breath, she turned towards the lake. "Listen Matthew," she said, her face suddenly flushed by sunlight, "I can see you're, well, trying."

Matthew's eyebrows shot up.

"But don't think that *trying*," she continued, "allows you to make fun."

"So, it's like last week's weather. You see some improvement?"

"Perhaps. Not too much though."

"C minus. Could do better."

"In the meantime," Sally cut in, "some of us out here are getting cold, aren't we, Paul?"

Paul, who had reverted to cool, put in a few words about it being early. It seemed he didn't mind.

Miranda was shading her eyes against the sun. Where she was looking, the evening was approaching, thinning out the sky. The colours were expanding to a cream and yellow wash. At her feet there were blurred reflections and a clear stretch of water, turned solid. Suddenly she switched her gaze back to Matthew. "I'd like to think—"

Matthew waved. "Go on, say it. Whatever's on your mind."

She squinted sideways, aware now of his eyes, blue-grey and challenging, and the sunlight shining bars on his light brown hair. "Maybe you've *changed*, but I'm not sure."

"Thanks, your view has been noted."

"Whatever," put in Paul, "don't let it get to you."

"I tell you what," said Miranda, "I'd rather it did."

"Get to *me*, you mean?" asked Matthew.

"*Naturalmente.*"

Matthew ran his tongue quickly around his lips. There was about him now a provocative, boyish defiance. He held out his hand, palm upwards, and took a step forward. "And you'd like to teach me a lesson, perhaps?"

Miranda shook her head then looked him up and down with a half-admiring smile. "Consider yourself punished," she said and touched his hand, as if in confirmation.

"And that's it? It's that simple?"

"As long as you've changed, of course."

"Which at present you think might be possible?"

"Well, I might need your opinion on that."

They both laughed.

"So, I'm in the clear," said Matthew, "no more pins in dolls."

Miranda pursed her lips. "It's more than you deserve."

"Hmm. 'Use every man after his desert and who should 'scape whipping?' Hamlet."

"I shall remember that."

Sally cut in, waving both hands, "Hello, I'd just like to point out that we're outside, it's actually cold – and I mean *perishing* – and some of us need to warm up."

Miranda made to say something then stopped.

"I think," said Paul quietly, "we ought to go."

Matthew stared at the lake then switched his gaze to Miranda. "See you then," he said, his voice dropping low. She looked him in the eye, echoing his words. When the women moved off hand in hand, he turned to Paul, pointing forward. Buttoning their jackets, they set off side by side, heading towards the bridge. As they walked Matthew smiled, staring thoughtfully into the last white rays of sun, without saying anything.

"A relationship," said Matthew, walking through the woods, "has to be fun."

"And free," added Miranda, dropping his hand as she scrambled up a bank that ran along beside the path. "Oh, and watch you don't fall in the pool!" she cried, picking her way over hollows and rocks. She swung around a branch then descended in a rush to seize him by the arm. "Or into mud," she cried, stepping in chest to chest, wrestling.

Matthew swore and battled her a few feet to a fallen tree trunk where they slumped down together, breathing hard.

"Idiot," he said, laughing.

"Pig," she returned, leaning back to cuff him around the ear.

"Bloody hell, that hurt."

She slapped again, harder, and he grabbed her arm, digging in with his fingers. Miranda squealed and shook herself free. "Matthew, don't do that!"

"Well I said it bloody hurt," he grumbled, rubbing his ear.

"Look what you've done," she said, touching the spot as if she'd been stung. Her flesh now was red-wealed and blotchy.

"You mark easily," he said, peering at her bruises. "Thin skinned," he said, feather-stroking flesh.

"Careful," she said, sucking in her breath.

A bird sang overhead, the lead note dropping then whistling in a round. It repeated, quick and ascendant, in an echo of itself.

She asked its name.

Matthew said thrush. He thought so, but wasn't really sure.

Miranda nodded.

The bird trilled briefly then dropped silent. A soft autumnal sun shone out beyond the path making the wood glow as if through curtains. There were colour spots and ridges, pools on leaves and a pearl-white tide, air-bright and soft, filling up the canopy. Where they sat was cooler, with dark green sphagnum, green-yellow spurge, and variegated patches of vetch and creeper. Immediately behind, autumn had begun: green to yellow and running into black. Over to one side, where the wood dipped away, there were weak sounds of water and a ghost cloud of midges, circling.

Here they were alone. Boy meets girl with a story between them.

Firstly, by the lake: Matthew walking early morning, with his thoughts set on Miranda. Wondering at the words, the mist drift and the haze (and did she really say that?). Matt, looking into water, warning himself off. And the white square and the grey, still walking.

Then the meeting, hot-faced in a bar, and the late-night invitation, returning to the lake, and *his* hand on her fingers. Turning to a clench in her bedroom afterwards, with Miranda teasing and Matthew throwing back her words. Then dozing till noon, to wake to the water fight, the door slam and shoes kicked off.

A week like a honeymoon, then a letter from Jenny, with an open invitation. Then travel arranged and welcome by Leon, Jenny and the girls. Soon outside, walking in the woods. To sit hearing birdsong, and Miranda, complaining.

"Still hurts," she said, rubbing her arm.

Matthew leaned forward, checking her skin. "Very much?"

"Enough."

He eyed her as if seeking further guidance. His ear still tingled from the impact of her hand.

In the wood behind the bird repeated, this time edgily, three long notes, a transition, then the notes again but shortened, and a quickly rising fourth. Matthew stood, peering into the branches. "I wish I *knew* what it was."

Miranda shook her loose arm as if she'd got it dirty. "You ought to say sorry." Her words were flat, matter of fact, definitional.

"What for?"

"For what you've done, you should apologise."

"Yes, if it was just me."

"Look," she hung out her blue-black arm like an exhibit.

"Nothing to do with you then?"

"It's about who got hurt."

"True, only some of us don't show the damage."

"It's simply a matter of facing up. Admitting."

"I see. Oh, and by the way while I'm admitting, can I ask for twenty-five other crimes to be taken into account?"

"Whatever you want, as long as you apologise. Say sorry and mean it."

"As should you."

"Ah, the old trick," she said, standing and brushing herself down, "turn it back on the woman."

Matthew looked away, feeling restless. It seemed they were in contest, face to face and pushing. He could hear their first argument and his mock-apologies, his la-di-da, posing on the walkway. It brought back Sally, the boasts, the smoking and the argument with the preacher. And now, was it so different? Driving in wedges to widen the gap. It did make him wonder.

"OK. What else?" he asked, grasping a branch and twisting till it snapped.

"How do you mean?"

"The charge sheet. I want it all. What else have I done?"

Miranda paused, sighting carefully as if she was a fielder about to make a throw. "Matthew," she said, pronouncing her words with deadly accuracy, "you're a fool. A complete fool."

178

He brandished his stick. "Great. Charge number one, foolishness. Anything else?"

She laughed, harshly. "Isn't that enough?"

"Not until it's all dealt with. Now, what else?"

"Lack of respect."

"What, for you?"

"For everyone, everything. Yourself included."

"Fine, number two. Continue."

"Arrogance."

"Same thing. Something else needed."

"Conceit."

"Ditto."

"Big mouth."

"Same old shit. How about being tall?"

"Oh, bloody hell," she cried, "can't you take anything seriously?"

"Number three."

"*Matthew*."

"Yes, I see. You just said it. *Matthew*, that's the problem."

"Oh—"

"Couldn't be you, of course. Never Miranda, that's impossible."

She turned and slapped him, catching his sore ear.

"Ouch!" he called and hit back, connecting stick to shoulder.

Miranda cried out in surprised disbelief. "That hurt!" she yelled, holding her flesh. She began to pace with one hand gripping her shoulder and her body angled forward. Something was holding her, head down in a tunnel. It kept her out of reach, moving slowly unable to settle, like a child in the dark. She was at the stairhead preparing to go down, groping for the light. And, as she shifted and muttered, her expression softened, her breath came back and the tears began to show.

Matthew dropped his stick. "I'm sorry," he said, looking down. "Honestly, I'm sorry, that's all I can say. I am sorry, Miranda."

He remained there at the ready. His will had gone down. Better, he thought, to be small and unnoticed. He watched till Miranda, who had pulled down her scarf to cover her red-marked shoulder, straightened, sighing. When he asked about leaving, she nodded saying nothing.

In the wood behind a bird sang. First up, then down, and then with a flourish the song rang out. The wood rang back as the call climbed to a peak and descended. It continued in a flow, extending and sliding into distance. The notes ran on, quiet now, as Matthew and Miranda, absorbed in their own thoughts, turned to the path and began their journey. They picked their way around tree roots and rocks, moving steadily and wordlessly through light and half-light as the last few bird notes lengthened into silence.

When they reached the house, it was hushed. They entered quietly, as if they'd stayed out late. Somewhere they could hear the muffled sound of voices. They paused to listen before shifting to the hallway. Between them now a purpose was gathering. As they passed by a door they glanced at each other, nodding like conspirators. In there, moving around, they could make out the girls: rising and falling, their voices came and went. They were busy being good.

At the bottom of the stairs Matthew signalled up. Already he knew. His heart was at pressure, his body in a flutter. No one must see them. Holding the banisters, he led and they climbed. At the landing, looking forward, he felt her hand squeezing his. He turned, kissed her hard and then, shifting like a dancer, drew her towards the bedroom. Once in, they faced up.

"Now?" she whispered, smiling.

"Yes, yes," he said, pulling at her clothes.

She helped him and they undressed. Moving silently, they hitched loose and lay out on the bed. Impatience made them calm. They teased and pulled and stretched like wrestlers, working each other until they came.

Afterwards they slept. When they woke it was evening and crepuscular. Lying still, they watched as the last soft rays of sunlight flared against glass. They watched to grey before getting up, summoned by the cries of Jenny announcing supper, the sounds of Leon counting, and the buzz of children in the next-door bathroom preparing to go down.

Later that evening, after talking with their hosts and seeing the girls to bed, Matthew and Miranda stepped out, saying they wanted to see the stars.

"You'd better take this," said Jenny, handing over a large black torch. She showed them how to shine it, pushing a square plastic marker along a channelled strip. "We've just had a new moon," she went on, looking at the sky, "so you'll need it."

They thanked her and set out together, walking along a field path.

"Careful, it's too dark, don't go in the woods," Jenny called, waving them off. She remained standing, outlined by the door, while they followed the path. As they picked their way forward the grass tops rustled. The ground was uneven and each step needed care. Above them the sky was open and starry with a crescent moon rising between trees. A thin trail of mist was already gathering, filling the hollows and spreading over grass.

"We're going to the river?" Miranda asked, stepping in tandem around a rock.

"That far?"

"Where else?"

The question sounded closed. In the dark Matthew was both joined to her body, feeling the connection, and oddly unreal. They walked within the beam and every little darting jogging thought registered between them.

He knew there was a tree line and was searching for the gap. On his own he would have circled around, using the cottage as his marker, but now he was coupled and drawn to go further.

"I think that's the route," he said, pointing to a gap where the torchlight yellowed into grey. As he swung the beam a mist-glow showed.

Miranda shuddered. "Down there?" she echoed.

The torch swung again, this time clearer. It circled through space, catching streaks of thread-like insects.

"Half a mile."

"You know the way?"

"Not so well in the dark, but let's try."

They set off. On the way down the torch arc began to narrow. As they passed through bushes it flickered like a candle. When the path opened out close to the river it weakened until it cut off altogether. Stopping, Matthew swore. He tried the switch, producing a short, glimmering flash. He shook it back to life, changed the setting and shone it on his hand. It glowed briefly then yellowed. Twice he repeated, cursing quietly. At each attempt the torch arc darkened, shrinking into grey. Finally, using both hands, he shook till it rattled, then struck it with his palm and the beam returned.

"Thank goodness." He shone the torch forward, seeking the river.

"Is it going to last?" Miranda asked.

"Maybe, if we use it sparingly."

When they reached the riverbank he warned her and flicked off the torch. They stood, blinking slowly till the world came back. Before them now the water glittered and turned, gleaming darkly.

As he watched, Matthew thought back. An image floated up of Robyn's last letter. He still had its drift, a dark-toned mixture of phrases and expressions singing in his head. In his mind he saw it all: bits torn and flaked and scattered downstream. White stars and promises; words against the flow.

Bending to a hollow, he tested for dryness. "Let's sit," he said, clearing a few stones. He spread out his raincoat and they lay down on the grass. The air felt chilled and lake-like. It held them in a pocket, an envelope of loosely-wrapped calm.

"Do you know why we're doing this?" Miranda asked, looking up towards the stars.

"The walk?"

"That, but more. Everything."

"You mean the big stuff? Whys and what-fors, all that?"

"No. I mean you and me, going together."

Matthew allowed her words to hang. He thought of Clarry and her talk about the moon. The sky above was filled with stars. At the centre they were clustered into wheels and spirals, at the edge they came in dots, and where the moon had ascended they were barred white and tinted, surrounded by haloes. They made him think of journeys. Forever dancing. Eye-bright and sleepless, following a star.

His reply came suddenly, appearing from nowhere, "Maybe because we want to."

"No other reason?"

"Depends."

"Depends on what?"

"How you look at it."

Miranda turned her head, observing his outline. His arms were folded, elbows out, pillowing his head. A question lay between them, something still to answer. It was almost as if he'd arranged himself with an eye for effect.

Sensing her inspection, Matthew turned. He seemed to have understood. "Well, you might say we chose. Or you might say it happened."

"Accidents happen."

"Or you could say we were ready."

"Like we were for this walk?"

"You mean—"

"Yes, I've regrets."

Matthew frowned. "If that's how you see it." He could feel her shifting up. "But you'll stay, won't you?"

"I might do," she said quietly, rocking back and forth.

"*Might* do?"

"Or might not."

"Miranda—"

She rose and walked towards the river. Her voice now had hardened, echoing back from water. "Here we are, out by the river, pitch black, torch no good, and neither of us seems able to come up with a reason to be here, or indeed any good reason to be together at all."

Matthew stood up. "Perhaps that's because we're too busy arguing to see what's important."

"What's important?"

He paused. In his mind he was touching her in bed. "We only have to look," he said gesturing upwards. "Look and feel. See the stars."

Miranda laughed. "Oh, Matthew—"

He peered into her face.

"There are times. I mean, there *are* times …" she said, her voice beginning quiet, rising at the end.

"Go on."

Miranda gestured heavenwards: "Look and feel. See the stars."

"OK, very funny."

"No, don't take me wrong, Matthew, you are *poetica*."

"You mean poetic or *posy*?"

"I mean you, what you're like. You're full of it."

"Hmm, I've heard that one before, too."

"It's true. You are."

"It's not what you called *Mr No-Apology*?"

"Ah, I see. That went deep." She gazed at the grey-streaked currents threading through water. "I meant full of *feelings*," she said, raising her head to face him squarely. "Feelings, Matthew. And I like that. I really do."

She drew one finger slowly down his chest. There were other words now forming, whispered low and maybe just imagined, so that neither could be certain that they'd really been spoken. Words such as *beautiful* and *crazy* and *out of this world*. Gently feeling words of endearment and surprise, touching on things hidden as they undressed quickly and closed against flesh.

He felt his hardness pressing on her hairs. They were tight-curled and soft. His hands felt her curves, her smooth, dark, contoured expressiveness. A song went through him *I'm so glad*. The song became a chorus, a feeling shared.

"Matt," she said, as he cupped a line beneath her breasts then tongued around her nipples. She was sighing and murmuring, making little noises. As he shifted lower, she pulled him to one side. "Here, here," she said spreading their clothes across the coats. "Quickly. The position. Here."

Miranda lay back while Matthew angled in and closed around her thighs. For him, she was willing. She had him with her, and her insides were warm.

As he entered, Miranda gave a jerk and shiver, breathing hard. The song was between them, more urgent now. They began to push awkwardly, then easing and lengthening with an occasional quick shudder and sideways kick. As Miranda began to clench he pushed in deeper, till he felt his own internal tingling brightness, a needle of excitement rising inside. It grew and intensified, filling him with uplift and wild expression then, burning in deeper, became full and extended and out there beyond him till they both fired up and they worked and they worked till her contractions brought him.

Afterwards they lay there briefly, with bodies pressed together, until Miranda shivered. "Cold," she said and twisted sideways, feeling for her clothes. Helping each other, they dressed in stages: a head, an arm, and trousers wriggled, then buttons and laces, and footwear fitted. Rocking back and forth, they slotted themselves in.

When they'd straightened and stood up, Miranda smiled. "Together," she said and took him by the arm.

On the route back they walked slowly with their eyes on the torch beam, talking as they went. They paused on the way, sometimes to kiss, sometimes to make fun, and then in amazement as they stood and viewed the stars.

Above them there was emptiness, high and impressive, an arch into nowhere. There were spot points, trails and flickers, and flight holes into dark. Wide and glittery, the stars were everywhere. They hung in drifts, spread in patches, glinted like splintered glass.

For a moment Matthew and Miranda stood together in silence, taking in the sky. When, at some distance from the cottage the torch beam died, they walked on together united by the dark and guided, it seemed, by the white-and-silver star glow.

On the next day Matthew and Miranda were, from breakfast onward, required by the girls.

For her it was a game, for him a show. He'd graduated now, from crazy-boy Matthew tickling her in bed, to the dreamtime man who rose to follow stars. Also, as the kids' MC, he seemed to know how to have fun and where to call a halt. In any case, he pleased her, so she joined in with the play and followed his lead with the girls.

For Rosa, Jasmine and Daisy the return of Matthew was an opportunity to bring out their paintings and paper-folded models, tour and name their very special places, update on stories and offer him, like a shopper, samples selected from their private collections. *Look* they said, pointing, as they showed him their pictures chalked on stones. *Play this* they said, running zigzags and dodging out of reach. *Shhh* they said loudly, crouching unseen. *Catch* they called at rounders as Miranda skied the ball and Matthew waited underneath. *Silly* they cried, laughing at both their faces.

And for Jenny and Leon, watching at the window, their guests were reminders of how they used to be.

"Time'll tell," said Leon quietly, seeing Miranda running races with the girls.

"She's good with the kids," Jenny said. "But her with Matthew, that's another story."

"When they battle, you mean?"

Jenny nodded. "Cat and dog."

"Some do."

In the game outside Matthew and Miranda were at the side of the track, claiming they'd had enough and didn't need to run. The girls were counting them down.

"Seven-a … six-a … five-a," cried Rosa, dancing around. Jasmine was sitting by Miranda, fingering her patchwork jacket and the grape-sized beads hanging from her hair. Daisy was counting too, descending from a thousand.

Matthew was feigning a stitch. When the countdown paused, he hauled himself up claiming he'd been tripped. "Rerun, rerun!" he cried then fell back in a huddle when the girls resumed counting. He continued in panto mode, huffing, puffing and threatening to get even. It was as if they'd got him chained.

A smiling Miranda declared him finished. "No stamina," she said, "the women win." Pronounced flatly, her words signalled closure and the girls fell silent, awaiting the next move.

Their wait was cut short by Jenny calling for lunch. Leon rang a bell and the girls ran in, vying with each other to be first through the door.

"Muddy shoes off!" their mother cried, causing a blockage while buckles were tugged loose. Once inside they were steered by Leon to wash upstairs and show both hands before trooping downstairs to occupy the table.

"Spaghetti!" they cried when Jenny placed a piled-up bowlful in the centre of the table.

The meal was in two parts: an open-mouthed, fork-winding pasta course, followed by jelly and ice cream. They all had second and third helpings, egging each other on. By the end they were exhausted.

"Full up," said Daisy, ballooning both cheeks like a hamster. Rosa held her sides while Jasmine leaned forward, complaining she was ill.

Afterwards, as a reward for clearing up, Jenny mentioned outings. "Wood-walk or biking?" she asked, glancing towards Leon.

"Blackberrying," he responded, "then we ride."

The girls were happy. They needed hair grips, bowls for fruit and Matthew to hold onto until Leon told them *no*. Then Jenny led out in the commune's direction, leaving their guests waving from the door.

"Time out," said Matthew when the girls had disappeared.

Miranda met his eyes. It seemed, without saying anything, that she'd caught his meaning.

They turned to face the house. On the open field behind, the afternoon sun was spotting little patches, each a kind of inlet, an inland sea. The field itself was thinning with bare earth in places and dried-out stalks filling up the hollows. At the end where the ground dipped away, a thick belt of woods curved around the slope, following the line of a sheep path.

"I'll take you down. That's our night route to the river," said Matthew, pointing.

"Can we go by the woods instead?" Miranda asked. Her voice tone was playful, with a slight edge.

"If you want to."

"Well, why not?"

He considered various answers, mainly rude, but no words came. It seemed she'd forgotten. Or perhaps, he thought, she was inviting some sort of replay, an attempt to settle scores. "OK then," he replied, pointing off, "the path's this way."

"The one we took before?"

He nodded warily.

Miranda inspected, taking in the house, the field beyond it and the sunlight playing over grass tops and stone. In one corner, where the woods thinned out, a vista opened. There were rocks both sides sprouting gorse and a ridge running parallel, topped with grasses and sea tides of heather. Further down an opencast area showed with dark, rust-coloured pools and gravel sloping off.

"*Andiamo*," she said, adjusting her hair-beads, and they moved off together.

When they reached the trees, Matthew touched her arm. "No fights," he said quietly as if he were asking her for ID.

"No," she said, and they entered hand in hand into the green-and-yellow silence.

In the forest they were explorers. At a stream they jumped the gap, balancing, goat-like, from one stone to another. When the path became faint, covered by evergreens, they kept their direction, pushing through the leaves.

They paused at a clearing where the sun shone in, spot-point on the grass. Underfoot was cushioned with small daisy-like flowers which Matthew squatted to examine. Delicate and filmy, they spread like lace.

Miranda joined him, touching the earth. "Come on Matthew," she said quietly, reaching round to finger his chest. "Our bed," she added, smiling.

Matthew felt the warmth. As he closed and kissed, his body took over, tingling slightly. Miranda leaned back, drawing him with her, and they stretched out, sprawled across grass.

"Undress," she said suddenly detaching, and clawing at his jacket.

"You as well."

"Yes, yes."

They dragged and pulled, kicking off shoes and removing tops. Exposed to the sun, their skin showed white, like children on a beach.

Matthew was breathing hard. A voice in his head was calling out her name. He touched both breasts and reached down to her waist. Everything now was running into one: the light, his fingers, the sun across her body. And, with the forest air pressing and the damp grass under, it felt rawly urgent. Then inside that urgency and rising on a wave, smooth and fleshy, he hardened.

"Nice boy," Miranda laughed, cupping around his cock.

Matthew grunted then, mounting sideways, climbed between her legs. Her name came back, tenderly. She was what he wanted; he was all hers.

Miranda took a breath. As he lowered and pushed, she winced with surprise. "That's it," she whispered. He paused in a hunch and shifted higher to find the best angle before he began.

He felt her insides fluttering tightly. Part of him was straining, held within her passage, but another was all soft movement – down and up, floating into dark – and the rest was gentle calculation. He was doing it in measure, balanced on a high.

Miranda tightened further. As they moved together the word *everything* went through his mind. She began to cry out and he quickened to a stride as they rose as one, edging to a fall. Then all at once the physical took over, he was blind to it all, he was out there and beyond it, and then he couldn't stop, the power moved up, Miranda grunted, and he went and he went and he went.

Afterwards he asked her if she'd come too.

"Nearly," she said, beginning to shiver.

"I'm sorry, I couldn't hold on."

She smiled, looking at him archly. "Now there's a thought."

"Sorry?"

"Ah, say again."

Matthew, who was pulling on his shirt, looked puzzled. "I said I'm sorry—" As realisation dawned, his eyes met hers. "Well there you go," he laughed, "it's the magic word. And not just once."

Miranda held up three fingers.

He grinned. "Caught mid-apology."

"Indeed."

He paused to consider, touching her hair. "Shall I bring you?"

"By hand?"

"If you'd like that."

Miranda reached forward, pressing his hands up between her legs and around her thighs. "Everywhere," she said quietly and laid herself back, staring blankly, while Matthew knelt by her side, reaching and stroking and going all over.

"Everywhere," she repeated, "everywhere, everywhere." On her chest now a flush was spreading and her areolas had darkened.

When she came, she was breathing like a sleeper with arms spread wide to the intermittent sun, warm and gleaming on the cream and white flowers.

When they returned to the cottage the back door was open and Jenny was visible. She was busy tipping carrots into a large iron saucepan. Arriving at the step, they observed, unseen. As always, she was occupied. Dressed in a worn-looking kimono, her movements were calm and brightly measured. Where the sleeves had been shortened, her arms showed pink and rounded.

When Miranda moved forward, she beckoned them both in. "The girls are still biking. I wasn't needed."

They joined her by the range, asking what they could do.

"Don't worry, I'm finished now," she replied, examining the red-brown mixture seething in the pan. Using a long-handled spoon she added the last carrots and topped up with herbs. Then she lidded the pan and reduced the setting on the air vent.

"In any case," she said, "I've something for you." She led them to the dining room, taking out an envelope from a drawer. "This just arrived," she said, handing it to Matthew.

The envelope was large, glossy and lightly scented. Matthew saw his name above *care of*, in gracefully looping swirls. The down strokes were extended and the uppercase letters were shaded into blocks. For a second, as he peeled back the flap, the room seemed to narrow. There were words coming up with a memory of vows and a bell tone ringing. He wondered where it might lead.

Inside was a photo with a message on the back. He scanned the writing and laid it on the table, picture side up. Large, expansive and detailed, it showed a bare bright shoreline acting as backdrop to a woman on a motorbike. Facing the camera in a purple helmet, she was holding up a fist-sized flower. The woman was tall, her face slim and dramatic with a wide-domed forehead, triangular cheekbones and a well-fleshed smoothness centred on her mouth.

"I think I might know her," said Matthew, noticing the woman's eyes. They were sky-blue, ironic, and deeply thoughtful.

"You do?" said Jenny.

He gazed thoughtfully at the photo.

"But do you know who she *is*?" Jenny asked after he'd turned to the message on the back, scanning the first sentence.

"She's a girl on a breakwater, pictured with my mother."

Miranda's gaze shifted from the photo to Matthew. She asked him to explain. Matthew, speaking slowly, described the picture at his parents' house. Miranda nodded: did he, she wondered, know any more?

"Other than that, not a great deal." He paused before turning to Jenny, "But do *you* know her?"

"Oh, yes."

Now it was Matthew's turn to act as inquisitor, "But who is she?"

"My children's godmother and a fellow artist. For you, close."

Miranda touched the envelope. "So the writing meant—"

"I knew it was from her," Jenny confirmed.

"But who *is* she?" Matthew repeated.

"A Perkins," said Jenny.

"Your aunt, I suspect," added Miranda quietly.

"But in that case …" Matthew began then stopped. There were memories pushing in of tidal scenes with seashells and pools between rocks. He could feel the wind behind him, smell the sun on canvas, hear the breaking waves.

"There's an invitation," put in Miranda, who was leaning forward, studying the message. It was signed A, followed by several kisses.

Matthew read to the end. Already he could imagine the white-painted houses, the back-alley doorframe and the long walks along the front.

He held up the photo like a transparency. Backlit around the edges by the window, it glowed. "Her name's Angel," he said suddenly, turning to Jenny for confirmation. Their eyes met briefly and he smiled knowingly: "I stayed with her a few times, when I was a child."

"You remember?"

"I do now."

"What can you see in your head?"

"I've got a picture of where she lives."

"Anything else?"

"Playing. Being a child. Different to me now."

"Different – why's that?"

"I can't go back."

"But in another way you are really there …"

"Yes. It was *those* days. When I was good – I mean good as in a picture. Just what people wanted me to be. A boy in a beach snap, playing all day. It all seems quite distant now. Like the tide's gone out a long, long way."

Jenny glanced at Miranda. An understanding passed, woman to woman. She cast her eye quickly over the photo. "You could go there tomorrow," she said calmly, picking up the discarded envelope.

"Tomorrow?" asked Miranda.

"Yes, she says asap."

"Is it close?"

"Not really."

"So how?"

"Same way as you got here. By taxi."

At six the next morning the taxi appeared. Climbing the valley in the early morning sunlight the large-wheeled vehicle looked like a cross between a jalopy and a tank. Heavy, uneven and rusted underneath, it moved in spurts. The front axle showed as it bounced up the track, pitching forward and back. As it approached the cottage it slowed and steadied, then swung through a gate and clattered loudly over a cattle grid. Once in, it circled the field, weaving left and right, as if in search of an opening. Finally, it straightened and approached the back door at 45°, sliding over mud.

"Two-three-four!" The call blared out from a trumpet-like address system strapped to the roof.

The vehicle pulled up. Grey and battered around the back and sides, the windscreen was tinted and the bonnet covered with sticker-designs. Underneath, the metal was rusty, caked with mud and torn-off branches. To the rear the paint was scored deep and abraded, while the radiator was hung with beads and bunting and a string-hung plaque naming it the MAGIC TAXI.

A man leaned out, inspecting. He was square-built with wrestler's shoulders, wearing a braided headband with a seashell attached. Pushing back the door he manoeuvred out to balance on the running board and hung there like a side-saddle rider. Peering in with his head to one side and holding the doorframe, he was nodding in time to amplified guitars.

When his passengers emerged, he stepped down in silence to open the boot. His face was round, his gaze was far-sighted and his chin was tattooed with blue spiral markings. He stood by watchfully as they said their goodbyes then removed their bags.

"I'm Y," he said as he loaded up. The three exchanged greetings, on their side verbal, on his side with arms in the air. "The sixth vowel," he added gently and held the car door open. They slid inside as he fingered one earring and smiled toothily. He checked their destination, pointed out the cushions stowed in the pockets, passed round a bag of boiled sweets and swung into the driving seat where he wound down the windows and increased the volume.

The music roared, a wave-break of sound. "Hit it!" shouted Y as the guitars closed together, running hard. The taxi turned, backing up like a heavy-bodied animal. Matthew and Miranda waved as the engine snarled, Y called "Go!" and the car leapt forward to swing off down the track.

On the route downhill the guitar sounds peaked then the music ebbed and slackened to a trickle. Y slowed too, cruising *a tempo*. Now tender, the sound was tidal, mysterious, and oceanic. There were percussive shivers, wind sounds and water dripping noises. It dropped to a close-up lapping sound then moved into echoes and low, rhythmic pumping. Lithe and dark, it was full of long-held riffs, swoops and stops and syncopated drumming.

They descended through trees, passing a pool, an abandoned building and a disused quarry, rejoining the main road at a junction. Turning towards the coast, they overtook a truck, gaining speed as the sky began to clear. They raced through a village with long terraced rows and a pit head behind, slowed where the road twisted through an open cast area then opened up the throttle, cutting through a flat-meadowed valley with cows and thistles.

"It's Longsands we're going to?" called Matthew.

Y leaned forward on the steering wheel. "Angel's," he said, adding they were expected.

"You know her?"

Y confirmed, repeating her name with first syllable emphasis in time to the music. An alto sax entered as he beat out time, one-two on the wheel. For a while the music stayed low and ethereal, spreading into riffs and occasional scat. Then the volume returned, switching speakers, and rising to a climax. "My band," he said, nodding proudly.

Miranda asked for a name.

"The Vowels."

"You guys playing somewhere?" asked Matthew.

Y reached forward, keeping the wheel locked inside one enormous palm. "Tickets," he said, scooping from the dashboard and passing back a handful. They pictured an ocean-going canoe with THE VOW-ELS above and speech bubble reviews at the bottom. "Free. Bring friends."

"You playing on a boat?" asked Matthew.

"Ship. Pirate radio. Fireworks Night."

The card gave details, port and vessel, with a warning, issuing from the mouth of a waving green frog, to keep it among friends.

"We'll come," said Miranda quietly as the music flattened to a pulse. It held with something low and Om-like playing around the edges while a high-up harmonic reached into silence. It continued at a hum, blending with the wheels, the air and movement and the first flush of sunlight.

"With friends," added Matthew. And he fixed his mind forward, picturing Angel with a hand-held flower straddled on a bike and behind her, running off, the long level line of the faintly glinting sea.

They entered Longsands, cruising between small blocks of houses and wide flat fields. The town came in clumps, beginning with outliers and single rows and a grey gasometer, followed by the station and the caravan park, leading to a sign, a church and rows of houses. To Matthew, who recognised everything, it was like leafing through an old photograph album.

Continuing to the sea they passed by a slag heap glowing with embers from a dump truck. Here the road dipped down and turned beneath a bridge, straightening to a tree-lined avenue and large Victorian houses. At the end they could see the beach and beyond that the sea.

Reaching a corner, they turned at a three-storey house, entering a side road just before the park. Passing by an overgrown wall they drew up at the entrance to a wide cobbled alleyway.

"Angel," said Y, looking right.

Halfway down the alley a woman turned to view them. Standing by a motorbike, she was wearing black-red leathers and a studded metal belt. She observed them in silence with an open-faced expression. Her gaze was welcoming. It almost seemed, as she walked towards the car, that she'd stepped out from a photo and was crossing from one space to another. And, as she approached, Matthew recognised suddenly that the figure now before him had absolutely no trace of eyebrows, eyelashes or any kind of hair.

"Matthew," she smiled, as he climbed from the car. "You remember?"

He flushed, wondering if she meant her baldness. "Rem—" he began, then realising his mistake, looked towards the house. "You still …" he began, casting around for words. "You've kept it as it was?"

Angel smiled, knowingly. "I'll show you. But first, introductions, yes?"

Miranda supplied her name.

"And you're happy," said Angel.

"I suppose … Well, yes, in a way I am."

Angel turned towards Y who was standing to one side with a bag on each shoulder. "I'm paying," she said softly.

"With carburettor."

"Yes, it's inside."

At her invitation they re-entered the alleyway, turning at the bike to lead in through a gothic-pointed archway. The heavy, metal-edged door opened to a recessed courtyard with awnings on columns and an overhanging loggia.

"My workshop," she said, pointing to a mixture of spare parts, instruments and stripped-down bikes. On one side was a workbench with a vice and power tools, behind it was a line of large-scale, wall-hung, colour-field photos. Picking up a part, Angel wrapped it in a cloth and passed it to Y. It seemed to Matthew that something special went with it.

Pocketing his part, Y pulled out a bag and offered round sweets. They all accepted, sucking and chewing while staring at the photos. The prints were of colour swirls, borders and meetings between elements. Textured, they glittered from within.

"Beach pics?" Y asked and Angel nodded. Announcing his departure, he peered at the dial of a guitar-shaped wristwatch, then leaned towards Angel and kissed her on the head.

Her eyes closed once and her face turned inward. She touched his arm and a charge seemed to pass, a low-key, wordless understanding. When her eyes reopened, a smiling Y was turning towards the doorway. "Fireworks Night," he sang out to Matthew and Miranda as he strode off down the alleyway.

Led by Angel, they entered the house through the kitchen, talking about features and when the house was built. For Matthew it had changed, and yet in spirit it was the same. It belonged to several eras, while pointing to one.

On the ground floor, the open-plan kitchen adjoined a living room with shelves full of shell finds and sea-print ceramics. Tapestries and posters covered the walls. A large metal stove warmed the back room while the fire in the front was tiled round and decorated with stucco amoretti. As they walked and looked, Angel answered Matthew's questions. "You were Christmas boy," she replied, when quizzed about the past.

"I remember that."

"Midsummer as well?" Miranda put in.

"Always," said Angel, smiling at the ceiling.

"She means I got excited," Matthew explained.

"Very."

"Ah, so he was a wild boy?" Miranda asked.

"A child, yes."

They continued talking about Matthew while they climbed the stairs. Angel led, walking to the wall side, speaking thoughtfully. She wore her leather collar up, red and black against bare pink flesh. Seen from behind, her head was shiny, angular, and absolutely hairless. She looked like a Middle Kingdom Goddess.

When they'd counted off the bedrooms and reached the second landing Matthew asked. "Angel," he said, holding himself calm while feeling for the words, "what happened to the …?" He gestured vaguely towards her head.

"You mean the hair?"

Unwillingly, he nodded.

"Alopecia universalis."

Miranda, looking shocked, apologised for Matthew.

"Not at all, I should have explained." She opened the door to enter the second floor. "I sometimes forget."

They entered a long high room with four central pillars, windows on three sides and two studio-style skylights. "My other workshop," she said softly.

The room was full. It had floor-mounted sculptures, some of them unfinished, with busts in corners and glass-cased constructions in plastic and wood. At the centre there were two long worktops holding rough clay models, fibreglass cones and reticulated frames. In one corner tie-dyed textiles hung like washing over a paint-stained bath.

Matthew noticed at once a collection of pictures pinned up on a display board. "They're Jenny's work, from the colony?" he asked, pointing to some blown-up photos of rock-sculptures and wooden constructions floating downstream.

"Using landscape," Angel replied.

"But the pictures are yours?" asked Miranda. When Angel confirmed, she looked them over, close-up. "They're *bella*. Emotional."

At the far end of the room a carved wooden roodscreen led through to a space with head-high windows running all around. To the right, the wall was recessed into shrine-like slots, each with a single grey photo sealed into a frame. Small pencil lights lit up the photos; they were old, grainy and rather two-dimensional.

Matthew felt the shift. These were more personal, a kind of private view. Moving left to right, he scanned them. In each he saw a motorbike with a couple in scarfs and helmets. They were alone on the road. He saw them in a blur pointing downhill then on a mountainside, the same by a lake, and in all a sense of wildness and high-up excitement, a worldwide view. "Who are they?" he asked, his eyes tracking to a bike shot where the couple cornered low, leaning into tarmac.

"No ideas?" countered Angel.

"Not sure." Suddenly he felt adrift. He had come here to visit, climbed to this studio, absorbed himself in looking and now found – or been guided into viewing – just what? Two chin-strapped riders looking like pilots or military despatch. What his parents called *ton ups* or *tearaways*. He searched for the lyrics to a song, rerunning *Route 66* and *Born to be Wild*. "Are they perhaps …" he began before cutting off into vagueness.

Miranda joined him. "In this one," she said, pointing, "I feel there's something special. As if I'd met them before." She glanced around at Angel who was watching.

Following his aunt's gaze, Matthew studied the photo. He could see a man and a woman riding on the beach. They faced out from the picture and didn't seem bothered. Suddenly he knew. "Are they …?"

Angel nodded.

"But they're so different."

"True."

Matthew gazed at Miranda. "You won't believe this."

She looked at him questioningly.

"It's my lot. My parents," he said, turning to Angel in outraged recognition.

"Certainly, yes."

"I don't get it. When was this taken?"

"Before you were born."

"But, like *that*. My dad? Were they really that way?"

Before Angel could answer, Miranda intervened. "They have to be, don't they, Matt?"

He drew back from the picture sharply as if he'd been stung. "How d'you mean?"

"There has to be a link."

"A link? You're not suggesting …"

"It's the only explanation."

"I'm like them, eh?"

Angel stepped forward. Her words were carefully considered. "No, Matthew, the reverse. They're more like you than you realised."

"I never thought …" he said, wiping the back of his hand around his mouth. "Well, if that's how it is … I suppose I ought to give what you've said a chance. Let it sink in."

Angel reached over and took him by the arm. "And now," she said, raising her voice, "I'd like you both to see something. It's the reason I invited you."

In reply to their questions she laughed, "No clues. You'll see, soon enough." She conducted them back down the stairs, answering Matthew's queries as they descended. Yes, she said, Harriet and Alan had led, with her there behind. And yes, she'd seen them race downhill, beating all rivals.

"So, what happened?" he asked, walking ahead. "Where's it all gone now?"

"You heard Miranda. There are roads we take."

Matthew, who by now had reached the courtyard, paused on the step. His voice flared slightly, "Biology is destiny, eh?"

Angel met his eyes. "Some things become part of us. We reuse them."

Matthew grunted and walked a few paces. "Are you saying I'll end up like them?"

"No, Matt, not if you don't want to," Miranda put in.

"Or maybe *like* them," added Angel, "but as in the photos."

"Have my parents seen themselves?" Matthew cut in. "Recently, I mean. Seen how they were?"

"I showed them last time they were here."

"What did they say?"

"They looked and said it brought back memories. They know things have changed."

Matthew's eyebrows shot up. "Changed—"

"At least on the surface … until you know." Here Angel paused. "Because I've got this thing waiting. A present they sent."

Matthew and Miranda looked around in surprise, as if it was a guessing game.

"I'm not sure …" began Matthew, slowly.

"Too late. *It's behind you,*" Angel quipped, leading to a corner where she pushed aside a curtain to reveal a recessed doorway. "You'll see," she said, taking out a key. Angel undid a padlock, pulled back the door and ducked in, clicking on a light. "Ah, yes," she said quietly, and her voice filled the space. As Matthew crouched, sighting something metallic, she invited them in. "It's a gift from Alan and Harriet, to their son."

When Matthew entered, wondering what she meant, the first thing he saw in the centre of the space was large, shiny and reflective. For an instant he stood, drawing in his breath. What he could see was almost too immediate and unexpected, too much to process. He wondered if he'd dreamed it. Or perhaps, he thought quickly, he'd got it all wrong. It was only when Miranda entered and she called out in surprise, that he realised. Before him was a bright, black and silver, square-framed motorbike.

"For me?" he asked, stupidly.

"Yes, you and Miranda."

"From them?"

"Certainly, yes."

He ran one hand lightly over chrome, grinning rather ruefully. "I suppose it's a lesson. I've things to learn."

Miranda, smiling, looked at Angel. "And you'll need a good teacher, if you're going to ride this thing."

Matthew pushed back his hair. "I'm grateful and I'm, well, amazed. In fact, I don't know what to say – to you, or my parents." Here he coloured. "And I'd be even more grateful if you could tell them—"

Angel cut in, shaking her head, "No, Matthew. I want *you* to tell them."

"You want me to?"

"Yes."

"But how?"

"Write to them."

He paused, head down, then flashed a smile. "Of course. A thank you letter."

"Lett*ers*."

"Yes, letters."

"And the bike?" asked Miranda. "You'll be his instructor?"

Angel gave a nod. Studying them both, her face softened. She appeared to have absorbed them into some sort of brightness, a quietly child-like, all-surrounding glow. "We exit this way," she said gently, pointing to a pair of wooden doors that led out into the alleyway.

"Open sesame," she said, handing Miranda the key.

"*Certamente.*"

After twisting the lock and pulling a bolt up from the floor, Miranda swung the doors open. The light that entered glinted on the bike, as if it was a model in a showroom.

Angel kicked off the brake and leaned against the handlebars. "Stand ready," she said, wheeling it out while Matthew and Miranda held the doors. Afterwards she asked them to lock up.

They gathered in the alleyway. "Lesson one will be peripatetic," said Angel, and she helped them roll the machine out to the road. "But before we get going, a few questions …"

She began by checking what they knew, taking them through the controls, the theory and what to watch out for. When she'd answered their questions and added a few points, they set off.

They wheeled and steered, advancing as a party past park and flagpole to reach the promenade and the view out to the bay, the wide-open seafront and the white-walled ramp descending to the beach.

They spent the day riding. For most of the morning, the sun shone and the tide was out. Curving away in a clean-edged sweep beyond the town, the beach was a blur. It was large and bare and empty.

They began with Angel riding just ahead, standing in the saddle. She scrambled with ease over soft sand and bladderwrack. The bike, a vintage Norton, was well-sprung and sturdy and slewed from side to side as it dipped into craters, kicking up a sand cloud. On reaching the hard beach, Angel remained mounted awaiting her pupils. When they arrived, she leaned out at an angle, checking the wheels. "Climb up," she said, nodding Miranda towards the pillion.

She rode up and down with her pupils taking turns, hanging on behind. The rides etched tyre tracks in the white-yellow surface. When she stopped, she gazed out to sea. There were tankers visible and wisp-clouds in patches. "It's another world," she said as if she was picking up threads from a previous conversation. The wind blew softly around her bare pink head.

Matthew nodded, following her gaze. Already he felt the life all around. The world seemed larger and much less personal. A distance was opening up and what had once seemed important was now, quite suddenly, out there and far away. He could see how much further he'd still got to go.

When they'd looked for a while, Angel turned back to the bike, mentioning time and purpose. She recapped her points, asking how far she should take them.

"We're new to this," said Miranda.

"And you know the machine," added Matthew.

"No problem," she said. "It's a beautiful bike, handles well." After talking, she coached them in turns to circle a few yards. By gradual extension, through widening arcs then straight lines speeding up, she developed their balance. Soon she was trotting to one side, calling instructions.

At lunch time they rode back landwards with Angel taking over when they reached soft sand. Bouncing for traction, she pressed on up the beach. Nothing seemed to throw her. Trippers who took notice were ignored, if children reacted and pointed she smiled, cameras she blanked. Encountering deckchair watchers, she passed between their camps or outflanked their defences by circling to one side. Leaving the beach, she revved up the ramp, waving at the top to a passing biker. Joined by her pupils, she slow-toured the front. Together they passed by the paddling pool and the yellow-painted shelter, pausing at the amusements.

"The funnies," called Matthew, "you remember?"

Angel confirmed.

They carried on past broken signage and red-painted doors to arrive at a chip shop with steamed-up windows and a sign saying *Not Open.*

"That's Longsands for you," Angel said. "But don't believe it. Rani'll be in the back."

She took them around a corner to an unfenced garden where she propped the bike against a yellow brick bunker. Waving them on, she advanced, peering at the building. "This way," she said. "She'll be in there." The back of the house was hollowed out and angular with off-true corners and cracks in the wall. "Rani!" she called. Her voice was clear and resonant and surprisingly loud. To Matthew it sounded charged, and rather operatic. There was no reply.

Repeating her call, Angel led in through a low door to enter a blue-wash basement. Matthew joined in as they called left and right, filling up vacant spaces. Their voices echoed strangely from plaster.

As they passed along a corridor, reaching some stairs, a reply came from above. "Is that you, my Angel?" The jaunty, singsong voice cut off suddenly and a round-faced woman appeared, wearing a blue kurti. "Glad it's you, my dear. Come on up."

They climbed a near-vertical ladder, gripping a rope. It took them through a hatch to emerge in a crowded, pub-like interior. "Now *there's* something," Rani said with a lilt, "I see you've brought company."

Angel introduced them. She explained the connection, saying they were students down for the day. Matthew mentioned childhood visits and Miranda added that they were biking on the sands. When asked about their morning, they answered brightly that they'd learned so much.

Rani established quickly that they'd not had lunch. "But before that, my lovelies," she said, beaming, "if you'd care to join me, please come this way for the quick, unofficial look-around."

"Lead on," Angel said quietly.

The tour began in the front room. It was wide and L-shaped with stones on shelves, painted feathers and terracotta models behind glass. It smelled of wax and fry-ups. Rani conducted Matthew and Miranda around by the counter flap and behind the metal-plated vats to show them a backroom full of sinks and towels and low-level cupboards. Tiled and wooden, it echoed like a church. They stepped around, admiring the brass plates and framed tapestries hung from nails. In one corner Rani showed them an ornamental table covered with a cloth. "My treasures," she said. The table was full of silver cups, mirrors and candles. At the back were some flowers and a pink-yellow image of Ganesh. As they re-entered the front room Rani pointed out the bell pull system above the door – a relic, she said, of the Edwardian owners. From behind the vats she showed them the lino-covered trapdoor and a hidden mirror that viewed around corners. She ended, grinning, standing by the counter. "Tour over," she announced, raising the flap. They passed under and out to see Angel, crouched in a corner peering closely at a miner's crystal.

"She's teaching you?" Rani checked, smiling at her friend.

"She's the big boss," replied Matthew.

Rani scanned all three. "And now, dears, since you've been out all morning," she said, glancing up at a large-handed clock, "I've something extra-special. Just for you."

She reached into a fridge, drawing out a paper-wrapped softness that she spread across a chopping board. It was grey and white and pink around the edges. "It's a cuttlefish," she called, taking a knife to trim back the ends. Adjusting her gloves, she spread three fish portions and some chips in a basket before plunging them into oil. The liquid hissed and frothed up to the brim. "One minute, my lovelies," she called, pulling out a long-handled spatula from a slot in a drawer. "You'll enjoy this," she said, shaking the basket.

They were served, at Rani's insistence, on a laminated table set back in an extension with a peace lily to one side and a fanlight above. She joined them to watch.

"Like it?" she asked, pointing with a fork to the lightly-browned flesh, and Matthew nodded.

"Surprising isn't it?" Rani added, exchanging a smile with Miranda.

"They say it's an aphrodisiac," she laughed, kissing Angel on the head.

While they ate, she asked them about college, their journey and their first-time biking. Everything to her was good, she welcomed what they said.

When they finished, she cleared up refusing all payment. "There's one thing though," she added as they rose to leave. "Something you *can* do." Half-closing her eyes she beckoned them to come with her. At the corner of the room she led through a door to a long, corridor-like lean-to with three walls plastered and an all-glass roof. It was tall and bare, echoed slightly and smelled of polish. The floor was tiled, the woodwork was glossed and the walls were painted in a blue-white wash.

She pointed to a line of empty frames stacked in one corner. "This, my dears, is my own private gallery," she said, glowing. "And I'd like you," she continued, turning to Angel, "to fill it up with snaps. Pics of these two, biking."

That afternoon, after picking up the camera, they returned to the beach and Angel took pictures. The wind had got up, the sun was raw, and they showed what they could do. Starts at first, then runs, then slow stops to order without losing balance. More runs later making turns, each quicker, leading to moves following a pattern, growing more difficult and complex, and always as a couple looking forward, overseen by Angel.

With Miranda steering and Matthew on pillion, they rode in a square, dodging around stones. With positions reversed they cruised, splashing through water. As the sunlight lengthened and the tide advanced, they merged, it seemed, into air and sound. The motorbike shook, the engine coughed and the tyres hissed contact.

There were photo calls too: pictures in profile, and head-on to camera. Angel took shots for all occasions, set-piece and snaps and what she called her "quickies". They posed in ones, in twos, journeying out across flat sand to ride into long shot past outfall and lagoon, then further to the point, then back to close-up in runs along a line.

As the sunlight weakened and the beach-strip narrowed, the bike became sluggish. With Matthew now riding and Angel on pillion, they were pushed onto soft sand. Her hands cupped his as they laboured by the dunes. At a stone and gravel slipway with a groyne for protection she slid to a stop. "I'll take over," she said, "this part's difficult."

As Matthew dismounted, she passed him the camera and closed on the groyne, pointing her front wheel at a wood-and-metal buttress. Angled steeply, it supported on both sides. Hunched over the bars, she dragged the machine up and sideways. It reared and kicked, twisting like a stallion. Sand sprayed out as Angel hopped forward to drop onto the buttress, where she held it balanced, shuddering slightly. Revving again, she stared towards the top and straightened in the saddle. With a roar and a snarl the bike shot halfway, paused, teetered, then leapt the last few feet, landing square.

"Yeehaa!" she called, laughing.

She pulled back into neutral, seesawing over and descending in stages. The slope down was longer with supports both sides, leading to a drop. There were four sets of uprights in rusted metal, sequenced like jumps. The first pair, being stubby, required her to slow, the second to lean back and the third to wriggle. The fourth at the end acted as a springboard for the drop to the slipway, where she landed on gravel, skidding to a halt.

"Wow, you wouldn't have thought it possible!" Miranda exclaimed, shaking her head.

"Encore!" Matthew chorused, jigging on the spot.

On the other side of the barrier Angel grinned like a pilot just landed. "Easier than you think. Of course, the bike's the thing." She glanced up the slipway and back to the machine. "And this one's the best."

"A good day's riding," volunteered Matthew.

Angel nodded. "You've come a long way, both of you."

"Loved it," said Miranda. "A learning experience."

"With plenty of pictures," laughed Matthew, holding up the camera.

Angel beamed and spoke about their first-time quickness and how proud she felt. "Star quality," she continued, pausing for effect. "I thought so when you arrived," she added, her voice dropping low, "and now I'm certain."

On the route back to the house they called at the chip shop, leaning the bike against railings. They banged on the window, summoning Rani, and posed for a photo. She clicked several times and asked about progress before seeing them off, watching down the street and waving goodbye.

At Matthew's request they made a few visits, stopping at the sweet shop, where they counted the rock sticks and jars in the window. They slowed to view the crazy golf before pushing on to the clock tower and the dried-out paddling pool. As they went, they passed a couple walking a dog and a small group of trippers. There were two children cycling who followed at a distance, shadowing their progress from the seafront promenade. On the road there were litter scraps and fine drifts of sand. They moved along a row of whitewashed houses, passing a garage, where Angel signed thumbs up to a mechanic, and continuing by a boarded-up pub until they arrived at the park and the road back to the house.

It was when they reached the alleyway, with the moon now out, that Matthew realised that the large car with multi-coloured stickers parked by the pavement was the taxi they'd arrived in. He peered through the window and turned to Angel, "Where's Y?"

"Out gigging. He parks here so I can use it."

A note on the dashboard in coloured pencil said BACK BY SIX. Angel read it and asked about their plans. It seemed they didn't have any.

She held up some keys. "If you need to get back, I can drive you."

Matthew touched the bonnet and glanced at Miranda. "I don't think …" he began then stopped to consider. Delivered quietly, Angel's words were a reminder of college. Suddenly he felt the distance, how far they'd come. He flashed back to Theresa waving from the van. "On second thoughts, maybe, if it's not too difficult."

"No problem," said Angel, "happy to help."

"You don't mind?"

"As long as we leave soon."

"Angel," said Matthew, his voice tone rising, "you're … what can I say?" He paused, as if in search of something scripted. "A truly amazing woman. And I owe you."

"Yes," said Miranda, "and a pretty good instructor."

Angel smiled archly. "There is of course a condition."

"Now would that be, by any chance, in writing?" asked Miranda, playfully.

"Conditions tend to be that way."

Matthew pursed his lips. "I know, the letters. I've started one already, in my head."

"And is it OK?" Angel asked.

"Yes, consider it done."

"Ten minutes, then we go," Angel called, wheeling the bike along the alleyway and unlocking the back door.

While she stored the machine, Miranda fetched the bags. Angel did a check, a quick look-around, mainly in the kitchen, where she parcelled up some apples and a packetful of biscuits before returning to the car. They all climbed in and set off into the dark with Miranda and Matthew curled up together and Angel at the wheel, singing quietly. In her hands the taxi seemed to move without effort, turning down the avenue and proceeding inland, meeting the odd car. The road soon emptied and they picked up speed after clearing the bridge.

As they left Longsands, Matthew saw wide dark spaces, road signs illuminated and lights against grey. There were street lamps at first, both sides, then at intervals, becoming scarcer with long gaps between them, and finally complete darkness. They were headed off into no-where.

During the drive Miranda fell asleep, resting on Matthew's shoulder. Her hair brushed his cheek and her breath came slowly. As the journey lengthened their balance shifted, leaning both ways as if they were on the bike. Imagining himself driving, he cushioned around corners and shifted with the movement, acting as her support. And each small turn, each limb-change and wriggle, was a partner thing.

As Matthew looked out, he recalled them on the beach. Boy and girl riders, balanced carefully with Angel close by. And with that came the photos of himself laughing and his father showing muscle. Sand-boy in the picture with family, larking.

The engine note dropped as they slowed behind a truck. They were passing houses, a gated level crossing and a station with lights.

He thought about college, the gatherings, and what they'd return to. People he'd called family. Minds without expression, all made up. He'd see and greet them and *be* there for the record, then get on his machine to begin the other journey, the long run into night.

At a junction, losing the truck, they opened full throttle and accelerated into dark. As the engine note ascended, Matthew counter weighed Miranda, push-pulling to the centre. When they arrived at a carriageway, he saw his parents as bikers, riding towards dawn. They'd kept themselves hidden and now had reappeared, all geared up and staring into camera.

And he knew as he dozed that he'd found himself somehow. He was there going forward with eyes to the horizon, moving through sunlight and shadow and air-bright motion in a soft glare of sand.

# EIGHTEEN

So, it comes back to family. Wave after wave, breaking on the beach. I can see it in the boys, the whole long line. My all-weather lads studying the signs, walking on hard sand. Jack's there at the front, chin out, braving the spray. He's mouthing his one word, "Don't." Behind him, Stephen's in overalls. His word is "Home." Stuart's there in tie and jacket, watching the horizon. He's not talking. And after them, I can see Edwin running, Alan picking shells, and sand-boy Matty with Richard and James, digging. They're the three musketeers.

And the women there, too. Grace standing, arms at her sides, saying "I-will-leave." Edith saying "That's over," packing her case. Doris calming Edwin. Harriet and Angel facing the waves.

And me?

I watched them all. They were my life. I was their voice, the story behind them. What they said and what they did, carried in my head. His name, her name, and what happened next.

Of course, it's how you remember it. You fit things to feel and make up patterns. There's a circle there, they grow up, they flower and they fade. Or back and forth, floating on the tide.

So, what stands out?

The Lavender boys and their line back, with knots. One strand Matty, in a tug of war with Alan, with Stuart as anchor. The other strand Edwin, tied to Dad, with a fishing line forward to Richard and James.

Not forgetting Grace and Doris planting their backyards with flowers and children.

But then, what next? And where does it lead to?

Well, there's always a story. Something left over, the sound of people talking, going around the head. Parts of a story, maybe. The last part, the bit under covers like a boat on the beach. Look below the tidemark and you'll find things hidden. What Stephen called diving into the wreck. Or like his postcards arriving from the blue.

I can feel Jack's hands on mine, chopping wood. I was in the coal shed, talking with Edith. It was dark like the inside of a wave.

The story, and the pictures. Beach snaps from a distance of Alan and Harriet with me, or asleep on the rug with Matt and Angel. Even now I can feel the brightness inside, the low sun and the seagulls circling. I was outside myself, looking down on life. I could see the dogs and the children playing on the beach. Matty smiling for a photo, digging tunnels. "Stop," I said, "before you get to Aus ..."

Heat, then cold. The words mixed up. Children's voices and cries on the wind. An ache in the chest and everything stiffens. And I see them again, with wreaths and crosses by the family grave. Washed out to sea and missing, presumed dead. As a shadow passed through me, I walked towards the waves knowing this was where I was heading ...

In the ambulance with Alan I made him promise. Put up the tent, the windbreak, look after the boy. Say it never happened.

Afterwards the tide came up, covering the rocks.

‡ ‡ ‡

"We're seeing the Old Year out," said Mia.

"What's your resolution?" asked Cass.

"No more shows," Joe replied.

"Joe," Mia asked, "why on earth?"

"Exactly. The Earth," Joe answered.

"Oh, really? But I got off on our show."

"That's nice," he said, "but now's close to midnight."

"Yes, we're running out of time," called Cass, checking her phone.

They were standing by The Minster, waiting for the bells. A few people nearby were gazing up at the floodlit façade. They were older than Cass, Joe and Mia. In the reflected light their faces were smoothly and gently worshipful.

"Aren't we all supposed to get drunk?" joked Mia. "Then sing happy birthday, or something like that?"

"Not any more," her brother replied. "It's about listening and regen."

"New Year's a turning point," said Cass, glancing at the other watchers, "when we cross a line."

"I've heard it called a tipping point," replied Joe.

Cass looked up at white stone. "Yes, if the people who built this had only known."

"And because of what we know," Joe added quietly, "it changes everything."

"And no fireworks," said Mia. "They freak out the animals."

"Bells are clean," said Cass.

At that moment the bells began to ring. A small cheer went up as their sound filled the square. Their long, up-and-down notes echoed from the walls and spread across the rooftops. While they rang, the air was alive; afterwards the air went on shaking. They were sounding the alarm.

"It's over," said Cass.

"The end," Mia replied.

"Or a beginning," said Joe.

♯ ♯ ♯

Over the next week Matthew and Miranda were on catch up. On the one hand they'd essays already close to deadline, on the other they'd people coming by wanting their story. So they stayed up late, talked through titles and sources and drafted several pages before they toured their friends. They put themselves out there. And their listeners were impressed. Whatever they'd imagined, this was something else. The story they heard had a getaway feel, a journey of discovery that went beyond the norm. It was beautiful to listen to and sounded like a film.

In Paul's view it was cool, when Sally heard it she wanted to see them saddled up, for Theresa it was *wow man-ish*, while to Jay it was *ultimate*, an ontological cameo with Sci-fi parallels in interstellar traffic and deep-space sprawl.

"This is my *Urtext*," he said darkly, reading from his novel, written in pencil on a rolled-up sheet of wallpaper. "My life as *Ouroboros*."

Kneeling on the carpet he pushed back the roll, uncovering his own words.

"Once and once only," he intoned, fixing his story with a wondering stare. He was humming contentedly.

"Worm holes, worm holes," he added, pulling out a penknife that he dug into the roll. Using its point and one claw-like hand, he hacked out sections from the text. As the bits came away, he slid around the floor, using his teeth to excavate further. Soon the floor was littered with torn and irregular wallpaper lumps. They were creased and lined and trickled with saliva. As the words blurred, he pulled out a crayon and began work on a series of illustrations.

"It's compositional," he explained dreamily to Miranda. He added several splurges, a mud-mess of wax then layered his sheets into packs. As he matched and placed, his face had the carefully composed expression of a small boy on the toilet. This was good business, an all-day thing. A portion of nirvana. He ended with a remark about time well spent while leafing happily through finger-smeared scraps of wallpaper.

Afterwards, when the gathering split up, Matthew led out, reminding Miranda of what he called their "walkaround" – a route they'd developed in their first week together to circulate venues and visit friends.

On their way he felt the change. At the gathering he'd seen the faces: self-regarding groupies hoping to impress. Suddenly, being there felt passé.

"I don't know about you," said Matthew as they passed along the walkway, "but this place looks different. Kind of unreal, like a film set."

Miranda took his arm. "You have to wait."

He knew she meant Longsands and the weekend ahead.

Later by the bar he looked in, unsmiling. "They think it's heaven."

Miranda laughed. "*You* used to say that."

This time there were parents in the background, long country walks and his battles with his father.

"To my mind," he said as they gazed across the lake, "there's too much image. It's all about looks and surface."

"And to my mind," said Miranda as they moved towards the bridge, "it's a stage."

As she spoke, Matthew remembered his own words in the dining hall about doing purple.

When they finished the circuit, they took a back path around the kitchens leading past a grass patch with bollards to a wired glass door and a strip-lit hallway. They approached silently, hearing voices issuing from windows and a couple on a bench quietly talking. Above them the moon rode high and clear in a grey-black sky.

At the door they stopped and kissed, first cheeks then mouth. A softness came between them, a pause before the show. "Shall we …" he said, half-questioning.

They went in smiling and passed along the corridor. Miranda stopped and pulled out the key. He closed to her waist, circling and exploring as she led through the door. Once in, they embraced and his lips reached her neck. Miranda shivered and drew him to the bed. She removed a layer and picked up a matchbox to touch-light a candle.

"*Artistico*," she said, inviting him to help. For a second he was stargazing.

Miranda took some candles from a box and they chain-lit several more.

"Better this way," she added, switching off the light.

In the half dark the candles glowed. Their line ran double, once around the bedhead and once, much darker, gleaming in the mirror. They were still and flower-like, blue around the base, honeyed above.

"Looks like a party," said Matthew, staring.

"Happy unbirthday," Miranda said, beginning to undress. She allowed him to take over and they counted off layers. His went too, with her fingers helping. When they'd peeled off, they gazed at each other in the mirror. With candles both sides they stood and looked as if they were portraits in a gallery.

"Sexy," he said as he finger-stroked her flesh.

"Hmm, good," she murmured, looking into glass. As lovers they were perfect; they enjoyed showing off.

When he pushed her to the bed, she went down smiling with Matthew on top and the candles to one side, bathing her body in an all-surrounding glow.

Next morning, they awoke to the clank of buckets and something heavy being dragged down the corridor. There was a knock at the door and a voice called, "Cleaner!" The knocking continued until Miranda called back, pulling on a dressing gown. She put her head round the door, promising a call as soon as she was ready. "Ten minutes," she told Matthew, after closing up.

They washed and dressed and opened the windows before retreating to the kitchen with Matthew brewing coffee and Miranda spreading toast.

"Best out of it," he said, touching her hair.

They ate to a background accompaniment of scrapings, taps and pneumatic gushes. There were doors being knocked and greetings delivered. As the cleaners advanced and the rooms turned out, the corridor became lighter and busier. To Matthew and Miranda, it felt like breakfast on a train.

When they returned, the room smelled of soap suds and linen. There were clean white sheets, vacuum lines in the carpet and the desktop had been dusted. "Quite a change," said Miranda. "Smells a bit like the seafront," she added.

Matthew kissed her brow. Her words were unintended reminders. "Time I wrote," he said, pulling out a notepad that he'd stowed in a drawer.

He opened at a double page of writing. It was dense and layered, full of underlined words with boxed-in sections in capitals and inserts in the margin. "As promised," he said, pointing to *Dear Mum and Dad*, which he'd crossed through twice, once to put their names and once in favour of *Hi there*.

"It's a start," he said and settled at the desk.

While Miranda read, Matthew composed, choosing his words for effect. Beginning with his thanks – warm and unreserved and implying, he felt, an apology – followed by his academic progress, a portrait of Miranda, the break at Longsands, and his impressions of the bike.

Writing slowly, he described how he'd come across their pictures and the difference it had made – and his recent awareness of how much he owed.

Often while he wrote he stopped to read out or passed across to Miranda, checking what she thought. "Do you reckon it's a con?" he asked her when he'd been through several drafts and was busy changing a few final phrases.

"You're in there," she said, grinning, "Matthew mark ten."

"So, it's false?"

"No, just revised thoroughly. Careful."

When he left off making changes, he read it back checking for feel, as if it had been written by someone else.

"I never fully realised," he said, "what writing, real writing, can do."

"Real writing?"

"An attempt, with your help."

Miranda looked thoughtful. "I liked what you said—"

Matthew glanced down at the newly dusted desktop. He knew what she meant. In his mind he saw them together, walking in the woods. He advanced one finger, tracing patterns in the wood grain. "You're thinking of what I wrote about you?"

"Well, yes."

"The description or the other stuff, the bits I'm not sending?"

She smiled, almost pityingly. "Which do you think?"

He spread both hands. "It's the truth. It may be kind of creaky and poetic, but it's true." And he kissed her on the forehead and down to her cheek then inserted his tongue quietly and firmly, filling up the softness of her mouth.

Their return to Longsands was late night on Friday. They packed the day before and when Matthew's essay was finished and Miranda had seen her tutor, the other life, the beach-life began. Y picked them up and delivered at speed, Angel received them and by early Saturday morning they were riding, continuing the whole day, Sunday as well. They biked back early on Monday to arrive in time for their first lecture, attending in leathers.

From then on they studied, lectures on weekdays – and between sessions lighting candles or walking around campus – weekends seeing Angel, where they rode out together and joined her in the workshop, diagnosing problems and learning to fit parts. She coached them through their test and paid for a licence. They also went exploring, following the coastline, climbing the sand hills and gazing out to sea. In the morning they rode timed circuits, while the afternoons were divided between off-road scrambling and taking snapshots with Angel. And when they went to Rani's the photos were there, mounted in her gallery.

"You look best in this, my dears," she said, pointing to a group shot outside the café.

"Because of the photographer?" asked a smiling Matthew.

"Well not because of *him*," said Miranda, pointing to an image of Matthew standing by the bike.

"You mean Peter Fonda?"

"Look again. That's Goofy."

Matthew rolled his eyes at the couple in the pictures, laughing at their poses and imitating their tics. "Guess who?" he grinned, mimicking Miranda as a wide-mouthed manikin clinging to her bike.

"Hell's Matthew?" she replied, leering madly and pushing out her jaw.

In the end it was Rani who shushed them, producing some paper-wrapped burfi for their journey.

They toured the district and visited the colony, where they took the girls for rides, turning slow circles with Leon on standby, walking within reach. They rode in the field examining the planets then accelerated off blowing kisses, returning to college. Back in an hour they quick-changed and washed before heading up an outing, with Paul and Theresa, to Y's boat gig and the night sea party.

Meeting on the road, with *Crossroads* blaring from the orange-striped van, Matthew waved, Paul signalled back and they set off, moving in convoy. Matthew and Miranda rode as escort, cruising just ahead, and when they reached the town, they directed with gestures to the car park by the sea. There they saw the boat all decked out in rainbow banners and flashing fairy lights, and from there they led out, walking by the quayside past fishing fleet and colliers, to step onto the gangway and watch the fireworks shoot while boarding in the dark.

"Remember, remember," said Miranda who'd paired herself with Sally when the crowd flowed in and around.

The display was front deck, in a glare. It began with a fizz, hissed for a while then spluttered and expanded, shooting into glow balls and clouds of pink mist.

Joining those standing, they oohed and aahed as three large rockets opened, spreading and unpetalling like flowers against glass.

The fireworks continued as the boat cleared harbour. When they ended, Y appeared wearing a long robe and holding a carved paddle. "Gig call," he announced and levered up a large metal hatch, dropping through his oar before climbing down.

Sally laughed, watching from the railing. "Who's he?" she asked Miranda. When her friend gave details, she peered into the hole. "So, they're *his* band," she said, flicking back her hair. "And they're all as mad as him?"

Miranda confirmed while reserving judgement on the sanity question.

"Well, let's go look. Say hello," laughed Sally, leading to the stairway and down into the hold.

Below deck was busy. There were people descending, some ascending, others at the bar. Several stood apart taking in the room, a few stray bodies crouched in corners, and a couple doing yoga were stretched out on the floor. There were groups around doorways and passageways off, and a flood tide of faces moving forward, drawn into a dimly-lit corridor where a counter-tide of music filled up the space, thundering and reverberating like surf. Joining the flow, Sally and Miranda advanced down the corridor, passing through a bulkhead, to arrive at a cave-like, fuliginous dancehall filled with smoke-wreaths and wave on wave of amplified music.

They spotted Matthew by his hair length. He was standing at the back, talking at a shout with Paul and Theresa. Noticing Miranda, he waved at her to come over. "Hey, beautiful," he laughed, putting out his arms, "you going my way?" She smiled and her teeth showed white and perfect.

They greeted as a group, throwing up their hands and jigging to the music. In the dark they were bound together by feel, the big line of sound sweeping the dancehall, and the impact rhythm pushing into flesh. They were at high volume, all raised up.

Matthew pointed and they formed a chain, moving forward through the crowd, first Matthew with Miranda, then Sally gripping hard, linking back to Theresa, with Paul as rear marker. They advanced to a gap where they stood, taking in the light show, the instruments and the great gale of sound.

On the stage ahead, Y stood tall. Stripped to the waist he was leaning forward, closed about the mike. His big bluesy voice was growly and strong. Inside and behind it there was a gathered-up feeling of damage and loss. He was struggling against the flow. Beside him two slab-faced guitarists were jerking around their instruments, a man with sax was dancing on the spot, a hand-clapping woman was harmonising scat and a big-bellied head-shaking drummer was hitting out all over.

The number was long. The all-out section had just reached its peak with Y on an up, the guitarists stretching, the others piling in, and the whole room standing, pumping, with hands high and all heads facing forward. At the climax there was a moment when the music hung, shimmering and percussive, with Y and the woman wailing, the lead guitar on feedback and the drummer in a sweat. Then came a time change, leading to a hushed, mysterious section with cymbals and sax making wind and wave sounds, Y on standby, the woman imitating bird cries and the guitars playing low.

While the band took over Y climbed down to pass among the audience. With his huge bare chest and gently rolling gait he moved along, raising his arms and mouthing silent greetings. He continued circulating, working the room till he arrived at Sally.

"Hi," she mouthed quietly, angling her face sideways. As Y stood admiring, she smoothed her hair, using her fingers as a hand brush. In the dark, her long soft ringlets glowed red-brown and chestnut.

Y remained fixed. His calm, unwavering gaze was trained on her fingers and on her hair. She was his Beauty; he had her in his sights.

Behind him now there were short jumpy staccato riffs, mixed with grace notes and cross-beat flourishes. The band began to cut from low insistence to wake up and stretch; they were calling for return. The insistence grew, the music tightened and the drum beat upped. As they moved into their intro Y, who was still looking, stretched out a hand to touch her hair. He drew down slowly and slipped his encircling arm in a loop around her back. Bending forward, he lifted her in a half-elevation. She was there in his arms, smiling; he had her as his baby.

As the intro came again, Y stepped back, placing her on the stage edge, and retook the microphone. Standing tall, he waited for the riff and took a deep breath. With his eyes fixed on Sally he began his song.

"A good match you'd say?" called Matthew, addressing Paul through the open van window. He was paused above the slipway, preparing to move off, with Miranda on pillion. The bike was pointing towards the sun and Longsands bay; the van was reversed with the engine idling, facing inland.

"Good for her."

"You think it won't work?"

Paul revved the engine. "Maybe he can sing about it."

"Unlucky in love, that kind of thing?"

"Something like."

"Well, that's the blues," Matthew said dryly, looking out to sea. "Poor boy in trouble. Woman done him wrong."

"Whatever it takes."

"But I'm on their side," said Matthew, suddenly, smiling. "I think they're well suited."

"Yeah, fellow travellers."

Miranda leaned forward. "You guys ready?"

Paul checked with Theresa, who nodded.

Matthew gazed around the horizon. The sun was spreading, white and clear on a diamond-blue sky. There were cloud streaks and contrails rising in wisps. The sea was flat: grey-green and slate, flecked with pewter. "OK. Meet you in the next world," he called, saluting.

Paul engaged gear. "And don't be late."

As the van moved off Matthew and Miranda turned and waved, watching the vehicle with its red-orange flashes bump over concrete and drop onto tarmac. The engine note deepened, a horn sounded, and a head and arm leaned out the window. Theresa carried on waving as the vehicle pulled away. Behind her the sky was lightly shaded with a few faint stars and, low to the horizon, the curve of a long thin moon.

They descended the ramp and rode out to the sea. As they cleared the sea wall Matthew felt a faint breeze blowing in his face. Overhead, there were gulls crying. From somewhere behind he could hear the sound of clock chimes and voices singing. All around were the scents of salted driftwood and dried-out plumage, mixed in with seaweed and water over rocks.

He reached hard sand and paused the bike. To the left, northwards, he could see the harbour breakwater and a low arm of land curving into softness. Out to sea there were ships backlit into blocks, and to the south the long level sweep of white and blue, shading into neutral and intertidal grey.

Behind him, Miranda shifted forward, pointing to a Canute-like figure facing the waves. "Angel," she said quietly.

Matthew looked, seeing bike, leathers and bare pink flesh. She had taken up position on a wide head of sand that projected seawards between a line of posts and a shallow lagoon.

Rolling forward, he noticed her posture: back straight, legs together, palms matched closely in prayer-position. "What's she doing?" he called back across his shoulder. Part of him, as he said it, realised at once.

"Isn't that rather obvious?"

Slowing the bike, Matthew laughed. "True."

They drew up and dismounted. The sun had reached them and the air now was yellowing. Faint patches of brightness were playing on the waves.

As they walked out to Angel, she turned. The bareness of her head, outlined by sun, was dream-soft and somewhat otherworldly. "How was your gig?" she asked, drawing them to her and kissing both cheeks.

Matthew, remembering that he'd shown her the tickets, talked about the music. Miranda added humour, describing Sally with Y.

As Angel listened, prompting them with questions she made encouraging noises. Her flower-blue eyes were attentive and focused. "I'm glad for them both," she said and her gaze travelled slowly, turning from their faces out across sand to the sea's edge and on to the waves, the bay in sunlight and the broad clear sky.

"Y took the photo," she said, hooding her eyes. "The one I sent you." Her attention switched back, measuring Matthew. "And he likes you, says you've got *soul*."

Miranda laughed. "My poet-man's full of it."

"And *heart* for you," said Angel.

"She's Ms *Appassionata*," said Matthew, slyly, gazing at the waves.

"You saw me praying," Angel said, shielding her eyes. "Maybe it surprised you, but I do, every day."

Pausing, she allowed her words to register before picking up a stone. She held it, cupped in her palm as if it was an egg. "I've a ritual. What I call my *observance*, anyone can do it." She scanned across their faces, questioning.

"You want us to get stones?" asked Miranda.

"If you've a mind to."

Miranda was willing; Matthew nodded. They looked around and selected, by size and proximity but also by feel. Then they joined her, facing seawards.

"What would Jenny say?" he asked suddenly.

Angel laughed. "I learned it, half of it anyway, by watching her."

"In that case, I'm in." He paused to check with Miranda and asked what happened next.

Angel explained that they were to begin by feel. A few seconds breathing, facing the sea, and what it stood for. "And then," she added quietly, "you must go deeper."

Following her lead, they looked towards the horizon. The sun was higher now and the sky had opened out. There was size and flow and river-bright divergence.

"And when you're in deep," she continued, turning her gaze to take in Matthew, "then you'll find the *stone*." She raised her arm higher, preparing to deliver. "And that's the bit," she added, flexing her arm, "that you need to get out. The bit that holds you back."

She aimed and let out a shout, propelling the stone in a long skimming line. It cut through the waves before dipping in a flurry, kicking up spray as it went under. "So now," she concluded, bending to the sand, "we do this one together."

"Follow my leader?" asked Matthew.

Nodding, Angel picked up a second stone and led them, step by step through her ritual, ending with a shout and three stones released. When they hit the waves, three white splashes shot up.

"And it finishes," she said, "with what I call my sea dance." She began to move, stretching tall and extending her arms. Circling, she advanced a few steps and swung to one side, then retraced to her spot. Here she held out her hands before dropping into stillness.

Next, moving forward, she body-swerved between imaginary walls. In a flurry of movement, she danced with imaginary partners, ducked and dived, then chased her own shadow to the sea's edge, where she threw up her arms in what looked like a rescue appeal. At one point she crouched, arms out tent-wise, and smoothed the sand, at another she beckoned and led around a maze. Finally, she slowed and turned inward, leading to gradually turning arabesque movements and statuesque pauses. When she stopped, Matthew and Miranda clapped.

Angel shushed them. With her head to one side, she turned on her heel pointing to the sea. Its bright wash of sound flowed over and around them. They were between lives, hearing the bird cries, seeing their shadows over sand.

Matthew looked out. The sea was calm. A sadness touched him as a cloud crossed the sun. "Where is she?" he asked.

Angel followed his gaze. "You remember?"

"I didn't before. It all went – even you."

"And now?"

"I remember my gran, and being here."

"Anything else?"

"Something happened, but nobody took any notice."

"She made us promise. Carry on as normal, she said."

"Ah, let's pretend …"

"Times were hard. That's how they did it."

"But is that what *she* was like?"

"No."

"Then why the cover-up?"

"Because Mary loved you."

"I miss her."

"She was a good woman."

"But where did she go?"

"Out there, where she wanted to be."

He continued looking. Where the light touched the surface, it rippled and shone in bursts. The tide was going out.

"And there's something else," said Angel, touching Matthew. She lifted her head. "A surprise." Her eyes now were dancing. "Your parents are here."

Matthew heard, or felt he heard. A thought ran through him and he saw – or he imagined – himself as a small boy laughing, pictured with his family, playing on the sands.

A motorbike was approaching. On it sat his parents: Alan, upright, careful, balanced, and Harriet behind, smiling.

He wanted to run forward, wave and make faces, calling out for notice. He could see them as they were, riding the high life, proud and calm and marked out as different. He wanted sun, air, wildlife, journeys. He also wanted (what else did he want?) to play himself as Matt, hold himself separate, call from a distance – to apologise even – or talk as an adult, go up man to man. He wanted and he saw; it surprised him really how much he was wanting, how much he had to say.

And then he saw them close. His long-faced father gripping the handlebars and his mother tucked in behind. They were bikers and travellers, no question. They'd ridden this far to join him. It felt like reinforcements.

When the bike pulled up and his parents dismounted, Matthew introduced Miranda and thanked his aunt. The sisters embraced, Miranda said hello, and Alan stepped forward to speak to his son.

"We saw your pictures. The photos at the café," he said, observing Matthew, trying to make him out. "Looks like you got somewhere," he added, gazing pointedly towards the Norton.

Matthew, while feeling the edge of his old impatience, heard the acknowledgment. This was shared, like a joke on the side.

"I was hoping …"

His words appeared to count. His father's look was questioning, definitional, preparing to receive.

Matthew shrugged. "Hoping to talk, I suppose."

"Hmm, talk."

"About everything?"

Alan's face clouded. "That's something you did a great deal."

"I see. You'd rather not?"

His father glowered, conceding nothing.

"Dad—" A quick, impatient breeze was tugging at his heart.

"What were you thinking of?"

Matthew twisted his heel into sand. "Biking for a start and the changes. And Angel."

"Very well, on that basis we will talk."

It seemed well meant. A balance had been struck.

"So, what has Angel told you?" Matthew asked.

"A great deal. She says you're a quick learner."

The breeze had dropped, the sun was returning.

"You read my letters?"

"Many times."

"What did you think?"

Alan hesitated, eyeing his son carefully as if he might bolt. "En-joyed them. Well written. You could try to get them published."

"Really?"

Alan nodded.

"You mean that?"

"No doubt about it, you can write."

Suddenly inside him, Matthew lit up. It seemed he'd been registered. This was his dad.

Behind him the sea had receded, exposing new levels. Something had emptied and opened, pushing up from below. There were outwash pebbles, worm casts, and tide pools with waders. Where a rock shelf had surfaced there were long green seaweeds running carpets to the beach.

The women joined them. Harriet led, touching Matthew's arm with a carefully measured look. She wanted something definite, a simple explanation, she needed to understand. "We rode down yesterday," she declared. "We said we'd like to see you. Angel put us up."

Matthew smiled. He answered at ease, thanking her for her letters.

Angel closed her eyes. Miranda, who had picked up a large pebble, weighed it in her palm. She examined it, drawing one finger lightly over stone.

Matthew took a breath. He was at centre: they were looking at him now. With sun and sky and sea and all-eyes attention. Fact or imagined, a circle that he danced. It might be enough, and an answer to their questions. Here with family fronting the picture, the small boy on the sands. And this *was* what he wanted, full circle on the seafront, himself come round.

"Let's ride," he said.

Angel nodded gently and they all saddled up. Led by the sun and the long curve of sand, driving forward through sea breeze and brightness with tyres drumming, they all rode out, headed to the light and the far points of the bay. They rode and they manoeuvred, three in line along the broad level beach, running on together, advancing steadily into air and light and movement and the big, bare trackless sweep of the yellow-white shoreline.

# NINETEEN

**Families, Imaginary Histories and the Silence of Gossip
A speech given at the 1992 York Big Ideas Award by the
First Prize Winner, Professor Matthew Lavender.**

Thank you so much for choosing my book for this prestigious award. Those of you who have only the title to go on may wonder how a history can be imaginary or how much silence there is in gossip. Of course, I don't see the past as "fact, fact, fact". My research suggests that accounts of family histories are best summed up by a phrase from the Sixties, "It's all in the head man".

You may know the experiment where a group of people are told to watch a bouncing ball while a man in a mini-skirt passes by. When asked afterwards, no one has seen the cross-dressed man. Similarly, families have a tendency to ADHD. Their guiding principles seem to be 1. Use gossip as smoke and mirrors to fill the gaps in the performance. 2. When recounting the past, follow the example of the Cheshire Cat – it comes and it goes.

In this lecture I hope to show that families rewrite history, and that their oral transmissions are the prime determinant of personal identity. Or to put it another way, family characteristics are the result of spin, shaggy dog stories and unreliable narrators.

I'd like to recount a personal illustration of this, taken from my own youthful attempts to write a novel. I soon discovered as I struggled with words and characters that they, rather than I, directed the show. To quote E L Doctorow, "Writing a novel is like driving a car at night. You can only see as far as your headlights, but you can make the whole trip that way".

What I came to suspect was that if the author is, in D H Lawrence's phrase, "adapting from life", the power of invention can upstage the past. So, in families what actually happened often gives way to the scripted. And the scripted, of course, turns out to have a mind of its own. Because any change in personal memory changes who we are.

Put simply, families are among the world's greatest storytellers. What they tell us about may be a fig leaf, a red herring or a wild card. They can also teach us about personal identity and the society that made us, or made us up.

‡ ‡ ‡

London 1992

It was Friday afternoon and Richard Lavender had taken himself off beyond the lawn and the shadow of the house to sit on concrete at the far end of the garden. With a wine glass close to hand, Richard was dividing his attention between two book collections, marking and transferring from one pile to the other. As he checked and sampled his eyes moved quickly, searching and comparing. At a fold-out page he paused, weighing up the evidence. At another he smiled, a couple he reread. For most he remained expressionless.

He wondered if now, after talking and trying and so much wasted effort, he'd finally had enough.

A cloud dimmed the sun and for a while he looked off, brown-eyed and thoughtful, examining the house. When the cloud passed over, he straightened in his chair and read a few more pages. As he checked his comments, he rolled up a sleeve and glanced at his watch before pressing in closer, bending to his work. Flicking over pages, he recorded marks. High-cheeked and definite with quick, attentive glances and firm-set lips, he was on task.

He'd really had enough. Enough for anyone.

From time to time he put aside his schoolbooks, closed his eyes and angled back his head, enjoying the warmth of the mid-May sun. Then he was himself: a boy, now man, not too old, not too young. At other times he gazed both ways, sighting the neighbouring gardens while taking in the sounds of dishes clashing, TV announcements and children crying. Occasionally he rose, topping up his glass from an unstoppered bottle, and stood beside the fence examining the wall-flowers. A plane passed over as he sipped wine. Glancing skyward, he yawned and refilled his glass.

Returning to his chair he placed his drink on concrete and spread both hands to finger-comb his hair. A dog barked, a window slid up and a radio sounded. When a voice called out, he looked across the gardens, then settled in his seat and picked up his ballpoint. Holding it cigarette-wise, he scooped up a blue-bound jotter from beneath the chair and thumbed through the pages, then stared into white.

Enough was enough. Enough, and too much.

In the house three doors away Vanessa Lavender was talking with her dear friend Ruth. "He's OTT," she said, sipping her tea.

Her host, who was wedged in with cushions at one end of the sofa, nodded. "Mine's the same."

"Doug? Surely not, he's more monkish."

"Can be fiery, though."

"Ah, but Richard—" Vanessa paused. There was so much she could say.

Ruth leaned forward. Her long, narrow face was flushed with awareness. Wearing sandals and a belted dress, she held herself at an angle with a *why-me* expression. With her watery eyes and red-blotched neck, she looked like a tourist just off the beach.

"He's obsessive," Vanessa continued. "Music, writing, the latest theory – it's all about him, his opinions. And each new one's the best, the most important, so nothing else matters."

Her friend tut-tutted.

"The men's club," said Vanessa, speaking slowly. "They're not like us."

Ruth raised her fingers behind her head. "Bloody Martians," she called, pulling a face.

Vanessa laughed. "I do wonder sometimes, Richard's so driven. It's all about what he calls *thinking straight*, which means, as far as I can see, putting things in boxes, labelling, having his own way. And

229

whatever he's into, it's that and that only. Day and night, nothing else matters. He's what you call *hyper* – life for him is one long campaign."

Ruth, agreeing, settled into silence.

Pausing between sips of tea, Vanessa kept up her talk. With her large eyes and firmed-up mouth she appeared to have things in hand. She belonged, at least in imagination, to those well-born ladies whose understated gestures, full of hidden meanings, are references off.

"There are things I could tell," she said, echoing her own thoughts. With her hand on the teacup, she sighed.

They'd been looking at photos in a frayed black album. It lay discarded on a low-level table with a double page on show. The pictures were arranged, it seemed, to illustrate aspects of two contrasting states. On one page, a wedding with Ruth in white, Doug by her side and Richard raising his glass to Vanessa, on the other page a beach-shot of children squatted, guzzling ice cream, with the women, now older, cleaning and wiping and directing to the tent. Then the children facing camera, seated under canvas, tucking into chocolates and coloured drinks. While beside that, pictured last, were the open-air husbands, one testing and tying up flaps, the other checking pegs; both ignoring the rain.

On the upstairs landing there was a scuffle, followed by a squeal and a door clicking shut.

Ruth eyed the ceiling as if it might cave in. "What d'you think is going on up there?"

Vanessa sighed, unhanding her cup. The answer she gave seemed to come from a long way off: *something*, she supposed.

"A death, I should imagine," Ruth replied, sounding as if she was reading from a script.

A child appeared at the doorway. He was high-cheeked and serious, with round brown eyes and a girl-smooth complexion.

"Stephan," said Vanessa, "what's wrong?"

"They locked me out."

"Locked you out?"

Nodding, he threw himself forward over her lap.

Vanessa smiled. "Oh dear, I'm sure they didn't mean it." She began to rub his back.

"They did."

"Well it's over now."

"They have to let me in."

"I'm sure they will."

His nostrils flared as he pulled back upright. "You tell them."

"I can try."

The boy began to push.

"All right, darling. Don't get angry."

"*You* tell them."

"All right."

"*Tell* them."

"I will."

"*You tell them.*"

"Yes, yes."

"Go on then."

He push-pulled her upright. "Stephan, don't hurt," she said jokily, as he herded her to the stairs.

Appearing on the landing, a girl called his name.

Vanessa looked up. "Charlotte," she said quietly, "let him in."

"He's not nice. He says bad things."

"Never mind, dear, just let him in."

The girl stood, shifting her weight from foot to foot.

Ruth appeared, calling encouragement from just inside the door. Vanessa repeated herself, patting Stephan lightly on the back. The boy stood head down, apparently resigned to whatever might follow.

Charlotte gazed without saying anything. Her eyes, like her mother's, were round and slightly otherworldly. Finally, she moved back, allowing access. "Only if he's good," she cautioned.

Stephan, after some hesitation, climbed to the landing, pausing to look back and throwing out a challenge as he headed for the door.

"Stephan!" his sister shrieked, lunging forward. There was a thump and shouts of protest as the two disappeared higher, fighting for advantage.

"Please, children," Vanessa said and took two steps up, requesting calm. Ruth hung back, calling instructions.

Upstairs the protests slackened as a door opened and two more voices joined in, followed by giggles then silence.

Vanessa remained poised, head to one side. Like a backrow spectator, she was straining to understand. "Are they OK?" she asked, turning to her friend.

Ruth gave a shrug.

"Should we go and see?" added Vanessa, descending to the hallway.

"Best not."

"You think they're safe?"

"As much as can be expected."

"I feel we ought to be *doing* something."

"Then call in Sir Richard," Ruth said sardonically. "*He'll* sort 'em out."

"God forbid."

They entered the lounge, shaking their heads. As they settled on the sofa, adjusting cushions, a shout went up from the room overhead.

Vanessa caught her breath.

"Don't worry," said Ruth, "it's probably a computer game."

Grinning, she offered more tea. As she topped up the cups, her eye caught the album and she pointed to the children eating. Woman to woman, an understanding passed.

"Kids."

"Husbands."

♩ ♩ ♩

Joe was MC-ing his show #loveandrage. Today his guests were Suzi, Lauren and Karl.

Joe: Hey guys, you remember our doomed youth stuff with OUTASIGHT?

Lauren: Yay. Sounds soooo dated now.

Joe: So what you up to now music-wise?

232

Karl: We're gigging climate.

Lauren: Yeah. Breakdown, chaos, runaway.

Suzi: (Sings) I'm on the highway to hell.

Lauren: And I'm playing feedback loops and tipping points.

Joe: Electric or acoustic?

Lauren: Solar when I can. Acoustic otherwise.

Joe: HTF do you keep going? I mean when you KNOW what's happening ...

Suzi: I just keep drumming. Always have. It's a tick tock thing I've got inside.

Lauren: Yeah, and I get on that guitar and scratch it.

Karl: And the more you scratch ...

Suzi: Seriously, we get the audience to clap hands, singalong and bang things.

Joe: So, it's up yours to big stadium rock?

Lauren: That's right. It's for the bugs, the insects and the birds.

Karl: And a wakeup call.

Joe: OK. Examples, please.

Karl: There's a bit where we get the audience to make buzzing noises.

Suzi: And I play Tinkerbell, making half of 'em shout I DO BELIEVE.

Lauren: And that's where I get the other half to shout AC-TION NOW.

Joe: All right – and the music? What sort do you play?

Lauren: Everything. Jazz, bluegrass, folk, soul, punk, indie – I even get to play Zappa and Django Reinhart.

Suzi: I like to mix it. Like Bill Bruford and Airto – if only!

Karl: And I'm Jack Bruce – in my dreams.

Joe: Last question. Where's the rage?

Lauren: Simple. We block roads. The drivers shout and stand on their horns.

Karl: And we get in the way where they're fracking.

Lauren: And we swear a lot. Lovingly.

Karl: 1-2-3-4. We get down. Go wild.

Suzi: Rock-rock-rocking it.
Lauren: And we like it.
Joe: You mean ...
Suzi: (Sings) Hey hey, my my. Rock 'n' roll can never die.

♪ ♪ ♪

It had seemed to Vanessa, when she'd first met Richard, that he kept himself apart. Her friends called him odd. He was tall and rather visible, but his manner wasn't smooth and he certainly wasn't trendy or easy to get on with. And although he was teacherly, giving off a measured air, he remained quite strange, switching between assurance and little-boy wildness.

They'd met on teachers' training: PGCE, London 1982, both young, seeking experience. For her, a teaching course was a way of giving back. It opened into street life, the real and present thing. For Richard it was more of a gap-fill: a way of killing time.

At a presentational seminar she'd talked about Illich, Holt and how children fail. Poised and definite, her voice marked her out. To Richard her interventions were of interest. Long-faced and poised, he thought she'd a mind – a body too – and held herself with a hint of something hidden, a brightness held back.

When the seminar ended, those who remained adopted her suggestion that they went for a drink. As she led off down the street Richard delayed, studying the pavement. He didn't like her *this is so* manner, her airs and graces.

Arriving down steps to a basement bar, he sat on his own, concealed behind a pillar. As critic and observer, he wasn't taken in.

At one point he'd passed close, on his way to the toilet, and heard her holding forth on political parties. She knew a few names, had inside knowledge, was up on gossip and who was knocking who. When he returned, she'd moved on to fashion and galleries and living in the city. As he walked to his table, he felt her inspection and the lift in her voice, the words pushed out, aimed at him.

"Some can and some can't," she said airily.

"And some teach?" came back, as if on cue, from her friend Bess.

234

"Or worse."

Richard refused to be drawn. He'd listen, gather evidence and plot what he could say. The more she talked the more he had her measure. And as the afternoon wore on, he felt a strange kind of flutteriness, mixed with irritation.

When the others had gone, leaving Vanessa to finish her drink, he put aside his feelings, slipped on his jacket and went up and spoke. "So, what d'you think of the course so far?"

She examined him slowly, smiling without warmth. "What do *you* think?"

His lip curled slightly. "The usual crap."

She gazed off unmoved. "That's it, is it?"

"How d'you mean?"

"It's worth four letters."

"It will be when we get to teaching and find what we've done is useless."

Vanessa continued gazing. Her long thin fingers, extended on the table, were fidgeting with a mat. "It rather depends," she said slowly, then stopped.

"Of course, we've all read the theory," he said dismissively, "for what good that'll do."

She pushed her way up, cool and self-contained. With her large brown eyes and quizzical features, she was facing him down. "I take it," she said, affecting nonchalance, "you will be leaving the course."

"What?"

She began to move towards the door.

"You going to explain?" he asked quietly, closing to her shoulder.

"Isn't it obvious?" She stopped at the steps that led up to the street. She was regarding him now as if he'd just arrived. "If you really think it's crap, then you know what to do."

"Not sure I'm with you."

"I believe it's called the honourable thing."

"What – fall on my sword?"

She laughed, sardonically. "I shouldn't bother. It might not do the job."

"I've offended?"

"Criminals offend."

"Bring back hanging, it didn't do me any harm."

She pulled a face.

"You think that's not nice?" he asked, goadingly.

"Just silly."

Stepping back, he waved her to the exit. "Have it your way."

Vanessa turned and climbed towards street level. As she reached the door she glanced back quickly with an expression of distaste. "I will," she said calmly, stopping at the threshold to button up her jacket.

"Then don't let me stop you."

"Do you imagine you could?"

"If I had to."

"But you'd rather talk and swear and make protestation."

"Oh, bloody hell, yes."

She laughed, without humour. It seemed, as she turned into the street, he'd had the final say. Richard withdrew, re-entering the café. It was bare and quiet. The chairs were pushed back, there were plates with slops, half-full glasses, unused cutlery and a litter of tissue-scraps – all of which the waiters were collecting, clearing, wiping over.

He idled by a pillar, marking time. Part of him was calm and satisfied at having stood his ground, another part was proud of his sudden insistence, while another part focused on what he'd done wrong. But mostly he wanted closure.

He'd just begun to leave when his hand brushed the chair back, catching on plastic. Looking down, Richard saw a creamy-yellow handbag that he knew, or reckoned, could only have one owner.

Checking an outside flap, he swore beneath his breath. Her name was there, *Vanessa Martel* stitched into the lining. He wondered what to do next. However he played it, he was damned both ways. Trying not to think, he lifted the bag. Light and rather fem, it marked him out. With the bag to his chest he climbed to the exit, preparing what he'd say if she was there.

Emerging, he blinked and looked around.

The afternoon was mild with sunspots on buildings, starlings on ledges and people walking coatless. To his left there was traffic, queued right back, on both sides stationary, mainly commercial, with taxis, a large white bus and cars between vans. To his right was a split-level office block and a one-way street: a channel for cyclists and walkers. Set back behind the block was a small rectangular park, half-screened by trees. Already the shadow of the building was touching their branches.

No Vanessa.

He peered at the traffic, checking for gaps. Recalling her long dark hair, he searched the pavements looking for a woman wearing jeans and a light blue jacket. In his mind, she was tall and precise, with a languid smile. He began to search harder, imagining himself being left with her property, and having to give it back in front of her friends.

No sign of Vanessa.

Looking straight ahead he focused in on a paved square. It was crisscrossed by pedestrians and grazing pigeons. In the centre was a statue of a long-robed man with a book in his hand; behind was the glass and metal entrance to the station.

Still no Vanessa.

Feeling the bag press against his chest, he turned to scan the end of a narrow lane. This time he was careful, examining every walker for something of her. He began to wonder if in fact he'd seen her but simply not noticed. Maybe she was watching from somewhere hidden, taking pleasure in giving him the run-around, leading him on. He knew, of course, that was silly and was just setting off when a movement caught his eye. Turning towards the station, he heard his name called and saw her approaching, pointing to her bag.

"You picked it up."

Richard acknowledged, trying to read her mood.

"Where was it – in the café? I must have left it. I never thought—"

He nodded, holding out the bag.

"It's a relief, thank you."

"No problem."

"Well I'm grateful, I was afraid it would have gone."

"All part of the service."

"But you could have left it. You might have been tempted, after—"

"Well, I didn't."

"I suppose …" she began, furrowing her brow. Her words hung fire while she stared off down the street.

Richard found himself looking with her. "You were wondering?"

She gazed around vaguely; a slackness had descended, as if they were dancers preparing for the show. "I don't know, maybe …"

Richard took a breath. He could see her watching, awaiting developments. "Shall we walk?"

"Hmm, the river," she said, nodding downhill to a lane beside the station. It was decided, a mood had taken over. Together they set off.

They passed into shadow, pacing quietly with a hand's space between them, crossing the road to reach a sweep of pavement that ran by a row of shops. The row was irregular with worn-down frontages, part-wood, part-brick, with fruit crates outside and windows surrounded by stickers. The doorways led in to dark, cavernous, piled-up interiors. As they walked by, they glanced at their reflections.

At a bookshop Vanessa paused, pointing to a photo that showed a thin-faced man peering from the cockpit of an open-topped biplane. "My cousin, stunt man Vaughan," she said, adding that she hardly ever saw him, but when she did, Vaughan wasn't that easy.

Richard laughed. "Behind the image, he's not exactly Prince Charming?" He stared at the book cover. "But presumably he can fly, that part's not managed."

"Yes, and he is a character."

"Peter Pan?"

"I do wonder sometimes."

They walked to the row end, emerging at a gateway flanked by railings. It led into a small public garden. Turning through the gates they followed a path that wound through a shrubbery. They were talking in snatches, exchanging observations as if they were the owners inspecting their patch. They had their favourite colours, knew most plant names and were aware of other walkers. Everything amused them, everything was a show.

"Do you walk a lot?" he asked, as they passed out through a gate and faced across a busy main road, looking towards the water.

"This way, yes," she confirmed, pointing to a bridge with a walk-way to one side. "It's exercise. My route, here and back … To my flat," she added, looking both ways before crossing.

Richard followed, passing between bumpers. In both directions the vehicles were queued up, waiting for the lights. He imagined she'd set off to avoid any further questions.

At the far side of the road Vanessa veered right, leading forward to some open-framed steps. She took the railing, and they climbed to the walkway. It ran out over water, divided from the trains by cross-barred girders.

They stopped at the centre. The sun had declined and the build-ings by the water were already part-shaded; behind them and higher, light fell in patches on walls and tiles, while higher still the domes and office blocks were bathed in ochre-yellow brightness. Halfway up a tall whitewashed building, a window glinted. Beside it, where col-umns rose to a carved stone pediment, a gull was circling and a collection of flags rippled in the breeze.

As they watched a pleasure boat appeared. Approaching, it skirt-ed a line of tied-up barges then hooted tonelessly as it passed be-neath the bridge. The barges continued knocking and jostling afterwards, shunting like freight.

"Ships in the night," said Richard. He'd spread both hands on the walkway railing. It was studded with bolt heads and hollow under-neath.

"You wonder what the barges are carrying," said Vanessa, looking down.

"Dirty British coaster …"

"Ah, we did that one at school."

He quoted the first line.

"And you have the words by heart?"

"Not sure, but I know it ends with cheap tin trays."

"Did you enjoy it?"

"Would've done, if it wasn't for the teaching."

"You remember how they did it?"

"Don't I just."

She pulled back from the railing. "We have to do better, find another way." She was speaking now with an offhand assurance, gazing past him as if he was only half there. "I read somewhere that teaching is about power-sharing. Knowing when to lead and when to step back. The book called it signposting. It's all about building skills, finding what works then bowing out."

"And that's it, sorted?"

Vanessa echoed his words as a statement. "It's what our course is about," she added. "Opening doors, learning new methods, making a difference."

Richard just couldn't buy that. "They want to fit us," he said slowly. "Line us up, all in one mould. The university knows best. Big Brother professors with nothing better to do. It's a kind of job creation scheme. Only dyed-in-the-wool academics need apply."

"You think so?"

"It's what they call process. They think they're counsellors or whatever. Always batting it back. 'And how do you *feel* about that? Isn't that rather *directive*? Are you *sure* of that?' It's a power game really. They keep us dangling till we see it their way."

Vanessa stared towards the far end of the bridge. She pictured their tutor: a soft-voiced woman whose frequent pauses were designed for effect. Her long-held stares and ironic questions kept them on the back foot. "Leading from behind," she said, surprising herself.

Richard nodded. It all seemed to fit. Her words, his, and suddenly they were *talking*, not just sparring but sharing their thoughts and adapting what they said. "Yes," he said quietly, "but we don't have to play that game."

As he spoke, a far-off shiver ran along the bridge. Beginning with a shudder, the sound moved closer. It became firmer, shifting up to a low percussive rattle. A slow, bumping weight of metal on metal filled the air, moving like a heavy-hinged door.

"Pullman," he mouthed as the engine passed by, dragging behind it a long line of carriages. Each was flashed purple, with curtains in the windows and self-absorbed faces behind tinted glass. Picking up speed, the train cleared the bridge. The sound went with it, dropping to a murmur as the last retreating carriage curved off between buildings.

"OK," said Richard, "it's gone." Suddenly he smiled. "So now, in the words of the song, should I go or should I stay?"

Before she could answer a second train appeared, this time incoming, and the bridge began to shake. As the noise level rose, Vanessa ducked forward, scanning the walkway. "Stay if you like," she said quietly. When Richard didn't answer she pointed forward. "Stay," she repeated, louder. When he raised both hands, pleading deafness, Vanessa shouted. As the train roar came close, she mouthed her word again before leading off to the bridge end, the steps down and the walk towards her flat.

"It isn't much," said Vanessa when they arrived at the door.

They'd walked the back route, cutting down streets with office blocks and flats and passing through a tunnel with the railway thundering overhead. On one side was a wall, on the other, pits and chambers from what looked like a dig. They'd emerged up a ramp, crossing an estate and a treeless park, continuing along a road with unkempt gardens fronting peeling doorways.

Her block, she'd told him, was shared. It was three storeys high with a bay at the front and a path leading around to a side entrance with window lights above. There were bells with name slips that he glanced at; they were handwritten and faded. As they entered, he saw a carpeted lobby, doors both sides and a staircase straight ahead. It smelled of cooking and polish.

"The downstairs used to be a surgery," Vanessa said, leading up. "A dentist's, I think."

The stairs were wide, turning twice and narrowing at the top to a skylight and a navy-blue door.

"*Chez nous*," she announced, pulling out a key.

The apartment they entered was a converted loft. Running the length of the back extension, it had a central corridor with four doors

241

off and, beyond that, a kitchen connected to a large, L-shaped lounge.

"My nest," she said, leading him around.

He noticed the shoes lined up on a rack and the clothes on chair backs. A string across an arch held a collection of photos. There were transfers on the windows, stickers on the fridge and piles of worksheets scattered everywhere.

Vanessa offered tea or coffee. When they'd settled, she tucked herself into the corner of a two-seater sofa; Richard sat facing in a chair.

He was calculating privately, turning over phrases. To be here and invited, it made him wonder how far it might go – though he also felt that anything further might prove difficult.

"I like your flat," he said, playing safe.

"It's a tip," she answered, wrinkling up her nose. "I try, but things go missing. You'd think it had gremlins, messing up the place."

"Looks like red gremlins," he laughed, waving at a poster with a shot from *Battleship Potemkin*. Grouped around a picture of people running, there were guns and flags, raised fists, a portrait of Lenin, and an outside border with heavily-typed imperatives.

He asked about her politics. Vanessa smiled. She had some, yes.

"Politics with a capital P. Where you stand on the issues of the day. Your beliefs."

"Ah, my Personal Manifesto. Now let's see … Should it be The People? Or Popularist? Maybe Proletariat?"

Richard pointed at the poster. "Or for some, how about Posturing?"

Leaning back and showing her neck, she laughed. Richard realised she was expecting more.

He checked her opinions and what she really liked.

"I'm a believer in style – all styles," she said when asked about revolutionary art, "especially the ones who had it."

"Anyone with attitude," she added when pressed for names.

"Groucho?" she countered when asked about Marx.

And she looked directly at him, as if she was on camera, as she talked.

For Richard it was a beginning. To be invited in after walking together and now talking so freely – they'd made the first moves.

At one point in the evening they stood at the window observing the garden and the blocks beyond, with their bodies nearly touching. They were pleased to take it slowly, to profit by delay. Later, at Vanessa's suggestion, they folded salad into pitta bread, adding in cheese and thin-sliced ham, then talked about places to visit. Both were against settling and wanted experience. They were world citizens.

Afterwards, when they'd moved back to the lounge, he said he'd wash up.

Vanessa shook her head. She'd rather he left it.

"Well, I ought to do my bit."

"No, I'll do it. It's the least I can do."

"What for?"

"What I owe."

"What you *owe*?"

"For what happened."

"Ah, you mean the handbag. Anybody would've done the same."

"Well, I'm glad you did."

"No trouble," he laughed. "If that's all it takes …"

"But just imagine, if you hadn't."

"OK, but you don't *owe* me."

"Oh yes I do."

Richard shook his head. "The other way round, I took against and pigeonholed you. I shouldn't have done that."

"Takes two, I thought the same."

"And now," he said, breaking off as the song *What now my love* sounded in his head.

She smiled, asking about drinks.

Richard declined. "I think," he said slowly, "I'd better get going."

"You're leaving?"

"What else?"

She sucked in her breath. "Maybe …"

Between them there were thoughts and suggestions; a balance to be struck.

243

"I suppose …" he said, indicating the door. "You see, I don't want you to get me wrong." Suddenly he rallied: "OK, it's simple. I'll stay, if you're willing, but we play it by ear, there's nothing required."

She nodded.

"In any case," he continued, "I think I'd like——"

Vanessa part-closed her eyes. A silent invitation hung between them.

Richard realised suddenly that whatever he said or intended didn't really matter, he was here and now, simple as that. "But then," he added slowly, talking to himself, "that's just theory, the stuff of books."

Vanessa smiled. Together they'd engaged.

He moved to where she sat and touched her lightly on the arm, stretching till his hand found hers. There were of course words: soft words, slow words, words of approbation. And also those words that passed beneath breath, heard but not said, the words that now guided. And the one word that remained, the feel word, smiling, as they closed together and absorbed each other in a long-held kiss.

When he left next morning Richard could hear her voice in snatches running in his head. Closing the front door, he heard her words on waking, their exchanges over breakfast and their goodbyes on the stairs. As he turned down the street the birds were singing and the traffic was picking up. He glanced at his watch. So early, and the air was fresh and clear. The city had its own sounds and rhythms.

He retraced his steps across the park. At a junction between paths, he stepped out onto grass, continuing forward with the sun to his right. Returning to the path at the end of the grass he noticed the light on unplanted borders. On the other side the bushes were draped with webs and torn plastic bags. There were pigeons strutting, dogs with owners and cyclists in Lycra. Here, he thought, beating out a rhythm, was a slice of life. Leaving by a gate, he crossed a narrow road. Lengthening his stride, he headed for the river. His route led through an estate, over concrete and tarmac, returning through the tunnel to downstream offices and the footbridge back.

By the river it was quiet. The light was still, the bridge was empty and the water below rippled slowly. Approaching the steps, Richard took the railing. He thought of Vanessa's cousin and again heard the words *a slice of life*. When he'd climbed to the walkway, he stopped to look out. Before him were the rooftops, leading down to the river's edge and the slowly moving water. He heard the sounds of traffic and bells in the distance. And behind that, half-heard and spreading, the gathering thunder of a slowly-moving train.

$$\ddagger \ddagger \ddagger$$

In the week that followed, Vanessa was surprised by how much she felt. At first, immediately after Richard left, she kept herself busy moving about the rooms, putting things in place. She heated up the kettle and toasted some bread, thinking of him while she ate. She could picture how he'd entered, looking from the hallway, taking in the flat. Of course, it was a mess, but then he hadn't seemed bothered. *Interesting*, he'd said, and looked straight through it. He'd even said he liked it, though to her mind too quickly, as if he'd an agenda. Either he didn't register or he'd chosen not to see it.

Turning in her chair, she gazed at her artworks. They'd joshed about the poster. Later, she'd heard him say he didn't like Impressionism. "Too many parasols," he'd said, or something like that. She supposed he'd found them *limited* – art he'd have to kick against or label as dull. He'd not seen her photos.

Rising, she crossed to the lounge where she occupied herself placing cushions. Standing by the window, she saw back-to-back gardens; they were bare and narrow, bordered by breeze blocks and half-rotted fences. Last night they'd felt deeper and wider, concealed within the dark. Now they were exposed. And she saw herself with Richard, standing at the window gazing into night. It was as if they were preparing, like her cousin, to step into air, kick away the chocks and take a leap of faith.

All that morning she slobbed around the flat, wondering at her state. Up till then she'd known men in passing and tried them for a while, comparing as she went, with quirks and styles and types to watch out for. She'd kept them as her *lads*, observing them for what they were made of. But now she'd a feeling, as she imagined Richard with her, that she barely knew herself. Because she'd had this persuasion that she didn't mind the guys if they knew their place. As long as she could play them and not get carried away then it didn't matter much, because most men just wanted to keep their distance.

But with Richard, she'd a whole new perspective. For or against, he'd said things and showed his feelings, pushed to keep it real. And she remembered how it felt, how they'd looked around and talked, and how they'd set out. A space had opened and a stretch across water. They were up there, first-foot, as they climbed the metal walkway, looked out into sunlight and crossed the bridge together.

On that first day she gave him a score, marked up an account, as she called it, of when and where she met him and what they said in public, how far, how much and what remained hidden. On the second day he came round and stayed over, leaving after lunch. The third and the fourth (she'd begun to make a rhyme, a variant on Solomon Grundy) they were already an item, declared at college and parading hand in hand. Day five was busy, with both visiting placements and Vanessa seeing parents, so they saw each other late, on overnight again. Six was for study, working on her coursework, so it wasn't till the seventh that they put aside everything, Richard stayed over, and they spent the day on a trip out together.

"It all depends on feel," she'd told him from the start. By that she meant not only venue but also the act of deciding. Because since day one there'd been ideas floating. Richard had talked of walks or boats upstream, she'd thought of shopping or maybe writers' houses, they'd both named parks with outdoor cafés. And each time they'd decided, or cut down to a shortlist, a new thought popped up or an old one returned or somehow they got side-tracked, resulting in more speculation. They'd too much to choose from, with nothing quite definite. Decisions were that much easier if arrived at on the day.

And since they'd time and leisure plus a promise of good weather, they decided to adopt a new suggestion, made by Richard and endorsed by Vanessa, to go with their cameras and join the crowds of sightseers who filled the city zoo.

They journeyed there by bus, talking of first times, of packing as a family and wet summer holidays. When they arrived at their stop, Richard led through ornamental gardens with a stream down the middle. On the way he kept up a commentary, observing the flower-beds and the groups headed zoo-wards. He noticed as he talked how his role today was to lead with words while Vanessa played audience. In fact, he felt the pull, an undertow of thought, almost as if he'd not made contact. Whatever it was, he couldn't help noticing a lag now between them, an obstruction. It was as if they were provisional, caught on camera, and his job was to talk and move the action on.

It wasn't till they got there that Vanessa, who was wearing moon-shaped earrings, declared one was missing. "It must have dropped," she said, checking both sides and scanning the tarmac. "Might be just anywhere …" she added, tailing off. Suddenly there was edge; her colour was up and her breath came slowly. For him, it brought back the handbag, and the hunt for her afterwards. This, it seemed, was a case for rescue.

"I'll help," he said.

"Do you think you can do that? It's not easy to find."

"Don't worry, we're the search party," he said and together they quartered the entrance, peering into corners, prodding around walls and checking into bushes. When nothing turned up, he suggested that they walk back.

"Not now," Vanessa said, pointing to a developing queue. "Don't worry, it's nothing," she added and fixed her gaze forward; she was struggling, rather. Richard joined her and they shuffled to the window.

He pulled out some coins that Vanessa supplemented, and an attendant issued tickets.

"Well, given we're here, we have to see the lot," said Richard. He was examining the signposts and the times of feeding chalked up on a board.

"You mean that?"

"We're on safari," he said, leading forward past a line of abandoned cages.

Vanessa smiled. Now they'd arrived and passed in through the gate, she wanted to be close. On the journey she'd needed him to be up front and make things happen. She didn't want him casual or taking advantage. Because already she could see him pictured with her family – all those briefings, meetings, stages up ahead – and *she'd* have to satisfy, play both sides, act as intermediary.

But this was different. A day, an outing, almost like a holiday, well, wasn't that enough? Because now she saw him out there, angled forward advancing on the green, he'd his own intended purpose.

The green led down to a long curving lake, set off to one side, looking almost ornamental. It was grey-green and vague, like a sketch for a painting. Intrigued, they approached behind a fence, glimpsing reflections in a still sheet of water. It ended in concrete with banks both sides and an overflow beyond. Here it bulged out with stone-dammed pools, winding mud flats and intersecting basins. As they came nearer, they could see, gathered in a loosely formed arc, shapes that resembled black-and-pink clouds, or a corps de ballet.

"Flamingos," he said, advancing slowly, camera in hand.

The birds were standing, half-asleep and sculptural, in ankle-high water. With their long thin legs, pod-like bodies and tubular necks they looked like they'd just landed.

"God, it's thick," said Vanessa, pointing to the water at their feet. "It reminds me of bone marrow soup. Only this smells more like those awful concoctions we used to make in chemistry."

Richard examined the yellow-green liquid. It was solid-looking and cloudy. "It seems to suit them," he said, lightly.

The birds now were striking poses. Some appeared to sprout, others jack-knifed, there were ones coiled like pipes and others standing tall. A group in the corner were head down poking in mud, a few were chain-linked, there were hook-shaped beaks and pseudo-plants and a number whose dream-like positions resembled half-finished artworks. "They look so strange," she said, thoughtfully.

"Surreal?"

"Gothic, I think."

"I suppose it works for them."

They circled the lake, arriving at a curved concrete area with a bench and signboard that overlooked the pools. At the front, a large man with a map was finger-tracing a route, while the woman by him was reading from the signboard. A family on the bench were listening to a radio while passing around drink cartons and chocolate-coated bars.

Vanessa raised her camera and waved Richard towards an unoccupied corner. "Best spot," she called as she chivvied and pointed, checking in the viewfinder before she snapped. Exchanging places, he took two more exposures then motioned to move on.

Vanessa showed surprise.

"Lots to do," he said brightly, waving to the slope.

"Well, yes ..."

He glanced at his watch. "It's a big place, have to get round."

"How far would that be?"

"I dunno, a mile, maybe more."

"You mean that?"

"Oh yes."

"Sounds like a route march."

"Sights to see."

For a moment she was thrown. There was nothing more she could say.

"The big five," he added. "That's what we came for."

"Well, if it's really that important—"

Richard confirmed, nodding vigorously as he named them.

"Are you sure they've got them all here?"

"They certainly used to have, when I came with my cousin."

"Ah, but suppose things have changed."

"What makes you say that?"

"Chances are, on average."

"Chances? Averages? Sounds like a lecture to me."

Vanessa stared past him. "It's what I think, that's all."

He looked at her oddly, grinning. There was challenge in the air. "OK. We'll go and find out."

Before she could reply he'd moved off uphill, climbing a path that curved through bushes. Vanessa followed, saying nothing.

She caught up in a dip where the path opened out. He'd descended to a double line of walls and was standing beside concrete, observing carefully through reinforced glass. The window looked out on a trench full of water, and beyond that some protective netting, a few scattered rocks and a broad savannah-like compound.

"One," he said, pointing to a large lion reclining on a platform.

Vanessa pursed her lips. "Four to go," she reminded, eyeing the animal as if it couldn't be trusted.

"I bet two's close," he said, wandering down a mall-like avenue with walls both sides and vistas through double-thickness glass.

"You think you'll find a leopard?" she said with an upward inflection, warming to their task.

"*Voilà*," he replied, moving to a window that had misted. Behind it a long, muscular, brown-white cat was slumped on grass.

Vanessa took a breath. "Well, I have to say …"

Richard kept staring straight ahead. He knew what she meant.

"I'm not sure I like it," she continued, touching his shoulder. "Doesn't look too friendly. You can see it in the face. It's all about power. Blind, unquestioning power. And if it comes for you, you'd better get going."

"If looks could kill."

"Do you think it sees us?"

"Hmm, I don't think it's interested."

"Too busy contemplating the next meal."

Richard tapped the glass. "I used to be a bit obsessed by big cats, when I was young."

"And now?"

He smiled, enigmatically. "Two down."

Beside them two small girls were talking loudly, quizzing their mother. It really wasn't fair, she'd made them a promise and they couldn't go much further. How long, they asked, before they'd see the gorilla? She stalled for a while trying to interest them in big-cat stories but when they persisted, she warned about the distance and steered them off.

"So, lunch break?" asked Vanessa.

"Aye, lass. Motion carried," he replied, flattening his a-s. "Feeding time at the zoo."

Vanessa laughed. "The sign here says the picnic spot's this way."

"That's champion," he said, deepening his voice. "Down tools, and lead on," he added, and they walked. They turned uphill, following a winding path that led past a rockery and a fenced-in paddock, emerging at a soft grassy lookout with wooden benches and a stone orientation table.

The sky had cleared and the crowds were building. Families mainly, but also busloads, a few distinctly old, some middle-aged, others twentyish but mostly schoolchildren. A tide-flow of children everywhere, wave on wave filling up the zoo, so much so that the place was sounding and looking like a break-time playground. There were groups of children in lines and gaggles, some linked with parents, some sitting on grass eating, others on breakaway missions, and still others gathered by cages and compounds. All busy, they ranged from very small children with toys or sweets, through older children asking questions, older still wriggling or dodging or pushing to the front, and ultra-keen children carrying rainbow-striped pens, followed at a distance by costumed children and yah boo sucks kids wearing oversize T-shirts and mud-splattered trainers.

"The human zoo," said Vanessa, gazing out.

"You don't like them?"

"*Adore* them, children are wonderful."

Surprised by her vehemence, Richard chose to say nothing.

They ate. Vanessa had packed two foil-wrapped pasties, each with a napkin and fork. Richard reached deeper into his backpack to add in apples, bottled drinks and a bag of peanuts. They spread them on a mac and lay out on grass, talking over what they'd seen and where to go next.

When they'd finished eating, Richard moved closer, fitting to her mood. They smiled and kissed, then stretched out side by side, touching each other and dozing in the sun.

"What are your thoughts?" Vanessa asked.

"Maybe you can guess."

"Well, I suppose I could try, but only if they're nice."

"Oh, they're nice all right."

"Ah, but *how* nice?"

"Triple tick I'd say."

"That much?"

"How else can I put it? A plus, plus – or eleven as in *Spinal Tap*."

"Well, let's see," she said, sitting up. "Your thoughts – are they about *now*, the zoo, the sun, where we're sitting?"

"Could be."

"Could be?"

He turned and levered up. "That's part of it. They're definitely warm."

"Yes, I appreciate they're warm. Anything else?"

"Oh lots. I'm full of ideas – crazy things, projects – things that might never happen."

Vanessa drew one hand lightly over grass. "That's good," she said, leaning forward. The grass was thick and tufty, and mixed in with weeds around the edges. Reaching sideways, she touched and tested, selecting stems. Choosing the tallest, she pinched out from the bottom then straightened to a bunch. "Very good," she said, arranging her grasses.

Seeing her absorbed, Richard cast around, selecting his own bunch. He pulled up a some chickweed and some dock leaves and a twist of ivy. "Mine's rough," he said, waving them for show.

She looked up, surprised. "Don't tell me that's my bouquet."

"You like it?" he asked, adding in some shepherd's purse and offering his bunch.

Vanessa eyed it carefully. "You take them both," she said, counter-offering hers.

Richard hesitated.

"Go on," she urged. "Take."

"You sure?"

"They're all yours. And the task," she said, passing over her plants, "is to arrange them – well."

Richard put down his collection. After sorting and combining, he doffed an imaginary cap, "England expects."

"Today's good deed."

"At your service, ma'am."

"Well, if you don't want—"

"No problem," he cut in. "In any case, we can use them as feed."

"Feed?"

"That's right." Richard leaned to one side, fishing in his backpack and tugging out some string that he wound around the stems. "Some animal will be glad of this lot."

"But you can't. Not in a zoo."

"Hmm, you don't think so?"

Vanessa shook her head.

"Well I do remember ..."

"I believe it's not allowed."

He stood and stretched. "I suppose you're right."

Before she could reply he picked up his backpack and moved to the orientation table.

"I know what you've been thinking," he said when Vanessa joined him.

"You do?"

"What you said, about the route march."

"Oh that. It's nothing."

"But there is a point," he replied, placing the plants at the centre of the table. "I mean you must have thought – why does this guy have to rush so."

Vanessa said nothing.

"After all," he continued, "it's a whole day free."

She nodded.

"But I'd thought, you see, if we came here, that I'd do it like before." He smiled to himself. "But now I see it's not that simple."

As Vanessa shook her head, he raised his camera and, positioning carefully, sighted the bouquet. Leaning forward, he clicked several times from all angles. "And now," he announced, waving her to him, "both of us, for the album."

"Both of us?"

"It's on time release," he said, balancing the camera on the bench head.

"You think it'll work?"

"Believe me," he said, pressing the button and drawing her close. "Just smile."

The shutter clicked as they embraced.

"But how do we know if we're in the picture?"

"We don't, so we'll try again."

Vanessa laughed.

"And we'll keep on trying," he added as he button-pressed, moving position, "and again," he insisted, pressing and positioning, "and again, till we bloody well make it work."

For the rest of the day they went with their feelings, talking habitats and sharing observations. Following the signposts, they ticked off the five, visited the reptiles, spent time bear-watching, saw the seals feeding and ended late afternoon surrounded by children, viewing monkeys.

Vanessa enjoyed the babies, cooing at their eyes and how they rode their mothers. "Perfectly formed," she exclaimed, pointing her camera.

"Great circus," said Richard, watching their parents' tricks.

"Gymnastics," called Vanessa, as they tail-swung and danced across ropes.

And they went with the crowd, enjoying the spectacle as they peered from all angles into glassed-in cages with Vanessa taking pictures.

Richard liked the chimps. "There's my Big Sis," he said as a heavy-jawed female slid along a beam and dropped to a crouch.

"Hi there, Old Man," he called when a male climbed down to join her.

And it was when they'd seen the gorillas, Vanessa's favourite, with their long slow rocking movements and penetrating stares, that they agreed to call it a day.

On the bus back they talked about what they'd seen.

"We did it all," Richard said as they walked towards her flat.

Vanessa touched his arm. Had it changed, she wanted to know.

"Some things have changed."

But in *himself*, she insisted, was he any different?

"Older and wiser, you mean?"

Vanessa looked into his eyes.

"I think," he said quietly, "it's better now."

His voice dipped and rose as they turned into her street and stopped at the corner, touching.

"Much, much better," he added and kissed her on the cheek then the forehead, and finally with hot-tongued passion, deep into her mouth.

♩ ♩ ♩

For the first few months it seemed to Richard that what they'd found together was as good as it gets. Not just their outings and their ideas as teachers, but also their romance with its bright turns, its dramas and all-night sessions. In Vanessa he'd met his match. As an up front, independent woman who knew her own business, she mattered.

At college people liked them. With everyone on teaching practice their friends – mainly Vanessa's, but now Richard's as well – called out greetings, shared what had happened, and wished them well. Being in school was a shock to the system, far more difficult than anyone had expected, and in one case at least, had split a relationship. Also, people were surprised, given the history, that *they* should get together.

But together they were good. They were at the front, talking and asking questions, making themselves felt. And they got through their placements, with effort and persistence, and showed the others how.

When teaching ended, they went out as a foursome with Ruth and Doug, Vanessa's friends. Meeting at college they walked to the market to browse and choose bargains. There were records for the men, jewellery for Ruth, and Vanessa's "collectables" – mainly posters but also small art objects and what she called *tat*. It felt like something shared, but also individual.

When they'd toured the side aisles examining prints and listening to bands, they moved into the concourse. It was a wide, steel-framed hall with red-tiled avenues and strings of bunting. In one corner a metal flight of stairs rose to a gallery supported by pillars. It led to a corner café where they sat down together, overlooking the market.

They ordered coffee and Doug pulled out a newspaper. He held it up, blocking out the company, as if for protection.

Ruth stared across the table shaking her head. "Bit antisocial, isn't it?" she said loudly.

Doug, who was wearing sports gear, looked up. Brown and round-faced, showing hirsute legs and prominent forearms, he was wedged into the railing. His eyes strayed vaguely out across the hall. "What do you mean?" he asked quietly, colouring.

"Nose in paper, when we're supposed to be talking."

"Not really."

"It's what people call rude. Very, if you ask me."

Doug returned to reading his paper. A ball-shaped stud gleamed in one ear.

"There you go," Ruth continued, addressing her friends, "it's carry on regardless. Seen but not seen."

"Nobody's getting hurt," retorted Doug, peering around his print-screen. With his hair cut short and shy, boxer-like grin, he appeared to be in training.

"Hey, no. I should have known, don't bother me, it's fine. And I'm just a silly woman."

Doug carried on reading. His hand on the paper was shaking.

"Stupid, like most women."

When Doug remained silent, she poked at his broadsheet, "'Ello 'ello, is anyone there?"

Twisting sideways, he pulled it out of reach.

"Anyone at home?" Smiling falsely, she screwed one finger to her head, "OK, OK, blank us. Read your bloody paper. No one else counts."

Doug, still reading, raised his head and started to reply. When Ruth cut in, calling him a boor and a me-only type, he put aside the paper and fixed her with a stare. "Stop it woman," he grunted, and sat back. He'd better things to do.

Ruth grimaced and turned to Vanessa, inviting her views.

"It's all right," she replied, avoiding Ruth's eye.

"A man's gotta do," put in Richard, grinning.

The coffees arrived and were passed around the table, cappuccino to Ruth, black for Vanessa, regulars for the men.

Turning to Ruth, Richard enquired about her time on practice.

"Oh that," she snorted, reaching for her cup. "Well, all I can say, if *that's* what teaching's about." She shook her head savagely, staring around the hall. "I mean the staff were great, really helpful, but the kids ..." Gulping down a mouthful she pushed up to the table with a calculating stare: "'Ere miss, you one of 'em students? One of 'em weirdos. Cos if you is, then you better be careful." She pulled back with a shiver. "And that, by the way, was on a good day." She cut to her coffee, draining quickly. She was observing Doug more gently now.

When Richard prompted, asking how she'd coped, she launched in again, putting on voices and taking parts before declaring loudly that school was not for her. She ended, white-faced, staring at the table. Her gaze returned to Doug and she ran one finger lightly across his arm. "He knows. He's seen me afterwards."

Doug confirmed. The set of his face lifted as Ruth reached for his hand. In her eyes there was gratitude and a hope of understanding.

"Because he's my Doug," she added, coyly.

When they left, she was tucked in to his body with her eyes half-closed. Beside her Doug stepped out, narrowing his gaze and facing forward with a slightly child-like, self-absorbed smile.

Afterwards Vanessa asked Richard for his verdict.

"Surprising," he said, fingering her hair. They were occupying the corner of a long, sprawling sofa positioned at the end of the student bar. In front, a table contained them. On one side was a window, while on the other a spotlight fell on a broad-leafed cheese plant.

She pressed him again.

Richard eyed his glass. "Some people throw plates, or cheque-books, or even rocks. They use words."

"You mean she does."

"Lots of 'em. Whereas Doug understands the power of silence."

"Absolutely."

They carried on drinking and chatting until Vanessa spotted Ruth, wandering alone on the far side of the bar. She rose to flag her down, warning Richard with a touch on his shoulder.

Ruth came over, greeting as she sat. When Vanessa asked for news, she grimaced. "Pissed off."

"Oh?"

Ruth's gaze became fixed. Suddenly she pushed forward. "You want to know a fact?"

Vanessa assured her she was listening.

Breathing hard Ruth launched in. She'd had it with Doug bloody Barnard, she said, gripping the table and shaking her head. It was too much, she really couldn't bear it, always dodging, always putting off, and God knows she'd tried, made every effort.

Vanessa was attentive.

Ruth continued, speaking hoarsely. Doug, she insisted, was use-less, hopeless, so much out of it, she couldn't gee him up. In fact, she declared herself really at *that* point ...

As her words fell away, she looked around in search of something. Reaching out, she picked up a coaster. It was head-and-shoulders shaped, sun face above, beer barrel below. Pressing her thumbs against the back, she pushed. A fault line appeared, running around the neck. Drawing breath, she held it, twisting both ways. As the coaster doubled, she bent to her task, worrying at one side until, with a final wrenching tear, the head pulled away.

She held up both parts, naming Doug. Fitting them together, she looked and laughed. MR SILLY MAN, she called, waggling the head. He really was absurd, she muttered ... He had this knack of putting her in the wrong.

She laughed again and put down her coaster. Her face had con-tracted, as if she was in pain. "It feels like a setup. Like one of those kitchen sink dramas where they fight over everything. Whatever I say, he has to go against."

"Do you find that surprising?" Richard asked, cutting in.

"How d'y' mean?"

"What I said, is it so unexpected?"

"Explain, explain. Don't understand."

"The point is, do you *really* think Doug's that bad?"

Vanessa's face fell.

Ruth looked up. "I don't see—"

"I mean, how fair is it?" Suddenly, before she could answer, he fired up: "Because if that's how you see him then I, for one, think you've got it all wrong – completely, absolutely wrong – and *you* need to back off."

"Richard!" cried Vanessa, as Ruth turned white.

He shrugged, rising from the sofa without saying anything.

"Richard, apologise!"

He waved his refusal, moving to a distance.

"What gives you the right?"

Still he ignored her, gazing at a spot at the far end of the bar.

"Look, Richard," Vanessa said, and stood between them, inviting retraction.

"Oh, don't bother," muttered Ruth as she, too, rose to take her leave.

"Richard …"

He looked, without interest. One shoulder dropped as he backed off. With his gaze now directed elsewhere, he pushed towards the door. As he left Ruth reached for the coaster. Picking up the head she laughed softly before throwing it to the floor. She watched it land and, holding her breath, heeled down hard into cardboard.

Next day, when they caught up in the market café, Richard spoke quietly between sips of coffee. "OK, I got worked up."

"You know Ruth loves him, don't you?"

"But what she said about Doug …?"

"That was letting off steam. She won't be like that with him face to face. You hurt her."

"You think so?"

"I know so. I'm her friend."

"Has she told you that?"

"She was crying. Yes."

"I didn't mean it like that."

"Sometimes you're more powerful than you realise."

"I am?"

"Ruth's vulnerable, she needs Doug. You were harsh."

"Well, I did say a few things."

"It would have been better if you hadn't."

Richard gripped the table edge with one hand. "I can't always hold my tongue."

"I'd noticed."

"That's me. Just get that way sometimes."

"It's Ruth you need to speak to."

"How about if I write to her?"

"In a letter?"

"That's right. An apology."

Vanessa held her gaze. "No, Richard, anybody can write, but that's just words on paper. It's not that easy."

"You mean I have to go further?"

"Certainly."

"Public self-criticism, that sort of thing?"

Vanessa pursed her lips. She examined her cup edge then ran one finger around the handle, saying nothing.

"Say what you think."

"You have to tell her, to her face."

"You don't think a letter's enough?"

She shook her head slowly and paused. It was like taking pictures. She needed it to be clear.

"You think she'll want more?"

Vanessa stayed silent.

He asked again and her expression hardened.

"OK, I'll speak to her."

"You will?"

"Definitely."

Vanessa gave a nod, saying she was glad. Returning to her coffee she stared across the hall, mentioning Doug and inviting comment.

Richard followed her gaze. "That's what I don't understand. Why does he put up with it?"

She smiled to herself. Her eyes were round and brown and full of enquiry. Below, seen through the bars of the nearby railing, the shoppers moved in crowds.

"It's how things are," she said. She was leaning forward, sighting faces, as if Doug and Ruth might be there amongst the shops. "Some people throw words – remember? It's her way of saying, *show me your feelings*. She wants to break him down, force him to declare. You have to see it as a kind of play-fight. She's like the girl in the playground who slaps the boy and runs off. He's meant to give chase."

"You mean they *want* it this way?"

"I believe so."

"But like *this*, her in a rage, him blocking?"

"It's how they are. They fill each other's gaps."

"You sure about that?"

"Oh yes. Seen from their point of view, it's successful."

"But surely you don't really think it's good?"

"It works."

Richard turned impish. "OK, so what's the evidence? Can you back it up?"

"You mustn't tell anyone."

"Go on."

"This is between us – promise?"

"Promise."

Leaning forward, she drained her cup then threw back her head, smiling. "They're engaged."

At the end-of-term party, held at Vanessa's, it occurred to Richard how many of their friends were already committed. For them it was settled; they'd agreed the whole package. What surprised him was how early they'd concluded, gone for what they knew: a life within limits, a quid pro quo. He noticed how they worked, or in Ruth's case with Doug went through with actions that kept them together, up and dancing as rivals in a ring. He saw too, the differences: how one couple were physical, others shared smiles or sat talking quietly, still others were all hype, while some kept their distance, barely taking notice when the partner grew restive or took themselves off to seek other company.

There was Lisa and Gary who talked health-and-lifestyle with friends Kate and Will, comparing conditions and most-used treatments, Bess with her man, jiggling in a corner with a small group of dancers, and Hugh and Penny who struck up with anyone, playing out school scenes and telling off kids. They were joined by other friends: the JJ sisters sampling wine, a couple shouting jokes, another pair snogging, several eating, and even those who came alone were busy making out, smiling often and finding things in common as they listened and shared and put themselves about.

Richard, while he hosted, played fly on the wall. The music and drink upped the volume, stories were called out and laughter filled the flat.

"Funny people," Richard murmured, alone in the kitchen with a bright-eyed Vanessa.

"Sorry?"

"I've been watching. Good cabaret."

"Richard, do you really have to—"

"Quirky. They know their parts well."

Vanessa shushed him and they returned to the lounge.

A group had arrived who occupied the hallway, smoking and drinking and greeting other visitors. Male and thin, they were sharp-eyed and excitable. For a minute or two they acted as unofficial doormen, directing to the drink, the toilet and the coat-pile. While they quick-talked and pointed, they passed around cans, dug out from a backpack. The cans, plus a few handy-sized bottles, were scanned for date and checked by label before being swigged. The group continued swigging and greeting until, when refills were needed, they reached into the sack, to find it empty. A mood-change set in. Suddenly they were angry, couldn't believe it, they needed their brew. Search parties were sent out, one to the kitchen, another to the lounge, while a third checked the tables. Their return, empty-handed, led to outrage. There were shouts of "Bloody Norah!" and "What-the-fuck-d-y-mean?", an exchange of catcalls, jokey exclamations and exit.

As they crashed downstairs the group could be heard joshing. They were debating parentage and the whereabouts of the nearest "offie". The last sounds were whoops and yells and footsteps running off.

"Do you think they'll be back?" Vanessa asked Richard, shuddering.

"Unlikely. Didn't get their booze."

"Is that all they think about? Drink?"

"It's important to them."

She rolled her eyes, saying nothing.

"You're not impressed?"

"Who would be?"

"I suppose it's a choice. Makes them happy."

She snorted. "Huh, it's carry on lads, regardless. What I don't understand is why anyone would want to behave that way. You'd think they were sleepwalkers. It's as if they've got some of their senses permanently switched off, so other people don't count."

"And not in front of the guests, eh?"

"I don't think," she said, gazing around the room, "*anyone* here is interested."

Richard smiled, allowing his thought to register unsaid. Of course, he could see that. They were, he imagined, too busy to take notice. Much, much too busy with themselves.

Over the next few hours, they stepped up the hosting. He served food and filled up glasses while Vanessa did the rounds, asking after health and news of absent friends. For her it was social, a balance that she struck, for him a task. A stage for one, a window for the other. And for Richard, partly as a game but also by design, his role was undercover. So he people-watched with interest, taking note of ground rules, agreements and what made them tick.

But also, he noticed how they looked off towards windows or hung around doorways, filling up time with deliberate exchanges.

Poised and careful, *they* made the effort, or at least they knew the script. And their lives were full of disappointment.

During the evening he returned to Vanessa on regular report-back, sharing updates on relationships and how people felt. Someone was "off", a partner was "loose-ended", there were people who fitted and those who stood apart, talkers with supporters and a number of oddballs who relied on entertainment, taking off themselves with self-mocking anecdotes and all-smiles remarks.

He'd just begun telling her about Hugh and Penny when the voice of a woman, cutting through the flat, stopped him mid-sentence.

"Sounds familiar," he said carefully, avoiding further comment.

Vanessa suggested that they viewed, and they moved to the living room where a crowd had gathered.

As they came closer they saw, in the middle, a red-faced Ruth with a drinks tray, raising a toast to the crowd. "Trouble is," she declared, her voice tone lifting, "men."

She paused then pointed around the room and began probing and challenging, inviting response. "OK, OK, OK, so give me something, anything, a-n-y-t-h-i-n-g at all about men that's even half-decent. No, not even that. A quarter'll do, less if you like, one point above zero."

The faces close-in showed nothing. At the back they were grinning. Stood to one side, Vanessa was watching with her mouth hung open like a child behind glass.

"See, you can't bloody do it," Ruth called, glaring around, "because that's how they are. They're all 007 and my bloody dad. All so bloody blokey. Bloody, bloody men." She snorted, tipping back her glass and reaching for a top-up. "And another thing," here she spun around, swaying forward, "have you ever listened in? Heard what they call us? 'Birds and bits and hits and fucks and hey man what you're getting' – it's like we're just *there*, objects, pick-ups, throwaways, like so much stuff."

Putting down her glass, she seized a bottle and began to wave it, walking the floor, pausing every so often to toss down a mouthful. Her audience now were shoulder to shoulder, giving way slightly wherever she walked. "And you know, they feel so sorry for themselves, so damned sorry – I mean can you believe it – they got it made and all they do is moan about women, call us naggers or slags, my bitch, my teaser or some such stuff. Because I tell you, if it comes to men take my advice just forget 'em, drop 'em, throw 'em all away."

A man by the door joked that he knew what *she* wanted. Swearing, she called him out. When the man called back, she invited him forward: head to head, their own war of words. He shrugged, went silent and moved off to the kitchen.

Ruth laughed, swigging from a bottle. White-faced now, she was gazing towards the door. She was speaking in asides with occasional pauses, repeating what she'd said. Turning to her listeners, she beckoned them closer. They had to share, she said. Wide-eyed and smiley, she passed around the bottle, followed by some glasses, some tumblers and two more bottles with extra plastic cups. She moved down the line, filling and replenishing then stood to attention with a tumbler in each hand. "You ready?" she called and a few people nodded. "OK, folks, don't look now, it's raining men." Suddenly, raising both arms to a point above her head she let out a cry. "Because it's such a bloody mess," she shouted and, turning her wrists, upended quickly.

All around the room people began to laugh.

The wine splashed out, soaking through her hair and staining flesh. It ran down in spurts, filling out her clothes. It spurted and overflowed, dribbling sideways, spotting the carpet and puddling around her shoes.

As realisation came, she put down her tumblers. "Ha, ha, ha," she called, seizing a full glass and sluicing again. The wine trickled down and she threw back her head, spluttering. There was pain in her face and a floaty kind of smile. Her eyes filled up and her head dropped sideways. Calling and shaking, she pushed through the crowd to reach Vanessa. "It's a mess," she repeated, breathing hard. She stood there, crying quietly. Then she hunched herself forward to put down her glass and turned to walk out silently through the door.

‡ ‡ ‡

For most of the winter it was Richard who visited, crossing the city and walking to Vanessa's, returning the next day to stand looking out from the walkway on the bridge. Rain or shine, the streets were quiet and he enjoyed the journey. It allowed him, while thinking, to go with the flow.

Of course, it was a trek. It did take time, and sometimes he was tired. There and back was an hour from college, further from his flat, and sometimes he had to leg it through wind and rain. But there was warmth one end and fondness looking back, and both ways a feeling that what they had was a line between them.

There were practical matters, too. Sometimes he stayed more than one night, which was when he found himself returning home to bag up books and clothes, or even, if he'd room, returning with his journal and cased-up Olivetti.

"My second home," he called as he arrived at the door with a rucksack full of worksheets.

"The man in two places," he quipped, living from the suitcase he'd stowed beneath the bed.

"Holiday's over," he said when leaving for his flat.

Vanessa thought him fun, enjoying his street-scene observations and talk of living life. She called him her reporter.

"Exclusive?" he asked, laughing.

"Sensational," she replied, accepting his kiss.

"Of course," he said afterwards, "it's kiss 'n' tell."

"What ... you're telling on *me*?"

"No, the other way round."

"Sorry?"

"Watching the world. What's out there, reporting."

"Ah, you mean you're undercover?"

"If you like. *Notes from the Underground*, that sort of thing."

At other times he'd talk about what he called *buzz* and *what goes around*, arriving with stories from classrooms and staffrooms and jokes he'd overheard, all played out with voices to keep her entertained. And when he left he was warm, saying he'd phone next morning, for cheer up, wake up and next day return.

From the start, he'd called her place *The Bird's Nest*, a room at the top that felt like a retreat. *The* Bird's Nest soon became *Our*, as his periods of occupation lengthened and he brought in more possessions. He began, at Vanessa's suggestion, to double on essentials, building up a *nest set*, starting with books and his own brand of coffee then adding in sundries: a notepad, a biro collection, photos in albums, old certificates and a selection from his tapes.

The fact of his presence, established with friends and increasingly obvious to visitors, pushed them to go public, and to clear it with her parents. Hers, not his, because they were nearer and wanted information. And the politics of telling included, as a sweetener, an attendance at lunch and transport to their house in a paid-for taxi.

"Why the cab?" asked Richard, when boarding.

"Appearances," answered Vanessa, "and because they're helpful."

"So, it's an act of charity – and meant to be seen?"

"Well, they *are* my parents."

"And the cost?"

"You'll see. It's a different lifestyle."

On the route there Richard was little-boy-defiant, dropping his h-s and flattening his a-s, while insisting that the visit didn't imply anything. He came to show willing and nothing more.

"I don't know if you'll get on," said Vanessa as they arrived at the street, "but you have to try. I'd like you to see them as they are. Rich, yes, but decent people."

"Don't worry, I'll play the game."

They cruised down a double terraced row of Edwardian houses with wrought-iron gates, wide bay windows and panelled front doors. Stone-built at the bottom, they were pillared around the doorways, rising to ornamental balconies, patterned brickwork and banded fascias. Vanessa named and pointed, and the driver drew up. They climbed out together, exchanging glances and smoothing their clothes. Entering the gate, they crossed a paved forecourt to climb a flight of steps. As they arrived at the top, the front door opened and a woman greeted them, smiling faintly. She was tall like her daughter, brown-eyed and poised, wearing a silk-sheen dress with matching accessories. She was all of one piece, full-length in blue.

Vanessa stepped forward, kissing her mother. "And this is Richard," she said, moving to one side.

"Pleased you could come," said Felicity, appraisingly.

A handshake followed and an invite to enter. Richard noticed how she kept herself braced, with a chin-up manner and an element of delay. She knew how to carry it off.

Behind her in the hallway stood a red-faced man with a serious expression. Introduced as Derek, he nodded in acknowledgement. Sounding slightly nasal, he enquired about their journey while taking coats. Vanessa thanked him, praising the driver and shivering slightly when mentioning the weather. She and Richard moved to one side while Derek shut the door.

Felicity conducted to the high-ceilinged lounge and invited them to sit, indicating a period sofa. When they'd made themselves comfortable, Derek wheeled out a rosewood trolley with glasses on top and bottles underneath. Orders were taken, poured on a tray and passed around – everything was measured and made up to taste.

Felicity asked about where they'd been to teach. "Not in this district, I imagine," she added, with slow-spoken emphasis.

Richard confirmed. "Closed doors, all private. Not surprising really."

Derek, who had repositioned the trolley alongside his chair, inhaled noisily. His face had darkened.

Felicity raised one eyebrow. "You have views?"

"Don't worry about it, Mother," Vanessa put in, "it's just an opinion."

"But I am interested, it's always valuable to hear ideas. We are all in need of a wider perspective."

Richard smiled. "Yes, I suppose it all depends on your experience."

"That's true," Derek shot back.

Felicity ran one finger around the lip of her glass. "I take it your teaching experience has been in the state system?"

Richard, watching carefully, formulated his reply. The father, he could see, was gearing up. With his small-jawed face and shaky hands

268

he was staring hard, holding his glass. His ears, which were prominent, had coloured up. The mother was different. Wide-eyed and stately, she held herself in readiness. Something suggestive of doubt or admiration played about her mouth, as if she wanted more. Vanessa was sitting upright on the sofa staring at the carpet.

"I went to a grammar school," he said. "Mind, you see the change when you go into comprehensives."

Felicity, nodding, invited further comment. It was as if she was in session, judging the case.

Richard explained, speaking with care, rerunning incidents, his schooling and its problems. "It's a choice," he said finally, "and a matter of conviction – though that's always personal. For me, there's an element of giving back."

His answer seemed to satisfy. Resuming direction, the conversation moved on, steered by Felicity into viewpoints shared.

After news and leisure talk, then observations on weather and plants in the garden, she proposed a move. "Lunch time," she said, leading them downstairs to a basement with a kitchen and a panelled diner. "Please make yourselves comfortable," she called through the connecting hatch.

Derek prepared to carve while Vanessa and Richard took their places at the polished wooden table. It was long and grainy, with a centrepiece display of African violets and a French window out to a courtyard garden. A wine rack to one side held a selection of bottles, all French, sealed with wax and dated. Vanessa was put in charge of serving them.

During lunch they kept up the talk about people they'd known, friends of the family and friends of friends, reporting on VIP contacts and what they'd really said. Mainly *faux pas*, told in detail, with a knowing smile. They were in the loop. And it seemed, as they gossiped that they'd passed over Richard; or perhaps, now he'd said his piece, they'd accepted his presence and made due allowance. It was almost as if he wasn't there.

When Felicity brought him in, he found himself speaking about travel, a subject that Derek warmed to, talking about footslog and overcoming barriers. "It's character forming," added Derek, rubbing his hands together. Behind the blah his voice was concessionary.

The meal went slowly. Partly it was helpings – large, repeated, with sauce and salad and a variety of meats – partly out of habit, but also because they could. To linger was more special; they ate and they *expected*. But also, Richard felt a sense of largesse; they were putting themselves out, doing things for him.

It was when they retired upstairs for coffee with chocolates and Amaretti that Richard became aware of Derek leaning in his direction, speaking slowly with an open-faced expression. When asked to repeat, he reiterated slowly. There was something, he said, that he'd like Richard to see. This was man-to-man.

Richard accepted, wondering what might follow.

Derek rose, mentioning the top room, and guided to the hall. He announced they'd be back soon and led upstairs, puffing as he went. "Three flights," he said, without looking back.

They ascended past Manets and Monets, up across a landing with photos of mediaeval chateaux then higher by brass-plate cathedrals and prints of vintage cars. At each landing Derek's hand slid across polished wood, before turning and gripping to continue upstairs. Pausing at the top, he pulled out a key, inserting it in a dark green door with a scroll metal handle. It opened slowly and he ducked in first, clicking on the lights. His voiced sounded hollow as he warned about the sill.

Following, Richard entered a high sloping room with bare plaster walls. The atmosphere was still and the light bulbs unshaded. Though large and dusty, the room felt lived-in.

In front and on both sides there were flat wooden tables with gangways in between. The tables were wide, box-room-size, with pit prop legs and surrounding ledges. Displayed on them were contoured landscapes, some flat, some rolling, and the winding metal tracks of a model railway. The tracks were zoned, beginning at the middle with bridges and cuttings and branch lines off. They filled up the tables, diverged over fields, looped around lakes and hills and forked together sharply as they returned to where they began. Each line or link or network included tunnels and viaducts and spans across rivers, each had its stations with nameplates and shelters and gated level crossings and each, where it reached open land, struck out past garages and factories, to circle into papier mâché fields and watercolour shorelines.

"Did you put this together?" asked Richard.

Derek confirmed. He was plugging in a circuit and adjusting switches. As he moved around the tables the street lamps lit up and the trains began to run. Suddenly the room had become a fairground.

Richard followed, looking closely at the models. He noticed how they varied. The landscapes ranged from alpine to desert, with small towns and villages built on the flat, farms between hills, buildings from all periods, and scaled-down versions of palaces and churches, many of them reminiscent of famous landmarks. Around and be-tween them, there were people walking dogs, commuters on plat-forms, tourists with cameras, mock-ups of weddings and even, on one table, an open-air theatre with audience and performers dressed as Roman citizens.

"It's like a film set," observed Richard, admiringly. Studying the detail, he moved between tables before turning to his host. "It must've taken years."

Derek held up five fingers. "Times three," he added, flashing up his hand like semaphore.

At the far end, in one corner, Richard noticed there was a small gate-leg table partly covered by a dust sheet. The material stood chest-high, squared in the middle to a tent-like block. It looked like a boxed-up wedding present. "And what's that?" he asked, pointing.

"Ah, that's the most recent," Derek said, weighing his words carefully. "It's actually rather specialised. But if you'd like to look …?"

Richard was pressed into service to lift off the sheet. They stood both ends, raising it to head-height and walking themselves clear. While removing and folding Richard became aware of what was underneath. He could see an edge of brickwork, a strip of painted wood and something architectural. But it was only when he turned to examine it in detail that he realised he was looking at a perfectly produced miniature version of a late Edwardian, three-storey, mid-terrace house.

Leaning forward, Derek removed the facade. As he pulled it away, he glanced at his guest. "You recognise anything?" he asked.

Richard looked. What had seemed like a toy was, in fact, a mock-up: a well-worked, room-by-room copy of the house they were standing in.

His eye searched the floors. "So, we're here," he said finally, pointing to the attic.

"Yes, all present and correct," said Derek, following his gaze.

"I'm impressed."

"You'd care to take a closer look?"

Richard nodded and his host reached in, using a wedge to lever up the floor. He drew the room out carefully and placed it on the table, inviting comparison, model and original. The correspondence was exact.

Richard crouched down, level to the table. "It must feel good," he said. "Seeing this, knowing that you did it. That's quite an achievement."

Derek grinned, staring at the model. "Well, yes, it is indeed ..." He blushed, adding his thanks. As his words tailed off his hands took over, raising and positioning the floor he'd extracted and switching off the circuits. Pointing to the dustsheet, he suggested quietly that they cover everything and head downstairs.

As they emerged to the landing, Richard heard the voice of Felicity rising from below. Her long level calls, projecting up the stairwell, filled up space. Derek replied calmly, stepping back to the door. Searching for the key, he glanced inside. The covers were drawn; the models were still; the dust was settling. Joined by Richard, he paused at the doorway, checked all around and snapped off the lights. Felicity called again and he retreated from darkness, gripped the metal handle and closed the door behind him.

On the drive back to the flat Vanessa wanted details. "What did you two do up there?" she asked, teasingly.

"What d'you think?"

"No idea. Major bonding, judging by the grins."

"Boys will be boys."

"True. It's the locker room effect, DIY and how's your father."

The vehicle turned a corner and halted at the lights.

"But seriously," she continued, "you scored a hit."

"I did? Was something said?"

"No, but I could tell. Mother has this way of *giving off*. You were approved."

Richard waited until the taxi pulled away. "Have you seen the top room?"

She stared out vaguely through glass. A fine haze of mist had gathered on the window, softening what she saw. "Not really, it was like that song, *Behind the Green Door*. One of those places I just didn't go. Somewhere upstairs where my father did things. Even now I feel it's all a bit abstract. I believe there are models."

"A gallery full. I think you'd be surprised."

"You liked them?"

"Admired them, yes. In their own way they're perfect."

"With a capital P?"

"Lifelike I'd say."

"And do they actually do things? I mean move, light up."

"Yes, lots of that. But it's not all fairground – or if it is, that's not what really matters."

"You mean there's something else?"

"I believe so. It's important, to him."

Vanessa raised one hand, rubbing a hole in steamed-up glass.

"And for you?" she asked, gazing out. "You found it interesting?"

"Oh yes, he's done so much. Just half that and I'd be proud." He lapsed back into silence. They were queued in traffic, moving slowly between shops and offices. There were other vehicles joining from side roads and a bus stopped ahead with passengers disembarking.

"So perhaps you," she said quietly, "being a man, can tell me why he does it."

Richard sat back. It seemed she'd looked over, pointed to an item and asked him what it was. "I think," he answered, fingering the upholstery, "it has its own logic. He's building models in the way people put up monuments. It's all about scale and ownership, and fixing things in memory."

"Well he certainly has been working at it, for years now. It's *La Grande Obsession*." Their eyes met. "Maybe, Richard, if I'd been there. Actually *seen* it—"

Sensing her doubts, he paused. The interior of the taxi was cross-barred by small spots of light. "It's good. You'd be amazed."

"It's always been his *project*, his own way of being Derek. All his own, till you came along."

"Ah, so I've joined the Martels. Honorary member, hitched to daughter, and well in with dad."

"But don't talk school."

He laughed, "True."

"Or if you do, old school."

Again, he laughed, gazing out.

She stretched out her hand, "Well, my dear, you did well."

For the rest of the journey Richard sat in silence, taking in the route, their closeness, the lights in darkness and the prospect glimpsed up ahead of becoming, like their friends, committed and spoken-for, partnered for life.

The next day at college, although they'd a seminar, they went in without books or files. They'd not checked the brief and hadn't read around. For once it didn't count who said what, whether it was honest, and how much their tutor expected. Both were out of sorts or they'd not slept well. They'd taken a step backwards.

At the end of the seminar they joined a serious-looking Ruth over drinks in the bar. She was wearing dark glasses and had tied back her hair. Speaking quietly, she talked about change and resolutions she'd made, mainly about Doug, but also a schedule to get through her studies. When Vanessa mentioned teaching, she spoke about possible retakes while hunting, she said, for non-school jobs, anything with people, outside the classroom.

Soon afterwards she rose to leave and hovered by the table, breathing hard. "Feeling pressured," she said. "Too much to do."

"Nonsense, you're fine, Ruth Draper," called Vanessa.

Ruth shivered slightly. "It's a no pain no gain situation, and I'm feeling the pain."

Vanessa shook her head. "You're you, and can cope. You always have."

"You're going to the library?" asked Richard, pointing to the door. Ruth nodded.

"You can afford, you know, to give yourself a break."

"Not for me, not so."

"Really? Well, don't overdo it."

"Not likely," she persisted, grimly, "Not in the here and now." Frowning, she stepped away. "No way, not now," she said, dropping one shoulder and removing her glasses. As she left, she carried on mouthing, like an actor learning her lines.

Vanessa waited till her friend was out of earshot. "You see what she's like?"

"I do, now."

"Ruth needs a boost, people being positive."

"Yes. Like you said, she's vulnerable."

"So, did you speak to her?"

"The apology? I thought she would have told you."

"Nothing's been said."

"It's done. We're on a temporary truce."

"Temporary?"

"Working towards permanent ..."

"Anyway, you spoke ..."

"We did and it was fine. The tongue is mightier than the sword."

Vanessa sighed, then touched her empty glass. "At least that's dealt with," she said and, rising from her chair, suggested that they go. When Richard joined her, they crossed the lobby and stood waiting by the exit while a crowd pushed in. The group were all male, long-limbed and noisy.

When the doors finally cleared, Richard and Vanessa passed out into daylight, en route to the market.

Outside was grey and damp. They walked along a row of blackened buildings with dirt-streaked woodwork and windows encased by bent wire mesh. The pavement was uneven and the road they followed was full of potholes and patched-up surfaces. As they walked, Richard changed the subject, replaying the seminar and their tutor's comments. "She bats it back, every time the same," he said, frowning. "And it works. Puts everyone else in the wrong."

When Vanessa didn't answer, he laughed. "Mind, Ruth's just the opposite, a bit of a leaky tap."

"What?"

It was his turn to be silent.

"Richard."

"Yes?"

"I thought you were on a truce?"

"Face to face we are."

"*Did* you apologise, Richard?"

"Yes, as promised."

"Then don't say that."

"What do you want me to say? She's doing fine?"

"You don't have to say anything. She's my friend."

"Look ..." he began then stopped. "But if that's how you want it, OK, enough said, I rest my case." And he led off down a side street, imitating their tutor and her way of twisting words. Vanessa followed, flashing him a look.

At the market hall entrance, Richard paused. "Shall we browse the books?" he asked, waving forward to a corner full of trestle tables and stacked-up boxes.

"If that's what you want."

"I thought, in a way, it might be——"

"Might be?"

"I dunno, a change, I suppose. Because all of a sudden it's nothing but problems."

"What problems?"

"Tutors, friends, whatever."

"And you'd rather look at books?"

276

"I can read *them*."

"What are you suggesting?"

"That we talk more. About what matters."

Before she could answer he led off to the tables, greeting a bearded man with a wave of the hand. The man was short and round with pink, blotchy skin and hair to the collar. His light blue eyes were small, alert and vaguely ironic. When Vanessa approached, he folded his arms and put on a smile. It was as if he knew exactly what she wanted.

She leafed through a few volumes, skimming for content. Richard, meanwhile, was peering at some verse.

"I can't seem to read properly today," Vanessa said, looking baffled. The man with the books unfolded his arms and stopped smiling. "I need to know, Richard," she continued, "what *is* it we've got to talk about?"

Richard put down his book. "Well, for one thing, my parents."

"Ah, back to that—"

He confirmed, narrowing his eyes.

"You're worried what they might say?"

"I don't think they're bothered," he replied quickly, returning to the tables and lighting on a hardback copy of her cousin's book. "As far as they're concerned, we live in a foreign country."

"Because they come from *up north*?" she said, imitating his voice, flattened at the end.

"Well, it keeps them at a respectable distance." He turned a few pages, reading out a sentence in lugubrious, mock singsong. "Pretty bad, isn't it," he said, addressing his words to the man behind the table.

"Not everyone in the family has my father's level of talent."

"Sorry?"

"It's nothing, just a remark."

"You're not happy with something?"

She shook her head and moved off down the aisle.

He exchanged glances with the bookseller, then followed her to a corner, beneath the awning of a flower stall. It was seaside-bright and pollinate. There were step-levelled displays with trailing baskets, made-up window boxes and mixed bouquets in wrappers. Here he found Vanessa with her head to one side, staring at a bunch of rust-red dahlias. The stems filled up a large glass jar. "Not much to smell," he said, as if to warn her off.

"These are my colours," she replied. "They suit."

She hadn't brought her purse so Richard stood by while she picked out stems, adding in orange, yellow and purple. Then Richard paid and helped with the carrying.

On the way back he reverted to the question of moving in. It had come up this morning in relation to his parents. He'd begun with a remark that his stay had, for the first time, extended to four nights. He'd used words like *habit* and *belonging*, jokily of course, but also as a marker. In the talk that followed Vanessa had sidestepped or minimised; he felt she'd begged the question. She'd like it when it happened but wondered about timing, because he'd put things in a way, she said, that felt quite closed.

Now, as they walked back, he returned to the subject. He was using his *cornering* technique, posing questions and asking supplementaries, then suddenly declaring that he'd go along with anything in order to settle it. "Maybe," he said quietly, "it's better – even if we both said *move in* tomorrow – if we wait."

Vanessa showed her surprise. She was carrying her dahlias, bunched at an angle, almost touching his. "But I thought that was what you wanted?"

"Not if it upsets things."

They walked on silently, crossing the river and turning south.

"There could be a case," he said slowly as they entered the park, "for a trial period."

Vanessa looked down at her collection of flowers. She was smiling vaguely, as if for a picture. The flowers, or her thoughts, had taken over. "How would that work?" she asked.

Richard frowned, adjusting. Though the walk was familiar, it felt much longer today. If he was honest, when they talked like this, he made the running. "Suppose I hung on to my place, but moved everything in. Then we could try, but there'd still be a route back."

She continued walking, looking from the flowers to the path. There were grey-brown patches where the borders had died back. At the end the path turned past a boarded-up kiosk and a bare, fenced-in patch with swings and a sandpit. "Richard," she said quietly as they passed out through the gate, "do you think we could manage?"

"Perhaps," he began then cut off. They were turning into her road, walking slowly, connected by a need to find common ground. "I think," he said finally, as they arrived at the door, "we should make a decision, now."

"What, right here?"

"Yes, it's time we did."

Vanessa held up her dahlias, as if they might protect her. "Does it have to be now? These things are difficult."

Richard shook his head and waited. "I need to know," he said, taking Vanessa's flowers when she offered. With the blooms in one hand he stood beside the step, half-smiling. "What do you say, move in or not?"

"Yes would be good," he added, laughing.

Vanessa remained silent.

"Please say something," he said.

"I think …"

"What?"

She returned to silence.

"If it's easier, you can just nod your head."

Vanessa coloured slightly.

"You don't have to *say* anything."

Their eyes connected.

Richard's gaze was encouraging; her large round eyes were already saying it.

Suddenly he straightened. "While I, being a man," he announced, holding out the bunch of multi-coloured dahlias, "will say it with flowers."

In reply Vanessa smiled, stretched out her hand to accept the bunch and slowly, with deliberate emphasis, nodded her head.

‡ ‡ ‡

Over winter they talked more about moving in.

"When it happens, we need a plan," said Vanessa.

"A plan?"

"We have to be prepared."

"Prepared for anything – that sort of thing?"

"You could say that."

"Meaning, it's a big deal."

"No, just something to get used to."

"You're not having second thoughts?"

"I wouldn't say that. But it takes time."

"Ah, understood. Time to adjust."

"Yes, and talk. Probably that, more than anything."

So, they gave themselves time, planning the move in stop-go fashion, with Richard asking questions about where this might lead and Vanessa talking about things she'd throw out. For him it brought back their friends at the end-of-term party – what he called the *whole package*. For her it was a question of clearance and getting things in place.

By spring they'd decided it was best if he gave notice. That way was simpler, fairer on everyone, and more cut and dried. It also seemed more practical. Living with a couple and their friend, the owner, in a three-storey house, Richard had books and equipment but very little furniture, so his move was more of a room-change, a step across a corridor carried off quietly with a minimum of fuss.

Once decided, Richard made it happen. He boxed and bagged up, taped around breakables, then arranged things in piles. And to do it in a weekend he fitted his journeys into morning and evening, walking the essentials, sorting both ends, and ferrying by car.

He completed on a Sunday with the help of Doug, who arrived after breakfast in shorts and a sweatshirt declaring himself "set". Checking and taking measurements, he examined what needed moving. "Let's see what goes in," he said, while manoeuvring boxes to fit in his Ford Estate.

After packing and securing the back doors, they drove to Vanessa's, taking a detour to avoid the city centre. On the journey Doug asked about breakables. At the door he directed, checking before lifting and positioning carefully. "You happy?" he asked as they pulled out a pair of speakers, wrapped in plastic and conjoined by wires. Richard grunted as they shuffled them upstairs.

"It's a big step," Doug said, reaching the top landing and glancing backwards down the stairwell.

When the last few items had been safely carried in, Vanessa thanked him, offering food.

"That's kind," he replied, glancing towards Richard for guidance.

"Well, there you are, please be seated. Guest of honour."

Doug stood quietly, looking doubtful.

"Go on, it's on the table," Richard beamed.

"I'm not sure. I just don't want to put you out."

"Doug Barnard, you're so bloody unassuming."

"You think—"

"I wondered," Vanessa cut in, "*if* you'd prefer, maybe we could do something, as a foursome."

The men fell silent, awaiting developments. "Perhaps," said Doug slowly. "What would it be?"

"I've an idea." Her words remained hanging as if she'd lost the thread. Whatever she'd intended, it could wait.

Richard smiled. By now he knew her habits. This was Vanessa.

"And your idea?" he asked.

"Just something," she replied, as if it didn't matter.

"Yes?"

"A thought."

"Which is?"

"I wondered about visiting a garden."

Richard remembered the horticultural monthlies seen at her parents. They'd leafed through photos of flower shows, colour-themed borders and woodland walks. "You've one in mind?"

"Yes, if you like. We'd have to check it's open." She turned to Doug. "It's quite some distance, and you'd have to drive, but *we'd* do the honours."

"The lot," added Richard, catching on. "Our treat."

Doug stood smiling, shifting his gaze from one to the other. His round, boyish face had filled to a glow.

"Is that all right?" Vanessa asked him.

Doug took a breath. "Accepted," he said, "I shall await instructions." Before they could reply he added, "Whatever Ruth says."

They visited *Manor Gardens* the next weekend. Doug drove and Vanessa directed, taking the scenic route, climbing through fields and descending sharply into leafless valleys. As they journeyed south, a grey-yellow sun appeared between clouds. When Doug grew tired Ruth took over, revving on straights and braking into corners. As she drove, she swore repeatedly. Beside her, Vanessa provided the directions. Her task was to calm things.

They turned west at a castle and ran past farms in an undulating district, cruising by fields and tree-topped outcrops to arrive at a final line of hills. Here they did a loop to descend beneath a scarp and enter the beginnings of a flat coastal plain.

"Soon be there," said Vanessa, aligning her map.

At a sign for *Manor Gardens*, Ruth slowed, swinging right into a winding country lane. The lane was narrow and muddy, with passing places.

"Well, it's a fun place to find," said Richard, gazing forward.

Close into the hills, facing south, they entered a bowl-shaped valley laid out in terraces with steps down, dividing hedges, and early spring borders. "Cheers everyone, we're here," said Vanessa as they turned right through a gate.

"Mind your bums," called Ruth as they bumped across a cattle grid.

"Drrrrrr," cried Richard.

They parked on grass and followed a track that dropped to a lodge where Richard paid, then passed in through an arch.

"It's south facing," said Vanessa leading along a gravel drive with banks both sides dotted with narcissi.

The path continued by a lawn and up steps to a terrace by a house to reach a low-walled square with a small pool. Here Ruth took Doug's arm. "Oh yes," she said gazing quietly at a large red camellia, "don't you just *feel* it." Crouching down, Vanessa took a photo of petals on water.

For a while they walked the square, taking in the sunlight, the stone, the first shows on wood.

The square led to a narrow zigzag path with railings and log steps descending through trees. Here the grounds were wilder. They filed downhill past overspreading bushes, mostly just in bud. Vanessa led, taking pictures of plants, shadowed by Ruth who kept asking questions. The two men followed, saying nothing.

At the bottom they came across a flat grassy spot and a dried-out pond. It was bare to the front and bushy around the edges. In the centre was a thick green awning with a swing bench beneath. "Rest spot," said Vanessa, rather grandly. They approached, exchanging glances.

"Come on, all aboard. Room for everyone," cried Ruth, who was first to climb in. They packed the seat with Ruth and Doug in the middle, Richard at one end and Vanessa at the other. The view forward was panoramic.

For a while they talked gardens and childhood holidays until Ruth, losing interest, began pushing out. One leg to the floor, she was using her body as a counterweight. "It sags," she laughed, foot-rocking harder. The seat began to sway, creaking quietly and scraping at the sides. When she pushed again, using both feet, Vanessa joined in and the seat began to lurch.

"Careful," called Doug as the frame started to shudder.

Ruth lifted her legs, leaning with the movement, and the seat became a gondola. "We're flying," she called and threw herself back, breaking into song.

"Hey!" shouted Doug, flushing.

Vanessa laughed. The seat was in motion, dipping and chopping like a rowboat. "Flying!" she echoed pushing at the frame, and the motion shifted sideways. She pushed again and the seat began to tack, corner to corner. It rose up, describing a parabola, hitting on metal and jerking forward.

Doug called again.

At one end a wing nut flew off, clattering to the ground.

With a shout of "Flying!" the women kicked out together.

"This is silly," said Richard, gripping a bar.

"Very!" Ruth called, laughing.

"Bloody silly," he insisted, forcing the seat downwards. He continued, gripping heavily and swearing intermittently, until the seat came to rest.

Silence followed. In the bushes there were birds, rustling and calling. An elderly couple appeared, descending the hillside, holding the railing. Their voices sounded muffled, absorbed by wood.

Richard stood up and began searching for the nut. His expression was focused and purposeful. "Should be here," he told Vanessa, peering into grass and poking around the frame. Ruth joined in, turning up stones. Doug remained in place, feeling into corners and checking where they'd sat.

In the course of the search Ruth offered Richard an apology.

"No problem," he said.

They carried on looking around. Apart from Ruth touching a spider, and a few old coins found by Doug, nothing turned up.

"Best leave it," said Richard in the end. "Head for the hills. Vanish."

Ruth laughed. "You mean the Indian rope-trick?"

He grinned and licked his lips.

Vanessa glanced up the slope. "Shall we go?"

"One more look," called Doug, reaching sideways. As he moved, the seat shook and slipped, keeling sideways. "Wha—" he called, reaching into air. The bench went down, tipping still further. Doug cried out, one end collapsed and the canvas imploded like a badly-made tent. As it fell it rebounded, tipping him forward. He grabbed for the frame, missed, yelled and landed in a heap, rolling his eyes like a punch-drunk boxer.

"Oh my God!" squealed Ruth, hand to mouth.

"You all right?" asked Richard, crouching down.

Doug lay hunched with his back to the questioner, shivering.

"Is he injured?"

Richard touched one arm, "Not sure. You OK?"

Doug continued shaking.

"Are you all right?"

No reply.

"Doug—"

Ruth pushed forward. She peered at him, craning to one side, seeking a reply. "Hey there?" Almost as she spoke, Doug turned suddenly, ballooning his cheeks and levering himself up. For a second he appeared hurt. Then, with a gasp, he stood pointing to the seat, doubling forward. "What a— What a—" he whooped, spluttering and shaking and dancing about. Arms out, he was windmilling both ways, as if he'd been stung.

Ruth stepped back. "You're all right then?"

Doug turned to face her, struggling for air. Before he could reply the others joined in, giggling and snorting. Even Ruth, after expressing surprise, was drawn into laughter.

They continued, high-stepping about and eyeballing each other. They'd entered, for a moment, a kind of charmed circle.

It was Vanessa who moved first back to the path. "Uphill?" she asked, pointing. Her face was flushed, her body set forward.

When Doug began another dance, she pointed harder. "Ladies and gentlemen," she insisted, "calmly please. We need to go."

Richard responded first. "Come on you lot," he said, looking upwards.

"Now," said Vanessa.

"At the double," said Ruth gripping Doug's arm, who repeated the phrase as a question. When Ruth pointed uphill, he squared his shoulders and led off smartly, climbing through the trees.

The path back was steep and they moved in a line, throwing out comments and laughing wildly. At each turn in the path they grabbed the railing and tackled the reverse slope. As they neared the top Ruth stretched up, one-finger-shushing, cautioning them to silence. Suddenly they were children with a secret between them.

On the upper level they looked about. The air was still, the paths were clear and the flower heads were motionless. They set off and explored, circling around borders and passing through a wall. In this part of the gardens they were alone. Moving slowly and taking observations, they walked past flowering bulbs mixed in with brilliant white cherries. Here Ruth came across a plant bearing her name. "Oh look, *Magnolia Ruth*," she exclaimed, showing Vanessa the label. "You're so beautiful," she added, pressing her face into a wide-open flower. At her insistence, Vanessa took a series of shots of Ruth touching the petals and embracing Doug. "I'm in a purple love haze," she said afterwards, picking up a flower from the ground. It was pink-purple and everted. "Oh yes, I could eat you," she added and clamped it between her teeth. With that, she knelt by the tree, posing for one last photo. Seeing her looking up, Richard was reminded of a saint in a picture. At the back of his mind, as if he'd skipped an era, he heard his cousin breaking into song on the beach. The words were about kissing the sky.

They left by a doorway in brick. Passing through a kitchen garden and a shrubbery, they made their way to the house, where they entered a conservatory through a half-glassed door. Inside, the air felt thick. A fine layer of mist had collected on the windows and the pipes. A tap in the corner was dripping onto tiles.

"It's like stepping into a sauna," said Doug, squaring his shoulders.

An attendant stood close by. She was half-concealed behind a large pot containing a butterfly palm. Beyond her was a glass and metal gallery with climbers on one side and a café at the end.

After agreeing they were hot, they asked the attendant about serving drinks and walked the full length to pull up chairs around a metal table. Richard took orders and set off to collect. During his absence the others gazed about. The corner they had occupied was tall and bare and painted white. Green around the edges, it was damp and echoed like a warehouse.

They were linked now by the occasional word with a grin and a hand-rocking gesture. After bringing the coffees, Richard made an effort to switch to plant talk, but when Ruth mentioned flying and

Vanessa began to splutter, the laughter took over, coming in waves. Small waves at first, then overlapping, ending in hand-gripping snorts as they rose and straightened and gazed out to the terrace, spluttering.

"Silly," said Richard, keeping it low.

"Bloody silly," whispered Ruth.

"Bloody, bloody silly."

"Silly, silly, silly."

"Bloody, bloody, bloody—"

They continued pacing, repeating in chorus. Behind them Vanessa and Doug had dropped out. They were in the audience, playing statues.

Seeing the attendant advancing from the doorway, Ruth pulled back. "I think," she said, steadying herself, "we may need to go."

Richard laughed. "And when you gotta—"

"Shhh," warned Vanessa, following Ruth's gaze.

"Careful," added Doug.

The attendant stepped around and back, staring at a point just to one side. She was tall and severe, wearing tweeds and a hat. Her movements were bird-like and edgy. When she'd finished her beat, returning to the doorway, Richard broke the silence. "Right," he said, "we'd best leave."

Ruth smiled thinly. "Pretend we weren't here?"

"Whatever it takes."

He began to walk and the other three joined him, moving back along the gallery. They advanced without looking left or right, ducking out through the garden door.

As they emerged a bell rang and a voice called out, echoing slightly.

"I think it's closing," said Vanessa, looking up at the sky. Beside her Richard drew one hand across his brow. Ruth and Doug brought up the rear, arms linked together.

They advanced silently along the terrace. The sun was low, striking their faces and the air was still. In the square to one side the shadows were lengthening; on the other side, the walls of the house were bathed in brightness. In front were steps down to the path beside the lawn.

The bell rang once, twice, and the voice called again.

"Time," said Ruth.

They descended the steps and crunched across gravel. When they reached the main drive, the light had weakened and a breeze was moving gently, shifting over grass. The bell rang again, followed by the voice – a single syllable. On the banks both sides, the flowers were closing.

As they passed out through the lodge Richard took Vanessa by the hand. "The voice in the garden," he said quietly.

Smiling gently and feeling connected, she walked back along the drive with the last rays of the sun in her eyes. They were hand in hand and together.

♱ ♱ ♱

The trip to *Manor Gardens* became one of their stories. As inner-city teachers they needed an escape. Told in company, it acted as a lift, cancelling out the dull days in the classroom and the late-night preparation. It stood for how they'd been.

"People say we must've been crazy," said Richard one evening, while marking.

"Yes?" replied Vanessa.

"Well, we were a bit, sometimes, weren't we?"

"I suppose."

"Sounds like you don't agree."

"Oh yes, we were. It's just ..."

"Just, what?"

"It's nothing, not much. Things change."

"You think it's different, now."

Vanessa stiffened.

"But it's still a good story."

"Yes, a story's useful, it gets you through."

"That's how you see it?"

"What else?" she put down her pen. "Look, Richard, all we do is talk about what people *said* and *did* and what *happened*. It's all about the past. You'd think we were pensioners." She closed her books, sighing. "Mind, I suppose we need to talk about something. Tell stories, if you like. They're a way of saying no."

Richard understood. She meant no to what was happening. It was better than going under. Because school, for the first few terms, had hijacked everything. They'd worked and they'd delivered as if nothing else mattered. It filled up their lives with lesson plans and long lists of equipment – what he sometimes called *fiddle* but at other times *crap* – while remembering as he said it, their battle in the restaurant and how she'd walked away. School, full-time, main-scale, had completely taken over.

On teaching days they'd a pattern, a way of getting through.

"*We don't need no education,*" he'd hum, as he rose in darkness, washing and dressing long before school time.

"Starting's always hard," mused Vanessa over breakfast, and again on the journey.

"Think free periods," he told her at the gate.

"Not sure I'm up to it," she said quietly, as she rested over lunch.

"One lesson to go," was his mantra, called across the staffroom during afternoon break.

Because his job was to lead. If a lesson went badly, he picked it over afterwards, reckoned pros and cons then stayed up late to work on improvements. If Vanessa had problems he acted as advisor, and when management observed them, he made the running, speaking of dynamics, of what made for interest and how kids learned.

Also, there were stories: joke scenes from classrooms, blunders, confusions and off-the-wall incidents that outdid *Manor Gardens*. It seemed that teaching was full of them. Lines said by kids, failures of equipment, parental interference, senior-staff cockups and a whole raft of anecdotes, apocryphal mainly, about life-and-death experiences and nightmare classrooms where kids ran riot and teachers practised moves in unarmed combat.

But when it came to stories, one, a dream, returned so often that it displaced all others, taking on a quality of quiet actuality. And although Richard tried ignoring, or riding it sometimes, he couldn't shake it off. Its persistence and mimetic detail made it seem, like a story heard in childhood, both all-too-familiar and *arrived* from a world where things just happened, at random, without apparent reason.

The dream usually began with kids in the classroom, third-form, oversized, pushing to the front. All on their feet, pulling faces. Bunchy and punchy, arguing behind glass. With a group at the back throwing paper darts and climbing on chairs. But it also included views from the corridor, footage of football matches and blue tits pecking fat, quick snaps of wrestlers and puppets dancing. Largely silent, the dream continued with a time jump to the stockroom where Richard saw himself double-checking shelves. He was looking for a collection of red-spined paperbacks, an examination set. Fumbling at first, with a panicky awareness of the wall clock above, but also secretly relieved to find an excuse. Slowing gradually, peering under desks and deep into cupboards, but now as a diversion, killing time. Keeping himself occupied, tidying and arranging and looking into space. Finally, with ten minutes left, leaving the stockroom and pacing the corridor, before returning for the register. A delay here too, hunting around. Then out past classrooms, arriving at the doorway. Pip pip pip pip. Saved by the tannoy, surrounded by bodies …

> In the really-real world he managed. He negotiated challenges, set deadlines and batted back their comments.
> "You do this," he said, keeping it simple.
> "I'll have a page," he told them, when they wanted targets.
> "Here's a start," he added, pointing to a sentence written on the board.

But the dream was different. Full of muddle and mishap it went its own way, with false trails and sequels and a series of sketches, set in classrooms, where kids took over and teachers lost their bearings.

In the first, the Sunday-evening-one, he was standing looking out at a dead-silent classroom and his mind had gone blank. He was gaping, fish-like, at puzzled eyes and faces. The audience were fidgety and were beginning to gear up. A group at the back were exchanging whispers, preparing to call out. He was humming and hawing, gazing around the room; the joke was on him. Searching for papers, he tried to head them off, but their comments turned nasty. Still his voice was silent as the class began to heckle. Shouting now, they were challenging him to a fight. His teacher-self was about to do something violent when quite without warning the storyline changed ...

And between each dream, sandwiched like an ad break,
the do-words and imperatives:
"That's enough!" called without warning.
"Volume down!" sung, with authority.
"Try this," quietly, smiling.

The second situation was the *perfect classroom*. In this, punishment was electric with students strapped down to wired-up chairs and the teacher at the front, with one finger raised, firing questions. The finger was the threat: poised over buttons it administered a jab, sometimes repeated, resulting in shocks at various levels. A moment's inattention could earn a tickle or a prod, an answer off the point might lead to a jolt, while rudeness or rebellion was several-times-blasted, leaving pupil and desk charred and incinerated ...

"Good," with dignity.
"Well done," with feeling.
"Your best yet," enthusing.

Then there were the dreams that cut back and forth, or switched between endings. In one – or one version – he wiped out the class, in another he issued orders that they jumped to, smiling. In some he bargained, exchanging work for no more shocks. In a few he ignored them. And in one, the most common, the class became hardened, laughing wildly and sparking and buzzing till their skins shone like angels. (And in that one became addicts, insisting on shocks with ever-greater voltage.)

The other dreams were vaguer. Set after school they were odd or quirky, moving at whim through zoo scenes and boxed-in episodes with attackers jumping out and well-known troublemakers confined behind bars. These too varied, including runaway moments, dives into caves and footslogs through jungle, all of them desperate, but also inconsequential.

So he dreamed, or he dreamed he dreamed, because after the beginning – the start of term, when the thoughts took over, and each successive term, each more pressing – he found himself surprised by the hollowness inside. Because, with time ticking down and things still to do, he'd realised that teaching and its dreams was a world in a box. An all-out, tasked-up dance without meaning. A battle to make out, to keep himself alive and not go under. And it led him and forced him and kept him chivvied up.

For Vanessa, school left her frazzled. Outwardly calm, still talking pedagogy and the university of life, she coped, but inwardly she distanced. At school she marked time, made do, and denied all problems. When the kids played up, as they did most lessons, she looked straight through them and carried on regardless. While she talked and appealed, they pushed harder. And as the noise level rose, she dished out worksheets, wrote up instructions and tutored the front row. "Working independently" she called it when they played cards at the back, then told on the boys when they spent the whole lesson doodling, chewing down rulers and dismantling pens.

But the act of reporting simply made them worse. Next lesson they sulked, and threatened to shop her to their mates.

"You know how to behave," she replied, when they claimed she'd got it wrong.

"It's up to you," she countered, when they contested what she'd said. "You can discipline yourselves."

"Because I know," she went on, ignoring their objections, "you can behave like adults."

But her words didn't wash. The more she appealed the more they obstructed. When she asked them questions they slouched in a corner, complaining she didn't help; whatever tasks she set, the work was too easy. In any case school was pointless, it didn't lead any-where – and as nobody paid them, why bother?

Then there were the girls. For them, it wasn't worth the effort. School, they announced, between glancing at mirrors and leafing magazines, was a bore. There were teachers not listening, boys being stupid, and a problem with Vanessa who spoke too much like a lady, complained about manners and wore the wrong clothes. They didn't like her voice, thought her fussy, rated her low on strictness, fairness, experience and how she did her hair.

And for Vanessa, marking late at night or searching early morning for material to please them, it felt so unequal, so much a matter of us against them – which didn't seem right. Because she'd only ever wanted to give what they needed: a hand up, an opening, a broader understanding.

"Does it ever get easier?" she asked at dinner parties attended by colleagues who'd all been through it. Her guests – hand-picked individuals, super-teacher types who really knew their stuff – were usually forthcoming. They drew a line at this, said it and meant it, took no prisoners. Survival, they said, was what mattered.

"The thing to do," said Frank Watts, their senior staff friend, "is keep 'em guessing."

Slim and dynamic, Frank was what Vanessa called "very Robert Redford". He spoke with finality, pausing for effect and emphasising his thoughts with a stagey grin.

"Because if they're kept in the dark," he added, sipping his wine, "they stay frightened."

"You really think so?" asked Vanessa, maintaining her gaze.

Frank confirmed. Beside him, his wife Jackie nodded her agreement. Tall and gaunt, she sat hunched forward, inclining her head to get a better look. Side to side and umpire-like, she followed what was said. Next to her, Vanessa's friend Bess was perched on the sofa arm, watching. She was there as backup.

Smiling, Vanessa pointed to their glasses, suggesting top-ups. "Isn't what you're describing all rather mediaeval?" she asked as she poured the wine. "After all, why not parade them in the town square, or put the leaders in the stocks and pelt them with rubbish?"

"But it works. Scares 'em rigid," Frank said. Pursing his lips, he quickly looked away. It seemed he'd said his piece.

They were talking after dinner, grouped around a low table. with music in the background. It was late, the night air was hot and the sky was lake-like and still. Through the open window a grey-white moon was clearly visible.

Richard called through from the kitchen, he'd nearly finished.

Vanessa called back that she'd do the rest. "Just soak the pans," she added, airily, lighting a circle of candles. When Frank cracked a joke, she threw out an anecdote, a bike shed story leading to thoughts taken from her essays about learning from experience and the hidden curriculum.

"The big lesson is who's in charge," said Bess. "We learn that by example."

Jackie took her turn, speaking about her time in secondary and the relief she'd experienced, moving to college. "More civilised," she said wryly, fingering her drink. Her face by candlelight looked care-worn and painterly.

While she was talking, a stretched-out Frank murmured his agreement. He was informal tonight, in jeans and T-shirt with his hair slicked back and a look-at-me expression. As Jackie finished off he leaned forward, wiping one hand across his face and offering support.

Richard entered, announcing he'd finished. After topping up glasses, he took up position squatted on the carpet.

Vanessa addressed Frank, asking a supplementary about controlling kids.

"You want the formula?"

"Tell us."

"Start off tough," he said with a foxy grin, "get tougher."

"Really?"

"It's who's on top, you or them."

"But isn't that bullying?"

He paused, looking down into his glass. It was as if it was a pool, and somewhere at the bottom he'd find an answer. "Well, you know me …" He smiled, fixing his eyes on a flickering candle, "Insecure … need to impress."

Bess laughed. "You're saying it's an act?"

Frank confirmed, backed by Jackie.

"But, Frank, isn't that difficult?" asked Vanessa, frowning.

"Why?"

"To keep it up – isn't it hard work? Don't you wish sometimes you could just be yourself, let down the barriers and *talk* to the kids? Isn't your method all rather stressful?"

"Once you get used, it's fine. Pure practice, and body language."

"Sounds awfully strenuous to me."

He shrugged, looking off.

They returned to drinking and exchanging stories. Frank told one about his old school. It involved words like "taming" and "training", was quietly spoken with pauses for effect, and invited his audience to laugh more at the teller than what he had to say. During the story he finger-wiped his face, sometimes backwards, sometimes forward, and often all over, kneading into flesh. Prompted by Vanessa, he talked about the acts he used. These included *The Bastard*, who spoke low with menace and said things only once, *The Revenger* and *The Grudge Pursuer*, both relentless, keeping notes of everything, and *The Madcap Clobberer*, who struck when least expected, joked as he punished and behaved as if possessed.

"So actually," said Vanessa, widening her eyes, "behind it all you're afraid – same as us?"

"Yup, terrified they'll see through me."

"True," said Jackie wryly.

"And I thought it was just me," Vanessa said, holding her drink out towards a candle.

Richard knelt forward. At the top, her glass glowed blue-yellow. He noticed, lower, a faint spread of orange, and where her fingers held the stem, a near-white axis. "The harder they come," he said, registering the song playing.

Frank smiled. "Now that's what they call real fighting—"

Vanessa shook her head. "Only if you're macho and think it's about what you're *against*. A man is a man, and all that ... There are other ways."

"But do they always work?"

"They can do," put in Bess, quietly. "I use rewards in the class-room. Lots of them. The results are bril, particularly with boys."

"Yes, positive reinforcement ..." said Vanessa. "Not just the praise-blame sandwich but policy, over a long time."

Frank grinned. "You mean if we had a be-nice-to-the-kids week?"

Jackie shuddered. "God forbid."

"You wouldn't fancy that?" said Richard.

"Too many yucks. I'd rather not think about it."

Richard turned his gaze on Frank. "What's the secret, boss? What goes through your head when you're hammering kids?"

"Not much, if I can help it."

"But behind that, what're you thinking about?"

"Misspent youth, and my father."

The room went quiet. Richard reached out, replenishing his glass. The song's last notes issued from the speaker.

"It's about what you can get away with," Frank added. He reached forward, cupping his palm and bringing it down slowly on one of the candles. Hissing quietly, the flame spluttered out. He removed his hand and a wisp-line of smoke curled towards the window. Outside, a plane passed over droning quietly. Its navigation lights moved across the sky, winking on and off.

"The trick is," said Frank quietly, "to keep 'em looking the other way." He reached again, facing his hosts and grinning as he passed his hand through yellow spurts of flame. "Of course, it'll get to you," he said, slowing one finger till the flame licked the skin. "But that's nothing, an illusion."

A faint sweet smell drifted around the room. Frank smiled, un-flinching; his flesh had darkened. "And however much it hurts," he added, withdrawing his finger and smiling even harder, "make 'em think you enjoy it."

The evening with Frank and Jackie was, as it turned out, both an end and a beginning. From that point on the first shock of teaching, with its panics and exhaustions and its all-out demands, began to ease. They'd learned how to handle it, to think on their feet, give orders and build a reputation. Known by name, with a year group to tutor, they were listed by department and appeared in the bulletins as established staff. Their presence was accepted. And with experience, they knew what to watch for, how to dodge, how to deliver and gap-fill as necessary. They were in the clear, judging and presenting as qualified teachers, looking back where they'd come from, looking around, sometimes for worksheets and equipment, and forward to the holidays. And as they moved into the break, they saw how they'd changed.

They developed their downtime, so that they were on the A list for contact, pop-ins and late-night entertainment. And being always busy, although it raised the tempo and left them feeling breathless, blocked out the day job. To work exhausted overrode their feelings, especially for Richard who found he'd lost his bearings. He'd gone in committed, and now he needed a true sense of purpose, a long-term view.

He'd no words for it. Whatever it was he'd sensed it all his life. A feeling that behind the actual, tricked in and hidden, concealed within the flow, was a pattern and a code, a hang-thread of meaning. It was something understood. A signature and a pointer felt within life, a shadow line of being.

In the past he'd tried to block it out, telling his teenage self that it only ever happened when he went *looking* – usually on walks where he made himself feel it – so that the uplift he wanted only ever touched him because he'd made it so ...

"Breathe deep," he told himself, walking.

"Too much chatter," he repeated, standing.

"Just be *quiet*," he hissed, choosing to move on.

In fact, his walkouts were not that remarkable. The paths were quite narrow, fenced and overgrown, sandwiched between opencast and newly-built estates. And where he struck through fields or climbed through trees there was still the sound of cars and shouts from pitches. And even on the walks when he moved beyond habitation, there was a suspicion that he pumped himself up, his vision was contrived and that the transport he experienced was of his own making.

In any case, he'd things to control. A number of obsessions, and aspects of self he'd tried to hide away.

The Odd Bod was there, putting on different voices. Odd Bod and friends, the cartoon menagerie, he knew them well. He'd a whole crew of commentators, whispering leery comments and cutting in often to rerun his worst moments and point out where he'd failed. One day it was The Moaner, another The Jostler, then came The Haggler; Babel-like, his head was full of them.

"Oh no oh no no no no no," he heard (or imagined).

"Ugg-ugg-ugg-ugg-ugg," his inner voice stuttered.

"Da da da da da da," echoed in his head.

Later, in the sixth form, he'd found it again, this time in his jottings, his song lines and wordplays and automatic writings. He wrote them down on envelopes and loose bits of paper that he added to the reminders stuffed into his pocket. When his notes built up, he transferred them to a bag, then archived to a drawer where they lay piled up like unread letters. Occasionally he sorted, chucking some, wincing over others and attempting rewrites where a line or expression sounded promising. But somehow that was all. Once he'd turned a phrase or juggled with a sentence, he couldn't see beyond it, a block set in and however hard he tried the words remained shy. The whole thing was diversionary. It was as if he'd run himself out, had reached the home straight and anything further was more than he could do.

So, when teaching started, he forgot about the words and worked in the present. And for a while his life was taken up with marking, instructing, looking around for extracts and rehearsing lessons. He'd no time for thoughts about life-choices or truths about self and what really mattered.

And he managed, or put aside his feelings. He kept himself busy and very much aware – balanced and directed, always on the case. He'd always had presence, and now he'd added know-how and what passed for judgement. He called it *doing Frank*.

In private with Vanessa he called it *reckoning* and in public *presenting*. Sometimes playing host, he called it *juggling*, as he settled down guests and traded stories. Out drinking he was floorshow; late night, talking, he was up for it; and when it came to dinner parties or drop-ins he was on the case.

In fact, he made it happen – words he repeated, internally, when hosting Vanessa's birthday with guests arriving bearing gifts. Inviting them to sit, he led off. "Eyes closed everyone!" he called from the kitchen, bringing out a shop-bought cake, topped by candles.

He placed it in the centre of the fold-out table. Looking around the living room he counted faces: seven in all, arranged on four sides, bench-like as if they were in session. Jackie sat at the head. One side was occupied by Ruth, then Frank, then his own empty chair. At the other end Vanessa had the window seat. The fourth side was occupied by Doug and two friends of Vanessa's: Lorna Bell, a smooth-faced narrow-lipped beauty, and Gabby Joseph, a short, round-faced woman with wide cheeks and dark, expressive eyes.

With their tightly closed eyes and candle-lit faces they looked for a moment like a group-shot from a film. "Open sesame!" he cried, taking his seat.

"Oh, look!" said Ruth. The cake was white and brown, ribbon-wrapped and studded with Smarties. The candles lit the room.

The other guests opened their eyes and there were laughs and gasps and expressions of surprise. Vanessa was tearful and thanked Richard, squeezing his hand. "You did this for me?" she said quietly, and he nodded.

Richard led the singing and the call for blowing out then orchestrated the applause that followed. He also produced the knife, presented the cake and helped Vanessa to pass around slices.

"Did you make this?" asked Ruth, as she picked off bits of chocolate.

Richard grinned. "Don't ask."

They ate, chatting and comparing. The room was busy and warm and full of shifting voices. There were people calling out and chairs drawn together with glasses raised. As the evening progressed subgroups formed, telling animated stories and debating issues. Occasionally everyone stopped talking as if it was a theatre, and someone took the floor.

At one point, Vanessa produced her camera and held up her hand for silence. "I must have pics of you all," she said, "but natural, just as you are. No group shots or posed photos. So, pretend I'm not here and chatter away," – then she waited her chance and snapped them discretely as they talked.

Richard found himself sparring at first with Frank and others, then acting as link-man, passing on messages, dotting here and there. Later in the evening he played the role of interviewer, probing for their views. Still later he picked up on threads and summarised back. In the end he returned to sparring, putting down markers with a narrow-eyed Frank, fishing for *inside* on policy and plans.

"Sworn to secrecy," the other replied.

"And when you're Head ..."

"He'll sack the lot of you," Jackie put in, expressionless.

The two men engaged in banter about hard-man tactics and taming classes. When they moved on to politics Richard leaned towards Lorna, asking for her views. "We need a different agenda," she said, flicking back her lightly-frizzed hair. It was hazelnut brown and fell to her shoulders.

"Different – how?"

Lorna glanced towards Vanessa, who was listening in. "Women in the lead, supported by men."

"Fat chance," Gabby snorted.

"You never know," said Frank, "it could be popular."

"I'd like it," Vanessa said brightly. "We could be the trainers. Operant conditioning, the Skinner approach."

"You like rats in cages?" Richard countered.

Gabby cut in. "I object," she declared, "rats are super-intelligent animals. It's the experimenters who should be caged."

"And throw away the key," added Frank, grinning.

"I'm serious. How would you like it, being locked up and given shocks?"

"Sounds like my childhood," he replied, wiping one hand across his face.

"I heard," interposed Richard, "that rats are cleaner than humans."

"That's a fact," said Gabby.

"And so much more cuddly," added Frank.

"Unlike men."

"That's true," echoed Vanessa.

"Indeed," put in Jackie.

"Exactly," said Lorna.

"Absolutely," concluded Gabby.

Next morning Richard called in sick. As he told himself quietly before Vanessa left, he really wasn't well. Whatever it was – something he'd eaten, a bug, or simply lack of sleep – the effects were unpleasant. His answerphone message, giving name and timetable and describing the work, was carefully worded. Though precise it came out, even to him, as hollow-voiced and strained. What he didn't give was background or any kind of reason, mainly because if he said "migraine" it might invite suspicion, and in any case what he was experiencing went deeper than that.

Five hours earlier at the end of the party, he'd been on a high. After seeing people off and pinching out candles, he'd drifted bedwards. Undressing slowly, he'd slipped beneath the sheets, where he lay thinking back. Hearing Vanessa washing in the bathroom he'd rerun the evening, matching words with faces. When she'd flicked out the light and joined him, he'd squeezed her hand lightly, returning to his thoughts. The dark was his screen: it brought things closer.

As her breathing slowed, he'd pictured her surprise. The evening had gone well. In the dark he shifted on his side, matching her breathing. Despite his thick head and the blur around the edges, he saw it all happening; he was awake and in the picture.

The clock tick, magnified, seemed to fill the room. Voices and footsteps echoed on pavement. Somewhere in the distance a siren circled.

Knowing it was late made him restless; he'd only a few hours. Although it was dark, a brightness held him, a backlit feeling, as if the room's outline was a curtain, a veil across the actual, soon to be lifted. He could sense already the bodies moving, could feel in himself the start of something stirring, the shift between modes. Soon they'd be yawning and collecting their things – then last words in hallways and doors clicking shut.

For what felt like hours he moved positions, trying different angles. He felt there was a grip, a pressure-lock and tightness building in his head. For a while he lay still, hoping it would pass, but the ache had its way. The more he resisted, the stronger it became. Head pains like this, he remembered from childhood, came on without warning and could remain for days.

Rising, he slipped out into dark. In the hall he was cornered. Mixed in with the outlines was an unseen brightness, what he called the migraine flare.

For a while he sat then stood up again. He visited the kitchen, boiled up a kettle and sipped at coffee, returning after dawn to lie beside Vanessa.

When she woke, he smiled, touching her lightly and limiting his expression. He wondered about school, gauging his own fitness, then told her that he wasn't that good.

"You feeling ill?"

"Pretty yuck."

"Hangover?"

"No, not that. Just not good."

Vanessa sat up, switching on the side lamp and examining him.

"Really. I'm not ..."

She raised one eyebrow.

"I'm poorly."

She asked about symptoms and he repeated.

"Oh dear, are you staying at home?"

He nodded.

"I'll get ready then," she said, "hope you get better."

Feeling awkward he nodded again.

"You'll manage?" she called when she was ready, standing by the bed. "I mean by yourself?"

Richard sat up. "I'll be fine," he said, waving her off. She asked again and he sighed. "Poorly," he added, sliding down.

He repeated his watchword, once as she left, twice on paper then often, during the day, as he lay on the sofa imagining what people would say. He could see himself in the staffroom answering carefully, alert to what they said. It seemed he'd become subject, stepped back from the classroom and taken himself out of it.

That day made it clear. While he picked at biscuits or lay on the bed listening to the radio, he imagined Vanessa's chalk-face efforts, and how she might feel. He came to see himself as a stranger or oddball who didn't quite fit. Of course, he *could* have taught but had chosen to dodge, and in faking or simply ducking out he'd entered a shadowland feeling; he'd touched on meaning.

When Vanessa returned, late and tired, pushing through the door with a bag full of books, he'd asked about her day. Had anything happened? Not much, she said, mentioning an incident, an event, and naming children. She added that people had wished him well.

In reply he'd thanked her. They'd not discussed feelings or gone below the surface.

During their meal, which consisted of leftovers, they'd talked about housekeeping. Later it was next day's school and whether he'd get there. Then, after clearing and watching television, she'd suggested, yawning, that they moved off to bed.

Whatever had touched him had pulled back for a while.

It was much later, when Richard found himself lying awake, that he saw, or glimpsed, his life in replay. He was in there, in his thoughts, as a shadow on the wall. Marking up the images, he saw them as they were. They were moments from the past, items in the flow. Counting, he recalled them: Frank's finger in flame, nights by the window with plane lights and stars, then car drives and talk and the accident in the garden. One by one, he saw them all: train sets, covers and pictures on the stairs, Ruth at the party, then bookshops, stations, markets, and – filling up the darkness – his search for Vanessa, the handbag, the river-bridge and the slow-moving train.

It had all passed over. He'd been there and done what he had to, made things happen. Now nothing seemed to matter. The part he'd played had gone.

Richard felt sad.

*‡ ‡ ‡*

In her dream Mia began her walk for the planet. Her feet ached and her heart was heavy. It was a long trek past sodden fields and abandoned buildings. The footpath was overgrown.

Beside the path she could see dog's mercury, rest harrow and woody nightshade. Seeing pineapple weed among them, she crouched down to smell it. She walked on past broken fences and muddy pools. Thistles and nettles sprouted where crops had grown. No birds sang. The bushes to one side were blighted, as if they'd been burned.

She heard people talking as she went.

The Earth is sad.

Tread lightly, lightly.

There are no accidents. Everything is connected.

Give thanks for life.

Stop, look, listen.

We have this one home.

Our mother is dying.

On all sides there were things missing. The creatures large and small were in hiding. The bees weren't busy, the birds and insects were silent.

As Mia walked, she began to recognise where she was. The track she was following led to the sea. There were echoes of *Kubla Khan* in the voices she could hear. As she descended, the stream she followed was in spate. At the bottom of a waterfall she came across a dead sheep. The trees by the path had been flattened.

When she reached the beach, she took off everything. Barefoot on sand, she felt the wind in her face. There were ghosts all around, walking beside her. Everywhere was unreal. There were storm clouds out to sea and slime underfoot.

"We've brought this on ourselves," she told herself.

She was crying.

# TWENTY

## Families, Imaginary Histories and the Silence of Gossip by Professor M Lavender (Cont.)

I'd like to say few words at this point about method.

We began with a non-linear approach, convinced that innovative research needs to challenge what Foucault calls the episteme of an era. The families we interviewed were too complex to be summed up by a spreadsheet or plotted on a graph, so we went for insight rather than stats. Accountancy is, in the words of Blake, "a rich, ugly old maid courted by incapacity".

Our in-depth interviews showed that families, like butterflies, are both fragile and amazingly resilient. To observe their dynamic transformations, to hold a single specimen, even fleetingly, in the palm of one's hand, requires a novelist's skill. And any attempt to foreground one characteristic necessarily backgrounds another. So, we focused on the development of families step by step, beginning with initial contact between partners, where we found that:

- There was a high-risk, lucky dip quality in most first encounters.
- During the romance phase, sub-vocalised expressions such as "dream girl" (or "dream boy"), "the one" and "the look" were effective triggers for trance and involvement.

305

- In other cases, couples came together as part of a slow process of habituation, remaining semi-detached even after years of cohabitation.
- Quite often in the romance period there were warning signs pointing towards later conflict.
- A method some couples used to deal with these signs was The Nelson approach, "I see no ships".
- A true picture of a couple's past, shared between them, was a strong predictor of a sustained relationship.

It was in the later stages of relationships that the stories diverged. We identified two main strands of involvement, one conflicted, the other less so. We classified them as *the pressure cooker* type and *the bubble*.

In *the pressure cooker* type:

1. Couples had a constant need for strenuous activity on a par with athletes or soldiers in training. They played the roles of hunter and hunted or adult and child, frequently switching places. We called this tendency "churning".
2. Some couples developed tight, exacting routines and rigid timings. These acted as defensive walls, marking out private patches and heading off disputes.
3. Other couples played the game of insecure parent. For them, being in company was an opportunity to co-opt others into corrective remarks directed towards the partner.
4. There was widespread use of blocking tactics such as pretending not to hear or feigning illness.
5. Silence was used as a weapon in some *pressure cooker* marriages.

*Au contraire*, the pattern in *the bubble* was to:
1. Spend quality time together.
2. Maintain physical contact.
3. Declare affection openly.
4. Publicly approve of the partner.
5. Share positive memories of the first meeting and early romance.
6. Regularly celebrate the relationship in many ways, both small and large.
7. Make frequent use of the L word.

To sum up, we found that beginnings are often significantly charged in a relationship and that initial greetings and gestures can signpost what follows. Rather like stones dropped in a pond, they can resonate for years afterwards. In problematic relationships the waves generated frequently overlap or clash, while in more settled relationships their successive movements are best described by Basho's famous haiku:

"Disturbing the waters of an ancient pond,
a frog jumped in water
– a deep resonance".

We also conducted pair-bonding awareness studies, asking respondents to describe how and when they changed from partners to couples or families. The majority of our interviewees selected two events – moving in together and visiting parents. We did find that the underlying significance of both was routinely concealed behind rationalisations, so the first was often described as an economy of scale while the second fell into the duty/etiquette category. But when probed, we found there were deep and complex psycho-politics behind both labels.

Finally, we explored Altman and Taylor's disclosure theory, looking at the onion metaphor for personality and whether the "stripping off" process proceeded most rapidly at the start of a relationship. It appeared that shared confidences did indeed build a joint identity, so that couples saw themselves as a unique single person. In the words of The Beatles "I am he as you are he as you are me / And we are all together". Or, as one interviewee put it, "we soon began carrying on like Tweedledum and Tweedledee". Later in relationships we found an equal and opposite force came into play, driving couples apart or turning a marriage into an *égoisme à deux*. This became most marked in a few open relationships, although these situations were hard to encapsulate within a single theoretic framework. Like systems involving $H_2O$ at different temperatures, their sudden unexpected twists and turns made them episodic and unpredictable. In the realms of affection, these families were apparently capable of all three independent states of being – solid, liquid and gaseous. And as in quantum physics, it was only possible to measure their current state or their dynamic development, not both at once. So, we used an adaptive, complex, non-linear methodology in order to take account of the multifaceted nature of many modern families.

We now, I'm told, have a pause for refreshments and book signing. In the second half I will return to the role of imagination in shaping family histories. Before that, as a taster, I'd like to send you off with a short, illustrative story. Near the end, it touches on Alice Rossi's seminal work on expressiveness and instrumentality in families.

## MARRIAGE À LA MODE

A young man and a woman begin, soon after meeting, with a week-long domestic celebration of their newly-discovered love. Let's call them Jack and Jill. They eat, sleep, insult each other, engage in play fights and make love, repeatedly. Afterwards they tell stories and read books together. In one of the books they come across an eponymous couple who are married with jobs and children, living at the top of a hill. Jill and

Jack Mark Two are both writing post-modern fictions about the breakdown of modern marriage. When Jill(2) shares drafts of what she calls her anti-love story with friends, they ask her, tongue-in-cheek, about the autobiographical content. Jill, of course, replies that she's writing a morally-relative, intertextual meta-narrative. Jack(2), on the contrary, keeps his novel close to his chest. He's only finished two pages that he keeps redrafting, longhand, daily.

After much argument, Jill and Jack start a readers' and writers' circle, managing to engage other, similarly challenged, couples who swop stories and laugh over their own peccadillos. But one day total writer's block hits both of them. They struggle with their condition for weeks, avoiding each other, with Jill sitting in her room, listening to sad music, watching TV and sipping wine, while Jack throws himself into obsessive DIY activity, fixing up the house for sale.

And the outcome of the story? Both couples and the reading group all split up ...

*† † †*

When she first heard Richard say it, Vanessa wasn't pleased.

Enough. ENOUGH, with emphasis, then muttered as an aside, or *Enough is enough*. The phrase or word pronounced as given, then repeated with edge. A word of dismissal, a quick word with a frown, a no-reply statement with force and teacher-like assurance.

Enough, or too much.

Because when he'd first said it, huffing and puffing as he decorated the lounge, she'd repeated to Ruth, telling her with a grin and a throwaway gesture, and echoing how he'd spoken. For him it was definite, he'd got that straight.

He'd used it on the children turning their marriage, until then an up and down business, into something close to war. A small war in bits, struggling not to say things, shifting into blow-ups with shouts and silences and claims of obstruction. He'd implied it daily in how he took offence, making out she'd said things or alleging intention – and he'd kept it in reserve, hidden behind jargon, when they took things to counsellors, speaking about listening and investing time.

He'd said it that morning when he came down hard on Charlotte and Stephan, who were arguing. He'd said the same thing when asked at the table to exercise patience, repeating it at the door. It was, after all, as she'd reminded him, *her* turn with the children and *his* to go to work.

During the day she'd ticked off past mentions. The second on a seaside outing, the third after school, several in the car, others at random and various interruptions cutting through her thoughts, either bossing children or shouting downstairs while she chatted on the phone.

"Richard's got problems," was what she gave out, at least to those politicos, women like Lorna who wanted explanation.

"He has this agenda," she said, speaking slowly, when visiting friends.

"It's textbook really, the XY factor," she added.

And part of her held it as established, a fact of life. He needed control. Ever since marriage he'd adopted *positions*, theories about work and the treatment of children that she needed to counter – though she also recognised the pleasures of obstruction.

Of course, she understood the patterns, the line they had to take. And Richard wasn't that easy or relaxed, or at all like other people thought. He'd his own fads, his ways of fitting everything; whatever was the latest, well, that was it. And when he'd pronounced or named or fitted, then suddenly without warning he lost all interest.

So, she was ready when she returned to the house. The children led in, occupying the lounge and switching channels as they squatted on the carpet. For a while she watched, feeling safe, surrounded by her brood. She appealed about volume, then idled on the sofa listening vaguely before retreating to the kitchen. On reaching the door, she looked down the room.

She knew he'd be sitting in the garden with a drink, marking. By now he'd be on concrete, moving with the sun. Perhaps he'd be relaxed, maybe even Friday-ish, but also he'd have *thoughts*. About supper for a start, but mainly about the children, with his own expected timings, his whims and theories: a point-by-point, one-way, laid-out plan. And because she knew him well, she made herself busy and brewed up a pot, greeting as normal when he entered.

"You're home then?" he said quietly, glancing about the kitchen.

Vanessa confirmed.

"How've they been?"

She answered off the point and offered tea.

"Uh-huh," he continued, expressionless.

While pouring, she talked – vaguely, filling in time. Every so often the dark brown pot in her hand had to be shaken.

"Don't mind," he replied when she asked about milk. "Same old, same old," he said when school came up. "Done for today," he added, pointing down the garden.

Following his gaze, Vanessa gave a nod. Outside and at a distance the air had thickened; close-to, there were patches of grey and green, shading into blue. Crosshatched shadows had spread across the lawn.

Richard drained his cup and asked about her day.

"Not much to report."

When asked again she topped up his tea and went through in detail, missing out Ruth. She'd delivered the children, mailed out to contacts, cleaned and shopped, then collected them from school. "And now ..." she said vaguely, looking around the kitchen.

"I'll do it," he said, meaning supper.

She started to say she'd help, then thought better. "OK. I'll be upstairs, in my room," she said, setting her mouth.

In fact, when she arrived at her office – after pausing on the landing and listening to the children laughing – she sat by the table considering what to do. She could still hear him talking. In her mind he was the presenter. The sound of his voice, magnified back, echoed like a jingle running in her head. Underneath the casual was a charge; words inside words, sounding correction.

But up here it was quiet, a space for doing tasks. Tucked into the eaves, with a cast-iron fireplace and two shallow alcoves, she'd made it her own. Her hideout, workshop and camera obscura. She'd filled it and used it to put up her pics. Because this was her home; a room of her own.

Sitting in silence, she ran her hand across the desktop surface. It was wooden and split-level, with a wide central area, surrounded on three sides by a low containing edge. At the back it thickened, where a row of handles gave access to pull-out drawers.

They'd found it in the market, bought it for a song and humped it back for Richard to work on. He'd stripped and sanded and stained as required. Putting it in place had been after a week or so of scraping, and banging up and down stairs with paint pots and rags and large mugs of tea. He'd occupied the room as if it was his studio. Getting up early, he'd worked all weekend, DIY-obsessed. She remembered as she sat there: his hair pushed back and lips pressed together. He'd that look of *Richard*, of doing his own thing.

Drawing her fingers lightly around the edge, she remembered how they'd carried it, lifting and turning then resting on the landing. Forward and back, she could still feel the weight. And Richard, calling out: do this, do that, whatever he said.

She rose to look out. The light was bright and watery. In the gardens it had pooled, on the walls it was blocky, while above that, and advancing, it planed off into blue.

As she pulled down the sash, cool air entered. In one direction there were sounds of taps running water, voices in the garden and party-ish music; the other way a dog. Further off she could hear a TV theme tune and a baby crying. Beyond that again, like a low-level argument, the sounds of traffic.

It seemed as she listened that her thoughts had expanded. They'd come here, renovated, made this place their own. They'd played the perfect couple, done what people did, made their moves. And now, after talking and trying and so much effort, they'd arrived at this.

Downstairs, Richard was calling. His voice, rising in snatches held around a note. She was required.

His call made her shiver. From here she could see it all: a contract, an exchange, a textbook case. What they used to call settling, a norm-referenced thing. Mainly, of course, for purposes practical. And soon – here she scanned the gardens – she'd be down there at table, back within the narrowness, with demands they eat up, then the after-supper battles when he cut through protests and forced the kids to bed.

While outside, in the garden ...

For Richard, Vanessa's retreat made it easier to regulate the kids. He didn't have that feeling of being watched, with an eye to what was wrong. It also avoided issues that rankled and how things were decided. The rules, and how to apply them.

So part of him hoped, when he called her down, that she'd delay her appearance or regard it as optional. Because when in fact she showed he had to admit that he didn't really like it. Her presence was unhelpful. She put in, cross-called, encouraged opposition. It was her and the kids versus him.

During the evening there were several ups and downs. Firstly at table, when the kids appealed against the food, followed by a quiet period when they picked and complained, leading to a go-slow stretch full of gloom, then a sudden turn-around when Vanessa agreed to let them go before they'd finished.

"Just wait," he said, taking a knife to each plate. "I want you to eat a portion each," he insisted, dividing both down the middle. "Right, you both have to choose – one half."

"But Dad!" protested Charlotte.

"Which one?"

"I'm full," complained Stephan.

"Choose."

The children fell silent.

Vanessa took their part.

"One or the other," he said, grimly.

Frowning, Vanessa pleaded their case.

"Oh, Dad ..." Charlotte added.

"What I said. Choose."

Vanessa, looking pained, tried again.

"It's necessary," he shot back.

"But is it working?"

Richard scowled. He wanted to make her see what was happening, how she set it all up. But also, he wanted to take himself off, shrug and walk away. It was oh-so predictable. And yet, he wondered … the kids were out there in the middle, caught between camps.

"You tell me," he said, glaring.

"I don't want them … to have problems."

"Problems?"

Vanessa gestured behind Charlotte's back. She was refusing food.

"They have to get used to eating, and without a fuss," said Richard, frowning. "You know what Ruth's boys are like."

"But this is a fuss."

"Maybe it's fuss that works."

Later in the evening, when the kids had been bedded and she'd tidied the front room, Vanessa took her turn to watch TV. Switching channels, she settled on a film. Although not exactly chosen, it fitted her mood and could be watched as a filler, without close attention. Set in the Fifties, it was clipped and rather upper, with the kind of mannered style that Richard called "ha-ha stuff". As she lay back and viewed, she could hear his dismissals. It would be "lightweight" or "clichéd"; he didn't know why she bothered. His opinions filled the house.

In any case, with him in the background, busy with his notebooks or playing the piano, she was happy. It allowed her to breathe. There was no need to battle or present a point of view.

When the film finally ended, after meetings by chance on harbours and yachts, she flicked between channels, sampling different shows. She knew, or hoped, that he'd be in bed. That way, when she joined him, he might stay asleep. As she lingered at a half-familiar sitcom, her attention wandered. A smoothness entered, a feeling of immersion, as the screen began to blur.

Divided now, she was drawn to bed, but an edge of indifference kept her on the sofa. It was as if she was on night watch and had to see it through. She'd go upstairs *when* she was ready.

Finally, after sampling a soap and a holiday taster, Vanessa switched off and climbed to the bedroom.

As expected, it was dark and quiet. The door was creaky and a corner scraped on carpet. Once in, she adjusted. His breathing had stilled, and for a moment she wondered … There were words she'd like to say, plans and agendas, things to discuss. As she moved to the bedside, she talked herself through. She supposed he might be listening and calmed her expression, imagining what he'd say. Perhaps, she thought, observing a light-streak falling on his hair, he wasn't that bad. She sat on the bed edge, peering at his face. Caught in the light, like a reprint from an album, his boy-face had returned.

As she slipped between the sheets, Richard stirred.

"Time?" he asked sleepily.

"It's late," she answered quietly.

His hand touched her waist. "How late?"

"One-thirty."

"Aren't you tired?"

"A bit. Did I wake you?"

"I'm not sure. Maybe."

Vanessa weighed his mood. In the half-dark he had softened. "It's weekend."

He grunted and his hand found her breasts. "You OK?"

She allowed. A voice in her head was asking about choice and whether to say no.

He continued stroking and touching. While they exchanged kisses, Vanessa felt her body taking over. She was herself, given into feeling.

His hand found her hers, guiding downwards. "Nice," he said as she cupped around flesh. She was playing with him now, grooming him as if he was an animal. "Hmm, that's it," he said and began to shiver. Suddenly he hauled up and mounted. A force took him over, he was squeezing into dark, feeling his way in. A rhythm set up, jerky at first but gradually lengthening. She could feel him in her, short-breathed and urgent, making it happen.

The rhythm gathered pace. Vanessa was awake and alive and filled with softness. The thoughts kept interrupting – random and scattered – but her body was in action, rising and expanding, firming itself up. She wanted and had to, and yet she was deliberate, willing herself on, and then with a wriggle and a jump it really didn't matter. Everything ran together, the dark took over and she clenched, and when she came it was short, involuntary and repeated.

Richard followed on. He stiffened, pitching himself forward. His body came down and for a second he sprawled, then side-rolled, panting.

They lay there, side by side. Vanessa was breathing deeply, like a swimmer on her back. Richard was leaning on the pillow with one elbow dug in. His face had smoothed and his hair was matted. "Enough?" he asked quietly.

In the dark Vanessa nodded.

That weekend they made a fresh start. While the children watched television, they occupied the kitchen, with Richard sampling poetry while Vanessa scanned the paper. Between reading out lines and one-off observations, they kept themselves in touch and almost, it seemed, returned to how it was.

Later they'd a meeting, an invite from Lorna to *the group* – a collective set up, she said, to talk about the struggle and support women's feelings. Richard thought it of interest, while Vanessa was more definite. Lorna, she felt, was on the same wavelength. They both put women first.

So when Lorna phoned, confirming timings and who would be there, Vanessa took the call, talking of "warmth" and "shared experience" while Richard bowed out. Adopting the role of observer, he sat on the stairs two steps up. It meant he didn't have to sort things, and for that he was thankful. He'd rather sit back and play the role of audience. In any case he could tell that the process of decision was seen by the women as important.

As the call continued, Richard moved into action. When it ended, he was smiling, the television was silent and the children were upstairs, dressing.

Vanessa looked around. "How on earth did you manage that?"

"Just told them."

"Told them, that's it?"

"That's right."

"What did you say?"

"Oh, a few suggestions."

"But you actually *told* them?"

"Uh-huh, I made them an offer."

"You mean—"

"Followed by a clip round the ear."

"I hope not."

"Shouted and yelled."

"Richard—"

"Then threatened them with death."

Vanessa set her mouth. She knew of course what he was doing, but she wasn't backing down.

"I gave them ten to dress," he added, glancing at his watch.

"Seconds?"

"Hours, of course."

Vanessa furrowed her brow, switching to the weather and what Charlotte would wear.

"The red skirt, I suppose," he said. "But I don't think it matters, as long as she wears something."

"Yes, provided it's clean and sensible."

"Ah well, best if I pass on this one."

Vanessa's eyes glazed over. "As you wish," she said.

"Not my thing," replied Richard, turning away. Reaching into a drawer, he took out a large canvas bag. "Going to the shops," he said, pulling on his jacket and unlocking the front door.

"Anything wanted?" he called as he stepped outside.

Vanessa didn't answer. Although there were items, it was better if he just went. His absence would be a breather.

As she climbed upstairs, Vanessa had the feeling that she was viewing everything from somewhere on the inside, very private, as if she was on a journey looking out the window on scenes she didn't recognise.

And what she found upstairs wasn't as Richard had said.

Stephan was in his bedroom; he was not doing well. It seemed he'd been picked on and bad things had happened. In fact, the word *unfair* was written all over him. There'd been a dispute with Charlotte, a battle over programmes and a wait for the bathroom, so that by the time it came to dressing he'd given up. Vanessa encouraged him, then left. He had to learn, she said, to do things by himself. But when she checked back later, he was still in his night things, fingering the buttons of a hand-held game.

"Come on, darling, dressing time."

Eyeing the screen as if it might be dangerous, he went on playing. Strange bleeps and whizzes issued from the consol.

Vanessa repeated, examining the display.

Stephan twitched, pressing buttons. Something popped, followed by repeated explosions.

"We're going out."

"Just finishing."

Vanessa asked how long that would be.

"One minute."

She smiled and air-gazed quietly.

Charlotte entered, brandishing a hair band. It was a thick elastic loop with blue-and-gold stripes.

"Mum!"

Vanessa turned, widening her eyes.

"Can you do this, the way you do ..." Reversing and tossing back her hair, the girl held out her band.

Vanessa shaped it to a hair-knot, which she secured with the band. "How's that?" she asked, manoeuvring to the mirror.

Charlotte looked and approved until, noticing Stephan, she pulled a face. "What's he doing? Why's he not dressed?"

"In a minute," said Vanessa evenly. She turned to the boy. "That's what you promised, isn't it, Stephan?"

The reply was a crunch and a series of metallic hits.

"Then why's he got that game?"

Smiling, her mother referred the question on.

"Take it off him. Take it, or he'll never get ready." Charlotte hovered her hand forward, threatening to grab.

Stephan rocked back, shielding his game. Battlefield noises filled the room.

318

"See! You must stop him!"

"Don't, darling," Vanessa said, glancing back and forth.

"Turn it off!" Charlotte demanded, covering the screen.

Stephan squealed and pushed her away. As they struggled for possession the game slipped sideways and dropped to the floor. The boy swung down, attempting a save. Before he could reach it, the screen gave a clatter and a high-pitched whistle, then cut off into silence. He gathered it up. "Look!" he cried. "First time ever. I was winning!" He turned his attention to his mother, brandishing the game and demanding reparation.

Vanessa listened, expressionless.

"It's just a stupid game," his sister cut in.

Stephan scowled. "Not yours," he muttered.

Returning to the bed end he sat, switched on his screen and began jabbing buttons.

Charlotte pouted. "Leave him to his *game*." She turned to the mirror, "We can go without him. *He'll* be happy anyway."

Stephan flared. "You'd like that!"

The girl stepped behind her mother, poking out her tongue.

"Stop it!"

She pushed it out further, rolling her eyes.

"No!"

Curling her tongue, she flicked it in and out.

Stephan pointed. "See her! See her!" he cried screwing up his face.

"See her!" Charlotte echoed, grinning.

Looking baffled, Vanessa appealed again.

"Not nice," he said, more quietly, putting down his game.

"Not …" his sister began, then cut off.

Richard appeared. Expressing his displeasure, he asked about the noise. His enquiry, which was delivered flatly, had a calming effect. When no one answered, he checked his watch.

"I don't know what you lot think you're doing. We should have left already."

His gaze swept the room as if in inspection; he'd set his expression to a warning smile. Seeing Stephan, he paused, finger-stroking his chin. "What're you up to?" he demanded quietly. When the boy stayed silent, he repeated his question, more sharply.

"Best just leave it," interposed Vanessa. "Things will sort out."

"No, no. He's not happy," Charlotte sang out. "It's 'cos of me."

Peering at his son, Richard raised one eyebrow. "That right?"

Stephan glanced at his sister. His face was white.

"What's she been doing?"

The boy shrugged vaguely; he was close to tears.

"I know," said Charlotte, "I can do it." She sat down on the bed and turned to face her brother. "Sorry Stephan," she said.

"That's good – very kind," chorused Vanessa.

Stephan looked doubtful.

"I mean it," said Charlotte. "Sorry Stephan."

Her brother nodded.

"Well," concluded Richard, "*when* you're ready—"

"Shall we leave?" asked Vanessa.

Standing, Stephan picked up his game and placed it on the bedside cabinet. After pressing several buttons, he peeked at the screen saying he was getting ready. He'd do it in five. As his family left the room, the game gave out a series of whacks and crunches, followed by a bang, a high-pitched whistle and a bell-tone, ringing.

On the drive to Lorna's, Stephan played his game, Charlotte divided her time between colouring in and staring out of the window, while Vanessa guided. Richard drove, complaining they were late and blaming Vanessa.

They passed through the city, shaded by its plate glass offices. There were pubs with bunting, and the odd small café selling drinks and snacks. Richard named the churches – often only towers, or walls with plaques – while Vanessa looked for road names. At a station concourse there were couples with suitcases and men hailing taxis. As they moved beyond the centre they drove past a market, a cinema and a large municipal building, turning left at a station to follow a one-way road between tall Victorian houses. Near the end Vanessa called a street name for the kids to spot, "Combination Row. Should be last on the right."

Charlotte saw it first, naming from a distance. "We've been before," she said.

When they'd arrived and parked, Stephan led through the gate. He marched up the path and banged on the knocker. Charlotte joined him and the two stood waiting, pressed against wood. Stephan banged again then peered through the letterbox. He rattled the flap and his mother shushed him. When Lorna appeared, embracing Vanessa, the boy slipped through. Calling to his sister, he led to the back room where two pink-faced girls were squatted on the floor surrounded by playthings. Behind them a pair of French windows led out to an overgrown garden.

"Hi," said Xena, the older girl, who was leaning forward, eyeing the television as if it had offended.

Charlotte entered, and the other girl looked up. Echoing her sister, Melissa said hello. The floor was spread with picture books and comics and see-through plastic wallets filled with ribbons and heart-shaped stickers. On the couch behind there were collected soft toys, a games compendium and a scattering of tapes.

Xena picked up the remote and started channel-hopping while Melissa reached for a wallet and fished out some pairs of tinted glasses.

"You're all in blue," she announced, holding up a lens and covering one eye. She switched between glasses, calling out colours before spreading them on the floor. "Try them," she said, scooping up pairs. "More than one," she said to Stephan, fitting them together.

The boy tried out different combinations before passing them to his sister.

Charlotte sucked in her cheeks. Taking the glasses, she waved towards the door. "I'm going outside."

The other two girls glanced at each other. "The garden?" asked Xena, addressing herself. "Yes, why not ..." she continued, smiling.

Her sister laughed, repeating the phrase.

"Yes, outside," Xena said, getting up and taking some glasses. She moved to the French windows and they all followed, pushing through the doorway wearing multi-coloured lenses, before advancing in a line on the overgrown garden.

In the front room, where the adults had gathered, it was talk time. Seated in a circle, they were taking turns, describing what had happened since last meeting. The circle was informal, some seated, some squatted, eight along the walls and two more in the bay. Beside them, positioned on a low-level table, was a collection of pamphlets, some stacked-up newspapers and a vase of red tulips.

This was their time, a pause for catch-up and exchange.

They'd begun with introductions. At this stage, although they were in session, the remarks were glancing, offered ad hoc. It was almost as if they were trying out an act with a few connective phrases before walking off.

When the full session began it was led from the corner by a thin-faced man in a frayed denim jacket. His hair was spiky and his expression rather fixed. He introduced himself as Justin Peters, father to Xena and Melissa, and Lorna's partner. Working his hands and gazing at the floor, he set out his position. There were, he said, complications and difficulties – but truth in what they'd experienced. As a man he'd resisted and set himself up, so he'd needed to be broken (here he glanced at Lorna on the sofa). But now he was focused on women, on giving space and backup. "We're *all* political," he added, "especially where it hurts."

Rocking side to side, his listeners nodded. It seemed he'd struck a nerve.

For an hour they talked about relationships and the wider network. The commitment was to change and what Lorna called, glancing at the friend sitting by her, *absolute recognition*. The aim, she declared, was "total awareness", staying on top and seeing the problem. "It's all about correctives," she said. "Matching theory and practice, getting it right."

Her friend, Caroline, a large woman with close-cropped hair, murmured her agreement. "Right theory, right practice," she mused, shifting closer. The two were arm in arm, squeezed to the front of the soft-backed sofa. They appeared to be hosting, introducing topics and inviting comment.

One that Lorna led and her friend endorsed was *coupling*. It went with *divisions* and *emotional weakening*. *Coupling* was exclusive and not good for women. It involved being owned, kept from each other and bossed by men. The opposite was *open* – a state of mutual support that centred on people sharing partners.

As Justin explained, fixing his eyes on Vanessa, "It's all about the women. They have the choice."

She smiled. "Of course. Mother knows best."

Richard asked a one-off question. Used as a cover, it marked him as present. But he wondered as he spoke if he'd come here to be chosen.

As the meeting progressed, the extent of choosing became apparent. Of the ten there present, eight had *networks*, mostly triangular but also linear, with a group around Lorna, including Caroline Lee, Justin Peters and a small man called Ken who also partnered Gabby. There was also another, looser group, consisting of Lorna's half brother and Justin's two girlfriends.

At the break, with some people wandering, others debating and Vanessa in the garden checking on the kids, Richard found himself chatting to Gabby. Her hair was a big curly mop, banded at the front, and her rounded, heavy-set face looked almost matronly. She peered up and sideways, flashing him a smile. Realising she was interested Richard lowered his voice to ask what she thought about the session.

"Me?" she said with a lilt. "I can't believe it."

"You were surprised, then?"

"Not at all. People talk. And talk."

"Ah, so you don't buy into it."

"It's all for show," she answered. "Peacock stuff. Covering up."

"But what's there to hide?"

"Ego. Bullshit. Some people here just want it both ways."

"I see. So there's a problem."

"Could say."

"I did wonder."

She looked him over carefully. "But what do you *really* think?"

"I'm not sure. But it does sound all rather perfect and wonderful ..."

"Ah, so you're not that keen."

"Still taking it in, at present."

"But really, you can see—"

"There are questions I'd like answered. And things I'd like to know about how it all works. Vanessa would say I'm hypercritical."

"I call it being straight, reading signs."

"I suppose it's only first impressions. After all, they can be wrong."

Gabby shook her head. "You feel it, then it's there." She appeared to be studying something that only she could see. "The first twenty seconds, that's when you know."

Justin approached, greeting them as if he was stewarding an event. He was touring the rooms, checking on feelings. "You caucusing?" he asked, grinning.

"Yes, against you," Gabby shot back.

"You're not happy?"

"Not so you'd notice. Better things to do."

He licked his lips and considered. "Well, it's in your hands. If that's how you feel …"

"You mean, I can go?"

"Not necessarily, only if that's what you want."

"Translation, *we can do without you*."

"No, it would be much better for everyone if you stayed."

"But don't rock the boat."

Justin's eyes closed slightly as he began to walk away. "Think about it, Gabby, think about it. You know you're always welcome here."

As he moved along the hall and out towards the garden, Gabby grimaced. Turning to Richard, she crooked her thumb. "Justin the lech," she said quietly.

Shortly afterwards, at a call from Lorna echoed by Caroline and relayed by Justin, the second half began. It started with people exchanging surprised looks. The front room had changed. The chairs and the table had gone and a large coarse-grained rug dotted with cushions had been stretched across the carpet. The patched rug had double-thickness borders. At the centre, a chequered cloth was spread with assorted dips in see-through containers, veg sticks in mugs and a bowlful of fruit. It looked like an improvised picnic.

Invited by Lorna, people took their places. Ken did a headcount, Gabby scowled, Caroline nodded and Justin ate, while Vanessa and Richard gazed around expectantly. After words from Lorna, reporting on the three who had been claimed by other commitments, the meeting started.

The second half was less ideological. They spoke with passion or sat saying nothing as if they were in transit, observing things passing. A few talked in code, considering all sides, the factors and the wider issues, some spoke often, others were receivers, all showed interest.

"It's about *sharing*," said Lorna, passing around food.

For Richard it was strange. It all felt quite inward, a self-defining world made up of thoughts and voices in succession; an event they'd set up. Just being here, he realised, was a gesture of intent.

"And entitlement," added Caroline, catching Lorna's eye.

Later in the session Richard's doubts returned. Glancing about the room he saw that things were disordered. It made him think of living rough. The finger-food at centre had been tried and discarded, the rug was stained, the cushions showed marks, and the empty fruit bowl was full of peelings.

A phrase about *after the party* passed through his head, followed by music. He wondered why he'd come here. Without showing any-thing, he was studying the group. There was Justin playing guru, Lorna making waves, Caroline agreeing, Vanessa questioning and Ken speaking up. It all felt rather stylised, something they'd arranged, a form of demonstration.

But then, of course, there was Gabby.

She'd wedged herself in, sunk between cushions. Judging by her movements, she wasn't very pleased. At the start when Justin spoke, her expression had hardened. Later when Lorna took over, she'd gazed out the window. When Ken said his piece – a breathless kind of pitch about balance and support and being torn both ways – she'd cut in more than once, stating her case. At one point, when discus-sion developed about *owning problems*, she'd added her comments, mainly barbed. Later she reacted by grunting or sighing or fidgeting with the rug. Towards the end she sat and looked, frowning occasion-ally and refusing to speak.

The meeting wound up with Justin talking about feelings and theories of the self. He delivered his remarks slowly, referring to himself in third person. At the end, after quoting from a pamphlet he'd written, he moved on to fixed business, introducing Ken by surname.

"So, Vladimir Ilyich, what is to be done?" Justin asked, grinning.

Ken Gorst took over. Speaking quickly, he pulled out a pen and a torn piece of paper and ticked off a list. His points concerned *Activist*, the group's newspaper that needed jobs done. There were production days, distribution runs, sellers needed, subscriptions to collect and articles to be written. Moving on to things in the movement he reminded them of scheduled meetings. In response to Lorna asking about women, he counted up selections with female shortlists. When pressed by Caroline he named the seats, denounced the opposition and sketched out their response.

When he'd finished, Justin gave an update on an issue, current in the party. It centred on some words he'd used in *Activist 29*. The leadership didn't like it, there'd been a spat, some nasty allegations and talk of expulsions. "We must understand," Justin concluded, "it's a smokescreen. They want to turn the clock back. Our answer needs to be unequivocal, we have to hold the line."

In the debate that followed references were made to past leaderships, historical parallels and lessons to be learned. Words like "opportunists" and "defeatists" circulated the room.

"Together we are strong," said Ken, holding up *Activist*. "That's this week's headline."

Justin wrapped up, speaking of personal closeness and pointing the way forward. The last words were Lorna's, backed up by Caroline. There was an outing to arrange with a date for diaries. Everyone was invited. Whatever the weather it would be, she said, a shared experience.

Afterwards, as they took their leave, Richard held back. Vanessa, he supposed, would handle their goodbyes. He collected the children and kept them amused while she worked the room. She did so with poise, like her mother; it seemed she knew how.

At the end of her round, Richard became aware of something new; she was talking to a man who'd appeared from the garden. He was solemnly attentive, with dark curly hair and metal-rimmed glasses that he adjusted by applying his forefinger to the bridge. He seemed to be thinking in his own private space.

When Richard came over Vanessa introduced him as Lance Roth, a community activist who ran the local crèche. They'd met through Lorna – here she laughed – who held him up as some sort of hero, a man she approved of. Because he'd stepped in last minute to entertain the children, replacing the actor who hadn't turned up.

To Richard he came across as an unlikely stand-in. Back-foot and watchful, with dark brown eyes and a wrinkled brow, he appeared to be taking mental notes. He could have been an academic, or a junior doctor.

Vanessa, to finish, circulated the room chatting about kids, laughed with Lorna, re-engaged with Justin, and didn't appear to notice Richard, or the kids' impatience. She was enjoying herself. Her voice was raised and she was in the flow. It was almost as if she was on tiptoe peering over a wall.

Lance said almost nothing. He followed her, smiling quietly like a minder; he was there for her.

It was Gabby who cut things short. Noticing Stephan in single combat with imaginary intruders she called to Vanessa. "Looks like we're front line," she laughed.

"Are you winning?" she added, addressing the boy.

Stephan glanced around and switched to fly-swatting.

"Does this mean you've nothing to do?"

The boy paused, looking slightly lost.

"Been here long enough?"

Stephan gave a nod.

"Well then—"

As Gabby spoke, Charlotte pushed forward. "We have to go," she said firmly, addressing her mother.

"That's what you want?" asked Vanessa.

Charlotte confirmed.

"You mean now?"

Her daughter frowned. "Go home."

Vanessa stared. "I think—" she began, before falling silent.

"Go, Mum. Stephan needs it. Go now."

"You sure?"

"YES, Mum. Please."

"There's a TV programme," said Stephan.

Richard grinned. "And when there's something on the box."

"OK, we'll go soon."

"*Mum*!"

"It's time – now," put in Gabby quickly. "You all go. I'll count you out, starting from ten." And she stood in the hallway, pointing and waving as she descended the scale, calling out numbers.

The last thing Richard saw, as the kids reached the car, was Gabby standing in the doorway signalling encouragement. She seemed to be placed there for effect. Her expression was heightened, as if for camera. She was grinning and gesticulating in a way that recalled Vanessa several years back, waving into sun in their holiday photos.

Next morning was Sunday, and a once-weekly meeting, gathered upstairs. A small group lie-in, with the following present:

The Lavender family, Charlotte, Stephan, Vanessa – father, apologies.

Pyjama Party members exchanging feelings, with no set tasks. Holiday-ish.

In terms of place: main bedroom, early. In terms of those present: comrades and supporters linking arms. In terms of women's power, this was giving audience. In relationship terms: making a point.

Minuted as follows.

With the curtains half-closed, a sleepy-eyed Vanessa received both children, taking them in bed to play games and snuggle. The games went through stages: cards that slipped under pillows or fell beneath the bed, ROCK PAPER SCISSORS beginning three-way but petering out when Charlotte lost interest, under-sheet-hiding games with ghost calls and giggles, I-spy games, word games and joke games and pen-and-paper games that involved joining up the dots and colouring in pictures.

Vanessa made them welcome, asked questions and directed. This was the good life, their own special time.

When their father returned from piano practice, the games had ended and the children and their mother were enjoying a three-way hug.

In terms of parenting, this was happy families.

# TWENTY-ONE

*Activist 30*

## THE PERSONAL IS POLITICAL –
## TWO SIDES OF A RELATIONSHIP

Editor: This month for our centre spread, *Activist* invited two comrades, V and R, to talk about sex-typing in their upbringing and its effects on their current relationship. Below we print what they said, written up in summary form, minus questions. Their responses document the politics of contemporary relationships with unswerving honesty. For further reading, *Activist* recommends Alexandra Kollontai, *Love of Worker Bees* and Anja Meulenbelt, *The Shame is Over*.

### A WOMAN'S VIEW

I come from a family of career women. As a child I was aware that my mother was employed in publishing. She told me that my grandma had also worked in books. I knew, of course, about The Queen and I liked Helen Shapiro, Dusty Springfield and Shirley Bassey, even though I had never heard them sing. I remember at an early age writing a story about women ruling the world. I

### A MAN'S VIEW

I've never really known my dad and he's never known me, beyond a certain point. I suppose it's a male thing we do to keep ourselves hidden, safe behind a mask. Dad would sound off about the bosses or whistle the red flag while I'd go for country walks or read in the corner. With other men he was one of the lads. He'd put on an upper-class drawl or take himself off as more northern than thou. He knew had noticed how my mother ran the house and my father carried out odd jobs as and when required. Of course, today we have a critical view of traditional sex roles, but in that generation the women did it all. They were the managers in the house, at work and with the children. I think they were stronger than the men.

To me my father, like most men, was a mystery. Without saying anything, he would mend things around the house or disappear upstairs to the attic where he'd build his models. He is a fairly strong and silent character, and I suppose shy of women. In my experience that is how most men operate. It keeps them apart.

As I grew up, most of the young men I knew were what my friends called stiffs. They were public school and all fingers and thumbs, with no idea of how to talk to women. Or they were physical specimens, only really interested in coming first in their own chosen sport. And they all had their own hobby horses like space exploration or racing model cars or collecting badges. Looking at them and my father, I came to think that most men are obsessives. Some live for their team, others for DIY

lots of jokes and on April Fool's Day he'd kid us with his straight-faced claims that a neighbour had died or he'd won the pools. He had to go one better than anyone else. Even today my brother and I joke that Dad has the world's biggest chip on his shoulder. His message to me was that fathers, like boys, are rebels and that men are defined by what they are not. So, a *real* man insists loudly that he ISN'T weak, small, dependent or female.

My mum was feminine on the surface but knew what she wanted. She was quiet and practical and did all the chores but she wouldn't let him swear and made him hand over his wages on pay day. She's a calm, determined woman who believes in *making the most of things* and always told me I had to do well at school.

I think as the younger son I wanted to outdo my brother, so I tried for Cambridge but didn't get in, and ended at York, where my cousin went in the late Sixties. Funny enough, his research on families includes findings on sex-typing. He's told me how some men used the so-called sexual revolution as an excuse to bed lots of women. I think what I picked up from him was that men don't

330

and some for their music. Maybe like my father they are just better at doing rather than talking, but when I was young that was less than obvious. All I knew was that men were non-communicators, they had to make their mark, and rather than come second in anything they would refuse to take part at all.

To be fair to my partner he is rather different. For instance, he is domesticated. There are hidden things I organise, but I have a much better deal than previous generations of women. We both work, we share household tasks and take turns with the children.

But parenting is where the problems begin. If things are shared, then everything is wide open to debate and different opinions. And as those debates escalate, the sex roles become more entrenched. So, with us the irresistible force of male single-mindedness meets the immovable object of female resistance. The man blames the woman, the woman blames herself and then blames the man for making her feel that way. It all tends towards closed doors and long telephone calls.

And the arguments are circular. The first hint of a familiar phrase leads to a sinking feeling: *not that*

change much.

My brother's a different sort of man. I used to call him My Big Brother Valentino. I suppose I see him as the romantic type who women like because he says the right thing. He's not like me.

I've always been a driven kind of man. It's to do with not fitting in. As a boy my favourite word was "Why?" It got me into trouble with teachers, so I learned to think "Why?" rather than say it. I'd an idea that the world was a jigsaw with one piece missing. As I got older, I remember searching for something deeper by staring at things until they looked strange. Or I'd repeat a word till it lost all meaning. For a while I became my own pursuer, playing pistols at dawn in the mirror. I still like that phrase about pulling up a daisy to see how it grows. That's what I've always been like. I think it's a man thing, going for it, questioning everything. Riding alone in the saddle, you might say.

Relationships can be difficult. What I brought with me was my home-maker mum and my oddball dad with his cut-and-dried talk. At times it's as if I'm two people. There's the socially-conditioned man about town and the awkward *again*. Then an over-reaction sets in as every word becomes charged with hidden meaning. In the end it all becomes rather predictable and exhausting.

There's a strenuousness about men that makes them quick to judgement but slow to give support. Solving problems in what they call a rational way is more their style, rather than being patient and understanding. And being in a relationship with one can feel at times like an uphill struggle.

I think the problem with sex typing is that it takes a conscious effort to overcome, and that can lead to overload. Nothing can be settled without a long debate, and sometimes on-the-spot decisions have to be taken. It was simpler in the past when the lines of demarcation were clearer.

In the end, I find myself divided. I want to be strong like the women in my family but not in the same way. What that new way might be seems unclear, but I believe it involves self-definition rather than seeing ourselves as second-class men. To achieve that we need strength, time to think, and the support of other women.

customer. And in private, if I'm honest, the second can get the better of me.

The issue of men controlling women makes me think about my own behaviour. What I notice is when small decisions have to be made there's a power struggle. It's a question of who knows best, but also who's tough enough to get their way. And in terms of the decisions, my male training usually wins out. Though of course everyone loses, because the battles are never-ending and each small struggle just sparks another.

Perhaps I regret writing this piece. The difficulty is I don't see myself as an all-male go-getter. And work and promotion are, let's face it, what men do. Without them they feel useless. But for me, the grind of work just doesn't satisfy. It feels like wasted time. On the other hand, domestic life can be isolating. You begin to lose confidence and question everything. Also, conflict at home goes much deeper than at work.

So, yes, I'm male and I'm driven – but towards what? If I don't want to "follow in my father's footsteps", what role do I adopt and what do I want to achieve?

# TWENTY-TWO

"A get together," Vanessa announced as she worked in the kitchen slicing veg and warming pans, "that would be good."

Behind her Richard, who was watching, had a matchbox in his hands.

Vanessa paused to look down the garden. "I think it could draw things together." Her thoughts were in the words, appearing slowly. "Invite round everyone, all the different groups."

Even as she looked, the garden was darkening. She could see it in sections, divided like a map: a sun strip at the back, shadows halfway and twilight closer. Long and bare and worn at the edges, it was functional: a run for the children, a corner shed, a patio at the end and grassed in the middle. This was the place, she thought. She could imagine it arranged with fairy lights and chairs. A summer evening sit-out for drinks and a chat.

Richard showed interest. "All of them?" he echoed.

Vanessa confirmed. A guest list was forming: Ruth and Doug, *the group*, politicos, some teachers, a few students from college-days and others in the network. They'd mix and mingle, meet new faces and find things in common.

At her request, Richard passed over some herbs in jars. "But what about the kids?" he asked.

"My parents will take them." She returned to her pans, frying and arranging her mixture in a dish for the oven.

"Sounds good. When?"

"I'll ring and see."

"You mean they'll sleep over?"

"The children like it."

Behind her words Richard sensed something more, a statement of intent.

"I think," he said quietly, "we should book them in, asap."

That evening, after Vanessa spoke to her parents, Richard did the ringing. He went through his address book, cross-checked with hers and dug around in drawers pulling out numbers he'd scribbled on paper. He resumed the next day, listing acceptances and using contacts to lead to other numbers. By the end of the week he'd talked and invited and left so many messages that he'd lost track of names and who might turn up. But he'd done what was asked, covered all the groups. As Vanessa always said, when Richard took on a job, that was it.

"He has his uses," she told Ruth on the day of the party as they plumped up cushions and turned out cupboards in search of glasses. "Richard's a byword for action. I wonder sometimes if it's in the genes, that kind of single-minded one-track thinking, like a runner near the tape. It's all about getting it done, and PDQ."

"The male of the species."

Vanessa busied herself wiping down surfaces.

"But it keeps them happily employed," Ruth added. "Occupational therapy."

"Well, I suppose they like being useful."

"Yeah, like skivvies they need to be given tasks."

Vanessa continued, placing mats while resisting the urge to answer in kind. With Richard and Doug out collecting drinks, it felt somehow off, an act of disengagement. In any case she'd a view that they might find things easier if they looked for a change in how they functioned.

"The obsessive sex," added Ruth curling her lip, "that's them."

Vanessa stood back, examining the cleared-out lounge. "Well, whatever happens, we'll just have to see ..." she said, and wheeled out the vacuum cleaner, beginning downstairs and working up the house.

By party time with all rooms cleared, lights in the garden and music playing, Richard and Vanessa were united briefly, playing hosts.

First to arrive were some college friends, followed by Frank and Jackie, wearing jeans and T-shirts. Richard led them in, conducting to the kitchen where they picked up drinks en route to the garden. Outside they stood talking, discussing Frank's imminent move to head up a school.

"It's a chance," said Jackie. "He's busy making ground on the inside lane." She was eyeing her husband with an edgy stare, as if he was a racehorse that might gallop off.

Frank grinned. "It's a big job. Super-heavy stuff. They want the place sorting."

"So, you'll be the main man," said Richard.

"More like a bouncer," Jackie countered. "He's been given what they call special powers."

"You mean of the hey presto sort?"

Frank wiped one hand slowly across his chin. "I think that's what they're looking for."

Richard introduced them to Hugh and Penny. When it turned out they were teachers, Frank checked where they worked and invited their views. How much were they suffering, he asked, grinning. Soon all four were sounding off. Schools, they agreed, were pretty much in chaos. Messed up places falling apart with too much pressure and not enough backup.

As they moved on to salaries, Richard nodded. He'd heard their talk and knew what followed. More gripes, of course: a long list of them passed around staffrooms with eyebrows raised and feelings aired, *first this … then that … and would you believe it?* And he wondered when they might call time, imagining teachers sitting on the toilet or talking in their sleep repeating their mantras about stress and tiredness.

Though of course they'd got a point, everyone felt it. It was only, he thought, that he'd lost all interest.

By now the group had turned their attention to politics. They were complaining about cuts, identifying councils who'd sold out. It was, Frank said, a problem of will.

"It's about who you put there," added Jackie quietly.

"And what sort of lead you've got 'em on," Frank replied, wiping one hand across his face.

Waiting for an opening, Richard pursed his lips. What they said sounded scripted. He'd a feeling they were playing with words, trying out effects.

When the group fell silent, he gestured towards the house. "See you all later," he said casually, "have to play host."

Moving indoors, he welcomed members of the collective then joined Doug who'd taken up position, covering for Vanessa halfway down the hall. He'd been asked to keep an eye out and to help with directions.

"On guard?" asked Richard, raising his voice above the wall of music issuing from the lounge.

"Awaiting developments," said Doug, glancing down the hall.

Richard followed his gaze. Seen through the doorway, the kitchen was busy. Looking towards the middle he could see Lorna and Caroline with their arms linked together, surrounded by drinkers. Both were giving forth, working their audience. Behind them, Ruth was throwing out quirky comments while mixing drinks. Beside her Ken was launching into speeches. Beyond that there were others, both known and less familiar, calling greetings and sharing one-liners. It was standing room only.

"You mean the percentage proof," he said, nodding toward Ruth.

"You think that's a problem?" Doug asked.

Richard could see her laughing and exclaiming; this was Ruth the performer. "I don't think so. She's doing well."

While they'd been looking, Doug had moved to the stairs. He was sitting, peering through the banisters, checking from front door to kitchen. "Let's hope so," he said. "I keep telling myself, fingers crossed it might never happen."

"True," said Richard. "Belief's the word. At least I think so. You know what they say, *I drink therefore I am* – it's called self-harm. And if there's one thing likely to bring it on, it's too much thought."

"I see. So that's what you *think*?"

Both men grinned.

"I mean," added Richard, "don't accept any kind of ideology. Question everything, including what comes first into your head. Stay outside the box."

"I did it *my way*, eh?"

"Maybe. The Sid Vicious version."

"Ah yes, what *they'd* call revisionism." Doug waved one arm in the direction of Lorna and friends.

"Them?" Richard laughed. "I suppose they would say that. You could call it enlightened self-interest."

"You agree, then."

"To be honest I'm not really sure. Mind you, they are pretty keen on slogans."

"Hmm, platform talk."

"Well, yes. They're not exactly *listeners*."

"Of course, they're VIPs."

"I don't—"

"Otherwise known as head-bangers."

Richard supposed so. He added a few qualifiers and attempted softeners then returned to playing concierge. Doug joined in and they worked together, meeting and greeting with Richard leading. After several more arrivals, mainly allies but also friends old and new, he excused himself.

By now the party was loud. The front room had filled up and a wall of music mixed in with shouts flowed through the house. There were queues for the toilet, people in corners and couples dancing. Passing through the kitchen, Richard topped up his glass and sought out Vanessa by the garden fence. She was talking to Lance.

"Hi there," he said, "party's going well."

"Oh yes," Vanessa responded vaguely.

"You enjoying it?" Richard asked, and Lance nodded. "That's good," he added, conceding nothing.

They were joined by Ruth. Vanessa introduced Lance, and her friend acknowledged, nodding and smiling.

Ruth put down her glass. She said she was on best behaviour, trying to please everyone, especially Doug. "It's FHB," she added, which Vanessa translated speaking to one side, for the benefit of Lance.

"I see," he said, adjusting his glasses. "Family hold back. Now I understand."

337

Richard noticed a catch in his throat and a mannered smile. Though young, he carried himself seriously, on stand-by. It seemed he wanted to be helpful.

Ruth was enjoying herself. She had to know the names, who was with who and where they all came from. She also quizzed Lance about his job and how he put up with it, drawing out his thoughts about bringing up kids. "You wouldn't care for mine," she said. "They're all over the place, just like their mother." Before he could reply she rolled her eyes and launched in again, imitating their *baby-wants-niggle*. Of course, she said, the joke was on her. Food fads and moans, day-long battles. "It's what you get when you spoil 'em."

Lance asked after names and ages.

Ruth gave details. "As you know," she added, "boys are impossible."

"XY," quipped Richard. "We just can't help it."

"Otherwise known," put in Ruth, "as *not me guv.*"

For a moment no one spoke. They were standing, facing each other, awaiting the next move.

"What do you think?" Vanessa asked, turning to Lance. "Do we accept that boys will be boys and this is the planet of the apes, or is the future female?"

He eyed her intently, without saying anything.

"The male mindset," she reminded, "is it fixed?"

"She means, are we doomed," Richard interjected.

"Not in children," Lance responded, speaking slowly like a diagnosing doctor. "Or just the first phase ... and then only in some."

"But otherwise," said Richard, "it's terminal."

"I think," Vanessa said, measuring her expression, "that boys, given a good example, with the proper upbringing ..." Pausing, she considered. Her eyes were large and round and directed towards Lance. She wanted his endorsement.

"Will turn out just like their dads," Richard said quietly.

Vanessa gazed off, smiling to herself. "What we're debating is the big question," she said. "Temperament versus conditioning, and do we make a difference. We all believe in self-improvement, but when it comes to it, family *don't* hold back."

338

Ruth snorted. "Too true, it's always the way. You start off trying to be different, and end up willy-nilly like your folks. It's the law of life." Her voice hardened: "Take my dad. I used to call him the world's biggest bastard. One of those ultra-brutal military types. I thought of him as the enemy to everything I stood for. That was until I met *his* bastard father, and he was a communist. You'd really think, to look at 'em, they had nothing in common." She paused and shook her head. "But, like it or not, folks is folks, they make you who you are. Whichever way you go, it gets passed down."

Richard held back. He was looking at Vanessa, remembering their first meeting, her short blue jacket and glimpses of waistline. Then her theories and pronouncements, leading back to her flat.

Both women nodded.

"Together with the genes," said Vanessa quietly.

"And the surname," Ruth added.

"*Plus ça change*," Richard said, gazing at Lance.

The other man smiled; he was agreeable.

Ruth raised her glass. "What comes round—"

"Indeed, so it's party on," Richard concluded, bowing ironically. "Because that, at least, seems to be going well."

The garden was dark now; its area had softened. It was bright beside the house, shadowy further out, and black towards the back where the last few yards had disappeared. At the centre, gathered on the lawn, there were people in groups, some listening, some gesturing and others playing observers.

To Richard, who had moved towards the kitchen, the party had the feel of good times past. It was as if he was an unattached visitor observing couples at a student party. He could see how they operated and understood their habits. It also gave him something immediate, a close-up on life.

He crossed to the counter and filled up his glass. The kitchen was full of wide-eyed people, talking brightly with deliberate animation.

As he entered the hall, he thought of Vanessa. He could picture her face with Lance as sidekick. She was wide-eyed and reactive and full of supplementary questions. What they'd talked about was happening.

Reaching the front room, he glanced in the mirror. The person he saw had changed. Age had made him stronger, at least in appearance. He'd life-lines and experience and a mouth set firm. Seen from a distance he gave nothing away.

The room was filled with music. There were bodies moving slowly, some bopping, others clenched, and a number sprawled on cushions, nodding to the beat. The volume held them in.

As Richard stood watching, he heard himself called. The voice said his name briefly, then again, followed by another, longer call. Realising where it came from, he put down his drink and stepped outside. There by the gate, waving and smiling, with her hair curling out and a rucksack on one shoulder, was Gabby Joseph.

"Hey," she said, "I'm late?"

"No, not especially, it's open house." He glanced at his watch. "And in any case, the night is young."

"How's it going?"

"The party?"

"Yes, what's it like?"

"Oh, it's great, really gr—" He pulled up, frowning hard. "No. That's wrong." Suddenly he found himself changing tack. "It's nothing really, nothing at all." He waved towards the house. "The truth is the air's a whole lot better out here."

He paused and they both stopped talking. The sounds of taped music filled up the gap. It felt as if they'd got in touch without saying anything.

The dark was his cover as he studied her closely. She was wide-mouthed and cheery with a slightly awkward stare. She wasn't, he thought, what you might call beautiful, though the street light gave her presence. With her dark brown eyes, lightly burnished skin and prominent features she looked like an Expressionist portrait.

"Just back from a walk," she said.

He asked what she meant.

"You'll think, that's crazy-crazy."

"Not as much as me," he said, examining her thoughtfully.

"Well you'd better watch out, it's infectious."

340

"You say walking is catching?"

"Very moreish."

Again, they both went quiet.

Noticing her sun sign on a chain and heavy-duty sack, Richard smiled. He could imagine her as a new age traveller. He pressed for details of her walks.

"I can show you," she said, suddenly little-girlish.

"Show me? What would that involve?"

"Night walks, mostly in parks, if I can get into 'em."

"You walk in the dark ..."

"I'm a night owl."

"By yourself?"

"That's so."

"Isn't that dangerous?"

"Not if you're careful and know where to go."

Richard frowned. He was trying to make her out. She was half in shadow, staring into darkness. He could feel her warmth.

"So why do it?"

"To see. And because I can. In any case, once you've got the bug ..."

"And the sack?" he asked, pointing.

"That's for food."

"It's an expedition, then?"

"Gentler. More about self-discovery."

"A kind of mind thing?"

"If you like—" She turned, inviting him to join her.

"OK, where to?"

"You'll find out."

Gabby led off and Richard followed. They were adventurers, stepping into shadow. This was unknown.

They crossed the road, turning both ways and cutting through a gap between houses to emerge on an unmade-up track. At the end, reaching some concrete blocks and a corrugated iron fence, she waved him close. "There's a hole," she said, pointing to a gap between an elderberry and crumbled brickwork. "I came this way a few minutes ago," she added, levering herself up to crouch cat-like on the wall, checking both sides before disappearing over, calling for him to follow.

341

Surprised by her agility, Richard scrambled up. When he reached the top, she helped him over, warning it was dark. On the other side he dropped down, landing against her. "Richard," she cried and pulled him to her. Suddenly he was hotly breathless and held to her body. "Is it OK?" he asked, feeling the glow and picturing Vanessa on the lawn, angling her comments towards Lance.

"What happened?" she said quickly, and unhanded.

They were standing on the edge of a disused railway line, lit from a distance by street lights. On their side it was backed by fences, on the other side it was bounded by brambles and a head-high bank. "Let's go, it's our trail," she said quietly, pointing forward to the levelled sleepers. "Take care," she said when they came to a section where the street lights had failed. She reached out to steady him and they shuffled forward, hand in hand.

As he went Richard tried not to think. It was, he supposed, a childhood game, an episode in the dark. If it was happening it wasn't that serious.

Gabby squeezed his hand and drew him to her.

"We're the railway children," he laughed.

They continued through shadow and around a bend to a lit-up patch at the back of a factory. Gabby led to where the track dipped into a cutting. They were standing together, blocked to the sides by rocks and weeds, and sloping ahead to a bricked-up tunnel.

"What happens here?" Richard asked.

"It's up and over," she said, pointing to a line of overgrown footholds. "Follow your leader," she called and began to climb, digging each foot into mud. Halfway up, they reached a ledge that led sideways across a drop. "Seems harder this way round," Gabby said, stopping.

Taking the side by the edge, Richard squeezed into the lead.

"We need to take care," she said.

At her insistence they positioned themselves side-on, facing outwards. Then they walked the ledge acrobat-style, with one arm linked, hands to wrists.

"You all right?" she said sharply when Richard stumbled.

"Fine," he replied, straightening. In the dark below the slope fell away to a grey-green mass of weeds and nettles.

"Keep going," he insisted, as she too slipped. She pulled back and they moved more slowly. By now they were short of breath and sweaty. Their hand-grip had shifted; palm to palm they were squeezing hard.

At a point close to the top, where the path curled back, Gabby lost her footing. "Richard!" she cried, lurching sideways. The ground gave way and she began to slide. Still holding, Richard flattened to the bank. For a moment they hung, his weight against hers, then both went down. With a short yelpy shout they rolled and plunged and tumbled to the bottom, landing side by side.

"Ugh," she cried, struggling for breath, "nettles."

At first, he didn't notice. The fall had shocked him and his blood was up. He heaved against Gabby, grunting. Then suddenly he was wild, he was grabbing for her, squeezing and pressing, kissing cheek and mouth.

Gabby grabbed back and they clenched. As their mouths closed together, he felt the stings. Hot around his neck, hotter and more painful on arms and sides. A peppering of stings, aching all over.

He was hot and bothered. Everywhere tingled: the backs of his legs, his thighs, his shoulders, his hair roots and scalp, even his tongue. It was as if they were kissing in a dust storm. And yet he didn't care. All at once he was alive, he was wild and he was in touch. A red-raw, burning kind of wildness, an overflow of hurt.

And then just as suddenly as they'd begun, they stopped and rolled apart.

Richard sat up. In the dark he was shaking. Part of him was amazed, another part was ashamed, while a third part wondered what would happen next. "My, my, my," he said as he stood up. "What can I say?" he added and leaned forward, helping her to her feet. Even in the dark he could feel her burning.

Gabby took a breath. "You don't have to say anything."

"But it hurts, yes?"

"Only when I laugh."

"Me too."

"Or move," she added, wincing.

He looked back up the bank. "I think we'll both have some explain-ing—"

"Don't fret, I've fixed it."

"Fixed it? How?"

"I phoned Vanessa. It's allowed."

He stared, taking in her words. What she'd said broke through everything. He'd known of course, somewhere subliminally. "You mean it was a setup?"

"I thought you wanted it."

"Nettles and all?"

"Ah well, when you're busy, things can happen …"

"So, it's been okayed. But where does that leave us?"

"Outside our comfort zone."

"True."

"With two scratchy bodies."

"Indeed."

"Stung head to toe."

"Absolutely."

"But then, of course, some like it hot …"

‡ ‡ ‡

After the party Richard and Vanessa told each other that their marriage had changed.

"It's like opening a window," said Vanessa, "and taking a deep breath."

Richard smiled. For him, he said, it was more open-ended. Though when they used the word "open" they meant a new beginning, a different way of living.

The rules had changed. Whereas before they were held in by family and habit and established routine, now they were on the lookout. It felt more up front and flexible, a bigger kind of structure; and it freed up hidden feelings. "Better out than in," was Vanessa's view, a remark that Richard echoed, quoting from Reich. But he wondered about their marriage. Together they'd reached a cusp or limit where things might end, or break open suddenly. They'd walked out to a bare bright spot where anything might happen, a point of no return.

In reality, of course, they were constrained by life, by jobs and kids and what could be fitted. So they needed a balance, a quid pro quo. Which meant, when it came to it, that they arranged their lives around a once-weekly swop where they took it in turns who stayed and who went.

They began with Vanessa and Lance meeting at his house. Just them, to avoid the children knowing. Richard was willing – after all, he'd agreed to an open relationship – and Vanessa was careful. She spoke about parity and testing how it felt, and whether they could handle it. In any case, she added, she wouldn't stay over.

She left that evening, promising return. As she walked out, she'd told him not to worry. But after her exit he could still see her eagerly awkward look. Her aim wasn't him.

While she was out, he'd tried making tea then listening to music, but his heartbeat was up and his thoughts wouldn't settle. He saw her with Lance, talking in the garden. It seemed they shared a view.

In an effort not to think, he went to the back room and practised on the piano. The notes came and went, like reflections in water. When he arrived at a key change he broke off, moved towards the hall and stood facing the doorway. When he switched off the light, the street lamp through the fanlight lit up the stairs. Following its glow, he climbed to the landing and paused, overlooking the hall. Its emptiness struck him. Although there were feelings, no one was there. Suddenly he felt as if this was a prelude, a first step into otherness that would soon take over and might well be dangerous.

He checked on the children, preparing what he'd say if they woke and wanted Vanessa. When he tried their doors, one was stiff, the other squeaky. Prising them open, he heard the sound of breathing. Both were asleep.

Climbing again, he entered the bedroom and clicked on the side light, directing its beam to pick out a photo of Vanessa. She was standing by a lake with flamingos behind her. He recognised something about her faraway look.

That night he tracked her, picturing her journey and seeing her with Lance. He supposed that they were watching and could read him from a distance. They had their own intentions. Whatever he did he couldn't shake the feeling that he'd wake one morning soon with a note on the cabinet signed by Vanessa saying she was leaving.

In fact, when she returned it was just after three and she entered quietly and pressed up close, asking how he'd been.

Richard remained still, murmuring vaguely. But inside, he was shaking.

She asked again, touching his arm.

He pushed himself up. "To be honest, I was worried."

"You don't need to be."

"You sure?"

"Absolutely."

"It's OK then?"

Vanessa confirmed. There was, she said, nothing to worry about.

"I get ..." he began, then shifted down. "Well, it's all very new."

"But OK."

Richard paused and pulled up the covers. "Yes, OK." Suddenly quite boyish, he leaned into her side.

"It's OK," she said, stroking his neck. They were together, and everything between them was calm and considered and full of sudden warmth.

Their sleep was short. When they woke it was half-dark and quiet. After talking and touching they rose as a couple, ate with the children and moved into action. Suddenly they were in step and had found something more personal, and all that day Richard felt himself liked. He'd regained his shine.

For Vanessa it was a new way forward.

"We've chosen," she told Ruth later, sitting in her neighbour's garden, "and we're going to try. It's a challenge."

"Makes for interest," her friend replied, stretching on the bench, "but I'd go nuts."

Vanessa raised one eyebrow.

"Too jealous," Ruth added, pulling a face. "My insecurity levels would go sky high, especially when it's all so open. I couldn't cope with being public property like that. I'd imagine everyone was watching, waiting for their chance."

"But don't you sometimes wish—"

"In any case, I'd be worried stiff Doug would clear off."

Vanessa gazed out across the unkempt borders. They were seated with the shed behind them, blinking into sun. The lawn in front was bare and grey in patches, the path was uneven and a tangle of rubbish had collected by the shed.

"Could be a way of forcing his hand," smiled Vanessa.

"Love me or leave me?"

"Well, it might at least gee him up."

"In your case, maybe."

Vanessa shook her head. For them, she said, glancing at the gaps in the fence, there was nothing definite. "It's all a bit up and down, a kind of adventure."

Afterwards she wondered. She knew her words had their own dynamic. *They* were what counted. It was words that steadied her: she needed their delay, their power to make good.

Because what she'd called an adventure soon became a slog. Suddenly there were pressures. It was partly a matter of timing – how often and where, and when to disengage – and partly balance, but also there were gaps where the feelings didn't fit. It was as if she'd been dating and found herself caught between rivals with a case to answer.

So, her next time away was daytime and brief. Arranged while Richard took the children to a film, it was afternoon-only. In fact, he thought he detected a slight hesitation once they'd eaten, as if it was a task she had to get through. She was only gone two or three hours, and when she returned her interest was up. Her focus was on talk and living together. And even with the children, things had cleared up between them.

From then on they were paired, with Gabby and Vanessa making the arrangements. They fixed on Fridays and worked out timings, aiming at balance and stability, especially for the children.

This time it was Richard who went overnight. Taking the car, he set off for Gabby's and suddenly he was up, aware of himself and what he had with Vanessa. It felt like a new way forward. Though for him it was also positional, he'd accepted her wishes and now it was his turn. This was what he wanted.

It was dark when he arrived. "Good journey?" asked Gabby, welcoming him in.

Richard confirmed. When Gabby met his eyes, he smiled. "You all right?" he said moving forward and they embraced. Her mouth came up and his closed over. Something automatic began beating up. He was hot and warm and breathless; they were kissing as if it was a party.

Gabby broke first, easing herself back and down. "Let's chill," she said, leading to the front room. He followed, saying nothing.

They settled on the sofa. It was worn into hollows and smelled of incense. There were tables both sides, one with flowers, the other displaying ointments and herbal remedies. Dotted around the room were polished stones, ornamental lamps and Goddess figurines.

She asked about the children.

"You know what they're like, ultra-lively."

"You could say."

"I suppose it's in the genes," he continued. "But then again, I always *wanted* them to stand out."

"Only feisty children need apply?"

"Uh-uh. Naughty but nice."

Gabby stroked his hand. "They learn by example."

He drew her to him, kissing again. His tongue entered slowly, pushing and curling. He was beginning the journey.

"I think," she said afterwards, "I'd like to walk."

"Ah, the call of the wild."

"*Without* nettles."

"But somewhere crazy?"

She touched him on the arm.

"In that case … ready when you are."

It was dark in her street as they passed out through the door. Gabby led, turning at the end beneath a broken street light and following a path that passed between fences. The path opened out to a tree-lined road with a garage on the corner. Beneath the trees ahead was a sweep of grey, visible through the bars of heavy iron gates.

"The park – no, *our* park," she said, crossing the road and peering through metal. It looked like a film set.

"We're going in," Richard said, as if it was obvious.

Taking his hand, Gabby confirmed and moved along the railings to a corner where a twisted tree trunk had thrust through the bars. She waited for a traffic gap before showing him where to grasp. "There, it's easy" she said, placing his feet. Richard grunted as he shinned up and over, followed by Gabby.

They were standing on grass, panting slightly. "Uphill," she said, pointing to a slope that rose into darkness.

As Richard's eyes adjusted he made out a path, some shrubs by a wall and steps to a terrace. Above that a wide swathe of grass spread towards a hilltop. "Lead on," he said and they set off hand in hand.

The light changed as they ascended. They passed from silver up through grey and beyond in darkness, to bare black space. Here they were unseen taking in the roofs, the street signs and office blocks, the lit-up city centre.

"Unreal," he said quietly. Overhead, a plane passed over.

They clenched by a tree. They were high up and floaty, lost in darkness. The sky above glowed like a pre-dawn flush.

Gabby drew back, breathing heavily, and her arm described a circle, taking in the city. "I come here to get away from it all. Belvedere Park, my island."

As Richard looked, he heard the beginning of *Island in the Sun*.

"It also has," Gabby continued, "its own walled garden."

Before he could answer she called out, "This way," and set off towards a tennis court and a high brick wall. Keeping in its shadow, she turned downhill at a corner. "The garden's inside," she said, passing through a gap with a chest-high gate propped against brick-work.

Inside was secret and warm and richly-scented. In front of them there were paths forking off: gravel to the sides; in the middle, crazy-paved and bordered by chicken wire. The sky above them showed clear and dark and overarching.

Gabby moved forward, choosing the central path. Her breath came quickly. She was holding her body close to Richard's.

At an arch with roses they paused to embrace, taking in the scents and the sound of running water. A dark, scrawny shape wheeled above their heads. "Bats," she said.

Richard tipped his head back. "Strange animals," he said, watching them loop and turn. "In a different world."

They were close by the pond. In the centre was a stone lit from above by a small solar light. A curve of water was issuing from a metal nozzle set into its side. "I spy fish," she said, pointing. Three silver-and-brown carp were circling in the glow. Moving slowly, they looped around each other. Their bodies were knotted like scarves. "Got something for them," she went on, slipping off her backpack. She pulled out a plastic bag of food sticks and examined them by the light of a torch. Each was brown and pellet-like. "See, feed," she said, picking out a small handful and scattering it on the surface.

As the water stirred, Richard saw an image of sun on grass and his mind flashed back to eating at the zoo.

The fish idled in circles, then shot to the top. Their mouths sucked in then twisted sideways to gulp down more. Finally, when all the sticks had disappeared, they dived.

"Watch the large one," she said quietly. As the leader nosedived, it bubbled out food sticks. They drifted to the surface, chewed up and sodden.

"Fussy eater," said Richard.

"Knows what it likes."

"Like children, wanting pudding first."

Gabby laughed. "Pretty cool kids." She looked up at the sky. A moon had appeared. It was half-sized, cut down the middle, as if it was a fold-out. One side was hard-edged, the other was hazy. She began to hum quietly to herself. "Walking on the Moon," she said, breaking off to clear her throat.

Richard looked up. The moon seemed painted.

"Land of shadows," Gabby continued, speaking slowly then looking away. She was full of feeling. "There's a shelter," she said, pointing, "over there."

She led around the pond and they approached together. The building was low, pillared both sides and open at the front. Inside was curved, with crumbling brickwork and a full-length bench. Gabby entered, examining the bench and peering into corners fingering the slats. "Clothes off," she said, suddenly.

Richard searched her face. "You mean you want to—"

She shook her head. "Better without, that's all." Her everyday tone surprised him. It was as if she was an agent, showing him a property.

"If that's what you want."

"It's best."

She began stripping off. As her flesh became visible Richard joined her, laying his clothes out across the slats. He noticed her folds, her heavy-set breasts and the broadness of her body.

When they were naked, Gabby stepped out into moonlight. "Come on," she said, extending a hand.

Richard paused. Compared with her, he was stick-white and bony.

"There's no one watching," she said, beckoning him out. With her large round arms, she looked like an oiled-up wrestler. "Think beach." Her voice sounded relaxed and completely alive. Drawn by her calm, he emerged and took her hand; it felt warm and comfortable.

"Have you ever done this before?" he asked, thinking of youth-talk he'd used in parties.

"Not with anybody else."

He grinned picturing her as a solo naturist, patrolling the night.

They followed the path that cut across the garden, placing their feet carefully, as if the stones were hot. By a corner they stood looking, scenting sweetness. A jasmine was sprawled across a head-high trellis. Pausing at a bench they hugged and kissed, then slipped out through the gate, finding grass.

Gabby began to sing. Her voice, which was soft, filled the dark. She was moving in step to her held notes. "I'm tuning," she said, breaking off.

"Tune on," he said, quietly.

Gabby started to circle, lifting her arms and craning her head forward. With Richard as audience she skip-stepped sideways, then pulled up suddenly. "What we must do," she said taking his hand, "is celebrate."

351

The moon was higher and its glow had hardened. The light it gave out was blue-white and reflective.

Gabby led back into the walled garden, taking the path to the shelter. "I've remembered," she said, picking up her sack, "something I brought along." She fumbled in canvas, pulling out a fist-sized pot. "Ointment," she said, taking off the lid and sniffing it. The mixture inside was grey-green and gelatinous.

She pulled out two more, levering off the caps and placing them on a birdbath just outside the shelter. "Green, gold, red," she announced, counting on her fingers. She paced a few rounds, circling her collection. When she urged him to smell, Richard bent forward smiling. The aroma from the pots was richly herbal.

"Plant stuff," she said, "mixed with oils."

The pots glittered dully in the moonlight. Balanced on stone, they looked like melted candles. "Good for special occasions," Richard said, allowing his eyes to stray from the birdbath to Gabby. She was broad and chunky and heavy all round. He could see her as one of her Goddess figurines.

Gabby glanced skyward. "Ms Moon's watching."

"And what does she see?"

"Oh, everything. A world, a city."

"Anything else?"

"A park and garden."

"And what else?"

"A man and a woman."

"Who are doing what?"

"Enjoying themselves."

"Like children …" he began then paused.

While they'd been speaking Gabby had thrust two fingers into a pot. She stirred and scooped, sniffing the bouquet. Her fingers were coated with thick green blobs. Before they could drip, she blinked shut and covered her face, rubbing in slowly.

"Creamy," she said, opening her eyes as if she'd been asleep. Patches of green were smeared across her brow; there were stains around her cheeks and mouth. In the dark she looked like a cross-channel swimmer.

"Let's mix it," she said, finger-stirring the gold. She smeared her chin and neck then switched to red for her shoulders before stepping forward, smiling. "Your turn."

Richard grinned. This was party. "You can start on my back," he called, turning and squaring his shoulders.

Gabby rearranged the pots and began to smear. She oiled down his spine and circled to his sides. From there she shifted to his arms and then to his chest. Here she used both hands. As she moved up and down, his body took on a painterly texture.

"Nice," he murmured.

She descended to his legs, brushing them downwards. "Life model stuff," he added as she worked down to his knees. She was crouched down by the pots with her head forward, breathing hard. When she reached his ankles, he touched her on the head. "Enough," he said, "I'll do you."

"When I'm finished," she muttered, beginning the return movement. Her face became set as she kneeled to her task, spreading around his thighs. She completed with a flourish and stood back, measuring him with a gaze. "That's you," she said, triumphantly, "in your own element."

Richard nodded; his body felt warm. The ointment had sunk in, leaving him sheathed in colour. "Now you," he said.

He reached for the pots, rubbing down her spine, oiling her front and around her waist, mixing colours. He skimmed her flesh lightly, butterfly-style, as he kneaded her sides then spot-touched her arms, her wrist and her fingertips. When he moved to her hips, he lingered thinking art, then descended to her legs before stepping back to admire. "Painted lady," he said, gazing.

Gabby narrowed her lips. "You mean *that* sort of woman?"

"Not exactly, I was thinking ..."

She faced him and their eyes connected. It seemed, in the moonlight, that she could see right through him.

"It's a type of a butterfly," he said.

"Oh, I see. And you reckon the name fits?"

"There are other types."

"Such as?"

"Peacock."

She laughed.

"Or fritillary …"

She laughed again.

"Or skipper."

Gabby smiled archly.

"But I shall call you beauty," he said, "because you're gold, green, red and," here his voice dropped low, "very beautiful."

They embraced and their mouths met again. A cloud passed over and the moonlight paled. They continued in a clench, touching and kissing. When the sky cleared again, they half-stepped back, drawing breath. Exchanging looks, they smiled. And they knew they were naked.

When Richard returned home early next morning he entered quietly, in a state of readiness. Ever since the party the house had changed. It had got out of hand. There were stains on the carpet, handprints on walls, and paper piles on surfaces. The house was a kind of drop-spot or repository where things seemed to lie, and remained there unnoticed. Not just the things but also, and mainly, the undisclosed *feelings*. It really was a mess.

Checking his watch, he slipped along the passageway hearing television sounds issuing from the darkened front room. In the kitchen a half-dressed Vanessa was sitting by herself drinking coffee. Her face was smooth and calm.

Her words, when they came, appeared from somewhere else. "I thought I'd wait with the children, till you got back."

He wondered what she meant. There were questions he'd like to ask about her and Lance. "That's fine," he said, pouring coffee.

"Things are OK," she said.

Richard took a mouthful. It was dark and strong. "You have plans?"

"Not really."

"Play it by ear, eh?"

"That's right."

"So, it's all down to us …"

At that moment the phone rang. "I'll go," said Vanessa, putting down her cup. She crossed to the hallway where she picked up the receiver. As she greeted, she paid out the wire and entered the back room, talking. Even as she spoke, Richard knew. And he wondered as he listened, hearing Vanessa, low-voiced and whispering, trying to turn the talk, whether he should tell her, not about the night walk, not about the garden, not even the painting, but just about Gabby, about life and energy and feelings and being there together and how much easier …

When Vanessa finished talking and returned to the kitchen, the back door was open. The sun was coming up. Looking down the garden she saw Richard at the end, sitting on the patio. He'd positioned himself at an angle, with his back to the side fence. A small plastic table was balanced between earth and concrete. He was doubled to the table, pen in hand, covering the pages of a soft-backed notebook. On the ground beside him was his coffee.

Light-spots appeared and the sun grew stronger. Its whitish-yellow beams, crossing the table, picked out the notebook.

Richard continued writing. Leaning forward, he was mouthing the words. It was as if he was addressing someone imaginary, a secret correspondent.

Even as she looked, Vanessa knew.

ǂ ǂ ǂ

Joe was reading the science.

He saw glaciers calving, forests burning, the Tundra giving way. Birds and insects were falling out of the sky. The beaches were full of plastic and dead fish. It was terrible to see.

In his head he saw children stepping over cracks on burnt-black savannahs. The last few trees had fallen and the herds had disappeared. Even at night the earth smoked.

Reading on, he saw people crouched in dugouts. The cities they'd lived in had become ovens. They'd fled when disease spread and the food gave out. Now, living in caves, they shared their last supplies and prayed.

Looking northwards, the land was flooded, southwards there were people on the move, to the east armies were fighting, to the west the lights were out.

Joe closed his eyes. To be alive and thinking like this was hard. The pain he felt went deep. It came between him and sleep. It was as if he was dying.

He talked to Suzi.

"My grief hurts," he said.

"That's bad, but quite normal, Joe. This is not personal grief."

"What is it then?"

"It's grief without stages."

"But what does that mean?"

"It won't go away."

"Really?"

"I believe so."

"So how can we deal with it?"

"Adapt."

Joe tried it. He found, by breathing slowly, he could lessen his pain. But it was like holding down a button: before long the effort became too great and it popped back up. Then he did things. By switching between tasks and not taking breaks he made himself forget. But again, the feelings returned. Soon he discovered there were good days and bad days. And he began to notice how his grief changed shape. It was always there, but sometimes large, some-times small. On a good day, if he closed his eyes, he could blank it. And although it came in waves, he was learning to live with it.

But then he saw, when he walked down the street, that other people weren't thinking like him. They were wrapped up in being happy or angry or looking good, or simply busy for the sake of it. When he listened in cafés they talked about sport and properties and making money. They all took holidays where they flew to the sun. They said they were stressed and feeling overlooked and didn't believe anything.

Joe went back to the science. It told him to watch out. The figures and graphs went off the page. Whatever way you looked at it, this wasn't good. To survive we'd have to change everything. Nothing less would do.

Joe decided to put aside the science and take action.

# TWENTY-THREE

"It's a matter of consciousness," Justin pronounced.

He was addressing members of the collective, standing by a fence overlooking a gully and beyond that, a steep grassed hill.

"And this," he continued, waving to the hill, "is where they did their thinking."

"You mean their theoretic base?" asked Ken, eyeing Lorna.

"A seat of learning."

Richard pulled a face. "Where they stood around listening to lectures—"

Angling her head sideways, Gabby laughed. When Justin resumed, she interrupted twice. He acknowledged her feelings before repeating his quote. "My own words," he added, beaming.

"So, this is – was – a temple, you believe?" asked Lance.

"More than that," put in Ken, "base and superstructure."

"And entirely person-made," said Justin.

A shout went up and someone started singing. Moving forward, Lorna pointed towards a path. "The top's that way," she said, tossing back her hair, "let's go."

With Caroline's help she coaxed her children through a gate. Vanessa joined, with Charlotte and Stephan. The others followed on, debating.

It was a clear, bright, late-August day. The fields were dry and powder-brown around the edges. Small spiked stems could be seen by the path.

They'd left from Lorna's about two hours earlier. Squeezed into cars, recalling the weather on last year's outing, they'd arrived mid-morning to walk through what Justin called *The Temple of Stones*. Leading down an avenue of winding sarsens, he'd talked about snake-lines and computational patterns. At a rough-cut ring of jumbled stones, he'd lectured on the Goddess. Naming various rocks, he'd guided past earthworks and out along the Ridgepath to visit the hill. After talking women's history, he'd moved to the observation point. It was here he'd mentioned dreams and university archives. "A hill of the unconscious," he'd called it, quoting his own writings. And when Lorna led off, he'd followed with Ken, discussing workers' power as they passed through the gate.

The hill was terraced, ascending in tiers. Rising abruptly, the ledges were connected by a series of steps. Sharp and angular but softened by grass, it looked like an overgrown pyramid. Led by the children they followed the path, circling around the back before climbing steeply. At the bottom there were butterflies and wasps, halfway up the drone of grasshoppers filled the air, at the top there was wind and brightness and skylarks on thermals.

They looked out from the summit. Crumbled at the edges, it dropped away suddenly: on three sides in terraces, on the fourth hollowed-out. The view was panoptic.

The children toured the edge shouting then descended to the hollow. Here they ran up and down, laughing and waving their arms like spooks. Their voices were magnified by the cut of the hill. Vanessa called a warning, but the children took no notice. "I suppose, really, they're perfectly safe," she said, turning towards Lance. When he nodded, she switched her gaze back across the top. "Now, that looks good," she said slowly, advancing towards Lorna who was laying out food on a large plastic sheet. Beside her, Caroline was digging out boxes from a backpack, opening them to display their contents like lucky dip prizes.

"Looks good," echoed Lance.

Ken approached, waving his arms. He wanted to know when they could eat.

"When you're told," Lorna snapped.

"And not beforehand," added Caroline, grinning.

Richard, who was stood at the edge next to Gabby, cut in. "We were thinking we'd go exploring."

"What about the food?" asked Vanessa. Her words, though quiet, carried clearly on the wind.

Before he could answer Gabby intervened. "So, what gives?" she asked, looking around and blinking. "Because I'll do whatever people say."

In the debate that followed Lorna decided, backed by Caroline, that eating came first. "But there's one condition," she said, staring at Ken.

"Which is?" he asked, colouring slightly.

"The men clear up."

"Unsupervised?" asked Richard, grinning.

Vanessa tut-tutted. Her eyebrows had creased up.

"Don't worry," cut in Justin, speaking hurriedly, "it will be done."

"Terms agreed," added Ken.

After they'd eaten and the men had cleared things, Richard and Gabby went off to explore. They climbed downhill, pausing to wave to the children. When they reached the observation point, they stopped and waved again before setting off along the Ridgepath. The sky was patchy as they climbed out of sight, following the track. They'd talked, and knew what they were looking for. "It's hidden by trees," Gabby called, pointing to a side track that dipped behind the hill.

They forked past grasslands dotted with small pink and blue flowers. At the bottom of the slope they passed through a gate and entered an old oak wood. The light levels dropped as they followed a route that wound through groves, enclosed by leaves and branches. The forest floor was dark and mossy in places. Walking hand in hand, they passed by overgrown mounds and dried-out hollows. "It's a time since I've been this way," said Gabby, peering around. "I'm thinking, follow the main path."

"You're sure it's here?"

"Definitely."

The path now was rocky. They walked down the middle, led by Gabby with Richard at her shoulder. The trees were twisted; some were low and sprawly, others were grotesque. When they came across a pool she stopped.

"We're near," she said.

The water made a break: a still, calm space.

Richard pointed. "I think I can see it." Through the trees a mound was visible. It was fat and long, and bulged out at odd angles.

"The passage grave," she said quietly.

Stepping over roots they approached. The mound was grassed, with bare rock showing through. It was the size of a garage but much longer. Rising sharply from the forest surface, it curved towards the top, which was ship-deck flat.

"And this must be the entrance," said Richard, as they walked up to three large stones set across one end. They were twisted sideways and gapped like teeth. Hidden behind them was an uneven stone doorway that came up to Gabby's shoulders.

"Surprised they haven't blocked it off," she said, bending to peer in. It smelled of quarried earth and rock. Beyond the doorway the chamber opened out into a stone-lined aisle with niches both sides and light holes above. It looked like a rough-hewn crypt.

They ducked and entered, then stood to inspect. Inside the air was dense and charged, either with silence or something pitched beyond hearing. "It's large," said Richard.

Gabby took his hand. "I'll guide."

Moving sideways they advanced along a tunnel that led to a stop. They were facing a wall of undressed stone, all of one piece. In the grey they could make out two large side-chambers branching off. Turning right, Gabby led along the rock face, stopping at a corner where the wall fell away. "It's a second chamber," she said, "the big stone's a screen."

They pushed through to find themselves surrounded by darkness. It was deep and still and closed-in on itself. "It's all right," whispered Gabby. She was crouching down, fumbling in her backpack, tugging out a matchbox. She struck a match and the chamber came back. "There's a candle in there," Gabby said, pointing to her backpack which had dropped to the floor.

360

Richard crouched down, groping into canvas. As Gabby chain-lit one match to another, he drew out a burnt-down candle. "Nice," she said as he handed it over.

Watching carefully, she applied the flame. The wick curled and spluttered into life and a waxy-yellow glow filled the air. As she lowered it to the floor the candle flickered.

Richard glanced around. The chamber was corbelled. He recognised the shape from one of Vanessa's photos. Compartment-like, it ran along the back of the large front stone. At the far end, where it widened to a square, he noticed that the floor was higher and contoured around the edges, with some sort of raised-up covering. "What's that?" he asked, advancing.

The square was padded with inch-thick bundles of dried vegetation. They were crossed and inter-woven like hair extensions. The air smelled sweet.

"A place for ceremonies," said Gabby quietly.

As she stepped out on the covering, it rustled like silk.

Richard stared. "What kind of ceremonies?"

"It's a marriage bed."

He hesitated.

"But it's only *called* that. It isn't really for vows."

"What's it for, then?"

"People who get on."

"Ah, comrades."

"Brethren, in the old way. Having that connection."

"And that's us?"

"A bit like blood brothers."

"You're saying we're kindred spirits?"

Gabby reached out. "Soulmates."

Richard stepped forward. The vegetation sighed and crackled as she drew him to her. Whatever his doubts, they dissolved at a touch. Their mouths came together, his tongue pushed in and they stood there in candlelight, rocking back and forth.

When they broke for air Gabby was trembling. "Undress me," she whispered.

Stooping slightly, Richard pulled at her clothes. Gabby helped, releasing her top then kicking off both shoes and undoing her belt. As he rolled down her jeans she leaned against the wall, repeating his name. His expression softened as he fumbled to remove her underwear.

"Your turn," she said, unbuttoning his shirt.

When they were naked, they kissed. Gabby drew him down and they stretched out on the floor. At the centre, where they lay, the plants were thicker. They were overspread with petals and live green stems.

Richard touched her, delicately at first. A slow, searching insistence possessed his body. She was all he wanted: his strange, wild, shy, runaway woman. He kissed her breasts and directed her hand down onto his penis. As she worked and teased, they both began to shiver. A gently moving excitement was filling him up. She had him in her hand.

"Ready," he hissed, and rolled up to mount. He paused, suspended, then fumbling and flexing, entered.

Gabby shuddered. "Yes," she sang, and grabbed for his back.

Richard kicked forward, beating time. Inside her body, he could feel her glowing as if they were naked in the sun. The thought came alive and suddenly he was willing and hot all over: his body was hers. Something was rising, pushing and filling up the chamber. For a second he slowed and hung in the air before accelerating towards climax. When Gabby shouted, he felt himself leap, then shake and shake and shake.

Afterwards they dozed, lying side by side.

Gabby stirred first, levering herself up to rest on one arm. "Not so warm," she said, touching his face and kissing. When they broke, she crouched up and turned. "My back," she said, "can you see it?"

Richard looked. Where the candle lit up her flesh, she was light brown, blotched and streaked all over. Her skin was crosshatched and marked with multi-coloured flower heads. "You're a Matisse," he said.

"Feels itchy, like wearing wool."

"It's the plants, they've taken to you."

Widening her eyes, she reached around to touch.

"You're a garden," he laughed.

"In that case, they stay."

"You're going to keep them?"

"As much as I can."

He checked her back again. It was textured like wallpaper. "But how d'you … what's your plan?"

Gabby stood and gathered up her clothes. "If you hold the stems," she said slowly, "I'll dress over."

"Won't that pull them off?"

She reached down to her sack. "Not if you rub this in," she said, holding up a jar of ointment. "It's good stuff, should do the trick. After all, they're much of a muchness, a mishmash of oils and leaves and fibres. Everything should run together."

Richard hesitated then smiled. "It's herbal glue," he declared, hitching on his shirt before taking the jar. "Full treatment?" he asked. Gabby nodded, and he began.

Working slowly, he picked off a few stems then started oiling. The colours ran and fused with her skin, releasing a gentle earthy fragrance. "Back to nature," he said, working on the curves at the base of her spine.

When the mixture had sunk in, she started dressing. "I think we ought to show our faces," she said as she leaned against the wall pulling on her jeans, "otherwise they'll be wondering what's happened."

"Perhaps it's best …"

"Yes …?"

"Well, we really don't want them to realise."

"Ah, I suppose that's a thought. So d'you think we need a story?"

"Something like that."

"OK, we'll work it out as we go. Now, shall we get ready and head on back?"

Shivering slightly, Richard finished dressing and picked up the candle. "Lead me the way," he said holding it high and putting out his hand. "The candle's getting hot," he said, stepping forward.

When they'd cleared the doorway, he turned and blew it out. The darkness was instant. "Kiss me," she whispered, "before we go."

He put down the candle and they embraced. The chamber now was visible, outlined in grey. The closeness of her body made it seem both bright and shadowy. Hearing her words repeating in his head, Richard squeezed, Gabby squeezed back, and their mouths came together.

When they left the mound, the weather had changed. The afternoon had closed up, the air was colder and a few light stipples of rain were drifting through the trees.

"We'd better get back," Richard said, holding out his hand. Inside himself, he was still in the chamber. A calm, soft glow lay between them.

"I smell like a potpourri," she laughed, allowing him to lead her.

Richard could make out a light skin smell, a mix between body and oil. The scent, which was watery, came and went. Already the rain was damping it down. "Look out," he said. The forest had darkened and the path was uneven. As they sidestepped rocks and skirted hollows, the rain picked up.

Bending forward, he caught a whiff of plant; it set off a picture of vein lines on flesh. As he walked, the image faded. "It's getting worse," he said. The air became thick and damp with side-drifts, gusting, and water-splashing falls, followed by gaps.

"And worse," Gabby called out.

They sheltered for a while, crouched beneath an oak, until the wind got under, making them shiver.

The rain intensified as they passed beyond the trees and climbed uphill. It fell in sheets, bathing their heads and soaking their clothes. They were half-running now, shouting to each other. By the time they reached the Ridgepath, the wind was in their faces and the air was thick with flying water.

"Oh shit," cried Richard, pushing on. As they neared the observation point, he could just make out the flat-topped hill: it was bare and grey and blurred around the edges. He peered across the fields, aware of something odd. Suddenly he realised that the gulley around the hill had vanished beneath a ring of standing water.

"There's an underground feed," cried Gabby. "Cuts off the hill."

"You mean …?" said Richard, looking puzzled. "Remember, the path's at the back."

"I'm sure—"

"They could be still around."

The downpour continued, working into everything. "Look," said Richard suddenly, pointing to a corner where some figures were emerging, stepping through water. "It's them," he said, waving.

The tightly-bunched group cleared the pool and pushed uphill. Richard descended with Gabby, closing the gap. When they met, the rain kept them head down and purposeful. Their clothes were wet through.

"You all right?" Richard asked the children, who were hand in hand with their mother. As he spoke the rain slackened off.

"We need to get them back," Vanessa countered. Charlotte and Stephan shivered, saying nothing.

"How come you stayed out? Didn't you realise?"

Vanessa bridled. "Realise what?"

"When it started. You needed to leave."

"No thanks to you."

Lance, at her shoulder, looked startled.

Richard frowned and fell in behind, muttering.

As they passed through the gate, Stephan slipped and fell against his mother, crying.

"This is stupid," Richard snapped.

"*Tais-toi*," called Vanessa, speaking into air.

"What did you say?"

"Richard," she called warningly.

"Come on, tell me."

Vanessa repeated his name.

"Don't *Richard* me. Tell me what you said."

"Shush. It was nothing."

"Bloody—"

"Richard!"

"Bloody, bloody …"

"*Tais-toi*."

"What?"

"*Tais-toi.*"

"You mean that?"

Vanessa sucked in her cheeks.

"No. No. You don't have the right …"

"*Tais-toi.*"

"No, you shut it. *You* bloody shut it."

The rain cut him off. It returned full-force, falling on the earth, the path and on the grass. The rain ran things together, beating on their skin, their hair and clothes, going in deep and slowing their movements. It filled up their eyes and trickled into mouths. Deluge-like it spread and covered everything.

The picnic was over.

♯ ♯ ♯

Afterwards when Vanessa looked back, she could see how all their talk about open support and wider structures hadn't really worked. They'd returned to Richard late at night on piano mouthing words like "crap", while she took photos and kept up with the latest news. As a couple, their positions had hardened. Not only hardened but taken on a slowness, a dead stop feel that she called The Block.

The Block was on everything. It concealed itself in the silence and the edge behind his words and charged up the breaks, introducing a shortness between them that affected all they did. The block was in their hearts.

And then, quite suddenly, after a session with Ruth and a long phone call with Bess, Vanessa decided. What was needed, she said, was a new agenda. Something to get a sense of purpose and find a different way.

"What was that you were saying about a break?" asked Richard standing in the doorway after bedding down the children.

"A chance to catch up," said Vanessa, "and find out what we want." She was sitting on the front room sofa reading a newspaper. Every so often she angled forward to sip her herbal tea.

"How d'y' mean?"

"We need to know where we stand."

Richard looked doubtful. "Isn't that about talking, or not talking?"

"Maybe, maybe not, we'll have to see."

The silence returned. Vanessa eyed her paper while Richard leaned against the doorframe. "It's up to us," he said finally, stepping into the lounge, "*we* have to talk."

"Does that *we* mean me or both of us?"

"I think you know the answer to that."

"I do?"

"Well, if you don't—"

"Who does? Is that what you think?"

"I don't get your point."

"The point is ..." she began with a sigh, then switched. "It's how you operate. Everything's decided from the start. Whatever it is, even what I'm saying now, you've made up your mind beforehand. It's all slam-bam, cut and dried and fitted into categories. You *assume* all the time."

"And it's all my fault, of course. Always."

"I didn't mean that. Just if you could put it differently some-times ..."

"I see. It ain't what you say but the way you say it, eh?"

"It's true. You need to talk, not give out."

"Well, if that's what you believe," he moved towards the door, "then I can only suggest we see someone."

"In any case, talk has to be equal. It's not a one-way street."

"Absolutely." He stared her in the face. "Absolutely so."

Vanessa flushed. "What are you suggesting?"

"We need help."

"We?"

"Yes, we."

"So, in your opinion, what should *we* be thinking of?"

"A counsellor."

She pressed one hand against her newspaper. "Ah, I see. But it wasn't that long ago ..."

Richard stood back. The tempo had dropped, allowing him to think.

"Well, if you ask me," he said, 'it's still worth a shot."

Reaching for her tea, Vanessa drained her cup before speaking. "You want to go back to that man? What was his name – Chris? You called him The Q and A man, the one who kept asking how we felt."

"Someone new would be better."

"What makes you say that?"

"Well, partly money. But also, what we got out of it. In the end he didn't do much."

"That's one way of looking at it."

"I reckon that kind of counselling is a con. It's all about dodging and staying on the surface. Don't rock the boat and don't, whatever you do, get too close to the problem."

"Hmm. I see your point."

"So, we need a different counsellor."

"Seems so."

"And who's going to look for this person?"

Vanessa thought it over. When he repeated his question, she made to speak, then sighed.

"How about if I do it?" he asked, more gently.

"Would you?"

"You want that?"

"If we could."

"So, in this case *we* means me. But I'll be doing it for me *and* you – yes?"

Vanessa confirmed. Picking up her cup and paper, she rose from the sofa and walked out to the kitchen. "*We* have to try," she said, depositing her cup and returning to the hallway.

Richard was waiting, saying nothing, at the bottom of the stairs.

"And we do what we do," she added quietly as they climbed past the kids' bedrooms and along by a short half landing to their curtained front bedroom.

They arrived at the counsellor's house just before 2 p.m. Leaving the car Richard led across a green, surrounded on three sides by flat-roofed blocks. At the main road he paused, Vanessa pointed, and they crossed between trees to arrive at the building.

It was low and set back from the road. Last but one in a long, terraced row, it had steps with railings, casement windows and a paved front garden. Richard glanced at his watch then pressed the bell, while Vanessa stared down at the basement.

The door was answered by a short, ginger-haired woman wearing a blue sequinned dress and white, ballet-shaped pumps. She was pale-skinned, with soft expressive eyes and a small, round face. Her eyes and lips were lightly made-up. Vanessa judged her to be nearing 40.

"Mr and Mrs Lavender? Pleased to meet you. I'm Letitia, do come in." Her voice was warmly upbeat with a playful edge. Richard noticed her Home Counties' accent.

They entered a hallway with dado and features. There were glimpses through doors of wall-to-wall bookshelves and period furniture. The house smelled of polish and flowers. Their host led in to a short flight of stairs where she stepped to one side. "I consult in the lounge," she said, pointing. "Up there." The arm she raised displayed a thick gold bracelet.

She followed them up to a softly-furnished room with a key-pattern carpet, gold-flecked curtains and abstract paintings hung in pairs. "If you'd care to sit," she called, "sofa, chairs, on the floor if you like."

Vanessa chose an armchair and Richard sprawled on the couch. Between them, positioned on a low glass table, was a water jug and glasses.

Letitia mentioned the loo and hanging up jackets then drew up a chair. It was high-backed and wooden with a small central cushion. She perched there, watching.

"So, introductions …" she said, smiling. Her tone had become ultra-bright and unequivocal. "My name, as I think you know, is Letitia Cauldwell and I've been a fully accredited counsellor for fifteen years. My background is interdisciplinary, but my main approach is encounter, which I'd say is more direct than most." Pausing, she adjusted her dress, sending small flecks of light dancing across the carpet.

As she moved on to fees, Richard found himself comparing her with Chris. Mouse Man, he'd called him. A still-life character allowing things to drift, a man of no qualities leading from behind ...

"And I may set you tasks," concluded Letitia, "homework, you might call it." The smile that followed was torch-beam-directed, taking them both in. It was as if she was preparing them for a part.

Neither answered.

"In that case," said Letitia, "let's talk." She began with Vanessa, asking about facts: how long they'd been together, children, status, employment, interests shared, and what they did together.

"You mean films, meals out, that sort of thing?"

"Anything. Visits, chats, television programmes, whatever you both enjoy as a couple."

"There's not much we enjoy."

Letitia fixed her gaze on her client. Her hands were in her lap, and her features had rounded. "Tell me," she said, "what really *happens* between you."

Vanessa sighed.

"How would you sum up your marriage?"

"Oh, I don't know. Disappointing, I suppose."

"Anything else?"

"Not much."

"Tell me how it disappoints."

"It's full of problems. Too many to name."

"But if I asked you to name them."

"What, all of them? You want that?"

"As many as you can. I'd like you to spell them out. It's important."

Vanessa frowned, studying the carpet. "Well, lack of communication, that's one. Assumptions, that's another. An attachment to being right, that's all the time. Sometimes intolerance, sometimes hype, and a certain relentlessness. Male stuff, really."

"And what do you want out of a relationship?" The counsellor's question, delivered softly, filled the room.

Vanessa shifted in her seat. "I'm not sure, these days I don't really think about that."

"But if you could have anything at all, what would you have?"

370

"Well, I might have more freedom, that sort of thing."

"And anything else?"

"Not sure."

"I'm thinking of the full wish list, everything you tell your friends you want."

"Well, I suppose I do need a bit of peace and quiet, and care if you like. A different approach where things happen slowly, so there's a chance to relax and not feel pressured. And enough time and space to feel there's someone there listening."

"And how about you?" Letitia asked, switching to Richard. Her gaze was direct and challenging.

"Well I don't agree with anything just said," he flashed.

"You don't? What in particular do you disagree with?"

"Everything."

"And when you were sitting here listening, what were the hot spots, the things you disagreed with most?"

"The things about men. And about me. Which was all of it, really."

"So, can I ask you, what *exactly* was said about you?"

"Oh, that I'm no good, falling short, running the show. There's always something."

Letitia held up a hand. "Very well, I'm going to set an exercise. It's to help you to get to grips with my question." She rose and faced them. "All you have to do is keep silent. No words or gestures or looking around. Just three minutes thinking about what you want from your marriage, simple as that." Letitia stood back, glanced at her watch and reached down a small silver bell from a shelf. "And to remind you, every minute I shall ring this," here she shook the bell. "So that when I ring, it means 'keep thinking about what you want from your relationship'."

She checked them for readiness. Vanessa was happy, Richard noncommittal.

"And now, I shall start you off." Stepping forward, she shook the bell so it tinkled brightly. As she rang, she called out a reminder.

Silence filled the room. With it came a closeness, a walled-in feeling – suddenly it was as if they were in a crowd, squeezed into a corner, trying not to touch.

After one minute, Letitia called and rang quietly, after two she was louder, and at three she rang full volume. "Time!" she cried, returning to her chair.

"Very well, what do you want from a relationship?" she asked Richard.

"It has to match somehow," he answered slowly.

"I see, so what's involved in a *match*?"

Richard glanced over at Vanessa. "I suppose," he said, "it's all about overlapping circles. Getting the right fit, not too much, not too little."

"Anything more?"

"Not really," he answered. "Except we don't."

Letitia leaned to one side, watching him closely. "What you're saying is you don't have any shared interests. None at all, is that right?"

"None that work."

"But you did have some in the past?"

He hesitated then nodded almost imperceptibly.

She swung around in her chair. "And if I asked you both, could you name them?" Her tone now was light and upbeat. It was as if she was chairing a debate.

They stared, saying nothing.

"In that case," she continued, standing and pushing back her chair, "I'd like us to try exercise number two, downstairs."

Vanessa raised one hand halfway to her cheek then allowed it to fall. Richard remained still, awaiting developments.

"It's OK," Letitia said, addressing Vanessa, "I do this with lots of clients." She walked to the door. "If you'd like to come this way, please."

As she moved to the landing, the sequins on her dress glittered. Her moon-soft face was round and inviting.

Her clients waited until she repeated, then they looked both ways, as if to check the traffic, and rose to join her. "Down here," she called, leading to the steps and turning left through a pair of double doors.

Inside was an oblong area with whitewashed walls and a bare wooden floor. It was barred on one side, with ropes in the corner, coiled like snakes. The other side was cluttered with balls in nets, a collection of sticks and a heaped-up pile of rubberised mats. "The games room," Letitia called, walking to the centre.

Glancing around, her clients joined her. She examined them with a blandly attentive expression. "But for us," she said quietly, "it's a place where we step outside ourselves."

Vanessa inclined her head to one side.

"Don't worry," said Letitia, "it's simple. I'll talk you through it so you understand what's happening."

She pointed to a line drawn across the floor. It was white and glossy, blurred around the edges, and marked off an area by the far wall. "We're going to play. But it's more than a game, it may change how you think."

Richard and Vanessa stood looking.

"You know *What's the time Mr Wolf?*" she asked.

Vanessa confirmed.

"You know it also?" she checked, staring at Richard.

The yes she received sounded matter-of-fact, like a name check.

Addressing them both, Letitia developed her thoughts briefing-style, as if she was their trainer. "You sneak up from there," she said, waving to the line. "While I'm Mrs Wolf, up there," she added, indicating the door end. "Now when I call out a time, for example three o'clock, four o'clock or ten o'clock, then you take that number of steps. But if I turn around – freeze."

"And if you call supper time …" prompted a deadpan Richard.

"Then scoot. Get behind the line before I can catch you."

She had to repeat herself, fielding questions from a doubtful-looking Vanessa. After a short trial with Richard as wolf, during which he broke out twice without proper cueing, she invited comment. Receiving none, she placed them behind the line and retreated to the door end. "If anyone cheats, you tell me," she called sharply, turning her back.

Her clients exchanged glances.

"So, can I hear you? Your words please. Now."

Richard rolled his eyes. "What's the time Mrs Wolf?"

"One o'clock."

They both took a step forward. Richard, a big one; Vanessa, a shuffle.

"What's the time Mrs Wolf?" – Richard's voice leading, Vanessa's joining in.

"Three o'clock."

Three more steps, all middling.

"What's the time Mrs Wolf?" – one voice loud, the other soft.

"Four o'clock."

Again, they advanced. At this point they were two yards away from her with Richard in front and Vanessa close behind.

"What's the time Mrs Wolf?"

"One o'clock."

Richard took a small stride then stopped dead as Letitia whipped round. "You're moving," she said, pointing.

"He's not," Vanessa countered.

Richard's eyes widened. Neutral was best.

Letitia stared suspiciously. "Tongue and lips," she said, quickly.

Vanessa shook her head. "It's only feet that count."

"I see, and that's the rule?"

"It is," replied Richard.

Letitia, looking hawkish, turned her back. "Your call."

"What's the time—"

Before they could finish, she was round and staring. "Supper time!" she laughed, lunging forward.

Richard skipped off and away. "Behind the line!" he sang as he dodged her outstretched hand.

Vanessa scrambled her way back, side-gripping the bars. "Off the floor!" she cried when Letitia tagged her.

"Over the line anyway," Richard put in.

Letitia drew back. "Very well, we begin again."

She returned to her post. This time she answered all their calls in ones and twos, spinning around sharply at unexpected moments. Realising her tactic, Richard slowed his approach, stopping when he sensed movement. Vanessa stayed close to the bars, advancing in spurts. When Letitia called *supper time* they both flung themselves backwards, twisting out of reach. In the end, after several rushes and a number of freezes plus a couple of send-backs, it was Vanessa who reached out and successfully tagged her.

"Well done," Letitia called. "Now, let us conclude."

Breathing hard, they followed her to the lounge and sat down. Her eyes flicked side to side, like a medic taking observations. "So how do you feel?" she asked.

"Surprised," said Richard. "But quite stimulated." Vanessa gestured into air without saying anything.

Letitia drew out an A4-sized whiteboard. "And this," she declared, holding up a pen, "is my magic marker." She leaned down and up, uniting the two. "And do we have anything from today to put down?" she continued, demonstrating a tab that rubbed out words. "Anything we *can* do together?"

"Counselling," said Richard dryly.

"True," she said, printing his comment. "Anything else?"

"Children's games," said Vanessa.

"Yes, anything more?"

"Working against you," Richard replied softly.

"And?"

Vanessa pursed her lips, "Running away?"

"That's so," put in Richard, pulling a face.

Letitia transcribed the comments. She asked Richard to hold up the board and stepped back, measuring it carefully like a prospective purchase. "One more," she said.

"Another?" said Richard, returning the board. "There are five?"

Letitia nodded.

He locked his fingers together. "I think you mean, when you challenged us."

"Go on."

Vanessa leaned forward, wrinkling up her nose. "It's like Vaughan."

Letitia sat back. "Explain please."

"My cousin, he's not easy, but he likes adventure."

"So, number five?"

"Risk taking."

Their counsellor copied out. The board was full of neatly-printed words.

Richard unlocked his fingers. "I've two more. Six and seven."

The women stared.

"I'd like to write them up."

Letitia smiled, passing him the pen.

Approaching the board, he crouched down and pulled the tab, erasing the words. "They cover all the rest," he said, raising the pen. "When you challenged us," he said, "I thought of this. It's political, of course."

Richard wrote slowly and awkwardly in a badly formed scrawl *1. Backing up*. After it, in brackets, he wrote *each other*. Finally, after some hesitation, he raised the marker again and added underneath:

*2. FINDING*

*A*

*MATCH*

He paused then repeated it on the right, using identical capitals. "And," he said, half-circling both statements, "there's the question of overlap." He completed the circles, creating an empty space in the middle. "It's in here," he added quietly, pointing to the centre, "where we don't ever go – that's the place."

"Don't ever?" asked Letitia.

"Don't usually," corrected Vanessa.

"But maybe we've been there today?" Richard put in.

"In theory, yes," Letitia said. "And that's where we'll be next week," she concluded, "looking at the detail. Seeing what you share, or could do if you chose to." She stood up with a flourish, inviting them to join her. The session was at an end.

Richard paid in cash. Vanessa checked her diary and booked in the next visit. Adjusting their expressions, they filed out through the door with Letitia behind them. "And your homework," she said, "which you can do individually or together, is listing what you share."

She watched them out to the gate. When they reached the pavement, she turned back to her door. Outlined against the building Letitia paused there, smoothing her hair and adjusting her dress. As they set off down the road, she raised one hand to wave them off. "Next time, the overlap," she called out smiling, and stepped back into the house.

As she turned, her hair coloured up, the sequins on her dress shone and sparkled, and her bracelet gleamed gold in the afternoon sun.

# TWENTY-FOUR

### Families, Imaginary Histories and the Silence of Gossip by Professor M Lavender (Cont.)

Welcome back to the second half of this talk. I hope you all feel adequately refreshed. In this part I shall present an abstract of our main findings, relating some of the key ideas to actual, lived experience. Apologies for using universal first person as my expositional style. I have adopted this for rhetorical purposes and in order to reduce the many team discussions we conducted to a single thread. The inclusion of the personal also reflects the conventions of a lecture, with its emphasis on oral directness and immediacy. In Marshall McLuhan's famous phrase, The Medium is The Message.

Detailed evidence for the assertions that follow, and a full account of who led the various sub-projects, can be found in the appendix to my book.

I first formulated the idea of imaginary family histories after reading Benedict Anderson's analysis of nationalism. In his model, people in an area bond around a number of defining incidents, passed down as gospel by print-capitalism. These shared incidents are, of course, projections. Like the Libet experiment, rather than being *out there* they are shaped by unconscious impulses. In a similar way, families doctor their pasts, employing some of Freud's dream-mechanisms such as distortion, displacement and secondary elaboration.

To give a few examples:

377

1. Events or people can be written out of family histories. I first encountered this with my grandmother. Her death, which I now know happened in hospital, was a mystery to me. Nothing was said. All I knew at the time was that she'd disappeared from the beach. For a while I just supposed she was taking a nap or walking in the garden, and from then on, our paths didn't cross. As time went on, her unexplained absence threw a blanket over everything. My life became unreal, like walking in fog or being wrapped in cotton wool. It may have been a factor in my late development.

   As my research widened, I became aware that friends and acquaintances can also be written *in* to family histories, becoming known affectionately as aunts and uncles. Some interviewees described being closer in childhood to these quasi-family members than their true blood relatives. They found it helpful to talk to an open-minded adult who could offer non-judgemental advice.

2. Families often scapegoat one or more of their members. The *bad 'un* and the *black sheep* cropped up in several interviews. The exact reasons for exclusion weren't always articulated, but words like "rivals", "tearaways" and "daredevils" were often used. My family contained a Prodigal Son, an Angel and more than one rebel.

3. In fact, some of the families I studied acted rather like casting agencies. They fitted each other to parts such as *good woman, policeman, naughty child, funny girl* or *perfectionist*. For many, the part was linked to a single squirm-making anecdote or one embarrassing physical characteristic. Reinforcement was achieved through daily teases and reminders.

4. In all the families I interviewed personal names were subject to whim and caprice. Nicknames were used, joke titles or single-letter epithets, and sometimes a family member was assigned a pseudonym. For example, my great-grandmother was christened Jane. At the age of three she was told by an outspoken aunt that she looked like a Grace. The family were told so too, repeatedly, and the new name stuck.

5. Denial and issues of control were to be found in all the families. This included young people denying wrongdoing, couples denying feelings and the elderly editing the past. Some forms of denial disguised themselves as kindness. For instance the faux-sympathetic phrase, "I'm only saying this to help you", said with a smile, was intended as a cheek slap. It sanctioned rudeness in the name of authenticity. Other power plays such as "don't tell me" and "it never did me any harm" came with large keep-out warning signs. Their purpose was to avoid any possible comeback. Finally, the we-tell-it-as-it-is families often seemed to require higher fences and more no-go areas around their lives than anybody else. The role of Honest John is always open to question.

   Reversals and trust-me declarations are essentially more of the same. So, I went through a no-denial-no-bullshit phase myself where I practised baring the soul in a robust, Blakeian fashion. This, of course, was the ultimate cover-up. I was stridently honest, using what I call diversionary denial, much like the panto call, "It's behind you!".

6. The legitimacy question did arise in my studies, often over family property and inheritance. But it was also used to define children, usually through phrases such as "where did he/she get that from?" Or "oh, he/she is so like x or y". Other variants were, "this isn't like you", "you're not really like that" or "no son of mine".

I remember turning this trope on its head and convincing myself, for a while, that I was living with the wrong family. I imagined a hospital mix-up or that I'd been adopted. Fortunately, I took a good look in the mirror.

7. Families make free use of the words *always* and *never*, as in, "you *always* do that" or "you *never* listen" and "you *never* understand". This is a tactic teenagers employ often, upping the stakes through phrases such as "look what you've done to me", "you've hurt my feelings" and Eric Berne's UGMIT (You Got Me into This).

8. Many families have gaps. Like holes in a CV, they are the omissions that excite special interest. In view of their frequent occurrence I probed for reasons. Sometimes this was to do with things being taken for granted or seen as unimportant – they didn't get a mention because they were always there. Sometimes the emotional charge they carried made it easier not to talk about them. For example, I recently discovered that my father's father was a keen chess player. He and my father played every day. When my grandfather left for the war, he was two moves away from checkmate. That position still sits on a table in my parents' bedroom. Similarly, my aunt has a jumper knitted by my grandmother. The pattern on it is a white dove.

Other gaps are more practical, like lost keys. But of course these things – keys, coins, photos, keepsakes – all disappear for a reason. There's a hidden noire meaning behind it. For instance, I found myself investigating stories that suddenly cut off. The family split or a character went missing and when they returned, they were either the same as if nothing had happened, or they'd changed so much they were no longer recognisable.

9.  One part of my study focused on gossip. Here it was important to distinguish between reinforcement talk, aimed at strengthening already existing ties, and subversive talk such as "I don't know why you put up with it". Both had a pressure-release function designed to render any further action unnecessary.

The original, working title for this project was *The Team Family and the Castle of Dreams*. This was intended to highlight the protective and aspirational roles of two different types of Team Family.

a)  Firstly, the horizontally-aligned *togetherness* families. These were made up of homemakers who marked birthdays and paid close, careful attention to get-togethers and protective shielding. In these groups peer solidarity was more important than jobs, qualifications or material possessions. Often these families were nonconformists with a preference for long-term values based on the expressive arts or religion. For this group, keeping in touch with other family members was a priority. They were, however, described by a few interviewees as "hard to live up to", "pie in the sky" or "overprotective".

b)  Secondly, the vertically-aligned, aspirational families whose primary focus was upward mobility. These groups were perfectionists and heavily driven by praise and criticism. Like high-performance sportspeople, they were rarely satisfied with an achievement and impatient to move on to the next challenge. Relationships in the group were often described as "difficult", "fraught" and "stressful". Many of these families either separated or drifted apart. In the ones that stayed together frequent spats and fall-outs were the norm.

One interesting pattern that emerged was that people who came from vertically-aligned families frequently chose partners from collectively-minded families, and vice versa. It would appear that the frisson of opposites can hold a marriage together. This pole-to-pole dance is a dialectic observable in my own family where unlike partnerships, including my own, have been common ...

At which point I'd like to move on to Deci and Ryan's notion of self-determination, with its core values of competence, autonomy and psychological relatedness, and introduce a few final observations along similar lines, based on first-hand experience ...

‡ ‡ ‡

Richard.
Yes.
Shall we make that list?
What list?
Letitia's. About what we share.
We could.
You'd like to do that?
If you want.
You don't sound very keen.
I don't mind.
But do you actually *want* to?
I'll do it, as long as you think it'll work.
Well, we could do it separately, if you want.
I choose – together or apart – yes?
Well, if that makes you happy. You decide.
So, let's be clear, if I say yes then that'd be me, doing it *my way*. Correct?
If you say so.
You sure? Aren't all men like that?
Like what?
Individualistic, competitive, wanting their own way.
Listen, Richard, that's not what I said. I just asked if you wanted to make a list.

382

OK, let's look at this – suppose we do it together and it all goes pear-shaped then it'll be my fault. And if we don't, then guess who's to blame …

Well, if you carry on this way …

I'll spoil it, of course.

Richard, don't be awkward.

Because I'm the spoiler.

Only if you want to be.

But isn't that my job? I say the things you don't want to hear.

Oh, this is impossible.

Exactly. Like I was saying, it's all because of me.

¶

Vanessa.

Yes.

I've thought about what you said.

You have?

About making a list.

Oh, that.

And doing it together.

I don't really think …

I know I wasn't very helpful.

You do?

I think it's a good idea.

Then as far as you're concerned it's back on?

Well, we could try. Are you up for it?

Maybe.

Maybe?

Maybe not.

Uh-uh, so it's like that. Maybe and maybe not.

Yes, that's what I said.

Meaning, it's up to me if we do it, but you're opting out.

No, you can go ahead, if you want to. I'll listen, but I don't guarantee anything.

I see. I'm left hanging while you do the grand lady thing.

Richard, there's no need to talk like that.

*Tais-toi*?

This isn't working.

And whose fault's that? Mine, of course. The nasty Richard does it again.

All right, whatever you say. It really doesn't matter.

OK, forget it.

Richard, have you made your list?

Ah, so we're back to that.

I just thought I'd ask, but if you don't want to talk …

No, you're right, we should talk.

Yes, but you know how it usually ends.

Well, we have to try. How about if I say what we share? Things in common.

If you like.

OK, number one, stroppiness, me a bit more than you. But only a small bit, I have to say. Number two, the children, though we can't agree on much about them. Three, politics of course, though again I think there are differences. Four – no, I've said enough. What about you? What do you think we share?

Well, I'm not sure. An education, I suppose, and we're both teachers. We used to watch films together.

Now that's what Letitia was talking about. What we *do* together.

Or used to.

What if we made a list?

We could, and do it as an exercise. Like one of Letitia's games.

And we could put in ratings. Stars, that sort of thing.

Then give it to her?

Yes, that sounds reasonable. Now, who's going to scribe?

You can.

You're happy with that?

Happy.

OK, I've got pen and paper …

```
┌─────────────────────────────────────────────────────────┐
│                  IDEAS FOR SHARING                         │
│ ****    BIRTHDAYS – V likes surprises. R likes outings to new │
│         places.                                            │
│ ****    GARDENS – Colour/scent/shape/sensual. An escape.   │
│ ****    ZOOS, good memories.                               │
│ ***     FILMS, Satyajit Ray, Sembene, Bergman.            │
│ ***     ART EXHIBITIONS – esp Photographer's Gallery,      │
│         V&A.                                                │
│ ***     WALKS in the city. Markets, florists, coffee shops.│
│ **      VISITING FRIENDS, some helpful, others can         │
│         separate/stir up.                                  │
│ **      TV WATCHING, addictive, like sweets, but different │
│         tastes.                                            │
│ *       DINNER PARTIES – a job to prepare. Can be grand-   │
│         standing/ combative.                               │
│ *       HOLIDAYS – extra work. Detail, detail. LOTS of time│
│         together. Can blow up.                             │
└─────────────────────────────────────────────────────────┘
```

Richard?

Yes?

Should we add something?

Like what … More ideas?

No, a conclusion.

If you think that's needed. Saying what?

Talking about *shared* things, a description.

Another list, you mean?

I was thinking more about the patterns. What they have in common.

You mean doing stuff together?

Yes, and what that's like.

I see …

And how we make those things happen.

Ah, I get it. A how-to guide.

How-to and how it feels.

Right. Let's talk about it.

And you'll write it up for Letitia?

If that's what you want.

CONCLUSION

We decided,

DOING THINGS TOGETHER is like:

    1.   Learning a new tune.

    2.   Housework or gardening.

    3.   Small actions to reinforce progress.

    4.   A walk in the park.

To explain:

1. Learning a new tune takes practice in small chunks, following the notes and counting. At the start, it's about going slowly. When you get up to speed, that's when you add in expression/feel. The method is to practise with no mistakes. And if you slip up, go back to the beginning, like Snakes and Ladders.

2. Housework or gardening

a) Because both keep returning day after day.

b) What you don't do today will be bigger tomorrow.

c) You have to keep at it.

d) Even a small change can freshen things up.

3. Small actions with transitional targets. The waymarked approach. How far we've come, how far to go.

4. You can walk in the park thinking about what's just happened or where you have to be. Or you can do it hearing the birds, noticing flowers, enjoying the sun. Even the most ordinary walk is an adventure, if you see it that way.

*Richard Lavender*       *Vanessa Lavender*

# TWENTY-FIVE

When school began in September, Richard and Vanessa knew what to expect. There were all the usual problems – photocopier break-downs, books gone missing, rooming clashes and too few chairs – plus a long list of duties. There were groups to organise, tasks to dish out, lessons to plan and of course, issues of control. But by now they'd made their mark. Known to the staff as *activists* and accepted by the kids as *all right teachers*, they understood the score. Because they'd fixed on a style: a blend of cool-talk and tough-talk where they stayed in charge but showed themselves willing to fit where necessary.

For Richard it was an act, a well-practised scenario where he signalled what he wanted. It kicked in usually as he walked into classrooms, and he felt himself taking on a character, a kind of second self. In he came and laid out his terms, giving order and direction without a pause for thought. He was up front and on it, simple as that.

For Vanessa it was a struggle, a fragile, thin-lipped battle against school rules and procedures that made each lesson feel like an exam. There were books and extracts and equipment and worksheets and tasks to give out, all of which involved detailed preparation – like entertaining family or setting up an art show – and talking pupils through. Because behind what she did was so much hand-holding and childminding and jollying-along.

"You carry everything with you," she once told Ruth. "A bagful of supplies, pens, pencils, paper, rulers, rubbers, whatever they've for-gotten, usually everything, you'd better have it."

So school, with its coded assumptions and all-too familiar prob-lems, kept them together. But it also kept them separate. They'd other things to do, some pressing, some political and some just intended … but also what moved and touched them, and underpinned their lives.

And for Richard it was the emptiness behind everything, the sense of missing out. He called it his *otherness*, his Richard-boy-self, con-cealed behind the teacher he glimpsed in the mirror. And although he could block it out by keeping busy, he wished for something firmer, a feeling of connection.

But for Vanessa it was practical. She'd rather, she said wryly, change what she did, because teaching was a bore. What should be a job had turned into a calling, an imposition really, so that everything else was pushed into the background. It felt too much like a burden.

And then Lorna rang up with a proposal. What she said came as a surprise.

"It's a breakthrough for me," Vanessa told Richard afterwards. "A women's exhibition with people Lorna knows."

"Really? That's a bit of luck."

"Are you pleased?"

"Why wouldn't I be?"

"I can think of a few reasons."

"Maybe. But it doesn't have to be like that."

"You sure?"

"It could be just what we need."

"Is that the royal we, perhaps?"

"More like getting in on the act – a bit. The trickle-down effect."

"Well, I'm not sure about that. Are you saying something about me?"

"Not at all. I'm just pointing out it's all a bit random. You never know. Anyway, I *am* pleased."

"You are?"

"Absolutely. Now tell me about it."

She gave him the details: a large mixed-media show featuring several artists, run in an East End warehouse.

He listened, nodding. Already he could see them stepping clean through the door to a gallery. He imagined it as a walk-through chamber with graffiti-ed walls and improvised furniture, a punk-art-emporium where those with attitude came to make their mark.

He asked about arrangements.

Vanessa beamed. "It's soon, next month. Lorna's got the contacts and they want me near the entrance. They call it *Seeing Red*."

"It's political?"

"Yes. Also arty, I think."

"And you've got enough photos?"

"Mostly. A few to finish."

"Perhaps I can help with transport, setting up, that sort of thing."

"Well, that's kind …" She paused, meeting his gaze for a second.

"It's something for both of us. Doug could be useful as well."

Vanessa's eyes widened. "Ah, you mean Barnard and co, man with van."

Her words took him back to the move-in and the outing that followed, and how absurd they'd been. He laughed. "Well, not the same vehicle. But in principle, much the same thing."

"Very well," she replied, "in principle, yes."

During run-up to the exhibition, Doug and Richard DIY-ed the show. After finding the building they brought in spare doors and palettes, using them as display boards. They drilled the floor and screwed in supports and connectors, building what looked like a makeshift compound. Inside was a viewing area with crenellated walls, made good and sanded. During construction, Vanessa painted the surfaces and screwed hooks into the panels, ready for hanging.

It was while she was deciding her arrangement that Vanessa was visited by two mid-thirties women, one wearing denim covered with badges, the other in dark glasses. They introduced themselves as the organisers, Sophie and Lanya.

Moving closer, they examined Vanessa's photos, which she'd spread like newspaper across the floor. "Important stuff," murmured Sophie.

"Political – right?" asked Lanya.

"More left."

"Dead right, if you ask me."

Vanessa, who was clip-framing photos, paused to look up.

The two women continued their exchange.

"Not centre, definitely not centre."

"Oh God, no. Anything but."

In the background the men were busy fitting supports to a door-frame.

"In any case, not *just* left."

"Or right."

"Or even centre."

As Vanessa's eyes widened, Sophie stepped back. "It's broad front art," she called out triumphantly.

"But vanguard."

"Yes, avant-garde."

"And important."

"A woman's view."

Dropping silent, they both gazed in Vanessa's direction.

Sophie smiled hard. "Oh, welcome to the woman's show. Your pictures are important, very important to us."

Lanya joined in, repeating the welcome as they turned and walked off.

Their last words echoed around the warehouse. They were busy getting it out there. For them this was art.

It was Richard who planned the opening. At first, he'd not volunteered. A women's event – even one where he looked after children and constructed the area – well, it needed careful handling. There was politics involved and a man who stepped in, even as a gap-fill, was a ready-made target.

But then, as the date drew closer and Vanessa didn't seem to register, impatience took over. "What do you want?" he asked her, at least twice daily.

She responded vaguely and withdrew to her studio.

"Is there anything you need?" he asked sounding uppity, when she appeared downstairs and hovered by the phone.

"Only a title. A few words that say it all."

He made various suggestions but nothing seemed to fit. Vanessa simply smiled or looked without interest and turned the other way.

"It's all right if I do what I like for the opening, then?" he said.

Vanessa nodded, ignoring the edge.

When he switched, trying to talk it over, she said she'd be happy whatever he did.

"You mean that?"

Vanessa confirmed.

"In practice as well as theory?"

Vanessa answered with a carefully-worded formula talking about effort and added value.

"All right, I take that means *go ahead*."

And go ahead he did, producing an invite and circulating everyone before following up with reminders and answerphone messages, then working with Doug at the warehouse, arranging lighting and commandeering tables that they stripped and polished and covered with cloth.

On the day, Vanessa was glacial. Dressed full-length in a close-fitting dress, she welcomed all-comers.

Lance appeared first.

"You're early," she said avoiding his gaze.

"This is right? It is the opening?" he asked, sounding hoarse. He stared about short-sightedly, as if he'd just landed.

Richard, who was working on the floor, grinned. Beside him, Doug stopped driving in screws to a link-plate.

"Ask a stupid question," Richard said quietly, keeping his head down.

Sensing something, Vanessa turned and stared. "Did you say you wanted to view?" she asked, addressing Lance.

"A tour would be helpful," he said, looking rather lost.

She walked him around the central pillar. On each side her photos were arranged in clip-framed batches, pinned up like posters. One wall showed demos and meetings, another displayed museum items and toys in close-up, the third held pictures of houses and gardens while the fourth was for portraits, mainly of women, caught walking or working or feeding children or pointing to a view.

Lance circled the pictures, asking questions. He needed information, clear lines and specifics, a theory to hold on to.

Gazing into air, Vanessa didn't answer. When he pressed her, pointing to a photo of faces on a beach, she smiled, claimed it didn't matter and quietly turned away. And when more guests arrived, she excused herself, citing other business.

The collective appeared, minus Gabby. They came in discussing a political event with Lorna speaking loudly supported by Caroline, and the men all vowing action.

Ruth entered next carrying a card and a bottle that she presented to Vanessa. She was followed by a suited Frank, accompanied by Jackie who walked him around the pictures. "Unless it's about teaching," she joked, "he needs it explaining, ABC and first guide. Says he doesn't understand."

"You mean he's a nervous boy?" Ruth called out.

"Pretty much," put in Frank. "Failed my art exam, bottom of the class."

The organisers showed up, debating between themselves, and ignoring the photos. Other guests arrived, including friends and colleagues, fellow ex-graduates and long-term contacts, all admiring, all giving out.

For Vanessa and Richard, it offered added value.

"The show's a success," was Richard's verdict when he caught up with Vanessa halfway through.

"My parents still haven't seen it," she said, checking her watch.

"No problem. Remind them it's family, then they'll approve."

"I shouldn't count on it." Her eyes met his. "But I know you're being helpful. It's just this exhibition means a lot to me, and I want them to like it."

"Don't worry, I'll talk them up. They'll enjoy."

"I do hope …" she began then cut off suddenly.

"Just watch me," he said, lowering his voice. He was half-turned to the entrance, where Felicity and Derek had appeared, leading the children.

Charlotte and Stephan ran to their mother and surrounded her, vying for attention. While Vanessa shushed them, Richard stepped forward saying he'd show her parents around.

"You are so kind," said Felicity, gazing 180°. She was dressed in a grey-flecked suit with light blue trimmings and padded shoulders; her chin was high and her colour was up. Beside her, Derek appeared to be awaiting orders. She cheek-kissed Vanessa then scanned the pictures. "My dear, you have done well, you must have worked ever so hard."

"It was all a bit last minute," said Vanessa, "but in the end we got it up. Everyone's been very kind."

Her mother lowered her voice, glancing around, "Now, please do what you have to do, I imagine you are busy-busy. There must be lots of people here you just *have* talk to."

Vanessa was about to deny when Lanya, who was talking to a man with a camera, called her over.

392

Richard stared. "Do you think it's the press?"

"I believe so," Vanessa replied. "I was told they might appear."

"Well, it looks like they want you. This minute," he said, turning to her parents and explaining quickly.

"Oh indeed, you must go," called Felicity, "*carpe diem*."

As Vanessa slipped off, Richard took over. Pointing to the photos, showman-style, and pitching his voice, he invited them to view.

"It is all suitable?" Felicity asked, nodding towards the children.

"It's good for all ages, yes," responded Richard. He waved one arm. "Please. If you'd care to step this way."

He led them to a collection of black-and-white photos. Arranged in sequence, they showed a woman cycling. The lines around her limbs were blurred, giving the impression that her body was in action. "The name's Athena," Richard said. "She's a colleague who teaches sport."

Felicity smiled. "She certainly looks the part. I suppose she is a typical modern woman."

"In which case …" Derek began then stopped himself.

Richard, as tour guide, moved them to a display of cityscapes. It was spread across the top half of a double-sided panel. There were concrete landscapes, pigeons on buildings and snaps of people reflected in shop windows. At the bottom were close-ups of borders in full bloom.

"Different landscapes," said Richard.

Derek stepped closer. "Interesting," he said, "it's all very carefully done." Richard's mind flashed back to the upstairs train sets.

"It certainly is a lot of pictures," Felicity added.

Richard led past clip-framed photos hung on wood, arriving at an end point where the walls gave out, leaving a hole. The gap between was blocked by a heavy wooden table. "Vanessa's desk," he said, "taken from her studio."

He drew their attention to a collection of photos displayed on the desktop. They were propped on wedges and printed on card with black and gold borders. At the front there were A5 portraits of Stephan and Charlotte taken in parks, escorted by their grandparents.

Derek coloured, staring blankly at the picture of himself. "I didn't expect this," he said.

Felicity said his name, warningly.

"I really don't think …" he added, shaking his head.

"You're not happy?" asked Richard.

The other man shifted his stance, not saying anything.

"I thought you'd be pleased."

"Well—"

"It's meant as a tribute."

"If I'd wanted …"

Felicity intervened again, cautioning.

"I do think we should have been asked," Derek continued, unsmiling.

"What do *you* think?" Felicity asked, turning to the children.

"Grandpa looks nice," Charlotte responded quickly.

Stephan backed her up.

"And the pictures of yourselves?"

Charlotte grinned. "Oh, we've seen those before."

"But what about the show? Do you like your mother's photographs?"

"Oh, yes-yes," said Stephan.

"Will they make her famous?" asked Charlotte.

"I don't think so. Not quite yet," Felicity replied.

"But one day …" put in Richard.

"One day," echoed Stephan.

"One day," called Charlotte, who was standing next to a portrait of Vanessa, "she'll be famous and *I'll* take pictures."

"Are you sure of that?" Felicity asked, laughing.

Stephan protested. It was meant to be him. That was the truth.

"Both of you," Richard said quietly. "You can both be in the pictures *and* take them." He reached towards the table, turning a handle and flicking open a drawer. Inside was a camera.

"I thought so," he said, drawing it out. "It's an instant."

Examining, he declared it ready then checked another drawer. His search produced a few frames that he propped to one side.

"And now," he said, "starting with Stephan, *we'll* take photos while *you* – if that's all right," here he turned and indicated the grandparents, "take centre stage."

Felicity was charmed, Derek blushed but the children insisted. Richard took charge, on the one side grouping Derek by Charlotte with Felicity just behind, on the other side guiding Stephan with the camera.

The children took pics, the grandparents smiled and no one walked between. Richard kept them with him, feeding them positives. Even Derek was persuaded.

Soon they'd several prints, rolled out slowly and spread across wood.

"The children must choose," said Richard crouching at their level, "two each."

Four were selected. Richard added two more and placed them, one to a frame, grouped around the portraits.

"Take a look," he said, standing back. "You're up there playing your part."

He smiled; the grandparents stood looking; the children laughed. Suddenly they were together, centred by the camera.

It reminded Richard of Vanessa and him pictured at the zoo, embracing. Even now he could hear the shutter click and the words he'd used, joking as he'd held her, that he'd bloody well make it work.

When Gabby arrived it was late, the parents had gone, and the gallery was empty except for a few remaining women who had gathered around Vanessa.

"I brought you these," Gabby said, presenting a large bunch of chrysanthemums.

Vanessa's eyes widened. "Oh, they're lovely," she said, raising the blooms to eye-level. She examined them closely like a photographic subject. They were rust-red, brown-yellow, and flecked with blue. Below they were green, above that orange and from centre to petal tip they shaded light to dark, red through purple.

"Sorry, I'd have been here earlier," said Gabby, "but the meeting dragged on – and on." She waved an arm towards the pictures, "Did the opening go well?"

Vanessa glanced about shyly. Beside her Ruth and Bess declared their support, talking as if the show was a contest and Vanessa was in the lead. "Everyone loved it," said Bess. "She's our own up-and-coming star."

"I think it was appreciated," Vanessa said, addressing her bouquet.

"And you've seen all this?" said Ruth, pointing to the walls. "We call it the farm."

"Why the farm?" Gabby asked.

"It's all bits and pieces," said Ruth. "Overnight stuff, cobbled together."

"It wasn't here already?"

Ruth shook her head.

"Somebody built it, then?"

"It's like all these things," said Ruth, "there were bodies. We're deeply indebted to Doug Barnard and Richard Lavender."

"They put it up? How come ...? Mind, must've kept them busy."

"Ah, but you should have seen us supervising. Flat out we were, keeping them on task."

Gabby considered, frowning, before returning her gaze to Vanessa. "They could do with some water," she said, glancing at the flowers.

Ruth laughed and moved to a table, picking up two bottles. Finding a jug, she poured in the contents. "I'll deal with that. Just give me the bunch." She took the flowers from Vanessa and held them aloft. "So lovely, aren't they ..." she beamed. "You're special," she said, addressing the bouquet. "And you deserve only the best ... Yes, the very, very best," she added, lowering the stems into the jug.

For a moment there was silence.

Bess's eyebrows shot up. "That's wine," she said quietly.

"That's so," Ruth shot back.

"But is it ...?"

"Suitable? Harmful? Probably not."

"Plants can filter," said Gabby. "They take what they need, leave the rest."

"Sounds like my kids," Ruth returned, "picking out the veg from anything you give 'em."

Vanessa laughed. "I suppose if *they* can survive on sweets and Shreddies."

"In any case," said Gabby quietly, "chrysanths can live on, for weeks or months, even. They're toughies."

"Flower power, eh?" quipped Ruth. "I'll buy that."

Vanessa pulled out a camera from her bag. "I think I've got it," she said.

"She's really got it," sang Ruth, inconsequentially.

Vanessa ducked into the strap and directed her gaze at the flowers. "Hmm, that's right," she said, pointing the lens and circling her subject. "Yes, yes," she continued, clicking. "That's it," she said, leaning in to get a few close-ups.

Ruth, inspecting, asked what *it* was.

"What I was looking for."

"Which is?"

"These," said Vanessa, pointing to the flowers.

"Yes?"

"They're the point."

"Explain please, Vanessa my dear."

Vanessa put down her camera. "My title," she said.

"Ah, I see."

"Flowers," said Vanessa, lifting the jug as if it was a trophy, "flowers and drink." Two-handed, she held it high. "Flowers in wine, a woman's view."

Hearing her say it, the other women smiled.

"I believe it fits, a classic still life," said Richard the next day.

He was examining a shot of a jug with chrysanthemums posted on a board at the entrance to the show. Headed in red by *Flowers In Wine*, the picture was signed in blue, with a caption announcing: *Vanessa Lavender: a woman's view.*

"You like it?" asked Doug, who was crouched behind the board. He was fixing the stand to a floor hole.

"I think it's good," Richard said, glancing around the empty warehouse. "Effective and eye-catching."

Doug grunted, leaning hard on a screw head. "You mean it's OK." He straightened, keeping his eyes fixed on the stand. "But lacking?"

Richard looked, shifting his weight from one foot to the other. Behind his friend the jug with flowers was standing on its table. Switching from subject to photo, Richard frowned. "Well, possibly a bit conventional."

He knew what Doug meant. Throughout the period of construction, he'd been aware of his own reservations. Of course, in the rush to put up he'd kept them hidden, but now he'd a sense that it might be better if he stepped back and examined what he saw.

"Though, if they *are* that limited ..." he began, then stopped.

"Then what?"

"Well, I don't know, it feels like a let-down."

The conversation dropped and Richard began a tour, studying the photos. Varying his angle, he paused in front of some and passed by others, switching between displays. Of course, he knew them well which made them all-too familiar. He supposed it was like looking in a mirror. "So, *you* think *I* think," he called, "they're not much to write home about."

Doug came across and they both gazed fixedly at a line of political portraits. "They're all smiling," he said evenly.

Richard grimaced. "That's more than I'm doing."

"Well, it is politics."

"You mean the show, or how I'm supposed to react?"

"Both. But don't tell the women."

"Or men. Just think of Justin and Ken."

Doug nodded.

"I imagine," added Richard quietly, "it's the effort of being right all the time."

"The art of *having something important to say*."

"Which they call agit-prop."

Doug pointed to the portraits. "So you're not impressed?"

"Well, I do admit, they feel rather *meant*."

"But you liked them only yesterday."

"That was when I thought—" Richard cut off. He knew his next words: *it might lead somewhere*. A chance to go places, a kind of special pleading. "I'd hoped," he said quietly.

Returning to the entrance, Doug checked the board and poster, and sniffed the flowers. "I hadn't realised," he said, wrinkling up his nose. "They really are in wine."

"In wine?"

"Yes, that's why they smell."

"Stinky, eh?"

"No, a sweet-smelling bouquet."

"I'd say pissed."

"Certainly, they're jolly."

"Over the limit."

"Just merry, I'd say."

"Rank, sozzled, smashed."

Richard grinned. "Flowers enjoying themselves." He picked out a few stems and held them up by the poster. "You never know, this might go big, like the water lilies." He brandished the stems. "O happy hour flower," he called, twirling, "icon for our times." He was grinning and declaiming with one elbow out, crooked like a waiter. Suddenly his hand slipped and the flower heads twisted. His grin became fixed as a line of dark red spots sprayed across the poster.

"Oh shit," he called. The poster surface had already softened as the wine spots started to trickle. He applied a finger, then dabbed one-handed with his cuff, but the smears remained.

"It's a mess," said Doug, pulling a hangdog expression. Both men laughed.

"And may not go down well."

"True."

"Vanessa won't like it."

"I expect Ruth'll have something to say."

"I imagine."

"So, *quo vadis?*"

"Wherever," said Richard, returning the stems to the jug, "preferably another planet."

"Better stand your ground."

"You mean take the road to Rome, face the consequences?"

"Get it over with."

"OK, let's go greet the women's army."

"You're in for this?"

"Bring it on."

"One for all?"

"All for one."

The story, when delivered to Vanessa, was offered straight. Richard told it, backed by Doug who corroborated detail with grunts and asides and confirmatory nods. The men agreed that the damage, though it showed, wasn't too extensive.

Vanessa responded with a few curt questions. It was almost as if she'd expected, or known all along, but she wanted Richard to show her, and she needed Ruth to be there.

Doug took the children while they drove around to the show. Arriving, they unlocked the warehouse and entered silently. The women were here to pronounce.

The poster that faced them looked like a cross between a painting and a map. The surface stains had deepened and soft, grey run-spots had developed around the edges.

"Maybe we need a reprint?" suggested Richard quietly.

Vanessa shook her head. "It took over a week …"

"Did you do this?" cut in Ruth.

Richard drew back.

"But did you?"

Silence.

Ruth softened her tone. This sort of thing, she said, wasn't good.

Richard scratched his head. "It's certainly not a pretty sight, no doubt about that."

She suggested cleaning.

"I've tried that already."

"The problem is," put in Vanessa, "it's the first thing you see, as you enter."

Richard acknowledged.

"And people go by that."

He used the word *accident*; speaking low, shaking his head.

Ruth, who was circling, touched the surface. She set her jaw forward and stared towards Vanessa. Her colour was up.

"It's bad," she said, addressing herself. She was finger-dabbing the corners and pulling faces. "Really bad," she repeated, shuddering.

Richard looked, saying nothing.

"I can't believe that happened," she said, sucking in her cheeks, "it's horrible."

"What you suggesting?" Richard asked, frowning.

"You messed."

"Say again."

"Messed."

His mouth set hard.

"Badly."

"So you say."

"No use wriggling. You did it."

"Yes, and put up everything else. The whole bloody lot."

"I don't see how that makes any difference."

"No, you wouldn't."

Vanessa intervened, talking them down. What's done was done, she said. The real point was how to fix it.

"Or who's going to fix it," called Ruth.

Richard coloured. "You offering?"

"You joking? Look at this," she said, fingering the picture. "Isn't it disgusting? How does *anyone* make a mess like that?"

"It's easy." Richard's fingers closed around a corner of the poster. "You just set your mind to it …"

"Richard!"

"Watch him do it," sneered Ruth.

He smiled as his fingers tightened. "I know what you think," he said grimly, "but I wouldn't give you the satisfaction." Dropping his grip, he walked away. "But who the hell cares anyway?" he called out from the exit, "because it's OK this show, it's good enough, but nothing to write home about." He turned in the doorway, facing Vanessa. "It's conventional, safe and middle-of-the-road, and that's about it."

That evening, when Vanessa returned home, she found an unsealed envelope positioned on the mat. At first, she didn't want to touch it.

Whatever it contained, she'd rather not know. But seeing her name on it, she picked it up. After checking on the children, she took it to the kitchen where she laid it on the table while she brewed up tea. This, she realised, might take time. What he'd said had hurt but now, with hindsight, she was calmer. Bracing herself she sat, pulled out the letter and began reading. With each sip of tea, her mood shifted. Although he said sorry, the words came across as forced. She'd a sense of something hidden, a level of intention, as if it was an act. But as she read on, the line became clear: an apology, unconditional, his comments withdrawn, and a wish to make amends. It appeared he'd thought better.

But also, while reading, part of her stayed separate: she'd rather not go there. On the surface there were words, but behind that there was nothing – a phrase here, a phrase there. So she read and sampled, in a state of indecision, skimming out content while sipping at her tea.

When she'd finished, Vanessa put aside the letter and stood to face the garden. While she'd been reading a feeling had developed. Richard, she suspected, was out there.

Opening the back door, she peered into the dark. At first, she saw only a strip of concrete, lit from the kitchen, and a path leading off. Beyond that were the tops of fences and houses outlined against a grey sky.

She switched off the light. Like water in a lock, the light levels equalised. She could make out a tree, some trelliswork and a few low bushes. Stepping out, she closed the door behind her. The path led forward, past a lawn and flowerbeds to arrive at bare earth. Peering ahead, she followed. As she cleared the house the path became wider, the light levels rose and she could make out a seated figure. "Richard?" she called, approaching.

"Here," he said, sounding hoarse.

"What are you doing?"

"Not much. Thinking."

She stood, staring into darkness. "I read your letter."

Silence. Richard shifted forward. "What did you think?"

"I'm still taking it in."

"What I said …" he began, standing up, "wasn't right."

Vanessa took a breath. The air was coolly calm and still. She wondered what might follow. Something, she supposed, where he'd find a line, a way of turning it around. It was all about angle.

"It's politics I'm sick of," he said suddenly.

Inwardly, she sighed.

"It's all so one-dimensional," he continued, "and full of people with no person skills, no understanding. They judge by rhetoric and voting record, nothing else."

"Well, it's practical." she answered, breathing calmly. "A matter of action, getting things done."

"And as for soul—"

She turned her head to stare across the fence. Greys and grey-blues played across darkness. The gardens were hard to make out.

Richard shook his head. "Politics is full of know-alls. They smile and decide, but never listen."

"You think so?"

"People who all reckon they know better."

"Those people try. It's not easy. They do their best."

"The activist tendency. They do and they do. It blocks out thought."

"OK, it's a struggle. But progress is made."

He snorted. "I imagine *that's* what's called a Marxist analysis."

Suddenly she felt weary. They spent their lives arguing. On and on, finding difference, pushing and declaring, crossing each other. Every day, the neighbours could hear them. "I think you're missing the point," she said, stepping away from the fence.

Richard took her place, staring down the gardens. "I don't know about that," he said, quietly.

"Whatever you say, politics *is* important. However difficult or unpleasant, somebody has to do it."

"Ah, the dirty hands argument."

"Politics is like that. You can't just magic it away."

"You mean like rows between couples. However bad they are, you have to live with 'em."

"Maybe. But people still have choices."

Richard leaned forward propping himself, spectator-like, on the fence. The expression on his face was adversarial. She could see he wasn't finished. "Marriage is what you make it, eh? I'm sure Samuel Smiles would agree."

A picture flashed through her head of a university seminar. She could see Richard talking, adopting positions, building up a case.

"I mean it's in our hands," she returned.

"Precisely. Which is why we don't need political ideologies."

"What's the alternative? The *Übermensch* or something?"

"The alternative is people, as they are, outside the box. And bugger the theory."

Vanessa shot him a look. "That's one way of putting it."

"You don't like it?"

"Not much."

"Ah, it offends."

"Some might say so."

"That's the difference between us. I say it, you go round the houses."

"In your view."

"It's true. You're like your mother, all airs and graces. A cut above."

"And that's personal."

He shrugged. "Well, as they say, the personal is political."

*Flowers In Wine* opened to the public the next day. During the morning, after seeing off Vanessa and walking the children to school, Richard practised his scales, wrote a few lines then rang Gabby. He described the accident, the photo at the entrance, mentioned arguments – lightly, in passing, without too much detail – and asked for ideas. After talking about the problem, Gabby volunteered to help. "Half an hour, I'll meet you there," she said. "With toolkit." Asked what she meant, she laughed. "You'll see. Ms Fixit, on the way."

When Richard arrived, the warehouse was empty except for Lanya who was sitting in attendance, and a red-faced Sophie who was pacing the floor. They were both in a fret, exchanging comments about a journalist who'd promised, and when they'd get a write-up. Seeing Richard, they greeted without interest and retreated to the end.

404

When Gabby appeared, she was well weighed down. She'd a sack on her back, a pouch-belt around her waist and a bag in each hand.

"Looks like you mean business," he said, helping her to unload.

"I've brought the lot. Paints, cleaner, cloth, patch-up materials, first aid for everything. This is the full, all singing and dancing photo doctor."

Their hands touched briefly and he smiled.

She crouched by the picture, humming while she studied the surface. Applying one finger, she dabbed lightly, then stood back and straightened. "Not as bad as it looks. Fixable, I think."

Richard watched her as she pulled out some thick glass paint pots, a soft cloth and a collection of brushes. Unscrewing the lids, she dipped and tested before applying. "Best begin from the top," she said, shading carefully before stopping to change brushes. She flicked and dabbed, filling in the surface. When she'd finished, she stood back asking what he thought.

"It's much improved," said Richard, squinting forward. "I don't think anyone who didn't know could tell."

"It'll do," Gabby said, beginning to pack away. "As long as it lasts out the show."

"You're not satisfied?"

"What counts is how Vanessa feels."

"Even more so, Ruth."

"Is it like that?"

"She's what's called an opinion former."

"Like Justin, you mean?"

"Justin and Ruth, leaders in their field. I can just see it."

Gabby finished packing.

"You've done a wonderful job," he said, shifting position. "Whatever angle you look from, it's great."

They stepped outside, with Richard carrying her bagged-up paints. "Don't worry," he said, checking his watch, "I shall give you a lift." When she began to object, he opened the car door and deposited the bags. "More, please," he said, nodding to her sack.

They drove back to her house and unloaded. "No call out charge, then?" he asked, standing in the hallway.

405

"Friday's payday. But I'll take a small deposit," she said, presenting her mouth.

He lip-touched, lightly, then closed to a kiss. "I'm in your debt," he said afterwards, laughing.

"How long's Vanessa's show?"

"Two weeks."

"That short?"

"I believe it's to do with the rent."

She gazed at him closely. She was watching him like an artwork. "I think you had hopes from this show. Maybe a change in direction?"

"You realised?"

"I did."

"I'd not thought it was that obvious."

"But why? Is it something you have to hide?"

"I don't want to be Mr Leech Man, living through Vanessa, hoping for an out."

"You think her show might go somewhere?"

"Maybe. Who knows?"

"And you've an idea that if that happens it might help you …"

"Absurd isn't it, I thought it might be helpful. A kind of escape, or even a main chance. I know that sounds stupid but we all believe in it." He sighed and dropped his shoulders: "It's all about keeping busy, looking the other way, so you don't have to think. Putting off, and then putting off ... And behind it you're a child, still secretly believing that somehow, without any effort, everything will change."

"Ah, the watcher angel story."

"And you still think there's a reward for being good."

"As if—"

"Or at least for showing willing."

"Which there isn't."

"Or you believe in fair-dos."

"Which *would* be very nice."

"But it doesn't ever happen."

Gabby eyed him warily. She was closing now, drawing herself up. "What you're talking about is experience. You go in feeling you've

406

got the measure of things, you know how they work, can handle anything. Then you find out."

Richard snorted. "Yes. It's more of a closing down. The dreams you had, the silly lost causes, even the smallest, stupidest inclination, it all becomes you, the last little bit left standing." He threw out a hand: "You hear it in your mind, repeating, *Stayin' Alive*. Suddenly all that trivia and indulgence and messiness takes on a different feel. You want it back, whatever it was, want to throw life up in a spin, go for broke, run off somewhere and never come back …"

Gabby laughed. "True," she said fiercely. "Too true. And one day we'll do it."

‡ ‡ ‡

Cass wrote a story. It wasn't history but it wasn't made up. It was a pick 'n' mix sampling of fact/fiction/ideas. She called it her lyrical essay.

Writing it had taken weeks. At the start she couldn't imagine herself writing anything at all. Just looking back was unreal. It was like peering through cracks in a wall. On one side there was darkness; the other side was lit by flashes. To try to see it all was like staring into the sun. What she remembered was beautiful and wild, but hard to write about; and even the looking took effort. In any case, she was soooo tired … All she wanted to do was lie down and sleep and sleep.

But then, as a record, it was important. And like a trailer, it needed to hit the highs, but also cover everything. So she put it together slowly between sleeping and eating and doing nothing then edited, edited, edited.

Her story went like this:

### BURNOUT

In my mind I keep replaying images from the second *Extinction Rebellion* London occupation. One scene stands out. It's a meme. What I see is a young man in a park leaving his bits and pieces on a groundsheet and going over to a nearby tent, calling for its owner. He's left behind a clothes pile, a sleeping bag, some food, a collapsed tent and a black-and-white snare drum. All around the park the police are closing in, uprooting empty tents. They advance to a sound of rebels banging metal and crying out – but no one is sweary or pumped-up. There's an invisible stand-off between the police taking the tents and the crowds made homeless. It's as if they'd all been placed there by a director as walk-on extras, telling their stories in mime.

The young man I see is thin-faced and skinny. He wears his brown-ginger hair tied up in a bun. To me, he's an avatar of frailty. Although he's young, his movements are shaky and his face is lined. He stares into the tent with a surprised expression, like an animal in headlights.

As he turns away three policemen appear and pick up his stuff.

"Please. That's mine," he calls, rushing over.

"Mine," he repeats, pointing to the drum.

One of the policemen answers, but I can't hear his words - although I know what's coming. It's all part of a silent film running through my head. The officer is leaning forward, holding the drum in front of his chest. The expression on his face is firmly, sadly parental. The young man's lost everything.

Eleven days earlier I was sitting in front of a computer, sending out emails to performers at 3.00 a.m. In my role as stage programmer I had to fill two weeks, eight hours a day, with climate talks, protest music, group singing, interviews, drama and eco info. I'd become artistic director for a full-time performance venue with a week to fill the space. If I stopped to think about it, my task was off the scale.

Our stage was one of ten. It was due to go up on the edge of the park, blocking the road behind the government buildings. As in our earlier occupation, we'd carry in wooden blocks and solar panels then camp in the road for a fortnight, singing and calling out and chanting, with one big watchword: EMERGENCY.

Behind that word was my first reading of the IPCC 5th report. Years back, but I still remember the shock. Up until then I'd viewed climate as a story that might or might not happen. I thought if I closed my eyes it would have disappeared when I opened them again. For me, climate was an underlying condition, close to the surface but unmentionable. To think too much about it might well trigger the nightmare I was trying to shut out.

Today I'm full of images, words, feelings. There are figures passing before me in the dark. It's like waking in a strange room, living a life I didn't choose with only the knowledge that everything has to change. Everything.

There's an impossible feel about our situation. It raises questions about who we are and why we're on this planet. It's as if we're heading into deep space without a map and nothing to protect us. Again and again, I ask myself why.

The first time we occupied, Joe made it happen. Without him, Mia and I might have bottled out. That was in Spring. We arrived at the bridge and walked up the slope in broad daylight with people wheeling in tents and equipment and plants on trolleys. It seemed we weren't that many, but rebels kept appearing from steps and ramps and we took the road together, surprising ourselves and the police. It was a blast. Mia held my hand and Joe sang – although for a moment, we went into freeze-frame mode. Breaking the law is scary, but once you've done it nothing can stop you.

I also remember rebels holding a big green banner, blocking one side of the road. Mia joined them and stood behind it singing. The wind from the river got up and the trees in pots had to be roped together. The rebels doing it were super-fit, paying out their ropes like climbers. Afterwards, they watered the trees every day. I thought all the trees would die, but they found good homes afterwards.

I can still picture the lorry we used as a stage. It came racing up the road and skidded sideways to a halt, blocking the other carriageway. A woman and two men jumped out as if they were staging a raid. They threw open doors and rolled down shutters and positioned the gear, two solar panels and steps at the back. The woman did most of it. She was built like an Amazon.

For the next ten days I was part of that stage. I stepped in without preparation, filling between acts while the two guys fixed up the sound. It was a scramble. I was working with a short, quietly-spoken woman who'd brought in acts, mainly musicians. They would turn up or fail to show, some arrived late, others overran, but mostly they were pure gold. When Joe came on with Suzi, Lauren and Karl, Mia danced.

Our camp on the Garden Bridge was a carnival. People hugged and laughed and shared their fears and hopes. There were deep mind moments, callouts for arrestables, love shouts, training and political speeches.

We sang.

> People gonna rise like water
> Gonna turn this system round
> In the voice of my great-granddaughter
> Climate justice now.

We all made friends.

I was arrested on the Garden Bridge. The police lined up in rows facing the heartline, then sent in snatch squads. When they surrounded the lorry, I hung onto a wheel thinking if they wanted our stage they'd have to take me. It was a long hot wait and my neck was burning. We were in a group, some of us glued-on, some of us chained to the cab and others camping on the roof. When an officer crouched down and warned me, I spoke about climate, she repeated her warning then four of them lifted me. I was cheered and whooped to the van then sat there for an hour with my officer. The police stations were all full.

When I was finally taken in, they removed my bag and its contents. *Just doing our job* my officer said, spreading my possessions on the desk. The woman behind the computer logged and bagged up my stuff, then I signed for it. Later in the photo room, an officer told me that he supported us 100%. That was during fingerprinting and taking my DNA.

The cell was cold. It was a blank space where I switched off. But it was also noisy. A high-street-type flow of police and prisoners kept passing the door. I didn't sleep and when I got out it was

410

early morning and I was well past it. I was helped by two rebels waiting in the lobby who fed me, then I set off. My journey home was on empty trains. When I arrived I slept.

I learned so much from occupying the bridge. About crossing lines and stepping up. About people being generous and loving and giving themselves to a cause. I also learned how to organise, improvise and use a mike. The Garden Bridge gave me hope.

I go back to the frail young man. I can still see him in the film in my head. There's a second on camera when his anger shows. But then his face falls and he's sad. Though he's lost his tent and all his possessions, what hurts most is the snare drum. It was taken without warning while he was helping others, and in front of him. But he's bigger than that. The planet is what's hurting.

Why do I remember him? Probably because he was bullied. The police had taken our lorries, our tents, our food, even our toilets. We'd moved our camp twice already, but like him we wouldn't give up. We were un-pro-vok-able. And I wanted to hug him, but the police were close and we had to shift our stage.

In the movement, we talk about sacrifice. People locking on, glued to buildings, climbing on aeroplanes, doing time in jail. Giving what we can. But whatever they took from us was nothing. We came back later, red-handed, and retook the streets.

In the burnout afterwards I kept that young man before me. He helped me through the lows and the whiteouts and the dead-end feelings. When I couldn't face anything, I saw him standing like a statue in the park. He's the peace activist, the Gandhi in us all. The quiet resister they can't overcome. He's why I'm a rebel.

They also serve who only stand and wait.

# TWENTY-SIX

*Activist 33*

## SEEING RED

Editor: This week as *Activist* goes to press, the exhibition *Seeing Red* opens at Stone Street Warehouse, London. With its subtitle *The Politics of the Heart*, the show presents artworks by a group of radical women with very different visions. What unites the artists is their resistance to male hegemony. To mark this event *Activist* proudly presents the artists' full statements below. The front and back covers of *Activist 33* carry photographs of the exhibition.

### *Flowers In Wine* by Vanessa Lavender

Clip-framed photographs

My photographs are urban. The pictures I take are of women in struggle, but also of the buildings and gardens we live in. I want to combine elements of the everyday with images of direct action.

As a photographer, I try out angles in my head, framing everything. I believe part of the mind operates like a camera, picking up on appearances. There is a wealth of hidden detail in everything we do. Mostly we censor it out, for practical reasons. In my case, in order to avoid filtering out experience, I remind myself of childhood fantasies of being present, but unseen. The effect is like being backstage looking out from a darkened room.

I am interested in museum pieces, particularly Victorian children's theatres. With their stylised action and figures on sticks they represent mini-worlds. I use them as models. My task is to capture the costumes and gestures, while hinting at what lies behind.

I see my work as a record, like a photograph album. I am intrigued by my memories of old pictures that are vaguely familiar, even when the names and places have faded. I aim to put together something similar, a gallery, with a personal feel. The exact nature of that feel might be unclear, but I do know that what we see, and what we miss, says a great deal about who we are.

My photographs are an attempt to capture the patterns behind appearance. To this end, I blow up my prints to change the perspective. They are my Book of Hours for the city, recording its day-to-day changes. My actual title *Flowers In Wine* celebrates this principle of mutability, an idea all woman understand because of our involvement in the everyday and the personal.

### *RED-RED-RED* by The Bacchae

Spraypaint, wool, card, cloth, photographic prints

"Insurrection is an art, and like all arts has its own laws," *Trotsky.*

What we enjoy:
- Plastering bridges and underpasses with feminist graffiti.
- Full-colour-decorating billboards and boundary walls.
- Scribbling pavements, painting dumped cars, giving sex shops the blackout treatment.
- Spider-winding wool around lampposts.
- Planting wooden women-symbols in parks.
- Writing out great-women lists and clipping them to windscreens.
- Flying purple/green women's flags from trees and buildings.
- In the night, slapping stickers on glass and overpainting sexist adverts.

Look at these images and originals, they show our work. It's a festival of the oppressed.

### *Whose Side Are You On?* by Wimmin On Top

*objet trouvé*

Our art is co-owned and co-created. We workshop it together, mixing and matching. It uses found objects. We choose subjects from myth and history, switching gender roles. All our pieces are outsize and mixed-media. They include David as a woman built out of copper piping, knitted clothes and car parts, and unisex Madonna images stuck onto wall-to-wall mirrors. We collect toilet signs, nappies and hard hats and hang them from washing lines. We make plants out of golf clubs and masking tape, wrapping them in men's ties, and sometimes ribbons, or bits of silk curtains. Our manifesto is:

1.  All numbers divide by one.
2.  Use what you find.
3.  Gender is a trick of the light.

### *Expression Rules* by Clarry Wilson

Pen, ink, paper

Art is about flux, so I draw what I see, changing my line as my subject changes. If I sketch a flower it includes growth & development. Every subject has an arc & a shaped pulse that directs my drawing. It's a matter of finding the right gesture, rather like Paul Klee's idea of "taking a line for a walk".

With the women's poetry I illustrate, I listen out. I'm trying to catch the right note, the exact concrete shape for sound & movement. There's a pattern there & I have to find it. In the same way, if you study a waterfall for long enough it seems to stand still. I'm always watching, always moving on. Each subject for me is a one-off, to be tried out & enjoyed. I want to capture the energy & indifference of nature. The way I work is best described by Szymborska's line, "Nothing ever happens twice".

### *Women First* by Herstory

Card, ink, coloured ribbon, double-side tape

Anon. Celebratory. A list of strong women, past to present, running like ticker tape around the exhibition walls.

### *Living with Imagination* by Angel

Stones, ceramics, textiles, plaster, wire, paint, photos

(Dedicated to Y who made all of this possible.)
I aim for *truth to materials*. A bare head with nothing hidden. And an open heart and mind. I call it thinking without words.

My catalogue:

1. *Underwater City*. A half-size replica.

The marble original is cemented to rocks and covered twice daily by the sea. It has a waymarked route, inviting the visitor to travel out and back in stages. The outward journey symbolises past difficulties, the centre focuses on things present and the return suggests ideas for change.

In the gallery, white stones and blue-green lighting imitate the original.

2. *Over the Rainbow*.

Multi-coloured textiles from my workshop hung on clothes racks.

3. *Chapels*.

The holes in these Venetian plaster sculptures lead the eye inward. The frames inside are intended to suggest the muscular/skeletal system. Within the body of each sculpture is a miniature of itself.

4. *Scent Trail*.

In this interactive piece, the square glass jars are made of rock crystal. All the olfactory substances they contain are natural. After smelling each, the visitor is invited to choose from a range of coloured straws, leaving them in dishes by the jars.

5. *A Stone's Throw Away*.

A meditational tool using stone and water. Each stone has been hollowed out and filled with chalk and scented dye. When dropped into bowls of diluted acid, the mixture froths and colours up, giving off a bitter-sweet smell. It's a flower opening on a busy street corner.

6. *Silence*.

Four night-sea views on floor-to-ceiling canvasses to be looked at wearing glasses and headphones. The glasses are dark, streaked with violet. The headphones play a recording of silence.

7. *Alopecia Universalis*.

Photographs and paintings from all angles of my own bare head.

♯ ♯ ♯

Vanessa decided, before the exhibition ended, that she'd like to go away.

From the first day of visitors she'd been in attendance. During the show she'd existed in her all-go mode: a sleepless state where everything was a whirl. People had wanted, and she had delivered. It was all about presence, the organisers told her, about face and impression and putting yourself around. Later, in the second week, she'd started to wonder about Richard's comments. Suddenly it seemed no one was interested. The gallery was empty, her pictures were flat and there were no smiley faces. When she looked at the other artists, their work felt much more adventurous than hers, and a voice in her head pushed in with questions. Was it as he'd said? *Safe, political, middle-of-the-road?* Or just so dull that nobody cared? And she wondered if his help was an act of condescension, a sop to keep her in her place.

When the fortnight ended Doug and Richard appeared again. Working systematically, they collapsed the walls and removed the show, as if they were roadies and did it every day. But their efforts had a downside. She knew they were saying things, if not directly then by implication, particularly Richard whose words and actions were designed, she felt, to open up a distance. *He* was considerate, knew his code of practice, played the role of nice guy, while *she* was the diva taking everything for granted. They were one thing in public, quite different on their own.

Then there were the words, the ones he'd read up on. Talk of repression and what he called "definers" with more about syndromes, shadows projected and hostile formulations.

*I'm feeling overrun* was how she put it when rehearsing in her mind for their next week's counselling. In the head-talk that followed she ran through various formulae, plotting her defences and practising what she'd say.

It seemed she'd had enough.

"A complete change," she told Ruth, "where one doesn't really have to do anything. A kind of health-farm break, that's what I need."

"Without men," she added, smiling.

With Lance she was cool. She needed to take stock, challenge how they did things, and that might, she warned, affect their Fridays. With Richard she spoke quietly, proposing that he and Gabby spend time with the children. With Lorna she was upbeat. "What *was* that place," she asked on the phone, "for women-only weekends?" In herself – after picking a date and packing – she was happy. She would go there for a rest and spend more time with women she could bond with. Together they were strong.

They left on a Friday soon after school, five in a car, with Caroline driving, Ruth taking turns, Lorna singing, Bess on maps and Vanessa looking out. The house they arrived at was an hour's drive south then longer westwards. After searching for an entrance and bumping slowly down a potholed track, they drew up at twilight. Standing alone in rolling hills, it was steep-roofed and quirky with leaded windows and a door around the side. A sign on a bush said *Welcome to The Hen House*.

They were met on the step by an ample, round-faced woman with pale inquiring eyes and a smattering of freckles. She was wearing a wide-brimmed cap set at an angle, and paint-streaked overalls. Ushering them in, she conducted them to a bicycle-filled hall where she introduced herself: "Hermione would like to say, how pleased she is to see you." Speaking as their guide, she pointed and directed: to the right, a door to where they'd eat, behind, a passageway and above, a dark oak staircase. "But first, you get to settle," she said, advancing to the stairs. They were shown to their bedrooms, then invited downstairs to gather in the lounge. On the way back she pointed out a wall map, a collection of horse brasses and a door key on a hook, before leading into a soft-furnished space, linked by an arch to the dining room. "Supper," she called, waving to a spread arranged on a heavy wooden table. It was piled up with strange mixtures, scented and garnished on top and spread on paper plates. Here Hermione, promising return, went off on business. She left them to Victoria, a willowy, dark-eyed woman wearing a green silk scarf and two-tone jacket. Victoria had style. With her shoulders held back and long S-shaped spine, she looked like a dancer. "Welcome," she said, "I've prepared a beanfeast. I believe it will surprise." When everyone was seated, she circled the table, naming dishes. "Be bold," she said, "and don't be afraid to try things."

While they ate, she asked them their names, talking and listening with measured attention and without too much pressure. Vanessa recognised in her what her mother called *je ne sais quoi.*

Afterwards, when they'd helped her to clear up, Victoria suggested they went in search of Hermione. They found her in the hall, fixing bikes. "Herm has been in struggle," she told them brightly, "one woman, many machines." The guests exchanged looks. "Hermione would also like," she continued, "to show you the workshop where the battle began." In proof she held up her hands, which were dirt-streaked and bruised all over.

Smiling politely, the group followed to a hole in the back wall. A step down and they entered a shed-like room littered with broken appliances. There were backless televisions, eviscerated Hoovers, doorless fridges, clocks in pieces and a corner full of broken mowers and fragments of what looked like agricultural machinery. "It's the local rescue centre," Hermione said, wiping her hands on a pile of torn-up sheets, "for reassembly and rehabilitation."

They nodded blankly, looking where she pointed. "There's more outside," she said, waving towards a dirty French window with a view out to blackness.

"So, this is how you live?" asked Vanessa, pointing to a leaflet featuring imaginary plants and a Rousseau-like drawing of the house with a green and purple flag flying from the roof. Above that, a fish on a bicycle was riding Santa-Claus-style across the sky, holding up a placard saying *Hen House Repairs.*

"Come," said Hermione, directing them back to the hall, "and be shown." She led to a door beneath the stairs that opened to a flight of steps dropping into darkness. Flicking on a light she invited them to enter.

Vanessa was first. A faint chemical smell met her, strengthening as she descended to the cellar. "Well, well," she said quietly, "this is what you might call *la grande cave.*"

The area was large and white and tiled like a bathroom; it was clean, surprisingly warm and lit by old bike lamps and rear reflectors. Near where she entered, Vanessa could see racks of bottles lining the walls. As her gaze adjusted, she made out bell jars with valves, some plastic vats and a clear space with what looked like a large children's paddling pool. It was filled with a dark aromatic mixture that she realised from the smell was fermenting grapes. "Beautiful spot," said Hermione, inhaling. In the silence after she spoke Vanessa could hear the slow pop and bubble of aerated water.

"What's in the middle?" Bess asked, pointing to the shallow pool.

Their host smiled, "That's where Hermione treads."

"Softly?" asked Vanessa, walking forward.

Ruth joined her, peering at the mixture. "You make your own wine?"

Hermione confirmed, adding they'd a vineyard just behind the house. "And now," she said loudly, taking off her shoes and removing her overall, "Herm will demonstrate." She crossed the central area to a footstool and a bench beside a low sink. Here she ran the taps and washed her hands before perching on the seat to soap her feet. After splashing back and forth, she invited them to admire and drained the basin, pulling down a towel. "Everyone, do what I do," she said leaning on a tap that gushed cold water. "Everyone," she repeated, mixing from the hot and calling again. "Footwash, everyone, foot-wash."

The women approached, Ruth first, followed by the others. They removed their shoes and bared their legs, piling their clothes on the bench. Some were smiley and some were edgy, but they lined up as required. Encouraged by Hermione, they dipped and splashed and rubbed themselves down, then gathered by the paddling pool. "Tread-ing is an art," she called, reaching out for a grape-filled basket and tipping it in. "Best done in twos," she added, leading Ruth to the edge, where they stood, as if they were at a crossing looking both ways. Then, on the count of three, Hermione stepped up and in, taking Ruth with her.

"Hey-hey, that's squelchy!" Ruth called as the liquid flowed up to her ankles. She leaned into her host while they promenaded once, twice, then a third time, separate. Their legs now were red: wine-splashed and streaked all over. "Come on in!" called Ruth, waving to the others. "Step up, my lovelies, you'll enjoy it." She caught on to Vanessa and conducted her in, one arm raised. The two women laughed as the grapes began to bubble, frothing up to their calves.

"It's alive," said Vanessa as the surface peaked like whipped meringue.

Ruth giggled. "It tickles your toes."

Behind them, Hermione swung heavily to the floor, dripping on the tiles. She rounded on the other three. "In, in, in, in, in," she insisted.

They began to move, stepping up and over, entering the pool. As their feet touched the bottom, the surface rocked and shuddered. "Oh," cried Lorna who was holding onto Caroline's arm, "it's like treading jelly."

"Or frogspawn," put in Bess, grinning.

The women all laughed. They had filled up the pool and now were holding each other, promenading in short half-circles. Ruth made quacking noises as they waddled back and forth.

First out was Vanessa, followed by Ruth. They sat by the sink, examining their legs. "Like wearing coloured tights," laughed Ruth, wiggling her toes. She was bright red around the sole, red-tinged to the ankles and pink above.

"Reminds me," said Vanessa, "of childhood, jumping in mud."

"Or worse."

"Worse?"

"Ink or paints." Ruth ran her hands up and down her calves. "Or blood – when you gashed your leg."

"I think a few childhood games …" Vanessa broke off when Hermione, who had cleaned herself up, called to the women, inviting them to wash. "But first, it's best if we can …" Vanessa said, fingering a tap.

Ruth began to wash. "*I* think a few childhood games would be good, a whole weekend of 'em."

The water in the sink ran red to pink.

"We'll make a list."

Vanessa smiled. The water now was clear and colourless.

"And work out the rules."

Vanessa echoed Ruth's words, turning off the flow. Together they began drying.

"And we'll do it together."

"Yes, because it's a change."

"And time out."

"And fun."

"And incy wincy spider-ish."

"And character building," concluded Vanessa, stepping dry and refreshed from the tiles into her shoes.

The first game next morning was I spy. They played outdoors, exploring around the garden and the road they'd come by. They tried it with variations, sometimes by last letter and sometimes by syllables. When they'd spied a few abstracts and began to repeat, Ruth held up a hand, calling time. "We'll rename," she said, smiling. "I used to do that, pretty much all the time."

"Rename?" asked Vanessa. "What's that?"

They were standing by the back gate, looking across hills. To one side was a fence and a farm track, in front was a grassy slope leading across fields to a wood, while to the left, and curving right around, was a brown-green patch of staked-up grapes.

Ruth pointed upwards. "It's custard, lovely custard."

"The sky? Grey and cloudy, if you ask me."

"Yellow, in a bowl, custard."

Vanessa raised an admonishing finger. "I name you grey sky, custard."

"And that," said Ruth, pointing to the ground, "is flimflam."

Vanessa narrowed her eyes. "Whereas that?" she asked, pointing to a bush.

Ruth tore off a leaf and sniffed. "Fool's gold," she said, pursing her lips.

They advanced to the vineyard edge, looking down the rows. There were unpicked grapes, hanging in clusters, and staked-up branches twisted into wire. The ground beneath dropped off sharply.

Vanessa waved an arm. "I call this land Cockaigne."

"I've heard that somewhere. Isn't it a *Sir Richard* word?"

Vanessa shivered slightly. "Is it?" she said, feeling vaguely blocked. It was as if Richard was present, asking awkward questions. Suddenly she was weary, caught out by thoughts she'd hoped to sidestep. She was remembering playing happy families, with Richard downstairs practising the piano. She missed her children.

"Did I say the wrong thing?"

"I don't know, maybe. It's certainly his sort of word." She looked down the slope. The vines bulged out; they were thick-leaved and snaky; beneath their mass, the earth was dry and furrowed.

"What, him? The enough-man?"

"Don't remind me."

Ruth returned to her game, picking out the house and calling it cake. She continued pointing and renaming, taking in the gate, the fence, the farm track and the wood. When she'd worked around the view, she turned back. "See me," she said, "putting on an act, trying to sound jolly."

"It's like that?"

"Yes indeed, rah-rah-rah, to keep from thinking."

The two women looked out. The hills were divided into different areas. With their hedges and fencings and farm tracks leading off, they looked artificial.

"That's a bit like teaching," said Vanessa. "Keeping up to keep them down."

"Now that's one thing I'm thankful I didn't stick with." Ruth began to saunter along the field edge, kicking at dust.

Vanessa joined her. "What it is to serve," she said, glancing down the valley.

"Well, you managed. Give yourself credit, I couldn't possibly have done it." Ruth was humming now, stepping side to side.

"Let's say you saw it coming. Take it from me, teaching's one of those jobs where you have to stay on top. You can't duck anything. Every day, it's pure front line." She laughed: "In a way, it's like a marriage. Nothing comes easily, you can't dodge, you can't bluff, and every mistake comes back to haunt you."

"Ah but Vanessa, no regrets, *ma chérie.*" Ruth leaned back and raised one arm across her brow. She began to sing in a croaky, barely

422

audible imitation of Edith Piaf. As she sang she half-closed her eyes, swaying back and forth like a drunk at a party. "You have to believe, even if it never seems to happen."

"Is that another line from a song?"

"Could be, it certainly feels that way."

"I think I know what you're saying."

"Love love love love love," Ruth half-sang, half-chanted, "that's what I want."

"Love and affection?"

"And more. Whatever it takes."

"We do need something." Vanessa turned to face the view: "Maybe it's out there somewhere. Somebody's got an answer, only they're keeping it very, very quiet."

Ruth's face stilled and concentrated. She moved up close to her friend. "And that was another childhood game," she said, slowly.

Vanessa gazed around. The sun was showing through. A flock of sheep had filled up the field below: they looked like scattered stones. "And what was that?" she asked.

"Staying quiet. Holding your breath so no one could see you."

"Ah yes, I played that."

Ruth took her friend's hand. "Shhh now," she said, raising their clasped hands towards the wood. "Let's go down there, playing it. Absolute silence, walk not talk."

Vanessa put a finger to her lips, stepping forward. They were hand in hand and wordless.

At first the slope was gentle and they followed a sheep track, with their arms linked and swinging. The sun came out and a skylark sang. It climbed and climbed, carolling wildly, then cut off altogether. Silence followed, as a light breeze fluttered the grass stalks. A sheep baa-ed and a horsefly circled. As they descended further, a gate they passed through creaked, but the quiet still held them. It was as if they were attached, roped together by an invisible cord.

When they reached the wood, the silence changed. It deepened and closed up. The leaves and branches acted as a wall; inside were whispers, rustles, light-plays. Their footsteps were cushioned, advancing softly, measuring earth. At one point a squirrel scrambled up a branch and disappeared into leaves. After its departure the branch went on shaking. As they ducked past an elderberry, a blackbird clacked a warning.

They pushed on through stillness, brushing against ferns. In the gaps there were light spots and patches, with birdcalls and insects circling. Where the wood closed up, the quiet returned. They walked through calm, following the path. At a fork in the track they paused, gestured both ways, and set off side by side. Still they were silent, feeling the strangeness, the all-surrounding hush. The air was pure thought, it had its own medium, a long-held quality of persistence and delay.

As they circled back, Vanessa found herself watching. It was as if she was taking pictures, recording life. There were webs between bushes, a ditch, a fence-strip then the sky around the wood edge. On the climb uphill she took in the field, the footpath, the view to the vineyard and, close to the top, the gate towards the farm. When they reached the house, she turned to look out.

"Well, I reckon that's it," said Ruth, breaking the silence, "game, set and match."

Vanessa continued to stare across the hills. Her face was pale and slightly abstracted. Something inside her wanted to stay dumb.

"You all right?" asked Ruth, raising one eyebrow.

"Fine."

"Sure?"

Vanessa gave a nod.

"I think the game has had an effect."

"The walk did, certainly."

Ruth pointed: "Ah, Vanessa's taken her vow. I can see it in her eyes. The notice says, *do not disturb*."

A wry smile touched Vanessa's lips. "But what's behind the notice?"

"What indeed, that's the biggie. The Mona Lisa question."

Vanessa hesitated, gazing thoughtfully at the landscape. "I used to think life was all about style, almost like a stage show. As long as you delivered then that was enough. And I believed I had style, or the words and the outfits. So I convinced myself, kept up a front, made it work, at least on the surface."

"Yes, it's funny when you look back now. We all thought we could strut our way through."

The women exchanged glances. Their expressions had set to a long-term kind of puzzlement. They looked like jurors weighing up a case.

"I think we're getting in deep," said Ruth, "and I'm feeling hungry."

"But I know there was something," said Vanessa, "about that walk."

"And the silence?"

"Well, yes. Definitely that."

"Silence is golden."

"Maybe, but not in the way I remember that being said."

"Ah yes, girls, button your lips. The double standard."

Vanessa stood back. She was half turned to Ruth, half towards the view. It seemed she was gazing down a path, a route into being that led both ways. "But it's still important, the game – and the silence. However you look at it that had a meaning."

"So, you're back there with the birds and bees?"

Vanessa shushed her.

Ruth laughed. "Well, I have to admit it *was* an experience. Something you don't forget easily. Spooky if you ask me."

"True, you don't forget. Though what exactly it was about ..." She glanced down the slope. "But I suppose, with time ..."

"In the mean*time*," Ruth replied, "I need to grab a bite to eat."

Vanessa made to speak then, thinking better of it, offered Ruth her arm, Ruth linked in and they turned towards the house. "Well, we'll see what we can nosh," she said. "Love, silence or whatever it takes." And they walked down the garden, with an eager-eyed Ruth singing *Yummy yummy yummy I got love in my tummy* and a tall and silent Vanessa smiling to herself.

That evening, at Hermione's bidding, the group gathered for supper in the front room. When they entered, the chairs had been pushed back, the sofa removed and the floor had been spread with coconut matting. A large patchwork cloth, fitted around the edges of an oval-shaped table, occupied the centre of the dining room. The cloth had been painted with two large staring eyes and an O-shaped mouth. Piled up with fruit bowls, leaf-shaped plates, flower-patterned cups and bottles of wine, it looked like an Arcimboldo.

"Fruit and wine," said Victoria quietly, "please partake."

With Hermione's encouragement the group filled their plates then sat around on cushions chatting their way through drinks and second helpings.

"Home brewed and handpicked," said Caroline, licking her lips.

"Drink up, fill up," cried Hermione.

"A toast to women's power," called Lorna.

"And let yourself go," added Bess, draining her cup.

"A bacchanal supper," said Vanessa, thoughtfully.

"A woman's right to booze," laughed Ruth.

As the evening progressed the women passed through stages, beginning quietly with stories and anecdotes, getting louder with political debates, turning shouty with songs in chorus, then returning to quiet in private conversations. When a red-faced Lorna dozed off in a corner, it was suggested by Victoria that they'd best turn in.

After seeing Ruth to bed, Vanessa found she couldn't sleep. Part of her felt what her mother would call squiffy, but another part was wakeful. She tried lying down but couldn't quite settle, tried sitting up, looked at a book, then rose and descended to the hallway.

Entering the front room, she came across Hermione spread across the sofa. She was examining the label on a green glass bottle. "Herm's brew, and still plenty left," she said, "Drink deep. Enjoy."

Vanessa smiled. A familiar aria passed through her head. For a moment she was floaty, and enjoying her detachment. "That's very kind," she said, squatting on a cushion, "but I think I'm happy as I am."

Hermione rolled her eyes. "The truth my dear. Swear to tell the whole truth, nothing but."

"I'm not sure I'm with you."

Hermione held up one finger like a baton. "Wait," she said as she rocked forward, leaning across the spread, "there's a lesson to be learned." Selecting two large apples, she put one in her lap and shined up the other on a corner of the cloth. "Take," she said, examining what she'd polished. "You don't have to eat."

Vanessa accepted.

"In the story," said Herm, holding up her apple, "it stands for what you might see in the mirror."

Vanessa, who was watching at an angle, gave a nod. Her words, when they came, were directed to the floor, "Well, if that's how ..."

"No, it's simple," cut in Hermione, "the truth's in there, if you can bear to look." She was gazing pointedly at her apple. "Observe, it's the Atlanta factor. Stoop to pick up and you'll lose the race."

"I mean," she added quickly, turning on her guest, "I can tell, it's written all over you. E for ego, my dear. Ego. You came here to escape, thought you could beat it, but it – or you – can't let go."

Vanessa's eyes widened. "I don't know ... Well, I'm not really sure." She met Hermione's gaze, it was pale, unsettling and directed at her.

"You have a domestic problem and you must let go. Allow what happens, don't hold on."

Vanessa thinned her lips. It was as if she'd been spotted, approached by a stranger and taken into confidence. "I have to admit, it's much as you say. There's a major business, long-standing, and rather messy."

"Concerning?"

"It's a question of two people fighting and if there's a solution, how's it to be done."

"Ah, the old, old story," Hermione said, "over and over. You must make it yours."

In the pause that followed Vanessa flashed back to her wood walk with Ruth. She knew that was important.

Hermione sighed and raised her apple like a toast. It was red and green and polished to a glow. "You as well," she said, touching Vanessa's elbow.

Two arms went up, each holding fruit.

"Now eat," said Hermione.

They both bit in. As they chewed and swallowed, the flesh of the apple appeared. It was white and uneven and soft around the edges.

Pausing between mouthfuls, Hermione laughed. "The apple of your eye. That's what you want."

On the next day it was Ruth's idea to end their stay with selected party games. "We'll play them as a send-off," she said. "Goodbye and all that."

At her insistence, after a morning doing nothing, existing on aspirins and large cups of coffee, the women came together. They were gathered in the lounge, sitting on arm rests and squatted on the floor. Ruth, who was positioned at one end, acted as MC.

"Animal, vegetable, mineral?" she asked, working around the room. If they paused she grinned, if they guessed she corrected, if they ran out of chances she awarded extra tries. She jollied them along, switching into deadpan when the next round began.

When their attention wandered, she changed games without warning. "For this one," she said, turning to Victoria, "we have paper and pens to give out."

After grouping the women in a rough half-circle, Ruth explained. "We're playing Consequences," she announced, supervising the distribution of materials. "All the normal rules, so you write an answer when I call out, fold down, pass on. The same for the second round and so on, but no peeking at answers!" She paused, checking their faces. "*Except*, there is a twist. I'll also ask for some to be read out."

An objection was raised by Lorna. The game, she said, had multiple sexist issues about ownership and coupling. Caroline chipped in – she thought the point valid – but Vanessa backed her friend. The room went quiet when Hermione came in loudly, shushing them all.

"Ready?" called Ruth.

"That's right," said Hermione. "You go ahead."

"The man's name. Write it," Ruth called. "The man's name, now."

Six pens moved across paper.

After some seconds, Ruth leaned forward. "And your answer?" she asked Lorna, pointing.

The other woman shrugged, saying nothing.

"I know what," cried Hermione, "her answer's Larry the Lamb."

"Continue," smiled Ruth. "Now write the woman who Larry meets. Her name."

The pens moved again.

"When Larry the Lamb met who?" asked Ruth, nodding to Victoria.

"Salome."

A few eyes widened. Ruth herself laughed.

"Now then, location. Where did they meet?" She looked around the room inviting answers. "Don't bother writing," she added, "just say the spot."

"Larry the Lamb met Salome at a selection meeting," called Vanessa.

Ruth pushed her jaw out. "Right, that's good. Now you all know the rest. He said, she said, the consequences, the world said ... Let's have your answers. Firstly, he said?"

"You're so baaaad," cried a sheep-eyed Hermione, hunching forward.

"She said?"

"Heads I win," called Bess.

"The consequences were?"

"A gynocracy," said Lorna.

"And the world said?"

Raising her voice, Vanessa smiled at the group: "It just goes to prove that women can get ahead."

"While men," put in Bess, "are headless chickens."

Hermione began clucking, ducking forward and back.

Ruth clapped her hands. "Great stuff. Now forget what we've just said. We're going for a second round. This time on paper with no calling out. Let's begin with the woman's name. *Her* name, please ..."

They left soon afterwards, waving and calling their goodbyes. They'd shared addresses and thanked their hosts with a decent-sized whip-round before climbing in the car. It had been, said Caroline, a busy weekend. On the drive back they caught up on sleep. Ruth took the wheel, stopping frequently and swapping with Caroline while Lorna and Bess dozed in a corner, propping each other up, and Vanessa slumped sideways, nose against glass.

During the journey the sky darkened and rain started to fall.

As they entered the suburbs Ruth began to hum. Her voice rose and fell, hovering between notes before moving onto words. She settled on a tune with a throaty kind of chorus, repeated. At each repeat the refrain shortened. Gradually it became clearer as the words reduced and the voice became stronger. When she got down to five and the words fused together, she stopped, then resumed *da capo*.

In the back Vanessa, who was dozing, heard or imagined a song going round.

*All I'm askin' is for a little respect when you come home*
*All I'm askin' is for a little respect when you*
*All I'm askin' is for a little respect*
*All I'm askin' is for*
*All I'm askin' is for a little respect when you come home …*

♩ ♩ ♩

Over the weekend while Vanessa was away, Richard kept himself busy. He said hello to Gabby, who stayed and helped, then went off to see family; he took the children on outings, dealt with domestics and fielded telephone calls, mainly political for Vanessa. Later, when the kids had been bedded, he searched through his drawers and pulled out his notebooks then sat up, reading.

The notebooks were numbered. Small and bound in blue, they went back years. Their pages were full of what read like a logbook: a blow-by-blow account of struggles at work, over children and in their relationship. More about the relationship, as the notebooks continued.

There were thoughts about separation. First as an adjective, how they needed separate space, came from separate families, and were separate or different as teachers and parents. Secondly as an adverb, separately in things done and felt; thirdly as a noun, a line drawn and gap; and finally as a verb, intransitive, with clean break and cut-off, ending in a split.

Also, and related, what they called *their own*: their own distinct areas, their own rooms and possessions, their thoughts and theories and own clear space. His on the patio and practising the piano, hers in the studio and in bed with the kids.

Then there were the statements:

*We're basically territorial. Opposites attract, but we're out of touch. We bounce off each other. Whatever one does, the other contradicts.*

It was reactive stuff.

Reading to the end, he came across a book with some A4 paper inserts. Called HOW COUPLES WORK, it listed strategies in relationships, each with its definition and named example.

It looked like this:

### 1. *POWER-PLAYS*

a) Saying nothing, or a minimum. Giving f. all away. Helps force the issue. Whoever holds back can't be in the wrong. Example: most counsellors.

b) Saying EVERYTHING, or pretending to. Straight from the shoulder to demonstrate ultra-honesty and mislead (self-fooling, especially). E.g. Justin.

c) Compartmentalisation. Different person, different places. Everything in boxes. Has to be Ken.

### 2. *PROCESS-WATCHERS*

Those who obsess about how an action/decision was arrived at, ignoring purpose or outcome. Definitely V.

### 3. *BIG-SWITCHERS*

Ego-driven, both-way swingers. 'Now I like you, now I don't' playground-types. Fits Lorna.

### 4. *SWEAR BOX*

A comprehensive, permanent mental record of a partner's (or rival's) past errors, omissions and offensive remarks. Records everything and cannot be erased. Possibly Gabby towards Len.

5. *PAINTING INTO CORNERS*

The process (usually unconscious) where one partner takes up extreme positions, forcing the other to take up contrary (and equally entrenched) positions. Anything you can do I can do … Quick on the draw. Yours truly, pretty much 24/7, and V.

When he'd read all four sheets Richard replaced the paper, closed the notebook, and moved to the back room.

Positioned by a wall, the piano was waiting with its lid propped up and a spot-lamp above. His obsession, she called it, a way of blocking out.

He switched on the lamp and sat down. Taking a breath, he checked the pedals: one down, the other hooked under. He flicked through his music, getting ready. Always preparing. It never came easily. Tunes were like that.

And then he was listening.

Heard in his head, a voice cut in. It was Letitia, objecting. Like learning the piano, she said, if you wanted a relationship you had to give 100%. Something practised again and again. And the voice in his ear: a line, a phrase, a score to follow. *Where words leave off. That which cannot be said. Painting a picture on silence.*

When Richard began, he felt the notes, like his thoughts, building slowly. They seemed to be alive in his mind, dark and light and high up in the register – and determined, he supposed, by events from a long way off.

# TWENTY-SEVEN

"I think we should speak," Vanessa said after supper, with the children upstairs.

It was her first Friday back and they'd got through the week by keeping themselves busy, playing down differences and being what she called *spare* – meaning slimmed down and separate, contained within themselves. She also meant choosing what they did, and how and where they connected.

Richard looked doubtful. "When's Lance due?" he asked.

Vanessa shook her head. "He's not."

"Has something happened?"

"Yes. Things do happen."

"But what?"

She took a seat, colouring slightly.

Richard, who was preparing to leave, put down his sack and stared. "Is there a problem?"

"Not really, I just decided it wasn't working. He said he wasn't happy. In a way, it's a bit of a relief."

Sitting down opposite, Richard spread his hands in pianist position. "Does that mean it's over?"

Vanessa compressed her lips. In her eyes was an artificial brightness; something about her was close to crying out.

Richard asked again.

"Over? Well, I'm stepping back, that's for sure."

"How long for?"

"Oh, ages …"

"Is there a reason?"

"He wanted more."

"So, you've decided."

She straightened and frowned. Somewhere, at a distance, there was a struggle going on. "That's right. But no one knows yet, so keep it quiet."

"Well I can't say I'm—"

"Sorry or surprised?"

"No, just not clear about what happens next."

"Nothing really. You go, I'll be here. The usual arrangement."

He waited for her to finish. It was as if he was counting bars in his head. "Do you want me to stay?"

Her eyebrows shot up. "I certainly wasn't expecting. You go."

"But it does need to be balanced, we always said that."

His words seemed to prompt her. An imagined conversation came into her head. "I don't think that anymore," she said.

"Is that," he said, placing both hands palm-down on the table, "a new theoretic development?"

433

"If that's how you want to label it. There are alternatives."

"You've had some thoughts?"

She looked towards the hallway. A child's voice was raised, carrying down the stairs. "I want us to try an idea. When you get back."

"Well, whatever it is I'd rather know. Otherwise I'm going to imagine all sorts of things."

"Oh, it's nothing big, just a walk, by ourselves. That's all."

When Richard didn't answer, she waved towards the door. "You can go now. Really, it's all right if you go." As he reached for his sack, she dropped her voice, "And don't worry about the walk, it can wait. But ask Gabby when she can take the children. Tomorrow, if she's free."

His answer was cut off by another childish call. Vanessa moved towards the hall as the cry came again. It persisted, echoing itself. Perfectly balanced between song and dispute, it was blithe, repeated and slightly plaintive.

When Richard arrived, Gabby was watching from the window. The sun had set and the skyline had hardened. The pavement was empty and the air was still. With her head to one side she was looking down the terrace: it was dark and light and spotlit in places. Like a model, it didn't look real.

Sensing his approach, she descended to the hall where she slung on her backpack and stepped outside. "Welcome, comrade," she said as he parked and climbed out. They hugged then stood close, watching each other like long-lost relatives. His breath felt warm on her cheek.

"Could we drive some time?" she asked.

"Yes, whenever you want."

"Now, if possible."

"*Bien sûr*, where to?"

"You know, the playspace."

"At night?"

"Yes, you'll see it differently."

Richard nodded and returned to the car. "The same route as before?" he asked as they both took their seats.

"That would be best."

He manoeuvred out and off, switching on the headlights. The road opened before them, joining others as it skirted an estate. After reaching a carriageway he drove several miles through mock-Tudor semis and the odd tower block before turning off at a junction. Here they took a ring road. The traffic was light and Gabby kept her hand resting on his shoulder. While driving they talked and checked directions. They were a couple in the dark, together, moving on.

A mile down the road they turned into a lane sloping uphill. It led to a village with a central pond surrounded by half-timbered houses. "You know the way?" she asked.

"I remember," he replied.

At a bend by a church they forked left and began a gradual ascent. The road was narrower, holed in places, and Richard switched the headlights to full beam. On both sides there were woods.

"Here," said Gabby when they reached a P-sign with a metal-arched entrance and a clearing behind. "It's different after dark," she added, reaching for her sack as they turned in and bumped across potholes to park by bushes. As Richard flicked off the headlights Gabby shifted forward, talking to herself. Something about her tone suggested distance; their arrival had changed things.

Stepping outside, they took in the silence, the emptiness, and the dark perimeter wood. "Yours," she said, pulling out a black plastic torch with red-yellow flashes. Passing it over, she pulled out another, beaming it in an arc.

"They're headlights," he said, aligning his torch beam with hers. Ahead was a track, leading forward through rows of silver birch.

"When I first came," she said leading off, "things weren't planted." An echo in her voice made it sound unreal.

They followed the track through shadows and silence. The torch beams flashed white, catching on bark. It seemed the trunks were peeling from within.

Gabby led on, passing a fenced-off dip to reach a meeting of paths in a deeply rutted area with a moss-bank to one side. Ahead the torch beams cut avenues through air. "The fort," she said, directing her torch towards a sprawling wooden construction with ropes and ladders at the centre of a clearing. They approached across grass, flashing their lights all around.

Richard played his beam over a board on a pole. It was head-high, bordered with metal and looked like a traffic sign. The words *Adventure Playground* were cut into wood.

"Let's try the swings," said Gabby, pausing for a second as if she'd been blocked. She pointed to some split logs hung by chains from a bar. They approached, using the torches to guide them to their seats. The chains rattled and clattered as they took their places.

"Ready for off?" asked Richard. Gabby nodded and they switched off their lights. At first the blackness held them. It was dead-still, close-up and all-surrounding. "Can you see anything?" he asked.

"Depends," she said, grasping her chain and leaning back, "it's different upstairs." The sky above was grey and patchy. The moon was faint, hazed by cloud, and softened to a glow.

Richard sat still, adjusting slowly. The tops of the trees appeared, then the planks and walls of the playground construction. When he looked down, his feet were there, side by side and planted. He swung gently back, using his weight to work the swing higher. As Gabby joined in, the chain began to creak and the frame shuddered. "Did you swing here as a kid?" he called as they passed in the air.

Gabby confirmed, speaking in snatches.

"With friends?"

"Just me."

"But not at night, surely?"

That, she said, might surprise him.

He continued throwing out questions and Gabby replied, calling as they crossed. Like balls thrown up for practice, their remarks remained hanging, repeating in the dark.

After a while they allowed their swings to run free and their words tailed off. The clouds had pulled back and the moon, which was high and large, was in full view.

Richard was first off, landing on grass. Gabby followed, descending silently and walking around like a guard, flashing her torch.

The main part of the playground was built like a stockade. Vertical outside, it was cross-beamed and buttressed at the corners. Inside went

436

up in ramps and walkways and step-laddered blocks, rising to a platform with nets either side. It looked like the house that Jack built. They entered by ducking down and groping their way through a large metal pipe. The pipe was holed from the sides and above. It smelled of sand and water.

Emerging, Richard looked up. He was standing in a narrow walled-in forecourt with the stars in view. Three sides were blocked, the other sloped up towards a hole in a wall. This, he realised, could be an outtake from a film.

Gabby joined him and they began their exploration. The hole led through to an open-topped passageway that forked and doubled back repeatedly. "You come this far before?" she asked, taking the lead. Behind her words, a space had appeared.

"Not sure," he replied, "I do remember there being a maze." He was aware of her back, shadowy in darkness, and the need to keep up. Suddenly it struck him that he needed guidance. If she left him here—

"It's simple-simple," she said, clapping her hands, "as long I don't think."

Richard gave an uneasy laugh. "Eyes closed is best."

Gabby laughed too, but there was strain there, hidden. He could hear her breathing hard. She was all head and shoulders, moving at a shuffle, seeking out a route. Together they were infantry approaching the front line.

"Blind man's buff," he added, searching for words to settle down his thoughts.

"Or hide and go seek."

She led, he followed, and soon they reached a clearing with a central pole and a ladder to one side. It went up in stages, leading to a platform. "The eye," she said, turning her torch and flashing it about. The walls here were bamboo, strapped in by wire and slung between stays hammered into fence posts. In the torchlight they bunched and gleamed like wheat. "Uppity-up," she instructed, shining towards the ladder. "You first." Richard stepped forward, following the beam. With his hands on the steps he paused, glancing back as if he was posing for a photo. "Go on," she urged, "it leads out." Her voice tone was clear; she was speaking from a distance, talking herself up.

When they reached the top, she paced out the platform, flashing her light. It ran along one side of the playground, raised up like a gallery. The wooden floor beneath shook and flexed and shuddered like scaffolding. "I'm on guard," she cried, "up above, treading the boards."

Richard stood back, observing her pacing. She was humming quietly, skipping her hand along the top of the railing, contained in thought. Every so often she turned on her heel and threw back her head, muttering oddly. As she moved back and forth Richard had the impression that she'd come here for a purpose, and he wondered for a moment whether she'd notice if he ducked out quietly and slipped off in the dark.

Gabby turned suddenly. "Don't mind me. This is *let's pretend*." She gestured out towards the clearing. "I was a child-crazy. Still am, really." She laughed. "I came here to do people – doctors and patients, cops and crooks, neighbours, TV characters, anyone. In my theatre."

In the silence that followed the air remained still. The moon shone clear and pale, touching the tree tops with its glow. Realising what she'd said, Richard stepped forward, "I thought you just wanted to come back. If you'd said about this, then I'd have known …"

"But you might have run."

"Or I might have insisted – would have, without a doubt." He threw back his head. "So now it's a double act." Suddenly the positions were reversed: Richard was in movement, holding the railing and pronouncing into air. As he called out, he imagined himself addressing a classroom, reading from his notebooks, as if it was open mike.

Switching off her torch, Gabby stepped forward. "OK, you be teacher, I'll play nurse."

"I get to be myself, is that the idea?"

"Yourself, yes," she said quietly, "you do that well."

He laughed and she looked up: the clouds had returned. They stretched across the moon, softening its edges.

"The man in the moon's winking," he said, remembering her words, naked in the park.

"Or woman."

The sky glowed silver-grey, ringed around the moon. Dark and light, it seemed to overhang them. It was sea-like, shadowy and expansive.

They watched, then led each other around, partner-style, by the railing and the view.

"Showtime," said Gabby, grinning.

"Right, let's pretend."

"Mad stuff, eh?"

"Anything goes."

"Crazy, and how."

"Bonkers."

"Completely cracked, barmy, loco …"

"Looney," he ended, glancing at the moon.

Later in the night, after playing let's pretend and putting on voices, Gabby and Richard returned to the car. As they walked, they were silent. They'd had their time, made their statement and now were taking stock. It was as if they'd been there, done that, and this was their return.

As they drove back to the city the sky began to brighten. The fields came into view and the roof-lines stood out. Following the ring road they turned onto a carriageway, cruising the suburbs before exiting into darkened side streets. Here the sky was a grey strip flushed with pink; everywhere was getting lighter.

Arriving at Gabby's, they filled up with tea and biscuits then climbed to the bedroom, where they quickly fell asleep.

Two hours later the alarm clock rang. "That hurts," she said, clapping her hand on the red button. Yawning and grunting, they rose, washed down and dressed. Gabby made coffee and they stood by the window watching the sky. As the sun came up, they kissed.

"It feels like we're the last ones standing," said Richard.

"Us, and the animals."

"Maybe it's more Saturday morning. Slow to get going."

"We're the early birds."

"What my kids call previous."

Gabby shrugged. "At least it's quiet. And that's a change."

"How do you mean?"

"Oh, it's *here we go again*. The Ken and Lorna show."

"So, what's happening?"

"They've split, so they say. Truth is, he's been dumped."

"I see. And where does that leave Ken now?"

"Conferencing."

"But what about you?"

Gabby snorted. "I've got him back. We're all *coupling* now – just because Lorna-half-wit-Bell *has* to be monogamous."

"Meaning, Justin's the one and only …"

"He's vowed eternal love, it's the greatest story told, for at least a week."

"But what about the girlfriends?"

Gabby rolled her eyes: "Oh, they're just happy for everyone else. I call 'em glad-abouts. Glad to be with you, glad without. You know the type …" here she snapped her fingers, "*nice* political groupies."

"And Ken? How's he taking it?"

"He's heartbroken, the end of everything. It's like he's living on death row."

"While you think he's overreacting …"

"It's her playing games that gets to me." She paused, glowering. "Because in the end it's me who picks up the pieces. Every time, I have to deal with her mess. Get him into shape, do what I can."

"So, it's the same old stuff. The ups and downs and around each other's houses …"

Gabby laughed harshly. "Musical chairs. They call it women's power, I call it farce." As she stepped back, frowning, Richard checked the time and mentioned Vanessa. Remembering their talk, he relayed her request and suggested ringing home.

"She wants to walk?"

He confirmed.

"And you?"

"I'm up for it, as long you don't mind taking the children."

"Do you know what it's about?"

Richard shook his head.

Gabby brightened. "Tell her I can come round, now if she likes. Then you two can go off, long as you want."

When Richard rang, Vanessa answered calmly, as if she was expecting it. She asked how long, questioned about food and warned that the children might need some settling. She also thanked Gabby, asked what she needed and called to the children, telling them who was coming. When Richard checked on timings she fell silent then, when he asked again, answered suddenly. "Allow forty-*ish*," she said, then excused herself.

When they arrived, the curtains had been opened and the TV was off.

While Charlotte was getting washed, Stephan was in his bedroom. Downstairs, Vanessa was clearing up. The kitchen smelled of coffee and toast. A deal was in place.

There'd been some happy families involving a Charlotte story, featuring her as Beauty and Stephan as the Beast, followed by talk about likings, all-round cuddles and an agreement to get dressed. The deal had filled a gap, a channel-hop break with all four stations broadcasting news or sport. It had been helped by talking and listening and not inflating issues. And this particular Saturday, perhaps to make a point, the children had been good. They'd taken turns, waited for the bathroom, not called out, and now were busy dressing.

When Richard appeared, he asked where they were, then climbed to the landing.

Downstairs the women were talking through arrangements.

Mostly it was simple:

1. Reassurance – "I've told them you're here and we're going out," smiled Vanessa. "They seem to be pleased."

2. Guidance – tips and reminders with the odd quiet warning, followed by thanks.

3. Last minute checks – on clothing, health and mood.

If she was worried, Vanessa tried not to show it. After all, the kids might get upset. But when the children appeared and greeted Gabby it soon became clear that she knew about food, was quick to spot problems and had a knack of being jokey while not talking down.

"Are you sure you'll both be all right?" Vanessa asked the children.

"Yes."

"Yes, yes."

"Oh, *Mum.*"

Vanessa kissed them, Richard waved, and they set off together.

In the game of relationships, they were searching, looking for routes forward, trying to find a way.

Q: And what did Vanessa think?

A: Not much. She didn't want a struggle. If there was an agenda or points to be scored then walls would go up. She'd rather just look and go walkabout. For her it was out there, and social.

They walked.

The sky had cleared and shafts of sunlight cut across the buildings. A bird sang from an apple tree as they turned out into the street. On both sides there were parked cars, some with tinted windscreens, others with stickers and some with hanging mascots. As they passed by Ruth's, Vanessa looked up. A large wisteria, sprawling across brickwork, had reached the guttering. The bedroom curtains were drawn.

Q: And what did Richard think?

A: He wanted to take soundings, mark down phrase and meaning, know the ins and outs.

They walked to a small corner shop. It was piled to the door with batched-up newspapers and cardboard boxes. The owner appeared from inside, holding a mug and nodding a greeting.

Q: And what did both feel?

A: Vanessa: things floating and provisional. Richard: a journey into nowhere.

They arrived at a junction and paused, looking north along a long straight road dotted with trees. On both sides there were tall Victorian terraces with fluted woodwork and slate roofs.

"So, we're going somewhere for a walk," prompted Richard.

Vanessa confirmed.

"Do we have a planned route?"

Vanessa pulled out an envelope from her bag. "I had this earlier in the week," she said, passing over an A5 sheet of coloured notepaper. "It's from Vaughan. He wants us to visit."

In the game of relationships this was a wild card.

He held up Vaughan's letter, examining the handwriting. It was clear and regular, perfectly formed, and neatly centred. "I didn't know he was still around. It's a while since his book."

"He lives in a flat by the river. Top floor, he says."

"What do you think made him get in touch?"

"Because of the show, I imagine."

"And you suggest we see him?"

She stood, undecided. "I get the impression he's changed. He does say any time."

In the game of choices, they were at a crossroads.

Richard checked the letter. "Well, I have to say, he does sound different from the book. So why not give him a try?" He looked at the address. "Harcourt Tower. That's easy, it's right by where I used to walk."

"Before you moved in?"

"Yes. My route one."

Her voice dropped low and her eyes looked off; she was thinking into air. "That's strange. I was remembering that."

"You were? I still take it sometimes, in my head. It's a good way to get to the centre."

"And to Vaughan's it would seem."

They walked along the street, beyond the terraces to an area where the houses were set back behind overgrown gardens. They were square-built and detached, brick-and-stone-faced with high sloping roofs and ornamental chimneys. As they walked, a cyclist passed by followed by cars then an open-backed lorry carrying planks and poles. At a school with a crossing they turned left beneath a tree to enter a thirties estate. Facing inward, the different levels were connected by open walkways with plants in corners, window stickers and handmade gates. Named after battles, they were linked north-south in a series of squares.

In the city-game these were boxes, bridges, spaces.

Crossing the estate, they passed by men in overalls, a runner and a group of workers digging up a trench. Reaching an alleyway, they emerged at a small row of shops with blinds across windows and paint-dripped signboards. At a bare vinyl café called *Angie's Place* they turned through a gate into a park.

*Two, on promenade.*

As they walked, they exchanged thoughts about the weather, moving into teaching, politics and news of friends, then Vanessa shared some facts about Vaughan, leading to talk about family and children, all mixed in with periods of silence.

*Opposites, stepping out.*

When they reached the river the sun had strengthened, playing clear and bright across metal and concrete. "Harcourt Tower," he said, pointing downstream to a medium-sized block standing on its own with smoke-blue windows and an external lift.

In the relationship game, although they didn't know it, this was home.

They approached along a walkway flanked by a wall that Richard touched occasionally, playing his hand across stone. Beyond was a drop, the river and a view downstream; opposite, a jetty and slow-moving water.

*On foot, going forward.*

Reaching the block, they entered an all-glass lobby where a heavily-built man in a uniform greeted them. Vanessa named her cousin and they signed in. While the man rang upstairs, Richard studied a large abstract canvas and Vanessa eyed a vase. The painting and the flowers both felt artificial.

"Please go up. You're expected," said the man and showed them to the lift.

The ride seemed almost fairground, it was all air and sky and sunlit buildings. As they stepped out at the top a figure appeared in the corridor wearing a close-fitting suit. He was tall and lithe with jet black hair and aquiline features. His forehead was wide, mouth narrow and cheeks sucked in. He looked like a cross between a Greek athlete and an El Greco saint.

"Vaughan," he said, shaking hands and inviting them in.

Officer, on lookout.

The room they entered was long and light with coloured windows. Furnished with glass-topped tables, specimen cases and freestanding VDUs, it looked like a museum.

When Vaughan closed the door, the room became silent.

*Pianissimo.*

They sat by a blue-green window with an outlook on the city. Outside a plane passed over, taxis and buses lined up and trains crossed bridges. On the pavements people walked, holding bags and briefcases. It looked like a silent movie.

"Triple-glazed," said Vaughan when asked about the sound. The room held his voice in a close-up stillness, quiet and persistent. It was as if they were swimming underwater.

*Shhh.*

He took orders for tea or coffee then withdrew to the kitchen, moving quietly across thick-pile carpet. During his absence, Richard looked at the river while Vanessa screen-watched, using a headset. On his return, Vaughan served drinks and talked about his life. It was as if he'd heard the backlog of questions they wanted to ask him.

*Listen.*

Removing her headset, Vanessa asked about his book. Had he any more planned?

Vaughan sat, observing his guests as if they were specimens. "I decided," he said finally, "to give up the stunts." His eyes were round and deeply thoughtful.

"You mean flying blind, that sort of thing?" asked Richard.

He confirmed.

"So it's a different life here?"

"Let me show you," Vaughan said, standing.

*Quiet.*

Leading to a screen, he flicked a button to bring up a slide show, beginning with a bare steep drop, then a seascape, a treeless scrubland,

445

followed by mist clouds and jungle. All were unpeopled and strangely otherworldly.

"It's the silence," he said. "I wanted it to go on, forever."

Vanessa shivered. "You used to be …" she began, stopping herself to stare deep into the picture.

"Different. I know."

"But these places – they're *you*."

"No, *us*. What I call creative commons. We have to hold onto them."

The photo on screen was an icescape. Pure white and glistening, it stretched in ridges, rising from grey sea to an all-white plateau. It was bare, blocky in places, jagged around the edges and completely empty.

"One of my trips." he said. "Antarctica, as it was. Before it goes."

*Hush.*

They all looked. Vaughan pressed a button and the picture enlarged. They were staring at a raw, blasted landscape littered with uneven snow-lumps. Deep ice cracks zigzagged across white.

"Were you alone there?" asked Richard.

"By myself, but not alone."

"Who was there?"

"Hard to say."

They continued looking as the picture closed to a grey-white blur.

*Dream-space. Wilderness. Void.*

Vanessa asked a question about how long he'd stayed. As Vaughan replied he gazed long and hard, without expression. He looked like a pilot about to take off.

"In a way," he said, "I never left."

The screen they were watching dimmed and a long shot of mountains took its place.

*Unreal.*

"Were you ever frightened?" asked Richard. He was thinking of Frank, and the smell of burning flesh.

"All the time, that's what drove me."

"And the silence," added Vanessa.

Vaughan stood back from the screen. Narrowing his eyes and pointing, he led down the room, checking both sides.

*Watch-spot and gallery.*

They stopped to examine the tinted glass, studying the colours and peering down at the cityscape below.

"Like scenes with different lighting," said Vanessa.

"Or times of day," added Richard.

*Kaleidoscope.*

At the end of the room they reached a different view. A door led through to a dark space that ran the length of the second side of the building. It was bare, shielded by blinds and backlit by a strange glow that appeared from somewhere hidden. The effect was nocturnal. "My studio," said Vaughan.

Enter the darkroom.

The wooden floor was polished. Across it lay a scattered collection of stones, some large, some patterned, mostly lying flat. They were arranged in groups: a few in spirals, some in parallel lines and others heaped up in oddly-shaped blocks.

*Mindspace and thoughtbox.*

Encouraged by their host, Vanessa crouched down and picked up a rock. "This one's been polished?" she asked and he nodded. She handled several more, remarking on shape and colour before returning them to their piles. On one she found a quartz streak, another a fossil, there were holed stones, faulted rocks, and fragments of shale with hollowed-out clinker.

*Handfuls, pick-ups. Still lives.*

Richard joined in, fingering stone. "Are they all from your travels?" he asked, wondering how one man could have carried them.

"Some. Others are Victorian, from collections. Your father," here he turned to Vanessa, "provided several."

"Derek did?"

"He designed this apartment."

"Really?"

"He wanted it to last, regardless."

"Regardless?"

"I think of it as my Ark."

Richard put down his stone. "Have you seen his models?"

"I didn't know you knew."

"First time there, he showed me."

"And every time we go," Vanessa put in, "they spend hours playing upstairs."

Vaughan pursed his lips. "But he didn't say what he did here."

Richard confirmed, looking puzzled.

"Come," Vaughan said, "I'll show you."

Sidestepping rocks, he moved to the end of the gallery. "To the balcony," he said, turning the handle of what looked like a fire exit. As the door unsealed, the noise levels rose and a wedge of light struck into the gallery. It was as if he'd opened a hatch at sea.

The balcony was narrow and crammed with small plants. It overlooked long lines of roofs. Beyond, they could see arterial routes, a side branch of the river and, further out again, a large green park.

*Outsiders.*

Holding the railing they shuffled sideways, edging carefully by flower pots and folding chairs. As they moved, a gentle breeze played about their heads. They were high and bright and poised above the drop.

Turning a corner, they followed Vaughan to the left and up some steps that led to the roof, arriving at a bare open patio with paths leading off and a panoramic view.

"Your own secret garden," Vanessa said. They were facing a spare, geometric space with patterns in gravel, low box hedges and greenery in pots. A sign to one side said, *The Hanging Garden.*

"Based on the golden ratio," Vaughan said quietly. He stooped to pick up a rock. "And symbolic," he added, turning it over in his hand. The rock was flat, mirror-smooth and carved in relief. It carried two overlapping heads, one sun-rayed, one crescent-shaped.

*Find. Talisman. Artefact.*

Richard peered at the rock then around at the borders. Remembering their outings, an ironic smile played across his lips. "Annihilating all that's made …" he said.

Led by Vaughan, they explored the pea gravel paths, ending at a central, bare-walled building with a pillared entrance. Inside, light from above picked out a waist-high marble slab. It was square and plinth-like. Centred on top was a tall, cut-away, architectural model.

*Image. Symbol. Prototype.*

"Harcourt Tower," said Vaughan.

"By Derek?" asked Richard.

"His work," said Vaughan.

Vanessa circled the model, leaning forward to scan the floors and check the garden. On the outside it was a section, showing the flats' interiors in fine detail. It was exact, photo-realist and perfectly proportioned.

*Made in the likeness.*

Beside it, on the table, was a numbered plaque with a key below, naming various features.

"We're standing in the temple, looking at the 'gin," she said.

"And below is the cell," added Richard.

Vanessa looked up. "I didn't realise," she said, thinning out her cheeks.

As Richard responded she cut in with a laugh. "Are all his models like this?" she asked, pointing to the top floor interior.

Looking where she pointed, Richard nodded, "Crafted, I'd say, all of 'em, with amazing detail."

*Like for like.*

Vanessa gazed long and hard, moving her head from side to side and making appreciative noises. "It's like finding a photo album," she said finally, "with pictures of distant relatives. Ones you've heard of but haven't ever seen."

"An eye-opener?"

"Definitely. And next time home, I'm going upstairs …"

"Ah, but aren't they the product of male obsessiveness?"

He smiled a challenge and Vanessa smiled back. "You know best," she said quietly.

"I do?"

Vanessa made to answer then curbed herself. It didn't seem necessary.

"But thinking about it," added Richard, "isn't male obsession what we're looking at here?" He swept his arm around, taking in the model, the temple, and out towards the garden.

"Yes, everywhere," responded Vaughan, "magnificent, foolish, childish, absurd." He held up his sun-moon rock. "And this is what will remain. *Après nous, le déluge.*"

As she looked Vanessa thought of Ruth, the argument with Richard and the beer barrel coaster.

As he looked Richard thought of Gabby and her wooden sun sign suspended on a chain.

An hour later, returning to the river, Richard and Vanessa climbed to the walkway on the bridge. The water below them was calm. On one side was concrete with flag poles and tree-lined promenades, on the other, a road with traffic queuing up. The metal they passed as they climbed was grey, streaked with graffiti and bird droppings.

Reaching the middle, they stopped.

"There's something else," he said, "I meant to say."

"There is?"

"It has to do with your exhibition."

"Oh, that."

"You remember Angel?"

"Ah yes, I admired her work."

"I should've told you at the time."

"Told me what?"

"We talked together. She's related."

"Richard, what are you saying? Are you sure?"

"Yes, she's family."

"In what way?"

"More to me than you. She's my aunt's sister."

"I see, so why didn't you tell me?"

"I thought you might not like it, coming from me."

"Not like it … But Richard, you should have …"

"You're right. Are you pissed off?"

"Not really. A bit shell shocked, but glad it's out. She's a brave woman."

"I've got her card at home. You'd like it?"

"Oh yes, that would be good."

"And you'll make contact?"

"Definitely."

They gazed downstream. The sky was light and dark, with sunlight spotting over stone. The river was blue-grey and wrinkled like a cloth. Shadows had appeared around the buildings. Vaughan's block was there, looking like its model.

"I thought of her because of him," said Richard quietly.

"You mean my cousin?"

"Yes, because of the stones, and the silence."

"But Vaughan's quite different."

"More male you mean?"

"More crazy. One of a kind."

"You heard what he said about how his stunts began?" asked Richard. He was staring down at a barge through cross-meshed girders.

"Did he tell you about that? The schoolboy stuff – red flags on buildings?" Vanessa looked out at a dome with a column beside it surmounted by a uniformed statue. Both were flecked white and circled by pigeons.

"Yes. But did you notice who with?"

"I don't know if I heard."

"He said it when he brought the drinks."

"Oh, maybe I missed it, then. Anyway, tell me."

"I think the name says a lot."

She looked at him quizzically. "I hope you're not going to keep this to yourself."

"You know him."

"I do?"

"Know him well."

"And the name?"

"Guess."

Vanessa shrugged her shoulders.

"Shall I give you a clue?"

"No games, just the name please."

"You give up?"

"Richard—"

"Try again."

"Name. Now."

"You sure?"

"No more talk. Name him."

"Justin Peters."

Vanessa frowned. "Surely—" she began then turned. As she searched Richard's face a far-off shiver ran across the bridge.

"The boy is father to the man," said Richard, as the sound came closer. Metal on metal, it advanced with a shudder. "But in their case," he added, "something happened, or was there already. One grew, one didn't."

The approaching noise was filling up the air. Drumming hard, the sound locked them in. Vanessa raised her voice: "Meaning it could go either way, is that what you're saying?"

He nodded.

"And whatever game you play," she added, "you can never know what's round the corner." As Richard acknowledged, she turned a circle, taking in the bridge, the river and the advancing train. "So, it's see for yourself, stand looking out, and that's good enough …"

The noise cut her off. It was as if she was on a phone and the line had gone dead. She continued mouthing, panto-style, as the walkway shook and the noise took over. It flowed and echoed and pressed in from all sides. Inside it they were calm and alive and held in silence.

And they listened together to the sound of metal moving slowly, the carriages passing and the big booming silence of the last departing train.

♯ ♯ ♯

The Hen House<br>10th Nov

Dear Vanessa and Richard,

After you've read this I'd like you to burn it, put a match to the corner and watch it go up. And please don't tell a soul. See it as a message whispered, a voice in the head, rain against glass.

452

Or you could just chuck it. Take scissors to the corner to tear and scatter, then straight down the flush. Whatever the way, it has to be final, over and done with. I've said my piece, and I don't want them to know.

Here are my thoughts.

Begin.

What counts is who we are. I wanted it to work, did my doggie best. Do this, now this, best friend and supporter. Speak and offer warnings. Run, run, run.

*Who* we are, well yes, a leaf, a wind, bits from a star. I am what I am what I am.

Let me explain.

WHO? Gabby, crazy. Ever seen those drawings of a child's face popping up from earth? A small round-eyed girl appearing like a blackbird in a cat's mouth? The child peering out from the whale?

WHAT? Objections, contradictions … Can't stand the want-it-both-ways, about-and-about facers, Lorna, Ken, Justin, the whole fizzing lot of 'em. Too much dancing.

WHERE and WHEN? I've walked. Backpack, map, provisions and head for the hills. Or, to tell the truth, Belvedere Park, the railway line at night, then up and off, beginning the grand tour, to the Ridgepath and passage grave. Yes, if I'm missing, it's a gap I'm filling, you understand. Digging up roots. Revisiting the patch.

Where am I going? Brambles, hawthorns, gorse slopes, ditches.

WHY? Well, here goes …

When I returned to the house late Sat afternoon, there was Ken jawing on the phone. "Lorna?" I said, though of course I knew. The white face and hands, the attempted smile, bottom lip threatening. *This is not me*, trying to get out. Afterwards we had a row. "She's *allowed* you one hour," I said, "to make some sort of case?"

Excuses, evasions, talk about the struggle.

When he came back The Line had him hooked. Breathless and twitchy, words in the mouth. Women as vanguard, the right to decide, female and first.

The next day, on the phone, back on the case. Some whining talk about Xena and Melissa, needing sitting.

"What about Justin?" Whereabouts unknown, on *Activist* call-out, fighting the cause. Another row and exit.

Later, more of Ken, returned again. A decision this time, everything off and a second front opened. By now I'd reached super-cool rage. "Oh, you mean it's still all monogamous?" Not so, apparently.

And the upshot? Two more days with Ken in the air, jaw out, shaky, short-breathed on the phone. Crisis, crisis, crisis.

Surprise is a child gazing at a hill, disappointment is an adult looking from the top.

It all became clear at Wednesday's meeting with the inner circle group, Lorna, Justin, Caroline, Ken, yours truly, plus one other. Dreamy-eyed faces, gathered in a circle. Executive business, money, targets, *Activist* subs … then all hail and salute to welcome the new member. Lance.

The cat that ate the cream, Georgie Porgy, Little Boy Blue, butter wouldn't melt … And this is where it snapped, afterwards, chatting (and when you've read through this burn, burn, burn, burn), with red mist and hot blood and up gals and at 'em.

Lance + Lorna, the latest thing.

Words used, chuck, chuck out, upchuck, big chucking yuck. The mega-stink. Knee high in gunk. Bogus, phoney, rotten apples. Nettles grow from slops. I think you know the rest.

So, I'm on migration. A late summer visitor, here to stop off. By the time this reaches you, I'll already have flown. From where I'm heading this is all past. See me as I go, now high, now low, the nightwalk child. I'm in the shadows, looking for scraps, anywhere, nowhere, everywhere. What we do is send out a signal.

I'm out here in the wild, somewhere, walking. In the rain-streaks and mists, OTT. Crossing over water, down on mud, up into fog, stepping over feelings. Poor G.

While it lasted it was nice. Wants are to needs as head is to heart. All roads lead there.

*Stayin' alive.*

Gabby xx

‡ ‡ ‡

## Families, Imaginary Histories and the Silence of Gossip
## by Professor M Lavender (Cont.)

As an epilogue to this talk I'd like, for a moment, to step outside the conventional boundaries of social science. By way of illustration, and off the record as a social anthropologist, I want to tell you a little more about my own imaginary family history. If that seems anecdotally self-indulgent I suggest you respond to this part, as would some families, with a pinch of salt.

One route in to my only-child persona is the selective application of systemic therapy. In my case parental scanning, diagnosing and treatment activities began early, leading to the inevitable adolescent rebellion. My childhood experiences also align with Bowen's theory of family projection. All three of us occupied separate corners but, as in the story of The Three Apples, there's a twist. Most of the time I took two parts, both of them named and shaped by my parents. So, in an ironic reversal of Hansel and Gretel, my parents stood listening intently outside my bedroom door while I put off sleep. You could say we were in session and engaged in psycho-analytical surveillance activities. Of course, my parents couldn't look into my dream but if they could they would have seen me a) dancing wildly b) crying.

These two versions of me gaze out from upstairs windows across a suburban street, paired up like self and reflection in a mirror. The first, perhaps misleadingly, was nicknamed Christmas Boy. He was the gap-tooth child pulling faces at the camera who would have liked to spend his whole year playing outdoors. Looking at the family snapshots it seems he almost did. He's the boy on his own fronting the family group, the boy in the garden crouched behind the fence and the boy with a bat on the beach. I remember his high-as-a-kite excitement at holidays and birthdays, but oddly I don't experience being *him*. The feeling has detached from the person. He has become an unreal child from way-back-when who ran like the wind and clowned for attention.

The second self is the youth who followed the girl without a name seen at the bus stop. That boy was withdrawn. He carried her inside him like a secret picture torn from a newspaper and hidden in a drawer. He was the shy boy, the invisible admirer, the Boy Who Never Was.

These two me-s were shaped by the stories in which they played a part. Christmas Boy first came into being when I appeared in my parents' bedroom one Christmas at three in the morning asking for my presents. Shy Boy began after watching *20,000 Leagues Under the Sea* and crying uncontrollably when the Nautilus went down. Both events became part of the authorised version of my childhood, referred to often at birthdays and celebrations.

Later I came to see that I didn't quite fit the parts I'd been given. After a period of denial, I came to view myself, and my role in the family, rather differently. It's that process of adjusting the story that I'd like to turn to now.

While conducting this project I encountered an interesting cautionary tale. It's about how one man tries to escape from his family and himself. This version is retold in modern language. I shall move my lecture towards its conclusion by reading it out.

## THE GAME OF THE NAME

Giving people nicknames is a sport and a pastime in Kashmir. Everyone is given a funny, clever play-name, even the king. But there's a fine line between humour and abuse. And for one small boy called Mohammed his nickname was almost too much to bear.

Mohammed's pet name was Momma, meaning woman's breast. It was his father's idea of a joke. At first the boy tried to disregard it but a name, once given in Kashmir, has a life of its own. And as he grew up Momma began to feel that people either looked down on him or they were laughing behind his back. He was the runt of the family.

At home the only work Momma had ever been given were odd jobs and running errands for the neighbours. As a result, when his father died he had to take what work he could get. He began by carrying sacks in the market, later he pulled handcarts. It was hard, exhausting work and when he came home at night all he could think about was getting an easier job. So he turned to his friend the grocer for advice. "Why not raise chickens in your back yard," the grocer said, "I can sell them for you, until you get a shop of your own."

Momma liked the idea and went out and bought a white hen. His hen laid and laid, and within a year Momma became the proud owner of a small poultry farm. But either the noise of chickens clucking all day or the chink of coins in his pocket had a strange effect on Momma. He began to laugh and strut up and down in front of his neighbours, singing about his hen. His song went like this:

> Ha, ha, ha, you and me,
> Little white hen, don't I love thee!
> Ha, ha, ha, you and me,
> Little white hen, don't I love thee!

Momma's singing and strutting soon earned him a new nick-name, Momma Kokker, meaning Mother Hen. As soon as he heard it, Momma rushed indoors and locked himself away. He stuck his fingers in his ears, but nothing could block out the hateful name. He could hear it everywhere. It was shouted by the children, sung by his neighbours and even, it seemed, chorused by the birds. The name echoed in his head and filled up his dreams. So desperate was he to escape that one sleepless night in a fit of rage he went out in the yard and slit the hen's throat. Then he seized some belongings and ran off, stumbling into the dark.

As Momma reached the town gate, he began to slow down. In front of him, the first rays of sunlight were colouring the walls. A soft breeze was touching his face. Pausing by a young plane tree he listened. The words in his head had changed. A far-off voice was telling him where he should go. It said he wasn't alone. As he walked on to begin a new life, he heard the voice whisper something again and again, two words he knew well but couldn't quite hear …

Years passed before Momma, ashamed of what he'd done, returned to his home town. He was married, went by the name Khan Mohammed and was a well-to-do merchant. Reaching the gate, he stopped to rest beneath the plane tree, now grown large. Two young men passed by, followed by an old woman. "Pst," he heard. The men stopped, curious. The woman stared.

"Who are you, son?" she asked. "I can't place you. Damn my old eyes." Momma was silent, he didn't know what to do. Then the woman gasped. "You young rascal, don't you recognise me?" With a wide, wrinkled smile, she slapped him on the shoulder. "It's Momma Kokker! Where have you been all these years?"

The words stunned Momma. Now the men knew him too. Forcing a smile, he hugged his aunt and promised to see her in the morning. Then he hurried away, shaking all over. He would rather die than this. It was too much to bear. He was about to board a bus when he looked up at the mighty plane tree. Through the branches he glimpsed the faint yellow glow of sunset. In his heart and in the leaves' whisper he heard two words he would never forget. *Khuda Hafiz.*

*Goodbye, you are blessed.*

Thank you for listening. As a postscript I'd like to set out the hidden law of the family that motivated the research and writing of this book. It's the study of how selective labels and group patterning can lock us into the collective narratives of *Games People Play*. It's also about the personal shift from labeling theory to horse-and-rider adaptation. Or to put it another way, the past is an ever-changing story where we dream our way out of trouble using language. In the words of George Bernard Shaw, "If you cannot get rid of the family skeleton, you may as well make it dance".

‡ ‡ ‡

Joe, Mia and Cass were in a quiz show.

"What makes the world go round?" asked Joe. He was the quiz master, dressed in joggers and a rainbow jacket. "You have three minutes to answer," he added, placing an upended egg timer on the table. The sand began to run.

"Is it money?" asked Mia. She was wearing an animal-print tunic over black leggings.

"What do *you* think?"

"Well I know climate deniers can't think of anything else. They're culty, like Midas. And remember what happened to him."

"The addict's punishment, eh?"

"I'm guessing money's not the answer."

"No, money's out. So, what makes the world go round?"

"You want the science?" asked Cass, who was wearing a white lab coat.

"Yes, if we can. But remember, we're on countdown." Joe checked the timer. The sand in the bottom chamber was piling up. It seemed to be alive.

"OK. It's about gravity," Cass replied. "The Earth's like an ice skater pulling in her arms to spin faster. That's been going on a long time."

"Ah, but is it spotting as it turns?" asked Joe.

"That's what's called anthropomorphism," said Cass.

"Gravity, you just hold me down so quietly," sang Mia.

"The question remains open," said Joe. "Any takers?" He took off his jacket to reveal his printed T-shirt. In the centre was an hourglass in a circle.

"Is it wishful thinking?" asked Mia.

"Good try. But you know what they say. *Be careful what you wish for ...*"

"Got it! Everyone knows, LOVE makes the world go round," said Mia

"That's half the answer," replied Joe. He checked the timer. In the top part, the sand had caved in. It was draining fast.

Mia pointed to the T-shirt. "You're not thinking of the ten-year warning?"

Joe shook his head. "No. In any case the latest science says it could be much sooner."

Mia clapped her hands. "I know," she said, "it's LOVE AND RAGE."

"Correct," called Joe.

As Mia jazz-handed, the last few grains of sand trickled through. She looked from Joe to Cass. "Can we begin again?" she asked.

"We don't really know," Joe replied.

"But it could be difficult," her sister added. She pointed to the timer. The bottom half was full and the top was empty. Realising the quiz was over Joe, Mia and Cass fell silent.

They were out of time.

# TWENTY-EIGHT

### <u>The Girl Who Began Again</u> June 22nd 1960

Once there was a girl who thought there should be more sunshine in her world so she decided to start again with more smiling and plenty of fresh air. But her new life didn't have enough rain to feed the trees so the next day she started a whole new story. Every day she made a new beginning. But even when the sun shone and the rain joined in to make a rainbow, the girl wasn't happy with the day because she wasn't a proper heroine, and stories have to have one of those. Otherwise a mirror and a spell are not enough.

Every time the girl started a new life she tried to be bigger in her own story. She was a princess but the king wouldn't let her climb trees. So she became captain of the ship but she could never find the island. One day she was born a singer and the whole world was her audience with candles in their hands but the trouble was the birds sang a better song. In her next life she was a clever artist but nothing she painted was as lovely as the flowers. Then she started again as a doctor but she didn't know how to fix all the fighting, just the wounds.

By now the girl was a lady, but her knight rode off to battle leaving her asleep. Then she escaped flying on a swan and went up into nowhere. When she began a day as an angel by the end of it she'd forgotten how to be good. Every new day of each new life she had to throw her story away because the ending wouldn't come and you only know it's a wonderful story when it's over.

The End.

By Elizabeth Jarvis

‡ ‡ ‡

21.2.03

If Beth Jarvis had been watching herself on camera, or observing her actions in a book, she might well have wondered what could have brought her, a woman of fifty with a job and children, to wait for an hour in a busy city restaurant facing the door on a cold February evening. To sit there alone, shivering slightly, a figure on the lookout taken, perhaps, from one of her half-written stories and positioned there quietly, one hand on some papers while observing the tablecloth.

She'd come as promised, arrived on her own and far too early, made herself do it. A woman holding still, trying not to show.

Because really, considered carefully or looked at as fiction, it was what her friends would call crazy or silly, certainly eccentric, a rom-com or sitcom, something she herself wouldn't credit if she read it in a book.

And yet she was here.

To anyone who noticed she might have seemed strange. Sitting in shadow, she was easy to read but not so easy to pin down. They might, like her, have wondered why she'd come here or what she was involved in. They'd have registered her red-lipped look and noted her top – low-cut with sequins – but sensed something underneath, a feel for difference, for questions unanswered and why she'd travelled miles to sit there solo, a woman with a wine glass eyeing the customers as they came through the door.

Then there were her papers. Neatly folded and positioned on the table, a whole wad of letters. If stopped and questioned, or approached by the manager, she could show them as evidence. They were her best chance. In any case they were all she had. The result of contact, received after work and read straight through, they'd carried her with them.

The letters and the calls. For the last two weeks, daily on paper or lying on the sofa holding the receiver: his voice and hers. And now in person, their first face-to-face.

Hearing her thoughts, Beth pulled back. She knew her own silliness, how it pushed and pressed and despite her best efforts wouldn't let her be. To be feeling kept her up. Thin-skinned or crazy, that's how she was, or could be if she was allowed.

Because for so long now, she'd not been herself. She could feel it in the room. There was a cold bare space somewhere to one side, a place without warmth. Inside experience there was a door closed, a stop and a darkness.

And she'd lived there, hoping: late night in the kitchen, in the back room, writing, and alone in the lounge, staring at the TV.

Leaning forward, she pulled a mirror from her bag. Prising it open and turning side to side, she studied what she saw. The mouth was full, chin line sharp, the cheekbones high, the hair dyed brown with waves and thinning a little. Lines around the eyes and forehead, some of them deep, had been part-brushed out. The image she saw was grey-eyed, long-nosed, all rather *meant*, but also receptive and alert.

Folding the mirror, she glanced around the restaurant. To be here at all surprised her. She wondered quickly how many others were out there waiting. Dressed up women sitting in restaurants facing the door, believers and hopers rehearsing phrases, awaiting their cue. She wondered, too, if their mindsets showed or if, like her, they'd adopted stillness and presence as a shield to hide their thoughts.

Her attention narrowed, picking up on couple-talk with faces listening – and how she might present. The room was warm, almost pressured, and illuminated by candles. From where she sat it was divided in two. The front part, a square, was shined up like a studio, with long, varnished tables, flowers in vases and multi-coloured tablecloths, while her area, running widthways at the back, was darkly lit and private. The two sections were split-level, linked by steps. At the front, the lower part, there were groups dressed up and talking, people checking watches, others fingering or studying menus, some shedding jackets, others on mobiles, some by the window glancing around, while a few sat folding napkins and examining their bills. At the back it was empty, with spaced-out tables and softly floating, ambient music.

Picking out a letter, she unfolded it and spot-checked for phrases. The handwriting was large and filled up the page. In it she could feel an outline, a suddenness of presence, imagined in the flesh. A shoulder she looked over without being seen. It was as if she'd discovered a page from a half-finished diary; not real, of course, but quick and alive, present in the writing. He was out there somewhere, approaching.

Again, she saw the house with its clothes racks, hangers, dressing gowns and books in bed. Feeling for the light switch, then thinking in the dark.

She folded the letter, returning the wad to her handbag. Better, she thought, if no one saw it. There was too much there that might invite comment – odd thoughts, hesitations – those all-raw flights, many of them excessive. And now, for better or for worse, it seemed they were happening.

A waiter came up. He was short, neatly dressed and his child-round face was attentive and smiley. In one hand was a cream-coloured notepad that he held out like a gift. "Are you all right madam? Can I get you anything?"

Beth glanced at the drink she'd been sipping. The liquid had reached bottom. Somehow, without her knowing, her past was in there, hidden. "Oh, yes. Thank you." She paused, measuring her glass. "I'd like another. A small one, please."

The waiter confirmed, returning quickly with a glass on a tray. She thanked him, perhaps over-warmly. "Someone will be here," she told him and he smiled.

"Of course. Whenever you're ready, madam."

Noticing his accent, she shifted slightly and smiled back. She felt a brief connection. "That'll be soon, I hope."

"No problem," the waiter said, withdrawing.

For a second, as he left, she saw herself sitting forward holding her glass, and she wondered whether she should follow. Go up, make payment and slip off through the door. It might be the best way. Because after all, she couldn't be that certain, and being outside would be that much easier, without obligation. She'd just begun to imagine herself on the street and him arriving at an empty table, when the door opened suddenly, bringing her back.

The couple who entered struck her as unusual. The woman was small; the man stooped forward. They were careful and deliberate, with her head up to his shoulder and his face distanced, as if he wasn't there. Both wore long brown coats and heavy boots. Beth felt for them slightly. They reminded her of what she used to be.

A waiter met them, hands to his sides, speaking quietly. After stepping back to remove their coats, they moved to a corner. Beth noticed, as they shuffled into place, how quickly the woman picked up the menu, busying herself turning the pages. Her skin was red and looked rather sore. A small tight muscle in her neck flickered and pulsed. The man sat opposite, with his hands placed loosely on the table, awaiting her decision.

They exchanged some words, without much expression. Beth thought the woman was trying to connect. The man, it seemed, wasn't too bothered. She could already see them, husband and wife, struggling to make do. Going through the motions, avoiding conflict, playing their part. Together but alone, in a house filled with silence. She was glad that was over.

Beth checked on her phone. Cupping her hand, she eyed it from the side then from above, as if was a puzzle. Her friends had warned her.

There were no calls or messages, and her inbox hadn't changed, but having it close …

For a second time the door opened, this time a man alone, tallish, in black. Standing by the entrance and smiling vaguely as if on screen, he scanned the room. As she looked, Beth breathed in. His face was soft-skinned and open, with steel-rimmed glasses over rounded cheeks. Grey-white hair framed his face, curling around his ears and straggling at the back. His forehead was large, eyes reflective, mouth held firm. She noticed how he stood facing ahead; poised, it seemed, for things to develop. There was a brightness about his face, a pressure and intensity of nerves, or awareness, as if he'd a speech to deliver.

This, of course, was him. Feeling his doubt, Beth waved.

The man advanced, smiling. "Hello. You must be Beth?" he said, reaching the table. As she nodded he stepped up and touched her shoulder, lightly, descending to her arm before pulling back.

"And you must be James," she replied, remaining standing. For a moment, she was stunned. It was as if he was sizing her for a dress, or she was sizing herself.

"The same, as in the late-night telephone calls."

She remembered his first message. *James Lavender here*, he'd said, sounding slightly playful. She heard him now, clear and upbeat as in his recording, and her breathing slowed.

"Can I join you?" he asked, glancing at her drink.

Catching his irony, something Jane Austen-ly popped into her head. "That, sir …" she began then stopped, colouring slightly, and invited him to sit.

Returning to her chair, Beth felt looked at; mainly, mirror-like, by herself, but also, gently, by the man who now sat opposite. Seen in close-up, he was fresh-faced and watchful. Although he'd lines – mainly light, barred across his forehead – his eyes were young, grey-blue and direct, but also understanding.

She wondered what he thought of her sequined top.

"I hope I'm not late," he said.

"No, not at all. I was early."

James settled. "I was worried. This place was pretty hard to find."

"Oh, you mean my directions?"

"No, nothing like that. I just didn't allow … didn't realise how far it was."

"You came up from Trafalgar Square?"

"The long way round, after asking a few people. They all thought they knew but, when it came to it, couldn't quite remember."

Beth looked thoughtful. She hoped it hadn't been too difficult. "Would you like a drink?" she asked.

"Later, thank you," he said, unzipping his jacket. "Anyway," he added quietly, "I'm here now."

"You could have rung me."

James agreed, smiling wryly: it seemed he didn't mind. Leaning back, he talked her through his search, presenting his walkaround as an adventure. When Beth asked about getting cold he held her gaze for a moment. "Warm enough now," he said, rubbing his hands together.

Beth blushed. The expression in his eyes made her breathless. She was back there by the window, watching in the dark. "Shall we order?" she asked, picking up a menu.

"Good idea," he answered, scanning *today's specials* printed on a card. "We could share something. A menu for two." His voice sounded firm; it steadied and calmed her. All they had to do was choose, simple as that.

They agreed on an all-in meal, lightly curried, with starter and main. Beth wanted poppadoms and James, when the waiter appeared, ordered water and a sweet lassi. In the break before service they both sat back. The music in the restaurant seemed closer now. Soft and insistent it filtered in, mixing with their voices. It was as if they were audience, watching themselves; the moment held them.

They spoke about work, describing their day, then Beth spotted movement.

"Is that what you wanted?" she asked as a tall, ice-white glass with a cream head of bubbles arrived at the table.

"That's it, goat's yogurt," he said, and mentioned a student trip to India. "It's good," he added. "There's a salt version, for the heat. But this is tastier." He held out his drink for her to sample.

Beth hesitated, then accepted. As she took it in her hands, she felt the touch of his fingers passing and the cold at the bottom of the glass.

She drew down a mouthful. "Good," she said, compressing her lips.

"Have more if you like," he said, as she offered to pass back.

"That's all right, it's yours."

"If you want it, it belongs to you."

"I'm fine," she countered. "Really, I am," she said when he raised one eyebrow. "Really," she repeated, offering again.

James leaned forward. His eyes had focused and his expression had deepened; he was giving full attention.

"Oh dear," she said suddenly, pointing, "but I must do something about this." The edge of the glass was smeared with lipstick. "It's not nice," she said quietly, napkin-rubbing. A cold, hard ache was threatening to take over. Somewhere, on her own, she was running water, scrubbing metal, filling up cupboards.

"That's OK," he beamed, "I like it that way."

Beth double-checked his face; he seemed sincere. She finished her rubdown and held the glass up to the light, dabbing vaguely and tut-tutting: "Well it's gone, mostly. I'm really sorry."

James shook his head. "No problem." He took the glass, turning it both ways. "No problem at all," he added then ducked his head forward to half-drain the glass.

Soon afterwards the food arrived. Brought on a trolley by the round-faced waiter, it was richly-scented and heated from below, green and yellow, bathed in sauces, with rice and veg piled in layers on oval-shaped dishes. The spread was laid, two plates were polished and a candle was lit at centre.

"Shall I serve?" asked James as the waiter withdrew.

"Please," said Beth, and told him what she wanted. Checking as he went, James served them both, mixing ingredients. "For what we're about to receive," he said then stopped.

Beth examined his expression. His eyes had stilled and his mouth had tightened. "What is it?" she asked.

"Just the words."

"The words?"

"Well, I wondered …"

"You wondered? Something about me?"

"How you might feel about that phrase. Used as a joke."

"Ah, you think I might be offended."

"Not sure," he said, appraisingly.

"Is it something I've said?"

"Not *said*. But I do remember reading …"

"You mean my letter, the one about faith?"

James hesitated; he didn't want to spoil it. "Romantic faith," he quoted, "it sounded rather fine. I couldn't help noticing." He laughed to one side, as if he'd caught himself out. "I suppose I did think you might be vaguely churchy."

"Well I'm not. Offended, I mean." She unfolded a napkin. "So perhaps we can start?"

"You mean break bread?"

"Eat what's here. Pure enjoyment, that sort of thing."

"Well, if music be …"

"Play on," she returned, picking up her fork.

They talked as they ate, filling in gaps and quoting letters. They recalled how marriage had changed them – what had happened, what went wrong and where it had left them. Their stories, told slowly, were a mixture, some dark, some tentative and some quite upbeat, developing into sideswipes and tongue-in-cheek remarks about battles in private and versions put round for the benefit of friends.

"In the end you come to expect it," he said, "so you say to yourself 'OK here we go again' and push straight through."

"Yes, it gets to a point," Beth replied, pausing between mouthfuls, "where it doesn't really matter. Whatever you say, it's always wrong."

James put down his fork. They were together on this.

"And *that's* when you get out," she added, surprising herself. She'd said it as a try-on, without thinking. Because for Beth, things had moved on. Somewhere around her there had always been a gap or disconnection, a half-and-half feeling. Of course she'd had her moments – her children, her friendships, the café she'd built up – but behind that, in private, with the man she called her husband, it had never really happened.

But talking here together was different. It was as if, while reading a novel and turning the pages, she'd found the right place. The action had started and she was being heard.

When they'd finished eating, with James forking portions, remarking on blended mixtures and food for thought, Beth brought out her letters. "What you sent me," she said simply. "All of them."

"I wrote that much?"

She fingered them carefully: "Twenty-two pages." To her, these said it all. They were what had brought her.

"Ah, but *you* wrote even more."

"I'm not sure about that."

"Definitely. I'll count them when I get home."

"You've kept them, then?"

"Of course." He laughed. "And reread them. You're a real writer."

"Well, if that's so, it's because I find it easier …"

James nodded as she returned the letters to her handbag.

"I suppose it's about words, and getting them on paper," she added.

"Words, words, words," he said lightly.

"Yes, that's what I use," she continued, meeting his eye.

"OK, so what would you do if we couldn't speak?"

She raised one eyebrow. "Sorry?"

"No words, only gestures."

"I don't quite follow."

James repeated.

"No words at all?"

He nodded.

"You mean sign language?"

James gave a thumbs-up.

"I'm not really sure."

"It's a game people play. People like us."

Beth considered, staring at her glass. "You mean you want to try?"

"Well, why not?"

"OK," she said, "let's have a go."

James placed one hand palm-up on the table. He looked down and up. Raising the other hand he air-drew a circle around the room. A mischievous expression crossed his face. His fingers closed on an imaginary microphone and he mimed a chorus from a song. Breaking off, he looked both ways then waved to the gallery, jazz-handed. By now he was fresh-faced, beaming into camera. With a smile, he ended pointing to himself, to her, then down towards the lines in his palm. When Beth made a noise, he switched his finger to his lips.

Beth sat forward. For a second she blanked then, narrowing her eyes, looked right, looked left, dropped one shoulder and raised her arm in a rounded gesture. Her face shaped surprise. One hand came back to press against her forehead, feigning thought. She held her pose before straightening and turning out her arms to a chicken-wing position. She pushed herself to the edge of her seat. Her mouth dropped open and she froze for a second, looking down. When she flapped her hands, James began laughing.

"That's not allowed," she said, straightening in her chair.

"But I didn't speak."

Beth rolled her eyes. Folding her arms, she adopted a quizzical expression.

He shrugged. "OK, point taken. But does laughing count?"

"Yes."

"You sure?"

"Absolutely."

James laughed again, this time more softly. Pushing upright, he raised one hand to his jaw. Turning his wrist and starting at a corner, he zipped up his mouth. In the pause that followed the room came closer. Suddenly he leaned forward and touched her hand. "I've just thought," he said. "We can do it another way."

Beth's eyebrows shot up.

"Listen," he raised one finger, "you know this track?" On the speakers, a warm, darkly powerful female voice had just begun. Behind it, a deep bass rhythm was beating up. He rose, putting out his hand. "Dance?" The one word, said nicely, filled up the air.

Beth flushed, about to speak. When James placed a warning finger to his lips, she paused. His offer was a lift … she'd not imagined … it

470

was all so unexpected – but also, perhaps, a proof of commitment. It meant he was with her.

He asked again.

Beth looked around quickly then rose. The one word went with her, repeated. Dance, dance, dance, it was quite enough for her.

Allowing him to lead, she passed between tables to a floor space at the back. Here they took up position. In the half-dark, moving slowly, absorbed in warmth and breath and the closeness of flesh, they began.

As they slow-danced together, Beth felt his hands closed about her waist. She was touched and held and at one with herself, it was as if she'd come alive. They shuffled in step, rocking side to side and she was full-length in the mirror, trying out her moves. The words came back from a dance show – *such a wonderful feeling* – and an idea struck her. She'd watched and cheered and given her support, but always at a distance, and not like this: suddenly she was herself.

The music ran on. They turned and stepped, moving without thought. Their bodies, pressed close, were soft and loose and smoothly connected; it seemed they were afloat. And she knew, as she circled, what touch and excitement and bright lights and being on screen really meant.

When they sat down afterwards the waiters were laughing. Several diners had noticed and were turning in their seats. Somebody waved, calling encouragement. There was a brief, admiring smattering of applause.

"They like it," said James. "Floorshow."

Beth, catching her breath, poured herself a glass of water. She offered him the same and he accepted. Her body felt good, she wanted it to go on. "It's first night," she said brightly, sipping at her water, "and we're on the bill." She laughed, raising her drink; this was unreal, and yet it was happening. Watching from behind her hand, she smiled; he was warm and alert and full of excitement. With this man before her it seemed that anything was possible.

The waiter appeared, asking if they'd finished and how they'd found the meal.

"Just right," said James.

Beth agreed and the waiter cleared up. While the men exchanged remarks, she reached into her handbag, pulling out a lipstick. She twisted, and a red finger-sized cone pushed out.

James laughed. "Ah, I see it's colour time."

"You weren't supposed to notice."

He ducked his head towards her drink: "Remember?"

She smiled.

"Red on white," he said, "your mark."

Beth took a breath. Words like *bright spot* and *bubbly* ran through her head. His attentions said it all. She was enjoying the challenge. "You'd like a sip of mine?" she asked, raising her glass.

"Maybe," he said quietly, "if …"

Pouting slightly, she caught his mood. "So you enjoyed it – your lipstick?"

"There wasn't really enough to tell. Now—"

Beth's chin rose. Suddenly she was quick and sparky and alive. "Very well, if you like, you can have more." This time when she drank she circled the rim. Where her lips touched the edge, the glass coloured up. Smiling slightly, she offered without wiping.

"That's quite a mouthful," he said.

Beth half-closed her eyes. Her lips showed full and red.

"Which I shall have to sample," he continued, working round the rim and draining the liquid.

Camera-like, she watched him. His expression was little-boy, and impish.

James put down the glass. "Am I red?" he asked, touching his lips.

"Cherry, still ripening."

He held his expression. "Very red?"

"Pretty much, I suppose."

"Beetroot?"

She shook her head.

"What then, peachy?"

She pushed forward to take a good look. "You're part carrot, part rose."

Grinning, he met her eyes then dabbed with his napkin. "Then you know me already," he said.

They stayed an hour more. To anyone watching, they were oldies at a table. A fifty-plus woman wearing a pink sequined top, beads and bangles and contoured jeans, and a man in a leather jacket with a dad-rock look.

As the evening progressed their talk became a flow, a verbal retrospective, analysing marriage with nods and shrugs and measured observations, leading to comments about how much they'd learned.

For James things hadn't worked. He'd been so busy. With kids and job and household chores and problems to sort, all of them pressing and apparently *expected*. He'd been there in the centre, arranging weekends, playing hero and doing everything, without much thanks. In fact he'd been ignored, or seen as an embarrassment. It was just like him, he said, to get himself hitched to someone who took advantage.

Beth was more resigned. For her it was sad. She spoke about the patterns, the signs there visible if only she'd taken notice, the lack of real contact. Her talk was quietly thoughtful and full of low asides. She'd tried, and fitted; she'd given what she could.

"Not that it did much good," she added, wryly. Her husband had been, she said, one of those obsessives, a born-again type who wouldn't talk or give and, whatever happened, wouldn't open up. "I should have realised," she said, "it wasn't a marriage." A picture returned of curtains drawn, a screen, a mug, a half-written story.

Putting down his drink, James frowned. "It seems so weird …" he began, passing one finger along the tablecloth edge.

Beth raised one eyebrow. "Yes?" she said quietly, watching his finger.

"You wonder why people do it." Reaching the corner, he flattened his hand. "I mean what's the point? If marriage stands for anything it's about partnership. Hold back and you get nothing."

Beth nodded.

"So, yours was pretty much *nul points*?"

Again, she nodded.

"When you'd expected more?"

473

"I wish I'd seen what was coming."

"Was it bad?"

Her eyes remained fixed on a point beyond the table.

James asked what had happened.

"I suppose I wanted something he couldn't give." she replied. "I mean of course, affection – something personal – *human* commitment. What most people call plain straightforward love." Her lips pushed out. The final word re-echoed in the dark; it was soft and fully-formed. Like her mouth, it was inviting.

He studied his plate: "What you might call the missing ingredient … without which it's all tasteless?"

Beth followed his gaze. A quick bright calm was rising inside her. "But in the right mix," she said musingly, "preferably with lots of affection."

James raised his head to look across the table.

Though in my case," she added, "I'd have settled for less. A lot less."

"Really? But would less have been any good?"

She asked him what he meant.

"With some people you have to keep the bar right up there. Otherwise ..." he waved one hand, "you know what the kids say – don't ask, don't get."

"But there has to be a willingness—"

"On both sides."

"Perhaps you think," she asked suddenly, "I was to blame?"

"How?"

"By doing what you said, not asking?"

"But you've told me, there was nil interest on his side. With some people it's as if they want to make it hard. They just can't be bothered, or need the big stick. Whatever it is they don't *give*. In the end it brings the whole thing down."

Beth's forehead creased. "But I suppose it could have been different. I didn't make a fuss. Maybe if I had …" In the dark she found herself poised, halfway between doubt and some sort of defiant confessional. The words *soul loss* and *outcast* came up in her head.

474

Suddenly James reached over and took her hand. "You were fine," he said. "Fine, fine. Just fine. Really." The touch of his flesh was a comfort; the smooth cool pressure closed around her palm. Soft and firm, it brought her to a stop.

When they left the restaurant, they were hand in hand. The waiter thanked them, bowing slightly as they passed out through the door. Beth, who was smiling, answered politely. It was as if they were on curtain call and this was their show.

Outside was cold. The air was still and raw and the street lights glared. Walking slowly, they stepped past stone-fronted buildings with columns and porticos and heavy double doors. They passed by signboards and photos with illuminated cast lists and quotes in red then turned in through a metal archway. Before them was a square where people were emerging from a glassed-in forecourt. As they skirted a statue, a light wind got up and Beth huddled close. The square became a road with an arcade opposite. Reaching the kerb, she checked both ways. The road felt cold and bare, it was all brick and metal and shined-up surfaces. Her grip shifted slightly as they crossed between traffic. The headlights glowed silver on tarmac. White lines and streaks cut through the dark.

When they reached the other side, their fingers locked and they moved in step, arriving at stairs down to the tube. There were posters visible, a curved metal handrail, a dispenser with broadsheets, and tiles in rows.

"Which way are you going?" she asked.

"To Waterloo, like you."

"You're sure? I thought it wasn't on your route."

"It is now."

"I don't want you to feel you *have* to."

"It's *want*, not have to. Which means I'm coming your way." He glanced quickly across at the stairs. "In any case it's late, so we'd better get moving, jump on a tube." His voice broke off as a group pushed past, descending.

"Well, as long as you're certain."

"I am." Narrowing his eyes, he lifted her hand as if he was presenting her to an audience.

"I don't—"

James led her, palm extended, to the stairs: "Even if I have to carry you down."

Beth turned like a dancer, offering her free hand. "Well, if I can't persuade you otherwise," she whispered.

He pushed close, kissing one ear. "Allow me," he said and drew her to him. Arm-linked and smiling, he partnered her down.

Between tube stops he put his arm around her shoulders. "Warmer now?" he asked, and she smiled, squeezing closer. Looking across the carriage, he saw her image in the window. In the glass she looked different. She was head to his shoulder, smaller than he thought. Her eyes had narrowed and her mouth was full-set and rounded. She was all depth and mood and reflection. "Our stop," he said, as the train slowed.

They stood and pushed forward to the door, joining a sizable group of passengers, mostly young, who disembarked, some of them singing. When they reached the escalator James took the lower step and Beth half-turned, allowing his embrace. His hand felt her waist: she was smooth and supple and cinched in tightly beneath her coat. All the way up, absorbed in feeling, they stood holding on. At the top, the escalator cut off and they stepped onto the flat. Beth led through the barriers, turning down a short connecting tunnel with adverts on both sides. Arm in arm they climbed a slope to arrive at a concourse with screens above and platforms ahead.

"Ten minutes to go," Beth said, checking her watch against the screen times.

He followed her gaze. "That gives us a little longer." His voice had smoothed and dropped low.

She turned and caught his eye. "Till just past the hour ..."

James leaned close and they clenched. Now she was excited, her chin rose slightly and her mouth widened. She was all brightness and intention. The cold station air didn't touch her. "Ring me tomorrow," she said.

"When?"

"Evening. Early as you like."

"Of course."

Their mouths came close; something automatic was drawing them in. Meeting slowly, their lips made contact. As his tongue pushed in, she fitted and squeezed back and the kiss took over. Between them it was dark, dark-light and somehow reflective. Their lips shifted and held, turned both ways, then softened. They were suddenly one person, joined by the mouth.

For James it was immediate, a dip into flesh. Deep throat and pressure, repeated.

For Beth it was without-thought and wordless. She was kissing, that was all. Her body was all give and touch and lightly-taken softness.

For both it was a fit.

They hung there kissing, locked together, parting only when a clock chimed the hour. "I'll have to go," she said, pulling back.

James stepped up as she drew out a ticket and moved to the barrier.

"Early as you like," she repeated. He released her hand and she turned, slotting in her ticket.

"OK. Goodbye." For a second he wondered whether he should join her, disregard everything, push through to the platform and board the train.

Her ticket popped up. She called into air as she passed through the barrier, "Goodbye."

"Goodbye."

The train began to hum and a note sounded as lights flashed, the doors half-closed then shunted open. Beth called and ran. She arrived, turning, and held up her arm. As she pulled herself in, the doors hissed shut. Almost immediately the train began to move.

His last sight was her face at the window, waving and smiling as the carriage pulled away.

# TWENTY-NINE

6.2.03

Dear Beth,

So now I know what you sound like! I was standing at the top of the stairs when you rang. I remember wondering as I went down to take it, "Is this a reply?" As my father would have said, probably as he pulled on a pair of heavy boots, "Phones are like bloody bosses, they make you jump." I'll tell you more about him later. Quite a bit later, I imagine, because this letter's going to take time. But once I get started … I'll write when I can, bit by bit over the next few days, and keep posting.

Anyway, when I picked it up, I was rerunning my message. I thought I might have put you off. But you sounded oh my goodness so warm. Chocolate, vanilla, strawberry, cherry. I think, to be honest, a bit edgy as well. I suppose anyone in your place would have felt the same.

I really enjoyed our talk. When I put down the phone there were so many words and ideas filling my head that I just had to start this letter. I'm going to write as it comes, with a smile and a large cup of tea, and now. It's like that art quote: *the chance meeting on a dissecting table of a sewing machine and an umbrella*. There's a lot to take in.

So I'm going over what we said, all that info and life material, then back to the start, to your ad, dialling that number and hearing your talk. I rang back twice, checking what you'd said before I answered. Each time it got better. One particular phrase stood out. When you said you were an open book that's when I thought, oh yes, I'll leave her a message. I suppose the honesty factor's pretty well top of my list. Being up front, speaking from the heart, owning up, that's what my ex really couldn't do. Or we both couldn't, mainly because we brought out the worst in each other. We were dug in, victim/perpetrator swapping roles, running a campaign, but trying not to show it.

478

I hope you don't mind if I write head-on like this, and things come out. It's how I am, or I'd like to be. It's a risk, I know, but I don't do well with too much politeness and things unsaid. And I try not to dodge if I'm asked anything about myself. I felt we were definitely moving in that direction by the end of the phone call, so I'd like to push it a bit further. I just reckon at this stage of life it's better to get things on the table so you know where you stand. I suppose I also secretly hope that you'll want to read more. But if not, please say.

I'm writing this, by the way, upstairs in my flat. It's warm, cheap for London and really large, which suits me. The outskirts of Mitcham are unexplored territory, out of the way and pretty messy. I like the view over the Common, which is fenced off and industrial to the south but wild around here in a dirty kind of way. It reminds me of the North. At this time of night you can only see the train lines and the lights of the station. And the pink-on-black glow of the London winter sky. The sign we live under.

Sandra and I lasted seventeen years on paper but you could say it was all over in five. We did the sticking-plaster week-on-week counselling thing without making headway. I can't help thinking of the scene near the start of *Through the Looking Glass* where Alice sets off from the door and the path bends and bends till she arrives back at the house. Though in my view Sandra blocked and I did the pushing, but then you always blame the other side, don't you? Anyway, I'm divorced now five years on, no strings attached, done that and moved on, though we still argue about the kids.

I remember we talked about yours. I could tell how important they are. It was in your voice-tone, all hush-hush and soft-centred. Rose and Naomi you said, one a daddy's girl, one a nurse.

I've got two, Hannah, 16, and George, 20. They're sparky, inner-city, lots of friends, very oral, studying and working. Not kids really, but still willing to play off their parents, bid up for presents and holidays, and shift between houses. Seems they've got the best of all possible worlds. The way it works Sandra's too soft and I'm middling, but like you and yours, I love 'em to bits, really.

I'm tired now. If you want a thumbnail sketch I suppose I'm an up front type, pretty dogged but playful, with a fair dose of reflective. I enjoy talking, mainly deep stuff, meeting people, walking and reading novels like *One Flew Over The Cuckoo's Nest*, *Chesil Beach*, *The English Patient*, also I'm into classical music and indie rock.

So, what more can I say? Well one thing, perhaps, about this letter. I'm giving you an edit, a fair second copy. It's as close as I can get to the voice in the head but tidied for style. A mask that shows through. Which might seem a bit self-defeating, like the emperor's new clothes. On the other hand, it can feel overdressed. All rather artificial, reading and writing with a dictionary to hand when we can pick up the telephone and talk.

Yes. Talk, talk, talk.

Hope you get this soon. I'll continue tomorrow, after posting. I really did enjoy our talk.

Best wishes

James

8.2.03

Dear Beth,

Next episode.

I said I'd tell you about my father. It's early morning and I'm at the desk, even though I haven't any jobs lined up today. In my mind I'm already busy. It's how I function, a useful habit that gets things done. Because, in general, who you are shows in what you do, but also the reverse. With choices and habits, we make them, or they make us. Like my father when he retired from the railways. It was as if he'd lost an arm. Make or break, I suppose, which sounds like a bad joke when I think of him in bed with throat cancer. They kept him in hospital until there was nothing they could do, then my mother took over. He died six years ago.

I want to cross that out and start again. But I've decided to leave it. I had to do something so I walked around the house, sat outside and closed my eyes, but now I'm back.

Reading what I wrote, the truth is I wasn't reconciled to my dad when he died. Coming from Chester-le-Street, he took on that Northern aggressive black humour, the chip on the shoulder depressive stuff about them and us and better off dead, a kind of inverted *schadenfreude*. That was later on, after he retired. Before that he was a clown, and a family teaser. But the signs were always there. There was an edge of hardness to his humour, he was keeping a score. And he always disputed with bosses, shopkeepers, neighbours and especially with me, taking aim at anything creative, what he called bloody namby-pamby or airy-fairy. Sour grapes, I suppose. Because he knew he'd a brain and felt passed over. He was a man who read up on facts as if he was preparing for an exam, then turned them into weapons, taking on politics, war, history, North vs South, God and the church, till there were no truths left standing. Mind, hearing him now as I write, I realise it was an act, a put-on as he'd say – his own way of kidding or ribbing or reckoning. A part he played to impress the lads, even indoors where none of them could see him. It makes me think of Billy Elliot and bits of Lawrence. That all-out spoiler, bloody-minded, bring-down-the-temple business. So where did he get it from? Probably something passed down from big Daddy-O, his dad and his; men who stood apart.

But then Eddie Lavender had other sides as well. He'd a practical-joking, throwaway larkiness, doing *Carry On* voices and plum-voiced speeches … the Right Hon Harold Macmillan and The Queen … and a long-term passion for dogs. At various times he kept a spaniel, two collies, a red setter and a mongrel. I remember their names: Lenin, Trotsky, Stalin, Engels and Marx. When he walked them, he'd break into a whistle. Quick, fluting runs that I've not heard since. I think they were tunes he made up. We walked around the hills with him whistling and delivering speeches about Kronstadt and The Winter Palace while the dogs ran wild. He was, in his own way, a latter-day revolutionary, a *sans-culotte*. And he didn't want me to become a landscape gardener.

Well, I think that's probably enough about him. There are limits. Men on men can be such a bore. I remember watching *The Deer Hunter* and thinking how much blood, sweat and tears does it take to make a film? Two guys spilling everything. Talk about self-indulgent.

And I'm wondering what you're thinking about my first letter, or will be thinking as you read this. I'd like to be with you as you open it, to watch your expression, like a fly on the wall. Even better to climb inside, as in that film *The Fantastic Voyage*, and hear how you react, what you like and what you don't. Of course, it's speculation, but I still find myself imagining meetings and having those conversations with people in the head. Like those niggly, blow-by-blow, finger-pointing dialogues when you make up different versions after a row.

I remember in childhood playing back voices. I was the boy on the landing hearing little scraps, words and laughter caught through door-ways, imaginary dialogues running in my head. It took me to a world of thought, somewhere private, my own special place. A mirror-crazy land where I'd watch from the ceiling, slip out unnoticed through air vents and keyholes, picture myself sky-high, turning cartwheels or dancing on the roof. Pretty silly, eh? But then I was a soft boy and very much bottled.

Well, I think that's all for now. While I've been writing the sun has come up, picking out the frost on roads and cars. The sky's clear, bright and cold. Looking around, everything's hard-edged and made of polished steel. The pylons in the distance, the corrugated fences, the flat tin roofs on workshops and garages, even the bushes look like metal ... all cold hard sticks and stripped-back branches.

But inside it's warm.

Best wishes

James


10.2.03

Dear Beth,

Oh yes. A couple of days, a long letter from you and a chat on the phone.

Opening that letter was one of those moments. I could see it was fat and knew from the postmark it was you, but I was still apprehen-sive. There's always a doubt, an unanswered question when a letter arrives. It's that time taken opening, when you don't know what's coming. So much seems to ride on it. You imagine different things, mostly painful, ranging from cool and ultra-careful to downright rejection. But that all disappeared as I read your letter.

You wrote about your life so beautifully, I could see every detail. Page after page, I wanted to keep reading, and when I reached the end I went straight back and read it again. I hadn't expected that you'd say so much, or describe your family in such detail. I had a strong sense of light and line, with you in the middle, what you believe in, your friendships, interests, things you enjoy and what you might be looking for. I loved all the scenes … the country walks, lighting fires, drawing birds, your dad painting eggs … but the best bit was at the end, because it was what I'd hoped for but didn't want to say. Men, as you know, are supposed to make the running but not rush in, while women pull the strings. Though in my book, it's a bit of both. So yes, as you say, we should meet up. And I'm very happy, excited really, to eat out somewhere, so we'll sort out the details on the phone ASAP (but not, of course, rushing it …).

You ask about childhood. I've told you about my dad. My mum was what folk, aka people in the North, call a different kettle of fish. In any case, she was a southerner, met at the end of the war. Theirs was a marriage of opposites, Eddie uppity, Doris calm. Dark and light, a balance of forces. Even now she's inclined to fit in, to see the other side and adapt to being pushed, but behind that's an independent woman who knows what she wants. To me, in her own quiet way, she's always been there. I remember watching her sewing, her slippered feet pushing the treadle, her floral dresses and fresh-faced smile. A lady and a housewife.

Our small side-return with its plant pots and boxes was where she grew her herbs. She taught me the names, pinched out stems and made me close my eyes. "Can you tell which is which?" she asked, passing different leaves beneath my nose. Then she'd make herself busy planting, using egg boxes. When the seedlings appeared she'd separate the shoots and root them in bowls. Heart-shaped lettuces and sprigs of cress to put in our sarnies.

I think she could have easily been veggie, but not in our household, not with my dad. He had an idea that meat was brain food and that

483

grain made you fat. Given his style I imagine he insisted, but my mum either provided or took no notice. She remained herself. What mattered to her was keeping people fed and clothed and happy and healthy, so she made do and put off and saved what she could, and when we moved she chose the house, what we took with us and how we handled money.

That move made a difference. Hastings never suited him. For her it was home, with family close by. For my brother Richard and me it was my playground, and his teenage hangout. Full of wind and sun and seagulls, it offered its cliff drops, its walled-in steps down to the sea, its lights and rides and pier-cum-promenade with views of the bay and France. Mystery and adventure.

I always feel there's something special about the sea. Nostalgia if you like, but I think it works for our family. I remember I got my first sea legs visiting my gran. She was called Mary and where she lived the sea was everywhere. It was big and grey like an ice sheet, and took away your breath. That was the North East coast. I can still picture the huge bay, the miles of sands and the beach games with my brother and my cousin Matt. Not much else, except my gran in a deck chair telling us swimming would toughen us up. She said it nicely but straight. And she was right. It was freezing. After that, a dip at Hastings felt like a warm bath.

Looking back, Hastings was South; it had a continental feel with flags on painted houses and exotic plants. Even though Dad called it his exile, and told us so, often, for me it was like being on holiday with my brother. We played at being child detectives, listening round corners and tracking down suspects. Away from the adults, we knew all the secrets. We were young and crazy and acted out scenes from films with me as cop, him on the run. Nowadays he's an inner-city type, a thinker and a teacher, and a bit of a rebel like Dad. If I'm honest, we're hardly in touch, which is my fault as much as his. But I still remember beach combing for evidence and following footprints in the sand.

When Eddie moved back to Chester-le-Street, we lodged for a while in St Leonards with Mum's parents, Henry and Isobel. And when Doris and Richard returned North I stayed on. After that, through youth, I paid regular visits to my grandparents over Easter and summer. I remember them as old-fashioned boarding house owners who provided quizzes and puzzles and soft toys and full English breakfasts, and were sweet on me. Whenever I'm by the sea I think of them.

Wish you were here.

James

13.2.03

Dear Beth,

I'm sitting at home playing Nirvana's *Nevermind*. It's probably not your kind of music, but when I listen, eyes closed, it perks me up. I remember a stage when I'd drive to work singing along to John Lee Hooker, Buddy Guy, Howling Wolf, foot down, volume up. Nirvana's like them: strong, and power-packed. "The bigger the problem the bigger the pill," as George Clinton said. If you ask me why I do it, I'd say it keeps me young. It's the kind of music that exposes all. But please don't worry, I know I'm not seventeen! Or if I am, that's a choice, something I accept in order to use it. To taste but not swallow. It lets out the child so I can be an adult.

I got into Nirvana in my first big gardening phase. That was when we moved. I'd rise at six to go out digging and planting, with music in my ears. Front and back, with headphones, to the sound of crazy guitars. I still have those tracks on tape: *Rock the Casbah*, *Rebel Rebel*, *Voodoo Chile*, hard-driven, swinging-from-the-gate stuff. And I know from travelling that The Stones can keep you going – energy, energy. Sandra always said I couldn't sit still. It was one of her not-now-dear remarks. Anything I did made her feel threatened.

Now the music's stopped and the flat's gone quiet. And I'm happy with that, too. I can hear the rumble of a train, traffic passing and birdsong in the hedge. Someone next door is talking on the phone while high up above, a plane drones over. Yes, in the quiet times I'm comfortable. Where the action pauses, the self can be heard. And after that music it's one-sound-at-a-time, like an icicle drip, or a stone into water.

So, I sit listening out. I'm waiting for a call. I've a project to start on a walled garden, working for what my dad would call "the other side". I'm designing for a rich CEO. As it happens, he's a rock fan, too. He has a roomful of electric guitars. Gibsons, Fenders, Les Pauls, they're his trophies hanging on a wall.

When I look at my vinyl collection, I remember Hannah as a baby. She'd crawl towards the bookshelf, chuckling, and drag them out. Before I could stop her, she'd scattered LPs across the floor. When I called out, "No, Hannah!" she ignored me. If I tried putting up a fireguard and blocking with chairs, she climbed around the side. When I upended a table and cross-tied the legs with string, she simply burrowed under. I attempted distraction with toys and games, but she set off again. And every time I hauled her off she crawled back, chuckling determinedly.

Hannah was fearless. You couldn't take your eyes off her. Before you knew it, she'd be up on a chair digging into cupboards and smearing cream all over. The bathroom was her play zone where she'd squeeze out tubes and chew down brushes. Out in the garden she'd pull up plants and hide behind bushes. I remember finding once, out shopping, that she'd escaped from her pushchair. The shop was small, it was a hot day and the doors were open. When I realised that she'd turned the aisle and was already halfway through the exit, I ran calling out. I could see her outside, crossing the pavement, heading for the road. Fearful images ran through my head. A car came close, and I shouted. She hesitated slightly and I just had time to scoop her up.

Later, in the middle of the night, she'd cry for hours. I'd pick her up and stroke her head till she nodded off, nestling in my arms. But when I put her back, she'd stir. As her head touched the pillow, she'd take a breath then break out crying. Very soon she'd be yelling and I'd have to start again. I can still see myself sitting there, stroking, lowering, then drawing her back up. In the end I'd creep out like a thief, willing her to sleep. Afterwards, lying awake, I'd picture the animal shapes and cartoon faces printed on her wall.

There were other struggles, too. I remember how Hannah would climb out of her cot and push into our bedroom, wanting to join us.

For Sandra that was fine. She liked the warmth and could sleep through anything, but I'd had enough of nocturnal visits with George. He'd appear, crawl in between us and kick me awake. Weeks of that and I was tired out. So when Hannah came in I'd a mattress on the carpet, ready to receive her. And when I intercepted, to my surprise, she settled without complaint. I think it might have been how I moved, maybe how I spoke, or the near-total darkness. Whatever it was, she slept through peacefully, and so did I.

Looking back to that period, I can still feel the urgency and the exhaustion. Having kids takes over completely. It's about non-stop juggling and stamina. Before having children I'd so much time on my hands. But, as you know, once you're a parent you have to make choices. It's a question of what you want to hold on to. Above all, of course, you hold on tight to your children. After that, listening late at night in a small dark corner with the volume turned down, I held on to my music.

And the kids are all right.

James

16.2.03

Dear Beth,

Your letter this morning was a shock. I thought our meeting was definitely on. Now it's off, or might be. I'm confused and, I have to say, feeling sore. I've read what you wrote, recognise it's difficult, but I thought we'd agreed, and in any case …

But then again, I suppose if that's how you want it. Or if it's *mañana* … and I see you're not giving a date … well, maybe that's best. Or maybe not, who knows?

I've made a cup of tea, it helps! I've so many thoughts going around, mainly attempts to make you change your mind. Rereading your words I see it's not definite, the door's not shut yet. So, OK, OK, reasons for/reasons against, one side/the other, I'll draw up a chart.

Best wishes
James

| For | Against |
|---|---|
| Having got this far, everything's set up. | It might be a disappointment but then it might not. |
| Adventure, what's around the corner. It's worth a try. | Yes, there's risk and you're right about families, |
| I'm a decent guy. It doesn't hurt, could be fun. | But we know so much already and we're not blind. |
| OK it's a challenge but there's no obligation. | If we put off it may never happen. As adults we choose. |
| You really shouldn't treat me this way. | |
| You owe it to me and yourself. | |

17.2.03

Dear Beth,

I see now. I'm glad we talked. Of course, I do understand, a phrase you used often, and your apologies. Yes, glad. Genuinely so, for now it's clearer and I think it's like standing on the beach … the long lines ahead, the view, blue-white to grey.

The sea's so uncluttered, it reminds me of youth. It bears down in a rush, or slowly in a clean-sweep to the horizon, where ships go by.

I'll be there on Friday.

Best wishes

James

# THIRTY

Beth loved her dad.

From the beginning John Jarvis was there, a bookish man in tie and glasses standing by the window. Tall and slight, with prominent ears and a toothy smile, he listened and explained, so she understood. But also, he picked up on why, why not, and what really mattered. And for Beth he was always there, an all-weather man taking in the garden, observing plant growth, with a life-interest in birds. All sorts of birds, mainly blackbirds but also dunnocks, starlings, robins, finches.

"Watch carefully," he said, speaking quietly, as they nodded and danced, hanging on the feeder. "Birds are fierce," he told her, pointing.

Pecking into brown, the birds drilled the feed.

"It's a different world," he said, touching Beth's shoulder.

Wingtip to wingtip, the birds wheeled and spun.

"They all have their stories," he added, playing with her hair. And she looked across the lawn, taking in everything. His words were what she needed.

Another day she joined him just outside the door. They were sitting on a groundsheet, spread across the wall. Her dad had a sketch book open in his hands. It was brown and cream and filled with birds, all hand-drawn and copied from black-and-white photos.

"Rara avis," he said, finger-tapping a picture.

Beth smiled. She liked his words; they gave her ideas. Strange as they were, for her they had meaning. She waved into air: "Are there r-r-ravis here?"

"I think not. Or if so, like angels they're invisible."

"Come on cheep-cheeps."

"And no birds sing," he said, looking up.

Beth followed his gaze, saying nothing.

"Ah well," he added more brightly, "just have to wait."

The sky was grey, silver at the edges and softened by mist, the trees were still, the air felt damp and a few green-yellow weeds sprouted around the borders. The garden was empty. Exchanging glances, they scanned the lawn and peered at the telegraph wires then tried imitating calls. But the birds, it seemed, were fast asleep or in hiding.

John marked the page, closing the book. If you were patient, he whispered, they all came out. Hidden in leaves or gathered around the feeder, they were biding their time.

Close to his shoulder, Beth looked ahead. He was her dad; he made things happen.

"They're my *flights of fancy*," he told her, quietly – a phrase he repeated, on wet days watching by the window, and on half-and-half days, sitting together just outside the door.

Afterwards, remembering his face, Beth realised that he'd something more, a depth of sadness, a down-mouth in his smiles. Behind it all, he wasn't of this world. He observed, he spotted, he imagined and, like St Francis, talked to the birds. He knew all their names, told her how they lived, made up anecdotes about soul-birds on fire and journeys from the north, and invented conversations that he tried out at bedtime, adding to his stories from one night to the next.

Often long and sometimes unfinished, his tales developed into Aesop-type fables with worldly-wise animals offering life-thoughts and commentaries, and humans who took no notice. The stories were fun, but gently barbed. Using nicknames and jokes and unlikely settings that half-mirrored life, they filled up the evening with improvised plot twists and verbal adventures.

And it was his stories, invented on the spot and delivered in private, together with his characters – both animal and human – that Beth kept with her, hearing him often as she played out her life. He was always there.

From the start she was Beth. Christened Elizabeth Ella Jarvis, she was the first of two, born near Bury St Edmunds to nonconformist parents.

She was B, the beautiful daughter of Louise and John, a well-respected couple who were seen by those who knew them as "the double act" and "the perfect pair". Paired by habit – likeminded, vegetarian, anti-materialist and involved in causes – but also by choice as lifetime partners, their closeness kept them different. Not just different but pacifist, Methodist and, in their own way, independent thinkers: John researching local history that he turned into pamphlets while Louise collected Victorian sayings that she stitched into cloth.

And Beautiful Beth, who had brains as well, was their joy. They called her Elizabeth after Louise's mother, a wide-eyed woman whose sepia-tinted photo stood on the cabinet beside Beth's bed. She, too, was different. Big-jawed, high-voiced, impassioned, she'd written several stories – *kiddies' stuff* she called them – and shared them in stop-go episodes where she closed her eyes waiting for something more to come, then flicked on several pages to end with a frown. A woman of feeling; Beth's jolly gran whose OTT gestures resembled the young-girl heroines who appeared in frocks, dancing or declaiming on the covers of her books.

But for Beth, when older, rereading those books brought back something hidden. Because behind those pages was a woman whose husband, sitting in the background playing cards, had never really taken notice. Or if he did, wasn't that bothered.

"Blooming books," Jim called out, yawning.

And Beth took against. She didn't like his voice, his tics and narrow-eyed quips, his self-regarding grin. In her thoughts and in hindsight this man wasn't good.

"Give us a pint," he declared, scanning his cards. "More use than *making up*." – a phrase she'd been surprised by, hinting at differences Beth didn't understand.

At other times he seemed puzzled. What, he asked, was the point? Chapters, sequels, words on paper, he'd had that at school, kept quiet at the back, got lost off.

Pushing out her jaw, her gran thought otherwise. Books, she said, were a pleasure, they fed the mind. For children they were everything.

Beth agreed. Her gran's words, heard and memorised and repeated quietly below her breath, then written up in round-script in felt-tip pen and displayed, by way of reinforcement, behind her bedroom door, were what she called her sayings.

They were:
1. YOU ARE WHAT YOU READ.
2. STORY BEATS REAL.
3. MADE-UP IS SO.
4. WITHOUT STORIES WE'RE BORING.
5. A BOOK IS AN ADVENTURE.

When asked where they came from, she coloured slightly. When pressed by her dad, she smiled. "It's what *we* think," she said, inviting him to view them. "All of us," she went on, standing at the bed end. The pronoun included herself and John, her mother, her brother, even old Jim, but most of all the image of her now-deceased grandmother.

"She wrote because of you," her dad said another time, pointing to the photo.

Beth fell silent as she looked. The big-eyed woman with swept back hair had a thoughtful expression. Framed by a window, she was gazing out on an overgrown garden.

"It was her gift," added John.

Touching the picture, Beth smiled. Her gran belonged, it seemed, to one of Beth's own stories: tales of daring and one-time adventures that she'd written in her sketchbooks then back-flipped and spread to begin a new story.

And as Beth grew older, she voiced her tales, setting them outdoors. Under her direction, with herself as protagonist and featuring her brother, she imagined situations and staged them in the garden.

"Toby," she called, "this bit's for you." And if he didn't want it or walked off to a corner, she simply delivered solo then started something else.

Because outdoors she could do anything. As Beth she was half-lady, half-outlaw, switching between stories and mixing genre. Her parents didn't know it, but she'd air-drawn horses and spacesuits and teacups and binoculars that she conjured up and named, directing their use as prompts in her story.

The main game was *Shipwreck*, with Captain Beth, standing on the rockery, sighting dolphins and navigating channels as she directed forward. "Land ahoy!" she called and Toby echoed, leaning into the wind. As the waves became taller, they swayed side to side and mimed their parts. When the water took over they ran downhill, taking to the lifeboats.

"Abandon ship!" she shouted. Reaching her boat, Beth began air-rowing, advancing at a crouch. "We're washed up!" she called when she arrived at the lawn.

Toby joined her saying nothing. Without even noticing he'd walked untouched across a wide stretch of path. In the story this was water.

"Toby!" she cried, pointing. "You drowned."

The boy flushed.

"You can't do that."

"Can."

"Well, you shouldn't."

The boy stepped back, planting both feet on the path.

"You're spoiling."

"No."

"I'm the captain and I say so."

Eyes down, Toby returned to the lawn.

Beth sighed. "Now we'll explore inland," she said, leading down the lawn to a wild spot at the back. Toby followed silently. Here they took shelter beneath some overhanging branches. Screened by leaves they peered across grass. Blackbirds and finches were hopping around the edges. "It's an island," she called, "with treasure and wild animals." The patch beyond was damp and leafy and spread with growth. There were fruit trees and climbers, weeds under bushes and mildewed roses.

Toby blinked. "And that's HQ," he announced, pointing upwards. In the tree above, a series of ladders with halfway landings led to a wood-and-canvas platform.

Beth shook her head. "It's the Wendy House, where the castaways live."

The boy made himself busy. He was jerking at a branch.

"So now," she added, approaching the ladder, "we're the lost boys. Which means, yes, we can fly ..." Beth back-swung and began to climb. With a springy, bunched-up movement, Toby followed.

They clambered up to a flat run of boards divided by a wooden partition. There were support struts both sides, a door between, and a grey, stretchy canvas roof. It looked like a cross between a hut and a tent. Ducking forward they passed through the door. Inside was messy. In the centre was a bamboo table covered with flaking chalks, two battered slates and a blue plastic tea set. Beads on strings hung down from the sides. Two orange box seats were stacked underneath.

Beth pulled out a crate then picked up a pole from the floor. Mounting the crate, she held one end of the pole to her eye, turning a circle. "Nothing on the horizon," she said. "Or on the island," she added, swinging round.

At the table, Toby was spot-testing chalks, breaking them in half and scrubbing the ends, before drawing.

Beth continued scanning then dropped her head.

Toby had completed a scrawly, pear-shaped outline with shaded-in areas. "It's a map," he mumbled when questioned from above.

"That's where we are?"

Toby carried on drawing.

"Of course, it's a story," she said slowly. "And this is how it goes …"

Speaking quietly, she named her characters as Beth and Toby and described a shipwreck with the girl rowing clear and the boy treading water. The Wendy House followed, with treasure and wild animals. Next was their landing, the move inland, an island tree house, leading to a bamboo table with chalks and crates. Here her expression softened as she spoke about the place, the castaways together, mentioning the boy, the maps, and the girl as captain, who made it all happen …

"And that's their story," she ended with a lilt. "And as long as they keep telling it, they'll never leave the island."

$$\sharp \ \sharp \ \sharp$$

The morning after her meeting with James, Beth had what she called her Desert Island Dream. It was just before she woke. In the dream she and James were radio guests. Speaking into an old-fashioned mike, they described their tastes and answered questions about what they valued most. Although it was a dream, Beth could feel James's hand touching hers gently.

When she was young, she'd had much the same dream and shared it with her dad. He'd read her *Treasure Island*. Later they'd played at *Survival*, inventing crazy uses for objects that they imagined being left over from a shipwreck. While Beth had drawn rope-and-plastic wings, John had made up a game using keys and coins. When Toby joined them, a coconut-football had been added.

In the dream the radio presenter, who wore glasses like her dad, asked them a question. "If you could choose," he said, "what two objects would you take with you on a desert island?"

Beth smiled. "One each?"

"That's right."

"Easy," she said, "my lipstick."

"And your … choice?" asked the presenter. Although she couldn't be certain, Beth thought she heard the word "husband's" slipped into the middle of his question.

"The letters," James said, drawing out some stacked papers. He selected one that he folded and tightened at the corners, till it sat in his hand like a bird. There were four exposed surfaces, divided by two crossing slits. Inserting thumb and finger below, he moved it back and forth. It gaped then closed. Beth thought it must be hungry.

"Give me a letter," he said.

"J," she replied.

"Now two letters."

"A-M."

"Two more."

"E-S."

Each time she spelled out a letter James finger-shuffled his whirly-bird. It stretched and collapsed, then pulled itself tall, bowing to an imaginary audience. It was his puppet.

"Now choose a flap," he said, holding it wide open.

Beth looked down into the folds. The paper inside was covered with writing.

"Any flap?"

"Yes. This is your time."

There were four to choose from so she ip dipped, selecting one that she peeled back. The paper felt alive. It reminded her of opening a window on the advent calendar.

Inside were four words, printed in red, with green and purple highlights. Leaning forward she read them to herself. The words said: YOU WILL FIND LOVE.

‡ ‡ ‡

As a schoolgirl, Beth wrote stories for her friends. Tales of children who sneaked out of houses and ran through woods, children who camped out or time-switched nightly into Victorian schoolrooms, oddball children with super-sight and wings or youthful savants in touch with other worlds, and simple everyday children in stories where small events mattered, loyalties were strong and just-so things were said. "It's all true," she said, if asked to explain. "Really-real."

And to her it was. Writing often, she told of incidents in the classroom – objects disappearing, ink marks and scribbles and whispered messages – and playground spaces where strange things happened.

Head down, she made up what she could, thinking of her gran.

And people liked her stories. Written at speed and added to daily, their twists and turns and unexpected shifts impressed her friends. *Their* friends liked them too. Word got around and Beth wrote more. Mysteries, mainly, with thick fog and ice and faces at windows, followed by footsteps leading nowhere and strange disappearances. And everything she wrote was creepy or puzzling or absurd or full of crazy action.

"Surprise, surprise," she hissed, as she produced her latest.

"Horrible, isn't it," she teased, huddled with her friends.

"You have to b-e-l-i-e-v-e," she added, pointing to a just-written story, "whatever it says."

Later still, in the lower fourth, she told her friends she'd stopped. The stories, she said, weren't there. She read, of course, and wrote in class, producing as required – mainly exercises and tests on meaning – and kept up her marks with an emphasis on corrections and preparing for exams.

But in secret, in her bedroom, most evenings, closing her eyes and picturing her friends, Beth was a writer. It recalled, in shadow form, her dad's stories.

And she wrote from what she knew: school and home scenes set in small towns with girls who went together. Hers were clever girls who read, said things and looked around seriously, while talking *people*.

First off was Charlene. Wide-eyed Charlie with her short hair and freckles, the all-go girl with her tales of inventions and records broken, using coin piles and card towers that she balanced on tables.

"It's magic," she claimed proudly, siphoning coloured water to run between glasses.

Sometimes she sent messages written in reverse or coded by reference to well-known books. She could add up in a blink, drew well, sight-read on piano and had reached grade four.

In the story she was C, the jump-in expert, whose feet-first reactions made everyone laugh. Her clown-girl mishaps occurring everywhere, together with her tendency to appeal to the gallery, made for entertainment. "Can't help it!" was her catch phrase, or: "Watch O … Watch O … Watch Out!" which came out straight, in a single breath. As madcap joker she overshot the mark, went into overdrive and got by in a tangle. But also, by degrees, she changed and developed, taking on the role of tongue-in-cheek commentator and clever-clever watcher who saw, took stock and signalled by example.

But in life she was different. The real girl Charlie gave up her interests to focus on what she called her *types*. Past sixteen, she said, you could straightaway tell. Either they'd got there or were promising. Whichever way, boys were it.

At other times she had it taped; as a girl of the world, she could hold her own. "I like them simple," she said confidingly – meaning, she said, office juniors and bookshop assistants who knew what a girl needed, how far and how much, and what was expected. She wanted boys who went deep.

Beth sat listening with her head to one side. Although they'd placed themselves beneath trees at the end of the garden, her friend's talk, half-boastful, half-breathless, wasn't really safe. What if Charlie's words got back to her parents? If someone told, or they overheard in passing? And what if something happened, if her friend cut off or fell ill, or even, as in the newspapers, her nice girl Charlie ran away to get married and ended as a hostage, tied up in a basement by one these boys?

Charlie smiled. "I'm a choosy girl," she said, narrowing her eyes. Reaching to one side, she teased out a grass stem and bent it round her finger.

Beth stared into the distance.

"See, it fits," her friend said, binding her flesh.

Beth's expression had flattened to a politely-held smile. The thoughts she'd had now seemed rather foolish.

Her friend repeated the word choosy.

"That's how girls should be," declared Beth.

Charlie held up her finger. "Look. It's my ring," she said, knotting the stem.

"That's nice."

"See, I'm engaged."

"You're engaged?"

"Oh, yes."

"Who's the lucky boy?"

"You."

"Me?"

"Ha, ha, not really."

"So who is it?"

"Oh, I don't know. Anyone you like."

"Anyone?"

Charlie considered, tugging at her ring. "Any boy as long as he's tall, owns a car and isn't called Fred."

"And that's all?"

"Oh, he has to be a fab kisser. And a virgin."

Beth remained still. The last word wasn't nice; it was one of those expressions found in dictionaries that she'd seen girls looking up. A conversation stopper, certainly with parents. A word like a timer, set to go off.

That evening, addressing the photo of her gran, Beth told her story. What she said was a summary, changed in certain parts; it gave the true feel, the air-light surface, and the shadow underneath. Because life had its dangers. Something unseen was approaching, as if she'd been out walking, alone in darkness, and heard someone following. And Charlene, she realised, wasn't there to help her.

So, Beth preferred C. Her on-the-page protagonist, though clumsy and reckless, hadn't that self-willed edge or it's-me presence. C in the story was brightly engaging and framed within limits. Seen as a character, her words and appearance were that much more attractive than her boy-obsessed friend. For Beth, as a teenager and secret bedroom writer, the story was the person.

There were other friends, too. Girls of spirit with individual view-points, get-up-and-go types with spark and life, whose stories filled her notebooks. Girls like Meg in her hand-designed frocks and multi-coloured hair bands who took on parts no one else wanted, stepping in to sing if someone dropped out at the end-of-term service.

Meg Daly was sweet. Round-faced and fringed, she was every-one's friend, a listener and supporter who advised on hairstyles, helped out with homework, gave little presents and asked about feelings. She put herself last. Quick at Art, she would dish out stock, sketch in outlines for girls who couldn't get started, mix paint with water in just the right proportions, then complete her own work with a few rapid brushstrokes. "That's lovely," she'd say, as she pinned up a picture by a classmate. "It's the sort of thing you do really well." Then she'd put her own work away in a drawer in a cupboard at the back of the storeroom where nobody would see it.

In the story Meg was wild: a Pre-Raphaelite siren living by the sea in a tide-swept cave. Between songs she'd improvise melodies, run-ning her fingers through her all-gold hair. As Morgan Le Fay she came in with the mists and appeared on beaches where she lay in the sun. When she swam out to a rock her body turned silver. She was finned and scaled and gleamed all over.

Beth called her Selkie – a name she'd learned from her dad – imagining her friend switching persona from wild-girl explorer to fresh-faced helper. As Selkie, or Silky, she was hard to read.

And once, in a contest, Meg had been both. With Beth there watching, she'd swum freestyle for the school, breaking a record and passing all her rivals.

"Hey hey, here comes the dolphin!" cried Beth, as her friend climbed out to the poolside.

"You think that was fast?" Meg said, turning her head. Her cheeks were flushed and her hair was running water.

"You beat them all."

A cheer went up as Meg waved to the crowd.

Beth laughed. "I think you enjoyed that."

Meg smiled sweetly. As she reached for a towel her eye caught another swimmer flopped across a block. The girl, who was thin and shivery, was staring into water. She looked worn out. "Are you all right?" Meg asked quickly, crouching down. When the girl said she felt ill, Meg offered her towel. "Here, take this," she said, wrapping it around the girl's shoulders. Patting the towel, she examined the girl carefully. She didn't look good. "And listen," Meg added, "I'm going to give you a present."

The girl's eyes widened. "For me?" she asked.

"For you," replied Meg.

"A present?"

"Something that will help – yes."

"Oh, thank you," the girl said, as Meg helped her up.

An announcement boomed out, calling for the winners.

"Just wait," said Meg, "I'll be back."

She returned a few minutes later, holding her medal. It was gold and polished, with a red silk cord threaded through a hole at the top. "Here," she said, throwing the cord over the girl's head, "I want you to have it."

The girl blushed. "But I can't, it's yours."

"It's yours now," said Meg, gazing across the water, "I'm not racing anymore."

"You don't want it?"

"No."

The girl considered, fingering the silk. "You really don't?"

"Not any more."

"And you won't be swimming?"

"Oh, I'll swim all right with friends. But only for fun."

When Beth arrived, Meg was sitting with the girl, dangling her feet in the pool. They were both wrapped in towels. Meg's face, reflected in water, was calmly smooth. With her gentle, unthinking smile, she reminded Beth of Ellie in *The Water Babies*. And the girl beside her with a medal, whose watery image seemed joined onto Meg's, was a Selkie.

Two other girls were close to Beth. One was Rachael, a tall thin girl nicknamed Brainbox who bike-rode to school wearing long grey socks and a Macintosh. Everyone knew Rachael. She was the girl who could calculate without paper and measure by eye, recite the periodic table, and name all 190 countries, with their capitals. To her what seemed obvious and straightforwardly interesting – numbers, science and all things factual – was simply how it was. She *knew*, didn't see the gap, and took herself, without any real evidence, to be some sort of norm.

Rachael entered Beth's stories as a teacher-lover. She sat at the front training her 20/20 vision on the new maths master. She viewed him like a specimen, logging all his habits. She verified his timings and routes down the corridor. Writing in her notebook, she recorded what he said, repeating his words and checking all the facts, before scanning him for shape, bit-parts and physical make-up. His dimensions were marked off, plotted on axes and turned into data. His looks were formula; gestures equations; his self made up the universal theory.

In the end, as herself and as a character, like all of Beth's friends, Rachael was different.

Then there was Amy who appeared in both worlds simply as herself. She was what the others called plain. Young and slight with soft grey eyes and a down-to-earth smile, she talked about lessons, ticking off her homework and preparing for exams. As *Eveready Amy* she kept her own notes, recording her marks and filling up daily schedules. She was the girl who organised quiz groups and debates in the library, and issued handmade cards, using expressions such as *bona fide* and *fully paid up*. She put things in place, was reasonable, thoughtfully pragmatic and functioned well. *Ordinary Amy*, in story as in life.

And for all Beth's friends, to figure in her stories made them more alive. Inside her books they could quick-change, test for possibilities, and switch between acts. They could be anyone: lead, support, good girl, bad girl … for them, like her, a book was an adventure.

*† † †*

"What's your favourite colour?" asked James.

Beth was back in the Desert Island Dream. After three hours' sleep and a full day working in the café, she'd left early, intending to write. Her excitement had carried her until she reached the sofa but then she'd nodded off. In her dream she was warm. The studio was comfortable and softly-cushioned. Images rose up of flesh in water. She could have been floating in a fish bowl.

The show was live. Its theme was relationships, and how pleasure and survival were linked. They'd talked about shared interests and now, with James as the presenter, they were discussing likes.

"What's yours?" she said quietly, inviting his gaze.

"Any colour?"

"Your fav."

"Pink."

"Pink?"

"The colour of your top."

"Any others?"

"Red."

"Like my lipstick?"

"Yes, mine as well."

"On your glass?"

*"On my collar …"*

Beth's face was glowing. "Mine's grey-white-blue."

"Eyes?"

"Sea, skies, as well."

"Anything else?"

"Hopkins."

"Hopkins?"

"Like *Pied Beauty*."

"Mixtures, combinations."

"Clashes as well."

"But what about the blues?"

Beth's gaze softened; she was giving him the look. "Music, you mean?"

"Oh *yes … yes … yes.*"

"They're sad."

"Very."

"You often feel sad?"

"Sometimes, when I'm alone."

"So what do you do?"

"Play music, or sing."

"You sing?"

"Singalong, bathroom stuff."

"I think I'd like that."

"*O Sole Mio*, that sort of thing?"

"If that's what you sing."

"Or *Straight from your heart*, perhaps?"

"Ah, I love those lyrics."

"*Keep us so near while apart …*"

"Yes … *I'm not alone in the night …*"

"Is that your favourite song?"

Beth coloured as she shook her head. "Blue Moon."

James said a few words, wrapping up the programme. He switched off the microphone and let out a breath.

Beth was watching him carefully. "Who do you sing to?"

"The girl of my dreams."

♯ ♯ ♯

When she was fourteen Beth became Saffron. "Call me Saf," she said to Meg, examining an art book spread across her bedroom floor, "or Saffy. Saffron if you have to."

Her friend turned a page. "Saf's best," she said, pausing at a print of a raven-haired woman with one hand wrapped around a pomegranate.

"You like it?"

Both girls stared at the picture. The woman was red-lipped, blue-eyed, wearing a loose, grey-green robe. Her skin was smooth and pale as water.

"Why Saffron?"

"It's a girl in a book."

"Like her?"

Beth shook her head. "One of my gran's books. She wrote it, about Saffron."

"Your gran wrote books?"

Beth confirmed. "For children," she added, "with girls dancing and poetry."

"Were they fun?"

"Jolly – or meant to be." Beth bent forward peering at the picture. "But not jolly." The long-necked woman in the art book was gazing at smoke rising from a burner. Her double-jointed hands were artist-thin and wasted. Behind her the light from a window spread across some ivy on a wall. "Supposed to be. But sad … very sad to me."

"Don't say that."

Suddenly Beth was crying.

Meg placed her hand on her friend's wrist. "You loved your gran."

*Saffron Alexander* was the title of Beth's first book. She wrote it for herself, alone in her bedroom, staying up late then rising early and putting pen to paper. Written as it came, quickly, then divided into sections, it fell into three parts, each headed in red, with boxed-in paragraphs and arrows back and forth.

The sections were:

A. SCHOOLSCHOOLSCHOOL – a close-up study of friendships and incidents and exchanges about families, particularly brothers (How Annoying They Can Be) as well as teacher profiles and homework set (not explained) and UNEQUAL TREATMENT. A succession of rumours and fall-outs and larks between lessons with moments touching feelings and cheeks sucked in while fingering notes found in pockets and hair stroked gently while lying in the sun.

In this part, the longest and densest on the page, Saffron was a mix. When she led from the front, her assembled cast – a bit-part collection of faces from the classroom, book-life, shop life and remembered family members – were subject to her whim. But when she played spy or classroom assistant, her characters, who jumped all over and never seemed to listen, went off at tangents and made themselves the story,

504

filling up the pages. Either they fidgeted or wouldn't stop talking. As characters they were out there, on paper, both independent and shaped by the story.

B. THE ROMANCE (PART 1) – the tale of a family appearing two doors down, beginning with a boy seen passing, returning from school. A boy without a name, soft-faced, light-haired, with thin arms and shoulders and a loose-limbed walk. A boy Saffron liked, watching daily for his fresh-faced blushes and eyes looking around. And the story developing, with her overheard comments, leading to a name, a school, and some sort of background. Then a meeting by chance, Saturday in the park, with the parents shaking hands, while the boy (called Tom) was sent off with Saffron to buy ice creams.

In the weeks that followed she showed Tom her *places*. In her mind they did it all: walking the garden on out-of-view paths, visiting the churchyard then crossing the playing fields to the mill, the stream and swans by the lake. As they toured she talked, the sky cleared and he admired her. Their story was a dream, a song at a window, a lightly-crooned ditty that she'd picked up from the radio, a boy-meets-girl, low-volume, summer-sun ballad that repeated and repeated ...

C. THE ROMANCE (PART 2) – suddenly a page break, a large-print heading, a switch in style and shift up tempo, with Saf and Tom as fugitives in a runaway story, outside time. At first by train, full speed to the sea, arriving in a mist where they slipped along the front then out across sand in thick clouds of spray. Finding a beach hut sheltered by rock; warm inside, with tinned food and candles, and the boy listening carefully to her whispered stories. Then sleep, then dreams.

Next on horseback, a Lorna Doone gallop, riding to a hideout in an ivy-thick wood. And the under-leaf darkness following a path leading to a waterfall and an iris over green, where they dismounted. Then words in the margin, a list, a box and arrows all over as the writing faltered and boy plus girl walked off into shoulder-high ferns ...

The book's last sentence was a single-line statement describing Saf waking, surprised and safe in her white-walled bedroom, returning from her dream.

*Saffron Alexander*, signed by the author, was finally completed in June 1967. By then Beth had lost all interest. She missed the task, but as a first-time attempt, it had served its purpose. Sealed in an envelope marked *strictly private*, it went to the bottom of a box beneath her bed where it lay around for years.

Because Beth was moving on. She was changing in ways she wrote in her diary, using as headings a long list of qualities that described her growing up.

- *Physically*, in the mirror she was taller, slimmer, with breasts and curves filling out. But also uneven with far-from-perfect teeth, hair she couldn't manage, skin-flush patches and a tendency towards voice loss when talking with boys.
- *Emotionally* she watched her own habits, found herself out, reacted and covered up, was driven, impulsive, get-up-and-go. But also sympathetic, she listened well.
- *Socially* aware, with a conscience, she held her friends close; they were her lifeline.
- *Intellectually* she counted her marks, topped most subjects and picked up at once on anything heard.
- *Report-wise* Beth, they said, was promising, conscientious, a pleasing pupil. Her mock exams were good. She was on target.
- *Imaginatively*, in herself, Beth progressed. She changed her approach from twice-daily drills – a tightly-controlled, necessary succession of tests, dates, memorised facts and thumbnail answers – to options, and a new stage of learning.

She'd entered a phase that took her from studying O's to developing her own taste, particularly in reading. She was quick and adaptable, switching between magazine short stories, classic novels and a short-list of poets – Wordsworth, Hardy and Edward Thomas – following leads that her teacher suggested, approved by her dad. And, as her taste developed, she branched out in verse, picking out favourites that she copied to her notebook, reread daily, and studied like a script.

Poems she recited, at first to herself mouthing in the mirror, next with John together in the garden, then tried out on her friends, beginning with Meg, then accompanied by Amy, ending with Rachael. Their responses ranged from listening carefully, to joining in the chorus, to talking about puzzles and formulae to unpick.

And during that period Beth wrote poems set in nature, looking at landscapes and the passing of the seasons. Composing daily, she recorded her sensations: sunrise and birdsong, the changes in the light, her indoor routines, and the movements of her family with their keepsakes and photos and the feelings that they shared. Everywhere, everywhere there was poetry.

And in verse she could say things in a glow, about truth and intercession and global inequality. Because what she called poetry, with its sing-song uplift and feel for loss, was very close to worship. It touched on something larger. Her poems were for God.

There had always been poetry in what Beth felt in church. It showed in the candles, the flowers on cloth, the light through glass. The people who attended, all friends of her parents, had an elevated, child-round softness to their smiles. Of course they were ordinary as well. Her mother always said that they were free-thinkers, who saw all sides, and the church was a home where they gathered as friends. There was beauty in that, as well. In the small things large, the everyday talk, the lack of all pretence. As her mother had said, it was rich and colourful, but not overdone.

"Church is for family," Louise said, as she entered the porch with an armful of flowers on a Saturday afternoon. Behind her, Beth was carrying two tightly-wrapped inflorescent bunches.

"So here we are," called Louise. Her voice was firmly expressive with a vaguely northern accent. With her big hips, rounded cheeks and wide-mouthed smile, she filled up the entrance.

Inside the building was large and light. It was brick-built and carpeted in red. There were rows of cushioned seats, a central font, and an apse at the back with children's playthings. At the front was a huge, polished wooden cross that hung above the altar. It was ship's-figure-head-size, handmade, and fitted exactly into a projecting ring of bricks.

"We'll take them to the hall," Louise called, shielding her flowers as she stepped through a mock-Gothic door. She held it open with her foot while Beth followed. The room they entered was high-walled and recessed on one side with blue felt boards full of children's artwork. Their pictures included paper-cut rainbows and glitter-smeared angels, moon-faced flowers, stars with arms, houses with teeth and strange-looking animals in multi-coloured inks. The next wall was plainer, with typed-out notices, a cork board with photos and a shuttered hatch. The other two corners held furniture.

"Now," said Louise, when they'd laid out the flowers on a table, "do you want to help me? Or ...?" She glanced sideways towards a glass door that led upstairs.

"I'd like ..." Beth said and paused. She wanted and intended, but when she was with her mother she found herself thinking other things.

Louise smiled. "You go along up there. Then I'll know where you'll be."

When Beth didn't move, Louise called, waving gently, "Go on. I'll be in and out with these." She pointed to the flowers. "And you'll be upstairs, so we can always see each other and call if we need to."

Beth said her thanks and went out to the staircase. As she climbed to the gallery she could hear Louise winding up the hatch and entering the kitchen. The sounds were familiar: a key in a lock, a cupboard being opened, vases on tiles, a gush of water then a knife edge, scraping. It made her feel oddly restless.

Halfway up, by the hall above, Beth paused to think. She felt her mother's presence, like a hand on her arm. She could hear her below, singing to herself. A sense of separation was urging her on.

At the top, where the staircase doubled back, Beth entered a white-walled corridor. It was cool and narrow and twisted slightly as it ran back to the church. Her bag scraped the wall as she passed by a cross-shaped window; it looked like an arrow-slit in a fort. Reaching the end, she turned left to arrive in a dusty, double-seated space. This was the gallery. It was narrow, barred in front, and hung above the porch like a theatre box. Seen lengthwise from here, the whole church was visible. Beth called it her *crow's nest*.

Sitting, she unzipped her bag and drew out a notebook with thick, grey-grained pages. Fingered lightly, they felt like tissue. She leafed through, sampling. The book began with poems, some short, some unfinished, others extending over two or three pages. Carefully decorated with scrolls and stars, they were dated and signed *Elizabeth Jarvis*. After that it was empty.

Her heart fluttered slightly. She could feel the quiet.

In the church below, her mother appeared. She was carrying two cast iron stands with projecting, tray-like ledges. Green squares of oasis filled up the trays. Holding the stands both sides, balanced like torches, Louise placed them near the pulpit. "All right?" she called.

Beth called back, repeating her mother's words as a statement. She didn't want an audience. Louise nodded then disappeared off.

In her absence the church-hush returned. The air was cool and still, and Beth, feeling the silence, returned to her notebook. She stared at a page. A poem was coming.

Downstairs her mother reappeared with a spray of brightly-coloured flowers. She laid them by the stands and began arranging. On the balcony Beth was fingering her pen. Beginning slowly, the words began to form: they were shy and evasive but invisibly strong.

Below, using long-stemmed trailers and bulbs, Louise was placing colour against colour: red and red-pink, offset by white. Her stands were filling up. Upstairs there were words, in a line. The poem was developing, with a space around the edges.

"Nearly done," said Louise, stepping back. She considered, then picked out some orange-yellow stems that she moved elsewhere.

Beth kept writing, trying out words. When the last line came, she signed and dated, then put down the pen.

Placing her last flower, Louise faced the altar. "A thing of beauty," she called softly, with an understated smile, "is a joy …"

The lines came back, filling Beth's mind. She knew them by heart.

For both, for now, this was their offering.

# THIRTY-ONE

12.2.03

Hello.

Is that you, Beth?

Yes.

It's James. How are you?

I'm fine. And you?

Pretty good … in fact, very good. And how's the weather?

Not so great, really. Misty, dull, then dull again. What about yours?

Much the same, cloudy and wet. I did some work, but rain stopped play. So how were things at the café?

Very quiet, hardly saw a soul. But that's normal, this time of year. Things don't pick up till nearer Easter.

Yes, I remember, you said. It's a bit like that with gardens, you know. People have to see things flowering before they'll call you.

They do? Well, maybe you should try down here. We've got crocuses and snowdrops everywhere – oh, and the daffs are up.

Sounds like Folkestone's quite far ahead. You've got primroses as well?

Hmm yes, we've had them for a month or two, growing wild around the café. We pick them and put them on the tables. I know we shouldn't, but there are so many. Sometimes I feel a bit mean about it. But then I look out the next day, and they're all flowering again. Maybe it brings them on. What do you think?

Well, it rather depends. With my gardener's hat on I'd say be careful this time of year, don't take too many off. With my own hat on I'd say, go for it.

So, you think if we're careful …?

But I'm sure you are.

Well, I'm not so certain about that. The plants get damaged.

Why – are you telling me you're *not* careful?

510

I am, very! But sometimes, when I'm picking on my own, they get squashed.

Ah, I know the business, I do the same. You have to remember, though, plants are survivors, especially in winter. But are you, if you don't mind me asking, right *in* there amongst the flowers? Can't you choose where you put your feet?

You'd think so, but not really. You see, don't be surprised, but when I pick flowers, I dance. I mean really dance, wildly, all over.

You do? What kind of dance?

Oh, nothing with a name, just bits and pieces. I make up the moves as I go along.

Without music? So what do you hear, I mean in your head? Is it like that tune in *The Nutcracker* – just trying to get it – *The Waltz of the Flowers*?

Not really. More Cha Cha Cha with the crocuses. Expressive dance really, my own kind, with the sea and the gulls. Sometimes in slow motion.

Wow. Does anyone see you?

I hope … Well, no, I don't think so. Not too many, anyway. I do it early morning, and the café's under the cliffs. The staff know, they've told me, but they don't mind. My deputy Sarah's joined me a few times.

So, it's party-on. But seriously, is it every day? Even on a day like this?

Not always, but I did this morning. It was clear first thing, and the moon – I think it woke me up – so I danced – I know this sounds crazy – reciting a poem. Keats's *Endymion*. A few lines, anyway. It's about the imagination.

Yes, I know it, and I can just see you there. Spring with dancers. Like that Botticelli picture, what's it called … *Primavera*.

You like that? My dad used to show it to me, in a book. It's very special.

My dad would call it arty-farty. He'd say bin it or chuck it on the fire.

He didn't like it?

Never heard of it. Or maybe that's unfair, because he did read in his own lefty kind of way, but only what *he* wanted to hear about. Anyway, whether or not he'd seen it, he reckoned all art was rubbish. Absolute, total rubbish … He did like Lowry, though. Called it proletarian. I told you about him in a letter.

Yes, I remember. I'm sorry.

That's OK, no need to apologise. I remember I went through a *who the hell does he think he is* phase – my daughter's going through it now – but in the end, it's just fathers and sons. As he would say, "It's about bringing 'em up, then getting 'em out the door". That reminds me, have I told you about the youth project I work for?

No, I don't think so. Is that a second job?

Not exactly, I'm there once a month on a Saturday. It's a scheme for what they call disaffected youth, meaning kids with tags, that sort of thing. Nearly all boys, of course. Some of them have done time in prison. They're on probation and have to attend, or go back inside, at least that's the theory. Mostly they do as they please, while I do the gardening.

That sounds rather difficult. What are they like?

Well, they're not as special as you might think, just ordinary kids. You'd be surprised how sharp some of them are. Half the time they've been bored at school, and that's how they've got into trouble. They're the kind who've bust through everything, so you don't really have anything over them. If they don't feel like it they'll walk away and there's nothing you can do about it.

And you're alone with them?

No, that's not allowed, we're always in pairs. In any case they generally don't turn up, so it's usually just the keen ones. We've been down to one at times, and then we end up talking. Which is what they want, really. There's one boy in particular, I can't say his name, but he's a character. We see him quite a lot. Shall I tell you about him?

Go on. Please.

OK, let's call him K. K always turns up late – one hour, two, it varies. Often we call his mobile, or we knock him up, literally door-step him, like the press. K's a clown. A gangly, toothy joker. He sings

James Brown, badly. The others yell at him to shut up or tell him to rap, so he does, and goes into mime. K's a break-in kid. I remember one story he told about being out all night squeezing through windows, getting so tired he fell asleep in someone's living room. When he woke up he found he'd broken into his own house. I don't know how true that is of course. I do remember him bringing in a stag beetle that climbed all over him, even his face. K didn't seem to mind. He called it Archie and claimed it crawled into houses to bring back jewels. He fed it on cake and dark chocolate. In the end they fell out. He said they'd had a row and Archie did a runner.

Archie sounds a bit like him.

That's true. When K sings, he sticks his arms out like a beetle. I reckon that's how he squeezes into houses.

And how does he do with gardening?

Not much, if he can help it. But he does have his methods. He talks to the plants, seems to want to get to know them. I think they're a substitute family. But you can't get him to pick up a spade. Not that I really care what he does, but you have to go through the motions. My dad used to talk about showing willing, and now I think he had a point. You know, how things come round. I hear myself saying "kids these days", and "no respect", and I recognise it's *his* voice I'm using.

I think it changes once you've had children.

Absolutely. You see yourself differently, and them. You know that Bette Davis quote, "If you've never been hated by your child, you've never been a parent".

No, I can't say I've heard that one. But I do like her line, "It should all be bigger than life".

Yes, "We don't need the moon, we've got the stars already" – something like that. She's a classic. I can't say I ever liked her, but then she's there to be admired, not loved, I suppose. A bad case of what they call inflation. I hope you're not a fan?

Not much. I do like that one line, but the whole relationship with Joan Crawford was awful.

Bad, bad, then worse. It's the danger of living out your art. Like Ted Hughes and Sylvia Plath – do you like them?

Oh yes. Which reminds me of something I didn't tell you. I wrote a story based on their first meeting and got it published, in a small magazine.

Wow, you must be proud. So you write?

I did, years ago. I suppose I dabble occasionally, even now.

You do? Tell me.

Well, it's not something I think about much, just another of those habits. I write notes to myself about people I see in the café. It's a bit like I'm secretly filming – though I wouldn't do that, of course.

Casting them for parts, eh?

I'd call them pen portraits. Quick sketches, really.

That sounds fun. What do you write about?

Appearances, and the odd habit. Things they do.

Anything else?

Sometimes I imagine who they're with and what they're like away from the café. I give them lives.

So, you're telling their stories?

Doesn't everyone? In their heads, I mean … I just use paper and write small, so I can stick them on playing cards. I've made up a whole pack. It's a kind of patience where I shuffle and deal, matching them up. Pairs, I call it.

That's interesting.

It's just a game, really.

Sounds like something I used to play. A memory game. Only now, of course, I've completely forgotten … It does have a name.

*Pelmanism*?

That's it. Thank you, I needed that. Though there's a certain irony there, of course. Anyway – and I hope you don't mind if I say this – I think, with the cards and the dancing, you've got something important, your own private world, and that's great.

Thank you. But James …?

Yes?

Please understand, I'm easily hurt. And that means, be careful.

Oh yes, understood. It's all or nothing. That's another thing my dad used to say that I've come round to as I've got older. You show who

514

you are, then it's take it or leave it. But perhaps I should say I want to be careful as well. It does take time.

That's right.

And one other thing …

Yes?

I'm not easily put off. Knock me down and I bounce back.

I think that's good.

And once I commit, that's it.

Me as well.

So, on *that* note … As I'm getting tired, and I'm sure you must be, I shall think about everything … But for now, goodnight.

And you'll sleep?

Not for a while, probably. But tomorrow's work so I'll have to. Will you ring tomorrow, or shall I ring you?

I'll ring.

OK.

Goodnight, James.

Goodnight, Beth. By the way …

Yes?

No dancing in the dark. Those crocuses deserve a night off.

Yes, I run them ragged … Tomorrow, then.

Tomorrow.

Goodnight.

Yes, goodnight.


# THIRTY-TWO


When Beth first saw the boy, she was seated with Meg and Toby around a fold-out table in the upstairs hall. Placed at the centre of the space, the table was bare, the chairs pushed together and the group – five in all – were gathered like rest-stop travellers. Snatches of organ and voices in unison drifted through the walls.

They were being led in discussion by two softly-spoken women. Annie, the taller, was pale-skinned and watchful with light grey hair and perfect teeth. She spoke about the Bible as if it was a picture, a story full of love and passion that she witnessed daily. Clare, who was younger, interjected quietly about world inequality and the efforts of the church.

They'd arrived at the point, usually towards the end, where Beth found herself arguing with her brother. "I know what you think," she called. "You see him as some sort of super referee, up there with a whistle and a book, taking names and sending people off."

"You don't know."

"But isn't that what you think?"

"Not much."

"So how *do* you see God?"

"More like a big sis."

"Oh, Toby, that's not fair."

Annie intervened, explaining that people in the world held different views, mentioning the Gospels and inviting reflection.

Clare, who was polishing her glasses, replaced them on her nose. "Of course," she said quietly, "for some football's a religion, they worship their team."

"But isn't that all wrong?" asked Beth. She looked quickly about the room, checking for listeners. When she was with the group, words popped out before she knew it.

"Quite harsh, yes," responded Clare. "I'm saying it's a vanity, which isn't very nice."

Beth coloured. "I was talking about football – it being so important. I wasn't criticising what you said …"

Again, Annie mediated, talking about feelings and strongly-held views.

"But it's *so* competitive," said Meg, wrinkling her brow.

"What do you think, Toby?" invited Annie.

The boy hesitated. He was round-faced and serious with brown curly hair and a rash across his forehead. "You want to know about football?"

"About football and faith. Do some people take it too far? Are they using it as a kind of religion?"

Toby stared at his questioner. The whites of his eyes were veined red. "Football's a game," he said slowly, "but religion's different. One's in two halves, the other's all the time."

The group dropped silent.

"Short-term, and long-term," said Clare.

"That's good Toby, good," put in Meg.

"So, one's for show," added Beth, "the other's hidden."

And it was then, as she spoke, that the new boy arrived.

He was light-haired and slight and held himself forward, at an angle, with his grey-green eyes turned to one side. His face was narrow, long in the chin and slightly mischievous. As he entered he ducked, in a semi-humorous gesture, as if the door was low. Behind him, his mother followed. She wore a pink knee-length dress, cut to her figure and tightly belted. Her small face was moon-soft and gently smiley.

"Ah, Mrs Bright?" asked Annie, rising in her seat and extending her hand. The women greeted with Clare joining in and the mother responding, waving vaguely towards her son.

"So sorry. I'm Vera, and this is Conrad. So sorry if we're late!" Here she directed a look towards her son, who had steered to one side and was leaning against the radiator.

Clare drew up an empty chair, urging Conrad to join them. Beth watched the mother apologise again, and offer her son a coat, coupled with a caution, before bowing out.

"Please join us," Clare repeated, gently.

Looking surprised, the boy came forward. "May I?" he asked, glancing around.

"Please do."

He dropped his head. "Thank you," he said, confidingly.

Annie welcomed, using first names, and reminded the group of their discussion. "So what do we think?" she asked. "Is sport these days all fine and healthy, or far too aggressive?"

Beth felt the pressure to answer. She'd views of course, mainly about tennis, and she knew the other two probably wouldn't take part, but the new boy's presence made her wary. She wondered how her words might sound, taken out of context. Or what might come up. Even though his eyes were turned away, suddenly she was out there, in public.

"What do *you* think, Beth?" prompted Annie.

The question brought her back. "It depends on the person. Who's doing it and why."

"I see. Do you mean it's a matter of temperament?"

"Well, I think so. A lot of sport is against the clock, isn't it? Or it's about doing it super-well."

Conrad looked up. "When I run, I run against myself."

"That's interesting," said Clare. "Do you run a lot?"

"I do, when I feel like it, but sometimes I don't."

"I see. Would I be right in thinking that you run alone?"

"Yes, when no one's around," he replied, and Beth felt the pause. There was a coiled-up silence somewhere inside, a wait in the dark.

Annie put in a thought about training, comparing it to prayer. "It doesn't always come that easily," she added. "Sometimes you have to build up to it."

Meg chipped in, "I swim with a club," she said, looking at Clare. "It does us good, and we all get on. Anyone can come along."

"I like football," Toby grinned, "when we win."

Beth heard herself objecting. She began, using words like "tribal" and "ritual" then stopped. "But I suppose you could say football's just a game," she added, colouring.

The new boy smiled. "My mother says it's all about money. Money instead of God."

"But do you want money?" Beth found herself asking.

Conrad looked straight across the table. "Not instead."

She nodded.

"Because I'd rather run," he added, speaking quietly as if they were alone. "It's out of the ordinary." His voice sounded firm but also rather child-like. Behind his words was a range of possibilities, something with shape and promise.

They were the first line to Beth's poem.

*Out of the Ordinary*

Out of the ordinary,
you came
when least expected,
after the swordplay,
the brother-sister cut and thrust,
into the sunlight.

Autumn boy,
your colours came too soon
too rich for naming,
too soft to touch
too light to catch.

No fuss, no flourish,
your business
was as natural as the forest.
You're A to B
like season to season,
a steady pace,
oblivious.

I know you saw me
because as you ran
you breathed a "Hiya,"
that made your rhythm falter.
But I'm the one
left breathless
by the smile in your eyes.

Somewhere you're running on,
the silence behind you
is full now.

Your tracks
cut deep.

*Elizabeth Jarvis*

"So, it's nothing to do with competition – the other runners don't count?"

Beth and Conrad were jogging by a hedge along a brown-yellow farm track between a cornfield and a thin clump of trees. It was early morning, the sky was clear and the air was cold and still. A rabbit scuttled away beneath bushes.

"Not when it's distance," he called back. His thin, elastic body moved easily over stone and mud. Beth ran with effort.

"But you time yourself?"

Conrad flashed a wristwatch.

"So it's about difficulty?"

"Only a bit," he called.

Their feet broke step, taking turns to jump-stride a ditch. In front of them now they saw a single runner. They were catching him up, but before they drew level he turned off.

When Beth reached a low ridge, she dropped back. Conrad waved on and they cut across grass to arrive at a gate into trees. A thin yellow arrow painted on a post pointed forward.

"Or is it … about the route?" She was sweating now.

Conrad reached over wood to fumble with a metal catch. "Cross-country," he said, hauling back the gate, "is about getting there."

Entering the trees, they slowed slightly as they sidestepped a pool then ran side by side down a cool, shadowy avenue. Here they were alone.

"This way?" she gasped, as they arrived at a clearing and a fork.

"Long or short?"

Beth stood, hands on hips, gathering her breath. "Could you wait?" Her request sounded edgy.

Conrad stared forward, jogging on the spot.

"OK," she said, looking upwards, on weather-watch. There were clouds now with breaks, a low-level sun and a still-visible, gibbous moon. Like her feelings, the weather wasn't certain.

"The long way," she said.

They moved to the right following a line of twisted fence posts. The trees thinned out and they emerged above a scooped-out pit. It was grey and stony, tufted with grass. At the bottom was a mud-patch and a circle of standing water.

"Watch out!" called Conrad as he scrambled over a rotted stump. Beth followed, struggling slightly. They curved around the pit, following a rock-strewn track. On one side it was steep, on the other there were nettles and loose twists of wire.

As they came to a dip, Beth mis-stepped and stumbled forward. She gave a short, yelping shout as she lost her footing. The stones gave way and she slid into the pit. "Oh … oh!" she called, rolling sideways. Throwing out her arms, she slewed down, hitting rocks as she went. At the bottom she landed with one leg in the pool. Dust swirled up as she lay there, unmoving.

Conrad scrambled down, shouting. There was blood smeared across her arms and down her leg. Her breath was shallow and her eyes were shut. "Beth! Beth!" he cried, shaking her shoulder.

She groaned.

"Are you all right?"

Her face remained pale and closed.

"Beth! Say something!"

Her eyes flicked open. They searched across his face. "Doesn't hurt," she said softly.

His hand touched her cheek. "You've got to be all right," he said, fiercely.

A slow smile passed across her face. "Don't worry, I'm OK."

"You sure?"

"Yes. You helped."

"Thank goodness." His head dipped forward and he kissed her on the brow.

Beth's arms came up and closed around his shoulders. "Thank you," she said quietly, allowing him to lift her.

⚕ ⚕ ⚕

"But you don't run anymore?" said James, sitting by the window of *The Shorespot Café*.

Beth smiled. "Walking's good enough for me."

Outside the sun was rising on a silver-blue sea. The air was clear and they could see down the slope, looking out across trees and bushes to a long sweep of gravel and a concrete jetty. White-flecked waves were lapping around its sides.

"Well, this is the place," he said. "Just chill out and enjoy the scenery."

"You should have seen it before, it was a greasy spoon."

"Really? You must have done a lot to make it like this."

"Money, time, effort. I practically lived here when I set it up."

"Sounds hard. But I guess it was something else to think about."

"Could say."

"So, everything here is *you*, in a way?"

She nodded. "My business, yes."

James looked around the café. Where they were sitting, soft light flowed in from the long picture window, further back the chairs and tables were lit from above by a skylight. On the tables there were flowers in vases, scented candles and leaflets. The walls were hung with original artworks. "And those are yours?" asked James, pointing to a laminated photo-collage showing plants and birds, people laughing, and overgrown, sunlit paths.

"Taken on my walks."

He rose to take a look. "Customers, perhaps?"

"Those are my girls, at the front. Behind, friends."

She ran through the names then invited questions. Peering closely, James pointed to the background. "And these paths? Are they close by?"

"Why yes, all round the café." She looked out at the sea. It was stirring and shining. The horizon was streaked with white-grey sunlight.

"Would you care to take a walk?" she asked, head to one side. She was playing him now, judging his mood. "The views are good."

"Definitely. But first, I'd like to try something." Dropping his eyes, James frowned. He seemed to be looking inward, searching for a clue. "There's no music," he began, raising his eyes, "but then again, there is the sea ..."

522

They both looked out.

"Care to dance?" he asked suddenly, holding out his hand.

Beth smiled and accepted. She allowed herself to be led to a small, square-tiled dance floor.

"You have to imagine," he said. "Think, music."

Beth angled back her head: "I can hear the track." An arm went around her waist, and breathing together they began to dance.

"You remember?" he said quietly.

She answered, but her words seemed unimportant. Of course, whatever they said, it was all about feel – only that, and the actions. Her body, like his, was circling quietly. They were on the dance floor, moving in silence, watching the sea.

When they left the café it was still early. There was ice in the hollows concealed beneath bushes and the grass was white. They followed a road that turned into gravel. Reaching an uphill track they climbed towards the clifftops, stepping across patches of frost-hardened mud.

"Do you walk this often?" asked James.

"In the summer, yes. Not when it's like this."

On the way up they paused looking out then moved on holding hands, adjusting as they went. When the path narrowed they kept in touch by talking or pointing out features, sometimes stopping to look back where they'd come.

"It's a wild spot," said James, and Beth nodded. Walking with him was an adventure.

They turned a corner and entered an area full of boulders and mud slides and prickly vegetation. The path dropped suddenly. Looking down, they could make out a rock-fringed bay with a stream to the sea.

"Do you want to go on?" Beth asked.

"Of course, as long as you do."

The sun had clouded over. A wind had got up and the sea was cresting. The cries of seagulls echoed from the rocks.

Helping each other, they descended. The path was slippery and the ground in places had hollowed to a drop. At one point James stumbled, steadying himself against a tree, at another Beth led across a stream, halfway down they zigzagged over scree to arrive at a rest spot.

"Let's sit," she said, hitching side-saddle onto rock, "and enjoy."

James joined her. "Happy?" he asked, squeezing her hand.

"Oh yes."

"Mind, it's still quite a drop," he said, stretching sideways to peer to the bottom.

Beth leaned over, holding his arm. The rock here was sheer. Below, it opened to a thin strip of water caught between cliffs. At the sea end a huge, steeply-sloping block held out the waves. Behind it, the inlet was still. Its dark, enclosed surface seemed almost lifeless.

James looked up. "What's the story there?" he asked, pointing along a fenced-off spur. A faded sign said *Danger* and, beneath that, *Lover's Leap.*

Beth's expression flattened. "A woman who drowned, I believe."

"You mean she jumped?"

"Not exactly, the story is she climbed down to a boat."

"That must have been difficult."

"Her lover was down there. She did it to escape."

"With love's light wings, eh?"

"She tried."

"What happened?"

Beth shook her head. "The weather changed as they rowed out to sea, at least that's the story, and they both drowned."

"Doomed love."

"Well, romantic, anyway," she said, shivering slightly.

The wind was gusting. It came and went, funnelled by the rocks. A deep, insistent surf-noise was rising up the cliff.

"But do you think it really happened?" he asked.

"Possibly, but then does it matter? It's true to life, that's all."

"You think so?"

"Don't you?"

"Well, I'm not a cynic. But I do think we should take nothing for granted."

"You don't believe the stories?"

"Of course, all lovers *have* to die."

Beth laughed. "But not …" she said, cutting herself off.

"Or at least, it's like that in youth," he continued, "... *trust me*."

She smiled and pushed in closer. "But then sometimes ... not often, but sometimes ..." She paused, trying to find the words, "People meet and surprise-surprise, things happen."

James touched her lightly. At first on her hand, then stroking and smoothing down her hair, shifting to her cheek, her shoulder and dropping to her breast, as his mouth met hers.

They rocked back and forth, kissing; then repeated, in a clench. Their faces had softened and their movements slowed. They were there, together, and nothing seemed to matter. No one could see them and they touched and they kissed, searching for pleasure, simply, as it happened, and because they could.

The tide was going out when they reached the shoreline. They followed the stream, sliding on gravel. The wind now was blustery and the clouds were low. In the distance the surf was kicking up. Bare rafts of rock showed around the headland.

"We can go out there," said Beth, waving forward. A few spots of rain mixed with spray flew in from the sea.

"Is that wise?" asked James, holding out his hand.

"The café's that way, round a couple of points."

"If that's quicker."

Beth confirmed. She kissed him, once, twice and led onto the rocks. To begin with they simply stood, plotting a route, but when the cold drove them on they made their way out. Firstly, on the flat and then across cracked, uneven surfaces. There were flurries now, some of them hail, driving from the sea. They called out and laughed, braving the weather. At a channel they slowed, choosing a detour, by a stack they ducked down, when they neared the headland they looked about – mostly they kept on. Reaching the point, they were absorbed by sound: the surf-roar, the wind, the seabirds crying. They were out there, alone.

As they entered the next bay, Beth waved towards the cliffs. "There's a place here," she called, "out of the wind."

She steered to one side, closing on rock. As she pointed towards an overhang, the rain grew heavier. "This way!" she yelled, pushing on.

Water filled the air. Whipped up by the wind, it soaked through their hair, beating on their backs. They scrambled for the cliffs, reaching the overhang where Beth pulled him in. "We're here!" she shouted, and her voice echoed briefly. Suddenly it was quiet.

Blinking, James looked about. They'd arrived in a short, scooped-out cave with a double-pillared entrance. It was tall and egg-shaped, and level underfoot. Along one side the rock dipped to a shadowy pool. A small vase of withered flowers stood by the poolside. Beside it a burnt-down candle had hardened onto rock. A few dead flowers had fallen into water.

"What is this place?" James asked. "Does it have a name?" His voice echoed slightly in the dark.

Beth hushed him. She motioned to the opposite wall where a fold in the rock acted as a seat. Beside it a squared-off stone doubled as a table. At one end, incised into rock, the stone was decorated with an Ichthys.

*"The Chapel,"* she said quietly.

✝ ✝ ✝

A banner behind the stage read LIVE LIFE FOR JESUS. Stretched like a sail, it was gold on black, bordered by red. A web of wires, fixed to the edges, led back to wall hooks. Lit from all sides, the banner appeared to be afloat.

Front stage was the show. It had begun with recorded hymns, followed by an organ fanfare and the entry of a woman in a high-necked gown. She'd called on the Lord quoting scripture then welcomed the choir: all long-sleeved, smiling and shiny, in white.

"Oh yes, hear the Gospel," the woman cried, and the choir launched off into an upbeat number, driven from behind by floor-shaking notes punched out from the organ.

They ran through three more: a high-voiced solo sung by a boy in a suit, a foot-tapping, hand clapping acapella and a stand-up rerun of the big-tune opener.

"And now," cried the woman, unclipping her mike, "I'd like you to welcome the man you've all been waiting for, please put your hands together for your testifying preacher, Luke Patrick Martin!"

At the back, Beth and Conrad were applauding. The audience roar had brought them to their feet.

A dance of coloured lights wheeled across the stage, the organ struck up and a tall man with a long-faced stare strode to the microphone. He was wearing a white jacket speckled with gold, a loose red shirt and black flares. His thick, wavy, silver-blond hair fell to his shoulders. He raised one hand, pronouncing a blessing. "You are the children of light. Let the Love and the Truth and the Power of the Good Lord Jesus come upon you."

A man called out, throwing up his arms. His words set off others, shouting to the ceiling. A girl next to Beth went down on her knees, sobbing.

Backed by the organ, the preacher began. His voice was low-toned and deeply resonant, pausing between questions and inviting thought. As he worked his theme – the great clash of opposites – his delivery sharpened: there was danger in what he said. Repeating words like *shameful* and *unwholesome*, he spoke of exposure, of falling and failing and being cast out. Raising his arms, he issued warnings of the world led astray, the wrong path chosen and the judgement soon to come. "It has to stop!" he cried, standing tall. The organ faded as he invited them to pray.

Beth felt pressure in the gap that followed. There was power here and calm. The hall was full of fear and hurt and locked-down excitement. She wondered about Conrad: was he shivering like her?

The prayers were for healing. The voice from the front dropped to a whisper, delivered close-mike. Luke Patrick Martin's words filled the hall. Afterwards he stood back, deep in thought, while the long-gowned woman cued in the choir. They sang in parts, arm-swinging gently while a collection was taken. He blessed their gifts as some flowers appeared, added a few prayers then left the stage, waving.

When the interval arrived, Beth and Conrad stepped outside.

"What do you think?" she asked, sipping lemon barley.

Conrad grinned. "It's good. Very." His face, half-lit by a street-lamp, was focused forward.

"So, you think we're winning."

"How do you mean?"

"Just a way of speaking, that's all. You're enjoying it?"

"Absolutely. Aren't you?"

"If you are, I am."

"I thought you were moved."

"Oh yes. It's a bit footbally, but I'm getting there."

"I found it an experience."

"Well, yes, it *is* exciting."

"Yes, the Living Word."

Beth drained her glass, saying nothing.

Conrad smiled. "God's judgement," he said quietly, regarding her with a fixed expression, "sees all. Nothing, absolutely nothing, escapes him."

In her dreams that night Beth heard her dad talking about God. He was with her, by her side. They were together in the garden, sitting on the wall – but also in a painting, a scene from the past with eyes behind leaves, green men carved in stone and bird-faced creatures peeping out of holes. The lawn smelled damp.

"His wildness and wisdom …" began John, and she saw herself climbing. He was there as her guide, leading upward. "Silent and unknown," he continued as they spread their wings, rising up a cliff.

The dream switched to church. They were upstairs in what she called her *crow's nest*. Looking down they saw purple and red. An organ began playing, leading a hymn. "Many colours, many faces," her father sang, as balloon-mouthed notes floated up. The congregation followed, ascending slowly. Each in a bubble, they were shaped like flowers.

"The great as-if," sang John and the scene changed to water. There were images, reflections and shadows on the surface. Beneath that, in the depths, there were thin-faced ghosts. They swayed back and forth, touching gently. She was down there, and she wasn't, and the shades were all around.

A prayer began. The words were simple, but repeated, "We thank you Father for our dreams." Then John read the lesson. It came out as a story of birds and animals, talking together. A warm glow of candles filled the air, mixed with roses, richly scented. They were at home, at supper, and their plates were full of petals.

John stood up, reciting a poem, and took her in his arms. He was carrying her, lifted like a bride, up, up. Then air, then sun, then birdsong beginning, and eyes opening, turning slowly like the pages of a book.

"In a different world," said her dad, quietly, and they walked out in the garden, with sunlight all around, as they listened to the silence …

The next day, Beth's birthday, Conrad was there. He'd sneaked into college and slept on her floor staying there as a friend, without of course anything happening. They trusted all the way. Because what others called dating, they saw as sharing, an intimate, honest, truth-seeking openness. A togetherness before God.

When Beth first woke, Conrad was standing by the steps just outside the window. He was still and impressive with his face angled back and his eyes half-closed. There was uplift about him and a weight of intention, watching for the way. She was aware of him out there, calmly separate and self-directed. And when he came back in, he still seemed to be thinking. Hoping for a surprise, she didn't remind him.

Over breakfast Beth held back. The dream, though backgrounded, was still with her. It came between them, making her uneasy. So when they talked about the gathering, she was careful. It was almost as if the service hadn't really happened. The moment had passed, she'd been there, taken in the feeling, and now was moving on. "Well, it *was* an experience," she said, trying to catch his eye. "And I did feel the love, by the end."

"I'm pleased," he replied, and they shared a short reading before going out.

In the morning they walked. Beth led off, following a route that she hoped might interest him. They passed by colleges with Beth naming some and crossed a park, with the weather brightening, to turn down some steps and arrive at the riverside. Here they wandered by trees to reach a built-out platform with huts and a boathouse. She noticed how his mood seemed to lighten as they looked across water.

Conrad took a fancy to hiring a boat, calling "Watch me," when she asked about rowing. He paid a man in leather for oars and a ticket then pretended to be wobbly as they pushed off from land.

"Back by two," the man called, flatly. Conrad frowned and dipped the oars.

"So, you *can* row," Beth said slyly as they rounded a bend and passed beneath a willow. Its fingers brushed her lightly, like a web.

"Good exercise," he said, shifting position. His knuckles gleamed white where he gripped the oars.

Beth went silent. They were face to face, with Conrad pulling strokes. He was calm and easy and kept his breathing low. An ironic smile played about his lips, almost as if he was awaiting orders. Beth wondered whether the boat trip, without anything being said, was his way of taking notice. They passed beneath a brick-built bridge, forking off along a backwater to arrive at a lake. Screened by trees, its surface was absolutely still. There were small tussocks both sides, some flat-leaved water plants and an overgrown island at the centre.

Conrad raised the oars. As the boat began to turn, he gazed across the water. "To the island?" he asked and Beth nodded. He had rolled up his sleeves exposing flesh. His long, loosely-jointed body was whiplash thin.

"We can land there," she said, "round the back."

"You want to?"

"If you don't mind the rowing."

Conrad grunted. "Just tell me one of your stories."

"You'd like that?"

He dipped in his oars. "Go ahead."

Beth lowered her fingers into water. Its coolness tingled, slightly. The sun was there filling up her head. She sat back, picturing her other birthdays and her dad in the garden. It reminded her of worship.

"It's called *Shipwreck*," she began. "It's a dream about a brother and sister playing in a garden. They're sailing, with the girl as captain, on the rockery. When a storm gets up, the ship goes down. But the children, as children always do, escape. They end up as castaways on the lawn." She paused, watching the ripples, while Conrad pulled on the oars. "And because they believe, things happen. So, they climb to the tree house and while they're up there, a cloud comes over. And suddenly, as if they're asleep, everything blacks out. They hear a warning cry and the flap of wings, and realise it's a bird. A huge, fire-crested one that they've heard about in stories." She laughed. Conrad kept rowing. "Then the bird carries them up, up, to a boat in the sky. And they sail away for a year and a day, or something like that." She paused again, hand in water, while Conrad swung the oars. "Then the bird returns, the cry come back and a storm gets up. It all blacks out, and lightning strikes. Everything burns up completely, the ship, the bird, all wiped out in a fireball. But of course it's a story, so the children escape. They end up as castaways back on the lawn. And it all begins again with the girl as captain standing on the rockery, looking out across the garden …"

Beth's hand trailed in water. Conrad continued rowing. By the time they arrived, it was lunchtime, the sun was shining and they were alone on the island. When Conrad stopped to pray, Beth stood by thinking of her and Toby playing, and the dream she'd once had of the island sinking. It seemed best now if she didn't mention her birthday.

That night, Beth had her island dream again. In it she heard her story, told by someone else. It sounded sad but calm, like a sermon. The story was about children and animals looking for shelter. There were photos she'd seen in albums, taken of the war. Pictures of plants dying, beaches underwater and people setting out in long canoes. Her island was going under.

*‡ ‡ ‡*

When Beth and James left *The Chapel*, the rain had stopped. A thin white glare was spreading over water. There were faint flecks and spills on rocks. Further out, the sea was greyly smooth, like linen. "I'm drying out," she called as they scrambled across pebbles to the sea's edge. Their feet slipped and scrunched and they held on to each other with a sense of release, as if they'd been rescued. They were outdoors, the sky was clearing and they'd made it through.

Facing the water, James put his arm around her waist. "Tide's high," he said. "Soon be turning."

Beth examined the view. It was much like a painting. "It's as if everything's hanging, just for a second."

James laughed. "Well, let's keep watching." He looked down to where the waves were hissing and bubbling over stones. "The thing about water is, it doesn't settle."

"Yes," said Beth. She leaned into his side: "It makes you want to get into a boat and row – go way, way out to the horizon." A silver-grey shaft of sunlight cut across the bay. Birds called out and the air seemed to shine.

James squeezed her hand then crouched down, fingering the stones.

"What're you doing?" she asked.

"Looking for skimmers," he said, scooping up a handful of coin-shaped pebbles. Choosing one, he leaned sideways and flicked it across the waves. The stone hop-skip-jumped before disappearing into water.

"That's fun," she said.

He picked up another and threw. Hitting a swell, it bounced high, spun, and dropped out of sight. "Only one jump," he said, shaking his head. He tried a few more skims, kicking up a line of white splashes. Beth, counting the hits, urged him on. He varied his methods from underarm to overarm then curled a throw from behind his back.

"Tricky," she cried, clapping her hands. "But what about distance?" she asked, pointing to the horizon. "Can you do that?"

James scooped up a handful and rocked back on his heels. "Up and under," he called and scattered his pebbles in one clean throw. They sailed out and landed in a group, plopping and pricking the surface.

Beth laughed. "I couldn't do that. It's too far."

"Maybe you could, with practice."

"I doubt it."

"I think you could."

"Not me, I was never any good at things like that." Her mind flashed back to a scene in a field with her dad.

"Why not? I could show you."

"No, I'd rather … But wait – there is something, from childhood," she stepped up to the water's edge. "How about if I do this?" she called, shifting back and forward to avoid the waves. As she called and shifted a tongue of water pooled about her feet. "Can't catch me, Mr Sea," she sang, dodging. "It's a great game," she called again, as a white line ebbed and flowed, hissing on shingle.

A larger wave rolled in, driving her back. It broke in a rush, spraying her heels and causing her to jump. "Oh!" she cried, slipping on weed. As she went down, James stretched out and pulled her up. "Thank you, my knight," she called and dusted herself off. She was by his side now, breathing hard, with her eyes fixed on water.

"Shall we take a dip?" he asked suddenly.

"Isn't it freezing?"

"Almost certainly, but I'm willing."

She looked around quickly. The land and sea were empty and suddenly it seemed they were out there with the elements, alone and free, in a world without people. "You really want to?"

"As long as you're up for it."

"That's crazy."

"Brings back memories."

"Memories?"

"Hastings in summer. But this's my gran and the North Sea."

"Ah, yes."

A wave rushed in, rising on gravel. It filled and foamed and boiled over, then with an abrupt, gurgling hiss sank back to nothing.

"OK," she said, "you're on."

As they pulled off their clothes the sea swell dropped and a faint white glow spread across the surface. The sky was clearing and the air was thin and dream-like. Above them a small flock of birds cried out; their shadows moved like ghosts on water. James and Beth were alone.

When they waded out, the first shock of cold took away Beth's breath. Holding his arm, she stepped across stones. The stones turned

533

to sand and she moved more easily. As the water deepened her body firmed up. Her feet went forward, pushing into softness. Her toes and her fingertips tingled; she was in the flow. If there was exposure, it had left her now. She was out here with him, feeling the love, and the tide-change had begun. The cold below had become a kind of wrap-around warmth. The sea, and her excitement, was filling her up. It closed around her thighs and pushed her off. Suddenly she was lifted and her insides freed; the waters held her. For her this was everything – passion in action, desire for James and the fullness of God. She was swimming out naked, with the sun on her back, and only he could see her.

† † †

After leading all the way in the Baptist College run, Conrad stood on the seminary steps, bowing his head. The applause fed his smile, kept hidden, as he gave thanks through prayer. He'd done his personal best. It made him glad to be.

"You were great," said Beth as he joined her in the crowd. "I watched you from the roof."

Conrad towelled down his neck. He was half a head higher than her, his jaw was long and he'd part-shaved his head. With his sucked-in cheeks and faraway look, he seemed like a cross between a monk and a soldier.

He thanked her, unsmilingly.

"First by a mile. You must have flown."

"Good, eh?" he flashed.

"Nobody could touch you."

"I imagined I'd jets on my feet," he added. A little-boy niceness had entered his voice.

"They say it's a record," she said, taking his towel.

"Thank you. I'm grateful."

Beth glanced over. She wondered how he felt. He was staring rather blankly towards the ground. His face suggested prayer.

"Run with endurance the race set before us," he said quietly, rubbing his legs, "Hebrews 12:1."

His tutor came up, a small, unkempt man with horn-rimmed glasses, and they shook hands. Antony used the phrase *ne plus ultra*, eyeing his protégé. He hoped he would see him, he said, at the forefront of the movement. When introduced to Beth, he held out a hand and welcomed her. Two other men appeared, both young. Like Conrad, they were tall and rangy. Shifting foot to foot, they joked with Conrad, calling him "the kid" and admiring his fitness.

A bell rang. "Time to eat," Antony declared. His eyes were twinkly and directed towards Conrad. Beth thought him fun, and surprising.

In the refectory they all bowed their heads while grace was said. Over the meal Conrad answered questions, emphasising his thoughts with tongue-in-cheek gestures. "It all comes back," he told his tutor, "to beliefs and habits, and how we are with God."

Later, after eating, he went quiet. While the others told stories he played with his placemat then reached beneath the table and held Beth's hand. They sat there undetected, showing nothing. It was as if they were plugged in to an invisible circuit. They remained linked while the plates were cleared, until another bell rang and they unhanded. Conrad leaned close to her ear. "Shall we go?" he said quietly, as if he was asking her to a party.

They rose, made their excuses and walked off together, pausing by the door. "The garden?" he enquired. She nodded and they slipped out quietly.

He led, at first without touching, along a curving path between shrubs and borders. When they reached a building he turned through an arch and they entered a walled-in space. "This way," he said, taking her hand. "You'll see."

They walked between walls of bamboo and head-high hedges. Turning right, they climbed some shallow steps. Somewhere in the leaves a bird cried out. The path went deeper, arriving at an enclosure. Here, screened-off by branches, they came across a polished steel sculpture.

"This is where I come," he said, "when I want to think."

The sculpture seemed to glow. It was recessed on top with a small, bubbling jet and a pool of slowly turning water. The pool ran out, flooding down the sides to a basin below. It passed down the metal in a smoothly shifting curtain. They stood in silence, watching the flow.

Conrad lifted his head. "I've plans. Things I'm working on," he said. "Let me show you." Stepping forward, he rolled up his sleeves and shoved his hands into water, holding them there with a fixed expression. His flesh turned white, dividing the flow. "I mean to stand up," he called, "and speak out, make an impression, get people thinking." He spread his hands wider. The water spurted out, soaking his strong, sinewy arms. It bubbled and ran, dripping from his elbows. "It's a promise I made," he said, stepping back suddenly, "in the sight of God."

Beth heard his passion. It felt hot and cold and shivery all over. He was making his vow.

Conrad held his arms out, rocking slightly. "Do you think that it's possible, as a minister, to change hearts and minds?"

"Oh yes," she replied, breathing quickly. "Definitely."

"And would you – can you find it in your heart – to help me do that?"

Beth's eyes widened. "Of course, I'll do anything. But how?"

"A joint project, for life. We'd manage it together."

"Conrad, you mean …?"

He dropped his arms to his sides. "I'd like to ask – invite you, if it's possible. Can we be engaged?"

"It's a surprise, I didn't expect …" Suddenly she rallied, "A lovely one, though."

He stood there, unmoving. She reached out and placed one hand in the fountain.

"Together," she said, as Conrad joined her and they locked hands in the flow. "We're engaged," she said as the silent rush of water curled and bubbled, pulling at their flesh.

Isaiah 40:31 "But they that wait upon the Lord shall renew their strength"

Elizabeth Ella Jarvis
and
Conrad Mark Bright

request the pleasure of your company at the Christian celebration of their sacred union in the eyes of God

Saturday, the sixth of September
nineteen hundred and seventy-five
eleven o'clock in the morning
St Martha's Church
Old Lane Honbury, IP29OT

Reception to follow

It was God's will, he told her, on the first day of their honeymoon. "He chose us to be here," Conrad said as they left the hotel.

His tone surprised her. They'd arranged it in a rush, with talk about the deep clean water and runs to the point. He'd checked it with friends and knew it would be right. In any case, as he said, this was their moment. But when they arrived it had turned out rather differently. It seemed there was a week-long evangelical gathering, and suddenly they were booked in.

Their route to the meeting ran along the front. On the way there, Beth walked slowly. She looked over at her husband: his eyes were fixed forward, talking as he went.

Turning her head, she could feel the wind playing on her face. It sharpened her awareness. Last night's gale was gradually dying down. A fine drift of sand had lodged itself in cracks and was now blowing across the pavement. As they passed a shelter she noticed large-print posters with head shots of worshippers. They were all smiling nicely. On one wall, a half-torn white-and-red banner announced this year's line-up.

By Conrad's remarks she'd understood something: he'd come here with intention. "So you *know* where it is," she said as he led to a large glass building decorated with cloth-strip crosses.

"See, it's busy," he declared, pointing to the people on the steps. There was music issuing from a balcony above. Every so often a door opened and voices blared out.

"Conrad, please," said Beth, stopping. "I'm not sure I'm ready for this."

He angled his head away. "You're not ready?" he repeated, suddenly quiet. "You mean you don't want to go on?"

She struggled for words. In her heart she was divided, part of her was willing – this was their honeymoon so she wanted it to work – and part of her was uncertain. It seemed like he'd carried her off. "I'm just not sure."

He turned his grey-green eyes in her direction; they were red-rimmed and watery. "It's important. God understands everything we do. It hurts when we deny Him."

Beth bowed her head and held out her hand. Conrad took it, unsmiling, and they walked in together saying nothing.

It was God's will, she told herself for the next five years.

When she visited her dad, she didn't talk about *him*. Sometimes, on their walks, she touched on arrangements, on calendar events with readings and services and meetings in their house, or she told of vigils and late-night prayers. But when John took her hand and they looked out for animals and identified plants, she felt something moving – tears or something deeper – and, remembering her poetry, dropped into silence.

When she saw Louise, she didn't mention marriage. At church they kept themselves busy cleaning into corners and putting up notices. Now she was older she could see how things were: the new life, and the old. The church she'd come from was a home, a place she could sit and feel understood, where ideas were welcome and people shared. She saw it in her mother and in all those who took time to greet her, especially her old teachers, Annie and Clare.

Also, on the phone or in letters, she talked about commitment. To her brother she spoke about effort and the struggle to stay positive. With Meg she shared faith, how Conrad had the Call, how his ministry was expanding. To Rachael and Amy she made mention of the new house in Folkestone and having children. And even with Charlie she talked about girlhood, and the difference she was finding.

It was God's will, too, that Conrad was angry.

A raw, dark anger not seen by others, a spark of excitement or outrage, a sudden switch in tone and fist to the table. And immediately the words, the not-me excuses of a little boy wronged. Then the chair back and door shut, followed by footsteps on gravel and the car driven off.

And the darkness afterwards in a house in limbo with its tasks and its routines.

Then the next five years writing stories, in secret, for herself. Drafts on paper kept in envelopes and moved between drawers with dead-end settings and out-of-sorts talk. Stories of domestics that broke off mid-sentence, meetings with strangers, and one-page diaries about women abandoned. In them she was alone.

And then came a piece that she handwrote slowly, and kept well-hidden, a journey into otherness that she thought about so often it almost took her over, a place she'd finally come to, full of simple fear.

And that was God's will as well.

## A HOUSEKEEPER'S TALE
### by Saffron A

Christina was a housekeeper. She worked in her master's house but she lived below in a small dark basement. Often at night she heard him, walking overhead. It wasn't just the slow shuffling tread that made her shiver. She knew he was up there, eyes to the floor, peering through the cracks. In her dreams she saw a big-bodied animal, sniffing; the paws against ice, the claws breaking through.

She had never met her master. But in his absence she heard him all around. He was a singer who had trained his voice to imitate life. As part of his practice, he sang against the birds, and his grace notes were perfect. With the animals he could growl and go low, grunt warnings, chatter, purr, or trumpet in chorus. It seemed he was everywhere, rustling in the bushes or white-water gurgling, running with the flow. Not just in the footfalls and breathings that stirred the empty house, but in the other songs, more mysterious and wild. He could call across the hills, dark to light; by day he was the wind, shifting through branches; at evening, by the sea, he drifted with the spray.

His name was O. She'd read it on his letters. Holding the envelopes to the light and studying the postcodes, she wondered. People wrote, repeatedly it seemed. Sometimes she speculated about what they knew, or wanted. Were they admirers who had once heard his voice? Did they owe him or want some sort of return? Was he what they hoped for, without knowing why? It made her uneasy. In his own letters, did he tell them about her, and her life in darkness? Or was she his secret, one of many?

Christina never saw him. She worked around the house, cleaning, cooking, tidying, and in the evening she sat alone in the quietness, hoping he'd appear. She imagined him phoning with a word about work, a brief explanation, but the call never came. So she went to bed early, listened, but only ever heard him, or so it seemed to her, after sleep when his footsteps woke her, circling slowly.

For a long time she waited. There were messages about payment, notes and reminders, but all short and strictly instructional.

Christina wanted more. Taking his notes, she finger-traced the loops and curls. She whispered answers to questions he hadn't asked. She tried different ways of describing her feelings then, putting them together, composed a long letter. It was full of hope and belief and ideas for the future. The reply, when it came, was impersonal, merely pointing out that there were documents to check, a surveyor due and that the piano needed tuning.

So she searched the house for some faint sense of him, opening drawers and peering into cupboards. Nothing but clothes, shoes, socks, hankies and a broken watch. Checking the shelves, the books were old and vaguely theological, with a few historical volumes, all second-hand. She dared, for the first time, to lift the lid on the piano and press a key. But the sound was cold. Its hardness hung heavy in the silence it broke, but it told no story.

Upstairs she drew the curtains as instructed, and felt the coolness as she shut out the light. The bed was as she'd left it and the en-suite bathroom was bare and cold. There was nothing to go by, no trace of the spirit that inhabits a house when its owner is away.

It was as she cleaned behind the fridge that she found a feather, caught in the grill. She had to use a knife to prise it out. When she examined it, her hands shook a little. Its size surprised her. Long and soft, it was semi-transparent and almost weightless. It could have been a leaf, dried by the sun.

Later she wrote in her diary:

> Did I uncover it, or was it left for me to find? Either way, it was more than evidence. It seemed like paw marks in earth. But I could hold it and keep it safe, and when I stroked the softness, it felt like air. It made me think of beauty, colour and flight: of fable, or dream. It felt un-earthly.
>
> I kept it for a while underneath my bed where it was safe, and mine alone. Whoever it belonged to wouldn't know I had it. But now I've decided to put it out where he can find it. It's a kind of offering, a counter in a game. I hope my master will accept it …

That evening, after moving slowly to a spot above Christina's head, the footsteps stopped. In the silence that followed she could feel a kind of shadow pressing on her face. She imagined eyes staring through the dark, sizing her up. In a second, it seemed, the plaster might crack and a God-like claw might reach out and grab her. There was nothing she could do. Inside her, the fear cried out. There was some kind of mistake, a throwback or distortion. It would all pass over. Perhaps if she lay there, perfectly still, holding her breath …

In the morning, the feather had gone. In its place was a small, round cage with a silver handle, no bigger than a lamp. Wedged between the bars was a neatly-folded note. Opening it slowly, Christina shivered. It began by telling her not to fear and not to resist, for all would be well. Tonight, it said, her master would come. The rest was practical, mentioning timings, readiness, what she must do and what to expect. And finally there were conditions: the silence and the darkness must be absolute.

During the day she prepared without thought, keeping busy. As the evening approached, she started to count down. She could sense his closeness. The house was in his gaze, and she was his target.

That night, when he came, his presence filled the house. In her diary, she described it:

> I was shivering, hot and restless, intensely aware; the room seemed both close and open to the skies. I only wanted it over. My chest felt tight and my breath was straining.
>
> Suddenly it changed. The darkness of the room deepened and swelled. A breeze passed through and he *was*, I could feel him. Then he was gone.
>
> Afterwards I fell asleep, almost at once. In my dream I was drifting into a still, cold nothingness of glass, of space. There was no one there, only myself and the void.
>
> In the morning, rising, I went upstairs and stood by the window, waiting.

That evening, he came again. This time Christina was prepared. She'd changed the sheets and scattered a few petals on an extra pillow. As the air stirred she felt him enter. In the dark she could sense the tide of his breath. For a second the room quivered like leaves in a breeze. Then, again, he was gone.

Over the next week he came every night. Each visit was a single breath, a shadow on the wall, almost without contact. And each encounter, lasting only seconds on the clock, yet lingering afterwards, felt quite final.

And then she realised. There were no rules or limits. He was her master but she was his mistress too. She could hold on to him, if she chose, and only then decide to let him go. Because he came with her breath. He lived inside her.

So she practised breathing, like a swimmer. As soon as he arrived she took in air. They were there, together, floating in a bubble. She could live for two.

Her purpose made her proud. They were lovers of a sort, at night, in silence. And like all lovers they lived their connection, a brief, nocturnal moment of closeness that passed unseen, something other-worldly, a shot in the dark.

The next day was different. Christina had a feeling that someone or something was there, inside her mind. There were eyes trained on her, voices somewhere, shadowy figures just outside her view. As the evening came on, it seemed they were gathering. The house was alive with unseen watchers.

Awake in darkness, she could hear the music, singing in her head. Things passed before her: the piano, the birdcage, the notes through the door.

This time, when he came, she could feel him in there. When she breathed out he remained in her body, filling up her lungs. She wasn't in control. As he squeezed still harder, she knew this was final. He'd closed his arms around her, and left no air. This time his stay would be forever.

# THIRTY-THREE

What R U up to honeybird? Still awake? xx Sent: 03-March-2003 22:12:05
Wide awake 4 U *mon ange* xx Sent: 03-March-2003 22:12:57
U rock me baby aaaall niiiight loooong
B with me now my flower man xx
And U my queen B
Buzz buzz buzz xx
Crazy about your sugar, sugar mama
Branches of a tree, birds in a nest, peas in a pod
Shall I compare thee to a summer's day? xx
The garden of love is green without limit
U R strawberry mango guava peach

And U my green man
My iris lily night scented stocks
U John Brown me Queen Vic
A rose is a rose is a rose is U
Will dream of U 2night xx
Sleep well my sweet lady xx
And U my chevalier xxxxxxxxxxx

Next morning when he woke James checked his watch. Holding it up to the window he could just make out the clock face. The fingers were pointing down. He thought about Beth as he rose and drew back the curtains. He missed her. Picturing her mouth, he heard her voice faintly, like music remembered. The restaurant came back, with the feel of her body, close up, dancing. She was soft and smooth and hot to touch. Pulling on his dressing gown he imagined their next meeting and what they'd say. He'd ask and she'd reply directly, without hesitation. He missed her face, her quick shy smiles and hands held out, her clear-eyed answers.

He realised on the landing how much things had changed. Up till now he'd believed in mutual self-interest, in a calculated relationship where both sides made bids, held their ground then settled in the middle on what they called fair shares. With Sandra, it had been like that. All about balance and space and lines of agreement. They'd needed rules – then, of course, broken them. But now, quite suddenly, he'd returned to that place where the waiting ends, someone walks in and the couples start dancing.

In the shower he sang an on-the-road song. Though inside the flow, he sang quietly, in snatches, staying cool. In the bedroom, while dressing, he mimed to the mirror, playing air guitar. He enjoyed it as drama. This one was for everyone, his workday blues. On the steps down to the kitchen he high-fived and waved, imagined Hannah's comments, then smiled to himself as he switched to adult.

As he boiled the kettle his thoughts returned to Beth. She intrigued him. She made him think of candles and letters and poems in a drawer. Her goodness showed through. When they were apart he could still feel her in the room, a woman who spoke to him with back and forth messages, dream stuff, youth talk, kisses.

Picking up his phone, he examined the screen. He wondered what to say. Oddly, he could feel her. She was waiting for a message, or so he imagined, maybe at a table, reading his letters. A song went through his head, *Sun, sun, sun, here it comes.* Looking outside he could see it, beginning, a half-arc to the horizon. As his fingers touched the keys another line came back, *Little darling it feels like years* ... Not that it had been really, he thought.

When James pressed Send, the song was repeating, the sky was clear and their day was just beginning.

Morning oh girl oh!
*Bonjour. Comment ça va?* xx
Blue skies. Bright eyes. Coffee cup. *Et toi?*
Accounts. Invoices. Calculator. Ugh!
Just to try and earn a dollar (SHOUT girl HOLLER)
Working for a living
Yeah oh yeah. Bittersweet xx
What U doing 2day?
Down with the kids digging borders
With crazy K? xx
If and when he shows. No holding breath.
Love U. Have 2 work now xx
Get down! Me 2. Love love love xx

All that morning Beth was lit up. She carried out her tasks quickly, thinking of him. When Sarah entered the café, Beth greeted and planned the day ahead but didn't mention James. Partly she was shy – it seemed so sudden and hard to explain – but also Sarah might jump in and ask awkward questions.

Returning to the laptop she filled in her spreadsheet, feeling that today nothing could touch her. Hearing Sarah singing in the kitchen she tried out a few words, poetic expressions, running through her head. The words were enduring, she'd used them in letters and, though familiar, she felt their truth. She heard them, repeated with emphasis, filling up the song. They were all about love.

As Beth went around laying tables she thought back to their meeting. She remembered how she'd stepped in from the cold, and the wait inside. She could still feel herself glowing. Frame by frame, she ran through what had happened. His hand on her shoulder, their talk, his sudden invitation then circling the floor with the chorus starting up, *Oh show me heaven, cover me leave me breathless, oh show me heaven please.*

Holding a water jug she toured the room, topping up vases. The flowers had lasted: she'd selected them carefully at the weekend market. They were white and cream and faintly scented. Touching their softness made her think of him.

During the morning she unpacked orders and took turns in the kitchen. The café was quiet and when Sarah offered, she left her to serve and went outside with an apple and a sandwich.

On the footpath to the beach she sat down on a rock. Eating slowly, she looked out to sea. Since his first visit the weather had changed. The wind had dropped and the sun had come out. She remembered his remark about *Primavera*. He'd be in the garden working with his students. The kids, he'd said, were OK. It amazed her really the way he told it, joking about tags and criminal records. It underlined the difference between them. While she'd been on her own, dreaming of passages from a half-finished novel, he'd walked in. There was edge there and excitement, but uncertainty as well. And all of a sudden she wanted to hold him.

Taking out her phone, she held back, thinking. She wondered why she'd not told Sarah. Maybe it showed she didn't want to share him. Part of her was out there, felt the connection, and didn't want him spoilt. He was her flame: a quick, bright flicker, a light she'd walked into, concealed within her heart. And she loved him absurdly.

As she turned back to the phone remembering their dance song, his text arrived.

What U doing now crazy gal? xx
Lunch break sun by the sea holidayish

Sunny here no students (K ill!) thinking of U
Can C us walking madcap in rain. *Lover's Leap* from me 2 U xx
My my my. Loonie is good. xx
U2 love is the sweetest thing
Have U seen narcissi? White orange yellow gold
Dancers. They flash upon the inward eye xx
Good 4 names. U and Me. Milk and Honey. Billet Doux.
U know all their names?
Some. Lemon Belle. Lollipop. Lucky Dip xx
I can C U now Adam digging xxxxx
Who was then a gentleman? PS This Sunday outing 2 garden?
Oh yes. U decide where. Take me there.
Thinking. Kissing. C U Sun xxxx

# THIRTY-FOUR

During her marriage Beth kept up by telephone and letter with her school friends, arranging meetings where they shared their feelings, talking about home life and work life, and how they'd changed.

From the start their stories, and views on couples, made her think. Theirs were the voices that she heard in her head urging her to stand up. They told her to ask questions, be critical and measure what was happening. They also told her that she'd been treated badly: a thought she blocked, fearing it would show. But the voices returned, creeping into everything, whatever she did. They filled up a gap. And though they disturbed her, her friends' remarks, heard in the dark, couldn't be ignored. Looking back later, she realised that they'd helped her.

Of the four, she saw Meg the most. They'd kept in touch, going out to films and theatre and, after long engagements, acting as brides-maids, giving thanks for their blessings while helping with straps and adjusting hairdos.

After their weddings, when they met in a café, they both brought pictures. "Let's see yours," Meg said, leaning forward as her friend pulled out a plastic wallet. It was good to talk on their own.

"They're only a selection," Beth said, clearing a space on the table-top. "Most of these were taken by my brother," she added, spreading them out.

"Ah," said Meg, "you must be pleased."

"I am, though I haven't looked at them properly yet."

Meg examined the snaps. "Do you mind if I group them?"

Beth agreed. While she went the toilet, Meg held them to the light, matching and comparing, laying out two piles, with one photo kept separate.

"I see you've been busy," said Beth when she returned.

Nodding, Meg picked up a picture from the first pile. "See, the church ones are so-o-o romantic."

"You think so?" asked Beth, fingering a back view of herself with her dad. "Maybe she's running for it."

Meg laughed. "And here she comes again, the blushing bride." This time she pointed to a scene from the second group. It showed Beth in her bedroom half made-up, peering closely at the order of service.

It was when they turned to the separate photo that Beth, thinking it through afterwards, realised that something wasn't right. When she saw it, she recognised her pose, and the fear of going under. It had been taken by her dad a day before the wedding. In it she was kneeling by the font with her face cast down, reflected in water. The picture was romantic, a young woman waiting, or praying, in late-Victorian style. But what touched Beth – and, perhaps, her dad – was the sadness of the picture.

At the end of their meet-up the photos went back to the white-yellow wallet. Beth kissed her friend and then carried them off. Slipped in between plastic they felt, already, part of something invisi-ble. They remained there hidden, at the bottom of a drawer, only ever viewed behind closed doors when she told herself stories, alone with her feelings, on their wedding anniversary.

Years later she expressed it in a letter to Meg. Written late at night, it began with messages from the girls, then news about friends and parents, mentioning illness and matters of faith, then shifted abruptly.

She reminded Meg of the photo by the font. Asking for God's forgiveness and confessing how she struggled, she declared her unhappiness then admitted that she didn't know what to say. Finally, writing slowly, she shared her thoughts about the picture.

She wrote:

INTERCESSION

O Lord, hear my prayer.

Put your gentle arms around this girl. Whisper in her ear. Bring her close to the fullness of your love. Deliver her from loss, make her whole. Roll back the fears, raise her, lead her, tell her to stand up.

O Lord, hear my prayer.

Return her to life. Do not allow her promise to be taken and nothing given; but, hand-in-hand, show her the way. Give love, breathe life; lift her, gently.

O Lord, hear my prayer.

Comforter, Inspirer, Face-to-Face God, touch her there. Release her from the wait in darkness. Open your arms and move her to be strong. Warm her, delight her in your spirit, and in the flesh. Be with this girl, this woman, all-known, knowing, and known by you.

O Lord, hear my prayer.

Beth soon came to realise, when she met up with Amy and Rachael, that most of their talk was about money. They described themselves as ordinary, middle-income, and not at all showy. Compared to some, their needs were simple. All they really wanted was to wine and dine and have nice things, to spend and be happy. And being well off, even though they denied it, kept them on the lookout. Whatever was current – must-have clothes, tasteful decorations, handbags and accessories – it was never enough.

In the world they lived in, it seemed that everything was, or should be, theirs for the taking. So Amy was settled with well-schooled children, lived nicely in a beautiful house and went on holidays in Crete and Corfu, but wasn't at all pleased by the cost of her weekly shop-up. And Rachael had a liking for the latest gadgets, buying them from mags and changing them monthly. She called them her play-things, joking loudly she was OD-ed again on all her cards.

When they met up over coffee Beth listened carefully. She could tell, although they didn't say it, they saw her as odd. A church mouse woman married to a man of the cloth. She suspected when they left they'd talk about her as if she'd missed out. Because for them, she realised, it was obvious, a husband was a catch. His job was to provide. If he was fit he had to be sweet-talked, given his head then harnessed. In their world men liked *doing* things, the challenge was to train them.

"Blokes have to be handled," Rachael said, raising her voice. They were sat inside a roped-off area watching shoppers crossing an echo-ey, glass-roofed square. It was afternoon, the mall was busy and the air was full of music and passing conversations.

"And good to look at," called Amy, nodding towards an advert showing a larger-than-life sportsman.

"It's how you speak to them," Rachael replied, eyeing the advert. "You have to make what you want ab-so-lute-ly clear." She glanced sideways, checking on Beth and smiling encouragement. "You OK?" she asked. When her friend smiled back, she returned to sipping from her cup.

"Is your husband like that?" asked Beth, pointing to the picture. The sportsman was wearing a skin-tight outfit, padded in places. She knew he was a racing driver but not the name, and didn't want to ask.

Rachael laughed. "That's my man." She paused, examining Beth carefully, "Not really, of course."

Beth studied the man in the advert. He was blank-faced and serious with a slight twist of the mouth. Staring straight over the shoppers' heads, he seemed to belong to another age. She could see him in a film, giving orders as a Roman emperor.

"They like to be heroes," said Amy, rolling her eyes. "You have to laugh. They're all in the business of playing Terminator."

"Or Brad Pitt," added Rachael, pulling out a magazine.

"But yours is different?" asked Beth.

"Yes, as long as I remind him who he is, daily."

Beth held her gaze. Behind the bravado, her friend was reaching out. "So how do you do that?"

Rachael hesitated then held up a page from her magazine. It pictured models in black wearing expensive jewellery. "See this," she said pointing to a filigree necklace with a single iris-like stone. "If I ask him nicely, he tells me I can have anything. So I choose the best."

"Hey, that's top of the range," said Amy, scanning the small print. "Did he really say you could have that?"

Rachael confirmed then offered the catalogue to Beth. Suddenly her voice tone dropped, as if they were one-to-one. "I know it's not your sort of thing, but I do think it shows something."

*Yes, but what?* thought Beth, glancing at the pictures. There were stones in rings, on chains, embedded in bracelets and set into clothes. At the bottom of each page, they were shown in close-up. Blue-white and purple, or pink and glowing, they shone from within. She had to admit they were beautiful.

Handing back the magazine, Beth took a breath. "So, is he the man for you?" Behind her question was alarm. Was it really like this in people's marriages?

"Oh, Guy? He's a good man. I know. He respects me."

Amy grinned. "You can tell from his eyes. He looks at you that way."

"And he cares about you?" Beth asked, leaning forward.

"He knows how to keep me happy."

"But does he ever say I love you?"

"Oh no, he'd never say anything like that. It's in his actions."

"You mean buying expensive things?" Beth pointed to the catalogue.

Rachael laughed. "Yes. It's like that song, *diamonds are a girl's best friend.*"

"So, he plays by the rules."

Rachael confirmed. She stirred her coffee and smiled. "What you have to do is make a man understand ev-er-y-thing you want. Money, love, sex or whatever, as long as he gives it to you, then that's fine."

She gazed quietly at the photo of the necklace. "That way, what you get is what you want."

"It's a fact," put in Amy, "they have to be told." Checking her watch, she announced she had to go. "Keeps them on their toes," she added, glancing up at the picture of the sportsman.

Beth looked too. She knew he was important, people admired him, but to her, although he was up there, he wasn't of much interest. She saw him as a boy, coming first, winning races; he was all self-confidence and watch-me poses.

"Ready?" asked Rachael, closing her magazine.

"Or not …" Beth said, and her disappointment made her smiley.

When they left, the concourse had cleared and the high glass roof had darkened. The three of them moved across the square, talking. It wasn't till the door that Beth remembered something about the sportsman. It came back in a flash. Now she realised why all through their talk she'd felt him watching. His surname was Conrad.

But of all Beth's friends it was the one she saw the least who registered most.

Charlie Vass and her got together twice. The first was when Beth was taking time out, meeting at a music venue. To her the place felt exposed, but intimate as well. A lights-down basement full of talk and passion that her friend seemed to like. Charlie knew people, or they knew her because she'd been with a band touring America sleeping in hotels and living, she said, on chocolate and pills. For a while, she'd rubbed shoulders with celebs: men she'd fought off, sworn at, slept with and ended calling friends.

But Beth noticed how, despite her talk, Charlie wanted more. At quiet moments, she spoke of finding love. Backstage, all night, on the road, she'd been out there, looking. The street talk was her B-side, adopted for effect.

"It's weird, really," Charlie said, filling up her glass. "You should see me, I'm all over the place. I hate being mouthy, but I do it."

Then for most of the evening, Charlie talked tough. Beth listened patiently while she spoke about addiction and burn-out and ego and people being real. Near the end, they chatted about childhood and

Beth, when asked about Conrad, described her feelings. Then Charlie left, saying they must meet again.

After that she'd gone to ground. At first Beth thought her friend might be busy so she wrote a newsy letter, but nothing came back. As time went on she began to suspect that Charlie wasn't interested. Perhaps she'd been offended? Maybe she'd thought better and decided to cut off? But also there was the worry that something had happened, that Charlie was hurt or ill or even on the run. All she had to go on was her remembered voice and gestures. So for two years there was nothing. Then a birthday card arrived, and Beth was relieved. It was followed, at odd intervals, by a box containing sweets, some heart-shaped earrings, a child's worry doll and then, a year later, by a phone call from the station asking to meet up.

Beth, when she lifted the receiver, recognised the voice. She hadn't forgotten the stories, and had prayed for Charlie often, at bedtime and in the dark. In any case she was curious, and they met within the hour, sharing breakfast in *The Shorespot Café*.

Her first impression was that her friend had changed. Charlie seemed stronger and less hyped-up. "Now, let's talk men," she said, after touring the building and catching up. "So, Beth, yours is a reverend?"

"He's a low-church minister."

"You mean he's a happy-clappy?"

"Not exactly, he has his convictions, important ones."

"But he believes in saving people like me?"

"No. I think, in fairness, he does a lot to help people, no strings attached."

Charlie threw one end of a black-gold scarf across her shoulder. "All right, tell me then, what does he do to help you?"

"He tries."

"But what does he do?"

"Prays and takes services, visits people, goes around other church-es …"

"Who comes first, you or God?"

Beth felt her face tighten. "I really don't think that's a fair question."

"From the way you say that, there's something wrong."

Beth's eyebrows shot up.

"I know," said Charlie, "I've been studying with a psychic counsellor." She tugged at a purple-dyed plait woven into her hair. "Now, tell me, how does he treat you?"

Beth lowered her head, "Not badly."

"But not well?"

"I don't really know."

"Would you say he loves you? Really loves you, from the heart."

Beth declined to answer. Her forehead was hot and her palms felt swollen. Voices in the air were telling her to end this now.

"Or is he too busy with himself and being a minister?" Charlie was sitting back twisting the tassels of her scarf. Her darkly-shadowed eyes were closely attentive. "I can see there's an answer, you don't want to give." Suddenly she lifted the scarf above her head, leaned forward and wrapped it around her friend. "There, that'll help. Keep it. It'll protect you."

"Oh, but I can't."

"It's yours now, a gift."

"Really, I can't."

Charlie continued to watch her friend. She was speaking gently. "You've been upset by my words – is that right?"

Beth blushed.

"But you know, if you're honest with yourself, what I said is true." When Beth lowered her eyes, Charlie pointed at the scarf: "Go on, I'd like you to have it. Please."

Beth felt the cloth, it was super-soft and silky. She thought of saying no, but gratitude won out. "Thank you," she said as she adjusted it on her shoulders. "It's beautiful," she added, fingering the tassels, "like a prayer shawl."

As she watched Charlie leave, Beth touched the scarf, hearing a line from Keats sounding in her head.

When Conrad saw the scarf, he glowered. "What's that you're wearing?" he said, blocking the doorway. He was bright-faced and sweaty, just back from his run.

"It's a scarf, from a friend."

Closing the door, he stood and stared before peeling off his shoes and climbing heavily upstairs. He moved slowly, as if he'd been injured. Beth could hear a few heavy thumps and the swish of running water. The pipes rattled until the flow cut off, followed by silence. When the bolt shot back, she jumped. Taking a breath, she checked in the mirror: the image told her she was still there. She shook her head then, opening a cupboard, laid out breakfast.

When Conrad reappeared he was wearing a white shirt and grey flannel trousers. His expression was thin-lipped and very 1950s. Squeezing his long-limbed body between the table and the wall, he said grace and allowed her to serve him.

"Black and gold," he said frowning, as he put down his toast. Beth remained silent, waiting. She could tell that inside himself he was asking for guidance.

He rose, avoiding her eye. It was as if he needed to escape from what he saw. "From Charlene?" he asked, staring at the scarf. Wondering how he knew, Beth nodded. A wish to say something – anything – pushed into her head. She was about to speak when Conrad cut in. His voice filled the room. "Not her," he said, moving to the door, "not from that woman. Be warned, not her." As he stepped out, he repeated loudly, using her friend's full name. "Don't wear it," he added, standing in the hallway, then left.

The girls, on the other hand, liked it. Naomi called the colours cool and when Rose touched it she smiled. "It's lovely," she said, "like my friend's cat." Their approval was a lift. So she folded the scarf into her jacket pocket and kept it hidden, close to her body. In there, it gave her protection. Occasionally, when asked, she showed her daughters, but only for them, when they were alone.

But Conrad had his suspicions, and when he finally caught her, made his views known. "I particularly ask," he said stiffly, pointing to the scarf, "that you respect my feelings." He'd surprised Beth at the bottom of the garden where she went some evenings on her own. Thinking he was out, she'd left the girls to watch TV, slipped on her jacket and sneaked down the path. Guided by the house lights, she'd reached the corner seat and sat there, looking at the sky. It was quiet and cool and darkly poetic. She'd just pulled out the scarf when Conrad appeared.

His voice made her jump. It was as if he'd been there all along, hidden by the hedge. When she didn't reply, he flared up. "Give," he said, flicking his hand open. Beth stood up, saying nothing. "Give," he repeated, wriggling his fingers. Her lips had parted, showing her teeth. "I said *give*," he insisted, but his voice had thinned and his hand had closed up.

Beth cleared her throat then slowly raised the scarf. She stood there for a second at full stretch, staring into dark. "There," she said, dropping it. "Have it." The scarf slid sideways, caught on the hedge and hung there by a corner. "It's yours," she said quietly, stepping around and beyond him. As she walked up the path she could feel his presence. He was there behind her, watching. When she reached the house, he called, but she didn't turn back. Even at the doorway, when she heard her name and what sounded like *come back*, she went in without turning.

Next morning looking out, Beth saw that the scarf had gone. After breakfast she went outside to check around the hedge, finding nothing. Thinking back, she'd not seen it with Conrad. She was fairly sure he hadn't brought it in, but while he was out running she looked around the bedroom. Again, she drew blank. When he returned, she didn't want to ask; it was better she thought, after last night, to leave him be. But to her surprise Conrad asked over breakfast if she knew where it had gone. He spoke quietly with an inquiring smile.

Later when Rose asked after it, Beth said she didn't know. When Naomi pressed her she said it must have walked. "It's a mystery," she told them both as if it didn't matter. She did look again but, despite her search, it was nowhere to be found – except, perhaps, in her thoughts about Charlie.

But when she told Meg her feelings came back. "I was sad to lose it," she said as they climbed past the clock tower to the upper town gardens. "Charlie gave it, to protect me."

"That was kind," said Meg. She glanced quickly across the flower-beds. They were end-of-year and straggly.

"Conrad seemed to know who it was from," Beth said, passing through a gap in a low wall. "I'm not sure how."

Meg's face tightened. "I hope he's not—"

"Not what?"

"Oh, doing detective stuff, like listening on the phone or reading diaries."

"Conrad isn't like that. He wouldn't."

"No, I wasn't serious. That's for books."

"Well, I was upset when the scarf went."

"Have you any idea what happened to it?"

Beth shook her head.

"Perhaps he took it?"

Beth's head went back. "Really, I don't think—"

"You said there was an argument. He didn't want you to have it."

"I'd know if Conrad had taken it."

"But how do you know? He might've done it without you seeing. Because if it's really bad between you …"

Beth glanced round, seeking help. "Well, if that's so, I'm a bit to blame myself."

Meg stopped at a viewpoint. "You sure of that?" she asked. Below them some winding wooden steps dropped steeply down the hillside.

Beth looked out. Her friend's questioning came as a surprise. She and Meg were sharers: they swopped experiences, spoke the same language and read the same books. On almost everything they backed each other up. "You don't agree?" she asked.

"You take too much on yourself."

Looking down beyond the steps, Beth could see a line of shrubs and *The Shorespot Café*. A few faint wisps of cloud had gathered on the roof. "I do that?"

"Definitely." Meg moved closer. "Remember the photo, the one by the font."

Beth shivered. "Ah yes, I wrote about that."

"Your intercession?"

Beth compressed her lips.

"When I read that, I prayed for you."

"You did? Oh, thank you."

"I prayed every day after that. I didn't want to tell you, but I had you on my list for ages."

They embraced silently. When they separated, Beth looked back along the path. "Maybe, if you'd said … but I suppose you didn't know how I'd take it." She forced a smile. "When it's bad, it's easier just to close your eyes, forget about things and pretend it isn't happening."

"You needed help."

"But you've already helped me. A lot with the girls."

"No, Beth, *you* need help. In yourself."

"I do?"

"Definitely."

"Well, yes. I think maybe I do."

"You really shouldn't be so unhappy. It's not your fault."

Beth gazed out to sea. A soft grey haze was spreading over water. She felt it advancing. For a long time now, it had been creeping up. This, she could tell, was a quiet kind of crisis. "So what should I do?"

"It depends on how strong you feel."

They stood there in silence. The sea was still, the sky had closed up and the air was cold. Fine threads of mist were filling up the hollows.

Beth turned away. Her voice, when it came, didn't sound like hers. "You think I should leave him, don't you …"

"Maybe," said Meg, facing forward. "If you can."

"There isn't any other way?"

Meg shook her head. The mist now had covered the bottom of the steps.

Beth looked down. She felt invisible, and cold inside herself. The white advancing tide was blotting out everything.

"I suppose," she said, bleakly, "that's what I'll have to do."

But first, she had to see her dad.

She used, as an excuse, his recent condition. He'd caught a dose of flu that she announced, not untruthfully, might still be on him. She knew Conrad didn't like illness, claiming he saw too much on his rounds and didn't trust medicine, so she went without him, taking the girls.

Being on a journey was a lift. She had them to talk to and played games then slept part of the way, and when they arrived Louise was there waiting on the platform. She drove them to the house, talking cheerily and questioning the girls. It was as if they'd always been with her. When they arrived, John waved from the doorstep and everyone embraced. His welcome, though jolly, seemed slightly awkward. Noticing his stoop and his sad-happy smile, Beth realised how much she missed him. She'd not kept up.

Over the weekend, Naomi and Rose came first. Louise took charge, laying on hard-boiled eggs, jam sandwiches and bottled fizz, with elasticated hats and 3D glasses. Her taste was traditional, but the girls seemed to like it. They went with her to turn out cupboards and put on masks, wearing backless shoes and pleated dresses. They looked at old photos, picking out groups and asking about names. They even allowed Louise to read out loud from her mother's books, laughing at the outdated talk and sketchy pictures. With no one watching, they forgot their ages and played at being girlie.

Being back with her parents made Beth happier. They both seemed to know just what she wanted. With Louise making space and John there listening, she could have her say. And her opportunity came when she walked out with her dad, taking a route she'd followed on her runs.

"How's Conrad?" John asked, as they skirted a cornfield. Tall and slight, he moved quite slowly, almost as if he was half-asleep. He looked quite sad, but his eyes were quick and alive.

"He's at home," replied Beth, dryly.

They stopped by a cattle trough. On the other side, tyre tracks had cut a trench along the side of the field. A red burst of poppies showed above the wheat.

"And how is he?"

At first her answer wouldn't come. She remembered her runs. At that time she'd been younger and had done everything she could, but now she needed air – air and light, and someone to talk to.

"He's all …" She cut herself off. "You know, Dad, I want to be honest with you."

John stopped and peered over his glasses. "That's what you must be, my love."

"It's not nice, Dad, not nice at all."

"You mean you're having difficulties?"

"It's something we both struggle with."

"Then let's walk and talk. And don't hold back."

They set out, following the line of the trench. It led to a low hedge. Beyond the hedge was another field that was bare and stony and full of weeds. As they passed through a gate a flight of pigeons rose and circled.

For Beth, his presence helped her say things. She talked about their honeymoon, the day-to-day frictions, Conrad's demands, his putdowns and dismissals, followed by the silence. "It's impossible," she ended. "Either he either ignores me completely, or he's finding fault."

"I know," John replied.

"You know?"

"Yes, it was always difficult."

"You realised all along …"

"Your mother and I could see you were unhappy."

"When was that?"

"Oh, when you visited, without him."

"And then, when I stopped visiting."

Her dad remained silent.

"So, you understood, but kept it to yourselves."

"Yes. We had to, for your sake."

Beth nodded.

John took her hand. The bones of his fingers pressed lightly against her palm. It reminded her of when he'd given her away. He'd been so gentle.

"Remember the birds," he said quietly.

They looked out together across the field. The pigeons at the centre were head down, pecking for seeds. To one side a group of finches were swarming the branches of a low tree. At the far end some seagulls were rising and circling slowly, outlined by the sun.

"They all have their stories," she said, knitting her brows. Her thoughts were filling up with girlhood memories. Her gran was there together with *The Water Babies* and Rossetti's picture. In her mind's eye she could see the title of her own first story, *The Girl Who Began Again*.

John's eyes searched the field. "Like us."

"But not always happily-ever-after."

"It all depends on where you choose to stop."

"I wish I'd done that earlier."

He shook his head sadly. "As for an ending, you must decide."

Beth blushed. Even after her lack of contact, her dad was there on her side. His generosity hurt.

"I know I've not always been the best daughter," she said, "but I'm here now." Before he could answer, she drew back: "I've not been in touch, not nearly enough, and it's because of this …" she held up her hand. "Look," she said, turning her wrist to display her ring. It was silver, flattened on top and inscribed with a cross. "His choice, not mine. And useless. It never fitted. I tried hard – too hard really, and now I need to live."

John gazed at her. She was staring at her hand as if it hurt. "Very well," he said slowly, "if it doesn't fit, you know what to do."

A group of starlings passed close by. They were swooping and twittering like bats. It seemed to her they were urging her on.

Extending her finger, she rubbed and twisted till her ring came off. "Watch," she said, holding it up, "I shall give it back." She took a step forward and threw her wedding ring out, like a stone, across the field. "There. It's gone," she cried as it spun low in the air and dropped to the ground. It landed in a weed patch, kicking up dust and scattering a mass of wheeling pigeons.

They stood for a while watching. The pigeons circled then returned to their patch to resume their pecking. Their busy seesaw heads ducked and bobbed like puppets.

When Beth walked forward, the pigeons took off again. They continued circling while she crouched, pushing aside leaves. Using both hands she felt around until she brought up her ring. It was dust-streaked and grey. Squeezing hard, she fitted it back onto her finger.

She was crying.

Dear Conrad,

This letter may come as a shock. I hope not. But if it does, although this may not be easy, please read it several times. It comes from the heart.

I see this as the beginning of a new kind of relationship. A more open, honest one. As it says in Matthew, "A healthy tree cannot bear bad fruit, nor can a diseased tree bear good fruit".

For a long time now we've been out of touch. Although we share a house, children and a faith, we live as strangers, in different worlds. To me, it's like being in hiding, in a dark cave, cut off from life. As if the world out there is somewhere far away. It's a lonely, shut-in kind of place. It makes me think of Yeats's line, "Too long a sacrifice can make a stone of the heart".

I know your church life is different. I can see how it lights you up. It's what you call The Glory. But to me, light and shadow come together, and where it's dark the truth is hard to see. So please don't be angry if I say our home life is dark: very, very dark.

Before we married, we were full of light and energy, we ran together and trusted each other, living our beliefs. We were young and we were blessed. And equal in the eyes of God. I didn't agree with everything you said, but I respected your views and married with your kind of service. I wanted to make you a good wife.

But a shadow came between us. Whatever we did, we couldn't connect. Perhaps I should have reached out, made myself felt, but, starting with the honeymoon, it seemed as if everything was in your hands, and already decided. Maybe I pulled away or lost faith, but I knew you were busy and I turned towards the children.

I really didn't want to send this letter. I've been writing it for years in my head, while telling myself that it isn't true. I've tried, I really have, but now I know it is so, and I can't live this way. For years I got through by closing my eyes and blocking off. I was acting, of course. As it says in Romans 5:3, "we know that suffering produces endurance".

But denial, in the end, doesn't work. It sets up a barrier. So now I know that, right from the start, we weren't for each other. You were on a mission and I was afraid. Afraid of getting it wrong, of making mistakes and forfeiting your interest. And because of my fear I tried too hard, and did things that annoyed you.

So, I've thought and prayed, but now I know. Because I believe that if God had intended us to be together then it would have shown by now. We took a wrong turning years ago. And now we're lost, stranded in a place where God can't help.

I want us to separate.

Of course, it will be difficult. And we mustn't hurt the girls. But I do believe we have to be honest, more painfully honest than we've ever been before. If we can do that, then we'll come out stronger. Job 23:10 "when he has tried me, I shall come out as gold".

Beth

She left the letter in Conrad's Bible. It was a Saturday morning just before dawn, the girls were away and she went to work early. As she closed the door, she shivered. The letter seemed so final. Walking uphill she tried not to think, but the words of the letter kept running through her head and she wanted to go back to remove it. She could imagine him returning from his run, reading it then chasing after her. On the path to the viewpoint, she felt so exposed. As she stepped down to the café, the sky brightened and she began to slow down. Feeling a faint breeze, she stopped and looked back. There was no one following. The birds were singing and the waves were breaking quietly on the beach.

At the door Beth glanced up. *The Shorespot Café* – he'd not liked the name, said she shouldn't buy it and called it a vanity. There'd even been prayers and talk of Mammon. And yet she'd done it. Taken him on, told herself yes, made it her business. And people had liked it, she was Beth of The Caff. It felt like home.

During the day she kept herself busy. As Beth-in-charge she was brisk and cheerful, almost playful, but also the proprietor: judging, consulting, putting things in place. She laid out stock, chalked up specials, greeted everyone, cleared tables when necessary then sat down by herself to redo her spreadsheets. With her staff she was jolly, listening to all-action Sarah and agreeing shifts. With the customers, she served them with a smile. And with deliveries and enquiries her manner was attentively friendly but also managerial.

It was only later, when closing up, that she remembered the letter and her shakiness returned. She said goodbye to Sarah without revealing anything. On the way back she checked her bag and fingered her keys. Their coldness kept down the sweats. As she walked through the gardens she counted each step, trying to stay calm. Entering the town, she saw herself reflected in a shop window and wondered who she was. She prayed, too, as she walked, trying to build strength. Several times she imagined Conrad's rage, or how he broke down, asking God's help. She saw his eyes, fixed on her letter and imagined him pacing, his voice crying out. And when she arrived at the front door, she held her breath then stepped inside quickly.

The hall was quiet. As she took off her shoes she was aware of him there, somewhere hidden. The doors were all closed. Feeling like an intruder, she stood for a moment before choosing the kitchen. As she entered, the room seemed empty, but then she saw him, sitting at the table. The letter was in front of him, half out of the envelope. His eyes were closed and his hands were together. His knuckles were white.

"Conrad," she said, flatly. It seemed he'd been there, praying silently, for a very long time.

His eyes flicked open. "I say, no. It's out of the question."

"You've read it?"

Conrad stared. His long lean face was closed against her now. He'd said his piece.

"And that's what you think?"

"I said. It's impossible."

"I'd hoped …"

Conrad stood up. "Marriage is from God."

"And so is love."

"For better or for worse."

"Then you don't see the problem?"

"We must live with what we are, husband and wife."

She found herself shaking. "And that's all? This has to go on, just as it is – on and on – and that's the end of it?"

Picking up the envelope, he shoved the letter inside and held it out. "Take this," he said, "and put it with your stories."

"I didn't think …" she began.

"Because I've read enough," Conrad cut in, walking to the door. He stood there, tall and wiry, blocking the frame.

"What does that mean?" she asked, her eyebrows coming together.

Conrad's face had smoothed to a mask. Nothing here could touch him. "You're making up. Always making up." And he turned, strode into the hall and climbed the staircase without looking back.

They slept in separate rooms: Conrad sprawled full-length on the upstairs double bed, Beth curled up on the sofa. Although exhausted, she found herself lying awake, thinking. Their talk in the kitchen kept coming back. She was afraid of what he'd do, but angry as well. To be told she was making up reminded her of Jim. Like him, Conrad took advantage. She felt him prying into drawers, peering through darkness, overshadowing everything. For years he'd talked about God's call, while going behind her back. He didn't have the right.

During the night she heard him moving around. At first she just listened, plotting his movements then, as he paced round in circles, she became tetchy, wishing he'd settle; later, in the middle of the night, a creaky, scraping sound disturbed her; still later she could hear him opening a window; finally, when the cold and discomfort drove her up, she sat down in the kitchen and pulled out a notebook.

Taking a pen, she drew two columns. One was headed *Reasons to Stay* and one was headed *Leave*. Under the first she put Naomi and Rose and some capitalised words – names of qualities, a few Christian values and some crossed out feelings. Under the second she began with phrases that ran into sentences, continuing to the page opposite. When she'd finished, she realised that the writing had calmed her. Finding an envelope, she tore out both pages and slipped them in, adding a short covering note and addressing it to Meg.

Conrad, as usual, appeared at six, in time for his run. By then she'd had her breakfast and posted the letter. He was blank-faced and busy, saying nothing. As soon as he left she went to the bedroom. Taking a deep breath she stared in the mirror. The girls were at her parents' and she knew what she must do. Putting it on paper had proved it. Even so, when she pulled out the suitcase, she felt herself shaking.

She packed her clothes, her toiletries, a few books and her writings, and carried the case downstairs. Glancing at the clock, she wrote a short note. She was about to place it on the hallstand when she heard a cough outside. "Oh," she said, ducking forward as Conrad came through the door. A white mist was filling up her head.

He eyed her oddly, pulling at his top, then stepped back against the wall. "What's going on?" he asked, staring at the suitcase. Beth shivered.

"You can't be," he whispered. His face had creased and fallen. One hand was shifting uneasily across wallpaper.

"I'm going," she said, moving towards the case.

"You're leaving?"

She nodded.

"Going – leaving – now?"

"I've decided."

"No, no. You can't," he said, lunging forward and taking the handle. "You mustn't," he hissed, "I won't allow it," and he pushed past her, carrying the case. "It's all wrong." He was shouting now, calling out to an invisible audience. "Don't let her do this!"

Conrad turned on his heel, strode through the kitchen and out into the garden. As he headed down the path, she followed to the door. She was watching a scene that seemed unreal, yet couldn't be ignored; it forced itself on her, like the climax to a film. And he was playing lead role.

Reaching the bench, she saw him stop. He sat down abruptly with his hands together and his body bent forward. He was staring at the ground. For a moment she'd a feeling that they'd been here before. Maybe he was ill. She had to stop herself from calling out. Flashing back to a run where he'd thrown up, she stepped into the garden. It was when he began to rock and his shoulders started shaking that she realised that he was crying.

As she approached the bench, she felt the white mist, gathering inside. It chilled her right through. The case was by his feet and she wondered whether to take it. Part of her feared him and part of her wished she could make him understand.

"Conrad," she said quietly, standing a yard off.

He looked up. "No," he answered. His face set firm as he stood up, holding the suitcase. "You must go," he said sternly, pushing the case towards her. Beth hesitated, eyeing his hand. "Go, go," he repeated, irritable now. Taking the handle, she felt the touch of his fingers, then the jerk along her arm. As the weight pressed down, she turned and lifted, using both hands. Holding it at chest height, like a shield, she began walking.

"Goodbye," she said hoarsely and found herself crying. She was worn and shaky, but relieved. In her mind she could see the gravel path ahead, the road out to the station and, somewhere in the background, the last few strands of mist clearing.

Behind her she heard a voice calling out. The words were from a sermon. They brought back the darkness, the door shut, and the wait at the window. As she walked, the voice seemed to follow her. It was her master, calling. The voice was requiring her to turn back. "For a spirit of harlotry has led them astray," it cried, "departing from their God."

Beth walked.

# THIRTY-FIVE

The garden outing took Beth and James west on byroads, through unfamiliar countryside. They steered between hedgerows with blossom and green-leaf-shows, across single-track bridges, past cow pools and gates and piled-up manure – then up through gorse to drive along the hilltops with a view out to sea.

James drove while Beth checked the food, changed the CDs and map-read. Inside, she was warm and tingly. Already it seemed they'd come a long way.

The ridgetop route led to a square of gravel and a viewpoint. Here they left the car, walking forward with the wind in their faces. Two metal poles guarded the drop. "Like Thomas Hardy!" she called, pointing to cloud-shaped shadows spreading over downland.

James looked out. The hills were soft-sloped, with dry gulley strips and clumped-together thorns. At the bottom they were green, above that brown, streaked white in places, and treeless. He held up an imaginary camera: "And then, Julie Christie runs into view. L-o-n-g take."

"James."

"I'm only kidding."

She scanned the view. "Don't spoil things, it's beautiful."

"You're right." He took her by the hand and they began to walk. The sun came and went and the wind cooled their faces. "Do we know the name of this hill?" he asked as they followed the ridge, arriving at a circle of earthworks.

"I think it's called *The Castle*," she said as they passed between mounds. Her focus was ahead: this was her time.

The path they were following was chalk-white and deeply rutted. James led to one end where they looked out across a crater-shaped drop, bisected by tracks. Beyond that there were roads and undulating farmland. The sky was clear and they could see to the coast, and beyond that the thin grey horizon.

"Up here!" he said, pointing to a steep-sided mound. They scrambled to the top, reaching a flat patch with a few scattered rocks. "We're kings of the castle. Or queens!"

The wind was beating up the hillside, colouring Beth's cheeks and tugging at her hair. "It's like a fairground," she called, circling her arm.

"How do you mean?"

"All rather wild and windy and crazy."

"Yes, I can see that. Anything else?"

She paused, eyeing the slope. "Well, you feel, if you could leap, the wind might carry you down. Or up, up, into the clouds."

James followed her gaze, sighting a group of seabirds. They were wheeling and turning in loose formation. "That's the way to be," he said quietly.

She stepped to the edge. "Effortless, aren't they."

"You wonder how they do it. They just seem to hang there, as if they're afloat."

"Or asleep."

"Sweet … dream … babies."

"Well, perhaps. But they are *gulls*."

"I meant the song. How long must I dream, and so on."

"I suppose, looked at that way, they are a bit dreamy."

They stood, leaning on each other and swaying slightly. As James touched her cheek, Beth turned to face him. The wind blew raw and gentle around her face as she whispered his name. Their heads came together and suddenly they were kissing.

At the end of their drive they passed the main gate, turning after a mile at a notice saying *Deanbury Sculpture Gardens II*. The sun was shining and the air was fresh. After parking they paid at a kiosk then followed a signpost directing to the *Walkers' Way*. Starting down a path between shrubs and bushes, they came across a high rainbow arch, cast in steel. It was stem-like and twisted, painted all over, and resembled a bouquet. "That's great," exclaimed Beth. "Looks Art Nouveau."

James ran his hand across its smoothly-curved surfaces. "If you look up here," he said, pointing, "it's got a row of eyelashes."

"You what – eyelashes?"

"Eyelashes."

"Well, I don't know about that. Aren't they supposed to be branches?"

James shrugged. "It's hard to tell."

"Maybe they're both."

"It's possible." There was a lilt in his voice. "You could use them to climb it."

"Climb it?"

"Why not? It can be done."

Beth rolled her eyes. "Not me, but you could try. Even better, you could *imagine* it. That way it's bound to come off."

James measured her with a look.

"You don't think so?"

He pointed upwards. "It's an idea. Jack did it with the Beanstalk."

Beth smiled to herself.

"Now you see me, now you don't," he added, taking her hand.

"You'd like to try?"

"Don't know about that." James drew her to him. "I'd probably fall off."

They hugged, laughing, then stepped on and through to a sun-dappled wood. The light came in drifts, filling up the gaps. "What's it make you think of?" he asked.

She peered both sides. The trees were still bare, there was moss between them, and fallen leaves. Small spikes of green were sprouting from the branches. She thought of her dad and talking in the garden. "A poem – or story, maybe."

"Like Goldilocks?"

They had reached a grey, weather-boarded house with shuttered windows. It was built in two halves, high at the front, sloping away to a brick-built extension. A handwritten notice outside said *Woodland Cottage*. Suddenly Beth had a feeling of being watched, as if they'd entered into someone else's territory.

"Looks more like the house that Jack built," added James.

She shushed him as a broad, bent-backed man appeared wearing a padded jacket. He was shuffling sideways, carrying a spherical object. When he reached the path, he lowered it with a grunt and straightened, wiping his hands down his jacket.

"First time visitors?" he asked.

Beth confirmed. Beside her, James touched his forehead in a mock salute.

"I hope you enjoy this," the man said, glancing at the sphere. "It's *art*."

"High or low?" James called. He seemed to be addressing the object.

"You're thinking of music?" asked Beth looking puzzled,

"Art," replied James. He turned to the man. "Does it have a name?"

The man pulled out a programme to check. "*Child's Play III* – by someone called A."

"Sounds like a pop group," said James. "German, electronic."

Beth smiled. She could see him, head down at the keyboard, pumping chords.

"It says here it follows from Parts I and II," the man said, scratching his head. "You see I'm not much for art myself, but I reckon ..." He paused, eyeing Beth.

"Go on," she prompted.

"Well, it's not what it looks. You try. Touch it."

Beth ran her hand gently across the surface. "Am I imagining, or is it warm?"

"And smooth as well," James said, standing by her. "Baby's bottomish."

"I choose not to hear that."

"Struck from the record – yes?"

"With immediate effect." Beth turned to the man. "Do you know what it's made of?"

The man checked the programme. "It says here, graphene."

"But it feels like stone," James objected. "And what about the heat?"

"Some sort of mixture. I'm told it has chemicals stored inside."

James and Beth circled the ball. As they looked, sunlight touched it, revealing vein-like markings. Its surface was criss-crossed with hair-line tracks. "It's alive in a way," she said, "like an egg."

The sun disappeared and the ball turned grey.

"If you try playing doctor," said James, cupping the surface, "you can feel something. I don't know what it is, but it's alive *and* it's rock, or something like. It's all a bit left-field."

Beth placed her hands next to his. They both watched as the sunlight returned in a pink-white glow. "Yes, it feels organic," she said as the colour advanced, reaching her fingers.

The man nodded. "There are more. You'll see, if you follow the path." For a second he stood, outlined by the sun. "And they're all *arty*," he said, looking off. When the sun went in, he straightened his shoulders and walked back towards the cottage. At the door, he stripped off his jacket, hung it on a nail then disappeared round the back. In his absence, the stone had lost all colour.

"He was absolutely right," said James as they toured the garden. They'd seen several curved pink-grey stones appearing at intervals along the path.

"Looks like they've just landed," he said, walking the line. At the end he touched Beth's arm. "Do you think they're watching us?"

Beth shook her head. Her face was lit by sun. At her feet, a disc-shaped artwork was glowing faintly.

James turned. "Would you do something for me?"

"Well, if I can. What do you have in mind?"

"It's something you've *talked* about …"

"Oh yes?"

He pointed to a grassy hollow beyond the trees. It was soft and smooth and screened on two sides by bushes. "If we went over there, would you dance, like you do round the café?"

"You mean with you watching?"

"Yes, if you're willing."

"I could. I really don't mind. But I'd need to warm up."

James reached out. "Textbook method, of course." He drew her to him, kissing once, twice, a third time, then pulled back.

"Very well," she said quietly, looking in his eyes.

With his arm around her waist they began to walk. When they reached the hollow they waited while a couple passed then Beth stepped forward. She put down her bag, kicked off her shoes and took up position next to a clump of white and yellow daffodils.

Her dance began, arms in the air, stretching and turning both ways. With James as audience, her body came alive. She'd entered, it seemed, a marked-out space where she shifted foot to foot, waving slowly. The wave became a drift as she advanced, before stepping back, bowing slightly. "Imagine …" she said casually, extending once more, arms up, shaping an arch. Her fingers touched then fell to her sides.

Returning to first position, she flexed her shoulders and rocked side to side. "Just be," she said, glancing at James.

Gradually her dance widened; her arms, her legs, everything about her was signalling. She was at her best.

Reaching climax, she paused and drew breath. From here it was simple. The dance took over with a few backsteps towards the hedge then, touching the flowers, a full-body sweep and heel-down to a stop, facing James.

His applause brought her back. "That was great," he said.

Beth stood still, with one hand on her side.

"You out of breath?"

"Just a little."

He waited then asked if she'd had lessons. When Beth shook her head, he laughed. "But surely you must be following steps?"

"Not really, I just do what comes. Of course, being outside helps."

"But if I asked, could you do it again?"

"I could, if you joined me."

"Well in that case," he said, taking off his rucksack, "it's a deal." And he advanced, placing himself on the other side of the daffs. "You lead," he added, and stood waiting.

Beth took a breath. "You'll do as I do – yes?"

"In step, all the way."

"But now, here's an idea … Are you OK to use letters?"

"Sorry, letters?"

"Letter shapes, in the air."

"Ah, no problem."

"In that case, follow me," she said, raising her arms.

Hands above his head, he mirrored her pose.

"It begins with A," Beth called, narrowing her arms to an inverted V.

Again, James copied.

"And ends in O." She outlined a circle in the air.

James drew the same.

"Then, of course, there's B," she continued, pointing to herself, "and J, who is L who is U." Her back-and-forth gestures ended with a sweep of the hand. "Or it's a combination, ABBA or ROCK or even L-O-V-E." She spelled out each letter with a quickly-changing, double-handed gesture.

"Hey, hold on," called James, "I'm losing track."

Beth stopped. "It's all about feel. What you have to do is let go." Flicking back her hair, she crouched down to the daffodils, touching their heads. They were soft, yellow-white and fully expanded.

"So perhaps we should do our own thing," she said, fingering a stem, "that might be best."

"Or take turns."

She cupped one hand around a flower: "Yes, that's good. I'll do a letter, then you do a letter and we'll go on that way. Alphabetical, if you like."

"Right. But are we copying?"

"Not unless you want to."

"OK, let's see how we go."

In the dance that followed Beth began by calling, illustrating her letters with a move or a gesture before James took his turn. His moves were in parts – first one arm, then the other, then both-ways stepping – quickly developing to a foot-turn, a shake and a fist in the air. Hers were smooth and connected. Their styles were different, yet related.

And then, after joking about fitness and gathering breath, they changed.

"Let's try numbers," called James, leading briefly, ten down to five.

"Or dates," she said, "using fingers."

"Together, now," he said, after signalling birthdays.

"OK," she replied, "X Y Z."

Afterwards, as they walked downhill, Beth felt him by her. Being this close made her more herself, more connected and alive. She felt the air, the flowers, the green life all around. They were here together as lovers.

As they moved through the garden, the sun came and went. Unseen animals rustled in the bushes. Where the path dipped down they came across a stream trickling slowly into a brown-green pool. They stood by a bridge naming plants then crossed to a walkway laid across a bog. Here they passed by reed beds surrounded by mud. On the other side was a gate and a path uphill.

"You've been here before?" she asked, as they climbed to a view.

"Once, with the kids, and Sandra."

"Right here, with her?"

"The same." His head came up and he smiled.

"Oh look," she said, pointing downhill, "there are lots of them."

They could see, gazing down the terraced slope, a sculpture at each level. Mostly metal with wood and plastic add-ons, they were large, semi-industrial and glinted in the sun. Around them and between them in khaki and cottons, some nodding, some listening and others staring while talking on their phones, were the visitors.

"Now that's what I call popular," said James.

"Was it this busy, last time?"

"I'm not sure I remember."

She wanted him to say more, but he seemed distracted. "You don't remember anything?"

"Not much, just them running round. Oh, and Sandra talking."

"So, you haven't forgotten that."

"Certainly not." James put his head on one side. "Even at this age, some things stick."

"Yes, and some people stay with us."

"You mean the telephone ex? She goes on and on. Still does, when she can."

Beth breathed in sharply. She wondered if, behind his words, he was comparing.

"She annoys you?" he asked.

"Not exactly. Not her, really."

His eyes widened slightly. "There's a problem?"

"No, not at all. Only me," she replied, and wished she hadn't.

James stepped closer. "What is it?" He waited for a moment then touched her on the arm. "Is it something I said?"

"Not really, I think it's about this place."

"But I thought you were enjoying it."

"I am," she said shakily, "and I don't want to spoil it, but ..."

"But what?"

Suddenly her voice broke, "I keep seeing you and her. Right here, in this place. And I don't think I can make you happy." She was crying now.

James reached forward. His eyes scanned her face. "Beth, please. I've told you what it was like. It was impossible, every day a problem. This is different, and so much better, because I'm with you."

"But did you love her?" The question was a challenge.

"I told myself I did, that's why we married. But looking back, it wasn't love."

"So, what was it?"

"Convenience. And a great deal of wishful thinking."

Beth brushed one hand across her cheek and shook her head. She was swallowing hard. "But what about us? Are we OK?"

James smiled. "Really, we're a lot better than that."

"You sure?"

"Absolutely." He rocked her in his arms. "I'm with you, and don't you forget it. Absolutely." His hug was firm and gentle. It kept her with him.

"Thank you. I've been silly, haven't I?" She turned to her bag, looking for a hankie. It came out, white and lightly-scented, like a flower. Touching its softness was a help. When she'd dabbed her face, she kissed him. "It's over," she said, "I'm myself again."

"We all have our moments."

"It's when you see yourself in another person's shoes."

"But there are no repeats, you know that? Especially us."

Beth thanked him again. She packed away her hankie and checked her watch. "Shall we eat?" she asked, pointing to a flat patch with a bench. Below it the slope dropped away in terraced strips, each a platform, connected by steps.

"Well, *I'm* hungry," James said, untying his rucksack. Inside were some bagged-up savouries, an apple and a plastic food box.

Taking turns to dip into the sack, they shared the food and poured two coffee cups from a small metal flask. "Lucky dip," he said, pulling out a bag of nuts.

"I'd like some," she asked, cupping her hands.

He laughed and kissed her forehead.

They picked at the contents, one by one. The nuts came in all sizes, they were whole, lightly roasted and unsalted. Dipping and munching, they shared what they had.

Afterwards they cleared up then took the steps down the hillside. It was bright and airy and the crowds had thinned out. At each terrace level Beth and James circled the sculptures, comparing reactions. There were nameplates with signatures, usually dated, some with commentaries that they read together. A few, untitled, had the artist's name, several had signs with painted numbers, and one, near the bottom, had a plan decorated with bubble-thoughts and doodles be-hind screwed-down Perspex.

"This looks interesting," said Beth, eyeing the display board.

The sculpture was in parts, covering an area the size of a house. The gate was festive, with bunting and light bulbs strung between posts. A ramp led in to an open space. Behind it was an all-plastic dome covered in badges with a flag on top and multi-coloured, port-hole-style windows.

"It's like a kids' playground," said Beth, pausing at the entrance. Beyond the dome there were outlying sections with slides and rope nets and wooden enclosures, all at different levels and connected by tunnels. "Let's go in, see what we can see," she added, dropping her voice.

Inside was shadowy like a cave. A vague, silvery glow filled the air: it came and went as if through water. "I wonder how that's done," said James, as their eyes adjusted. He noticed, to his right, a big-bodied couple walking the floor. The woman held an old-fashioned camera, the man's arm was heavily bandaged. Something about them didn't seem to fit. It was as if they were actors who hadn't learned their parts.

Beth stood close to James; what she saw surprised her. The space ahead was filled with upended cardboard rolls tied in bundles. Between them were maze-like passageways that crisscrossed the floor. It looked like a carpet warehouse. "Which way?" she asked.

"Wherever you like," he said, quietly.

They chose a corridor between rolls. At a twist where it narrowed, James took the lead, putting out a hand behind his back. Beth held it, thinking of rescues. Reaching an intersection, they swung right to arrive at a white-walled chamber lit by lamps. At one end was a large, polished, concave reflector. It faced them like an eye. "Looks like a house of mirrors," said James. Moving side to side he peered at his image. Like a ghost at a window his reflection came and went.

"It's strange," said Beth, stepping closer. A line in the mirror thickened to a block. As James joined her and they hugged, their reflections fused and spread. "We're in there," said Beth, "if you look."

"So which part is you, which is me?"

"Whichever part you want."

"No distinction, eh?"

"Well, there *is* a quote," she said, meeting his eye.

"Yes?"

"It begins with 'Anyone can talk love …'."

"And how does it finish?"

"I can't quite say it word for word."

"Give it a try."

"OK. It ends something like, 'but it takes a real lover to be silly'."

"That's good," he grinned. "Two crazies are always better than one."

"You like the idea?"

"Oh yes. It's like The Beatles, *I am the walrus*."

"Not sure I get it."

"You don't have to. That's the point."

Beth leaned forward, watching her image.

"In any case," he added, as their reflections merged, "when you're on the inside," – he waved at the mirror – "you really can't tell one head case from another."

When they emerged from the dome James could see, looking downhill, the unlike couple. They were arguing. The woman was pointing to a path down the slope, the man had half-turned away. She was speaking quickly, with an edge of defiance. Her words appeared in snatches as if forced out. His replies, when they came, were angry and deliberate.

Beth pressed a fist into her side.

"They don't seem to be getting on," James said. The couple were now battling, with her voice up-and-down, his blocking, and both sides cutting in.

"I wish people wouldn't do that," Beth said, grimacing. The woman had turned and was walking off; the man was calling after her.

"Not in public, anyway."

"Not at all, ever."

"Yes, it's ugly," he said, "but some people seem to need it, or it's about having the final say."

"But that doesn't make it right."

"No."

Beth stepped back, breathing hard. "I'd like to go somewhere, anywhere – another part of the garden."

"You're not happy?"

"I just don't want to be here and listen to *that*," she waved downhill to where the couple were still battling.

"I see what you mean. It sounds like pistols at dawn."

The man was shouting and swearing.

Beth winced. "You wouldn't ever do that to me?"

"Absolutely not."

"You promise?"

"Promise. It's out of the question."

"I couldn't bear it."

He smiled. "Tell yourself, love talks."

"I will," she said, and they hugged.

Leaving the couple, they skirted the hill. A ridge led up through bushes to a hillside track that circled a lake. Here they were alone and they walked arm in arm, pausing at viewpoints. Seen from above, the lake was long and thin and rounded at one end. As they descended to a bank, a scattering of white and purple flowers came into view. "What are those?" asked Beth, pointing to clump. When James said fritillary, she asked if she should pick them.

"Best not, I'd say. The gardener might not like it."

She laughed.

Their path dropped further, entering a mixture of goosegrass, wood sorrel and dwarf silver birches. Close by the water there were sun-beams through branches and insects circling. Now and then small shifting ripples appeared on the surface. At one point a squirrel scrambled up a tree. As they approached the lake head an army of crows flapped into action, cawing. "I don't think anyone comes here," said James.

"Are you sure?"

"Not often, anyway. You can tell by the track."

They'd reached a point where the path split, one track dropping to water where it ended in mud, the other climbing straight into bushes. Both routes were overgrown. Beth looked uphill. "Do you think there's anything up there?"

James followed her gaze. "Trees, bushes, time on our own."

"It looks the kind of place …"

He nodded and their fingertips touched. Something passed between them and they set off together. They took the higher route, pushing through heather as they climbed to a wood. The trees were old and covered with lichen and ivy. At the edge there were elders and flowering thorns, further in there were oaks with twisted branches, beyond that holly and brambles and an isolated clearing. Here, in a corner, screened by laurels, they came across a large, tunnel-shaped shelter. It was barn-length and constructed entirely of woven branches. The wood had been trimmed and layered carefully, but was sprouting.

James led to an arch-shaped door. "I think it's a sculpture, or used to be."

Beth joined him. "You think so?"

He pointed to some paint-streaked branches. They had peeled and faded.

She touched the wood and a few loose grains of colour flaked off. "But it could just have been a place to shelter," she said.

"Let's take a look," he replied, taking her hand as they stepped inside.

The space they entered was cave-like and still. In the semi-dark they could make out the walls. They were covered all over by a rough plaster mix. A faint blue glow, spreading from the ceiling, seemed to fill the air.

"We could stay here for a while," Beth's question was framed as a statement. She was pointing past the entrance to a low, bed-style platform. It had a logroll edge, linked by wires; inside was dry and soft and covered with sheep's wool. Advancing, she prodded one corner then lay down. "It's good," she said. "This is what we've come for. Our rest stop."

James heard the lift in her voice. Her eyes were on him, inviting. "James," she said quietly. She reached out to be touched, repeating his name.

For him it was absorbing; they were all lips and tongues, kissing. For Beth it went deep, she could hang there forever, or so it felt. It reminded her of their kiss at the station.

His hands went free, circling her waist and down to her thighs. She sighed and they pressed in closer. "Yes," she said, fingering her buttons. As his hands began to fumble a rustle in the bushes made her sit up. "What's that?" she asked.

James rolled over. "It's a bird, I think."

"You're sure there's no one out there?"

"Listen," he said. The rustle continued, followed by an earth-ss-cratching sound. "That's close, and too low for a person."

"I wouldn't want anyone coming in."

He squeezed her hand. "You remember how hard it was to get here, and how overgrown it was?" Beth squeezed back and he drew her to him. "If anyone was coming we'd hear them way off."

"You really think so?"

"They'd have to parachute in, or we'd know it."

She lay back and listened. "Now you say it, that's a bird." She reached out to him. "I told you, didn't I, about Dad and bird watching?"

James said yes and touched her cheek, lightly. Beth turned sideways, while he stroked her hair. She understood him now – right through, completely. He was what she wanted, that was all.

"Darling," she said, and an urgency entered. His tongue found her ear, lightly, and they began to undress, fumbling slightly. Each garment was rolled either down or up and slipped off by hand. They did it together.

"You happy?" he asked as he lay on his side circling her breasts then reaching down to her thighs.

"Very," she said, and he touch-stroked lightly, while she explored his chest. Desire took over as he turned and positioned then climbed between her legs. As he entered a wave rose from below; it was as if she was underwater, swimming through light.

He began, moving in rhythm, rocking slowly. He eased in further, squeezing and pushing until he was deep inside, leading and led. He was in there, moving without effort. And then, driven from below, they tightened. His movement quickened, gradually building to a single, connected, all-in-one flow – speeding onward to a big-leap moment – and then they were squeezing and grunting and crying and shivering, till they came and came, releasing with a shout.

Afterwards they lay facing, in silence. Their bodies kept them warm. Above them a bird sang, whistling softly. The air through the door was cool and still.

When James reached out and pulled on a shirt, Beth sat up.

"Thank you," she said.

He smiled and hugged her. They kissed.

"Well, it's lovely here," she said, "but I suppose …" She began shifting about, gathering up her clothes.

James eyed her gently. As she dressed, he shuffled closer, handing over garments and kissing where he could.

"We're in a good place," she said.

"Home from home?"

"It's our house in the woods."

James murmured agreement, touching her hair.

"And from now, it's our story," she added, smiling.

# THIRTY-SIX

Folkestone/Papeete, fut.

Beth was awake in the dark, thinking about love. Or was she asleep? Certainly, whatever was happening didn't seem right. Although James was there, she couldn't quite reach him. She was the girl who began again.

The bed she was lying in had become her whole world. It felt like a beach with the tide coming in. She'd slipped on shingle and couldn't get up. Something heavy was filling up her body. In the distance, she could see James in a boat. She wanted to swim out, but the waves were too high.

Of course, she knew what was happening. Her Desert Island Dream had come back. But this time it was strange. Although it was her dream, it didn't seem to fit, as if she was watching from a distance, as someone else. She was at the vanishing point, outside life. "This is from the other side," a voice in the air told her. It was one of those dreams where things like that were said and anything could happen. There was a screen with pictures and an echoey voiceover that came and went like people talking underwater. It took Beth back to the reel-to-reel films she'd watched at a small local cinema.

The voice Beth heard moved in time to the pictures. Each word was alive and joined to the next. After being spoken the words changed colour.

Beth knew a lot about words. All her life she'd been writing. Her words came out as balloons, all different colours, just like that.

The colours she liked were combinations, mixtures, in betweeners. Blue-pink, violet, grey-white-blue.

But these weren't her words. They were deep and wild and alive but someone else's. And their colours were dark and stormy.

Returning to the screen, Beth followed the dream. It developed slowly, moodily, moving like tides in the grip of the moon. In it there were pictures of animal graveyards and empty cities with thunderheads above. Skeletons glowed and bears roamed through shopping malls. There were giant figures standing on ridgetops, casting long shadows on the valleys below. Sometimes the dream failed or went hazy, but the voice kept on. Smooth and cultured, it told a story of nature at the margins, extremophiles, microbes and random mutations. At one point in the dream the screen became a cliff, swathed in clouds. Soon after it was a frozen lake. Then it was a misted window with curtains drawn. When Beth cleared the glass, the images she saw were ghosts from the past. Some she recognised, others were new. They were very thin and twittered warnings.

In the film Beth was both presenter and audience. Her name had changed and she was standing on her island, in a spotlight, overlooking water. Behind her, the screen showed pictures of other islands. They were all going under.

"This could be the last time," the voice sang as the all-white screen paled into nothingness.

"Everything must go," it continued as the sun rose and set.

"We are going down-down-down," it cried and the words were stars. Black stars.

"This is the end of the rainbow," the voice called.

Then the screen opened like a flower. Inside the flower was a beating heart. The heart was inscribed with *Beth 4 James*. The words had been carved into a tree. And the tree was going under, too.

Suddenly Beth realised that the island she lived on was LOVE and James was on it, together with all the other people she knew and others she didn't.

Somehow her dream had been taken over. There were instruments in it and massed voices. No longer hers, it was shared with the living and the dead. It had the shape and power of history. It was for the Earth.

And if the Earth was going under, then they'd all hold hands.

♯ ♯ ♯

The piece that follows, winner at the last York Big Ideas Award, was staged and broadcast from Papeete, Tahiti. Described by its author, Elizabeth Lavender, as her "swansong transcribing people's lives", we reprint *A Dream of Futures* in its entirety. As the last in a long line of challenging, experimental pieces, it marks the end of a prestigious competition. The judges chose it unanimously, praising it as a lyrical journey combining elegiac speculation with truth to life. In their comments they drew particular attention to its reach, its super-personal content and the dramatic irony of its closing signature: *Ghost-written by E L.*

A DREAM OF FUTURES

1.

At the Deep Adaptation Conference it was fifteen minutes before lights out. At 8.30 p.m. Earth Hour would begin.

On the main stage a short, raven-haired woman was miked up for her talk. Standing in front of a curved screen wearing a brown tunic and rope sandals, Professor Hereiti Chaze was gazing at the audience, mouthing a greeting. With her prominent teeth and wide smile, she had the look of someone old who stays young. To one side, a signer was repeating her welcome. Led by Hereiti, their words and gestures came in waves. Both were lit up.

In the front row of the audience Hereiti's brother was checking his guitar-shaped watch. Beside him Joe, Cass and Mia Lavender had accepted his offer and were sucking on boiled sweets. Y leaned forward to tell his guests about his sister, reading from the programme. In it, her talk was described as a Regenerative Oceania Voyage. All four didn't look their age.

When Hereiti began she introduced herself as an indigenous activist and scientist – in that order, she said – and then, as the lights dimmed, she started her talk.

It went like this:

I'm going to take you on a journey. A *nekyia*. What my people call *te hoe tere*. It's a guided vision exploring what's to come and what's being lost. And to share that vision I'd like you all to close your eyes. Tell yourself, as you close them, that you're happily tired. But not sleepy. You've had a busy day and it's time to rest.

What you might be seeing are ghostly images or a small lightshow. I'll explain that later.

Now the darkness is clearing and your vision – true vision – is coming back. You're awake and you've walked into a different world. There are sounds all around of people singing and running water. You're lying on a floral bedspread with the windows open in a house by the sea. Warm rain is bathing the garden. If you listen carefully you can hear it swishing on the leaves. The air is damp, the grass is shiny and you're smelling flowers – beautiful, creamy, richly-scented flowers that open at dawn. It might be you've returned to an earlier existence. Maybe to what's called *illud tempus*, when the Gods were real. It's where everything's alive and charged with meaning. And that's where I'm hoping to take you tonight.

You can open your eyes now. But please take care. Do it slowly. Feel yourself coming back, but hold onto what you saw. Call it what you like, your third eye or dream state, but stay inside your vision.

At the same time respect the science. Because there are explanations. Those lights and flashes you saw were physical phenomena. Not stars or fireworks but what's called phosphenes. They're electrical sparks coming from the retina.

So, come with me into my world. It's a vast space, a wide ocean the size of a continent. We're on a long voyage from island to island, a dark crossing, a journey into emptiness. Firstly, in childhood standing with my father on Point Venus. Here the land's red, and the beach is black volcanic sand. The view takes in Mo'orea and beyond that the invisible archipelagos. To sail to them can take days or weeks.

A word in your ear about that voyage. The boat's cramped, you sleep sitting up, you're hot then you're cold, and your body hurts. When the food and water run short you start seeing things. It's like being shut into a small cell with the roof wide open. And when the seas get up, parts of the boat get broken. It's a physical state similar to breakdown. A condition or illness sometimes called *lysis*. The dark night of the soul. Like vision, navigation is hard.

But the star in your mind will lead you on.

Now, eyes closed but open, I'd like to take you on my first navigation. It begins at dawn, guided by the stars, the colours of the sky, the wind and the waves. Of course, there's science in that as well. But what my father taught me was that to find an island, picture its image. Keep that before you as your guiding light. Navigation begins in the heart.

Both my parents taught me about culture. How we're all linked – plants, animals, humans, the ancestors – all part of the chain. They saw our world as a gift, something passed on. I can still feel them in that garden, in that warm rain. I visit it often in my dreams.

I want to take you now to Vahitahi, in the Tuamotu Islands. It's a small atoll with a central lagoon. What you see as you sail towards it is a line of trees rising out of the sea. But when you get closer you realise that they're growing on low-lying land. The island's a raft of green with a blue eye in the middle. It looks like a paradise garden.

But when you step onto the beach you realise it's dying. Every year the waves eat up more land. The sea turtles and triggerfish aren't seen anymore. The corals are bleaching. A few people still live there, but most have left.

This is the loss I was talking about. A cast-out feeling, an abandonment. An unrelenting exodus.

As a people we've been left off the map. Paris, London, Tokyo, Shanghai, New York, they're the ones winning, on top. We're on the outside, going under. Keeping them afloat is what's flooding us.

Science tells us the oceans are warming. Thermal expansion, added to ice-melt, raises sea levels. The salt gets into plant life and eats away glaciers. The damage is to trees, insects, animals, birds, all of us.

The water's already up to our chests and touching our necks.

My ancestors were navigators. In these times we need their vision. The world is disappearing beneath our feet. We're all on Vahitahi losing our lives, our homes, our Gods.

So I invite you to open your eyes. See with your heart. Go out, be brave and set sail without compass to follow our guides – the birds, the sun, our inner vision. Do that, and find again that first time in the garden.

We will find a way.

As Hereiti stopped talking, the lights went up. When the applause began, she turned towards the signer, bowing slightly. In the front row, Y was standing, with his arms in the air. Beside him Joe, Cass and Mia were pressing their palms together. As a group, they were silent. When the signer presented her with a bouquet, Hereiti began to cry.

On the stroke of 8.30, the lights went out.

Listening on the radio, James and Beth Lavender were silent too.

2.

In a midweek session at the Deep Adaptation Conference, Professor Matthew Lavender was interviewing Hereiti Chaze. As a follow-up to her talk it was deliberately small and low-key. Held in a gallery, it was billed as an eco-journey to be followed by a screening of Hereiti's film *In The Earth's Last Days*. The audience, who were lined up on benches in two parallel rows, included Y and his friend Angel, sitting opposite her friends Jenny and Leon Deane with their daughters, Jasmine, Rosa and Daisy.

Photos of artworks signed by the Deane family hung on the walls. They included pictures of beaches with dry-stone herms going underwater; yarn-bombed fences and fallen statues; shots of rock-marked routes through burnt-out fields, ridged circles and spirals in sand, and bird's-eye photos of rock-cut troughs that looked like water tanks or coffins.

The interview, which was recorded, began like this:

ML: I'd like you to welcome our keynote speaker, Hereiti Chaze, who is going to share with us an overview of climate and bio-loss before showing her latest film. (*Applause*) Thank you, everyone. And now, Hereiti, I'd like to ask you about title of this session. You've called it, Intensive Care for the Spirit-Journey. What's behind the label on the can?

HC: Good afternoon, Professor Lavender and everyone. Thank you so much for inviting me. I will do my best to answer – in two parts, if I may.

Firstly, Intensive Care is a medical metaphor based on the Gaia principle. It compares raising the temperature of a human body to the same for the Earth. In both cases a small increase can be fatal. The dangers, too, are similar: dehydration, hot-cold spells and organ failure.

Secondly, The Spirit-Journey takes us elsewhere – which is a real place by the way, though it may be hard to discover. I had in mind skin diving or sailing into the eye of the storm. To do either without bravado or hubris takes us into the spirit world. It's about living as *the other* in order to grow.

If I could give you an example. When I was a child, I went in fear of what I called the Gods in the garden. I believed they'd taken cover under the leaves of the tiaré flower and were watching. At any moment they might jump out and eat me. I'd tried various ways of shutting them out – running past their hiding place or wrestling them in my mind or sitting with my eyes shut pretending they weren't there. In fact, without knowing it I was acting out the theory of fight/flight/freeze! But one day I did the unthinkable. Like Newton or Marie Curie, I experimented on myself. I pushed my way in under the tiaré bush and joined them. Suddenly the power I was afraid of was sitting inside me. I'd turned myself inside out, from victim to agent. It was then I discovered that our deepest fear is the gateway to our true selves.

ML: That's really interesting. Is there an overlap here with deep adaptation?

HC: Yes and no. The theory of deep adaptation accepts that the current emission levels will push us under. Effectively, the genie is out of the bottle. But within that process sticking points and refuge spots still exist. And each delay adds up, changing the story. It's like me talking to you now. If I stop and start again, even a tiny shift in the word order has a knock-on effect. Everything changes and it becomes a completely different story. The well-known example of this is Edward Lorenz, when he resumed on his computer after a break. Like him, we begin wherever we last left off – and that can lead to radically different outcomes.

ML: I think you're referring to limited predictability. Do you want to say anything more about that?

HC: Certainly. As you know, Edward Lorenz is the father of what's been called the *Butterfly Effect*. But it seems to me that his theory describes influence rather than effect. It also operates over great distances. You could say it's magic. The effect is large and small, random and purposeful. It's a theory of interconnectedness based on the idea that power is everywhere. That's what we call *Mana*.

ML: I see. So can I ask, as an Occidental, if I want to understand *Mana*, is it better to go through science or poetry?

HC: I'd say through poetic science. A holistic approach. For me, *Mana* is everywhere, but particularly in the wildness of nature. There's a hidden wisdom in thunderstorms, flowers, curious stones, rainbows. It's also about mirroring natural patterns. A bit like Shiva's dance. I think the Dylan Thomas poem, "The force that drives the green fuse drives the flower", expresses it well.

ML: I've heard you describe yourself as a Mental Traveller – perhaps after Blake. Could you expand on what Mental Travelling means, please?

HC: Well, to adapt a famous quote, *The mind is a foreign country*. All travel today explores imaginary space. The threat of The Event forced it on us. The people of Oceania were the world's first inner argonauts, which is one of the themes of my film. We understood the harmonies and how they'd been broken. We were people of the gift, passing on our necklaces and armshells, linked by respect and love.

It's like chain letters or pass the parcel, only each gift is different and what comes back isn't what you thought you'd get. The ripple that goes out today returns tomorrow as a song, a menu, a hand tool, or a message in a bottle. The circle is big. Anyone can do it.

ML: Thank you. I find that quite inspiring. Going back to your adapted quote from *The Go-Between*, are you implying a link between the past and navigating today?

HC: In a way, yes. The memories are imprinted. Each journey is a recapitulation of an inner calling.

ML: You also mentioned The Event. Could you expand on that, please?

HC: The Event is our current world phase, pushing us ever closer to breakdown. It's what Berlioz called *The March to the Scaffold*. When extinction becomes extermination. As you know, there are people behind it. Burners of the Earth. They cast their long shadow over everything.

ML: Do you see any hope for the future?

HC: Absolutely. We can enshrine Future Rights and Ecocide in law. We can replace fossil fuels, change land use, live simply and power down. But really it's about mindset. My ancestors knew that. They understood how to share and respect the Earth. Today, Indigenous People are in the frontline, risking everything to defend Nature.

ML: On a personal level, are there experiences that give you hope?

HC: The one that comes to mind is seeing a double rainbow, particularly at sea, where it looks like a huge gateway. Interestingly, the two arches are inside-out versions of each other. They're two worlds nesting, like Russian dolls. But the metaphor I'm thinking of lies in what's called *Alexander's Band* between the arches. It's the dark patch – and that's where the hope lies. In the unknown – and with the children, of course.

ML: Turning to your film. It's been said that *In The Earth's Last Days* enters the virtual realm through innovative filming. Can you explain?

HC: I'll try to! The film is projected as if it was running on the mind's inner screen. It's not intended as a dream or a fiction, but neither is it reportage or a documentary. If you like it's simply a series of panned shots across ocean, islands and underwater life. What's unusual is the pacing and the feel. It was put together during meditative episodes on long journeys. We filmed what we could barely see. Some of it is close to invisible, or was to us.

ML: And now, before we show it, the plug … I believe your film has already been accepted at several film festivals?

HC: Yes. We sent it out on Film Freeway and the response has been terrific. We now have 20 showings scheduled in the next two months with more on the way. It's coming to countries that might surprise you, so watch out for a local screening!

3.

When *In The Earth's Last Days* came to their home town, Beth and James Lavender were there. It was shown without a trailer as part of the Triennial Fringe, so at first neither of them realised how much they knew about it. Intrigued by the title, they'd chosen it as a category winner, but while watching they'd soon begun to recognise phrases taken from Hereiti's talk.

The film itself was slow and mysterious. The soundtrack included lengthy silences between far-off bird cries and water-slapping sounds, and even Hereiti's words seemed to come from a great distance, carried on the wind. There were establishing shots of sea and sky, long takes on islands with water washing over and dissolves of armshells abandoned on sand. As the film progressed it went from extreme close up on tattooed faces to wide-angle shots of flat horizons. The transitions were wipe shots and fades, switching scenes through thought-bubbles and dives into water. Towards the end the film became a single held frame with a succession of dream-like images. Mainly abstract, they were grey and ghostly, but somehow familiar. They resolved, finally, into a tall wooden statue with huge eyes and dragon-like teeth. In the background, heard faintly, were Hereiti's final words:

"But within memory is a core of rightness. Something left over from the Gods, the hive mind in us all. And my ancestors were curators of the spiritual life force sometimes known as *Reiki* or *Orenda* in other cultures. So, in the Earth's last days let us honour those who went before us. The Resistors. Those Still Standing. In their haste the colonists had overlooked the power of deep memory. Facing into the storm, we found ourselves."

After watching the film, Beth and James Lavender returned to their café by the sea. It was closed and silent. Looking out, they could see the waves in the afternoon sun breaking on the beach. The view was a reminder.

"This seems tame, compared," said Beth.

"Compared?"

"To the film."

"But what we're looking at is sea – right?"

"In the film it was more."

"Are you thinking of what's been called the *Oceanic Feeling*?"

"I'm not sure. It depends what you mean by that."

"As in Freud. A feeling of oneness and unity – eternity if you like – often brought on by looking at the sea."

Beth shook her head. "Not really. What I'm seeing is loss, the sea as a divider."

"True. But it's also connected."

"Well, maybe. It's certainly where everything comes from," she said. "I sometimes feel it's where I'll return."

"The sea's certainly powerful."

"A big space, a wilderness."

"And rising."

Soon afterwards, at James's suggestion, they walked. Retracing their footsteps, they followed the gravel path to a track up the cliffs. They climbed, talking in snatches about the film. Reaching the spot called *Lover's Leap*, they sat holding hands. Birds cried intermittently. It was bright and still and the rocks below gleamed in the sun. The water between them came and went. moving slowly as if it was hurting.

Looking at a nearby notice, James spoke. "What happened to the woman who was supposed to jump?"

"I think I said it was a story." Beth replied.

"Ah, that's right. Doomed love. But last time here you called it romantic."

"Not so romantic now."

"How do you mean?"

"She climbed down. They both drowned."

"I thought you said only *possibly*?"

"Yes. But the story's true to life."

"In what sense?"

"The sea took them. It all happened quickly, as in a dream."

"But what about everyone else? Didn't they notice?"

"They were too busy."

"Didn't the lovers, or anyone, cry out?"

"They all washed away."

"Like in the film?"

"Like us," said Beth.

"And the planet," said James.


# THIRTY-SEVEN

18.4.09

If I'd known, I'd have memorised everything at the time. For James, for John and Louise, for my girls, for everyone.

I'd have captured each gesture – a light shift on glass, a face in passing, the weight of words – caught the whole thing, in detail, as it was.

A book is an adventure.

How could I have done it? On cards at table, or phrase by phrase carried in my head? Maybe as a dance with finely-balanced moves, developed by feel. Or perhaps as a photo, a second's impression, then mounted with captions and stuck down in a book.

Once, with Dad, I named birds and talked. As we walked around the garden he told me their stories. I hear him now: his thoughts, and the dreams that follow. It's him and me in private, like characters in a book.

Without stories we're boring.

Where I am now isn't easy. I try not to show it, but there's so much to think about. The past and how I've changed. I hear a high-up voice singing "Demands my soul, my life, my all". It's like looking out of the window on the last train home.

So, this is my gallery. Beginning, of course, with my husband and lover.

24.5.09

Waiting in the restaurant, I felt him coming. The grey-blue eyes, the walk with purpose … he was looking for me. Of course your mind plays tricks, but this was different. What you remember is a glimpse, a pared-down image. The past is what we feel. But with James I knew straight away, as if it was now. In the restaurant he had presence.

I do remember the build-up. I thought of running because my nerves were singing out. Looking back, it all seems rather breathless. But it's one thing to say, another to be there. You try not show it, but you feel wide open. Turning up is a statement, and once you've done that, is it possible to back out?

I'd talked to friends beforehand. Of course I was starry, but I knew that trap. And Sarah had warned me, "It's the difference between shopping for a recipe and feeding kids," she said. "So *please* don't get burned."

That's how Sarah talks. In the café she makes a big entrance, calls out, says something quirky then sings from the charts as she cleans all over.

"You're dreaming what's on the menu," she went on, "but watch out for the bill."

We call her FSS: Full Speed Sarah. She's even more pumped-up than Toby at a match. I remember how she danced, first thing in the morning, calling, "*Olé! Olé!*" and crazy-hand-clapping while running up and down.

But with me she's different. Perhaps it's how we've adapted, our French and Saunders on-stage thing. Or maybe it's by contrast: the dreamer and the doer.

On this occasion we were standing after work on the beach and Sarah was pressing her toe into a clump of seaweed. I remember her calling it food for free. While she talked about its uses, I listened and looked out. The sky was grey, shading to black, rimming the horizon. The wind was changeable and the tide was half in. It felt like the beginning of a film.

I thought of *Dover Beach*. That's what happens, give me a seascape or a big wide sky and I think of poetry. Celebration and consolation.

"Shall I meet him?" I asked.

The light on the sea glowed white. I'd a feeling of something moving, a bright spot within.

"You want to?"

I see it as a picture. Two women on the shoreline, one large, one skinny, with a world behind them and a lifetime ahead. Or something shorter, now. It's like that song in *West Side Story, Something's Coming*. Of course, begin a phrase and my mind fills the gap – *Down the block, on a beach* – which took me there and suddenly it was obvious. "Yes," I said, removing my shoes and stepping into water.

She joined me in the shallows. The waves lapped around us. They were clear and cold and tickly.

"Yes, yes," she said, taking my hand and we danced.

3.6.09

Recently I've been looking at Dali's *The Persistence of Memory*. The soft watches describe how I feel: caught in the glare and melted, in a quiet way. The view out to sea is bright, while, in the foreground, the shadow of a mountain is filling up the picture. It's a clean bare place with sharp lines and spread flesh. A Gethsemane. It reminds me of my first experience of death.

I was eight at the time, the year I wrote *The Girl Who Began Again*. I was alone in the back garden. I don't know where my dad was, but I can still feel his absence. I was crouched down studying the path, seeing it as a jigsaw, an old one with bits missing. Parts of it didn't fit. It was cracked and patched and smeared with concrete. Small, spiky weed-tufts showed around the cracks.

Taking a stick I began digging. I was poking at the side, exploring a crack, when a lump fell out. I remember sitting back in surprise. I can still feel it now, like an extraction. I was numb, trying to work things out. Had I done this, I wondered, and if I had, wasn't it by accident? At the same time I knew the truth, and that made me jumpy. I had the stick in my hand and could see where the lump had landed, in the shadow of a bush. I hoped it wouldn't get noticed.

I glanced back at the house then checked the hole. Just one peek, I told myself, and I'd be done. But what I saw scared me. I could make out a rough, cave-like space filled with roots. It seemed to be alive at the bottom as if it was bleeding.

I looked again. This time I was prepared, but it still made me shiver. The roots were full of dark, wriggly shapes. They were running all over in lines and knots, filling up the cavity. It seemed like they might boil over.

Then I realised they were ants, nesting. And in the middle, where they were busiest and blackest, they'd seized on something large. I watched in silence as they tore it apart. Body bits were held up, twirled in the air and cleared like rubbish. They were relentless. I began to turn away then realised suddenly what they'd got. The creature they were dismembering was a large, hollowed-out, silver-winged butterfly.

I was deeply shocked. How could they do that to something so beautiful? As if it was their prisoner. It was hard to understand. But also, by being the only witness, I'd got myself involved. And ants were ruthless, I knew that from school where a teacher had compared them to armies. I'd read about captive explorers being coated with honey and eaten by ants. But this was worse, their oddly-shaped, ritualistic movements were fiercely territorial. In them, for the first time, I glimpsed a different world.

For the rest of that day I could feel them with me. They were hiding in the loo, inside the plughole and underneath the bed. Like the ants in Dali they kept reappearing, on plates, through cracks, and dreamed in the mirror. At night I could feel them, tingling in my flesh. Even today, those ants are still with me. I can see them crawling on a clock in *The Persistence of Memory*.

I've read that Dali wanted to illustrate the theory of relativity. What I'd seen in action was the second law of thermodynamics.

15.6.09

I'm making my preparations. They're for me, as a fall-back, but they're also for family and friends, if anything happens. I want it on record like a film or book. To be all in one place, like a CV. At the moment I've only told James. Telling the others would only set them off. They'd fear the worst, suppose I knew something and want reassurance, but there isn't much to say, just a gut feeling.

Fortunately, James understood. In good-guy mode he listened before making a few suggestions. That's why I love him. He's a man, wants action, but always hears me out. He did ask for details and we talked about feelings, seeing doctors and what might happen. Later he looked up the symptoms online. And he played escort. So he walked me to the surgery and, when he could, drove me to hospital or collected me after tests. If I'd let him, I think he'd have taken my place.

Encouraged by him, I'm preparing.

Firstly, I'm filling up a scrapbook as my aide mémoire. In it I've placed family snaps, magazine cut-outs, dance show programmes and catalogues from galleries. I've deliberately mixed it up, with a page for lyrics, a pressed-flowers page, another for cloth-scraps and bagged-up seeds, and a double-page spread with notes on card about people in the café. At the end I've added a section with certificates, a few poems and some ecumenical prayers.

Of course, it's all about character, seen through a window. And it's for my daughters, to pass on what I can. So, on the cover I've added drawings: early ones of theirs, and one by me. On the inside I've dedicated it, signed and dated, to Rose and Naomi. And I've given both a page, named at the top, with a one-line message asking them to fill it up.

Secondly, there's my bedside cabinet. It's rather fancy, striped and padded at the front with cut-glass handles. I think of it as my allsorts collection. Inside, it's full of red-yellow ribbons and black/purple stones, and packed with goodies, like a gift shop. Of course they're a selection, so my drawers aren't me, not exactly. They're more about things and what they feel like. Everything in them is there for themselves, but also as a surprise. Like art, they've been taken out of context, changing their meanings. Having said that, they are what they are and the history behind them is additional.

I keep up my drawers. I review what's in them, take things out, place them around the room, and make myself *see* them. Next I choose, returning some, putting others on display. Then once a week I add in something new: a toy, a meditational text or a found artwork. I do this as a ceremony, taking time, sometimes with James, in silence. When he's there choosing, we mime. So, pointing to items, we nod or pull faces. Sometimes we give a thumbs-down, or we wave and laugh, setting each other off. Afterwards we stay silent.

It's like lighting candles, one from the other, in church. It's like our first meeting.

25.6.09

Inside myself I've always been a nun. Nuns are wild. They are lovers of gardens where bees hover around mint. The places where they pray are full of lilies and scented herbs. Their walks are like turning pages in a book.

I keep my nun hidden, most of the time. She calls herself Lucy. In her mind she's a naive painter. She's the one who stops on the path to talk to the birds. When no one's watching she climbs trees and swings on gates. As Lucy she's a dancer. When she's moving the world stands still.

The nun I am now is older and tougher. She lives on the edge. She's reached that point where her body drives her. Her mouth is dry and her insides ache. Her face is hollow and her bones show through. I call this nun Amanda. She still has faith.

In the dark she breathes heavily. There's a man by her side who keeps her going. He's her angel, cheering her on. She's against the clock and keeping focus. But what she has to do seems beyond her. The distance is telling. Although he's beside her, her strength is fading. The thoughts she has seem to vanish into air. What used to be her voice has become a whisper. Her arms, her legs are all giving out. She's a woman beginning Lent.

4.7.09

When I was young it all seemed simple.

I thought I could change things, have it my way, do everything at once. I was on the look-out. Like one of my characters I'd put myself together: a bit-part collection of film clips, life observations and aspects of soul. And I believed my own stories, because the truth was in the telling, and I lived inside my head, in whatever way I chose.

Made-up is so.

Now I know better. You watch as it goes on, try this, try that and laugh at your own absurdity, because anything can happen. It's how you frame yourself, and then stay in there, with effort. It's a bubble you blow.

Take my life with James. We began by telling all, the dos and don'ts, the things we'd learned and what we'd been through. For me, if it's a marriage, then both sides are obliged. It's a variation on the self-fulfilling prophecy: looked at over time it's all about belief. Apply that theory to James and me. Right from the start we *chose* to be in love.

I think of it as a map, whatever route you follow, it's a one-way thing. The real risk is holding back, what they call *letting things be*. But for us, with our history, it was about looking forward. So we'd say things in public, flaunt it, if you like. And we still keep it up – kind words in the morning, a cheek kiss, the L word – really we're on stage. Making our mark, telling all.

Which brings me to family, Hannah, and the problems.

17.7.09 – 30.9.09

I first met Hannah at a South Bank restaurant. James had showed me pictures, so I knew she was beautiful. What struck me was her child-

600

round face and her scarf-like hair trained across one shoulder. She was long-limbed and slightly Romani. Young of course, and very photogenic. I noticed in a Facebook picture, posed next to her brother, how she looked into camera as cool as you like, as if she wasn't bothered.

James used the word "lively" to sum up his children; he said they were "smart kids" and "perfectly wised-up". The words that followed – London, the reconstructed family, college – should have made it easy. But maybe they were meant as a warning. After all, we do come from different worlds.

The meeting had been arranged on neutral ground. Not at James's and not by the sea. We needed space and an exit strategy. Also, we had to be careful. No looks, no handholds, and strictly functional talk. We knew we were on show.

"It's a bit like an audition," I told him, walking to our meeting along the riverside path. We were facing into sun, picking our way through groups of people talking into phones or pointing cameras, moving slowly, with a slightly distanced feel. On one side there was space with flags in the air and views over water, on the other side, glass and steel. In between were slatted benches and low concrete walls.

"Don't worry," James said, "they always like being paid for."

Looking at the crowd, I tried to spot his children approaching. I had their pictures in my head. Inside myself I was preparing what to say.

"In any case, I've told them," he continued, squeezing my hand.

"Told them what?"

"The rules," he replied, gazing ahead. A light, soft breeze was playing around our faces. "Don't worry, eating out will limit behaviour."

I know he meant well, but his words alarmed me slightly. I wondered what their unlimited behaviour might be like.

We arrived a few minutes early. The restaurant was modern with shop-sized windows and a view across water. Joining a queue at the door, we filed through an entrance into an open-plan dining room. A waiter directed and we occupied one end of a cushioned bench.

"What are they like for timing?" I asked. By now I was feeling nervous.

"They're young," said James, dryly.

George arrived first. He was tall and hunched and softly-spoken. He had spots on his neck, a hairless chin and attentive, child-like eyes. I felt for him.

We greeted, shaking hands.

"Han's coming, soon," he said gruffly, eyeing his mobile.

James checked for drinks, ordering juice.

I remember how they talked. They were deliberately low-key and careful of each other. There were gaps between phrases, words left hanging and the odd wry smile, as if they were side by side on a sofa, watching a film.

Then Hannah arrived.

"Is this, like, where we're eating?" she said, furrowing her brow.

"It's where you asked for," said James.

Hannah sat down, pulling out a silver-edged phone from her handbag. She laid it in front of her then touched the screen, sounding a bell tone, with her fingers dancing. While she was typing, I wondered just how much she noticed, and if she was with us.

"Shall we order?" asked James.

Hannah looked up, apparently puzzled. "You mean, like, now?"

"I intend to eat, I don't know about you."

"That's what people do in restaurants," put in George.

"You choose," she replied, returning to her phone. "I'll eat whatever."

It was a relief when the food arrived. I remember the rich, smooth smell and the soft/firm textures in piled-up bowls. It was fresh, slightly milky and herbal.

Hannah peered into her dish, shuddered, and pushed it away.

"You're not hungry?" asked James carefully. I could tell he was feeling blocked.

"I don't eat mixtures. You know that."

"Give it a go," he said coaxingly.

"Do I have to?"

"I'd like you to. Just try."

She glanced in my direction. Her eyes were dark brown and expanded. "How much am I expected to eat?" she asked her father.

"Whatever you feel like, and can manage."

"I might throw up."

"Well, do your best."

"Yes, I'm sure you can do it," I put in, and James nodded, but Hannah looked away. I realised then it was safer to play audience.

"Han," George called out, "you remember our game with Dad, *it isn't happening*?"

She looked at her brother, drawing in her breath. Suddenly there was interest.

"Well, do that. Eat, but tell yourself you aren't."

Hannah's face glowed. "Do you remember that, Dad?"

"As if it wasn't happening. Now."

"That means go for it, sis," called George.

"And do you, like, think if I say this's a virtual meal ...?"

James smiled. "If it helps, why not? Call it Zen eating. Do it for laughs."

Returning to her bowl, Hannah sampled around the edges, poked and prodded then stopped. "Feeling yuck," she said. A pink-red flush was spreading up her neck. I wondered for a moment if she'd some sort of allergy. Glancing over at an unconcerned George, I realised it was theatre.

"Gruesome," she added, sighing as she pushed back her chair. Rising to join her, James called her name.

"Need some space," she said, waving him off, "too hot." And she went to the loo, dabbing at her eyes and declaring herself sick.

In her absence, James asked the waiter to cover her plate. "Don't worry," he said, "Hannah's doing fine."

He said it as an aside, nodding slightly in my direction. It was one of his phrases. I knew when he said it, he wasn't happy.

"She's feeling it," said George, shrugging.

"That's Hannah for you," James said, waving his fork. "She'll be back, so eat up."

During the meal that followed, I remember thinking how well we played our parts. My role as girlfriend was all about appearances, and like any actor, my intention was to please. So I kept myself visible and agreed with things said. But also I was aware of how little I really figured.

The main show was at table. They took up their positions with James playing lead, putting up thoughts and suggestions, while George held back, saying very little. I could see, as a double act, how they set each other off.

We'd nearly finished eating when Hannah returned. She appeared from the back and sat down abruptly, looking at the table. Her expression had stiffened to a doll-like stare.

"How are you feeling?" asked James.

Hannah murmured something I couldn't hear.

George pointed to her bowl. "They kept it hot for you. We didn't even have to ask." I remember how he smiled: carefully, giving very little away. His face was deliberately bland.

She examined the lid, blinking slowly.

"You can eat it," added George, "Dad doesn't mind."

Hannah pouted.

"And *nobody*'s looking," he continued, slyly.

Her mouth twitched slightly and she sighed. I could see there was help needed.

"It's up to you," said James. "Your choice. Eat or don't eat, simple as that."

Hannah hesitated then grasped her bowl. "All right," she said, wrinkling up her nose, "I'll do it. Anything to keep you guys happy." And she took off the lid, picked up a fork and dug into her meal.

We stayed in the restaurant for a least another hour. I felt for them all. Anyone watching would have seen the fidgets and glances, the faces glazed over, while picking up on James's efforts, with the odd prompt from George. For James it was about leading, without too much pressure. He was the facilitator, the man-in-the-middle with a slot to fill, and he talked to reassure us, at an evenly-judged pace, switching between news, his job, TV programmes and accounts of things he'd read. But underneath everything, I could see he was struggling.

His main target was Hannah. Not obviously or head-on, but through choice of words and incidental gestures. He kept up the flow, varying his content, while she eyed her phone.

I remember when they left how suddenly and completely her voice tone changed. "Oh, thank you," she said, blushing. Although she said it quietly, it seemed directed towards me. Perhaps it was her way of saying sorry.

At the end James hugged them both. Standing just behind him, I thought about doing the same, but held back, waiting. George coughed, said bye, and reached out a hand while Hannah waved her phone in the air. As they left, picking their way around tables without looking back, James caught my eye.

"You OK?" he asked.

Returning his gaze, I nodded. His shoulders had dropped and his hands were spread. Even before we touched, I could feel him shaking.

From then on, The Hannah Factor became part of our lives.

The restaurant performance and our exchange afterwards brought us closer. It was as if we were pundits discussing a sporting upset, or a political event. We'd talk about her as an *issue* and almost at once, as if she'd heard us, there would be Hannah on the phone, questioning our movements, like a parent checking up. Her texts would come through saying *call me now* or *U doing stuff?* arriving, usually, just before bedtime. We called it HI DAD IT'S ME, or RADIO HANNAH.

And when she came on the line, she was reactive, complaining about boredom, bad thoughts and feelings of exclusion, naming names and quoting out of context then cutting off suddenly with a brief apology and silence.

It was when she visited, calling from outside and entering breathless, that the worst things were said. I'd be upstairs, staying out of it, but would hear every word. It was long, uneasy and wrangling, a set-piece dialogue of the sort that only really happens in private between families.

If it had been recorded, it would have gone like this:

Father: Hello stranger, this is unexpected. Nice to see you.

(*Father gives a slightly one-sided hug.*)

Girl:   Whatever. It's raining outside.

(*They enter a colourful kitchen with plants on the window-sill and posters on the wall.*)

Father: So, what d'you fancy, tea or coffee?

Girl:   Is that, like, all you've got?

Father: You want something else?

Girl:   Depends on what there is.

Father: Let's see. (*Opens fridge.*) Grape juice or water, that's about it.

Girl:   What about gin, or vodka?

Father: You serious?

Girl:   Gin with vodka's good.

Father: You know I'm not a big drinker.

Girl:   You think *I am*?

Father: I didn't say that.

Girl:   But that's what you meant.

Father: No, not at all. As far as I'm concerned you drink or you don't drink, it's up to you.

Girl:   So, you wouldn't ever consider, like, trying to stop other people. Except me, of course.

Father: Well, have it your way. You've heard what we've got. Tea, coffee or juice. Now, would you like something?

Girl:   Anything. Doesn't matter. Same as you'll do.

Father: Teabags it is then.

(*While the father makes tea, the girl is busy with her phone. He asks her questions about her course, her brother, her plans. She replies with a half nod, a word or a grunt. Sometimes it's unclear who or what she's addressing: her father or the phone.*)

Father: There's your tea, then. As you like it.

Girl:   What? That's for me?

Father: Yes. The way you like it.

Girl:   Oh, I thought you meant something else.

Father: Something else?

Girl: *As You Like It*. We've been doing it on my course.

Father: Ah, and *do* you like it?

Girl: Not much. Rather have something else.

Father: By the way, have you noticed something?

Girl: Noticed – what?

Father: Those words *something else*, you keep using them.

Girl: Me? Don't think so.

Father: You do, though.

Girl: Noooo-way. Not me.

Father: It's as if you're signalling something – looking for something else – permanently.

Girl: Lay off, Dad. I heard *you* say it.

Father: Yes, repeating after you, that's all.

Girl: So YOU know the problem. It's all about me, like, looking for *something else*. Weird or what?

Father: This is silly.

Girl: Yeah, you're right. Silly-silly. And you're something else.

Father: Your words not mine.

Girl: Bloody hell, Dad, do you have to be this way? Going on and on. Can't you just leave it?

Father: It's only an observation, that's all.

Girl: You know, Dad, I never feel, like, comfortable in this house. There's always something you want to get after. Like, you have to prove a point, have the last say, again and again. You think I'm not good enough or clever enough or nice enough to be your daughter.

Father: I don't think that's fair.

Girl: But it's what you think. *Really.* Ever since— (*She glances up towards the ceiling.*)

Father: If you mean what I think … Well, you're wrong. Nothing has changed. I'm still your dad and you're my daughter.

Girl: So you say.

Father: It's true.

Girl: Yeah, biologically. But what about how we relate? Do you believe we're like, compatible?

Father: Of course.

Girl: But let's say, let's just say we could both swop for something else, a different family, would you do it?

Father: Look—

Girl: So now – swop and you get something else. Would you, or wouldn't you?

Father: Hey, just slow down. You're missing something.

Girl: How? What's up?

Father: You said it.

Girl: Said, said, said, what's that mean?

Father: A lot when it keeps on happening. It means you're avoiding … But forget it.

Girl: Shit, Dad. You've got this obsession. OK just to please you, I'll say it: *something fucking else*. Happy now?

Father: Not really.

Girl: OK … (*She glances at her phone*) You like how I talk?

Father: It's not that important. Liking doesn't come into it, anyway.

Girl: But you really don't, it offends.

Father: That's not the point.

Girl: Is there a point? I mean, does any of this matter?

Father: For me, yes.

Girl: So what's, like, pissing you off?

Father: Not much. It does feel pretty uphill, though.

Girl: But you come to expect that from daughters, don't you? Yes, yes, Dad. I know how you talk together. (*Again, she raises her eyes to the ceiling.*)

Father: We don't. Not the way you put it.

Girl: But what do you say when you talk about me? She's such a sweet girlie-girl … so nicey-nice … knows her place …?

Father: Don't go there.

Girl: Oh yes? So what *do* you say then? And why d'you keep looking at me like I've done something wrong? I'm not some sort of criminal.

Father: Come on, this is all drama.

Girl: Yeah, and I'm playing psycho tonight.

Father: Really, it isn't like that. You're blowing everything up, out of all proportion.

Girl: That's what you think, isn't it? I'm some sort of OTT spoiled brat who, like, doesn't know her place.

Father: You know, there's a name for this. It's called going round in circles.

Girl: Meaning?

Father (*shrugs*): Meaning I'm tired, and there's nothing much more to say.

Girl (*rising to go*): You know Dad, it's always like this. Whatever I say you won't listen. You just think everything I do is wrong. And now you say you're too tired to talk.

Father: Knackered's the word.

Girl: And I'm just so … fru-stra-ted.

Father: That's what we do to each other. Sadly.

Girl: Dad, I need you to talk, I really do.

Father: All right, I'm willing. It's just …

Girl: Just what?

Father: Well, when I'm tired and, to be honest, pretty put off.

Girl: By me. I know.

Father: Could say. Not intended, but then …

Girl: All right Dad. I get it.

Father: You do? I hope so.

Girl: I do, really.

Father: OK, tell me what you're thinking.

Girl: You want to listen?

Father: Absolutely. Go ahead.

Girl: All right, look at it like this – in most ways we're the same. We're both stubborn, because, let's face it, most people are. And we're both a lot of trouble, we don't toe the line, probably you more than me. Listen Dad, it's true. When it comes to people my age I, like, fit in. And that's deliberate, for now. But when I'm adult, I'll be the same as you.

Father: You mean arguing all the time with your daughter.

Girl: Of course. On and on and on.

Father: But what do you do if she keeps arguing back?

Girl: Oh, that's no problem. I'll, like, tell her. The simple truth.

Father: Which is?

Girl: That dads and daughters, like, know best.

Father: And if they're, like, stubborn and troublesome and won't toe the line?

Girl: Then they'll both have to learn.

2.10.09

People change. In the case of Hannah, not too much. But after the first few meetings I came to see her more as she was, or the girl she'd like to be. There were moments of shyness, mostly in private, curled up on the sofa with James as listener, when she asked for help, usually with essays. Once, visiting the café, she sat silently at the back then joined in afterwards, clearing dishes and washing up. You never knew quite who she would be, Hannah Mark One, rough and mouthy, or Hannah Mark Two, little-girl-helpful. Perhaps she didn't know either. But I do think now that she was young, self-conscious, and needed to cover up. So she hid her nice-girl habits. But to us, in private, her true self popped out. As Good-Girl Hannah she sneak-watched quiz shows and costume dramas and listened, occasionally, to online talks. And sometimes she shared quotes, often her own but reworded, taken from films, or she sent us pictures with her own jokey captions. There was even one time when she brought round a friend's story and left it with James. With it came a note that said she'd like my comments.

"Why me?" I asked, gazing at the folder left lying on the table. It was covered with cartoon stickers and flying dolphins.

James shrugged. "I told her you wrote at her age. She didn't say much, but Hannah takes in everything."

"Have you read it?"

"Once. Be warned, it's bog standard stuff. What you might call a generic piece."

"You don't rate it?"

"Hard to tell. It's unfinished."

"But you don't like it?"

"Take a look yourself."

"You think it's bad."

"You'll see."

So I read.

I guess I'm the product of all kinds of forces I can't control. Some of them dark. And then there are my genes.

I don't know a typical all-American family, twenty-first century, but I know I don't come from one for sure. Although a mommy who's a drunk with classy social skills for cover may not be as rare as you'd think. I'm not exactly daddy's girl but plenty of others are, girls I mean, some of them friends of mine, past tense. Dean Dickinson likes to think he's hot but his belly tells another story and his jeans are one size too tight. Miami is the eldest of the Dickinson kids and she takes setting the baddest example possible really seriously, as in a full-time job. Her look is grunge with hairy armpits and flame-red lips, rips in her T-shirts and black fingernails but one thing she isn't aiming on is scaring any guys. There may be some hiding teeth marks with hoodies zipped up high because it'd be hard to find anyone more suited to the vampire life. Or death.

Next is Demona, taller, flat chest, braces, straight As. To look at her you might think churchgoer, virgin. No way. Demona can act the straight but she smokes more than tobacco, only gum and perfume hide it well. That leaves our little brother, the Junior Dean, and he's a shouter, always has been, only it used to be I hate you to his teachers with a teddy thrown their way and now it's fuck off with a compass. Except when he's cute and curly with his tongue hanging out stabbing anything small with more legs than him.

Which leaves me, Evangeline, the audience taking it all in and mixing it my way, making it pay, biding my time. Stockpiling grievances like weapons. Getting ready.

I closed the folder. "So what do you say to something like that?"

"Nothing, if possible."

"But I'm expected to comment?"

"It seems she wants it that way."

611

"Do you know why? Is it some sort of test?"

"No, not at all. In fact, I think it's a mark of respect."

Surprise overcame my doubts. I couldn't quite see it but maybe, I thought, there were other people involved.

I looked back at the folder. "And do you know anything about this friend?"

"I think we're not supposed to ask. Imaginary, I suspect."

"I see, extreme care needed."

"Indeed."

"Maybe if I ask about film deals, and who's going to play Evangeline?"

"As long as you approve, that's OK. But don't stretch it, or she'll suspect."

"So, what you're suggesting is no negatives …"

"And the odd positive thrown in, but keep them general and not too gushy."

"Ah, let me see. Forget style or content and talk about promise and appeal, only not too much. Yes, I think I get it."

"Can you manage?"

"Don't worry I'll do it, very carefully."

"And Beth …"

"Yes?"

"Thank you."

"Oh, that's all right. I like her, anyway."

"I know you do. Write what you have to. I'll read it over if it helps. Maybe you could see this as a kind of olive branch."

15.10.09

I write most days, it keeps me busy. On bad days I manage just a few words, on good days it's in three figures. Like my condition, it comes and goes.

Perhaps I shouldn't say *write*. A lot of it is mental. And there's a magic in it, as if I'm in the dark, talking myself up. So I imagine myself writing, chat to myself, challenge my own feelings and shape my own story, sometimes on paper and sometimes in the head. Often it's in the night, when I'm half asleep. That's when the story develops. The words run on and events take a turn I hadn't expected. It's like a novel in progress. For every small addition something else goes out.

In the morning I look back. If I've any notes I may just copy them and see what happens. But often it's a summary, without a written record. If it exists at all, it's like an image in an album, or a half-forgotten story that crops up in conversation when a friend comes round.

Sometimes I revise, try out different rhythms or switch around phrases. Then I talk to James, describe what I've been thinking, tell him where I'm up to. It's another kind of story with him and me together. I say to him it's for us, I'm trying to make it happen. But in my mind I'm less certain. It's all about survival, there's a hole, imagined or real, and that's what I'm avoiding.

It reminds me of what I'm running from. The detail's there as a cover. I'm alone in the garden, naming what I see.

It's like shining a torch onto see-through paper. The grains stand out and the whiteness shows through.

I've a strange feeling that what I thought was in the past never really happened. Or that what I'm living now is actually a story I've imagined while lying in my bed.

But then, if God is there, does it really matter?

26.10.09

The worst thing is doubt. For a long time there were shadows, sudden alarms, and a shifting, tidal kind of pressure, as if I was underwater. I was drowning, or I was stranded. Something worm-like and achy was filling up inside, then draining. It was in there I knew, but not so I could prove it. Which made me feel unreal. James of course listened, in bed, with his arm around my waist. I could say things together, in a room of our own. But outside that I didn't feel safe. I'd a creeping feeling that I was on a ledge where no one could see me. I was high up and exposed and all on my own. Though, oddly, I wasn't too afraid. It was like jumping between cliffs: I had my eye on reaching the other side, not on the drop. So when the blood appeared I saw it as a sign.

Not the kind of cross-on-the-door, avoidance sign, but an unfamiliar signal, something coded, with a message. It shocked me into life. But the darkness returned and for a while the tests showed nothing.

The odd thing was that during that period, I felt quite strong. On the surface, nothing seemed to trouble me. I went through the fasts and scans and samples and tests, ignoring their meaning. But underneath, I wanted closure, to have something definitive, no matter how unpleasant, to know where I stood.

When the diagnosis came, part of me wasn't that surprised. I did have a gut-shock level which kept me awake. My system was on edge and time was ticking down. But my main worries were what it would be like and whether I could cope. And I did have a hope that if I kept my head down it might go off. That the angel at the door hadn't come for me. But what happened then was I found myself having to explain. All at once I was the centre of interest. In fact it seemed to be my job to deal with everyone, other than James. He embraced me and said we'd face it and together we'd see it off. He put himself in line. Now I think he took too much on himself, but his strength helped me.

The real problem was my family. I do love them, of course, but this was too big or painful for them. They were either tongue-tied or only-too-keen to talk about anything else. I could see them from a distance, they seemed so unaware, but it did keep me occupied. Because there are times it's better to stay awake. I do know that, afterwards, when I'd told them all, I began to weaken and see it as a story full of personal suffering. In my mind there were clips, often from weepies, with black-bordered cards and white-faced relatives around hospital beds. I thought of myself as the subject of a painting, a sad, Ophelia-like drifter. I was Violetta or Mimi, dying in the snow.

Sometimes it's better to be in doubt.

12.11.09 – 3.1.10

I think, over time, we learn how to play things. Because with age you adapt, sometimes to the point where anything goes. You get to know how it works, that it's all interconnected. Also, you see the knock-on effects, the things passed on. In our case not just with the kids but right through the family. So, for instance, take my two: here was Rose at the centre, with Conrad one side and Naomi the other. I was on the outside, closer to Naomi, but available to everyone as a sympathetic listener. Most times they said nothing. If they were happy and comfortable then I wasn't on call. But once they were in conflict then I became their messenger and everything was an issue. It was all about challenges and complaints and finger pointing – which was what developed quickly around Rose's baptism.

I'd seen it coming but said nothing. For Rose at that time, church was her life. It was where she found herself in a strong place, somewhere she was known. Though my views were different, I understood her faith. It answered all her questions. The mood took over and she sang as she prayed and walked to the altar in step with others, and nothing was uncertain or shadowy or shot through with doubt.

But when news of a special service reached Naomi, the arguments began.

"Mum, did you know about Rose's baptism?" she asked, after chatting about work.

I recognised the tone. She was holding back.

"What about it, love?"

"Well, for one thing – did you realise when it was due?"

"Not exactly. I knew it was coming up soon."

"This week, just four days' time. Almost straight away."

"Yes, I suppose it is very close."

"And you didn't tell me. Not-a-single-word."

"I'm sorry love, I hadn't realised."

"But did you agree to her doing it, in the way they're going to?"

I paused before replying. Her voice tone had hardened: there was an RP crispness about it, as if she was speaking in public, for effect.

"You're worried about her?" I asked.

"Not worried, but alarmed, and with good reason."

"You needn't be. She'll be fine."

"You sure of that? I mean, total immersion, it's what we call invasive. A takeover job."

I recognised her objection. It was her urge to protect her patients. I could hear her in the ward wanting action.

"But it's what she wants. Her choice," I replied.

"You mean Dad's. It's all about him and his cult. They just want her brainwashed, and you have to stop it."

"I don't think it's like that. If you want it stopped you'll have to talk to Rose, or your dad."

"Oh, Mum. I don't think … I *really* don't."

It was at this point that the talk became charged. Up to then she'd stayed calm, at least on the surface. But at the mention of Conrad her voice suddenly turned and she was on us – me, it seemed, more than him.

"It's simply not fair," she cut in. "You do whatever you like, break up the family, close your eyes to *us*, and then you allow this stupid business."

"Naomi, please," I said, "this doesn't help."

"But it's true. It's an awful mess. You've allowed Rose to get into this, done nothing, and now … you've left it too late."

Her voice had dropped and turned inward, I could feel her pulling back.

"All right," I said, "I'll talk to Rose and see what can be done."

"You will, Mum?"

"I'll try."

"Promise?"

I promised. She received my words with a quickly-taken breath. It was just, she explained, that no one had told her. Pausing, she repeated then switched back to work-talk, distancing slightly. For her the argument was over, something more important had taken its place. Like her father she'd closed herself off.

I texted Rose and we met up the next day. At this point she was living at Conrad's, a choice, as she called it, that I saw as inertia. I think I'd rationalised away the hurt, I didn't want her damaged, so I hid my feelings. She was still a teen, my flat was out of town, and they'd beliefs in common. In any case I'd left him, and Rose felt he needed company. So we met after school at the sports centre café using *our table*, a small two-seater in a glassed-in corner that overlooked the pool.

As we talked our words seemed to drift, bobbing about like shadows on water. I couldn't quite tell what she might be feeling, but when I told her about Naomi she blushed.

"I really wish …" she began, gazing down at the pool. It was full. At the shallow end there were small children treading water, the centre was occupied by head-down swimmers, in a corner teenagers were splashing wildly. At the deep end, a lifeguard sat watching. He was short and squat and sat cross-legged on a fold-out chair. He looked statuesque.

"What, my love?" I asked.

Rose remained silent. Pale and self-aware, with her head to one side, she seemed to be waiting for something to happen.

I continued probing, "You want to go through with it?"

She shrugged. Her soft grey eyes had taken on a moon-like expression; she was focused inward.

From below a shout rose up. A chorus of voices joined in, repeating the first call. The hall was full of splashes and grey-white movement.

"I don't think anyone's got an answer," I added. "Maybe you could delay?"

Behind her, the waves were rising and falling in short, choppy bursts.

Suddenly she clasped her hands together and raised them to her chest. "No delay. This Sunday, I'll be baptised."

When I told Naomi, she took it better than I'd expected.

"Now I know what's happening, I've got used to it," she said, raising her voice above the sound of passing cars. Her mobile made her shouty.

"I'm glad," I replied, "I hope you'll come."

"When is it?"

"Oh, you don't know?"

"Just tell me. Time and date, so I'm clear."

As I gave her the details, I wondered why she asked. To have forgotten so quickly just didn't add up. There was something intended but left unspoken.

I finished, calling out against the background roar. I could make out the sound of tyres on tarmac and engines revving.

"So, you're coming?" I asked.

"I'll see. Maybe, if possible."

Before I could reply, the traffic noise peaked, her voice cut off and the phone went dead.

On Rose's special day I got ready early. I'd chosen a blue blouse, cream-coloured tights and a check-patterned skirt. Minus earrings and lightly made up, my aim was to fit. There were memories, of course: Conrad and marriage, living in his house, conflicts, refusals … Then the girls growing older, and dreams of walking out. But I made myself ready, focusing on the girls, trying not to think. Behind my carefully-judged looks, I was missing James.

When I arrived, I stood outside the black stone chapel, reading the notices. They were large-print and bright. On the wall behind, a pure white rose caught my eye. Above it an off-yellow light glowed through glass. I knew there were people in there, preparing.

When Naomi turned up, wearing jeans and a sweater, I greeted without question. If her clothes were a statement, I chose not to see it, hoping that others would take their cue from me.

"I'm glad you're here," I said quietly, kissing her forehead. I could feel her gearing up. She was tight around the face and breathing quickly.

"I had to," she said, "it's important."

Arm in arm we entered church. The inside hadn't changed. High and wide with folding chairs and darkened windows, it smelled of soap and polish. At the centre was a bare white altar raised like an exhibit on a low stone platform.

"Look," I whispered, nodding to one side, where a group were mouthing prayers by a roped-off area. Inside the ropes a woman was pouring water from a jug into a large metal bathtub. The water, as it dripped and splashed, seemed to mingle with the prayers. Every so often the woman half turned, catching the eye of a girl in a long white gown. The girl, who was seated and alone, was Rose.

"Where's Conrad?" asked Naomi.

I nodded towards a high-arched doorway. In the centre stood a robed figure with his back to the church.

"We'll sit as a family," I said as I led towards the front. Inside, I was groping in the dark.

Rose smiled when we joined her. She sat with her hands clasped together, pressed into her lap. Her stillness made me feel for her. I could see how much she wanted to please.

I glanced down at my watch. The woman had finished pouring, the waters were still and an organ had begun playing, quietly. The prayers, though audible, had faded to a low-level drone. The church was in readiness. The worshippers' faces were full of soft, gentle expectation.

Then suddenly it all changed. Conrad appeared, walking to the front. His long, flowing robe made him darkly impressive. He stopped by me, looking down. For a second he reminded me of a Tintoretto portrait.

"I'd like a word before our service," he said, waving a hand towards the vestry. "Girls as well."

To my left I could feel Naomi bristling, on the other side, Rose was what they call lifted, my role was to act as intermediary.

"Come on," I said, putting out a hand to both girls. For their sake I needed to be strong.

We followed to the vestry. Entering, we sat down as invited, lining up on one side of a table. Conrad took the floor opposite with his back to the wall. He thanked us quietly then switched without warning to what I call his prophetic mode. I'd seen him do it before: head back, eyes narrowed to slits, both hands outstretched. But this time, though familiar, I still wondered what was coming.

His breathing relaxed and his colour returned as his eyes opened in an otherworldly smile. When he began his voice was directed towards me, "I'd like you, Elizabeth, to join us, today."

Fixing me with a stare, he continued, "Come forward, Elizabeth, Mother of Rose," here his eyes strayed to his younger daughter, "enter together in total immersion, become one body in the love of Christ."

Looking back, I remember the feelings. They came up from nowhere and in no particular order. At first I simply stared ... my mind had slowed. He'd said something strange, an outlandish statement that didn't add up. I wondered if I'd misheard or simply missed the point. The experience was there, without the meaning.

Then came the shock as the phrases began to register. How dare he, I thought. The time, the place, in front of the children, the whole thing came back. Those years in private and the hours at the window then all that darkness and silence, under his surveillance.

I refused, of course, keeping it brief and stating my position, but I could feel the heat rising in my cheeks. Inside I was shaking, only this time I was determined not to show it.

I think I surprised him. There were words exchanged. Conrad and Naomi argued while Rose became tearful, asking for quiet. I felt for her then. I didn't want to hurt her but the situation called for something strong, a clear-cut statement to challenge Conrad.

I remember at that moment something else took over. Perhaps it was the backlog, or maybe there were voices – mine, or my gran's – but suddenly I told him. "You need," I said, "to do what we're here for and baptise Rose …"

In my mouth, unspoken, were the words, "and not me."

When we left the vestry, I could still hear their imagined voices, running in my head: Naomi protesting, Rose interjecting, Conrad sounding off. Without saying anything we continued our dispute, locked into ourselves. In the silence of the church as we sat down for the service, the thoughts kept flaring up. They were hot spots, sparking, in warning.

At least that's how I recall it. At the time we'd been through a divorce and the service, when it began, didn't feel nice. There were too many bad memories. In any case I was jumpy about the girls. It also brought back what I'd known all along: that Conrad was lead actor while we were audience. So, with all eyes on him, he called on God's *majesty* and *splendour*. "We bow down," he cried, "we honour, we worship." When Rose came forward flanked by two women, his voice took on an insistent, sing-song quality, as he spoke of being clean. I could hear inside his words the call of the little-boy-lost.

The actual baptism happened more quickly, I imagine, than Conrad really wanted. It began with Rose, wearing a one-piece costume, lowering herself into water. As she went down she slipped, a wave sloshed out and spread across the floor. Inside, I was with her, praying quietly. One of the women spoke and Rose ducked underwater, but almost immediately spluttered back up. Red in the face, she began to cry. Her moment of truth hadn't worked out. When the woman handed her out I wanted to hug her. She dried herself and left for the vestry, head down, avoiding our eyes. Beside me Naomi was staring and muttering to herself. I could tell that Conrad wasn't pleased. His words came out in a flow; they were bright and smooth with a rawness underneath. They sent me back to the times I'd listened, bowed forward in church, praying. But on this occasion his mood couldn't touch me, my heart was with Rose in the vestry …

4.1.10

Doubt and faith are two sides of a picture, dark and light, front and back, figure and ground. Or they're two opposite forces in a storm, and like pain and breath they come and go. Sometimes they're the same, or there's an overlap and the hurt and the confusion become a line of feeling, a waving running in from a wild sea.

Doubt, of course, is in everything. It's in this story, in my head, in my heart. And I can't tell sometimes what's real and what's imagined. I know I'm with James, he's my rock, but the world around isn't always there. It can be hard to make out, as in a dream, seen at a distance, looking out from the entrance of a cave. Inside the cave I'm safe, in prayer, with voices and song. But even in there the doubt creeps in. There's a blur around the words, an out-of-body feel, as if I'm listening for a call in an empty waiting room. I can hear my own breathing and the rhythm of my heart, moving quietly. Doubt's in there, hidden behind everything. It comes and goes like shadows in the night. I'm a child in darkness, knowing nothing.

To believe is to be alive, like Rose. It's what keeps her safe. For me, it's like swimming with one foot on the bottom. Something to hold on to, because I want things to be real. So I live my story. I've been out at the headland with James, running from the rain and I can see us from a distance, walking back into sunlight. Belief is everywhere. It's in the photographic image, the bird in the garden and the side lamp by the bed. In the stain in cloth, the wind against the face, the colour of a flower. Of course, my belief in these things is shot through with doubt. The two are connected. *Without doubt*, are the words I say in prayer. They ascend like smoke, dissolving into air. They come and go with the wind, and are nothing and everything. Doubt and faith make up my God.

I felt both forces when they wheeled me towards the surgery doors.

10.2.10

In my thoughts this week:
- Jiggling up and down on the bathroom scales to nudge the pointer higher. So strange after all these years: weight-watching in reverse.
- Dreams of being in the ward. The sleepless ache, grey skin and hair, voices in corners: a Place Left Out.
- Good days, bad days, one after the other. Struggling to stay strong. Knots and barbs and grits. Edges pushing up through earth. Then roses in a vase.
- Blood spots appearing on enamel. Painlessly pink. Floaty, like blossoms on ice.
- Grand Old Duke of York marches up to the loo – straining, spotting – and down again.
- Texting James with smileys and kisses.
- Examining my scar: purple-brown zipper, sewn into flesh.
- Rain as comet-streaks on glass, the sky as ocean, storming, angels in the clouds.
- Weighing out ingredients for cupcake and blancmange, my mum's recipes. Preparing gravy and herbal sauces. Rub a dub-dub, polishing plates.
- Sleeping all day in a litter of magazines, glass to one side, with pill packs on the floor.
- Matthew 8:17. "This was to fulfil what was spoken by the prophet Isaiah: 'He took our illnesses and bore our diseases'."

- Phoning my girls when I'm at my jolliest. Talking, smiling. Making sure the love shines through.
- A resolution: avoid talk of illness, appointments, doctors and me-talk. Instead face outwards, follow stories, ask everyone who, what, where.
- Sneak-feeding self: eyeliner, foundation and lippy. Long, multi-coloured dresses and silk headscarves. Two rings in a box. Photos of the beach. Reading love letters, one a day.
- A blue line on a piece of paper with a yellow ball above. I study it calmly, intently, under 60 watt pearl, without thought. It becomes me.
- 1 Corinthians 6:19-20. "Or do you not know that your body is a temple of the Holy Spirit within you, whom you have from God? You are not your own, for you were bought with a price. So glorify God in your body."
- Watching birds pecking on the lawn: seesaw bodies with needles darting cloth.
- Postcards to parents: Vanessa Bell, *Interior*; Stanley Spencer, *Resurrection*; Edward Bawden, *Lagoon*.
- Eaten inside by unseen mouths. Pelican feeding chicks. *The Nightingale and the Rose*.
- Ache. Coarse-grained, like sandpaper. Scraper, cheese grater, wire cutter.
- James stroking my body with softly-smooth hands. Sharing small-talk and deep-and-meaningfuls. Bringing water, joke books, fruit. His wise-owl eyes watching.
- Sleep.

27.2.10

I don't think God watches. It always seemed to me, from childhood on, that we're the ones looking out. In the garden, from a window, all across the night sky, wherever there's a view. If God's anywhere we have to look round corners, dig deep, go against the flow. And I try to avoid the words He or She or even It. I see God as metaphor, as *imaginary*, not real or here. Something we've made up. A story, if you like, that doesn't exist and is all about opposites, accidents, contradictory states. What's not possible is larger than life.

For Conrad, God was always *now*, and in action. He's the big man Father who brings down the rain. You can pray to him for health and success and building a church. There are rewards and, of course, punishments. The world is a classroom where you pass tests or learn by rote to win gold stars. And it's very personal. So from early on, Minister Conrad was a noise. He'd that power-in-the-Lord which impresses. Partly voice, with its flights and swoop-downs to a stop, but also appearance: his above-all-that, *Justice League* look. He saw what's what, without any question.

But I knew him better, my job was rescue. Because behind his grand words, Conrad struggled. Bad things, he said, attacked him, mainly at night. For most of our marriage he slept with a torch. He kept it by the bedside and used it when he went to the bathroom, saying it gave him protection. Even then he sometimes stayed up for hours. More than once I found him in the morning, asleep in a corner with his arms across his face. When I woke him, it was if he'd been hit from behind. I asked him to explain and he drew me a picture. It showed him small, crouched in a hole, with fighter jets above. The hole was oval, dipped at one end and looked like a section across a lung. He'd drawn in tunnels, appearing from below. One was filled with an enormous spider-like creature that reached out to grab him. He told me it was called Smoke.

Sometimes he was different, more willing to talk, and he spoke about his fears, how he woke thinking he was someone else, or that no one could see him. There were voices behind doors, things in mirrors. Mornings where he cried, saying he was finished.

On those days I nursed him. I patched him up, read to him, listened to his fears and restored his faith. And I joined him afterwards, praying.

For a while it worked, and he returned to himself, feeling good. I mean good as in sanctified. And for him, to feel was to do. So he launched out, fought for the poor, worked in shelters and distributed food. And I encouraged him, telling him he was doing Christ's work.

I knew that while he was giving he didn't have to think. While he talked about shaping and struggle and making people whole, he could ignore himself. It was what he needed. A salvation world where the spirit acted, where heaven and earth connected.

But then quite suddenly, he lost his footing.

It was Easter, the season of doubt. There was a vigil, at first with just Conrad and me, then with Derek, a church elder. To begin with, we sat near the high east window, beneath a cross carved on the wall. Bare and cold and alive with shadows, the church smelled of candles. At this stage I was recovering from flu so I didn't stay long. I left him with Derek. The two of them had blankets and food and prayer books and Conrad's torch, hidden in a bag.

Derek told me that just before midnight Conrad began to pace up and down. Apparently he was shivering and short of breath. From what Derek said, Conrad had been quoting Isaiah. It seems that as he spoke, he fell to the floor. I remember Derek's story, told quietly, how Conrad's body went rigid and he couldn't get up. It must have been awful. Midnight, in a church, with a man on the floor, having fits. Derek didn't say how long it went on, but when Conrad came round he was shouting. Maybe he'd banged his head or perhaps he was afraid but, once up, Derek described him dancing down the aisle, shadow-boxing, then lashing out suddenly, knocking over candles.

I'm not sure how it ended but I think it involved the torch. Derek just said Conrad found himself. What I do know is that when my husband came home next morning, he was red-eyed and stammering. All his private problems had come to the surface. He didn't want to eat, couldn't sleep and was pacing the house talking to himself. There were bruises on his body and blotches on his forehead. He kept wanting his torch, and crying.

I remember I was appalled. Upset for him and afraid of people knowing; it all seemed so extreme. So, like Derek, I covered for him. We put together a story about a virus that was dangerous and meant, we said, he couldn't speak. I didn't like the story, but did nothing to challenge it. At least it gave us space. Except for my visits to the shops, it kept us one-to-one and private. There were cards and prayers, but no calls or visits.

What I hadn't foreseen was how being together would affect me. Over the next three weeks all my feelings, which had been half-forgotten, surfaced again. It was us together in darkness, with Conrad angry and me trying to please. I'd gone back to that woman who wanted all but didn't dare ask. In hoping and waiting and praying for his health, I was hurting myself.

What I fell for was his wounds, and trying to make him happy.

5.3.10

There are so many metaphors for having treatment.

1. It's a garden where I'm in the bushes, with my skirt caught on thorns. I think of undergrowth and the hundred years' sleep. There are chewed down stems and webs in corners. It's a dirty place full of rot and mud. Bluebottles and flying ants swarm around concrete. There are thrips, fungi and knots in wood.

2. Running through a stitch, walking on blisters, squeezing muscles, fighting for breath – the highs and lows of pain.

3. Inside the ambulance is an underwater swim with a blue light flashing on the walls. There's a floatiness about it. A tunnel-like dreaminess, as if it was a capsule launched into space. It oscillates slightly like a needle pointing north. To be in there is a journey.

4. There's a route through the hospital that leads to *Oncology*. It's along a wide sunlit corridor with art on the walls. Towards the end there's a picture behind glass that I stop and look at. It's near where they operated on me. The picture is large, mediaeval, and alive with village life. In the foreground there are barrels on large-wheeled carts and steep-roofed houses. It's full of people bent over, busy in snow. There's a crowd around a building, peering in through a wide opening. Only those at the front can see what's inside. The house holds a secret, something hidden that changes everything. Somehow, it sums up my illness. It's Breughel's *Census at Bethlehem*.

5. Waiting rooms, consulting rooms, dressing rooms, rooms with machine-sized instruments, lab rooms, rooms full of beds and curtain-dividers, rooms that become corridors that turn into tunnels then stack above each other – they appear in my dreams, close in from all sides, force me to my knees.
6. Injections and cannulas are like threading needles. Taking blood needs a steady hand. The bedside doctor speaks softly, the nurse plays sister and friend. Pills and water are our communion.
7. The medical facts: cold, bare, moonlight walks, bright metals, rawness and strange possession.
8. Fallen from the nest. Sprawling. Broken wing.
9. Soft hands, new sheets, cool water, listening expressions. Careful touch, clean flesh smell. Naming and smiling, giving praise, healing.
10. Unless you change and become like little children …

21.3.10

Looking back, I couldn't have left Conrad without Toby's help. After teenage we'd grown apart, phoning sometimes and catching up at family gatherings, but even at a distance we had a way of sensing if the other was in trouble. So when I walked out, Toby offered help. I half guessed the reason, but accepted gratefully, out of fear of exposure and care for his feelings. I stayed for a while in his house: a large, draughty, weather-boarded bungalow with high hedges and a perpetually damp back garden. He lived there on his own with a collection of cameras that he used to take pictures of the town. Photography helped him, I think, with the loneliness. In his own words, he'd become a camera nut.

The house was a short walk to the station, which made it easier to commute. Of course, I was in shock. Nothing seemed to register. I slept four hours at most, taking the first train out and last train back. My life was a struggle, I'd lost my footing, I was going under, but Toby was my rock. Together with Meg, he kept our family going, helping with fares and phoning the girls, and driving to Folkestone to bring back my possessions. On his return he stuck out his jaw and lowered his voice. "God-squad, wants everything cleared," he said. The last word disturbed me, it made me realise how far we'd come. But I enjoyed his Conrad impressions and our talks.

While I was there, I came to know him better, mainly through discussing growing up. I pressed him about youth and then about his dreams, which led to talk about football. I learned about his team's colours, the names, and why he was a fan. It was the first time he'd talked about the subject as an adult. He called it keeping the faith, a blind belief in what comes round. In any case, he explained, he'd stood with his team through thick and thin and wasn't going to change. "The spirit of football," he said, "is hope for the best, expect the worst." And he transferred that spirit to my divorce.

I stayed for a month. Sleeping on a mattress in a damp back room made me understand how he hadn't had it easy. "I've been where you are," he said, pointing to a picture of his ex dressed in black. He told me about her, saying she wasn't what she seemed. A gentle, caring older woman who'd changed altogether when she joined a sect, renaming herself and sleeping separate when he refused to join. He'd moved out shouting, with her declaring she'd never forgive.

"I was too young," he told me, turning back to an earlier photo. "And she changed. A bit like Conrad, only mad cow, not bull." In that picture I could see him, little-boy Toby arm in arm with a woman in a hat. They looked like mother and son.

When I moved back to Folkestone, Toby was my companion, dividing his time between weekdays in Sidcup and weekends at my flat. "Pleased to be of service," he said when I thanked him, "just call me guard dog." And he bared his teeth, pretending to growl.

But when it came to divorce, Toby was my Best Man. Acting as my adviser he told me what to do, warning of solicitors and legal delays. "In the end," he said, "they'll make it run and run, like mine did."

In fact, without him we couldn't have settled.

What I know now is solicitors have to be watched. Mine was young, unsmiling and nicely-spoken. At the start she listened, asked a few questions and took what she called a view. I was given the impression, without too much said, that Conrad didn't have a case. From then on the costs went up. At each new turn I was consulted, informed of options, reminded of progress, and billed for what I said.

At the time I was upset and wanted it over, so I paid without question, hoping that would speed things. But after periods of silence and problems with letters and a botched disclosure I became less willing. It was all so ad hoc, so messy and uncertain, and I wondered how long it might continue and whether I could bear it.

Fortunately, Toby got to know. "Never trust a solicitor," he said. "They just want your bank details."

By then I'd changed as a client. My suspicions had grown and I was less afraid, so I made an offer. It came just in time, heading off a court case, and led to my solicitor, after an exchange between parties, advising in writing that Conrad could go for more.

"Oh yes," exclaimed Toby when he read it, "nothing like a U-turn. But if you argue, she'll charge you for her time."

Of course, I wasn't happy. I wanted to bin it and simply walk away. But Toby, when he realised, stopped me. He described his divorce and pushed for action. At his suggestion I raised the sum and came to a settlement. Together we achieved what the solicitor couldn't do.

Afterwards at the café, Toby brought his camera and we celebrated with friends, sharing ice cream and cake with elderberry cordial. Toby was jubilant, football-style, and snapped me with Sarah. He paired me with customers in celebratory close-ups. Later, on our own, he took some fill-in shots as we cleared up the café. Then we walked out to the beach and began to talk.

"I never really got it with Conrad," said Toby, aiming his lens at a thistle, "ever since that first time at Sunday school."

I understood. He'd said so before but I'd not been listening.

"You remember?" asked Toby, pressing the shutter.

In my mind, I was back there in the church hall, meeting Conrad. I could see him as he entered, clowning slightly, then at the table enjoying the questions. He'd played hard to get.

"I don't know what you saw in him," said Toby, pointing his camera at a rock. It was grey, cigar-shaped, and pitted with holes.

I shrugged. "I suppose he was solid, or seemed that way. With ideas of his own."

Turning the stone over, Toby took a few more snaps. There were hairline cracks and a band of crystals appearing at one end. "I always thought you looked up to him."

I didn't answer straightaway. I think, now, I took his words as a challenge. They made me feel I needed to explain, to myself as well as him.

"I did, but that wasn't why, or it wasn't the main reason."

At that moment I remember seeing myself in church, writing poetry, with Louise below. A picture came back of her by the pulpit, arranging flowers.

I pointed to the stone. "I mean, that's beautiful, yes?"

He looked and fingered his camera.

"But strange as well," I said.

Toby nodded.

"So, you take a photo because it's different, in a way only a picture can capture," I added.

He opened his mouth then, thinking better, closed it.

"And afterwards you still see it, in your mind."

Toby smiled.

"But it's full of holes and cracks, some of them nasty, and it seems to have fallen from somewhere else?"

He nodded again.

"Then that's Conrad, as he was to me."

4.4.10 – 6.5.10

Yesterday's hospital appointment was, on the surface, what we've come to expect. As usual, James took me there and we walked in slowly to busy corridors. There were people in gowns, patients on trolleys, lost-looking visitors, staff and nurses carrying files, and we moved through with rest stops, while keeping direction. As an outing it was familiar but tiring, though I liked the attention, the out-there feel. But not the waits. And the treks between buildings, sent round for testing. And not, of course, those stripped-down examinations behind curtains with students in attendance. You know when they mean business, with their skin-tight gloves and bowls to catch blood. Also, the trolley-beds trailing drip-lines and charts you can't see. But this was a routine examination, one of those white-wall appointments with joke-books and mags and views across the garden.

When you visit it brings things back: the scentless, weightless pills, the doctors with their notes and the courses of injections. They say it's necessary and you believe them. That is, until you begin gagging. And then you get that yellow paper feel, so you can't take food, and your insides wipe with what I call the snowstorm, and you have to lie down. It makes you wonder if the cure is worth it.

I remember those months, how it changes moods and makes you think you're someone else. And sometimes it changes the relationship, completely.

My illness took over, creeping into everything, closing us down, in a house full of silence. Not the kind of long-term silence of couples in touch who accept who they are, not the silence of absence or of reading a book, and not that silence of gestures or words-in-the-head, but silence as denial. Silence as cut-off.

It was a shock. I thought it wasn't happening or we were going through a phase. I persuaded myself it wasn't that important, or really wasn't so, using words like "adult", "realistic" and "normal" then allowing things to drift. I even told myself that we were simply being honest and we'd come out stronger. Looking back, that was a mistake, it kept me from thinking. So we passed it off, we were casual or teased each other, and my condition worsened as the moods took over.

"Thanks," I'd say, speaking without warmth, when James brought me tea in bed. When he asked how I was, I said nothing, and when he repeated, I pretended not to hear.

"I said, how are you?" he asked, raising his voice, and I answered "All right," avoiding his eyes. Next, when he served food, I objected to stains on the tea tray or I ate, complaining about portions and the unheated plate. I think my remarks annoyed him. He was on duty 24/7, so a single positive might have helped. But in any case, if *I* wasn't that easy, he played his part. He put on an act. He'd ask how I felt then change the subject or he'd tell me about work, describing an incident, usually unpleasant, while looking out the window. Sometimes jokey and sometimes calm, I felt at times he was going through the motions. "Is that what you want?" he'd ask, after bringing me the radio, or my phone and a book. "Anything else?" he'd add, and suck in his cheeks. Sometimes it felt as if he gave me support only because he had to.

From that point on, the silence was in us, whether we spoke or not. For example, while I was on the phone, he'd be playing music, full volume. Or he'd come to bed late, wake me, then fall asleep while I talked. In the morning he was there, still busy, dividing his attention between work and breakfast. We'd catch up in a fashion, but mainly about timings and arrangements. When he left he'd kiss my cheek and cut off. Though I do remember in the evening he'd sometimes bring me flowers, but then leave them downstairs.

I was hurt, of course, but in a way my illness came first. When you're cold and aching and shaky, you don't have much left for anything else. In any case, he was doing everything he could, it was just that the heart had gone out of it.

Later, when I was up and around, the not-now business began. He'd say "Not right now," then pause and consider. Sometimes he'd ask me, "Now?" or "Not really now?" then go back to his catch-phrase, adding an excuse. He had it off pat. So if I wanted to talk he'd not-now and go shopping or he'd need to ring someone then keep out of sight writing notes or calling from the kitchen, and when my girls came round he'd disappear into the garden with plants to chop or a fence to mend. He'd not-now, too, about gossip, exchanging news, or watching TV. It was all about avoidance and exchanges quickly taken.

I think we needed something to shake us up, what medics call a critical incident. Ours was domestic, small-scale, but important in its way. It happened on one of those days when everything goes wrong. We'd not slept well, a door handle jammed and the computer went down. It could have happened earlier, but we got through till late, despite a spillage and Sandra ringing up. But the strain was there, and when the TV blanked with James upstairs, things kicked off.

I called out, more loudly I think than I realised. Normally James would have not-now-ed me, but on this occasion he called back and when I didn't answer, he called again. I knew or half heard, but chose to cut off, I wanted him to show feeling. A third unanswered call, close now to a shout, and he sprang to the stairs. As he came down at speed he slipped, hitting the floor with a thump. I cried out in alarm and heard him groaning quietly as he pulled himself up. "Shit," he muttered as he hobbled into the lounge. He swore again and thrust himself down on the sofa.

"Are you OK?" I asked.

He grimaced and asked me the same thing.

I remember looking at him oddly. Rerunning his fall, I realised what I'd done. "I called out, didn't I ... It was fussing really. But what about you?"

"Bloody hurts," he muttered, rubbing his toe.

"I shouldn't have shouted."

"When you didn't reply I thought you were ill."

"Yes, I'm sorry."

"I was rushing."

"And I should have replied," I said.

He winced as he pressed down on his toe.

"Blame *that,*" I said, pointing to the TV. "Broken again."

He laughed, uneasily. "I was afraid ..."

Realising what he meant, I offered him a hand. This time the silence was shared. We were in touch, aware of what we'd said and what we really meant.

Afterwards he kissed me ...

I think yesterday in the hospital was another of those moments. It seemed we were there for treatment, waiting to be seen, but really we needed answers. Not what was happening or how to treat it but why. Why me? Why anyone? It's the first thing you ask. And it's there behind the blue lights and the bare white corridors and the sealed double doors. The question of suffering. Why it happens and who it chooses. Or how it does things, and how it presents. I sometimes think if suffering was a person he'd be on his own. No one would trust him. Dressed as a broker or a playboy, he'd be the sneak, the one who got away. I often imagine him strolling, picking out bargains, wearing something once and chucking it away. He's a flaneur type, full of self and doing what he pleases, a believer in nothing.

In the face of all that, I think we do our best. It's about getting by. For some that means luck, for others struggle and for most of us, being patient. I call it a thought-form. When you reach a certain point the outlook changes and you take a longer view. You live now, but more *inside* life, as it happens, whatever comes up. From experience you can tell, when to question and when to be still. And yesterday, in hospital, was a good example.

So we waited. James understood, and we sat close, keeping focus. I'd given my address, checked off my GP and telephone number, and was running through what to say. I needed to be ready.

A nurse called me to be weighed then directed us both to a smaller room. Here we sat between a fish tank and a boxful of toys. Through the open door we could see people passing. "It's all very public," James said quietly.

I remember feeling stared-at.

"Hospital's supposed to be confidential," he continued, leaning close, "but you can tell who are the patients, you just have to look."

He was right, of course, but his statement was a shock, I wondered what he was saying about me.

"But don't worry, darling," he added, smiling. It was as if he'd heard my thoughts.

"I look ill, don't I?" I said.

He put his arm around my shoulders. "I really didn't mean it that way."

"But I look bad – yes?"

"Don't say that."

"And you don't find me attractive anymore."

That was the defining moment. It was something, until then, I'd kept locked inside myself. I was too ashamed, but also I was angry – with myself, with James, most of all with my illness. If this was life, then I didn't want it.

His reply came slowly, "Beth, just tell yourself no. It's not true."

I looked away, shaking my head.

634

James began telling me how guilty he felt, not being ill. "There's so little I can do," he said, spreading his hands.

That was when I realised that he, too, was suffering. "But you're not to blame. How could you be?"

He looked into my eyes. "I'm lucky. Sometimes, I know this sounds stupid, but I feel I don't have the right."

"In that case, it's down to both of us," I replied.

He looked me in the eye and for a moment I was reminded of our first-time meeting. "But down to me especially," he said. "Though of course," he added, brightening, "you have to do the right thing."

"Which is?"

"To make sure I know what you want."

"That's simple."

"Simple?"

"Yes."

"Explain, please."

I smiled. "What I want … is for you to let me have my way. Always."

"Always?"

"Always and without exception," and I kissed his forehead, telling him I loved him.

14.5.10

Sometimes when I think back, I can feel those moments, they work like sightings. It's as if there was a light switch ready to go on. Or an automatic camera with a view out, and its own inner line. Often at an angle, they appear out of time, off-purpose, in a quick-release burst. They're sharp, like birds, and have to be watched-for. I call them my angels.

Of course, sightings are all different. I discovered that early on, with my dad. The angel of air that he spoke about in stories and rose at dawn; the angel of leaves that turned green then black; the angel of sleep that drifted downwards into earth. Angels had their habits. They were sad at night; colourless and invisible during the day. Once, in the garden, he talked about meeting them then made up a story.

He began quietly, with a finger to his lips. "Shh. Can you hear them in the bushes?" he said, widened his eyes. "If you look you'll see them. They're paper-thin and glowing."

I remember asking if they were birds. Smiling, he looked down the garden. "They're a bit like robins. You can lose them in the shadows, but they're always there."

Then, putting an arm around me, he began his tale.

There was once an angel no one saw. He was a big, fine angel made of dreams. At full stretch he was tall as a house and wide as a field. He was old, old as the Earth, and could fly above the moon. But there was one problem, no one could see him. When he was there people felt the wind or the sun. Sometimes they smelled flowers or heard music. On dark nights he was rain against the window. But nobody saw him – and because he wasn't seen, he didn't have a name.

But he *did* have a name, one he used alone, when he talked to himself. He'd tried it in the day, but the other angels didn't like it. "Too short," they said or "Not right," they said, then "Not for you," they said. Their words put him off. So he went around trying different names. He called himself Old in the sun, King by water, Young in the wind.

But no one saw him. So he disguised himself, coming down to earth as a bird. And there he found a girl, sitting by herself in a garden. "I am the bird No-name," he sang.

She listened, head to one side. "No-name, why do you call yourself that?"

"Because no one can see me."

The girl looked sad. "No one sees me, too. But I can see you, you're a bird."

The angel blushed. "No, no, that's not my name."

The girl stretched out her arm. "Come," she said and the bird hopped onto her hand, "let me take you to my naming place."

Then she walked, with the bird on her palm, along to the church. The door was open and as they entered the bird flew up. It landed on the cross and at once the church was filled with rainbows. Flowers appeared and the bird began to sing. The walls and ceiling lifted off and then the girl was alone, walking beneath stars. They were bright and silvery and shone like jewels.

"Now I know your name," she said quietly, "You-Are-Who-Is." As she spoke, she looked up. Above her she saw the angel, stretching from horizon to horizon, covering the stars. He was white and shimmering, glowing all over. Reaching forward the angel scooped her up.

"And you," he whispered, "are Queen of the Sky."

12.6.10 – 2.12.10

In remission.

Three months, then six. More than I ever expected, with green ticks on the calendar and time and people to catch up with, and my girls paying visits, and every day a prayer.

The prayers began as a result of walks. They were short at first but when we drove inland we went further, crossing fields with cowpats and flies around pools. In the past I'd wanted something larger, so I'd be counting steps or talking about friends, but now it was enough. Just to hear the birds and imagine my dad, to go with James talking flowers, to be walking free past fences and hedges: it filled and absorbed me. It reminded me of reading out loud from my gran's children's books.

As a prayer it wasn't fixed, it didn't have an order, and the words, if there were any, were more like colours, or the idea of colours floating in the head. But we walked, stepping over stiles and passing through gates, and the ordinary became special. We were in the fields, taking the air, hearing birdsong, following the path.

"Shall we try the woods?" James asked, pointing.

I agreed and we headed uphill, following a sheep track. As we entered, the trees cut us off. I was reminded of our walk at *Deanbury*.

When you're in the woods it magnifies everything. You're in a cave, sealed into quiet. It slows you slightly and you move through untouched, as on a screen. But you're *inside* the picture, observing. And, in there, the paths are all different: some narrow, some road-width, with forks and detours and crossings leading off. It seems, in the woods, life's older, less here and now, and oddly-patterned.

We didn't exactly pray. The silence had its voices, and the step-by-step progress took us further in. There were a few words: a gesture from James, a flower name and smile, and my thoughts about the place. Sometimes we stopped to embrace and that, too, was a prayer, a way of being present.

And then came one of those angel moments.

At the centre of the woods, I remember entering a clearing full of purple foxgloves. We stood still and admired as if we were staring at a painting. The foxgloves were close and snaky, rising to spikes above our heads.

I think the nearest I can get to what we said was "Ah," or "Oh." It was our own secret garden.

"Digitalis," said James, as he led down a path walled-in by plants. The path curled around, arriving at a bare earth mound. "But I call them Foxglove City," he added, smiling, and we climbed a short slope to a viewpoint. On all sides we were surrounded by a spiky, nodding sea of colour. It was plum-purple, yellow-purple, and purple-pink.

Then came the moment, as a line of poetry popped into my head. "I taste a liquor never brewed …" I said.

I remember the shift in James's face; he was reading me carefully. "What's that from?" he asked.

"Emily Dickinson."

"I see. Or maybe I don't."

"There's a line, describing a drunken bee at the foxglove's door."

"So that's why you thought of it?"

"Not exactly," I shook my head. "It's about spirituality …"

James smiled; the angel had arrived. "Ah, the point."

"Something that takes us out of ourselves."

"You mean," he replied, waving his arm, "all this …"

"Anything that makes us bigger."

"And thankful." James raised his hands to prayer position. Facing, I raised mine too and James placed his hands like gloves around mine. He closed his eyes and we prayed.

Prayer is a mode of being. A wide-awake, floaty clarity in which we live life, fully. We pray with our eyes, as artists, with our ears like an orchestra tuning up, with our bodies when we kiss. And we pray in ourselves when we forgive or listen or simply show interest. For deep prayer to happen you have to be yourself: the self in waiting on the path, in the café, and of course in the hospital.

I often think there's an angel inside, looking out quietly, with its face to the window. Someone we recognise walking by our shoulder, familiar but unknown. That figure is *us*, our real selves in the dream, not perfect but aware. It's what we see when we close our eyes and feel the touch of presence. And prayer, my kind of prayer, is about meeting that self, dreaming of the light. It's about thinking nothing and expecting less. And recognising that what's out there is larger than us.

With James and me, prayer was all about feel. It could happen in bed, warm and fresh, after sex, when we embraced. Or it could be on an early morning walk, looking out across sand, with the sea moving slowly. Or a violin solo, heard on a CD from the inside of a car. Sometimes the prayer was larksong climbing to an overcast sky. It could be time spent together in a wild spring garden. Or shared time in an empty church with scented candles and white light through glass.

It was James's idea that we went to services as well. Of course, his interest surprised me. I'd thought him too full of fun and irony and reluctant to commit. To bow down in church wasn't his thing. Or so I'd supposed until we talked, on an outing.

We were sitting together in an overgrown graveyard, looking out to sea. We'd come there at his suggestion, touring the coastline. The wind was fresh, and we had our backs to the remains of a stone-built chapel. James was talking about his childhood.

"Church was never part of my life," he said, "but I'm willing to try, now."

I looked at him, carefully. "You sure?" I asked.

He gazed across the weathered headstones, "As long as it's together. And the sort of worship that you – no, we – believe in."

I understood. What he wanted wasn't Bible. None of that little-boy-up-there, comic book God who has to be talked out of smashing things. Not too high-and-holy either, with or without incense. And not, of course, sin-fest or guilt-trip or getting loud for the Lord. For him, for us both, it was about metaphor, the word as symbol, and love.

So we went on Sunday, held hands in the pews, sang and exchanged glances then discussed it afterwards. Not as performance but in spirit, as a gift.

And now, two months later, still at peace, we celebrate as we eat, give thanks when rising and live life in the sun. There's an everyday rhythm that keeps us together as watchers and lovers. For us, this is praying.

So why James?

Or if not why, at least where, when, and what if …

If James was a singer, I fancy he'd be a song thrush. The New Year one as in Hardy: piercing, throaty, trilling in the dark. Or a woodpecker drilling down, tap-tap-tap. Then flying in a loop, hedgerow to hedgerow, flashing his colours.

But he's my James, my silver-haired admirer and crazy dancer. The man who listens and nods then talks about feelings.

A story about him …

We were eating out at our West End restaurant when, without hesitation, he told the waiters how we'd first met there. Later in the evening he told some diners about our anniversary. Each time he described it he held up his ring. And he told our story well: straightforwardly, warmly, as an adventure, without embarrassment. Of course I remembered how he'd said that during youth he'd seen speaking openly as another kind of mask, but now he simply shared. And he used the L-word, repeatedly.

If James was an artist he'd paint very large pictures, over and over. Theatre-like scenes with fireflies in the dark, or tenth-storey views with stars on water, some white, some grey, seen between branches. Or he'd overpaint photos and hang them in a series. They'd be Ernst-like, watery, in blues and greens. I imagine those pictures hung from strings and displayed like Christmas cards across the sky. They'd be up there, *made one with nature*, dotted around as fixed stars. His *autoritratto*.

Another story …

When it came to getting married we knew there might be problems. There were families lined up with exes in the background, views on who should be there, and questions about the service. Of course, at our age we arranged it all, which placed us, like officials, on the spot. It meant we had to be careful and think it through. In fact, I was happy with anything as long as it had the right feel and James just wanted to celebrate. But at the same time we believed in the poetic, in metaphor, not a checklist. So, after lengthy discussions and advice from Toby, we settled on two ceremonies, one private, in my parents' church, one outdoors, at *The Shorespot Café*.

On the day with close family. we went for restraint. There were low-key declarations, vows and readings, a kiss, and tea and cake afterwards. It was small, dignified and gently-worded, most of all it was simple. And, of course, private.

At the café a few days later, it was much more for show. We'd invited everyone and set up in the garden, I'd prepared a script and James had covered an arch-shaped pergola with an arrangement of flowers, combining them in stripes. They were purple and blue and spikily red. Some I knew, poppies and antirrhinums and veronica, and others had unfamiliar names and strange, insect-like blooms.

When the time came, I led James into the middle of the lawn to face the arch. The flowers were in place, woven in, with a tunnel behind and a ribbon tied across. We stood holding hands and said our script. The sky was clear and the guests were all around us, following every word.

It was when Toby cut the ribbon that James took over. As we entered the pergola he reached up, took a handful of blooms and wove them into my hair. I smiled back as he added more, pinning them to my dress. He kissed me then slipped some smaller flowers into his own hair and the pocket of his suit. Finally, we both gathered bunches in our hands and stepped out to the lawn.

I still have the pictures. When we look at them together we seem so alive. In spirit we were spring chickens.

With James I can still do that, step outside the box, invent things, do what we like.

So why James?

Firstly, his hair. He's happy with its length – not too obvious, layered at the front, longer at the back – but enough, a headful. After washing it's smooth and floppy and surprisingly strong. It feels like water.

For a while we shared a joke that he had all the hair. "It makes up for mine," I said, and I meant it. Of course, he told me I'd get mine back, but as long as I had his I was happy, or at least, it helped my feelings. He grew it for me.

Secondly, his James-isms. His teasing expressions, a joke or reflection then a quick double-take – with judgement yes, but straight, with feeling.

Also, his voice sometimes loud, sometimes gentle, intimate when low. Mature, as well, with his own chosen tics. And his hand in mine: warm, loosely-fitting, a garment to put on.

When we're out walking, he stays by me, and we go forward through the world. It's the red carpet treatment, everything in place, laid out for us. Or so he tells me.

James can cook, dislikes hot baths, has a passing interest in sport, and watches athletics and tennis, highlights only. He has his own mug with an author quote, a collection of vinyl classics and several sizes of multi-coloured badges.

Thirdly there's James-of-the-garden. Outdoors, working, he's *inside* nature, a doctor of the soil. There's a priest in him, too, bringing on flowers, planting fruit. He's the painter of roses. And when he designs, using metal and stone, he's halfway to an architect.

Yes, so why James?

The question brings back the restaurant. I picture him there with silver-white hair. On the table there's a newly-lit candle. It's leaf-shaped and pointed, like an upside-down heart.

I ask the question again and feel myself warming up. I'm in the sun and we're walking. In my head I can hear Beethoven's *Pastoral*. We're figures in a painting, passing through a gate. The garden we enter is alive with Cranach-like apples and exotic beasts. There's a labyrinth, marked out in stone, that we walk. Its twists and turns lead into the heart. And we're at the centre.

Recently I've been dreaming about dancing. The dreams come in two main types. In both I appear with James in *Strictly Come Dancing*.

Of course, we're fans. On Saturday night the sofa's our front row where we get in close and study every move. We're marking what we can, talking about content and feel, but our focus is on passion, what the judges call connection. In other words, we want to know who fancies who.

It's fun, that's why we do it. We recall past winners, comment on costumes and go to bed excited with our heads full of kicks and lifts and promenade runs. You'd think we were kids at an all-night party. But behind each dance there's another story.

And the dreams? Well, here are a few highlights.

In the first type of dream I'm a professional. My name's Constantia and I'm from the island called *Love*. Strictly Love, where women wear sparkle and feathered headpieces and play opposite masked men who are B-list celebs. In this dream I Waltz in white, Rumba in red and Tango in orange and black. The music's coloured too, ranging from Quickstepping silver and blue-yellow Jive to rainbow Samba and Lindyhop green.

James is my partner. In Series One he's on TV, possibly fronting wildlife, but mainly flower shows. He's won a silver-gilt at Chelsea and gold at Hampton Court. In Series Two to Five he's in rock, writing powerhouse classics for an indie band who everyone respects. From Six onwards he's in stand up, telling slaphappy jokes and truly, deeply, off-the-wall stories.

He's a natural, takes well to the dance, and we bond straight away.

There are others who appear, listed in the credits. Not surprisingly their names are familiar. My dad is voiceover, Rose and Naomi cheer from the audience, Meg designs costumes, George leads the orchestra and the panel's made up of Charlie as Bruno, Hannah for Alesha, Amy/Rachael standing in for Len, while Craig's part is delivered by Conrad and Toby, backed up by my gran. My mum plays Tess.

For several weeks James and I sweat and struggle, practising our moves. We're busy as flies in our glass-walled studio. We use affirmations like *nail it* and *staying in the zone*. On camera we're a hit, week on week topping the leader board, and of course we fall in love.

The second type of dream is slower and deeper. It's full of glides and turns and smoothly-flowing movements. The music's soft and Impressionist. It comes in waves, one moment close then drifting off. In this dance I'm at peace and I lie back on James, breathing slowly. I'm rising and falling in time to the waves. Our hearts beat together. There's a wild, abandoned siren song singing in my ear. It's for us. The tune's our tune: *The Power of Love*. It reminds me of an imaginary film I carried in my head. *My Dreamboat*, I call it. I rerun the last scene where the lovers fall asleep and drift out to sea. It's what you might call the dream behind the dream.

In all these dreams, when we reach the Strictly final we're in the lead. The public are behind us. The judges award us tens, saying we're amazing. The studio audience give us standing ovations. Then, on the last dance, in the final move, just when it seems we've won, my dizziness strikes. I lose my footing and fall. The floor seems to rise up and hit me. A hot needle shoots up my back. I'm lying, shivering in darkness, and something's grinding in my body. James is stooped over me, calling, but the blackness swells up and takes me in its arms.

I wake.

7.1.11

I've a name for my illness coming back. I call her Lottie. She's young, slightly-built and, behind her blushes she wants attention. She's me, in a way, but also she's a character. Partly historical, she lives in her own world. And she's a storyteller, which makes her both rash and afraid of shadows. Over the years, I've got to know her, and I've realised she needs my full attention. So I talk to her nicely, ask her how she feels.

Lottie's always there. She has her own story, beginning in the dark. It's like peering into water: to see her, you have to sit still. In one form, she's pondweed. Grey-green and clinging, she's smooth and has curves. But that's at the beginning. Later, when she's bigger, she makes herself known. She's behind everything, in the breath taken slowly, the unsteadiness, the red-marked sheets. But also, she's barely there at all. Hard to describe, the hollowed-out feeling, the bareness inside. Not so hard to describe the squats, the black blood, the ache.

So, I listen at night-time, I imagine her story, as a sister, and try to feel her there. I picture her with me, perhaps rather distant, in secret, then turn up the volume. "What's wrong?" I ask. I want to draw her out, find what we have in common, I also want an explanation. I'm angry. I tell Lottie she's not welcome, not this way. It's her habit of turning up, without proper warning, appearing, not asking, and just sitting there saying nothing. She's the face at the window, the looker, the old black hag, the one who keeps returning.

Like now.

15.1.11

I have two boxes inside me, a pain box and a beautiful box. I'm in the middle, caught between them. They appear in me without warning. I never quite know which one it'll be. Like Jekyll and Hyde they come and go.

The pain box is metal. Its lid is scratched and dented and heavy to lift. As it goes up it sticks in places and the hinges flake rust. Inside it's full of tools. There are two fold-out ledges, packed with drill bits and screws of all sizes. In the central compartment there are six-inch nails and saws with broken teeth, below that, sharp metal pincers and rolled barbed wire, at the bottom there are clamps and padlocks. The tools rattle about inside like broken glass. Some of them are twisted out of shape, others are cracked and splintered, all of them can slice through bone. I call them my instruments.

In the beautiful box there are deep blue pools where I lie looking up. The world around me is soft and slow and glows from inside. Down there I'm weightless, like a fish, not touching anything. My breath comes slowly and I'm floaty and free. It's as if I'm at a window watching things go by. I can see the ripples, the insects on the surface and reeds in mud. Stretching, I turn and rise to the surface. On the banks there are willows and people looking down. I can see myself through their eyes. I'm a woman in a picture, holding flowers, with a song in my head. Of course, nothing can touch me. I'm Ophelia.

When the pain box returns, I'm on stage. It's coffin-sized and curtained at the front. I'm standing by it, looking down. In there I can see what looks like a false bottom. As I reach in, my hand catches on a blade. It cuts deep but I don't feel a thing. There's no blood, and suddenly I realise I'm dreaming. I hear a drum roll and a shout as I climb into the box. The box is tight and its spikes and needles cut into my sides. I've just wedged myself in when I realise that the bottom is solid, the saw is approaching and I'm the lady to be sawn in half.

I realise as the blade cuts in, pain and beauty are fraternal twins.

1.2.11

James saw it first in the garden. I remember his words, though at the time I didn't really listen, not fully. It was out there and noted but not heard deeply or taken into my heart. There's a voice inside where everything lives, and for me, although it was the truth, I'd not allowed it in. But for James it was real. He'd told me that the plants were out of step, that they were shooting and flowering before they were due. In the past, he'd said, he could plan for year-round interest choosing plants that came at different times, but now everything flowered at once. With that, he said, came swings in the weather: one day hot, the next day cold, with floods and gales and frosts then droughts. But mostly, he said, it was about lives that went under. I think when he said that I should have listened. But for me it was easier if I carried on as normal, just as it was. As far as I was concerned, the sun shone, the rain fell and we were happy in the garden. When it came to bio or climate, that was too much to think about and wasn't going to happen. It was about as likely as children growing wings or falling from the sky.

But lives were being lost. James talked about disappearing birds, insects, animals and species going under. Everywhere there were casualties. The garden was on the danger list. Its body clock was broken.

So why did I deny? Mainly, I think, because the change was so slow. And when a big shift happened, I could see it as a blip, a one-off, something to be expected. Climate wasn't on my list of things to watch out for. Up close it didn't move. And if you turned your back it had gone when you looked again. Also, coming as it did in millimetre shifts and ppms, it was hard to measure. It was like walking in the dark. Everything was in flux, but unless you looked carefully you might not notice it.

But in any case, I turned away. There was something out of place, a glitch, a tear, a break in the surface. Someone was hurting, but I chose not to see it.

Climate is a mood, a condition. A tap drip, a knock at the door, a runaway ride. I feel it inside me as a shadow lengthening. It's in the system. The bad stuff fattens on itself; it knows no boundaries. It's my cancer, everywhere, all over, unlimited.

I listened to James. He'd shown where to look and now I could see it. I was with him as his lover in the garden. I'd found that place where the voice lives on.

And this is what I know now:
– Climate is our limit, our point of no return.
– It's our free fall dive, our race to the bottom.
– Count the carbon; it's our angel of death.
– The sun's too close, the UV is inside us.
– Don't look away from the burnout.
– It's what we've done to ourselves.
– It's the boy falling from the skies who no one sees.

15.2.11 – 20.4.11

What counts is people. I listen to their lives, what we share and who we are. Their stories keep me going, I know they mean well.

Rose, when she visits the ward sits on my bed. No phones, no gadgets, just a plain cotton dress, and a photogenic profile. She's vulnerable in a pale-skinned, unadorned, gently-compassionate way. With her slightly ethereal, Botticelli smile, she reminds me of my younger self.

Each time she comes she brings me a gift. I love her presents, they're always special. Often they're written: a quote recorded in a pocket-sized book, read out quietly, or a sketch and a poem. I did once ask her for a self-portrait but she found that difficult.

Rose is training to be a veterinary nurse. She's on placement just round the corner, so she visits most days. We have a routine: a cheek kiss, her gift, a few minutes' catch-up then an animal story. She tells me their names, their habits and how she came to nurse them. The dog that swallowed a key, the cat with wounds, a bird so concussed it fell into a pond. We talk about her course and the difficulties she's having. It's about the medical terms. So she brings in her textbook and I test her on words like adenoma and intussusception, sounding them slowly, syllable by syllable.

At first, when she said she wanted to be a vet, I thought it wouldn't happen. She'd always been ultra-particular, with an aversion to plug-holes and hairs in the bed. "Animals are dirty," I warned her. "And they smell."

"Mum, it's what I want to do," she replied, looking past me.

I knew what that meant, for someone so quiet she's surprising strong. Or to put it another way, she's a split personality, outside shy, inside defiant. She'd shown that at mealtimes with her sister. I remember them arguing, both wanting the same piece of cake and Rose conceding nothing. Naomi kept talking, giving all her reasons, but in the end Rose saw her off. She simply said "No," until Naomi fell silent. Then she took the cake and pointed to the garden, "*They'll* like it," she said, "and everyone'll be happy." We ended up at the window watching Rose throwing crumbs to the birds.

I suppose, thinking about it, the choice of veterinary nurse made good sense. I'd heard her call and talk to her animals by name, telling them stories, and I'd seen her standing, seemingly untouched, when they gnawed down her finger.

It's that side of Rose that Naomi finds difficult. She's a stickler for order, calling herself maître d'. And being older makes her more reactive. Naomi believes in sorting things, and says so. She's a born carer, so the passion is directed. In the past she was happy as long as she was clear about what was happening. She'd go along with games that suited her sister, be child-like, and stay upbeat. But once she was put out then we'd never hear the end of it.

I do remember Naomi on holiday.

Every summer, we went to the Isle of Wight. It suited us. There was something quasi-50s about the trees down to the beach, the boats and boat houses and old-fashioned bungalows, something both quaint and formal. It seemed to belong to Enid Blyton. We stayed on the east coast in a small hotel with a view out to a bay and yachts at anchor. I remember playing rhyming games, matching words like *Dolphin*, *Blueskies*, *Scheherazade*, and hearing rigging slapping in the wind. I also remember the girls on the sands, running and laughing. It always seemed sunny on The Island, and without Conrad, who was usually too busy to come, we stayed out late, building beach fires and baking potatoes.

It was after sundown, on our last night, that Naomi first told me she didn't want to go to church.

"Promise you won't tell Dad," she whispered, snuggling up.

We were sitting on a rug with our faces to the fire. On one side there was a low wall, on the other side Rose was asleep, bundled in a sleeping bag. Behind her, the waves were breaking quietly. The air felt both cool and warm.

"But why don't you want to go?" I asked.

Naomi looked into the fire. "It doesn't seem real. I don't feel it."

"But is that about church or how we do it?"

"No. I don't see the point. I need a change."

"You sure? It's not because someone's been talking to you?"

"No, Mum, I just need a break."

"So, what will you do?"

While Naomi considered, I listened to the sea. Its softly lapping rushes filled up the dark.

"Will you just stay away?"

She sighed. "I'd like to, but what do you think?"

I remember feeling torn. I was at a stage where my own faith had changed. In myself, I wanted to be alone, without restrictions, walking in the woods. In fact, for me, nature was the way into God. So I understood what Naomi was saying, but I knew that Conrad wouldn't like it, and I wanted to protect her.

"Could you be in church but think of something else?"

"Mum, you can't say that. It has to be honest."

I heard the pressure in her voice. For her this wasn't so easily dealt with.

I would have left it there but at that moment Rose opened her eyes. "Then don't go," she said.

In the dark, the waves pitched quietly against the beach.

"Rose, you're awake?" I said.

I could tell by her movements that Naomi didn't like it. She was leaning against my arm, breathing quickly with her head turned away.

"I don't think …" I began, keeping my voice low. I was determined to stay calm.

"What we said," cut in Naomi, "was private. For me and Mum."

I could see her eyes were fixed on the fire. Her cheeks were glowing.

"Naomi," I said, "Rose was only trying to help."

Both girls sat still, saying nothing.

"Listen, there's nothing to argue about." I pointed to a branch at the edge of the fire. "Because God's not just in church."

The branch was crackling, peeling as it burned.

The girls remained silent.

"You see that?" I asked, pointing to the flames.

Rose nodded.

"Now look," I said. The whole length of the branch was splitting open. At the tip it was oozing sap; each slowly-gathering drip was whiteish-green. When it dropped, it spat all over.

"You understand what I'm saying, about God?" I asked.

"I think so," Naomi said, quietly.

"Then let's not argue. Not in front of God."

I think there was something in my voice that touched her …

Of course, when she visits now, Naomi knows much more. I can see it in her face. She tries not to show it, but like most nurses, she's too much aware. In a way she's squeamish. She encourages me to be active, get up and walk, look out the window, do anything as a form of distraction. And there's a kindliness about her, a sort of super-niceness, which keeps her professional, in hospital-mode. In an odd kind of way, she's my patient.

But it's when my dad visits that I listen and see other things. What happens with him is closer to prayer. He arrives quietly, often when I'm asleep, and sits watching. Even if I don't wake up, I know he's there. When I ask him for a story, he hesitates, but I ask him again and he agrees. And I can't quite tell, as the words start, whether I'm awake or asleep. But I hear him talking, picking up on phrases from an earlier time. But then his voice drifts off and I'm left alone. There are no words now only images. As if he, too, wasn't really there.

The dream takes me back, but this time to a pool. It's summer and a couple of damselflies are circling the surface. They're electric-blue and tied together. They land on a water lily where they seem to be struggling. It's as if they're frying. When they lift off, they're still locked together. They tour the pool, skimming the surface then alight on a bank. The sun goes in and they lose all colour. Everything around them begins to thin out. The grass has faded and the water is icy. The sky has blanked and even the sun has paled. It's as if everything's rubbing itself out. And when I wake, or another dream begins, everything is clear and bright and weightless. I'm between walls surrounded by faces and my dad's voice is there.

Like him I'm fading.

5.5.11

I'm out of hospital, talking with Carmen, our minister. She's small and bright, like a pebble. Her face is round and simple, with light brown curls and a twinkly smile. She's warm and she's gentle. It comes through in her listening expression, her laughter, and in the pause before speaking when she goes into herself. She's experienced as well, which I imagine comes from visiting people like me. But there's no kind of pressure, I'm not in a queue or being judged. Although there's twenty years between us, she's a sister to me in an eye-to-eye way.

She's the same in communion. When she gives bread, she looks for a second into your eyes, and in offering wine she offers herself.

When Carmen comes round she's so glad to see me. I sit with her close up to the table and feel the glow. It's like letting in the sun. I'm back there in the youth group, sharing the time with Annie and Clare, but now I'm not tempted to say things for effect. So we talk. It's one-to-one, with me as subject.

Carmen, I know, gets alongside to give herself in any way she can. She's my companion when I talk about doubt. In what she says, she acts as a messenger. She wants me to believe but doesn't contradict. If she could, she'd be my servant, not literally, but in my head, as my conscience.

Compared with her, I'm struggling. I tell her about what I call my journey. It's uphill, I say, much steeper than I expected. She listens and I tell her how I feel. Not lonely in this world, I say, but very much alone in what's going to happen. I'll miss him I say, quietly, and change the subject.

We talk for a while about worship, and what I call the hole. The God hole, I tell her, is where I find faith. For me it's in the gaps and breaks, the nothingness. And I take her through my doubts questioning everything: the church, the creed, most of all miracles. I end up feeling bad because I'm attacking everything she stands for. I'm Thomas with my finger in the wound.

Carmen listens carefully. She's with me, mid-stream, going with the flow. When she replies she doesn't offer fixes. Her words are clear with a hint of sparkle. Underneath the surface they go deep.

She tells me a story about her own earlier life. It seems she used to climb mountains without equipment, until a fall one day and a year-long struggle with illness. She ends with words about surprises and the hidden face of God.

Afterwards, she asks me what would help. I notice her hands: they're red, shiny in places, and large for her height. She holds them half-cupped on the table, pointed towards me. She's so much like my mother that I cry. We pray together.

2.6.11

As a child, I loved our garden. It always seemed that being outdoors stirred me up. It was the kind of place on-its-own where anything could happen. Out there was wild, an unexplored heartland that I didn't call *garden*, or if I did it was quietly to myself, with its own private meaning. It was my hard-to-reach outback where I lived off the land, a place with tent-people and unknown creatures and its own bare life. A paradise of sorts, one full of sunlit corners and clipped shrubs and creepy-crawlies.

Now the garden seems like a picture seen from a long way off.

I shared the garden with Toby. He drew a map with contours and coloured-in symbols. I put in names, marking in *The Castle, The Swamp* and *Spooky Wood*. Over time we both added to our map. Toby drew rivers and mountains and a collection of trails, while I wrote on the back about the map's discovery. We made a copy in a scrapbook and I began a story in the pages that followed. Toby put in some cartoon-like animals and a key.

Working on our book brought us close. It kept us busy and, in a way, it changed us. In fact, I could almost say we imagined who we were. So sometimes we were well-spoken children calling the earth *white* and *bare* and *magical* when it was green and brown, and sometimes, as Mary and Colin, we entered our own secret garden through a door in the wall.

But also, there were outdoor incidents. Brief and small-scale, but revealing as well, usually happening as a part of something larger.

Here's one I remember.

We were twelve and ten, young for our ages, but quietly thought-ful. Looking back now, I see myself reading outdoors. Because the garden, for me, had become a place of study, a library, if you like. I was out there sitting on the wall with the scrapbook in my hand. A tin beside me held a collection of coloured pencils. Toby was opposite, kicking a football against the fence. He was grumbling in his throat, yelping sometimes and crying out "Ref!" I knew he was trying to annoy me.

For the second time that afternoon the ball flew in my direction. It skidded off the lawn and bounced up, hitting brickwork.

"Oh, Toby!" I cried, closing my book.

The ball had dropped to the ground and was trapped between a tree stump and the wall.

"Can I have my ball back please?" Toby asked. Underneath his nice-boy manner there was a mischievous smile.

I think that was when I realised that he was embarrassed by his own behaviour. I could read it in his squared shoulders, with arms pinned to his sides. He was making himself upright, as stiff as possible.

"Is that what you want, really?" I asked.

Toby shook his head. He was looking at my book.

I'd a feeling that he knew but was too shy to ask. Then suddenly, remembering *Shipwreck*, it came to me.

"You want me to read to you," I said.

Toby hesitated.

"Would you like that?"

When Toby stayed silent, I invited him to join me.

"Can I?" he asked.

I patted the wall and he sat.

I opened the scrapbook and flicked through the pages. Finding my story, I called out the title *Safari Adventure* then read right through, beginning to end. It had poachers, a chase and some closely-observed beasts. At the end Toby asked to draw the animals.

"Of course," I said, handing him the book.

I've still got the picture that he drew. Looking at it now, I realise what it shows. It's thickly-worked and messy with a close-up herd of animals and behind that two Moomin shapes peering from bushes. Their faces are balloon-shaped and dreamy. They're water-baby-like. Somehow they're blank: round and sagging, yet pointy as well. They could be angels or fish, but they're also slightly spooky. They're alive, alert, and yet out of it.

They're versions of Toby and me.

15.7.11 – 3.10.11

By teenage, looking in the mirror, I really believed I was out of it. It was the shape of my face, which I thought of as hollow, and my mouse-brown hair. Also, my teeth and my after-bath spots. Of course, I know now that the faults I saw were nothing, but at that time I almost *wanted* my blemishes. They kept me safe from what some boys were after. So I stayed apart, talking, both superior and exposed. But

654

secretly I'd my own I'm-special feeling, and a wire inside that sparked when a boy came in the room. I hid my blushes behind a clever-clever front.

But it was when I stopped talking that my desires showed through.

I realise now there's always chemistry when nothing's said. Silence is powerful, it makes things stand out. It's like a layered painting: underneath the surface something's signalling. Because I had my private feelings – moments on the quiet, with carefully judged glances and unseen looks fixed from behind on men who were older. Maturity to me was impressive. It went with saints in stained-glass windows, kneeling hermits and elders in stories, and included, without anyone knowing, a crush on our minister.

His name was Simon Fitzgerald. He was tall and thin, with blue, staring eyes and artistic hands. His voice was musical, slightly sad, with a soft Scottish accent. When he spoke from the pulpit I felt the power of his gaze. Like his words, it seemed directed. It was as if he was shining a torch on me. There were questions in the air, gentle invitations and a sun-like warmth creeping into everything.

After the service, when he spoke with my parents, I glazed. Underneath my politeness I was watching. And though I didn't say anything I had a feeling that his remarks were secretly aimed at me.

He made my Sundays extra-special and I went to church feeling light and unreal. I sat there lifted – and continued, afterwards, breathless and high until early evening, when I suddenly came down.

Then I had the longings, a kind of raw, obsessive itch that went on all week; he was somewhere close. Because if we went to the park or out in the town I kept seeing him. His name appeared on road and shop signs and in the books I was reading. Sometimes I felt him beside me in the morning, looking out of the window. He was there, speaking quietly, taking in the lawn, the birdsong, the sunlight on the path.

I knew my love was absurd, but I'd vowed, and wasn't going to let him down. So I worked on our connection. Sitting alone in my room, I imagined conversations. In my mind I composed Brontesque poems full of wind and wildness and ghosts crying out. Vaguely, in snatches, I relived his sermons. And I made up lists of what he liked, where he went, and what he secretly loved.

Then there was his wife, spotted from a distance, shopping in town. Small and dowdy, slightly overweight, with a worn-looking smile, I saw her as unworthy. Nothing about her seemed equal to him, and that gave me hope. It led to my stories of how she wasn't what she seemed. Maybe she'd trapped him through a promise he'd made, a youthful vow that he'd honoured out of loyalty. Perhaps she'd a rare disorder that could trigger collapse, and she used it as a threat. Or maybe they were related and the marriage was a sham.

Of course my condition couldn't last, but while I lived it I found it helpful, in a way. Here was a place where no one could touch me, a quiet, look-in-the-mirror, alone-with-my-fantasies world. I saw it as my territory, mine alone, a place I'd chosen away from anyone watching. Inside my love-dream I had him to myself.

And then my feelings changed. Or rather, they shifted from church to school.

It happened halfway through term, with our first exams coming up. For a while there'd been talk of a replacement English teacher. Our tutor, Mrs Coates, had been taken ill too often, so we were given the deputy head, a middle-aged man who tested spellings, followed by a music teacher, recently retired. They set work and supervised without much interest. The classroom became, in effect, a free-for-all, allowing us to copy model answers and cheat in our tests while feigning due diligence in whatever we had to do.

About that time, Mr Edwards arrived.

He was a short, broad-browed Welshman with long sideburns, a soft, sensual mouth and slightly starey eyes. He announced straight away, speaking with a lilt, that we had to aim high. We were young minds in the making, who ought to ask questions and challenge what we read. And he lectured gently from the front, analysing genre, types of character and the use of language.

Within a week I'd become a follower. I hung on every word, enjoying his long pauses and quiet intensity. His presence lit me up. It was as if I was standing looking out from a high-up window.

My task was to please. I became his best pupil, asking questions and memorising answers. And I filled up my essays with near-quotes and grand, speculative phrases intended to impress. I wanted notice. So my essays moved between sections, setting out theories and adopting positions, some of them quite extreme. But what they did communicate, regardless of perspective, was the importance of thinking.

Looking back now I believe he was aware but, unlike my minister, his response was to cut off and talk into air as if he was an actor. He delivered his thoughts and kept his distance. When I answered a question, he'd nod and move on. And when he marked my work, the most he ever gave me were one-word comments.

I suppose at first I simply followed. I thought I could read him, believing his indifference to be a trick, an outward show to cover his true feelings. Only I understood his signals. But after a while I began to question. I needed reaction, even if it was negative. So I laid little traps: words missing in essays, a name change or switch, the odd deliberate error or self-contradiction. But his comments didn't change. It was good or satisfactory, or simply left blank and ticked at the bottom with a single-figure mark.

I think in the end I needed something more. Gradually, without it really showing, I began to lose interest. My gentle Welsh dragon now seemed smaller, less the man he'd been. It was mainly his voice which, like the other teachers, had flattened to a drone. I noticed too, how often he repeated himself. In fact more than once I found myself wishing he'd stop talking.

I didn't look back when Mrs Coates returned. Mr Edwards had gone. And when, within days, our minister retired, I was two times relieved. I didn't need their love. I'd outgrown my fancies, I was stronger; and, for a while at least, I wasn't out of it.

25.11.11

There are ways of dealing with pain. It's about awareness, what I call *separating out*. And that means listening and knowing the difference between chronic and acute.

When it's an ache and keeps on aching, then it's all about mood. About taking action, and pushing on. Moving whatever hurts, regardless, but carefully as well, with judgement. Of course there's pressure, and more ache as you carry on. And as soon as it's a down-mouth you're struggling. You might think *I can't do this* and tiredness sets in. Or you might think *oh no, not again* and sink, or imagine a future where it never goes away. But it's thinking that hurts. The brain's a cover, keeping bad stuff out, but also a filter or frame we look through. So it needs to be flexible and choose what to stop, what to let through. Yes, there are days when the effort's too much, and not-now wins. But that's when you have to struggle. To talk yourself up, say *I can do it*. Every day, it's about putting in the hours, making the effort, fighting to stay up.

I've come to understand that illness, and especially cancer, is bigger than you think. To stay on top you have to be strong. And that can take everything. It may look as if nothing's happening, but inside's a battleground. It's what they call character-building. And especially when the pain is severe.

When it gets bad, you have to think. At first it doesn't seem possible as the levels go up. You say to yourself *What*— as the waves get higher, so much higher you fear you can't cope. It happens between breaths. Then you realise that your life has changed and you can't escape. The pain breaks through and what you thought was dangerous becomes an emergency. It's then that you use breathing. In your head you count. Talk yourself up. Say no to the red light, change it to blue.

But the real trick is to swim. I use words like *going with, not against* – and repeat them. It's about taking deep breaths and staying under. Then you float. The pain is everywhere, it's the world you inhabit, and where it goes, you follow. It's almost like a dream: you're watching yourself being hurt, and on the surface there's nothing you can do. But once you're inside then that gives meaning. You can make adjustments, guide and be guided, hold onto a rhythm.

Of course, morphine helps. At first I was afraid, but the doctors reassured me. And once I'd tried, I understood its calm. Morphine is a lake; its deep blue spring spreads underground. It's the blue of gentians and violets and Lawrence's last poems. And that's the blue, when I swim in it, that I feel when I pray.

The end of treatment was my decision, with James's agreement. We needed a cut-off, a line drawn. Of course, we knew what it meant. I don't believe in herbal or alternative or miracle cures. Everything's been done.

I told Naomi and Rose, with James over a meal, holding hands. The meal was simple: bread, thin soup, water – what I could manage without throwing up. We'd set out the table with cream-coloured candles. In the centre was a cut-glass vase of arum lilies. For us this was communion, though with Naomi there we called it light supper.

To tell them, I used the face-to-face method I'd seen on *ER*. But without the urgency. I waited till we'd eaten then lit the candles and spoke to them calmly. "The cancer's spread, so we've put the treatment on hold."

The girls were both silent. I could feel them trying to take it in. Rose was curling forward, Naomi was finger-twisting a ribbon about her neck.

"No more chemo," I added. I could see they were hurting. They were my children, trying to understand.

"It won't go away," I continued, "so I've decided to enjoy my time."

Naomi coloured. "Enjoy?" she asked, hoarsely. "You'll enjoy – what?"

"Enjoy what I have."

"… left," Rose put in, speaking automatically.

"And for how long?" whispered Naomi.

The candles part-lit their faces.

I remember James squeezing my hand. "No one knows, but it's about living with dignity. And choice."

At his insistence, we all joined hands across the table. "Don't worry, you don't have to say anything," he told them. "It's about living, that's all."

The sweet, waxy aroma of flowers and candles filled the room. We were absolutely silent.

Bad news is always difficult to tell. The story, that's easy. Things happen as you say them, it's about words, the feel, the people. But pain and illness get in the way. Everything becomes hand-to-mouth. So, it's where it hurts, it's noisy, it's hot, or the bed sheets are twisted and the food won't go down. Also, there's fatigue. Physical of course, and also mental, but mainly spiritual – and that's where it hits you. The soul's what's left when everything else is down. A leaky balloon.

But I had to tell Mum and Dad. And they needed the story, not just the hurt.

James arranged it. It was my birthday: my big six-o. We'd decided on a visit. James made the car ready, putting in blankets, drink and back seat pillows. "No need for an ambulance," I joked, climbing in. He drove and I slept, only waking when we arrived. I'd expected to see the house, so I was surprised when we drew up at the church. "What's this?" I asked when we reached the back entrance. James smiled and helped me inside.

The church hall was candle-lit, quiet and richly-scented. For a minute I thought we were preparing for a service. Then I realised. John, Toby and Louise were there, waiting by a square of tables. Behind them was a small group of locals. In front, on the tables, was a small, tiered, indoor garden. It was layered, like a cake. The flowers, which were purple and yellow and white, trailed all over.

"Happy birthday," said Louise. She offered me a bunch of roses. They were heavy-headed and darkly red. I accepted and James guided me to a large padded seat with flowers both sides. I perched there with space all around, smiling. He called it my throne.

They didn't sing. Instead my father said a prayer. At the end, Louise brought out a cake. Looking at its icing took me back …

I pictured myself on Christmas Eve crouched at the window, praying for snow. I'd wanted to wake to a perfect, trackless all-white world. I'd seen it in the glitter-cards and the Victorian prints and, like my birthdays, I'd hoped it would last forever.

I'd been told Christmas was an epiphany. I knew the word meant something like a birthday surprise. The only difference was the number of candles. And whose day it was.

I kept that Christmassy feel right through childhood. Most of all on my special day. I remember how happy I felt. Wanting to hold onto it, I'd fix my gaze on my cake with its circle of candles. "They're beautiful," I'd say, keeping everyone waiting while I counted.

"You have to blow!" Toby called.

Mum shushed him and I remained still, watching.

"Go on," he mouthed, looking pained.

In the end, after being urged and encouraged, I sat back in my chair, shaking my head. "They're beautiful," I repeated. Somehow, even back then, it felt like an angel moment, but mixed with hurt. I wanted to be helped.

"Shall I?" Dad asked. When I nodded, he licked his thumb and finger and pinched out the flames ...

I did blow the candles out on my 60th. I wanted my family to see I could do it. When Louise cut me a slice, I took the odd bite then left it as evidence on the plate. I thanked them, keeping my voice strong. I was holding back the tears – and the news I had to tell.

But this time I didn't say it straight. I'd passed that point and couldn't find an opening, and I needed to sound calm. When I'd told the girls, I'd first prepared it then taken my chance. But being in church made me more inward. In any case my mind had blanked and the wobble had crept in, so I asked James to explain.

He called for quiet. When they were silent he quickly told them then raised his glass. "To my lovely wife Beth," he said, gazing into my eyes. Behind his words I could hear a calm, level voice, repeating: ... *for better or for worse ... in sickness and in health ... till death do us part.*

7.6.12

Today I realised that sport and illness are two sides of a coin. Both are tests of endurance. They have to be worked at. What you have to aim at is your PB then hold out, right to the end. After that it's about how well prepared you were in the first place, and how you adapt. There are experts in the field – doctors and trainers – and recognised techniques. Your task is to dig deep, in mind and body. Most of all it's the effort that counts, how you see it and how you stay up. And, of course, you're playing against yourself.

I wrote a poem comparing the two. It came slowly, leaving me exhausted. I worked on it in snatches, taking rests then pushing on. It was like training a wild animal. Each time I thought I had it in my grasp, it managed to escape. In the end I had to accept I couldn't pin it down. So I left it like this:

*Getting closer*

Now we're in-deep, playing for extra time.
Reaching the spot, I'm sticking in. Ignoring.

With hints and flashes and bluelight warnings.

I'm defending. Standing where it hurts.
Judging distance, one shot to another.
It's a series of attempts.

And the strain, the hotfoot, the windup from behind,
I'm taking my chances.

Remember discipline?
First steps, learning moves, positioning well?
Keeping upright, regardless, I choose belief.

With bodyclock and chart and back glance at corners.

Now I'm crossing between halves:
mind and flesh, a thin white line.

And the effort to keep up, self v self,
when defeat becomes certain
    and everything centres
        on a new understanding.

                        *Elizabeth Lavender*

After reading it, I hid my poem from James. It felt like holding onto ice. Or touching something you can't quite make out. It came from a place I knew was there but wanted to avoid, an in-between state that I couldn't shut out. The sadness had taken over, filling up everything. Like one of those moments when the pill you've swallowed refuses to go down.

Some things, even between us, were better left unsaid.

29.7.12 – 15.10.12

Love. At last I know what's included in that word. Love's the martyr in glass, the patient, the child in darkness and the angel at the shoulder. You can walk with love through forests, seeing fungi and ivy or wild flowers shooting. Love's everywhere, in the bird tracks on sand, moonlight over grass and the portrait on the wall. Love's in the leaves and below earth, in the bulb and the fruit in sunlight. It's there in dirt and worms and bluebottles, circling. It's also in the sea, spread all over. On beach slopes and coastlines and tide runs and wave tops, and deep beneath the surface.

And the love I have for James is all this and more.

So, it's decided. We've talked it through. The story's ours, and we're back to the beginning, as lovers, reliving our first date …

As we entered the restaurant, I noticed how it had changed. Not a lot, but in detail – the red lighting and green tablecloths; the art, leaf-pattern and ethnic. I spoke to the waiter. His face had aged and his movements had slowed, but he remembered our last visit. We talked anniversaries and James held up his ring. We laughed. The L-word was used. We were in the warmth, enjoying life.

After ordering, we gazed about.

"It seems small now," James said.

I knew what he meant. When you revisit a place you've had in mind for a while it always seems different. You see it as a stranger. The perspective's changed. And you wonder if you're seeing it from outside or in.

Of course, I couldn't eat much, but we shared, and James helped me out. I hoped he'd have it all but didn't like to say. I wanted him to be happy.

After the meal James reached over. "You remember?" he asked, taking my hand.

The warmth of his flesh, doubled on mine, was a relief.

"Thank you," I said. "And, yes, I do." The last two words took me back to smiling faces, and signing the register. I'd been so lucky.

But inside I was cold.

We returned to the café. Now it wasn't mine. With my agreement, Sarah had taken over. We'd come to an arrangement, but the money didn't matter. What was important was the life of the place, the flowers, the pictures, the customers' faces. Because everything in the café had its own story. I'd bought it and filled it and arranged it, like a home. It all hung together, nothing was out of place. Only now I was a customer. What James had once called a *part of you* was out there and separate, in other people's hands.

Going there was an event. Led by Sarah, the staff asked us about family, caught up on gossip, and served whatever we wanted. They didn't say a word about health. I could see why. I suppose my wheelchair warned them. And my figure, of course. Even though I try not to look, I can see myself, reflected in the mirror. I look so old.

I write this with the feeling that I'm in God's hands. Somehow I'm there, in *The Shorespot Café* and at the same time I'm sleeping, crying, taking morphine, cuddling with James. And the writing finds me out. It has its own viewpoint, streaming in the head. I'm here, and I'm not, or so it seems. Everything is framed, like a film. Now I can hear *Swing Low, Sweet Chariot*. It's a matter of commitment. And of giving way, allowing what happens.

Of course, there are moments, especially at night, when the shadow takes over, times I feel the ghost, the at-my-back watcher. The stalker inside and the face in glass. Then I'm the victim, who isn't of this world.

At the café James and I talked. We listened. We smiled. Together we shared memories. I told him about fun times and the games I'd played.

One of them, with Sarah, was blind man's buff. "We learned to serve without looking," I said, and described how we'd gone about in blindfolds, before we opened up. I showed a few cards I'd made describing customers. I told him about shore walks with Sarah and dancing in the waves.

*The Shorespot Café* – I see it now, right behind my eyes, with James and me talking, like actors on a set. It's there when I'm asleep. I'm able to watch and be there as well. In the moment and in the story. Spirit and flesh, in both worlds.

I don't know if I imagined it. In a way it doesn't matter. What we dream is *us*, it shapes who we are.

So I believe we left the café and walked, following the path to the cliffs. We were in the sun, taking the air, hearing birdsong. James held my hand; he was smiling, naming flowers and it seemed I could walk.

"It's so calm," he said when we reached the top. We were looking down on a sand and gravel beach in a bare white bay. The tide was out and the rocks were glistening.

I remembered our first descent by *Lover's Leap*. "It was cold," I said, eyeing the path.

James seemed to understand. "You'll manage," he said. I believed him when he said it.

I don't know how, but I got down to that beach. I can't be certain but I think, for most of the way, James carried me. I know I was light enough.

When we reached the shoreline, I was relieved. James understood, he was my guide. He found me a hollow in a large flat rock and I sat looking out. "Thank you," I said.

The sea was quiet. It barely whispered as it pushed against stone. Somehow I felt the world was out there, waiting.

"You're comfortable?" he asked. I smiled. I was a child in his hands.

"We went round there," he said, pointing to the headland.

I listened. With the cliffs echoing behind us, I couldn't tell what was sea, and what was in my head. "We'll go again," I said.

James nodded. At our feet the waves came and went. We were on the edge, looking out. It was calm and otherworldly.

I don't think I went out to the headland. To walk out across rocks, even in sun with the help of James, was far beyond me. I don't think so. But an image remains of seaweed in channels and deep green pools and stepping across boulders. If we did reach the point, he must have helped me. Otherwise the tide would have caught up.

Looking back, I can see us out there. We're small against the rocks. I see it as a painting. The sea is silver, the sky white, the headland is grey. Insect-like, we're at the edge, turning the point. I see the gulls, they're V-shaped, hanging in the sky. In my mind they're calling: long, lonely, echoing calls. Out to sea is blank. All at once I feel the closeness of the waves. They seem to be inside, rising from within – James and me, lifted by the sea. Now we've turned the headland. And now, as James carries me across shingle, I realise why we've come here. We're close-in to the cliffs, inside the shadow, and the cave is here. I recognise *The Chapel*. Entering together, the light goes grey. It is quiet. We're sheltering in the body of God. James lowers me gently to rest beside water. The rock I'm sitting on is smooth. His arms are around me. A repeated drip spreads ripples, disturbing the pool. I see the Ichthys and the burnt-down candle. The stone beside us is an altar. We are praying.

Now we're kissing. James is inside me, kissing. Deep-tongued kisses, in the dark.

I am ready.

# THIRTY-EIGHT

Dear Beth,

At first I told myself it wasn't going to happen. I'd rather shout, break things, put a bomb under everything. I wouldn't allow it. To be taken from me so soon, and in that way. The injustice was too great. I imagined that if I willed you to get better then that might stop it. I thought of Job, Prometheus, Samson in the temple. If I could equal their suffering then, somehow, the story wouldn't end.

I knew, of course. But it's easier to look away. I mean to look hard at the picture and say, "No I don't see that." Like Hannah's way of looking, before her baby, where everything's decided in advance. And I did remain strong. For me to give up was too dangerous. The stars would go out. I'd be left in the cold. Not on my watch, I told myself, and kept awake, sometimes all night, willing you to stay.

I suppose I'm still a small boy with a box of matches, hunting for snails in a damp back garden. I always liked their softness, their stretchy-silky bodies and flower-like horns. I picked them off plants and put them in jars where I fed them leaves. I watched them browse. They moved without weight, like seals. I gave them names: Horace, Mary and Excalibur. Then I threw them over the garden wall. Out of sight, out of mind, so my father couldn't hurt them. At night, I heard his boots scrunching on softness and the blackness bubbling up.

And now I'm alone. Alone with the ache, the gap in my head.

Though not alone at all. I set out two plates, talk, ask questions. I still feel your hand. However much wasted, it's my drip-line.

I began this letter to bring things up, to find out where I am. But the memories take over and the damage is done. I want – I need you to read it, to receive it in some way. Like those first letters. But at the same time, the idea of you reading these words is almost unbearable. It's too much to take in. I want it all changed, to meet in the restaurant, kiss at the station, phone next day and have it all over again.

And I wonder what I could have done to stop it. I want to go back and find that moment, the split-second lapse where I turned away and your illness jumped in. When I didn't try enough and you sank. The backward glance that showed I didn't understand. My Orpheus moment.

If only. Every night I think how it might have been. If we'd met when we were young, if I'd known how short it would be, if I'd realised earlier. I search through the past, hear my own voice, my

667

denials. The fault was mine, my attitude was all wrong, it was head-in-the-sands. I wanted to run, to become invisible. I wanted something, anything. But I hid my feelings, and my distress turned to anger.

And yes, writing this, I realise I'm angry. I'm angry with you – how can I say it? – for leaving, for ignoring me, for giving up. I know it's not fair but that's how I feel. It's your fault, I say. I tried hard, but you let me down. But please understand, my darling, this is not me speaking. Of course I'm not angry, it's just a phase. And I love you, forever.

It's 5.00 a.m. and I'm tired. Maybe it's a vigil or a mood-shift, but I always feel I'm up against the clock. As if I'm on a run or climbing a steep cliff. It brings back youth. When you have to stay up, live life, be there for the action. It's about getting through. Only now it's alone, in silence.

But I prefer it this way. Our separation keeps us together. I still have you on walks, and when I'm by myself in gardens. No one can touch us. It's all quite Hardy-esque. And, yes, for me it's like stepping back in time. Because once we're together the longing eases, and I'm in the clear, facing the sky. It's then that I'm awake. Wide-eyed and alert. In the woods, by the sea or out on a hilltop you're there, in voice and presence. And though I know it's imagined, it brings relief.

Afterwards, when I'm aching, I remember those moments as late sun, caught between clouds, switching into rain.

In fact, I *want* my grief. I'm possessive. It holds me together. To be inside the shadow is prayer-like and alive but vulnerable as well. In an odd way it's an adventure, a hidden one, close to danger. It's like swimming under ice. I'm reminded of a dream you once described: a view over dark, grey waves, stretching into nothingness.

But don't worry, my love, I'm still with you in the angel moments, when I read your letters, or hear them in my head. It's something I do daily. They've taken over everything. Like a pianist in practice, I know them by heart.

So I spend my nights in a twitch, rerunning incidents, digging out things said and trying to fix what happened, keeping it in an archive. I'm a collector. I want it in a box, a glassed-in bubble. To hold you, like a statue, in the hope you'll come alive. And while I'm in darkness, that always seems possible. Because the bedroom's my museum, a place full of finds and reminders and precious bits and pieces. It's my vault. Things in their place, left as they are. Fragments of our story.

And I'm walling myself up. I've become my own experience: an event, and nothing more. So I dig and scratch and burrow beneath the sheets. My world has closed up. Like a stone inside, I measure and feel weight, touch on shape, reach for who I am. Which is blue-black and painful.

There's a song I keep hearing: "In a white room, with black curtains, near the station …" In a strange way it's joyful. Inside the song, there's an urgency, a circle of life. Plaintive as well, it goes round slowly. The guitar notes turn and peel off, they're a dying fall. We listen, and I tell you about it. In my mind, we're sharing how we feel. Now, as I write, I break off, find the album and turn up the volume so it fills the room. I listen, eyes closed, breathing slowly. It's certainly sad. But somehow in *this* room, it's smaller and more ordinary.

Sometimes it seems like I'm banging my head against glass. It's absurd of course, but my fear is that something will shatter. So I allow it, low-key, inside myself. I'm so fragile. I'm a cracked vase, badly taped together. Just walking down the street, or talking to George, or writing this letter: I'm full of broken-off thoughts. Small things irritate me – cars in a jam, blaring music, shoppers queuing, neighbours cooking – they try my patience. At home I swear at the computer, bang doors, V-sign the TV. I laugh at myself sometimes, I'm so teen-boy reactive. Outside I see red – literally, in flashes – but I blink and look away.

Really, I feel helpless. Like a climber hanging over a long drop I daren't look down. I wander out to the shops and people say hello. They seem fascinated by me. They want to help, but I can tell they're making themselves do it. Underneath they're afraid. When I walk away, I feel them watching. They're mindful of me, as if I might break. Sometimes a thought pops into my head, "what if I fall down?"

And I feel, in an odd way, they've asked for it. It's almost as if they're holding me up and one wrong move might throw me.

But I tell myself to keep going, as if I hadn't noticed. It reminds me of walking home from school in the dark. Like the *Ancient Mariner*, you mustn't look behind. Because, in the end, the problem's inside *you*. It's all about weakness, how you see yourself and the voices in the head.

I know those voices well. Or they know me. They fill up the air, acting as a wall, a glass one, double-glazed. They make me fearful of going wrong, of not measuring up. And they come between me and whoever I'm with. I collect their expressions, searching for an opening – a secret, coded, one-off gesture that might help me connect. I'm a castaway waving the only shirt I've got. And with some I'm lucky. Before I realise what has happened, a switch has been thrown and I'm with them. For instance, with church people. They're quick to understand, so with them one word can do it. They know how to get alongside. I think it's being older. I feel them with me at times in the garden or awake at night. I call them the weak force, holding me down. But sometimes, when I see them coming, I want to escape. I'm suddenly ashamed and want to disappear. So I duck down a side street and take the long way round. It's a gut thing. I just can't bear their wax-doll calm. Anything to avoid them.

Even with Hannah I seem to be at one remove. When she visits she brings her three-month-old. I hold him, make noises and stand him on my lap. "King David," I call him and we laugh. She's full of what she's doing, about night feeds and sleep times and bringing up baby. I share what she enjoys. But underneath I feel cut loose; I've spent too long on my own.

Feel, feel, feel. Writing like this, I think I've had enough. It hurts too much. I want to shout, blot out everything, put my fist through the wall. I'm a figure in a darkened room staring at a locked door. I feel sorry for this man. He's not me, he's a victim.

I see myself in third person. When I talk to him he's my imaginary friend. Teacher-like, I watch him from a distance: he's my K, an awkward, toothy kid. One of the lost boys, he's a follower, a used-to-be. Not like K today – a sing-along man with a bike and a job – but a child with a hurt. I think of him as a face in a window, an *invisible*: someone from the past who takes it all in and says nothing. He's me as I was, a shy boy on the inside, dreaming by the gate. I see him in the mirror and question why he's here. He doesn't say much. He's churlish, I think.

But sometimes I get closer. Mostly when he's working, when he's outdoors and watching. Then he's more giving. I see him in the garden, measuring perspective, designing views. He carries a spirit level in his hand. There's a map inside his head. He knows the life of the garden, its shape and its spaces. The areas he creates are full of hidden symbols. The dome, the crossing, the arch: they all point to you.

When I'm gardening I notice the small creatures. When I kneel, I'm close to their level. I feel, in a way, a part of their lives. Each day I see how they are. I keep a mental diary of their movements. Beginning with flight, they land and get busy, circle around colour, freeze for a moment then take off. For them it's a dance. I see other insects, scraping, crawling or poking into corners. They're bright and black and shiny.

I examine the spiders: their web-lines, crossing, and tightly bunched bodies. I name them: Itsy, Wriggler, Mr and Mrs S, then poke them with a stick. They run for cover. I'm God to their struggles.

As I'm digging, I turn up worms. Red-wrigglers, white-backs, purple-headed ones: they feed on darkness. In the evening they come out. When I crouch to look, they remind me of childhood. Together with snails, they're softly-softly. When I touch them they draw back into fists. Cut them and they heal.

I see them, filling up the garden. I have them in my sights, in map-view. It's like looking down a microscope. They're at the bottom, chewing slowly. Their mouths are full of rich black earth. What they bring with them is painful.

I found this poem.

*The illness bug*

With a buzz-fly's persistence
it charges and skitters all fours on glass,

it has a straw-suck mouth, bubbling air
through melted ice.

Inside-out, it's an ever-open eye
with a cord-pull reflex

and a loop to a point where it strap-hangs
doing nothing.

See there, where it jumps with a scissors-shut grin.
It's a tongue-tied kid
pulling faces in a sliver-chipped mirror.

Backhand swatted into corners
it plays dead,

then pops up again, hotfoot dancing
as the all-night baby.

It's our condition.

*Elizabeth Lavender*

After reading it, I sat in silence. The poem seemed to have come from a long way off. There was nothing else I could think about. I felt emptied out. I think in the end I went into the garden. I don't remember much, simply that I dug so hard it snapped the spade. I threw the two halves away. Then I sat down on the path staring at the ground. I think I must have stayed there a long time because the next thing I knew it was evening and the small creatures were back. The moths, the beetles, the slugs on the path.

They made me think of ants sorting Cinderella's peas, and bugs and spiders in my wildlife book. In their world, things were different. I'd a sense of how they have always existed, and their otherness. I remember how, in childhood, it seemed they'd been there forever. Even now I can feel them, watching. They're slow and inward but wild as well. I think of them as fragile survivors, short-lived and subject to climate. In a way, they're part of God.

So, I'm back to watching. The changes and the timings and where they fit. Day by day, keeping track, seeing how they do it. And this is my log, my book of sightings. *Mutatis mutandis.*

When autumn begins, the wasps fight to get in. As I draw back the curtains, they launch their bodies against glass. I can hear them scratching, digging into corners. It's hard to watch. Like standing by while someone drowns.

In winter there are caterpillars, snail tracks, teeth marks on wood.

In springtime, turning up a stone, the woodlice run. The roof's off and they're in a panic. The earth's alive. Their grey-silver bodies pack out the gangways. Someone's shouting fire.

Then summer, with flies. So many bodies, cutting through the air. Feeding, crowding, and crawling over earth. Struggling for space, they go on.

Today I sat down and reread this letter. I found it difficult. Some parts were embarrassing, other parts I wanted to tear up. I thought about stopping, putting it away, or even shredding it. I felt quite exposed. Was it me, I asked myself, or me acting a part? I wanted to wake up, break out and shake myself free. I'd allowed someone in, a dark, self-doubting, head-down avoider. Then I thought: if you could hear me, how would you feel? Of course I knew the answer. I could imagine your talk of flowers, the Gospels, a story you'd been reading. You'd be all light, like your parents. So I checked again and this time I read it differently. I've written simply what came up. My thoughts about you, or what you've become. Like a recurrent dream, you've taken over everything. An image so large, this letter doesn't matter.

When I close my eyes the displaced scenes keep coming back, like a film run backwards. Mainly of you, near the end. You beside me in your brother's photos, with life showing through. Painfully thin. A beautiful loss.

I think of you in blue, like Akhmatova in Altman's portrait. A poet and a lover. Your tight slim line and feel for colour. I can still bring you back.

The scene changes and I see you at the theatre, looking down the rows. We're there in the circle. The lights dim as the curtain rises. There are shapes on stage, moving in the dark. My arm's around your shoulders, touching flesh. The stage lights go up and the dance begins. It's a duet. The woman's antelope-thin, the man's an athlete. Their all-in-white bodies work together. The hush they create fills up the hall.

The pictures keep coming. I see us together, walking. Finding our way through gorse and mud. Passing the clay pit, the thicket, the broken fences. Hearing a car horn and a train moving off. It's us on the Common and I want it again. Our bodies, side by side. Your hand in mine – released for a moment as we duck past branches – in real time, as it happened. With sunshine, water, and the drumbeat of traffic.

And one mind between us, together in the wild.

We dealt with your baldness. No wigs, no pretence. I helped with your medicines, reading the labels and ordering repeats. There were visitors to greet, tea to make, cakes to pass round, and our minister saying prayers. When they'd gone away there were phone calls, or texts. You said your affirmations. We watched for birds. I taught you flower names then tested you, daily. Together we looked out, studying the garden. There were moments of discovery, small things shared: clouds like faces, dew on webs, light on the path.

Now I look back I see us walking into sunset. We didn't feel the cold.

Right from the start I've kept your pink top out. You must have seen it. The sparkly one, from our first date. I have it on a hanger, hooked on the wardrobe, like you used to. It looks much the same, though less bright, more special now. It's with me in the morning, all evening and when I switch out the lights. Even so, it still comes as a shock when I see it. For a second, with the mirror behind, I believe it's you. Each time's the same: a glimpse and a question, *can this be so?* then the let-down.

Afterwards, I'm shaken. It seems so unlikely. I tell myself it's a mistake, that I've projected, and it's all about me. But it feels quite spacey, as if I've seen a ghost. It reminds me of Tarkovsky's *Solaris*.

Mind, I suppose I'd be even more shocked if the top wasn't there. If it moved as I watched or turned up somewhere else. But my heart still jumps every time I see it.

So why do it? As a comfort, of course. Its faint rose-water scent reminds me of the restaurant. It's our secret. And it puts off the time when I have to open the wardrobe and sort things out. So it works for me. Though it does seem a bit crazy keeping it out, but hidden, like a holy relic.

Though not so crazy really, because it's up there as a portrait. It's between me and you, our private view.

But now I've begun to see further. Keeping it up there is superhero stuff. It's about me protecting you. I'm still in the business of holding up the temple, or trying to give back. And in my mind the odds are stacking up. It's the deficit model. All I can do is keep bailing out.

It's really a protection. A shield for us both. Because I think without it the house would fill up. Your presence would be every-where. And I need that distance, a room of my own.

As I write that phrase, I hear your objection. It belongs, you say, to women's history. But then you smile. Your reaction, you say, is really about you, and how you loved your gran. You talk about her books, and your stories. It's all made-up, you say.

Later you come to me in a dream, wearing your top. I've a set of books beside me. You're offering a swap, a book for a sequin. I know it's crazy but I agree. Soon it's a library, an imaginary one, with floral book jackets that we take out to the garden. You ask me to read, and leaves fill the air. I hear a bird scratching, digging in the soil. We're in the wood house, *Deanbury Gardens*, lying on wool. In there, you're protected. It's a dark, safe place, a seedbed of love. It's where I keep my heart.

You wanted a woodland burial. It was late on, remember?

I agreed, of course, and planned it as a party. It was what you wanted. For the kids, for the parents, for us. No quiet leaving, or talk about passing away. Music and flowers. Colour, poetry and bel canto. And Toby's Hawaiian-style photos, blown up on the walls.

"Would I want you unhappy?" you asked me from your bed.

"What kind of feeling would it give me, if I knew you were going to be miserable?" you said to your girls.

"I'm thankful for everything," you told your parents. "That's how I want you to be."

So we were all lined up. The funeral was about joy and life. A celebration. Only in my heart I didn't want it that way. It was too early. Black would have been better and truer – or a solemn, tender, darkly real service with Verdi's *Requiem* and the march from the *Eroica*. I wanted sadness and needed hurt. I *was* hurting, but pushing myself to be jolly.

Afterwards on the journey, I cut off. There was a wall between me and everyone else that kept me numb. At the committal I watched, sang with the others, then returned silently to a life emptied out. Everywhere there was the feeling that you'd not been buried: you were asleep or TV-watching or walking in the garden. I'd a sense of you locked out, on your own, a faded, unreal, weather-exposed ghost. And that where you should really be was a gap.

That gap was in me. Like a tooth gone missing, I needed you to fill it.

But that was then. Now I've been through it, had my dark night, and seen how you fit. As the song says: *Shine on you crazy diamond*. I can tell you this now, as if we were walking in the woods. There's a Beth-ness all around. A strong line running through everything. And when I look at a landscape I feel you there. You're a plant, a root, a solid thing,

> *Rolled round in earth's diurnal course,*
> *With rocks, and stones, and trees.*

And when I visit your grave, with its red-black sorrel and yellowed grass, walk the bare path through knapweed and toadflax, or pass by iris dying in the sun, I want to join the party …

Love

James xxxxxxxxxxxxx

✝ ✝ ✝

Here are a few of the messages that were pinned on the notice board at *The Shorespot Café* after Beth's death.

A note written in blue biro across an unstamped postcard. On the reverse, an old picture of an oiled-up cross-channel swimmer: "I come here every day to watch the sea. She always smiled"

A message in red on a cream-coloured coaster, she served me with ginger tea and cake. I liked how she talked."

A typed-out tribute on ultra-white paper: "Beth was truly a mother to me. She put up with my singing! We danced barefoot the gardens listening to the birds. Her cinnamon toast made me sw I feel her by me when I'm lighting candles. She found love." *Sara*

A scrawly, pencilled-in caption beneath a stick-drawing f a child pointing to an oversized sun: "I loved this lady."

A photo of pink and white flowers arranged in a vase. The flowers stand at the centre of a varnished table. Propped up in front of the flowers is a small folded card with *Beth* printed on it in S idge Script. All four corners of the photo are covered with felt-tip crosses.

And here are some of the intercessionary messages displayed at St Winifred's Church, Folkestone.

"Dearest Beth, we will always remember. Peace be with you."

"You go before us. A bright star."

"God bless you, Beth, and protect you. You showed us the way."

"From one world to the next. In the name of love."

"For you, the fire and the rose are one."

Also, arranged on a table below, a collection of greeting cards with crosses and angels. Inside each are kisses, heart-shapes and multiple signatures.

And this, a longer message, was left in an envelope tucked inside *The Book of Remembrance* at Lovecliff Woodland Cemetery.

"I came to know Beth when I was an elder at her former husband's church. She struck me as a woman of spirit, going through difficult times. I remember one Easter how I helped her to comfort her husband, who was ill. We worked together for the good of the church.

Years later we met by chance at her café. She welcomed me. If she had any concerns about the past she did not show them. Her gentle

directness won n nd. I told her I'd lost my faith, perhaps because
of things I'd se d she knew at once how I felt. That was when I
understood ho p she was, and selfless. She talked to me regularly,
usually after v There was a warm, softly-driven compassion in her
voice that I k came from her second marriage.

Through words I came to see faith as an ocean made up of
different c ts, some of them dangerous, some of them beautiful.
She was i those currents, alive and uncertain in an intense, joyful,
giving k f way. It was there that she met her wild, unknown,
imagina od.

Wh ne fell ill, we still talked on the phone about life as a flow
with n xed points. And how you could not pick it apart. When she
was c d, I imagined her in that ocean again.

T ugh her example I have reconnected to the wonderful, virtual
po of God. In my heart I call her, in private, perhaps absurdly,
Sa Elizabeth." *Derek Ward.*

se, found after her funeral, were some of the objects in Beth's
asure drawer.

Two chunky engagement rings with red glass centres and bronze
clasps. Wrapped in tissue, they'd been joined together by a few strands
of silver-grey hair.

A small knitted toy in natural and denim, reverse-worked in stock-
ing stitch, with polyester stuffing. The toy, shaped like a rabbit, had
ears, a white tail and a sewn-on grin. The body sagged in places. The
stomach was covered with what looked like bruises. It had been
patched round the back with green thread.

A collection of waxed leaves, stacked loosely like cards. They
were red-brown, yellow and purple.

A simple, unvarnished, hand-sized cross. Tied together by string,
it looked like a miniature mast. Beside it, a set of rolled-up napkins
were packed into a box. They were decorated with fishes and Chi-Rho
patterns. Each had a sewn-in signature, *Louise.*

A CD of Mahler's *Ninth Symphony.*

And these were some of the pictures discovered in Beth's scrapbook after her death.

A photo of Louise arranging a collection of wild flowers in a miniature watering can. The scarf on her head originally belonged to her mother. In the background, John's knitted beret was a present from Rose.

Cut-up calendars showing flocks of birds feeding and flying.

A photo of a field with James in the foreground, taken from their Irish honeymoon.

Several passport-size photos of James and all four children at different life stages, arranged in a collage.

A reproduction of Arnold Böcklin's *Isle of the Dead*.

And this obituary, based on a sermon, appeared in the St Winifred's church magazine. It was written by the minister, Carmen Higgins.

"Elizabeth Lavender was born in Honbury, just outside Bury St Edmunds, first child of John and Louise Jarvis, and elder sister to Toby. From her family I've learned about Beth the child, delighting in the world of nature and the imagination which she lived out in games in the garden and in the stories she wrote from an early age. Talking to Beth towards the end, I realised how happy that childhood had been, how loved she felt and how she valued the child in her that lived on in adulthood, making possible her openness and creativity. Beth did well at school, and some of her youthful friendships lasted the course of her life cut short. During her teenage years Beth's faith matured and deepened and she attended St Martha's Church, Honbury, where she met her first husband at the Youth Group. Beth studied English at university and, prompted by a social conscience, joined Tearfund and The International Fellowship of Evangelical Students. She married in 1975 and after her husband's ordination became a clergy wife, a role she tried to fulfil while remaining true to her own beliefs, which already embraced doubt and mystery. Like many good women she took failure hard, and was troubled by guilt as the marriage foundered and she determined to protect and nurture their daughters, Naomi and Rose.

Some of you will have experienced the pleasures of her *Shorespot Café*, where everyone could be sure of a warm welcome and where Beth herself liked to listen as well as serve. Meeting James was something she called a reckless act, driven by uncrushable romantic hope, but from the beginning they made a deep connection that brought her great happiness. They were married in 2004 but five years later she became ill, and cancer of the bowels was diagnosed. Surgery and chemotherapy followed on a regular basis, and Beth was enormously grateful for the medical care she received, but after a period of remission she died peacefully at home, where she wanted to be, on 19th October 2012.

During our talks through her illness Beth took a great interest in matters of faith and doubt. She talked about the power of imagination and the God of silence and absences. She was committed and adept in everything she did: gardening, work, dancing and motherhood. Nevertheless, I was told I was on no account to eulogise her just because she'd gone! Beth set herself high standards, but she never courted undue notice or praise. Flowers, the sea and poetry meant more to her than image or success. She loved her life with James and didn't want to let go, but she told me that she needed to learn to love death too, without fear. Beth liked learning up to the last, asking me to share what I'd discovered through my ministry about the big taboo and how people face and deny it. What she wanted above all else was to die honestly and bravely, in a way that would encourage others. Some of those who loved her might say that was what she did best."

# THIRTY-NINE

One by one, I see you.

My family, James, my friends. And with you, your stories. I see who you are, how you've changed, how you find meaning.

You're images now, in a blur. A dream procession.

Beginning with Meg. I hear you talking, as words in the head. You're with me now, a Madonna face, rounded, my closest friend.

Godmother to my children, you sat them and took them through. Smooth-faced and willing, you held my hand. At first in thought, growing together, adjusting hair bands, then in prayer, with faith. You were so good.

But your marriage wasn't. I saw you once, on holiday with Phil. He put himself around. A balloon face to your smile. Plastic, stretchy and close to bursting. Charming, charming, he wanted to figure. Raising a glass to people he'd sold to and their beautiful lives. You know of course where it led. That evening, in the bedroom, I heard his shouts. When a man's angry anything goes.

I know how he kept you. Men call it depression, make their promises, buy large bouquets. Strange isn't it? I left Conrad after we'd talked. But for you it was always about putting others first.

I can see you at the bedside. A picture by Manet. You were so patient. Good at being there, and lively as well. But really you were crying, right from the start. Only I didn't see it. Too much giving. A star behind clouds. Rain and more rain.

After Meg, others. Arrivals, departures, one by one, I see you as you are.

Beginning with Rachael and Amy, appearing with flowers. Faces in the dark. If I could talk to you now … A warning, a question, a simple explanation. It seemed to you I'd stepped out for a moment: a strange disappearance, somewhere off the map. It wasn't what you believed in. My friends, I can understand now how you didn't have much to say. You smiled, like children. You didn't know how I could bear it.

Afterwards you blanked. The world took over. I hear you at a table, talking prices. Enjoying coffee. Exchanging gripes.

And the words:

> It has to fit the scheme.
> You want it to look nice.
> Yes, good value as well.
> Have you seen his picture?
> Pretty good stuff.
> And how's your other half?

On business. Away at present. And yours?

Not much to say.

And your marriages … Separated or not speaking, heading for divorce.

From then to now, I notice the difference. Because where I am now gives me advantage. It's a screen, a great glass eye, and I've passed through. I'm at a place where everything's visible – a view, all-angles, out to the blue. Beyond that it's clear: a big space into nowhere. A sky-high island with dream-shaped smiles and faces from the past.

I'm looking into brightness, seeing who you are.

Charlie. Charlene. C. Strange how you come back. Always yourself, appearing without warning. Popping up late in purple and shades. I can feel you now, somewhere close, dreaming in the dark. You were the sleepless watcher, the made-up woman at the studio window. What did you see there …?

Stars and desire. Lights on water. A hand, an eye, an image of love.

"Look," you said and your heart was there, a dream of lovers, kissing.

You led. Wildlife and passion. Took me through the world and out into nothingness. You were the angel of flesh, the runaway woman, the underworld queen.

You were Psyche.

Then of course, Conrad. The man on his own, out of control, dropping. Over the edge and down into darkness. Grabbing for hand-holds like a dislodged climber.

I see you in youth. You were Mr Look-at-me Clever, clowning. Conrad Bright, on the run, my glory-be.

Or you on the phone, trying to make up. My strong-and-silent, now holding talks. Awkward, breathless, the one who wore black. *Regarding the girls … Changeover times … Necessary adjustments …* The man behind the mask. Without you I'd be different.

For you I need forgiveness.

Also, Toby with camera. And the pictures he gave us, the inside view. Blown-up large, what we agreed to. Each photo a statement.

I list them here, with captions.

Photo 1.

Two faces at table with linked arms, sipping water from each other's glass. The walls are angled, like a ship at sea. The picture's focus is sharpest on the glasses, which are lit from behind. Flowers in the background give a domestic feel. On the wall a glassed-in photo reflects the light. It's luminous, like a Vermeer. The faces seem far-away; they're hard to read. It's James and me at the café.

Photo 2.

A sea view with sun on stones. Semi-abstract and bare. There's a white line between yellow and greyish-blue. The surf is suspended in a low C-shape, like a Japanese miniature. It leads the eye to two pairs of feet, without shoes. Toes up, heels down, they look like plants. They come from legs that must be flat to the earth. From their size it seems they're male and female. The small pair, mine, are paper-white, like narcissi.

Photo 3.

A portrait of me outside the hospital. I'm sitting on a wall wearing a sleeveless dress. It's knee-length and floral. It makes me seem rather 50s. The hospital to one side is a wall of glass. There's a path between the wall and building. The gap between me and the hospital is about four feet. Looking carefully, there's a streak on the glass. I see that it's a shadow. Although the camera's at an angle, I know it's me. My shadow's pencil-thin.

Photo 4.

A close-up of my hands. They're held out, cupped slightly, holding something. They're thin and creased and folded like paper. They remind me of a late Rembrandt. But these are different. Round each finger, and wrapped in crisscross patterns across the palms, are web-like lines. They are my lost hairs.

Photo 5.

James and me in the park. We're together in a swan-shaped pedalo. We look like a picture on a pop-up card. It's our summer's end outing. James is holding up two ice creams. They're cornets, and look like upside-down party hats. One is dripping on his shirt sleeve. Behind us the trees are solid, opaque and two-dimensional, a wall of green.

Photo 6.

A body in water. Light in ripples, playing across flesh. The slack, seal-like body is half-submerged. It's seen from behind, head above the surface, feet out to sea. It's close to the shore and the waves are gathered around in folds. The smooth, shiny body looks like a sunken statue, or a diver, resting.

It's me, returning to the sea.

Photo 7.

James at the end of the bed, looking down. The bed is empty and the duvet is stripped back. The sheet is stretched tight. On one side, where the mattress dips, a child-sized outline can be made out. It's vague and shadowy like a watermark. It reminds me of a sweat-cloth, or Veronica's veil.

Photos 8 – 15.

Me and James, Hawaiian-style, surrounded by flowers. Blue-white ribbons and coral-coloured necklaces. Flowers as cummerbunds and sashes. Red and yellow headbands. Flowers in buckets and vases. Cushion covers with William Morris prints. Floral shirts and Matisse-like dresses. Buttonhole carnations and Queen of the Night tulips. Green-black wreaths and purple crosses.

Photo 16.

A woman in a car leaning her head on her mother's shoulder. The woman looks worn; her face is hollowed out. She's small and slight and lost beside her mother. The car's back seat rises above her head. Her mother's smile is tender, wistful and gently elevated. It's me with Louise.

Photo 17.

John at the bedside. He's leaning forward. His hands are white and clenched. A grey wisp of hair has fallen across his forehead.

In front of him, the sheets are in a bundle. They cover what might be a pillow, or could be flesh. If it's a body, there's hardly anything left. It's thin, white like the bed, and spread like dough.

John is head down, rocking back and forth. He's crying.

Photo 18.

My chair, empty.

So, this is me at the edge – the high up moment when the soul grows large. Look down: it's a challenge. The biggest; it takes you to the end, to not being so. Or rather, to being present while absent. I'm out there in the blue, my angel moment.

What I see is the story.

My children, firstly. They're wearing white, chasing butterflies. Naomi's singing, Rose holds a doll. They're walking in a meadow, waist-high in grass. The grass is dry as tinder. As they walk, it rustles. It's as if they were wearing thickly-layered clothes. The meadow gives way to hollows and nettle beds. When the doll falls in, Naomi pulls it out. Afterwards, they hug. While Rose does a dance, Naomi sits watching, saying nothing. Her ankles are white and blotchy. The sun paints her skin.

My daughters by a river, with thoughts running on. I can hear Psalm 23. They're in a gallery, looking at a picture. It's called *The Lady of Shalott*. I talk about Waterhouse, and Rose says she likes the picture, touching the glass. Naomi warns, Rose objects, and words are exchanged. An attendant comes up and we leave. Outside, by the Thames, both girls are silent. I use the word angry then stare down-stream. In my heart I hear snatches of the Tennyson poem, repeating. It's my story.

My daughters, eyes closed, in church. They're there with John and Louise, saying nothing. I feel for how they are. Their grief can't sing. The world they live in is a slow drip, a hole in water. The air isn't theirs. On the walls there are marks: dark spots and stains, it's not what they expected.

And now they're by the grave. It's mid-afternoon and we're close. They've joined me in the sun. This place where we meet is grassed over, with bright, wild flowers and insects passing. If you lie down you can feel the earth. It's damp and covers all. There's no fear now. The birds are singing, the blossom shows and the ants are busy. The faces of my daughters are daffodils, filling up with light. They are with me.

And secondly, Louise.

I imagine her, in church, holding up flowers. We're all in the hands of God, she says. Childhood hands, they bring back a song – *You need hands*.

She gives me her hands – large like hers.

A safe pair of hands, pencilling in dates. Busy hands opening packets of seeds. Hands-on hands, fitting flowers to vases, labels to parcels, pictures on the walls.

Arts-and-crafts hands, sewing in names to gymslips and hankies. Steward's hands, passing round Bibles. Hands on sheets and hands on heart.

A hand to my forehead, stroking gently as she whispers my name.

Mother, I stretch my hand to thee.

And now, a story for John.

It comes as a voice in the dark, a long-distance call. A story with a message, like a broadcast in the head. A dream of someone talking.

It goes like this:

### The Girl Who Didn't Like Her Name

Ania was a girl who didn't like her name. She wanted to change it, but when she asked her parents they told her she had to keep it. She asked them why. Her parents said because it was her name. When she asked again they said because they'd chosen it. When she asked a third time they told her she *looked* like an Ania. This answer puzzled her. How could that be, she wondered, staring in the mirror. Ania asked them what they meant. This time her parents didn't reply. When they finally spoke, what they said troubled her. They told her Ania was a name with two meanings. In Greek it meant grief, in Polish grace.

Ania respected her parents, but what they said didn't feel right. It wasn't what she wanted. In fact, she felt quite hurt.

Ania lived in a country where people felt hurt. She'd watched their faces, she knew how they talked. If things went wrong that pained them. They were shocked by what they read. It was in what they ate, what they believed, and what they spoke about. They said that the odds were against them, their luck was bad, money was a headache. They were upset by what they saw. What they didn't have bothered them. Other people let them down. Most of all, their feelings hurt.

Ania wanted to understand. She thought if she could share their pain it might help. So she set about collecting hurt-names.

When Ania walked out in the morning, she felt her first hurt. A bird sang quietly on a tree and a cloud passed over. Love-ache she called it, smelling a rose. All that day she was sad and troubled by things in the air. There were seed heads drifting and wind, sighing in the trees. At noon she was thoughtful, later she was cold. In the evening she was alone. When the moon came up she was afraid. At night she felt her loss. It hid together with grief beneath the stones.

She realised how it hurt to be hurting.

Looking in a book, Ania found other names for hurt. She read them out. They included discomfort, weariness and fatigue. When she went into shops she heard people talking. They used words like tired or angry. In church she heard expressions of sorrow and regret. When she visited hospital they spoke about illness, dysfunction, disease. In dreams she saw bodies. Looking at nature there were victims and outcasts. Hurt was in the climate, they called it breakdown, chaos, loss. In her heart there was emptiness. It seemed, once you noticed, hurt was everywhere.

Ania went back to her parents. She told them her story, and how much it hurt. Where did it come from, she asked them, and what could she do?

In answer they smiled. Tell us another story, they said.

Ania didn't answer. She felt too hurt.

Another story, they said. Still she couldn't speak.

A story, they repeated, and hugged her.

So Ania began. And the first few sentences went like this …

A girl lived in a country where people felt grace. They accepted hurt, and where it came from. If things went wrong that didn't upset them. They were not at all shocked by what they read …

As she continued, Ania heard her story, repeating in her head. Instead of hurt she said grace, instead of sorrow, joy, instead of pain, forgiveness. Then she heard her voice saying goodwill and kindness. She spoke about sharing and charity, and surprised herself with delight, happiness, care. At the end she was full of empathy, understanding, compassion, love.

When she'd finished her parents kissed her and gave her a blessing.

Promise you'll remember who you are, they said. She promised. And where you come from, they added. She promised again. Because from now on, they said, you can choose your name.

The girl thought carefully then smiled. "Sorrow and forgiveness." she said. "Ania."

And now I see James.

He's at the end of the headland, watching the waves. I'm out there, too, but not so he can see me. I can feel how he hurts. In his mind there are pictures. He sees us swimming out. We're on our own with the sun on our backs. The sea's all around, it's where we go back to. As we dive below the surface the past takes over. I'm with him in the dark. In dreams I'm walking by water, climbing to the view.

Now I'm at the window, watching for the moon. White and spread, it paints on water. A love song begins. The notes are messages. Sung low-volume, they're words of longing, from me to you. They're for the lovers, listening in the night.

A cloud passes over and I feel him getting closer. I'm writing to him now, telling him I'm waiting. I'm rereading his letters, urging him to join me. He's on the way, walking to our meeting. Appearing at the doorway, I see him looking around. The world's there before him. I want him to feel love.

Dearest,

If I could speak to you now I'd use those words: darling, paramour, heartthrob, my one-and-only. I'd take you on a walk with song thrush and lark. Dance with you barefoot on the lawn. Sit together on the swings, in the park. Then I'd sneak into bed as your girl.

There are no accidents. What we have is given. It's not me, not you, but an image.

You understood my pain. I was the instrument locked up in a case, you took me out, we sang. The case was in the corner of a dark, dark room. You opened the door, we walked out. In the sun we were crazy, nothing held us back, nothing went away. You watched over me as the shadows lengthened. When darkness came the ache came too. Bare-handed, you held the flesh together. Still, the ache found a way. It ran down the walls, gathered in shadow, filled up the cup.

Who are we? Lovers and children. Believers in the ancestors. Descendants from the stars, who suffer, who fight. Souls in limbo, one world to the next. Who dance back time.

And now? With music and voices I shall bind you up. I'm in the air, leading. What we share is the story. Where we come from and where we're going. Because unless they're imagined, miracles don't happen. For better, for worse, it's a bubble that we blow.

What more? The light shines through. Ask and it shall be given – in flowers, in the woods, in rain, still with you. Also, in the stone, in darkness, in silence. If love's for the taking then stay mindful.

And be as you are. James, my man. It's not about joy but fullness. Child of God, I love you.

Beth xxxxxxxxxxxxxxxxxxxx

Hannah wrote a story. It's for me, about me. I'm in there, invisible.

I see it now, large-print, with a stitched card cover. Like a picture book it has very few words. Where an image should be, there's just soft, thick, pure space.

The little boy looked up at the grey sky.

"It's meant to be blue," he said. "Why is it dirty?"

689

"Because," said his mummy, "yesterday a boy threw a stone at a swan."

The little boy felt the wind slap his face.

"Why is it so spiteful?" he asked.

"Because," said his mother, "it heard what the girl whispered at playtime."

The boy saw a daffodil hang its head in a vase.

"It stinks!" he said. "Why is it bad?"

"Because of lies," said his mummy. "Sweet scented lies." She smiled. "A man bought flowers for a woman he didn't love."

As lightning lit up his face the boy held his mother's hand.

"Why does it flash?" he asked.

"Because of the light that's inside," said his mummy, "hidden in the clouds."

"Why is it so scary?" the little boy asked.

"Because it's full of life," his mummy said.

Then the boy heard a siren screech on the street. He covered his ears till his face was red.

"Why is it so loud?" he cried.

"Because it needs us to take notice," said his mother.

"Where is it going?" he asked as the siren faded.

"Into the place where love makes us whole."

I closed the book at the end. The story was over.

‡ ‡ ‡

Welcome to *Beth's Garden*.

This memorial to Elizabeth Ella Lavender, laid out in the shape of a family tree, was started in 2013. When the garden began the idea was to use a small number of plants chosen by Beth's closest relatives, linking them to her life. As the project grew, the range of plants and their connections widened. The final design came about through the involvement of the whole family.

Your named trail is marked in blue on the garden map. You will find the same names, with numbers, painted on stakes beside the path. The full tour usually takes about an hour.

1. As you enter, look back at *The Shorespot Café* and the sea behind it. This is Beth's café.

2. On your immediate right, you will find *Spring Hollow,* an area full of scilla, white spring crocuses, anemones and Tête-á-Tête daffodils. This auditorium-shaped space is where Beth used to dance. Look towards the back and you will see a line of lilacs. Their colours range from Alba through shades of pink and mauve to Dark Knight. Lilacs traditionally symbolise love.

*Spring Hollow* is maintained by Naomi and Rose, Beth's daughters, and her brother, Toby.

3. Next on the right is *The Churchyard.* This has ivy-clad stones, a Judas tree and holly, underplanted with pasque flowers. Conrad Bright and his congregation look after this area.

4. Further up the path, on the right is *The Storyteller's Grove.* The eucalyptus trees here were chosen by Beth's parents. The trees' soft, rustling whispers have been compared to human voices. A listening seat at the centre is inscribed with an elegy by John Jarvis. At his suggestion there are nesting boxes and berry-bearing plants dotted around the grove. Underfoot, the peeling bark provides a rich mulch for trilliums and enchanter's nightshade.

The grove also contains *Cornus sanguinea* "Midwinter Fire" and a wall of black bamboo. The former was planted for Beth's grandmother, Elizabeth Turnbull, the latter as a tribute to Beth's great-grandparents on the Jarvis side. They campaigned to improve women's education.

5. As the path curls round we enter the *Wilderness Garden.* This dry, stony patch is covered with spurge, plantain, thistles and common ragwort. To soften the effect, blue-leaved rue and yellow field pansies have been introduced at the edges. In May the hawthorn hedge at the back is a white wave. This area represents earlier generations: in-laws

Jack Henderson, his wife Grace Henderson and their three children, Mary, Edith and Stephen.

7. A walk downhill brings us to the *Lavender Gardens*. Here we follow the descending family line, beginning with Mary Henderson, represented by a bed of sea lavender (Marsh Rosemary). Her husband, Stuart Lavender, has a single Iceberg rose planted in his memory.

At this point you will see the path forks.

8. Steps to the right descend to *The Old Quarry*. Due to subsidence, the surface here is damp and uneven. Follow the steps down to a dark pool, shaded by a canopy of purple magnolias and rhododendrons, and 'Purple Haze' camellias. This quiet, self-enclosed space is dedicated to Mary and Stuart's older son, Alan Lavender, and his wife Harriet.

9. At the end of the pool the path re-ascends, via the *Zigzag Way*, to dwarf maples, flowering quince and Pieris japonica. At the top is an insect area, planted with cornflowers, foxgloves and buddleia, leading to an open meadow. Tall grasses flourish here including Black Bent, Cocksfoot and Yorkshire fog. It was Alan's son Matthew who suggested the layout. His wife Miranda and their children Joe, Mia and Cass chose the planting.

10. Returning to the fork, the left-hand path descends through *The Terraces*. These vegetable plots are intended to be both practical and ornamental. A carved boundary stone dedicates them to Mary's younger son, Edwin Lavender and his wife, Doris. The first plot is a herb garden modelled on Doris's backyard. Here you will find the same herbs as she grew for her sons, Richard and James. Lower down, The potage-style plots mix flowers with vegetables and fruit. They are named after Richard's and James's children – Charlotte and Stephan, Hannah and George.

11. At the bottom the path passes through a gap in a hornbeam hedge to enter the circular *Love Garden*. Dedicated to Beth's husband, James Lavender, this is the heart of the garden. Set out in quarters, with a red-purple colour scheme, its arches and frames display clematis, honeysuckle and twenty varieties of rose. The radiating beds are full of catmint, iris, sweet pea and stocks. At the centre, a heart-shaped lily pool sprouts ferns around the edges. Damselflies can be seen

hovering in pairs close to the water. Behind the pool, a large, flat stone has been set into earth. On its surface a faint human outline is visible.

12. Pass out through another gap in the hedge and you will find yourself back by *Spring Hollow*. Return from here to *The Shorespot Café*. Inside you will find a framed photo of the stone beside the pool. It shows the artist Angel Perkins scraping the stone. The title of her sculpture is Beth.

‡ ‡ ‡

The message went out.

It began with a simple childhood game, *Pass It On*, played by school friends of Hereiti's. As a game it had been a hit. With its ins and outs and fun variations, including *Spread It* and *Chain Tag*, it had taken over life all through summer. Hereiti remembered the note by hand, the tug on the sleeve, the whispered message, and the rage of excitement running on grass linked in a chain. It brought them closer and more alive, connected to the birds, the trees, the earth and all things creaturely. Although sometimes the game was wild and could be dangerous, it touched on what mattered, as Hereiti well knew. So when the ground shook or a storm rolled over she stood by the door listening to the trees falling, the animals crying out, the surf on the beach.

As a fad it lasted about a year but then it changed. It became less visible, more subtle and hidden, heard behind everything as an imaginary broadcast sung at a distance by spirits of the air. For Hereiti it was still there, a line of intention inside her secret self, passing on meaning, as in families. Her direction in everything, seen in bird flight and the angle of the sun. And she practised how to read it and hear it and make it her companion in the garden and on her journeys.

Later, as an adult, Hereiti returned to her game. What had worked so well was the one-to-one contact. *Pass It On, Pass It On*, they'd said, linked in chains and dancing together. That was when the magic happened. With a shout and a laugh the pent-up energy broke loose, changing everything. So Hereiti put together a message from the heart, a life-first, bright-side, act-now manifesto. It read like this:

693

- All life forms are equal.
- We are more than the sum of our parts.
- Science has answers. The science is us.
- Poetry has no answers. It knows the way.
- Neighbourliness and affection exist in the mycelium, in flowers and insects and all things wild. Listen to their voices.
- Measure with the eye, work with the hands, journey using the heart.
- Transform, renew, be gentle. Turn your energies inside out.
- Friendship sustains; money divides.
- The secret lives of plants, animals and insects uphold everything.
- The children are the inheritors. Their time is now.
- Walk the new paths, sail into the wind; let the ancestors be your guides.
- Exercise your dream, it speaks the language of the rebel inside you.
- We are the tipping points. Go out, change the world.
- We all have a book in us: The Book of the Earth.
- Everything begins with imagination.
- There is no end, only where we stop to take a breath.
- Rebellion is a voyage into meaning.
- When stepping outside the box, set out at dawn.
- Read this. Take action. *Pass It On.*

When she'd finished, Hereiti sent out her message, beginning with activists, readers, scientists and small-scale gatherings of friends. It was carried on cards and in greetings on banners, it was written in slogans on placards and T-shirts, it was chalked up on walls and fences, and it could be heard in the lyrics of songs and talks on the radio.

And each sent message was similar to the original, but varied slightly for the person being told.

When the message reached Joe, he heard it in the voice on the mike and chants on marches. When Cass heard it, an alarm bell rang and an ambulance arrived. For Mia it was a face at a window and a cat, prowling in the garden. As it spread, it became a shape in darkness, seen by the fathers, a child's cry heard by the mothers, a red flag on the beach for walkers, a reflection in water for lovers on the bridge. For Hereiti and Y it was the sea's vastness and journeys by night.

The message went out. On foot, by hand, through books and pictures and in schoolrooms and museums – in all the old ways with tales on walkabouts of hands-in-the-air ceremonies and people meeting up. Everyone shared it. It was the story of lives on the edge, islands going under, of travelling into darkness and finding a way. But also of spirit-navigation, living in the round and gifts passed on.

And she called it Love's Register.

# NOTES

p8 *The Book of the Dead – The Egyptian Book of the Dead* by Anonymous.

p9 anamnesis – A recollection, especially of a previous existence.

p9 *We are the people your mother warned you against* by Nicholas von Hoffman.

p9 *Everything they say we are, we are* – lyrics from *We Can Be Together* by Jefferson Airplane.

p25 Sparky at keyboard – *Sparky's Magic Piano* is a 1947 Capitol Records children's audio story.

p73 *merci* – An extra card that can be played at the end of various card games.

p87 THC – a crystalline compound that is the main active ingredient of cannabis.

p96 *Peccavi* – meaning "I have sinned" was a punning mock-apology offered for exceeding orders in the ruthless British occupation of Sindh.

p145 Fat Freddy's Cat – a cat from the sixties' cartoon the *Fabulous Furry Freak Brothers*.

p146 IDL – I don't like

p147 WTFDYM? – What the fuck do you mean?

p193 *a tempo* – in music, resume normal speed.

p212 *Ouroboros* – an ancient symbol showing a snake eating its own tail.

p233 HTF – How the fuck

p249 The big five – African Lion, leopard, elephant, rhinoceros and Cape buffalo.

p305 episteme of an era – as described in *The Order of Things: An Archaeology of the Human Sciences* by Michel Foucault.

p307 Altman and Taylor's disclosure theory – *Social Penetration: The Development of Interpersonal Relationships* by I Altman & D Taylor.

p308 *égoïsme à deux* – a relationship in which each person is entirely focused on the other, to the detriment of other people around them. *The Art of Loving* by Erich Fromm.

p308 expressiveness and instrumentality in families – contrasting female/male behaviour patterns, as described in *Transition to Parenthood* by Alice S Rossi from the *Journal of Marriage and Family*. 30 (1): 26–39.

p377 Benedict Anderson's analysis of nationalism – *Imagined Communities: Reflections on the Origin and Spread of Nationalism*

p377 The Libet experiment – *Unconscious Cerebral Initiative and the Role of Conscious Will in Voluntary Action* by Benjamin Libet in *The Behavioural and Brain Sciences*. 8 (4): 529–566.

p380 UGMIT – from *Games People Play* by Eric Berne (see also P458).

p382 Deci and Ryan's notion of self-determination – *Intrinsic motivation and self-determination in human behaviour* by E L Deci & R M Ryan.

p408 IPCC – Intergovernmental Panel on Climate Change.

p430 *da capo* – repeat the music from the beginning.

p455 Bowen's theory of family projection – in *Family Therapy in Clinical Practice* by Murray Bowen.

p455 The Three Apples – a whodunnit from *One Thousand and One Nights*.

p458 Labeling Theory – a theory about negative labels causing behaviour changes.

p503 a print of a raven-haired woman – *Proserpine* by Dante Gabriel Rossetti.

p526 Ichthys – Jesus fish sign used by early Christians (see also p666).

p586 a *nekyia* and *te hoe tere* – both refer to spirit journeys.

p586 *illud tempus* – from *The Sacred & The Profane* by Mircea Eliade.

p587 *lysis* – a process of disintegration or dissolution (as of cells).

p590 limited predictability and the *Butterfly Effect* – how a minor change in initial circumstances can cause a large change in outcome: "Does the flap of a butterfly's wings in Brazil set off a tornado in Texas?" – Edward Lorenz.

p591 Future Rights – respect for the rights of future generations in environmental policy.

p591 Ecocide – the criminal destruction of nature by human activity.

p598 the second law of thermodynamics – over time the universe runs down to a state of inert uniformity.

p615 RP – Received Pronunciation, sometimes called a posh accent.

p640 *autoritratto* – self-portrait.

p647 the boy falling from the skies who no one sees – as in *Landscape with the Fall of Icarus* by Pieter Bruegel.

p659 *ER* – an American medical drama television series.

p661 PB – Personal Best: an athlete's best score.

p673 *Mutatis mutandis* – with things changed that should be changed.

p678 Chi-Rho – ☧, an early Christian symbol of Christ.

# Other Leslie Tate books

published by TSL Books
https://tslbooks.uk/facts-memoir-and-living/

*Heaven's Rage* is Leslie Tate's non-binary memoir that explores addiction, cross-dressing, bullying and the hidden sides of families, discovering at their core the transformative power of words to rewire the brain and reconnect with life.

*The Dream Speaks Back*, by Sue Hampton, Cy Henty and Leslie Tate, is a joint autobiography exploring imagination and the adult search for the inner child. It's also a very funny portrait of working in the arts, full of crazy characters, their ups and downs, and their stories.